GW00500754

ALIEN GENESIS

EDEN'S ANGELS BOOK 1

GARY BEENE

Published 2022 by Next Chapter

Edited by Graham (Fading Street Services)

Cover art by CoverMint

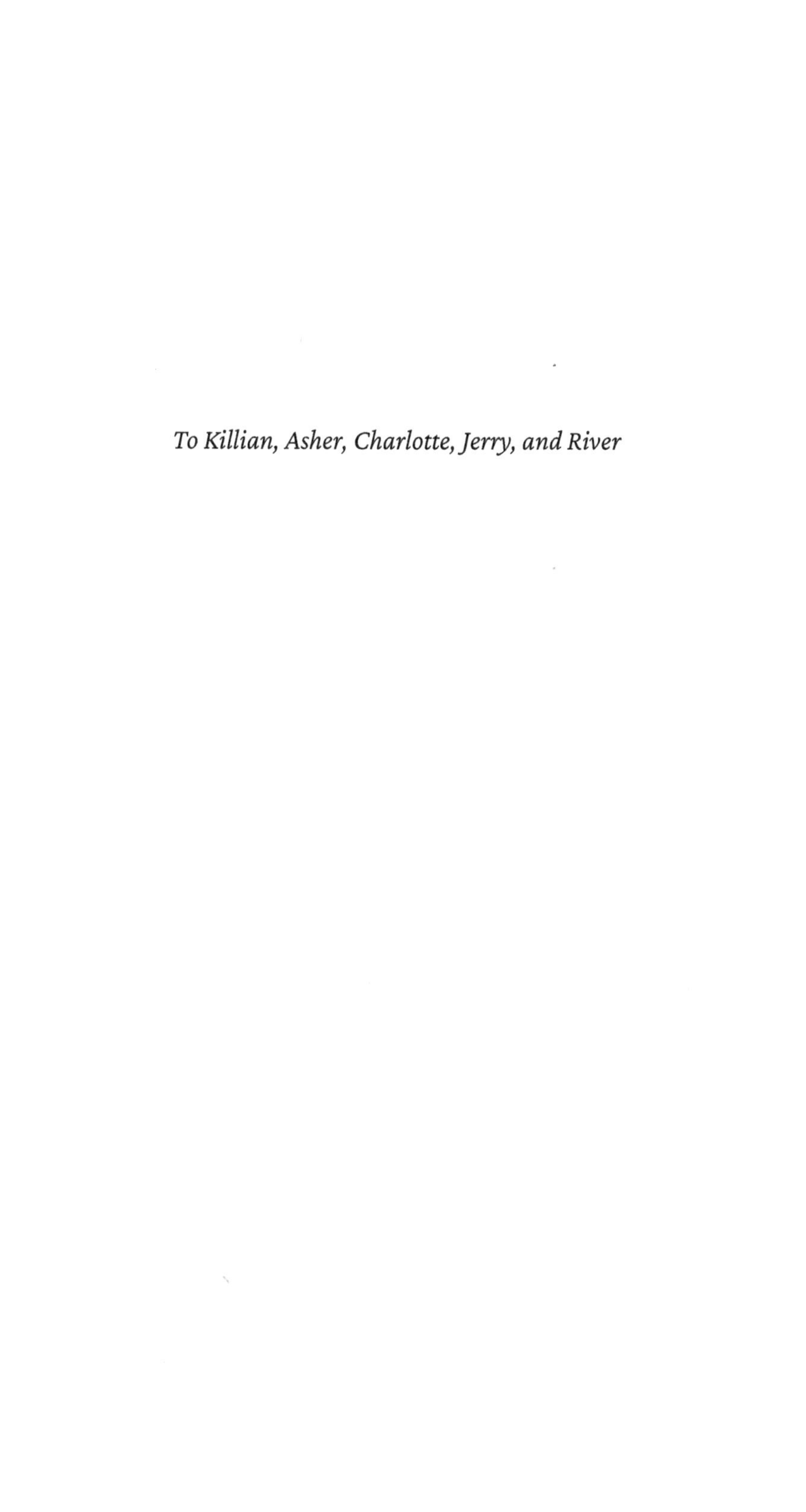

To Killian, Asher, Charlotte, Jerry, and River

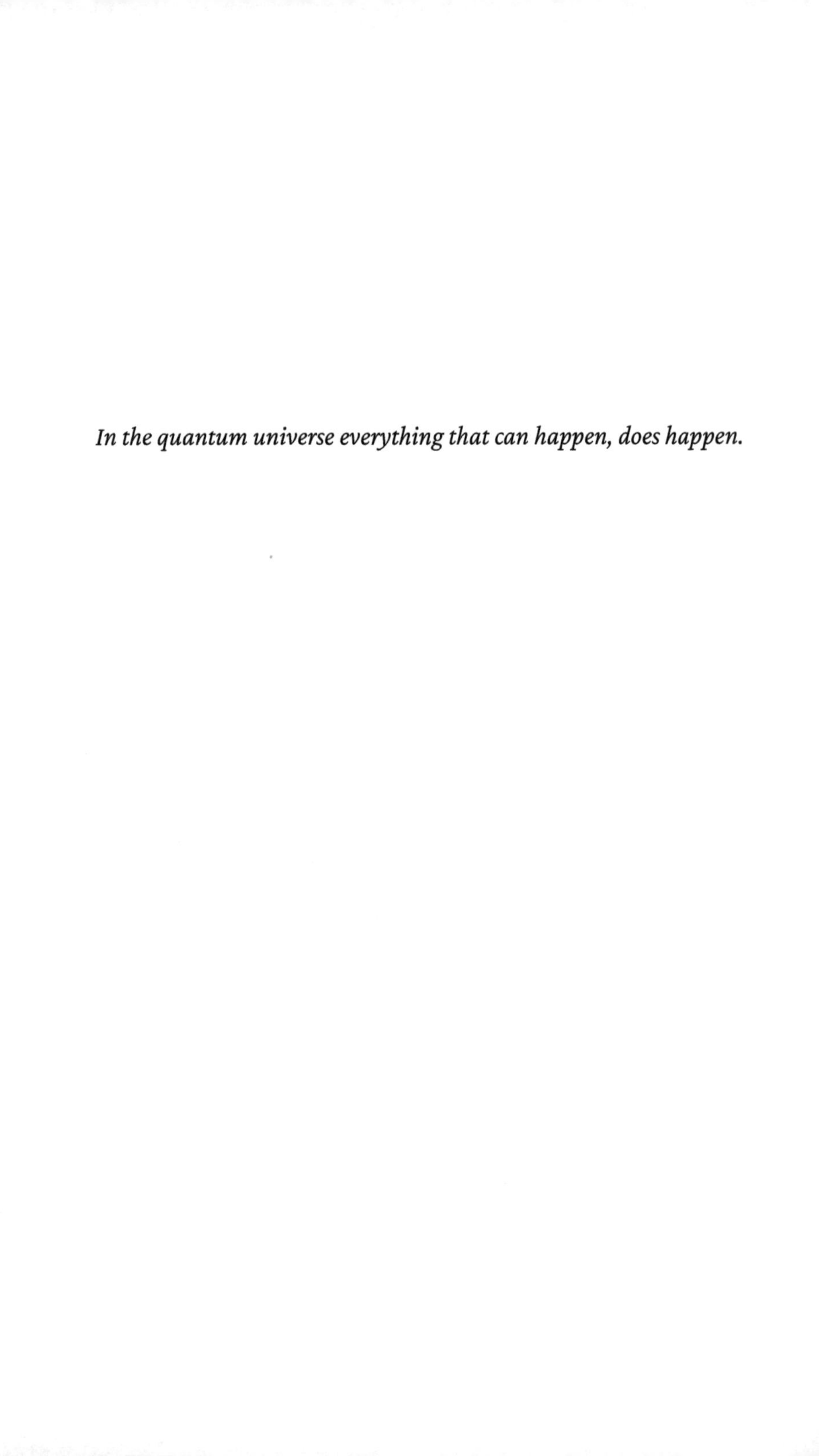

In the quantum universe everything that can happen, does happen.

CONTENTS

PART ONE

CHAPTER ONE

IN THE BEGINNING

(CIRCA 50,000 YEARS AGO)

THE AIR ITSELF CAUGHT FIRE.

Ramuell didn't know how long he'd been lying on the cave floor. He felt hollow, his chest ached, and he was unable or unwilling to move. Slowly he became aware of quiet rustling in other parts of the cave. He was not the only survivor. He lapsed into a fitful sleep, haunted by the horrors the people of Domhan-Siol had visited on the planet Ghrain-3.

A blinding flash and deafening roar had shattered the early dawn. Everything lying loose on the canyon floor was sucked violently into the air. Choking clouds of dirt, stones and ash boiled skyward. The portal canopies in front of each inhabited cave were ripped from their anchors. Instantly the pilings were shattered as they swirled up toward the canyon rim. The flying debris spontaneously combusted as it crested the ridges.

People and animals outside the caves were likewise drawn into the maelstrom. Every crow roosting in the nearby trees simply disappeared. Small children were vacuumed out of caves as if by a tornadic wind. People with enough strength anchored themselves inside by clinging to rocks, roots, or log structures wedged into wall cracks.

After those first few seconds, Ramuell's gasps couldn't fill his lungs. He realized that oxygen was being burned so rapidly several hundred metres overhead that he was suffocating. This understanding intensified his terror, and that fear turned to dread as the last image he saw before losing consciousness was Dahl staggering about the cave—blood oozing from his ears.

The next time Ramuell stirred, someone offered him water from a gut bota. His eyes were crusted with mucus and ash. He pried his eyelids open with his fingers and became aware of a yellowish light filtering in from the cave's mouth. He crawled to the entrance and saw the thousands of trees on the canyon floor were nought but smoldering stumps. Falling ash shrouded everything with several centimetres of grey death. He dropped his head and retched.

He could hear moans and voices from nearby caves. When a woman called out, Ramuell heard people scrambling to the front of their dwellings. He hollered, "Stay in your caves—until the sky stops falling." He knew breathing much of the ash would almost certainly cause illness or worse, it could be radioactive.

Standing just inside the cave's mouth, Shiya began a roll call of the Crow Clan's people: who was hurt, how severe were the injuries, and who was unhurt. Through the process of elimination she reckoned who among the Clan were missing, dead, or perhaps still unconscious. She also asked about food and water stores. By the time she completed the inventory, Ramuell had managed to prop himself into a sitting position with his back against a boulder.

The toddler Busasta startled Ramuell by climbing onto his

lap. He grabbed the little boy into his arms and began to weep. Busasta wasn't Ramuell's son or grandson, but he loved this child beyond all reason. Domhanian travelers had long since realized that their feelings for the planet's indigenes were, in fact, a phenomenon outside of reason, that those feelings were the product of a mysterious kind of extrasensory experience.

Shiya sat down beside Ramuell. "Dahl is dead," she said as she played handclap with Busasta who had wriggled into a sitting position on Ramuell's lap. Shiya began a meticulous recitation of the roll call information. Fourteen clanspeople had not responded to her calls. Three of the caves did not have any drinking water. It was impossible to know about adequate food stores, given that it wasn't known how long their sequestration might last – how long the ash would fall.

Having gathered his wits, Ramuell rose and went to his hollow in the back of the cave. He dug up a waterproof footlocker. The people of the Clan knew of the trunk buried beneath his sleeping furs. It was the subject of superstitious fear, which Ramuell did nothing to dispel. For the first time in over a decade, he removed the flight suit woven of metallic fibers. While not as safe as a hazardous materials suit, it would be better than only wearing the sapiens' leather clothing in the falling ash. He also had goggles and a breather.

Realizing this attire would frighten the already traumatized clanspeople, Ramuell wore the form-fitting flight suit under his leather clothes. He would remove the headgear immediately upon entering each cave.

Each cavern provided shelter for three to nine people depending on size, accessibility, and features. Ramuell had been sharing a cave with the Clan elder Dahl, Sinepo, her man Maponus, and their son Busasta. Shiya, the orphan who had grown up to become the Clan's alpha female, also lived in the shared cave.

Fortunately, Shiya and Ramuell had restocked their group's water supply the previous afternoon. They had three buffalo stomachs full as well as four botas that held about three litres each.

Taking the bota bags, Ramuell dashed from cave to cave to provide water and to further assess the situation. He didn't know what to expect and was unprepared for what he found.

Three bodies lay in front of one cave. They must have panicked and run out into the intense heat seconds after the explosion. Their fingertips and toes had ignited with fire spreading up their arms and legs. A pinkish liquid oozed from the scorched extremities and pooled on the ground. Ramuell was horrified and could only hope they'd lost consciousness immediately; it was likely at least a half-hour passed before death laid its final claim.

Inside Ramuell found six more people. Two were unconscious. Extreme heat had scorched their bodies. Blisters had burst and skin hung from their faces, chests, and legs like moss clinging to trees. These two had only hours to live. The other four people did not have physical injuries but were so traumatized they were unresponsive.

In the last cave Ramuell found Anbron holding her daughter on her lap. Sheets of skin were peeling off the infant's body. Anbron had been knocked unconscious and upon awakening realized the baby was missing. Panicked, she rushed barefooted from the cave and found her child's broken and burned body at the foot of the rock ledge, some four metres below.

Ramuell could see that the child had been dead for several hours. He cautiously took Anbron's hand and touched it to her baby's carotid artery. As tears rolled out of Anbron's eyes she exhaled a moan of hopeless despair. She handed over the dead body. Ramuell took the mutilated infant to the crypt cavern.

He returned and carried Anbron, whose feet were burned, to her sister's cave.

Upon returning to his own cave, he shed the loose-fitting clan clothing easily enough, but as he tried to peel off the flight suit his hands trembled so badly he could not grip the zipper pull. There were certain conventions about watching a person in their "private" quarters within a shared cave. Nevertheless, out of concern, Shiya was watching Ramuell's efforts. Though she had never seen a zipper and could not have imagined such a device, she walked over and after only a brief moment's inspection took hold of the pull tab and unzipped the suit from collar to crotch. When Ramuell looked at her with astonishment, he saw that she was not looking at the zipper. Shiya was staring directly into his eyes. She took his hand and gently pressed it against her gestating belly.

She held it there as Ramuell described what he'd found within the caves. He believed most of the injured clanspeople would likely survive, for a while at least. Of course, he had no way to explain that if the falling ash was radioactive none of them would be alive in a month. Madam Curie was yet tens of thousands of years in Shiya's future.

Ramuell had taken up residence with the sapiens of the Crow Clan following his expulsion from the Ghrain-3 Expeditionary Mission. The Clan inhabited a cluster of caves tucked into limestone cliffs near the bottom of a deep canyon. A dependable river ran almost due east through this section of the canyon. The clanspeople gathered fruit, nuts, roots and legumes that grew near the river's edge. They hunted and scavenged most of the meat they consumed and supplemented their protein intake with fish, insects, grubs and worms.

The Clan's canyon home was breathtakingly beautiful. It had been a good home, though the clanspeople lacked many things. Thousands of years would pass before the people of this planet would even contemplate what those things might be. They lacked any knowledge of germ theory. They had yet to conceptualize the tools necessary for agriculture. Medicine was a marriage between superstition and herbal remedies. Early death was a fact of life that the people simply accepted. They knew no better. Life was difficult, but it was the only life the Clan knew or could comprehend.

Ramuell had been the leader of a group of twelve Domhanian scientists assigned to study the sapien species. Anticipating their exile by Grandmaster Elyon, the group had "liberated" and divvied up a cache of equipment, weapons, and supplies from the orbiting station. Ramuell had buried his share of the materiel in waterproof boxes under enormous boulders in a side canyon a few kilometres downriver from the cliff dwellings.

As he lay on his bed of furs, with images of his horribly burned friends playing back-and-forth in his mind's eye, he contemplated the next move. If the fallout was from a thermonuclear device, retrieving his Radiation Particle Detector would be a death march. However, in his tour of the caves he had seen no symptoms of acute radiation syndrome. Perhaps a journey to the trove of supplies would be safe.

If either the Serefim Presidium or the Beag-Liath had detonated a device with low yields of radioactivity, the sooner the clan departed the greater their chances of survival. Even if there was no radioactive debris in the fallout, the tremendous volume of ash was contaminating the river, killing the fish, and poisoning the soil. Given the amount of heat they had experienced on the canyon floor, there was no doubt that the forest had been decimated on the plateaus above the canyon rims.

There would be no wood for cook fires, and flash floods would roar across the ash-covered ground and through the canyon when the early summer warmth melted the winter snow.

As Ramuell drifted into a tormented sleep, his last thought was that either by death or by banishment, their paradise was lost.

CHAPTER TWO
THE CALL
(2017 CE)

THE CALL CAME on a June evening just as one of northern New Mexico's monsoonal thunderstorms ebbed. It had been a violent affair with claps of thunder that sent the orange tabby to the safety of Carla's lap and the little black kitten to her hidey-hole beneath the covers of our bed. We had stepped outside to admire a spectacular double rainbow framing the Sangre de Cristo Mountains when Carla heard the phone ring. A few moments later I followed her into the house, and she handed me the phone. Eyes wide with astonishment she said, "The man said to hold for James Cortell."

Assuming it had to be some other James Cortell, I answered the phone with a casual "Hello." It was **not** some other James Cortell. It was the James Cortell who had served two terms as his state's Senator; Admiral James Cortell who despite his penchant for pacifism, had served his nation as Chairman of the Joint Chiefs of Staff; the James Cortell who had spent his life, both in public service and in retirement, trying to embolden humanity's embrace of our better angels.

"Can you put the phone on speaker, we'd like to talk with

you both. I have a proposal that I believe will interest you... No let's not go into details over the phone... If you're interested in meeting with us I'll have my assistant get your information in order to make travel arrangements for a trip to the farm in Puerto Rico, but we must insist that for now neither of you discuss this with anyone... Yes, I'm looking forward to meeting both of you too... Your first visit will only be for a week or so. After that we may be spending a good deal more time together. Hold on a sec, Mr. Williams is grabbing his tablet."

"Hello, Frank Williams here. So, how soon will you be able to get away? ... Rather than having neighbors watch the animals, perhaps you'd like to hire a house sitter... Now if you want to do that, I'll arrange to have some funds transferred to you to cover those costs... Late next week will be fine... We'll book you to Miami. Captain Roibal will meet you at the luggage claim. He'll fly you to Ponce in our plane. Following up on the admiral's comment, I cannot stress strongly enough the need for absolute confidentiality. We're placing a great deal of trust in your discretion." ...He chuckled, "Yeah, telling people you won a Caribbean vacation will be fine. Clearly you've mastered keeping secrets without telling lies... I'm looking forward to meeting you both next week as well."

Carla and I sat in the living room looking at each other in stunned disbelief. This kind of thing just did not happen. On that afternoon we as yet had little understanding of the true power of knowledge – nor the existential challenge of doubt.

CHAPTER THREE

TREES, GOLD, AND LSD

Two days later FedEx delivered an envelope with two $1500 First Citizens Bank prepaid Visa debit cards. The return address was the International Foundation for Sustainable Agriculture, 128 S. Tryon Street, Charlotte, North Carolina. The enclosed note was brief:

This should help with incidental costs you may have related to your trip to Puerto Rico. See you soon. – Frank Williams

The same day we received an email from Mr. Williams with our itinerary and flight confirmation. We would leave the following Thursday at 8:30 am from Albuquerque International Sunport, making connections in Atlanta and arriving in Miami at 5:00 pm. The return flight date was left "open."

We deplaned and got to the luggage carousel at about 5:20 pm. A strikingly handsome man with grey-green eyes, olive skin and lightly salted dark hair walked directly up to us and extended his hand. "I'm assuming you are the Beenes."

"Yes we are, but how did you know that?"

Grinning, "No other couples among the escalator stampede seemed to fit the bill. I'm Chris Roibal. If you'll follow me we'll fast forward to the next leg of your adventure."

Confused by how it was we looked like the couple that 'fit the bill', I asked, "But what about our luggage?"

"Oh, I took the liberty of having the Delta people transfer your bags directly to our shuttle—saves a lot of time. If we hurry we can still get to Havana in time for dinner with the boss."

In sync, if not harmony, Carla and I exclaimed, "Havana!?"

"Yeah, the admiral had a meeting with the Minister of Antiquities and some oceanographers from the University. He wants to mount another deep-water survey of ruins found some six hundred meters below the surface a few miles west of the Guanahacabibes Peninsula. He's convinced that site is much more mysterious than anyone imagines. Over the years his insights have proven uncanny time and again."

Carla looked at Chris for a long moment, then shifted her gaze to me, "Fortunately I remembered to grab our passports."

"Ye-ah!" Chris drawled. "When you come to see Admiral Cortell always, and I do mean **always**, bring your passport. You never know from one morning to the next where on this planet you might find yourself."

After the twenty-minute shuttle to the Airport General Aviation Center, the terminal used by business jets and small aircraft, Captain Roibal led us out onto the tarmac and directly to a Hawker Beechcraft King Air 250 with an off-white fuselage and a bright green tree painted on the tail. This was a good deal smaller plane than fit neatly into Carla's comfort zone, but the captain's businesslike demeanor during the preflight check bolstered her confidence – somewhat. I, on the other hand, was thrilled with the prospect of flight in this sleek twin-engine workhorse.

Once aboard we were feeling quite heady with the prospect of being the only passengers in the luxurious eight-seat cabin – and we were going to Cuba! We're old enough to have ambiguous childhood memories of Castro's revolution, the Bay of Pigs fiasco, and the Cuban missile crisis. Never had we dreamed that we might someday visit our closest island-nation neighbor.

Captain Roibal explained that we'd arrive at the Playa Baracoa Airport in under an hour. Only fourteen miles from Havana, the facility was a former airbase for the Cuban Revolutionary Armed Forces. Now it is used primarily as a VIP easy egress airport.

Chris, Carla, and I were met at the airport by a six-door "taxi" that had been fabricated by cutting two old 1960s era Russian Lada cars and welding the two pieces together into what came to be known as "embargo limousines." The ride, sans modern suspension, was a good deal rougher than our flight over the Straits of Florida.

After a few minutes bumping westward on the Carr Panamericana Highway, the Lada "limo" deposited us at the estate of Ricardo Gomez y Davila. We arrived just as dinner was being served. Señor Gomez y Davila jumped to his feet and waved us into the room. Arrayed down the length of a cherry wood banquet table was a buffet of seafood, green salad, red beans and rice.

Before we had taken even three steps into the room the spry eighty-eight-year-old Admiral Cortell had reached us. Captain Roibal stepped into our midst and adroitly made the introductions. "Sheesh, I wish I could do that." I joked. "I get up in the morning and check my driver's license to remember my own name!"

A quirk tugged the corners of the admiral's mouth. He turned to Carla and said, "Then it's good he has you around to keep him headed in the right direction."

The ice was broken and over the course of that dinner relationships were germinated that would lead all of us on a journey of exploration; a transformative adventure into the prehistoric past.

The following morning we were woken early and served a light breakfast and dark coffee in our room. Within an hour we were loaded in a Lincoln Town Car L and on our way to the airport. The admiral apologized for the early hour, explaining that he was a morning person and didn't like returning late in the day to the farm near Ponce, Puerto Rico.

Soon we were once again aboard the King Air 250, seated in plush leather seats on either side of a small fold-out table. Within minutes of takeoff, the admiral struck up **the** conversation. Carla said, "Hold on a second, Admiral. Would it be okay for me to move over and sit beside you? With this much engine noise, Gary's hearing aid is pretty much useless. I can use Sign Language to interpret for you when he doesn't understand."

"Of course, I'd be a fool to turn down an offer like that," the admiral replied, chuckling.

When Carla was buckled in her new seat, Cortell began again, "So, Mr. Beene, I understand you believe in angels."

My expression must have looked something like a video freeze-frame.

Mirth etched the admiral's crinkled face. "Okay, but you did write this article didn't you?" From his valise he pulled a copy of a 2009 "My View" article I had written for the Santa Fe New Mexican. One paragraph screamed from the page with neon HI-LITER. Pinning the sheet to the table with an index finger, Admiral Cortell spun it around and slid it toward me.

The paragraph read:

"The manifestation of the decision to embrace kindness as an attitude toward the world can be expressed only by our actions. The decision to be kind is the most powerful decision a person can ever make. Because of the butterfly effect, every individual act of kindness is passed and enhanced across generations. There are those who simply come to this life understanding this reality. They embody kindness intuitively. They are remarkable people. They are the angels who walk among us."

I looked up and said, "Yeah—I guess I was speaking metaphorically though."

"Suppose I told you a story that proves angels are quite real —that they do indeed walk among us and have been among us for many thousands of years. I've brought you here to determine if we might be able to do some work together. I'm contemplating writing about the history of those angels—more specifically a history of some fallen angels."

I glanced at Carla. Her expression was unreadable. Turning back to our host, I stammered, "I, uhm, I don't even know what to say."

"Hey, I'm an old man and you need to know I'm not a senile old man. I, on the other hand, need to know if you have the personality to take on a project like this. I've read your books. You have the capability, but there's a lot of distance between 'can do', 'want to', and 'will do.' That's not meant to be pejorative. It's a statement of fact."

"Well, the sales of my books wouldn't support the notion that I've nocked the 'can do' arrow," I replied.

"Nah, sales were not a factor in our deliberations. Anyway, there's a whole lot of crap that sells quite well and a lot of good writing that never gets discovered among Amazon's many millions of titles." The admiral grinned sheepishly and added, "But let's not sully our relationship this early with talk of money."

"Okay but let me ask a question. How did you find us, and why would you even consider us for this project?"

Sitting across the table from him I noted how the sandy blond locks of his youth had given way to the wispy white hair that now covered his head except for a bald spot on the crown. The admiral was not a large man. He may have been one of those men who had shrunk a bit with age. One thing that was striking was the size of his hands. They were much larger than one would expect on a man his size.

He leaned back in his seat and looked out the window, drew in a deep breath and said, "It would be true, but not the whole truth, if I said your style is what we've been looking for. It's more than just that. We've followed you on Facebook and read articles you've written for newspapers and journals. We've interviewed people you have worked for and people who have worked for you. I apologize for that breach of privacy, but we had to feel comfortable that we could trust you in terms of the confidential nature of what we have in mind.

"We've invited you to spend a week or so with us at the tree farm in order to gauge your interest and to determine whether you have the temperament necessary for this utterly implausible project."

The admiral stood and stepped aft to the refreshment center. "What would you like? We have tea, a few sodas, and some fresh hot coffee." With a proud grin he said, "I love this plane!"

The next morning we found ourselves in a spacious, modestly furnished hacienda. The front door opened onto a wide veranda appointed with swivel porch chairs. Carla and I found Admiral Cortell and another gentleman sitting quietly sipping coffee and watching the sunrise. When they heard the screen door close they spun their chairs toward us and rose to their feet.

With long arms that matched his 6’4” frame, the tall black man’s proffered handshake extended several inches beyond the admiral’s. “Hello Gary, Carla, I’m Frank Williams. We spoke on the phone a few days ago. How was your trip?”

“Hello, Mr. Williams.”

“Nope, Mr. Williams was my father. You must call me Frank.”

Grinning I replied, “Well okay then, Frank. I suspect due to your efforts, our trip was seamless.”

“We were shocked, in a good kinda way, about our Cuban detour,” Carla added.

Casting a sideways glance at Cortell, Frank responded, “Uhm, that was **not** on the itinerary I had arranged.”

“Hey, I’m a child of a twentieth-century military-industrial complex—you can’t have a good adventure without throwing in a few communists,” Cortell quipped.

“It seemed Señor Gomez’s villa was a bit too bourgeois for a communist,” I commented.

Turning to Frank, Carla said, “The Communist aristocracy notwithstanding, we do appreciate your efforts to get us here. Though we’re not exactly sure where ‘here’ is.”

Cortell said, “Just relax and let the experience wash over you. Soon enough you’ll understand our purposes—or not. If you do come to understand what we have in mind, you can decide if you want to join our little project—or not. Either way, be our guests and enjoy your stay."

Just then a lady rolled a cart onto the porch with a platter of steaming scrambled eggs, a bowl of papas fritas, a platter of tropical fruits, and a pot of coffee. Cheerfully the admiral commented, "Ahh, nothing like the arrival of food and coffee to punctuate a 'make yourselves at home' moment. Lupita, your timing is impeccable." Taking Carla by the elbow he guided her toward the veranda's oval table.

We were unfolding napkins when Captain Roibal walked onto the porch sniffing like a hunting hound and following his nose to the food cart. I couldn't help but think how unfair life is. A man should not be that good looking at any time, much less early morning. His charm and likeability were irresistible. I said, "Buenos días, Capitán. Quisieras café?" He held out a mug, which I filled from the thermos carafe.

———

Later that morning the admiral found me nosing around the farm's equipment sheds. He said, "Just exactly where I'd expect to find an old farm boy."

I looked up and replied, "Yeah, and I know enough to see that this is an impressive, well-funded operation."

Nodding, Cortell agreed, "Yes it is, and we're doing important work here."

"I have a question. What led a Navy salt to tree farming on the side of a mountain in Puerto Rico?"

"Now that is a question, isn't it? The short answer is, I know a great deal more than the average guy about genetic engineering. If you decide to join our project, you'll learn how that came to pass. In the meantime, let's take a walk and I'll explain what the Foundation is trying to do here. Our goal is to make long-term cultivation of hardwood trees a viable enterprise for family farmers in the tropical third world.

"You see, humans like wood. We do now and will continue to want beautiful woods for furniture and decorative building materials. Tree plantations have their place, but mono-species acreage has a minuscule environmental impact when compared to tropical rainforests. The current practice of razing and burning tropical hardwoods is unsustainable and just plain wrong. Tropical forests play an oversized role in our planet's biosphere, and biodiversity is a critical factor. Various species grow better during early life in the shade of other trees. Over a period of time they grow taller than the benefactor canopy species. That process may require a couple of centuries.

"Here on the farm we're trying to speed that dynamic by selectively planting and thinning several different species of hardwoods. The main problem with replacing deforestation with cultivation is lifespan. Most hardwoods grow slowly and live much longer than human farmers."

We were walking along a well-worn footpath lined with trees, vines, and flowering shrubs. It was hard to imagine that this forest was actually man-made. We stopped for a moment to take in the beauty. "We're addressing the lifespan challenge on two fronts," Cortell continued. "We're doing some of our work the old-fashioned way by selective breeding and grafting. We also annoy many of our environmentalist friends by aggressively pursuing the genetic modification of selected species." With a little smirk he added, "Of course we only engage smart environmentalists—the ones who understand that our efforts may be the only real hope we have for saving tropical forests."

We had taken several more paces when he turned to me and said, "Tell me what you know about junk DNA?"

"Only that the expression is a terrible misnomer."

"Right you are," the admiral replied. "In fact the phrase refers to a big bunch of material within DNA that doesn't encode protein sequences. The pejorative term, 'junk DNA,' was coined back in the 1960s—decades before we'd mapped the genome.

"A lot of really interesting stuff happens in non-coding DNA, but humanity has yet to even scratch the surface of what's going on in that so-called junk. I'm sure you've heard that humans and chimpanzees share 97% of their DNA. In an effort to bolster their world-according-to-Genesis nonsense, creationists claim that only about 75% of human/chimp DNA is similar. Actually, when we include junk DNA in the calculation, that figure is closer to correct than the 97% estimate."

"Really!? Next you're going to tell me that intelligent design theory is the truth and Darwin was smoking weed in the Galapagos!"

Cortell stopped in his tracks, fixed me with a penetrating gaze and said, "Yes I am. Now I don't know if Darwin smoked dope, but I **am** going to tell you that humans are the product of intelligent design."

My mouth must have gaped. The admiral chortled. "Don't worry, Gary, you're not in the company of a madman—though for many years I wondered about my sanity. When I say we're the product of intelligent design I'm speaking literally, but much to the chagrin of our creationist friends that design occurred over thousands of years and without all the theological abracadabra.

"Now you're wondering what in the heck I'm talking about. If you decide to come work with us, you're going to be astounded. You will never see life in the same way again."

That afternoon I told Carla of this conversation. She observed that the admiral's last comment was both intriguing and disconcerting. When I told her of his wish to continue the discussion on our next morning's walk, she insisted on joining us. She said hearing a summary of the conversation was "like smelling a neighbor's barbeque."

———

The three of us had walked in silence for a few minutes when the admiral said, "Carla, yesterday I was explaining to Gary that our Foundation is trying to address the issues of hardwood tree farming on two fronts. We discussed increasing tree growth rates in order to expedite the production of harvest-ready wood. Our efforts focus on modifying the trees' genomes as well as the development of feeding and fertilizing protocols. As you can see, we're making progress." He waved his huge hands in a wide arc at the giant plants towering above our heads.

Carla said, "A society grows great when old men plant trees whose shade they know they'll never sit in."

The admiral studied her for a moment then said, "Ah yes—some Greek wisdom." He paused, looking up into the canopy. "The thing is, tree farmers have to eat, which brings us to our second and perhaps more vexing issue—financing. How do we convince nations and the World Bank to up-front fund multi-generational agriculture endeavors? Even if our genetic modification efforts are a screaming success, the reality is that many species of hardwood trees planted by farmers today will likely be harvested by their grandchildren. So what are the generations of that family going to live on during the interim between planting and milling into saleable lumber?

"We must develop ways for farmers to earn a living during the years of work that goes into raising hardwoods. Our foundation has engaged some of the most innovative and brilliant economists in the world to pour their combined intellects into that beaker. Many of the ideas coming out of their think tank are elegantly simple—and simplicity may be the most important factor in selling the notion of raising rather than murdering forests.

"But articulating the economics of our project is made complex by our notion of wealth, which goes to the heart of what we value. And what humans were taught to value got **totally** screwed up many thousands of years ago."

We walked a few paces before Carla rose to the bait, "What do you mean?"

"**Gold**! I mean gold." He waited several seconds, letting the abruptness of his response settle in. "Have you ever wondered why we value gold?"

I scoffed, "Because the jewelry industry has convinced us that coupled with diamonds it is the forever expression of true love."

The admiral cackled. "Indeed they have, haven't they? Bully for them! But why? Why gold? Sure it's beautiful and makes lovely jewelry. It is a most wonderful and fascinating metal. It doesn't rust, tarnish or corrode. King Tut's gold mask was as lustrous when rediscovered in 1922 as it was the day the pharaoh was entombed some three thousand years earlier.

"Gold is remarkably conductive, able to transmit even tiny electrical currents in temperatures ranging from minus seventy to positive four hundred degrees. It's so ductile that a single ounce can be drawn into a wire almost fifty miles long. It's so malleable one ounce can be rolled into a three hundred square foot sheet. High purity gold can reflect ninety-nine percent of infrared radiation. The combination of malleability and reflectivity is why gold is used for our astronauts' space suits.

"Yet all of those remarkable properties cannot even begin to explain why humans have valued gold all the way back into prehistory. That litany of gold's qualities was not known and could not have been understood by our ancient ancestors. Hell, they didn't know about malleability, reflectivity, and infrared radiation. So, why have humans valued gold since time immemorial?"

"I suppose because it's beautiful and rare," I answered.

"I knew one of you would say that because that's the nonsense we've heard all our lives. We still see that explanation bandied about today. Take a look at this."

The admiral pulled a smartphone out of his cargo pants pocket and began tapping the screen. Within a minute he'd opened the '*History of Metals Timeline*' webpage. The top of the graphic began with '*Metals of Antiquities.*' It listed metals in an ascending order of "discovery." Gold was the first metal smelted about eight thousand years ago. Some eighteen-hundred years later came copper and two hundred years after that we began working with silver.

Pointing to the screen, Cortell said, "Look what it says right here—'*Stone Age man learned to fashion gold into jewelry. The popularity of gold is largely due to its scarcity, value, and mankind's fascination with the metal.*'"

Pulling his glasses off, he looked first at Carla then at me and said, "So there you have it, proof that humans have valued gold for eight thousand years because it's scarce and fascinating. What nonsense!

"How would ancient peoples have known gold was scarce? Though it has wonderful conductivity, ductility, malleability, etcetera, etcetera, what did any of those things have to do with the needs of hunter-gatherers? In addition to all its wonderful qualities, gold is too soft for tools, pottery, or any imaginable practical device our prehistoric ancestors needed.

"It was not until the late twentieth century that any significant industrial use for gold emerged. Did you know that we mine twenty-five hundred metric tons of gold annually, yet only about ten percent is sold for industrial applications? Fifty percent is sold for jewelry and about forty percent for investment; mostly purchased by people hedging against economic disaster. Does anyone really think we would eat gold if civilization collapsed?" he scoffed. "If you want to invest for a dystopian future, buy and preserve spices in vacuum-sealed bags. They would be a helluva lot more valuable commodity than gold!"

Waving a hand in front of his face as though swatting away the apocalyptic thoughts, he continued, "The point is, the value of gold has always been contrived, and it still is today. Which brings us back to the question, why gold? Actually, I suppose the question is both why and how."

"What do you mean by 'how'?" Carla asked.

Pointing again at his cell phone, "Look here, archeology tells us stone-age man began fashioning gold into jewelry some eight thousand years ago. We determined this from unearthed graves near Lake Varna in Bulgaria where people were buried wearing gold jewelry.

"As you know gold nuggets and flakes occur naturally and sometimes appear shining in streambeds."

"Sutter's Mill," I said.

"Correct! Now the alluvial gold theory proposes that prehistoric hunters and gatherers noticed the shiny objects in streambeds. At some point someone placed some nuggets on firepit stones, and voila, the gold melted. Seeing that it cooled and rehardened into the shape of the stone, these ancient peoples reasoned they could make casts of stone and shape the gold into aesthetically pleasing forms.

"While on its surface this theory makes some sense, the problem is gold melts at over 1900 degrees Fahrenheit, which is three times as hot as an open-pit wood fire. So, did our prehistoric ancestors build a forge? Or were they using coal rather than wood for campfires? Archaeologists have simply not been able to offer conclusive answers about how the Lake Verna gold jewelry was made.

"Even if you accept the idea that early civilizations were producing gold artifacts using alluvial gold, at what point did they begin mining ore? While there likely was enough gold lying around for small pieces of jewelry and sculpture, there certainly wasn't enough alluvial gold to mold the enormous pieces found in Egypt. Over four thousand years ago Egyptians were already producing about one ton of gold per year."

Turning to Carla, "Is this boring you to tears?"

"No, I'm fascinated."

Winking at her, he continued enthusiastically, "Thank you for humoring an old sailor. So, to produce one ton per year ancient Egyptians had to be smelting gold from ore. This fact raises all kinds of confounding questions. In its alluvial state gold nuggets or flakes are pretty obvious, but gold in ore sediments doesn't really resemble those eye-catching baubles.

"Did some hunter stub his toe on a rock, pick it up and say to himself, 'Hmmm, this rock has gold in it.' He coupled this remarkable observation with an epiphany that he could crumble the rock by setting it in a fire. He could then pound the crumbled rock in a stone mortar until it was reduced to pea-size gravel. Next, using millstones he could crush the gravel to the consistency of flour, then rub the powder on an inclined board, pouring water over it all the while. The crushed stone matter would wash away leaving gold powder adhering to the wood. Finally, he'd build a 1900 degree fire, melt the powder and pour the liquefied gold into molds made of God only knows what. That would be quite a remarkable set of insights, wouldn't you say?"

"Perhaps a bit too remarkable," I replied.

"Exactly! Downright preposterous! And that's why the question is not just why gold, but also how."

"And I suppose you're going to answer these questions," Carla suggested.

"I can, but it's going to take a good deal of your time. It would be better to think of this conversation, as well as that stuff about intelligent design, as a tease."

I chuckled, "So intelligent design was yesterday's tease, and you saved the really believable stuff for today."

By now we'd made a complete circuit and had returned to the hacienda. With a warm smile, the admiral waggled his index finger at us, turned, strode across the veranda and entered the front door. Class was over and we'd been dismissed.

We spent the next few days wandering around the farm, engaging in stimulating conversations, and savoring the delicious cuisine. On our sixth night I asked Carla, "So, what do you think?"

She replied, "I think the admiral probably has the most arresting eyes I've ever seen—I'm not sure if it's the bright green or the rings of gold flecks."

"Aww, come on..."

She laughed, "Okay, I think **if** the admiral and Frank are trying to sell us on the idea of coming to work for them, it's an exceedingly soft sale. Perhaps they've decided we're not a good fit and they're just too polite to tell us to go home."

During the previous evenings' dinners we had been joined by various combinations of neighbors and dignitaries, scientists and economists. On this night, the dinner table was set for only four. We arrived just as Frank walked in with the one martini he allowed the admiral each evening.

"Ah, just in time," Admiral Cortell declared as we entered. "Perhaps this will be a two martini night."

"Probably not," Frank responded drolly as he pulled out a chair for Carla.

"Well, you can't blame a guy for trying—or so they say."

The conversation was affable and stimulating, but it seemed something of great consequence was not being said. Quite abruptly Frank turned to the admiral and said, "I think it's time we talk turkey."

Without missing a beat Cortell pivoted to face us, "Here's the thing—I'm an old man. I have carried an extraordinary cache of knowledge in my head most of my life. I couldn't share this knowledge with anyone other than Frank here—and many years later my daughter. For over six decades I've made extensive notes and recorded hundreds of hours of what we might call recollections. I've come to believe it would be unforgivable for me to take these memories with me to the grave, but I have neither the skills nor enough years left to marshal a coherent narrative of this incredible tale."

Raising a hand and waving it slightly, he added, "Now I use the word memories loosely. Let me explain.

"When I was a young man, just a few months after returning from service in the Korean War, I became quite ill. It began with a fever, muscle pain, and then an excruciating headache. Rayleen and I were living near the Naval Base in Charleston, South Carolina. I'd been too ill to go to work for a couple days. I was walking back to our bed after using the bathroom when I collapsed in a heap at the bedroom door.

Rayleen called the base clinic, and they sent an ambulance." Chuckling softly, "I was a bit more muscled-up back in the day and Rayleen was just a slip of a girl. There's no way she could've dragged me to our car by herself.

"By the time we arrived at the local hospital, I'd slipped into a coma. Within hours the medical director had called my father in Annapolis with a grim diagnosis. I had contracted eastern equine encephalitis. The medical staff were extremely worried because back then almost one in four people who were infected died from complications of the virus. To make the prognosis even worse, an encephalitis coma almost always resulted in severe brain damage.

"As you know, it takes resources to access high quality medical care. That was true in 1954 and no less so today. Fortunately for me, my family had resources, namely friends in high places.

"Dad had been the commander of a battleship escort group in the North Atlantic during World War II. On one of his voyages across the Atlantic, a man named Leonard Scheele was aboard his ship. Colonel Scheele was a medical doctor en route to take command of the Medical Department of the Army in the African theater. Dad and Dr. Scheele became friends on that voyage. As fate would have it, in 1948 Dr. Scheele was appointed Surgeon General of the United States. I've never known what strings were pulled, but within twelve hours I was loaded on a military med-evac aircraft and flown to Rochester, Minnesota. Have you folks ever been to the Mayo Clinic?"

"Yes, in fact we were there just a few years ago in their GI Clinic," Carla replied.

"What did you think?" the admiral asked.

"The place is astounding. I was having some serious complications related to my rheumatoid arthritis. After months of daily nausea they nailed the diagnosis and got me back on my feet."

"So you know," Cortell continued, "if you're seriously ill, Mayo **is** the place to go. And that was the case back in 1954 too. I have no recollection of any of this and can only tell you what Rayleen told me. She, a doctor, and a nurse flew with me from Charleston. The medical staff were expecting us and immediately began trying to reduce the brain swelling that they assumed was serious, reduce my fever which they knew was dangerously high, hydrate, and nourish me. I don't know exactly what treatments were prescribed. What I do know is that I didn't awaken from the coma as quickly as they'd have liked.

"Now the electroencephalogram was not an altogether new technology, but it was not as ubiquitous or advanced as it is today. The Mayo neurology clinic probably had the most sophisticated equipment and qualified personnel on earth at that time. Yet from the moment they hooked me up to the electrodes the neurologists were stumped by my brain activity.

"As I understand it, they expected to see a particular pattern of theta and delta waves, perhaps even some alpha and mu waves depending on the depth of my coma. They would have been relieved with that EEG pattern as it would have indicated I was perhaps minimally conscious.

"Instead, what they found was a brain running four-minute miles. Hours of beta and gamma waves were interspersed with periods of alpha. Occasionally it would appear that my brain had gone to sleep for a couple of hours with the EEG recording only delta and theta waves. This caused quite a stir all the way from Mayo Clinic to the Surgeon General's office."

"You weren't really in a coma at all," I observed.

"I don't think there is a medical term that describes my

state of consciousness during those eleven weeks," the admiral replied.

"Eleven weeks!" Carla exclaimed.

"Yes. My brain was running in overdrive, but I didn't wake-up and do not recall hearing any conversations around me for eleven weeks. Then one day, and I remember this as if it happened an hour ago, I opened my eyes and saw a nurse marking the paper on the clipboard at the foot of my bed. I said, 'Good morning. What's your name?' She shrieked, threw the clipboard up in the air and bolted out the door. She ran down the hall squealing." With a falsetto voice Admiral Cortell mimicked the nurse, "He's awake, he's awake, he's awake! Get the doctor! Call Mrs. Cortell! He's awake!"

The admiral's affectations were so amusing Carla and I burst out laughing. Even Frank, who no doubt had heard the story numerous times, let loose a throaty chuckle.

"Now I'd say that moment of mirth calls for a second martini, wouldn't you?" The admiral held the empty glass by its stem and shook it in Frank's direction. Frank rolled his eyes, snatched the glass from Cortell's hand, and strode into the kitchen. "Yes, just so. I thought we might be able to prevail upon the always vigilant and ever so conservative Mr. Williams tonight."

"So what happened then?" Carla asked.

"Ah, everyone was either laughing or crying or both. The room was crowded with staff who were soon joined by Rayleen and a couple of friends. I was poked and prodded; my temperature and blood pressure were taken dozens of times. They looked at my toenails and massaged my feet. They made me demonstrate my grip strength and looked down my throat. They looked in my ears and up my bum. Looking back I suppose I was more amused than confused at the time.

"Soon it ceased to be funny. It's hard work getting your

strength back after lying prone for so long. Extensive physical therapy was required in order to regain the youthful vigor that had, to some extent, defined me prior to the illness. But the physical challenges turned out to be trifling compared to the emotional issues.

"Incrementally I had a growing awareness of thoughts that didn't make sense and recollections I couldn't place. I mentioned this to Rayleen and my doctor one morning. The doctor explained it was not unusual for people emerging from a coma to have thought disorders.

"At that time, our understanding of coma was still quite rudimentary. My doctor suggested perhaps I was just remembering dreams. Given how alert and articulate I was, he assured us I'd likely have a complete recovery. In other words, 'don't worry about these odd thoughts, they'll pass.'

"Rayleen and I were naturally relieved by his assurances. From that moment Rayleen became a rock of strength and the voice of reason. Perhaps that's why I was never able to tell her the whole **unreasonable** truth. The story I'm going to tell you was a secret that haunted our fifty-two year marriage. It nagged at me and vexed me in ways I cannot even now come to terms with. I tell myself if she is watching down on me, she understands and has forgiven my deception. I tell myself that, but I can only hope it is so. I suppose my feelings of guilt and ambivalence are because the deception implied I didn't trust her with the truth." The admiral's voice cracked, "...and for that, I haven't been able to forgive myself."

Frank had just returned with the martinis. He reached over and gripped Cortell's forearm, squeezing it reassuringly. We sat quietly for a couple of minutes waiting for the admiral to continue. "Perhaps because of that guilt I decided to tell our daughter, Kelsey, after Rayleen was gone." With a snort he added, "And she's been kind enough to be a skeptic without being a denier.

"During those days at Mayo, each morning I awoke with more and more recollections; more and more notions of things about which I could not possibly know. And it was not only after sleep that these images emerged. I would be reading something or watching something outside the window and suddenly an unbidden idea or memory would pop into my head.

"It seemed my only relief from the crazy thoughts came while I was doing physical therapy. So I tried to exercise all the time. At first the medical staff applauded my tenacity, but it became clear my regimen was too compulsive to be laudable. In actuality, escaping into physical activity didn't really work anyway. After I'd showered and relaxed a few minutes, the brain's floodgate would open to torrents of new ideas and memories.

"As is often the case with people in the middle of a crisis, I believed somehow geography would mitigate the fix I was in. Because I was making such good progress physically, and because I kept my mouth shut about the emotional turmoil, I was released to return to Charleston within a few weeks." The admiral chuckled, "As you might guess, American Airlines therapy wasn't successful. In fact the change of scenery only seemed to provide more fodder for new and increasingly disturbing thoughts. At some level I knew these ideas were not the product of dreams. But because I had no way to understand what was happening to me, I slipped further and further down the rabbit hole.

"While I could deceive Rayleen about the source, there was no way to hide the fact that I was in trouble. She talked to our doctor. I was too confused, proud, stupid—take your pick—to do so myself. He again assured her my progress was remarkable, particularly given that the medical professionals had believed I'd probably never recover.

"This time she was not so reassured. She had to go home and deal with a man who'd come out of a coma but didn't want to come out from under the bed covers. I was on extended medical leave. My commanding officers assumed that was because I was still overcoming the effects of the encephalitis, not because I was too depressed to work.

"I told Rayleen she needed to just put me in a psychiatric hospital." Cortell looked away and sniffed. "But she had an aunt who suffered with depression and was in and out of a facility over in Georgia. Back in those days a routine treatment for people with severe depression was electroshock. The protocol was to strap a person to a table and fire massive jolts of electricity through the brain, usually without the benefit of anesthesia or muscle relaxants. During one session her Aunt Tabitha had such a severe seizure she broke the ulna in her right arm. There was almost always significant memory loss subsequent to the treatments. I knew about the memory loss side-effect and was hoping electroshock might wipeout my unwanted memories. Thankfully, Rayleen was adamant that no one, under any circumstances, was going to hook me up to an electroconvulsive therapy machine.

"I was too confused and depressed to even have the energy to argue with her. I began to believe that brain damage was causing me to hallucinate. We talked about going to see a psychiatrist but remember this was 1954. Rayleen said she would support whatever decision I made. Then she asked, 'If it ever leaks that you've seen a shrink, are you willing to retire in twenty years as an Ensign?' Her question stunned me. I hadn't really considered the impact of mental illness on my career. I'd always envisioned someday being a ship's captain.

"So it was, I made the decision to get better—as if it would be that easy! The fact that I was able to make myself get out of bed, put on the uniform, and go to work did not make my "hallucinations" go away. I thought I was losing my mind. As the collection of memories kept growing I found myself having subvocalized conversations with people I could remember but did not know—people who didn't even look like us.

"I was able to do my job well enough I suppose. I smiled and spoke confidently. I laughed at the right kind of jokes and chastised sailors for the wrong kinds of jokes. People on the base went out of their way to welcome me back. I was liked and respected. I should have been awarded an Oscar. But by the time I got home each evening I would collapse in bed from the exhaustion of pretense. I lost a lot of weight because I often skipped dinner.

"Finally, I became so desperate I spoke to my father about what was going on. I didn't tell him about the exact nature of my hallucinatory thoughts, but I shared enough for him to understand that I was in trouble. I told him Rayleen was shaken but standing firm.

"Again my dad put in a call to Surgeon General Scheele, and again strings were pulled. I was assigned temporary duty at the U. S. Embassy in Great Britain. That was our cover story anyway. The real reason we went to Britain was to see a doctor named Ronald Sandison at the Powick Hospital near Worcester.

"It was about a two-hour drive from London to Worcester. Each time I had a couple of days off, Rayleen would get a car and we'd drive over and stay the night at an inn. I met with Dr. Sandison several times for what he called diagnostic assessment. His staff performed a thorough physical exam and he interviewed me and Rayleen extensively.

"It was not until our fourth or fifth visit to the hospital that he proposed a radical treatment. At the time we didn't appreciate just how radical. We'd never heard of psychedelic therapy. The only thing we really understood was that he wasn't going to pound my brain with electricity. Even if I had known what lysergic acid diethylamide was, I'd have agreed to the treatment. Partly because Dr. Sandison was an impressive guy, but mainly because I was just so desperate to make the bizarre thoughts go away.

"Sandison was an unapologetic proponent of using psychedelic drugs as a tool in the psychiatric regimen. Now he wasn't a Timothy Leary kind of nut case. He didn't believe LSD was the source of spiritual enlightenment. In fact, Sandison was a rather religious man, and a sailor too by the way.

"Some years later, just out of curiosity, I did some research on his use of the drug. He treated several hundred patients with LSD during the 1950s and 60s, but it was not his treatment of choice for most patients. He used it as a fallback therapy for the treatment of neuroses and depressions that were resistant to more traditional approaches.

"He believed it likely that I'd sustained some subtle but profound brain damage from the encephalitis. For that reason, he didn't consider me a great candidate for what was in that era the standard psychoanalytic approach. He seemed to understand from our interviews that I was on a slippery slope and sliding fast.

"Sandison invited us to his home. We arrived at mid-morning on a Saturday. He offered us tea and biscuits. Actually, he offered Rayleen biscuits and told me it would be better not to eat anything prior to ingesting the drug. His wife, Evelyn, joined us and we all sat in the parlor talking and relaxing for almost an hour. Evelyn asked Rayleen to ride into town with her to do some shopping. Dr. Sandison led me to a bedroom they had converted to a combination library-office. He put on a record of soft melodic music and asked me to take a seat on a

Victorian style couch. He began regaling me with stories of his sailboat adventures. Soon he went to his desk and produced a tiny vial of liquid.

"I drank the sip from the vial and sat back while Sandison continued his stories of sailing and fishing. As I listened I became aware of perception distortions and an altered sense of time. In fact, the complete buckling of time is what I remember most. I wouldn't say I enjoyed the experience nor was it a 'bad trip.' Psychologically speaking, I'd say the drug had no real therapeutic effect." Cortell stopped and held up his index finger and shook it dramatically. "Except for one thing—one very, very important thing. After taking LSD I knew what a hallucination was and how it felt. I knew for a fact my strange thoughts, the incessant internal dialogue with people whom I'd never met, my impossible recollections were absolutely **not** hallucinations.

"We spent the night at the Sandison's home and Rayleen drove us back to London the next morning. I can remember exactly where we were when the realization that I had not been hallucinating struck me. I remember the very moment my recovery began. That awareness occurred over a period of about thirty seconds. I spent the next thirty years coming to terms with what it all meant."

Cortell leaned across the table, his clasped hands extended in front of him. The barely touched second martini rested behind his interwoven fingers. He stared in our direction with a somewhat unnerving expression and said, "You see those bizarre thoughts—those mental images **are** memories. I remember a life that was lived thousands of years ago. I have vivid recollections of that life. I remembered more and more details of that life as time passed. Even to this day I continue to remember more specifics of events that transpired many millennia ago."

Carla and I could not take our eyes off the admiral. After a moment he continued, "With that I'm sure you think I'm a crazy old kook. Let me assure you I may be old, but I'm not crazy. I'm not saying that I lived before—that I am some kind of reincarnation. You see, I know enough of that long-ago life to understand how it is I have these memories. I remember the life of one of the fallen angels. That's the story I want to tell you. It's a story recorded in my junk DNA. It's the story I want you to write!"

Incredulously, I said only, "What!?"

The admiral and Frank were sitting directly across the table from Carla and me. They turned toward each other, then exploded in uproarious laughter. Frank crowed, "I told you that's all he'd say."

Carla and I were yet too stunned to join in the levity. With a toothy grin Frank added, "If you think that disclosure was bad, wait until he drops the next bomb on you."

Regaining his composure, the admiral continued, "What you must understand is the fallen angels were anything but angels. They were travelers. They were industrialists. They were scientists. They were scholars. They were many things. They were egotistical and fallible—oh God how fallible they were! As it turns out though, they were not just passing through. They came and they stayed. They're still living in every cell of our bodies."

"What does that mean?" I implored.

"Now you've heard the claim by the so-called pro-life crowd that life begins at conception."

"Of course," Carla replied.

"I absolutely assure you that is patent nonsense. Was the ovum not alive before fertilization? What about the sperm? Could a dead sperm swim upstream to find and enter an egg? Of course it was alive too. Life began long before the fertilization of any egg in a womb. You see, life has been surging forward in fits and starts for billions of years. What the not so angelic angels did was tinker with this planet's DNA. We, sitting around this table, are the product of their intelligent design."

We sat, each with our own thoughts, for several moments when Carla asked, "What did you mean when you said you continue to have new memories of that past life?"

The admiral looked into her ocean blue eyes, "I've spent a good deal of time over the years thinking about that. I've come to believe it has to do with the way human memory works. Let me give you an example. Tell me what you remember about second grade."

With no hesitation Carla responded, "I remember sitting for my school photo with cat scratches on my face."

"There you go," Cortell said. "For whatever reason, that was a profound experience for you and it created a powerful memory. Without even thinking about it, that image surfaced almost immediately in your consciousness. Now tell me everything else about your second grade year."

"Pfft, I don't think so! My kids have long accused me of having 'Carla's-heimers'."

Cortell laughed. "You make my point. We can remember some things almost instantly, but most of our memories come to us as the result of external stimuli. Sometimes memories pop into our heads because of something someone said or something we saw or read.

"But most memories are ephemeral and fleeting. The old bedrock of jurisprudence, eyewitness testimony, has proven to be horrendously unreliable. That's because over time our memories are altered by interceding events. They fade with age. We repress some memories. We change some memories to make them worse than the events really were. We also sanitize memories through a kind of mental alchemy.

"We cannot remember everything that happened to us in the second grade," gesturing toward Carla, "because we either lack the catalyzing stimuli or the memory has been altered. But perhaps more important than all of that, most of the events we've experienced during our lives are simply not recited to memory. Given all that, just imagine the problems with a human brain trying to recall a life lived thousands of years ago —the life of an extraterrestrial."

When we retired that evening I had little doubt what our decision would be. Nevertheless, the next morning at breakfast I had to ask again, "Why would you want us to compile your story into a book?"

"For the last several years Frank and I have been searching for a writer with the time and, more importantly, the temperament to take on this job."

Mischievously Carla asked, "And just what makes you think Gary's crazy enough for you?"

Laughing, the admiral asked, "Well he is, isn't he?"

"No doubt! But that hardly answers the question!" Carla teased.

Feigning insult I asked, "Crazy or not, what do you mean by 'the right temperament'?"

Frank shared one of his finely honed observations. "It seems to me that in order to do this story justice the writer must be open-minded enough to embrace the unbelievable, yet agnostic enough to ask the right questions."

The admiral pursed his lips and nodded. "That's quite good, Frank."

Turning to us he said, "Now if you decide to join us, you need to understand it will be a full-time commitment. Oh, we'll find some time to go to the beach and do a few scuba dives, but as I said earlier, I'm no youngster. While we never know when departure from this life might come, at my age one can be certain the end draws nigh."

PART TWO

We returned to Santa Fe, engaged the services of a house-sitter, and arranged auto-drafts for our recurring bills. Three weeks later we were back in Puerto Rico.

On our first morning back at the hacienda, when the admiral finished his second cup of coffee, he stood and said, "It's time for us to get started."

Following him into the library, we did not fully appreciate the enormous leap we were taking into the abyss of humanity's dark prehistory.

The narrative set down from the story told by James Cortell.

CHAPTER FOUR

RIDING NEUTRINOS

DOMHAN-SIOL IS the fourth planet of eighteen orbiting a yellow K-class star. It has an abundance of gaseous, liquid, and some frozen water. Life began its remarkable evolutionary journey on the planet some seven billion annum ago.

The sentient beings that evolved on Domhan-Siol wanted to believe the cosmos was teeming with life. Domhanian scholars proposed theoretical models that estimated the number of technologically advanced civilizations in the galaxy. The variables included: the rate of star formation, the number of planets per solar system environmentally suitable for life, the fraction of life-bearing planets that evolved sentient life, the fraction of civilizations that developed technologies emitting detectable signals, and the length of time such civilizations produced those energy signatures.

Initially this formula was merely a brain teaser, but over time Domhanians became obsessed with finding extraterrestrial life. The more focused they became on this quest, the more they refined the formula, and the more discouraged they became. Technologically advanced civilizations were simply not as abundant as they had hypothesized.

During the early centuries of Domhanian space exploration they invested heavily in extraterrestrial mining. They became increasingly dependent upon imports of minerals from planets, moons, and asteroids throughout their solar system. Enormous industries producing almost incalculable wealth grew out of these enterprises.

Though the search for extraterrestrial intelligence had been fruitless and their enthusiasm flagged, Domhanians did not abandon the effort. They were astounded and ecstatic when a spacefaring species visited the solar system of Domhan-Siol. They called the extraterrestrial visitors Natharians. However, Domhanians were crestfallen when they realized the Natharians would neither respond to nor initiate any form of communication.

They came to believe the Natharians were probably a lifeform so different that interspecies communication would be a difficult proposition, if even possible. They also theorized that Natharian space travel technology was based on a branch of physics unimagined by the scientists of Domhan-Siol.

Domhanians had for centuries understood that antimatter particles could coalesce to form antiatoms the same way protons and electrons form atoms. However, virtually everything they observed in the universe was made of matter rather than antimatter. So where was all that antimatter?

They were also aware of the existence of an electrically neutral subatomic particle that did not behave like any other type of matter. (*Tens of thousands of years after this discovery by Domhanians, humans on Earth would identify these particles and call them neutrinos.*) Even though neutrinos are infinitesimally small, they are so numerous they have approximately the same mass as all the stars in the galaxy combined. Every second, billions of neutrinos pass through every cubic centimetre of matter virtually everywhere in the cosmos.

Because they are neutrally charged, Domhanian scientists were unable to confirm the existence of a neutrino's antimatter correlate. Their search for the antineutrino went on for decades. During this time they continued to observe many dozens of Natharian spacecraft visiting Domhan-Siol's solar system. Applying known principles of physics, Domhanians were baffled by the frequency of Natharian visits.

Then a team of theoretical physicists was struck with an inspired epiphany. They proposed and soon proved that most antimatter does not exist in this physical universe. Rather it is deposited in another dimension of a multiverse. This discovery led to the realization that the matter-antimatter model simply did not apply to neutrinos.

The new science predicted that not only could neutrinos pass through other matter unimpeded, they also passed through the barriers between dimensions of the multiverse and through folds in the fabric of space-time. A neutrino could exist in dimension Alpha, cross over into dimension Beta for just a few days, then reenter dimension Alpha many trillions of kilometres away; the effect being that the neutrino had traveled an unfathomable distance relative to dimension Alpha.

Domhanians realized that neutrinos are the threads that knit the fabric of the multiverse together. Over the course of many decades they learned how to weave clusters of neutrino threads into interdimensional energy conduits. They came to see these neutrino streams as the neural pathways of the cosmos; an interdimensional corpus callosum.

Domhanian scientists theorized that Natharians were not only moving energy along the neutrino threads between dimensions, but they had learned how to fold additional mass into neutrino streams. If Domhanians could develop a technology to accomplish that feat, the pathways could become neutrino tunnels between dimensions and across the galaxy. This theoretical possibility underpinned whole new areas of study.

All the while there were dozens of pious sects zealously claiming that in the entire galaxy only Domhanians had been created in the image of an all-powerful deity. Among these cultists it seemed comforting, and even became vogue, to mock intellectuals and their scientific "mumbo jumbo."

Thousands of annum before they embarked on space exploration, a cultural homogenization had occurred on Domhan-Siol. Though there remained some regional eccentricities, for the most part linguistic and cultural differences were inconsequential.

This integration process naturally resulted in a blending of the genepool. Racial differences all but disappeared. Adults ranged in height from about 1.6 to 2.1 metres. There was no significant difference in gender sizes, though on average males tended to be slightly larger than females.

They were a symmetrical, bipedal species: two eyes and ears, one mouth, and one nose. They had two arms with hands reaching about mid-thigh. Their hands had six digits; five fingers with an opposing thumb. Likewise, their feet had six toes.

Domhanians had a fully developed forehead above thick eyebrows. The parietal area in the back of the skull sloped back in the shape of an elongated egg. Their skin color varied from darkish cream to light olive. They had scant facial hair though their heads were covered with thick curly locks, ranging in color from shiny sorrel to almost flat black. They also had fine, light-colored hair sparsely covering the rest of their bodies.

All in all, they considered themselves quite a handsome species.

INTERLUDE #1

August 2017
Santa Fe, New Mexico

Since the beginning of our project we had worked primarily in the hacienda library at the farm in Puerto Rico. We'd also spent a few days at Admiral Cortell's home on Lake Norman just outside of Charlotte, North Carolina.

Both North Carolina and Puerto Rico are muggy in late summer, whereas Santa Fe's seven thousand foot altitude makes for quite pleasant Augusts. Since Santa Fe's Indian Arts Market had long been on the admiral's bucket list, we decided to retreat to the high country of northern New Mexico for a spell.

Carla had been listening to Cortell's description of the Domhanian people. When she walked into our small office/library and set two freshly brewed lattes on the desk she asked, "So, Admiral, what did they **really** look like?"

"Why, thank you my dear," Cortell said as he leaned back

in the chair and wove his fingers together behind his head. "Egyptians! We looked like Egyptians."

I scribbled a note and dated it. This was the very first time he had used a first-person pronoun when referring to the people of Domhan-Siol.

Cortell chuckled and said, "Now that's not very descriptive is it? You know those five-thousand-year-old paintings and sculptures of the Pharaohs and Queens of Egypt's Old Kingdom?"

Carla nodded.

"Well, those weird head dresses they wore that sloped way to the back—that was the shape of Domhanian heads. And the skin color; most Domhanians' skin color was very close to the color of those ancient Egyptians."

"Mesopotamians also wore similar head coverings," I added.

"Yeah, many cultures did. Some even bound the growing heads of infants with cords to elongate the parietal area. You ever wonder what that was all about?" Cortell paused, looking out the office window at the aspen trees Carla and I had planted in the back yard a decade earlier. "But they got it wrong. Sculptures of the Anunnaki have little pointed or big square hats and long square beards—that was all wrong. The Old Kingdom Egyptians—they nailed it."

"Wait a minute—you mean the Egyptians designed headwear to mimic the skull shape of Domhanians?" Carla asked.

The admiral shrugged and again looked out the window at the leaves of the aspen trees quaking in the breeze. After a long moment he swiveled his chair around, inhaled deeply and said, "That's a great latte."

When Carla smiled he winked at her, then turned back to me and said, "Enough lollygagging, let's get back to work. And now I want to tell you a bit of the Domhanian backstory. You need to understand some things about their history."

CHAPTER FIVE
LIFE BELONGS TO LIFE

Admiral Cortell continues his story:

POLITICAL SUBDIVISIONS on Domhan-Siol were neither partisan nor geographic. In almost every respect governance was the outgrowth of corporate business structures. Though Domhanian culture valued and fostered personal liberty and responsibility, their government was a corporatocracy.

Workers were required to invest a portion of their compensation in their employers' businesses. Those investments were held in trust for employees and their families. Earnings from the investments were disbursed to provide for housing, retirement, medical, and educational needs. The principal amount invested by workers could never be withdrawn though it could be passed from parent to offspring. After a couple generations of corporate loyalty, the earnings from a family's investments often became quite sizable. Many families became rather wealthy, but offspring who chose a different career path lost any claim to the investment earnings from the nest egg held by the family's employer.

This investment model had its detractors. The most outspoken critics claimed it was a "golden handcuffs" scam. Nevertheless, given Domhanians' natural conservatism, this method of capitalizing corporate enterprises endured for centuries. As space exploration efforts became industrialized, frays began to rend the fabric of the multigenerational marriages between corporations and families. This, in large part, was due to extended off-world work assignments in environments that were quite challenging.

When it became obvious that jobs in low gravity environments took decades off one's life, volunteers for extraterrestrial postings shriveled. Corporations found it almost impossible to recruit for those positions. Massive investments in robotics and other labor-saving technologies had some impact, but did not eliminate the need for crews of live, on-site workers. Various systems of workforce coercion were attempted with limited success. What corporations needed was a dependable source of reliable conscripted laborers.

Meanwhile the quest to replicate Natharian technologies marched relentlessly onward. Over the course of several decades physicists, mathematicians, and engineers teamed up to develop a prototype 4D-Initiator. The device was designed to produce then hitch a ride on an artificially generated neutrino stream through dimensions and across the galaxy.

The first tentative steps into the interdimensional unknown involved the dispatch of various kinds of time and distance measuring devices. Microbial organisms traveled next, soon followed by more advanced lifeforms. Finally, the big day arrived. After millions of annum of evolution, sentient life on Domhan Síol stood on the threshold of leaving their solar system behind.

Most Domhanians were intrigued and cheered these

efforts with pride and awe. But in the background there was an undercurrent of doubt. The more moderate cultists found the specter of identifying other possibly far more advanced species existentially disconcerting. The most radical cultists claimed that space exploration was an affront to their god. They screeched that the 4D-Initiator would open an interdimensional portal through which all manner of evil might flow. They had no idea!

Early Domhanian explorers found life on planets orbiting stars within the narrow band where water exists in its liquid state. However after centuries of 4D galactic exploration they had discovered only fourteen worlds with sentient life-forms and none with technologically advanced civilizations.

Domhanian theorists coined the phrase, "Life belongs to life" to articulate a belief that life's prime directive is to reproduce itself. A philosophy emerged among many Domhanians that the enhancement of evolving sentient life-forms was a noble endeavor worthy of a great species.

When scientists began genetically augmenting extraterrestrial species, Anotas-Deithe Command implemented rigid protocols for the classification and release of information about those activities. The existence of that classified information just served to intensify paranoia among the deity cults. Most cultists remained steadfastly opposed to space exploration.

Social psychologists theorized this radicalism was the result of a fear response to the Natharians. Decades after their discovery, many cultists still refused to acknowledge Natharian existence. They refused to read, study, or even try to understand the evidence. To do so would negate one of the most basic tenets of their faith; that Domhanians sat at the apex of an all-knowing deity's creation.

While most Domhanians accepted the scientific evidence as irrefutable, among the more fanatical cults this acceptance actually exacerbated a xenophobia that had not been seen on Domhan-Siol for millennia. That fear behaved much like a recessive gene. It had lain dormant since the planet's "unification," but given the right stimuli, these anxieties manifested full-blown among a surprising number of people who carried the right combination of predispositions.

At the other end of the ideological spectrum were Domhanians who believed every morsel of new scientific knowledge had the potential to produce profits. At some level, this attitude was reasonable and even beneficial in terms of advancing galactic exploration. Corporations lavishly funded the development of technologies necessary to harvest resources from extraterrestrial sites. Over the course of several centuries, the values undergirding Domhanian galactic exploration veered away from its focus on science. Commercial opportunism drove most exploration decisions. Almost without notice, scientists and engineers within the upper echelons of Anotas-Deithe were replaced by entrepreneurs and industrialists.

As the people of Domhan-Siol became increasingly strident within their disparate clusters, hyperbole rather than reason came to typify public discourse. To wit, they labeled the philosophical conflicts swirling around their various points of view as "culture wars." Anotas-Deithe had long since fostered a "Pax Planeta" on Domhan-Siol. Insurrection as a means of initiating social change was a discarded relic of the planet's distant past. While suspicions and disagreements fractured unity among the people of Domhan-Siol, no actual "wars" were being fought.

Discovery of the Beag-Liath would change all that. In retrospect, it was likely not the discovery of a third spacefaring species that catalyzed the ripping of Domhanian social fabric, but rather the nature of that first contact.

CHAPTER SIX
ADVENTURE OF A LIFETIME

RAMUELL HAD GRIEVED DEEPLY when his parents failed to return from what was to have been a short-term survey expedition. For the next sixty-two annum he was raised by his adoring grandmother, but he remained haunted by Dr. Althea's and Professor Egan's mysterious disappearance. His fond memories were images of shared activities and events during the nine annum they had together. He could remember the way they looked but was unable to recall the sound of their voices. He had long since accepted the likelihood they were lost in another dimension or another time or perhaps dead.

Even given this heartbreak, Ramuell fervently hoped to someday travel aboard a 4D-Initiator ship. Being so young, he'd resigned himself to waiting a few more decades. Youth under the age of ninety were almost never allowed on Anotas-Deithe interstellar missions.

One evening Ramuell's grandmother, Kadeya, announced that her assignment to the planet Ghrain-3 had been approved. She was thrilled. Ramuell was mortified. He loved studying at the Institute of Science, Math, and Literature, but the idea of living on-campus for the next twenty annum was not appealing.

Toying with the beaded headband that kept her curly thick white hair almost in check, Kadeya looked at Ramuell and said, "Guess who's coming with me."

The lanky, auburn-haired boy launched out of his chair as if a rocket had been sewn in his pants. They hugged, laughed, and did a do-si-do around the kitchen.

The very next day Ramuell began reading everything he could find about Ghrain-3, the third planet orbiting a G class yellow star. He found quite a lot of information from the early surveys of the solar system and planet, but most information about recent work on Ghrain-3 was classified and available only to those with high-level security clearances.

A brief note in one report completely baffled him:

Genetic manipulation experiments to create vesicular monoamine transporters were suspended after certain enigmatic mutations were produced in the targeted species. Extensive interventions may be required to rectify the unanticipated results.

Frustrated with his inability to access clarifying information, Ramuell badgered his grandmother incessantly. Exasperated, Kadeya closed off any further discussion of the matter. "Look, under no circumstances will I discuss classified information with an excited seventy-one-annum-old boy. Can you imagine how much trouble we'd be in if you let even a peep slip while bragging to your friends? And yes, I know you'll be bragging—I was once a kid too you know!"

A taller-than-average female, Kadeya towered over her seated grandson. Gesticulating with her long left hand she added, "Only after we've made the jump and are out of contact with the homeworld will I discuss this matter with you again!"

———

Kadeya and Ramuell embarked on their adventure from the Nexo de Mando 4D terminal. Some two hours after launch into orbit, the 4D Initiator device was activated and the ship hurtled across a barrier between dimensions in the multiverse.

Kadeya led Ramuell to the ship's lounge after the jump. They drank tea sweetened with fruit juice and laced with a mild phenothiazine antiemetic. Both of them had experienced what was known as "the stretch." It's the sensation one's body is expanding then contracting during the interdimensional jump. Even wearing sensory deprivation suits, many people still felt a bit wrung out after jumping.

Neither Ramuell nor his grandmother felt horrible, but they didn't feel great either. They were lying back on reclining chairs and watching a comic movie as they sipped their medicine-laced tea. Several other passengers joined them in the lounge. Some watched the movie and others sat at a hexagonal table playing small-stakes games with gambling cards.

Later they went to their shared cabin. Ramuell flopped down on his bunk and once again began pestering his grandmother about what they were likely to find on Ghrain-3. Kadeya grabbed a pillow from her bed and affectionately, albeit not too gently, stuffed it between her grandson's back and the wall. Ramuell wriggled around to make himself comfortable. His long legs dangled off the side of the bed.

Kadeya eased herself into the cabin's only chair and pulled the tiny tea table up as a footrest. With an amused expression, she studied Ramuell. There was no known technology for transmitting communication signals from ships traveling within the interdimensional neutrino streams, so she now felt safe speaking freely with her grandson.

"I believe one of the main reasons so much information about Ghrain-3 has been classified has more to do with what we've learned about ourselves than what we've learned about the planet. There was a time during the early days of our interventions with alien species that the secrecy was absolute; releasing classified information was punishable by a life-sentence of exile on Tine-4.

"Over the centuries, tens of thousands of people have worked on other worlds. At some point when a very large number of people know a secret, it ceases to be a secret. That's what happened with much of the classified information about our genetic manipulation experiments. Today almost everyone takes this information for granted."

"Not everyone," Ramuell interrupted. "There are a lot of cultists."

Kadeya waved her hand dismissively and continued, "Never mind them—a bunch of ignorant reactionaries. The decision to genetically fast-forward the evolution of other species was made more than a thousand annum before I was born. Unlike the cultists, I've taken the time to actually read about that history. The people of my great-grandparent's generation didn't make the decision lightly.

"It was hypothesized, using credible scientific models, that our own genetic makeup may have been manipulated by some unknown spacefaring species in the distant past. The evidence was convincing enough to persuade a significant majority of that era's decision-makers that not only was genetic enhancement a justifiable undertaking, it might even be our obligation to sentient life throughout the cosmos.

"You know, Ramuell, we are such an extraordinary species. We love life. We can produce extraordinary works of art, science, literature, and we appreciate the beauty of all those things." She paused thinking of how to continue. "The fact is, at some point our society will collapse. Our species will inevitably become extinct. It would be an incalculable and unforgivable loss if we fail to figure out how to pass on our most important contribution to the cosmos—our love of art, music, physics, mathematics, literature—our self-awareness—our sentience."

"Do you believe our genetic makeup was enhanced?" Ramuell asked.

"Yes I do. It's likely some ancient species helped direct our evolutionary course. I just don't believe the fabled missing link exists." Kadeya rubbed her lips and chin thoughtfully. "Or rather the missing link did exist—it just happened to be from another world. Perhaps they were so good at splicing and dicing our ancestor's genome that now we can neither prove nor disprove their intervention."

Ramuell asked, "So on Ghrain-3 are we just carrying on a galactic tradition?"

With a slight shake of her head, Kadeya continued, "It's a bit more complex than that. As I said, on Ghrain-3 we've learned a good deal about ourselves. Early on there was considerable dissension among our explorers. On several occasions, they protested directives and at least half a dozen times scientists flatly refused to comply with instructions received through Anotas Command. As I understand it, only twice were those refusals related to technical issues. The other incidents of insubordination were about ethical conflicts.

"All of those cases were ultimately resolved through legally mediated processes. That's not to say everyone agreed with the decisions, but the issues were resolved. Then several annum ago philosophical and ethical disagreements on Ghrain-3 escalated from insubordination to insurgency. This occurred so quickly the authorities on Domhan-Siol hadn't even been alerted before a smattering of violent incidents occurred."

Ramuell exclaimed, "Violence!?"

The knowledge that Domhanians had actually resorted to violence made Kadeya decidedly uncomfortable. "Yes, as hard as that is to believe. Unfortunately, the unrest among our own kind has hardly been the only problem we've encountered on Ghrain. You might even say our efforts there have been a cursed enterprise. That is if you were a cultist and believed in their divine interventions and angels and curses and other such nonsense."

Ramuell could not possibly have foreseen how poorly his grandmother's spiritual skepticism would serve them in the decades ahead. Ghrain-3 would prove to be far more mystical and complex than either of them could imagine.

CHAPTER SEVEN

HOME AGAIN

CONSCIOUSNESS CREPT upon Althea much as an early morning's light filters through window curtains. At first Ramuell's mother was aware only of being cold. *Of course I'm cold—I'm lying here bare-butt naked. But, where am I?* When she heard a moan to her left, Althea slowly turned her head and opened her right eye ever so slightly. She was vaguely aware that it was either dawn or dusk as she could only make out her husband's profile.

A heavy film of postnasal mucus choked Egan as he roused. The sensation flooded his body with corticotrophin and epinephrine. He lurched toward awareness with a startled panic. Choking and coughing, he spastically rolled to his knees and retched. Though there was little in his stomach to purge, the heaving cleared the sensation of obstruction in his throat. He crumpled back to the ground facing his wife. Only after managing to see her body with his unfocused eyes did Egan realize he too was naked.

Instinctively the couple dragged themselves across the few metres of cold ground separating them. They clung to each other for reassurance and warmth. Within minutes they drifted into an odd kind of shared slumber. As the sun rose and bathed their bare bodies, their core temperatures crept upward.

By late morning they'd warmed enough to realize they needed help. Althea was able to drag herself through some bushes and small trees to the crest of a trough. Though unable to focus her eyes, she was certain she could hear the sound of water gurgling over rocks. Turning back to Egan, she was only able to croak the word, "Water."

Egan struggled to gain his hands and knees. This time his mission was to get fluid into his body rather than expel it as vomit. Althea managed to slide most of the way down the slope but lost momentum less than four metres from her life-sustaining destination.

Unable to grip with his numb and tingling hands, Egan slid a leg under the small of Althea's back. Clinching her between his legs in a scissors hold, Egan scooted on his side dragging his wife to the nearest trickling flow. After they managed to suck in a few gulps, Althea coughed then said, "Slowly."

Hydration helped, but they understood they needed food and clothing before nightfall. Once again they fell asleep in each other's arms. The sun had just passed its apex when voices startled them awake. Their situation was so dire that any notion of danger simply was not a consideration. Both began trying to call out for help, but their vocalizations came only as coughs and groans.

Egan picked up a fist-size rock and tossed it into the stream. The clatter and splash made enough noise to do the trick. Within minutes they were surrounded by several people rendering aid. As lightweight jackets were being wrapped around their naked bodies, Althea became vaguely aware of their rescuer's beautiful elongated skulls. *We're home! But how?*

The next time Egan and Althea roused they found themselves in a hospital room being treated for dehydration and hypothermia. They spoke for a few minutes, checking in with each other to set their minds at ease. Egan felt a huge flood of relief about his wife's condition. When he had dragged Althea to the creek's edge she seemed almost too weak to lean over and suck in the water her body desperately needed.

While they lay contemplating their extraordinary situation a doctor and two men wearing Law and Order Directorate identification credentials entered the room. With a kind expression and a gentle voice the doctor began, "Hello Dr. Althea—Professor Egan. Do you know where you are?"

Seeing the Law and Order officers confirmed Althea's conviction that they'd been returned to Domhan-Siol, though she couldn't logically navigate how that was possible. "It seems we're home," she said.

Egan was not so convinced. Though he remembered being rescued by Domhanians, he couldn't shake the notion that this might be an extremely vivid hallucination. Possibly these kinds of thoughts were the last a person experienced before dying. He believed that was as plausible as being in a hospital on the homeworld.

The doctor confirmed Althea's surmise. "Yes, you are home. We were able to identify you by your DNA signatures."

The taller Directorate officer pulled up a chair and sat at the foot of the two beds. He leaned forward and shifted his gaze from one to the other. "As I'm sure you can imagine, we're anxious to piece together where exactly you've been and how you got home. Can you tell us the last things you remember before waking up in the park yesterday? We know where you were sent, but we don't know if you ever arrived at that destination. And we don't know where you've been for the last sixty annum."

"Sixty annum!" Althea exclaimed. "How could we possibly have been gone for sixty annum?" She felt her throat tightening and managed only a strangled croak, "Where is our son? Where is Ramuell?"

The officer pinched his lips together tightly, glanced at his colleague, and then explained, "Ramuell is now seventy-one-annum-old. Kadeya just accepted an assignment with the Anotas-Deithe mission on a planet known as Ghrain-3. She made the jump just a few days ago and took your son with her."

Over the next few days Althea and Egan were subjected to a battery of physical and psychological evaluations. Though the medical personnel with whom they interacted seemed compassionate, no one could truly understand the couple's sense of loss: the lost decades, the lost opportunity to raise their son, the lost hugs and laughter and tears, and a lost sense of faith in the nobility of their species.

Learning that mere days before they were found at the stream's edge, Kadeya and Ramuell had made an interdimensional jump to a faraway world foisted an ominous sense of foreboding and a shared darkness on the couple.

CHAPTER EIGHT
ANGELS AND TEST TUBES

DURING THE FOUR-DAY interdimensional journey from Domhan-Siol to Ghrain-3, Ramuell almost never set down his foliopad. He carried it with him to the ship's galley, to the toilet-closet, and to bed where he read himself to sleep.

Kadeya thought perhaps she'd loaded too many Ghrain-3 documents on her grandson's foliopad. Had she only loaded a couple at a time, she could have monitored his reactions and insisted on conversations before providing the next document. *Oh well, that neutrino has jumped and there's no way I can reel it back in.*

Though the documents were fairly academic, Ramuell understood the gist, though not all the specifics, of what he was reading.

Ghrain-3 Archive Document 01:00492245-07

Intervention Rationale – Executive Summary

The surveys of Ghrain-3 paint a picture of a remarkably rich world with an extraordinary range of ecosystems. The planet is replete with a diversity of life forms that have made astonishing adaptations and are abundant in virtually every habitat.

Over seventy percent of the planet's surface is covered with water. Most water has a sodium content too high to be potable by land-bound species. The majority of the planet's organisms live in various water environments.

Hundreds of land and sea species have evolved sentience. The range of demonstrable intelligence is quite large.

A few species have developed rudimentary tool-making skills. Three have been considered for possible genetic enhancement. All three species are primate omnivores that cook their food. Their mastery of fire and their consumption of cooked meat has resulted in approximately a 20% larger brain and 20% smaller gut than herbivore, non-cooking primate species.

The denisova species has too small of a range and too few numbers to be considered a viable candidate for enhancement. Both of the other species have begun developing symbolic art forms and communicate linguistically. One species seems to have a somewhat higher degree of facility with language and has begun developing basic musical concepts. (It is theorized that musical capabilities may predict a predisposition for better spatial-temporal reasoning.) Live studies of six hundred individuals of both species supported the hypothesis that the sapien species is more advanced in this area than the neandertalis species.

Predicated on these findings, coupled with information obtained from over three thousand brain autopsies and sample gene manipulations, it has been determined that genetic enhancement efforts should be focused on the sapien species. It is believed, with enhancement, this species has the potential to develop technological societies.

Though interesting, this document and several others like

it didn't explain the secrecy and mysterious stories about Ghrain-3. Ramuell's disappointment had the effect of motivating him to read on with even greater fervor. While learning a great deal, he felt like he was trying to put together a jigsaw puzzle with many pieces missing. Then he came across a short document confirming his suspicions about hidden information.

Ghrain-3 Archive Document 11:44213570-14

After almost 700 annum of research, it was determined the most promising strategy for genetic enhancement of the chosen species was by engineering and inserting retroviruses into the sapien DNA. Some of these viruses caused immediate mutations impacting specific neurophysiological characteristics. Dozens of other retroviruses have been designed to lay dormant as inert agents of change within non-coding DNA. Over a few dozen millennia specific environmental and developmental milestones will act to catalyze these retroviruses. Once activated they are designed to produce genetic mutations that will fast-forward and leap over normal evolutionary processes.

The first enhancements targeted the sapiens' neurotransmitter systems. Retroviruses were deployed to produce genetic variations resulting in the production of vesicular monoamine transporters. That mutation dramatically enhanced intellectual functioning among the progeny of infected individuals. These results were observed within a mere three sapien generations.

The lifespan of the sapien species is quite short, with the age of female fertility beginning at about fourteen annum. This has proven to be a favorable trait in terms of evaluating virally activated mutations. Within one standard tour of duty on Ghrain-3, geneticists can observe and track genetic enhancements across four sapien generations.

It was envisioned that many scientists would return for

second and even third tours on the planet, thereby ensuring continuity of research and enhancing our ability to monitor and fine-tune various genetic interventions. For obvious reasons, many scientists have been unwilling to return to Ghrain-3 after their initial tour.

Tossing the foliopad on the bed, Ramuell slapped his hand on the cabinet above his bunk. "'For obvious reasons'—what obvious reasons?" he asked no one. Throwing open the door, he strode into the corridor between cabins and decided he had to press his grandmother to be more forthcoming.

Moments after Ramuell returned from fetching a snack in the ship's galley, Kadeya entered the cabin, towel drying her unruly locks. She had just showered in one of the ship's four small baths. A tall, strikingly handsome woman, her square jaw and smooth spotless skin belied her 489 annum age.

Ramuell immediately launched into an interrogation. "Grandmother, what in the heck is happening on Ghrain-3? What caused the violence? Why all the secrecy?"

Kadeya picked up Ramuell's foliopad and scanned the documents her grandson had read. Pursing her lips she nodded and said, "Yep, it's definitely time we had a talk."

"I understand what we're trying to accomplish, and I understand much of the science behind our efforts. What baffles me is why and how all of this became so controversial—how it led to insurrection. I just don't get it!"

Kadeya narrowed her eyes contemplating where to begin. "So, you know what the retroviruses are?"

"More or less, yes," Ramuell replied.

"The earliest Ghrain-3 Expeditionary Mission scientists spent centuries determining how to best proceed with the augmentation process. The decision to deploy retroviruses was well researched—not at all extemporaneous."

"Yes, I read about that in several of the historical documents. It seems they were thorough and cautious."

"That's correct." Kadeya sniffed and with an inscrutable expression added, "At least early on that was the case. You see, during the first two sapien generations the retroviruses performed almost exactly as had been predicted. Oh, there were some mildly anomalous results, but the undesirable manifestations didn't much concern our scientists. The unexpected mutations seemed minor, and the adversely affected individuals were easily culled."

"Culled?" questioned Ramuell.

"Hmm, I can imagine how that might sound. Yes, they were killed, and their corpses brought up to the labs for study," responded Kadeya.

"Killed? How?"

"Carefully! We mimicked the behavior of Ghrain's wolves. They don't attack a whole herd. They single out a young animal or isolate the sick or wounded and then launch their attack. We did the same thing. We waited until the specimen displaying physical or behavioral anomalies was separated from its clan then swooped in and took that individual."

"But why did we need to kill them?"

"For both safety and expedience. Our surface teams didn't want to endanger themselves or other sapiens by instigating a fight. The surest way to avoid that was to kill the targeted individual before it had a chance to cry out. We were never going to allow those individuals to reach the age of reproduction. We couldn't allow them to pass on the anomalous mutations."

"I see—I suppose that makes sense."

Kadeya heard the reticence in her grandson's voice. "Actually it does, on several levels. In retrospcct it seems major problems likely began as early as the third generation post-infection. We had not anticipated how robust the hybrid vigor among the offspring in the third generation would become. That vigor manifested primarily within the central nervous system, though the changes were initially quite subtle. We would not have learned about this had we not performed autopsies on dozens of culled specimen."

"I'm not sure I understand what you mean by hybrid vigor."

"And that's the point," Kadeya replied. "It's likely whoever wrote the papers you've read didn't actually understand hybrid vigor either. Physiological and behavioral changes among the hybridized sapiens were more profound and were occurring much faster than anyone had foreseen.

"At that point, our scientists began a second set of autopsies on preserved specimen from the first and second hybridized generations. When compared with the brains of non-hybridized sapiens some variations had either been missed or seemed insignificant during the earlier autopsies. Two in particular were considered the most likely culprits of the behavioral changes.

"Neurologists found more than twice as many spindle neurons in the ventral portion of the anterior cingulate cortex."

"Which means what?" Ramuell asked.

"We theorize the larger and more numerous spindle neurons may have been causing a more robust emotional experience. Brain scans on live individuals showed those neuron clusters were activated by stimuli believed to be antecedents of emotional responses.

"In addition to intensifying emotional responses, it's probable the spindle neurons enhance complex problem-solving. Some neurologists speculate that they also play a significant role in the motivation to take action, recognition of errors, and impulse control.

"The second significant change was the increase in size of

the superior temporal gyrus and a deepening of the lateral fissure above that area of the cortex."

"Again, which means what?"

"We know the superior temporal gyrus is the sapiens' cortical level speech and language center," Kadeya replied. "That's the reason expressiveness and linguistic skills exploded among third and fourth generation hybrids. It's also likely that area of the brain is where they process emotional perceptions."

"Ahh, so coupling those two mutations has massive implications," Ramuell observed.

"Yes it does. But what's especially important here is just how malleable the sapiens' genome proved to be. Within just a few generations our retroviruses were causing profound behavioral changes. It happened quickly and had a dramatic impact on intra-clan, inter-clan, and even interspecies relationships. Early on we were thrilled, but in retrospect it's clear we should've been alarmed."

"And why is that?"

Kadeya rubbed a knuckle under her nose. "All of this should have begged the question, what happens when something goes awry with a particular mutation of the brain? Suppose enhanced problem-solving leads to the ability to produce more complex tools and weapons—suppose it also gives hybridized individuals a leg up in terms of strategic decision making. Then couple those two changes with a more robust emotional response. Now if for some reason the impulse control mechanism is not fully developed or is flawed, the result might be hyper-aggressiveness."

Narrowing his eyes, Ramuell suggested, "...and if there are anomalies in those areas of the brain that would likely intensify violent behaviors."

"That's right." Kadeya massaged her temples. "What

happens when the superior temporal gyrus is over-stimulated? What if within the abnormally deepened fissure there are neurons that self-stimulate? Could that mutation set up a feedback loop that produces auditory and visual hallucinations? Pathological sensory experiences? Mental illnesses?"

Sitting up straight and stretching his back, Ramuell added, "And if so, who knows where that might lead?"

Kadeya said, "Perhaps we've observed where it leads—certain individuals violently imposing their will on others. When the numbers were not so great, we simply eliminated those individuals. It was at that point we should have acknowledged some potentially serious miscalculations. We should have begun damage control efforts immediately. That we did not is why we now have a host of devils to pay."

CHAPTER NINE
INTERROGATIONS

MEANWHILE BACK ON DOMHAN-SIOL, Anotas Deithe agents Chelt and Dyer had been assigned to investigate Egan's and Althea's bizarre disappearance and return. On the agents' third visit to the hospital another individual accompanied them. He was introduced only as Liam. At over two metres, he stood several centimetres taller than the Anotas agents. That effect was accentuated by the four centimetres of wavy grey hair piled thickly atop his head. In addition to intelligence, his amber eyes projected a gentle intensity. His presence made both agents decidedly uncomfortable. Liam took a seat in the corner and silently observed the interview.

The agents questioned Egan and Althea about their journey to the largest moon of the giant planet, Lume Morta. They'd been assigned to survey the moon as a likely source of terbium, a rare-earth metal required for all manner of solid-state and fuel cell devices. Extracting terbium from clays on Domhan-Siol required the use of highly toxic chemicals with serious environmental impacts; mining on a lifeless moon was far preferable.

The couple shared technical information about the interdimensional jump, but they understood sharing information about their first contact with the species they called Beag-Liath could be destabilizing, even perilous. They didn't know whom to trust.

Sensing the deception of omission, the agents interviewed Egan and Althea separately on several occasions. They compared notes after each interview and found numerous inconsistencies. When confronted, the couple explained they simply didn't have clear recollections about all that had happened.

Several days later Liam sat in on another interview. He noticed that after hydration and rest the couple looked exactly as they did in their file photos. Althea was a willowy beauty with a lithe gracefulness. Her long sorrel hair framed chiseled features and offset her teal-colored eyes. She was quite a striking head-turner. Egan was a more "average" appearing person – average height; average frame; average weight. It was the perpetual expression of amusement on his square-jawed face that set him apart. His eyes projected an engaging kindness and intellect. They were quite a charismatic couple. Liam was bewildered that they didn't seem to have aged during their six-decade absence.

In a debriefing session after the first undecim Chelt and Dyer discussed the possible use of psychoactive drugs to compel more truthful responses. Though Liam showed no overt reaction to this proposal, his heart pounded, his stomach churned, and his mind raced for a response that would curb the more aggressive inclinations of the Anotas institutional culture.

INTERLUDE #2

October 2017
The Farm, Puerto Rico

AT THIS POINT I interrupted Admiral Cortell's storytelling. "Undecim? I figured out what an annum is, but what's an undecim?

"Ahh, sorry, I should've explained all this at the beginning. Domhan-Siol doesn't have the same rotational speed as Earth, nor does it orbit its sun at the same rate. So naturally, Domhanian time references were different.

"Each day lasted twenty-six hours. Interestingly, their hours were almost identical in length to the way we calculate hours on Earth.

"Domhan-Siol circumnavigates its sun in three hundred and eight, twenty-six hour days. They divided those three hundred and eight days into seven forty-four-day kuuks, and each kuuk was divided into four eleven-day undecims. Does that make sense?"

"So, comparing that system to the Gregorian calendar, the undecim would be an eleven day week?"

"Yeah, I suppose so," the admiral replied.

"Four undecims is a kuuk, which is comparable to our month. And the Domhanian year has seven kuuks."

"That's correct," Cortell replied.

Grabbing an index card I said, "I better write this down."

Day = 26 hrs.

Undecim = 11 day week

4 undecims = kuuk (month) = 44 days

7 kuuk = annum (year) = 308 days

When I finished the note, he asked, "And I'm assuming you've figured out what the foliopad device was?"

"I'm guessing it's like our tablets or laptop computers."

"Yeah, probably like our best tablets on steroids. A foliopad could run a lot of artificial intelligence software, and they had an enormous memory—probably a couple hundred times more capacity than our best personal computers."

Cortell watched me make a notation then he asked, "Are we good?"

"Yep, got it. Please..." I gestured for him to proceed.

Admiral Cortell continues his story:

When under pressure Liam's mind processed thoughts in milliseconds. He decided a gentle assertion of his authority was better than a heavy-handed approach. "As you know, our mysterious surveyors have become quite the celebrities. Journalists all over the planet are calling them heroes almost hourly. From a public relations perspective we need to proceed with caution. Besides, we have no evidence to suggest wrongdoing."

"No evidence yet, but surely even you can see that they're hiding something," Dyer challenged.

Disregarding the veiled insult, Liam replied, "Nevertheless, approval for the use of chemical inducements under these extraordinary circumstances would have to come from the Law and Order Council of Governors."

"So, the Deputy Secretary of the Law and Order Directorate cannot authorize the use of a truth-serum?" Dyer asked derisively.

Unruffled by the agent's churlishness, Liam remained calm. "That is correct. I would not consent to any kind of enhanced interrogation absent a formal authorization by the Council."

Cutting off the tit for tat, Chelt rose and respectfully said, "As you say, sir. Have a good day." With a slight bow, he turned and exited Liam's office.

Dyer shot the Deputy Secretary a petulant askance as he followed his partner out the door.

Melanka was a small dark-skinned woman. The Chief of Security always wore the male version of the Anotas-Deithe dress uniform to work. The likely monotony of her wardrobe closet was a standing office joke. The rigidity of Melanka's attire contributed to an air of authority that induced an odd combination of respect and fear among her thousands of subordinates. Her only nod to femininity was an ever-present, delicately curved and sculpted ivory pipe. The fact that she too often puffed on a dried herbal concoction gave her voice a raspy quality.

After watching several of the interviews as well as the surreptitiously video-recorded meeting with Deputy Secretary

Liam, Melanka said, "I don't give a bloody damn about Liam's public relations sensitivities or legalistic caution. Those two people are keeping secrets. They were off-world for sixty annum and I don't buy for a minute that their memories have been wiped." Setting the pipe down in its holder she thrummed her fingers rhythmically on the desk's glass top. "Something just stinks!"

"Agreed," Agent Chelt said, "but given where Egan and Althea were found the Law and Order Directorate claims jurisdiction, **and** given that the Deputy Secretary's direct involvement, I'd say they're pretty dang serious about that claim."

"Yeah but there's more than one way to catch a fish. If they were up to no-good while off-world that makes it my business. The Law and Order Directorate's jurisdictional claims can go float on sewer water for all I care!"

"So what would you like us to do?" prodded the intemperate Agent Dyer.

"Threaten 'em!" Melanka snarled. "Put a vial and needles on the table before your next interview. Make it clear we think they're not telling us what they know. Make sure they see the serum label. They have no idea that we don't have authorization to use the stuff. Hell, it'll probably never occur to them we need authorization. Tell 'em we'll start pumping them full of chemicals and won't stop until we get the whole truth. Perhaps a bit of fear will revive their anemic memories."

Chelt scratched his jaw contemplatively and nodded. Dyer, on the other hand, was almost giddy about Melanka's belligerence.

Early that evening a courier delivered an envelope to Liam at his home. There was no note; only a flash-dot which he loaded into his foliopad. He watched two brief video files. The first was of his discussion with Agents Chelt and Dyer earlier that day; a meeting he didn't know was being recorded. The second video was a recording of the same agents' conversation in Security Chief Melanka's office.

In most circumstances Liam was, simply put, unflappable. For that reason Sean picked up on his friend's agitation. "Do we have a problem, Lee?"

"Perhaps—call the driver. I'll grab our coats. We need to visit our heroes in the hospital."

Liam had second thoughts on their way out the door. Sharing the videos with Egan and Althea wouldn't be prudent, given the certainty that they were under constant surveillance. In fact, any communication with the couple needed to be discreet – old-school discreet. "Wait, this is a bad idea, Sean. Cancel the car. We should take a walk."

While Sean placed that call, Liam sent a message to Captain Chosant, the hospital's security administrator. The captain dispatched an emergency vehicle to the waste bins behind the neighborhood food and sundries store, which was only a five-minute walk from Liam's and Sean's condominium. The two men strolled nonchalantly through the store and directly out the back door.

One of the hospital's security officers was driving the ambulance. Another officer met them at the rear door of the vehicle with two loose-fitting uniforms worn by emergency medical technicians. Loose-fitting was fortunate, as Sean would have had trouble squeezing his short stocky frame into a tight-fitting outfit. As he pulled the zipper from his crotch to his neck he asked, "So what's the drill?"

"The captain says we're to go in low profile—no flashing lights. We'll pull up in front of the cafeteria and stroll in like old friends grabbing a snack."

"Will Chosant meet us there?" Liam asked.

"No. After a leisurely cobbler and café we'll make our way to the gymnasium dressing room. He'll be there," the officer replied.

Noticing both men had removed their name tags Sean asked, "If we're supposed to be old friends, what shall we call you?"

"Oh—right, thanks for reminding me." Reaching into his pants' cargo pocket he pulled out two lanyards with scratched plastic ID cards. Gesturing toward the driver, "This gentleman is Hasp. My name is Toth."

"Okay, good to meet you. You can call me Lee, and this is Sean."

Amused, Toth said, "Yes sir. We know who you gentlemen are."

As they sat sipping café and feigning a relaxed conversation, Hasp startled slightly. With an uptick of his head, he pointed his nose out the huge cafeteria window. Three uniformed men were trotting across the lawn toward the side entrance of the of the hospital's East Tower.

After watching for a mere second, Liam looked down at his cup, shook his head and sighed, "We've been made."

They rose and casually walked over to deposit their dishes on the sanitizing machine's conveyor. Assuming the hospital's security system had been hacked, Liam and Sean kept their faces averted from the surveillance cameras as they exited the cafeteria.

They were met by a Medical Tech at the gymnasium door. With a gesture she directed them into a side hall. Sean nudged Liam and pointed at the ceiling mounted cameras.

None of the tiny yellow lights were lit – the cameras were offline.

They made their way to a service elevator being held open by a man whose name tag identified him as Officer Farris – Night Chief. As soon as the elevator door closed Chief Farris said, "We've had a change of plans."

"So you saw our Anotas-Deithe friends arriving?" Liam asked.

Farris replied, "Well, we saw some unexpected guests arrive, but we're not sure they're actually Anotas."

When the elevator arrived at the twenty-second floor, Farris warily peered into the corridor. Once he ascertained that the surveillance cameras were out of service, he hustled Liam and Sean out of the elevator and across the hall into a janitorial closet. Officers Hasp and Toth followed closely behind. Farris opened an electric power panel and tapped in a lengthy code. The closet morphed into an elevator! The lift only carried them one or two floors and upon stopping the back wall of the "closet" opened into a windowless room. Desks were mounted to every available metre of wall space. Above the desks was an impressive array of screens displaying live-feed video images of virtually every corner of the campus. As they surveyed their surroundings, images on two grey screens flickered to life as cameras in the previously blacked-out hallways were brought back online.

Captain Chosant stood in the middle of the room. "Liam, before you say anything, I've always thought this setup was overkill for a hospital security system, but it was here before I arrived."

Liam replied, "Perhaps, but tonight may prove your misgivings unjustified."

Sean's onyx-black eyes locked on the video-feed from the medical station near Althea's and Egan's room. "I suggest our first order of business is figuring out who those three men are loitering in the waiting area."

Agent Toth noted, "The man on the left is video-recording the area with his communicator. That can't be a good sign."

———

Melanka grimaced at her communicator. She was in no mood to take a call from Chairman Regan of the Business and Industry Council. "As you might imagine, I'm a little busy at the moment," she growled.

Regan said curtly, "Speak to me. What do you know?"

"Well let me tell you what I know—I know three men are standing in the hospital lobby outside our subjects' room. I suspect they are some of your dimension jumping goons who haven't the slightest idea what they're doing. Why do I suspect that? Because I watched them run across the lawn at the side of the hospital with about as much stealth as a herd of marsh bison."

Chairman Regan countered, "We believe Liam and Sean were spirited into the hospital in disguise."

"Oh, you **believe** so," retorted Melanka. "Is that why you dressed up your rent-a-cops in Anotas uniforms and had them storm the hospital, as if they were pursuing some off-world semi-sentient outlaws? Did you think that tactic would net you some cache of information my best people have yet to acquire? And if you had found the Deputy Secretary of the Law and Order Directorate conducting a private interview with Professor Egan and Doctor Althea, what would your oafs have done? Detain the Deputy Secretary? Really?" She paused for effect. "Now, given your associates' ineptitude, we'll never know what old Liam and Sean might be up to."

Being chastised pricked the Chairman's fragile ego. Testily

Regan replied, "We need information and it's your job to get it. But perhaps you're not up to the task!"

Melanka's raspy voice now took on a treacherous quality, "Mr. Chairman, let me stop you right there before you say something regrettable. We **cannot** know what we **do not yet** know. Perhaps you believe you're protected by the Business and Industry Council, but don't make the mistake of interfering with my investigation again."

"Is that a threat, Melanka?" Regan raised his voice, "I just want you to do your damn job!"

"Really? You just want me to do my damn job? Has it ever occurred to you if I do my damn job just a bit too well I may learn things you'd rather I not know?" She let the question hang in the air for a moment then said, "Have a good evening Mr. Chairman," and disconnected.

Melanka calmly pocketed her communicator and then furiously slammed her palms down on the glass desktop. Her pipe jumped out of its holder and spilled the half-burned herb all over the desk and floor. Her assistant rushed into the office. When Cubra saw the mess, he grabbed the handheld vacuum from the coat closet and without a word began cleaning up.

"Dammit! Everyone involved in this whole stinking affair knows more than they're saying. No one is telling lies, but no one's telling the truth either!" Regaining some semblance of composure, she added, "...and that can only mean there are things to hide."

CHAPTER TEN
ARRIVAL

DURING THEIR INTERDIMENSIONAL JOURNEY, Ramuell hadn't given much thought to what the orbiting station or Ghrain-3 would actually look like. Ramuell and Kadeya joined the crowd in the lounge to watch the docking procedure.

Kadeya had known what to expect, but Ramuell was thunderstruck by the enormity of the orbiting station's rotating toruses. The wheels within wheels looked like colossal white tires spinning around a translucent cylindrical axis.

Both of them were completely unprepared for their stunning first look at the planet. It hung like a blue and white jewel suspended on black velvet, offset by brilliant sparkles of light from distant stars. They had seen photographs, but digital images did not do justice to the extraordinary beauty of this planet with so much surface water and so little cloud cover.

During their first few days on the orbiter, Kadeya was occupied with meetings and briefings in various labs. Having little else to do, Ramuell spent most of his time on the observation deck. He couldn't get enough of the views of Ghrain-3 and its single moon. He also watched a couple dozen dockings and launches of transport vehicles carrying personnel and supplies to and from the surface. Time studying the planet through the orbiting station's powerful telescopes served to intensify Ramuell's excitement about their Ghrain-3 adventure.

One evening he noticed Kadeya's normal exuberance seemed uncharacteristically muted. "Is there something wrong, Grandmother?"

She waved a hand dismissively, "Oh, it's just that we have such a huge amount of work to do in the lab before we'll be ready for a trip to the surface." Seeing Ramuell's disappointment, she added, "But, that doesn't mean we can't begin acclimatizing."

Ramuell beamed.

Waggling her finger she continued, "Be warned, the process is going to be a tedious ordeal." She picked up her grandson's foliopad and loaded a flash-dot. "Here, you can get started reading about how we have to ready our bodies for surface assignments."

Eager to begin, Ramuell playfully snatched the device from his grandmother's hands. When she didn't even grin, he narrowed his eyes and studied her face. Sensing Kadeya was not telling him what really had her worried, he decided now was not the time to press for details. He flopped on the sofa and began reading about the acclimatization protocol.

Because the day on Ghrain-3 was two hours shorter than days on Domhan-Siol, surface assignments required an extended period of adjustment. This was accomplished by shortening each day by one minute, which meant taking each meal one minute earlier; going to sleep one minute earlier; rising from bed one minute earlier. For many, this was more taxing than one might expect. Almost 21% of Domhanian travelers were simply unable to compress their circadian rhythms into Ghrain-3's twenty-fourhour day.

Adjusting to the much lower humidity on Ghrain-3 was often even more challenging. The acclimatization process involved setting the climate control devices in their living and working quarters to gradually lower humidity levels each day. This in turn necessitated drinking incrementally more water. On their homeworld Domhanians required about one litre of water per day. On Ghrain-3 they needed to drink almost three litres of water each day in order to maintain health. This proved tricky with a urinary tract that had evolved to handle much less fluid waste. The resulting problems were mitigated somewhat with medications and diet, but again some Domhanians were not able to make this adaptation.

The gravity of Ghrain-3 was within 2% of Domhan-Siol. This difference proved to be insignificant. In fact, the artificial gravity created by the centrifugal force of the station's spinning toruses was set to equal the gravity on the Ghrain surface.

All told, 38% of Domhanian travelers were physiologically unable to endure long-term assignments on the surface. Most were allowed to make brief visits to the planet, but their surface assignments rarely exceeded an undecim. Perhaps it was Ramuell's great misfortune that he was not among those ill-suited for the environments of Ghrain-3.

The work they began in Kadeya's laboratory during that 120-day acclimatization process would continue for over half a century and would forever change the planet's destiny. Circumstances would dramatically accelerate Ramuell's maturation from an intelligent boy into a powerful young man. In the decades to come he would be called upon to implement Kadeya's stratagems with the indigenes of Ghrain-3. Likewise, Kadeya would do Ramuell's bidding with the administrators aboard the orbiter. Even now, dozens of millennia later, one would be hard-pressed to declare with any certainty whether or not their collaborative efforts were successful.

CHAPTER ELEVEN

WARNING

In the Nexo de Mando Hospital security center, Sean turned away from the computer screen and said, "Their uniforms are masterful replicas, but those men are definitely **not** Anotas officers."

Hasp, working at another terminal, added, "That's not all. Our monitoring camera in room 579 has been hacked and not by Anotas."

"Anotas has no reason to hack a single room, they've tapped our entire system," Chosant explained. "Liam, what do you want to do?"

"Obviously, someone has a vested interest in our investigation. They probably have Sean, Chelt, Dyer and me under constant surveillance. We must proceed cautiously until we figure out who they are. It would be unwise to have your people escort the faux agents from the premises."

Exhaling audibly Chosant said, "That's a relief—they're just standing in the waiting area. We don't really have a reason to boot them."

"How can we get a message to Egan and Althea without alerting our mystery guests?" Liam asked.

"What kind of message do you want to send?"

"They need to be warned to be even more circumspect, and not only with Chelt and Dyer but with everyone they talk to."

Sean snorted and added, "Yeah! They need to keep their mouths completely shut."

"Actually not—that would probably create greater suspicion and more aggressive questioning," Liam replied. "They need to continue talking and blaming distorted memories for any inconsistencies."

"For how long?" Chosant asked.

"Until we can get 'em out of here," Liam answered.

"That would be a good move. It looks like they're in someone's crosshairs," Chosant said pointing at the three faux Anotas agents.

With an epiphany's gleam in his eye, Sean asked, "Lee, did you bring the flash-dot?"

Realizing what Sean had in mind, Liam smiled and pulled a blue ditty bag out of his pocket. "I sure did!"

"Captain, can we transmit a video-feed directly to the television in their room?" Sean asked.

Captain Chosant turned a quizzical expression on officers Farris, Hasp, and Toth. Hasp swiveled his chair around and said, "Sure, it's actually not all that difficult."

Leeza, Captain Chosant's daughter, was a hospital radiologist. She was dumbfounded when her father escorted her from the janitorial closet/elevator into the security center. Stating the obvious, Chosant admonished, "You understand you can tell absolutely no one about this place."

Leeza nodded slowly as she took in the room, “Dad, I can’t believe you never told me about this place.” She knew the three security officers and extended her hand for palm-taps. When her father introduced Sean and Liam, her eyes widened as she realized she was meeting the Deputy Secretary of the Law and Order Directorate.

After everyone had taken a seat at the oval table in the middle of the room, Officer Toth led the conversation. “We need to deliver a message to Professor Egan and Dr. Althea. Do you know who they are?”

“Of course—room 579,” Leeza responded.

“They’re being watched, and we don’t know who the watchers are.” Toth pointed to the screen showing the three men milling around the lobby on the fifth floor.

Hesitantly Leeza observed, “They look like uniformed Anotas agents.”

Toth replied, “‘Look like’ is the operative phrase. Those uniforms are either stolen or replicas, but the men are **not** with Anotas-Deithe.”

Looking over at her father, Leeza asked, “Then who are they?”

Captain Chosant gave her a tight-lipped shrug.

Hasp took over and explained the plan to deliver a clandestine message to the couple.

Leeza stopped at the medical station and exchanged pleasantries with the medical technicians. After a couple minutes of small-talk, she announced loudly enough for the faux Anotas agents to hear, “I need to discuss the neuro-scan results with our patients in 579. It’ll only take a few minutes.”

This didn’t raise any eyebrows, as patient visits from

medical specialists were commonplace after dinner. The five men watching the video-screens in the security center saw one of the Anotas impersonators furtively taking photographs of Leeza as she walked across the circular lobby.

Under his breath, Chosant said, “Dammit!”

Patting the captain’s shoulder, Liam said, “Don’t worry, they only have a picture of a professional doing her job.”

“Yeah, but if they learn she’s my daughter it will put her on their watch list.”

Leeza had already met Althea and Egan. “Hi folks. I’m guessing you’re getting pretty tired of being poked, prodded, and cooped up. Other than that, how are you doing?”

“Poked, prodded, cooped up **and** asked the same questions over and over and over,” Egan replied sarcastically.

“I can only imagine and don’t want to add to your stress, but there’s something I’d like to go over with you. Let’s take a seat. I want to show you your neuro-scans.”

Looking a bit anxious, Althea gestured toward the table.

Leeza picked up the remote control to turn off the television while surreptitiously changing the channel. Upstairs, Hasp sat down at a terminal and began dictating code. Within a minute he’d created a secure link with the television in room 579.

Leeza took a seat with her back to the room camera and looked carefully at her patients. She noted their expressions of concern. *Perfect!* Sliding her foliopad out of its case she said, “I’ve got the images right here.” She turned on the device and opened the neuro-scan file. She also opened a blank window at the top of the screen. When she simultaneously pressed four keys a message popped up in the window.

You are being watched. You must be cautious, even in your “private” conversations. They are not private! Be

careful what you say AT ALL TIMES. After I leave, you will be shown two brief videos on your television.

Althea and Egan looked up with startled expressions. Egan began to ask for an explanation, but Leeza made a very slight gesture with her hand and subvocalized, "Shh, shh, shh." With her pen she pointed to the fourth sentence in the message on her screen. (Be careful what you say AT ALL TIMES.)

Leeza continued to play her role to perfection; pointing to various areas on the screen and explaining the neuro-scans. Knowing that Watchers were listening in on this meeting, Leeza was painstakingly accurate with all of her comments about the images.

Understanding Leeza's prompt, Egan and Althea played along, even asking questions about some of the technical information. Wrapping-up the session Leeza said, "I'm sure you'll have more questions after you've had some time to digest this information. I have to go do a spinal scan in a few minutes, but I'll check in with you tomorrow." She rose, picked up the remote, and turned the television back on.

Althea called out, "Thank you doctor," as Leeza exited the room.

Egan fluffed the pillows on his bed and invited Althea to sit beside him to watch television. To minimize ambient noise, the hospital's television audio was only available through earbuds. As soon as Hasp saw the couple settle in, he transmitted the message to their room.

It began with a text:

What you are going to see will be startling. Do not let your expressions give you away. Say nothing to each other or anyone about this video. We are your friends. Help is on the way – soon. Sit tight – remain calm – SAY NOTHING!

Next came the two brief video files that were on Liam's flash-dot. First Althea and Egan watched the meeting Agents

Dyer and Chelt had with Liam. They were distressed by how casually the Anotas agents discussed the use of psychoactive drugs.

They were surprised when Liam objected to injecting them with these powerful chemicals against their will. Surprise was replaced by astonishment when they heard Agent Dyer say, "So, the Deputy Secretary of the Law and Order Directorate cannot authorize the use of a truth-serum?"

They struggled to affect indecipherable expressions while watching Liam confirm that he wouldn't sanction the use of those drugs. Sitting closely on Egan's bed, Althea gave her husband a subtle nudge with her elbow as a way of communicating that they were sharing the same thought. *The Deputy Secretary of the Law and Order Directorate is trying to protect us!*

While the first video file was alarming, the second was much worse. They didn't know who Melanka was, but it was clear she was quite the firebrand; a person with considerable authority inside Anotas-Deithe. The couple was taken aback by Melanka's bluntness and frightened by her threatening statement:

"Put a vial and needles on the table before your next interview. Make it clear we think they're not telling us what they know...Tell 'em we'll start pumping them full of chemicals and won't stop until we get the whole truth. Perhaps a bit of fear will revive their anemic memories."

When the second video stopped playing the television screen went blank. Althea and Egan sat impassively waiting to see if there would be any further information or instructions. After several seconds Egan removed his earbuds and said, "I'm not really interested in this program, would you like for me to order a movie from the hospital's library?"

"Sure, that would be great. I'm going to use the potty while you do that." When she closed the bathroom door, Althea found herself shaking and tears spilling out of her eyes. Not knowing where spy cameras might be installed, she sat on the toilet and hid her face by looking at the floor. After a couple of minutes she regained her composure, stood, flushed the toilet, and stepped over to the sink to wash her hands and face.

Opening the door she saw Egan looking out the window at the city's lights. She walked across the room and wrapped her arms around him from the back and felt him shudder. Sensing it was going to be difficult to keep up the emotional masking ruse, Althea said, "You know, I'm awfully tired. Why don't we just snuggle in your bed until we fall asleep?"

Upstairs in the security center Chosant, Sean, and Liam were holding their collective breaths; hoping the couple would do nothing to give away the covert sharing of information. When the couple climbed into bed and turned off the lights, Sean said, "She's a shrewd one, to be sure."

CHAPTER TWELVE
OMINOUS PORTENTS

RAMUELL WAS a good deal more animated than his grandmother during dinner as they discussed Kadeya's list of job assignments. Though a 120-day acclimatization process seemed interminable, Ramuell was looking forward to working with Kadeya in her laboratory. He understood it was an honor to collaborate with a scientist of such eminence, even if she was his grandmother.

As they ambled back toward their cabin Kadeya said, "We should get to bed early. We'll be needing our rest for the acclimatization ordeal ahead."

Again Ramuell sensed her emotional unsteadiness. Kadeya was clearly not herself. This time he decided to be direct, "What's wrong Grandmother?"

Realizing she couldn't dismiss his concern a second time, she said, "Not here, we need a bit more privacy for that conversation."

Upon entering their apartment, Kadeya took a chair and Ramuell flopped on the sofa. She leaned forward, her forearms resting on her thighs with hands clutched between her knees.

As she stared silently at her folded hands, Ramuell realized he'd never seen her actually look old. He had never even thought of her as an elderly person, though she was now 489 annum. Kadeya always had so much vitality and playfulness. Naturally, her physical prowess was past its peak, but her mental acumen hadn't waned in the slightest. However tonight, silently stooping forward in that chair, Kadeya looked her age.

"Grandmother..." Ramuell prodded.

Sitting back and inhaling deeply, Kadeya looked up and for a moment stared silently at the photograph of the Ghrain-3 moon Ramuell had hung over the sofa. Turning her gaze to her grandson she began, "As you know, our efforts here have hit some snags. Those problems began to manifest significantly in the fourth hybrid generation. The sapiens' lifespans are short. So we're only talking about seventy to eighty Ghrain solar revolutions. When I received this assignment I knew the situation was bad. In the last several days I've met with members of the Anotas Science and Exploration Council. I've met with leaders of the Ghrain-3 security forces and representatives of the Business and Industry Council. I've met with several members of the Serefim Presidium and even had a brief conversation with Grandmaster Elyon."

Ramuell's eyes widened. He sat up, threw his feet off the sofa, and leaned forward. Kadeya continued, "To say things are bad is an understatement. The situation is worse than I'd been led to believe.

"We were like children! For over a thousand annum we studied the planet and its inhabitants. Our earliest surveys identified dozens of reasons to proceed with extreme caution —or perhaps not to proceed at all with genetic enhancement. Then our geologists found caches of gold lying like turtle eggs within a few metres of the planet's surface. We're using so much gold in all manner of spacecraft that our demand for the metal is running well ahead of supply."

"So we cast caution to the wind like a handful of flour—that's not to say our biologists and geneticists didn't endeavor to do their best. Early on it seemed luck was on our side. We were thrilled at how quickly the introduced retroviruses produced the desired genetic mutations. But we should have been alarmed. We were like children, eager to snatch up all the shiny baubles in the sandbox," she repeated with disgust. "And now we've got a planet-wide breeched-birth!

"It never dawned on us that our interventions would result in hyper-sexuality among the sapiens. It never dawned on us they would crossbreed with other primate species and those couplings would produce viable offspring!" She blew out a long sigh. "But perhaps most unforgivable, it never dawned on us to carefully study the long-term effects the planet would have on our own species."

"Wha ... what do you mean?"

Kadeya shook her head slowly. "As you know, Domhanians continue to have various types of sexual relationships well into old-age, but we've evolved to have neither the sexual appetites nor motivation of most other species on our homeworld. You've no doubt learned in your biology classes that only about thirty percent of our fertilizations are the result of intercourse.

"A millennia ago we hopped in our 4D-Initiator ships and plopped thousands of men and women of our species down on Ghrain-3 for long-term assignments. A few centuries later we learned our people were engaging in sexual dalliances with the third and fourth generation offspring of our sapien experimental groups." Kadeya's vexation hung in the air like dust motes.

"What in a holy-hell are you saying, Grandmother? That can't be true!"

Waving off Ramuell's denial, Kadeya continued, "Oh, it's true! I've been shown irrefutable evidence of the couplings!"

Ramuell winced, "That's disgusting! How can that be happening?"

"Figuring that out is one of our two assignments." Again she sighed, "We know some kind of bio-chemical exposure catalyzes a sexual response among a significant number of our people working on the surface. Our job is to figure out the recipe for that disaster."

Now Ramuell was also leaning over his legs looking silently at the floor below his folded hands. Had someone taken a photo of them sitting in mirrored poses it would have been considered endearing – unless one understood the depth of their angst. "You said we have two assignments. Finding out why our explorers are fornicating with the natives is one, what's the other?"

"Now let me correct what you just said. After being on the surface for relatively short periods of time many of our staff became attached to and protective of the sapiens with whom they were engaged. This was not considered a problematic development. Our people have not, however, been fornicating with the natives. Rather, sexual intercourse has occurred between some Domhanians and the offspring of hybridized sapiens."

Unable to suppress his revulsion, Ramuell declared, "Oh like that makes some kind of big damn difference. That's completely unacceptable—completely unethical!"

"Your attitude is what's been drilled into those of us employed in the various galactic exploration industries, which makes this phenomenon all the more perplexing. To my knowledge, this has not occurred on any other worlds. If we are to figure out how and why this is happening, we must suspend our judgmental and ethical certainties and replace them with scientific inquisitiveness."

Pressing the heels of his hands into his closed eyes, Ramuell grunted. "And what's our second assignment?"

"You're probably not going to like this one any better. When sapien-hybrids mated with the *neandertalis* species an unexpected mutation occurred. Remember, we didn't even believe the two subspecies could interbreed, but we should have been expecting the unexpected. At any rate, this mutation caused the pituitary gland to secrete growth hormones at more than twice the normal rate; the result being offspring that grew to **at least** half again the size of a large *neandertalis*."

"Good grief, they were giants!" exclaimed Ramuell.

"Correction, they **are** giants—they're called nefilim and there are a lot of them, and they pass the mutation on to their offspring."

"And our assignment is to figure out what to do about it?" questioned Ramuell.

"That's right. The Serefim Presidium is adamant we will not leave this planet infested with a subspecies of giants. We are to figure out a way to halt the passing of the mutation—the other alternative is just too horrible to contemplate. We must succeed!"

Looking quizzically at his grandmother, Ramuell asked, "Extermination? Are you talking about extermination? How many are there? How can we even consider mass slaughter?"

"Well, when you've had the chance to learn more about the abhorrent behaviors of these creatures you'll better understand the Presidium's point of view. You won't like it. I don't like it." Kadeya paused and studied Ramuell's face. "But it's not our job to like the Presidium's decisions. It is our job to follow orders and soldier on. Sadly, a good number of us have not done so, and now it's an unholy mess down there."

After a moment Kadeya clapped her hands and rubbed them together enthusiastically, trying to force herself to brighten up. "Anyway, with a couple of great minds like ours, we'll have this gigantism mutation figured out in no time! No doubt, we'll leave the planet better than we found it!"

Ramuell appreciated his grandmother's effort to lighten the mood, but he was only able to muster a wan smile. His eyes betrayed profoundly troubled thoughts.

CHAPTER THIRTEEN
DECEPTIONS AND THREATS

At the Nexo de Mando Hospital, Egan and Althea lay in bed dreading the visit they were sure was coming. They weren't surprised when Agents Chelt and Dyer arrived before breakfast.

They felt certain the Anotas agents would try intimidation but believed it was unlikely the agents would actually use psychotropics. Althea and Egan decided to continue the wile of claiming lost and distorted memories. This strategy was not entirely a deception, given that they could not account for how sixty annum had passed during their time with the Beag-Liath.

After cursory greetings, Agent Dyer announced they would be conducting separate interviews. He escorted Egan out of the room while Agent Chelt took a seat at the table and gestured for Althea to sit opposite him.

As Dr. Leeza had the night before, Chelt positioned himself with his back to the room's camera. He made much ado of reaching into his valise, pulling out a plastic case, and setting it on the left side of the table within the camera's field of view. He then removed from his coat pocket what looked like some kind of writing instrument. Concealing his actions from the camera the agent twisted off a cap and removed a miniature electromagnetic transmission disrupter.

Chelt looked sympathetically at Althea and said, “I’ve just blocked all audio signal reception within this room. Please be assured that regardless of how it might appear, you have absolutely **nothing** to fear from me.” With that, he replaced the disrupter in its case and returned it to his pocket. With his expression he made it clear to Althea they were again audible to the Watchers.

While opening the case and exposing a hypodermic needle and a vial of bluish liquid, Agent Chelt began the interview. “Dr. Althea you’ve claimed to have almost no memories of sixty annum lost in space. We’re wondering if perhaps you might now have some recollections that hadn’t been clear to you earlier.” He looked down at the box with the needle and vial and tapped it with his index finger. He looked back at Althea and shook his head ever so slightly. He continued, “For example, do you have any recollections of encounters with other travelers from Domhan-Siol—or perhaps even travelers from another world?”

Althea looked down immediately, believing her pupils had likely dilated. She was shocked by Agent Chelt’s warning that Anotas-Deithe suspected the truth.

Meanwhile, Egan’s interview with Agent Dyer was not prefaced with any assurances about “nothing to fear.” Dyer was more than just suggestive with his display of the hypodermic needle and vial. He went so far as to remove the cap and fill the syringe with serum.

At one point during the questioning Dyer became so agitated Egan thought it was possible the agent would go off-script and actually try to inject him with the blue stuff. The only thing giving Egan any sense this was not likely was the fact that he was not physically restrained. *Surely Dyer knows I'll fight back.* Nevertheless, Dyer was unhinged enough to be more than a tad frightening.

When Egan returned to room 579, his wide-eyed expression told Althea the interview with the zealous Agent Dyer had been stressful. He strode across the room and took Althea in a long, firm embrace. She said loudly enough to be picked up by the microphones, "I love you." Then burying her head in his chest she whispered, "Everything's going to be okay."

Having missed breakfast they decided to go to the hospital's cafeteria. Althea picked up her foliopad and held it at her side. She wanted it to be obvious to the Watchers that she was carrying the device. As the couple stepped into the hallway the guard stationed outside their room challenged, "And just where are you off to?"

Egan, having been exposed to enough bullying for one morning, responded curtly, "Your colleagues arranged for us to miss breakfast. We're going down to the cafeteria to get something to eat."

"Just call the kitchen to tell them you're back and have them bring your breakfast here."

Egan responded forcefully, "We're going down to the cafeteria, now."

"Hold on a second, I'll have to call and clear that with my boss."

Egan took a step forward. Standing mere centimetres from the guard's face he seethed, "We are not criminals, and we are not prisoners. Your job is to protect us, not restrain us. If your Anotas bosses don't like that we're going to the cafeteria, you can inform them where to find us—and I'll tell them to go suck swamp water!"

Pivoting on a heel Egan took Althea's arm and they strode away. She said, "I'm not sure that was wise, but it was awfully sexy—in a primitive kind of way." Egan just smiled as they stepped into the elevator.

Under the elevator's cameras Althea made a show of powering up her foliopad. "I've been reading a most interesting article on lost memories. I'm going to pull it up and you can take a look at it while we're eating." As they walked past the security cameras in the atrium Althea continued tapping the keypad.

After getting their food they sat in a small booth. With a couple more taps Althea exclaimed, "Ah, here it is. I was afraid I hadn't saved it." She slid the foliopad across the table to her husband.

Egan picked it up and was surprised to find Althea had actually opened an article about memory loss. He hadn't given any thought to the likelihood that their Watchers were also monitoring their electronic devices. *She's a smart one!*

On this particular foliopad model, sidebar notes were not accessible on the cyber-net unless intentionally transmitted to another device. Egan read the note his wife had entered.

It seems Chelt is on our side – but that may just be an Anotas trick. I also think they suspect the truth about our time with the Beag-Liath. He asked if I had any memories of encounters with "travelers from another world." We must be VERY careful!

While the folks at Anotas-Deithe had their suspicions about the possibility of the couple's encounter with an extraterrestrial species, the Business and Industry Council intelligence operatives were convinced that had occurred.

At this point Liam and Sean were still out of the loop. It had not occurred to them that extraterrestrial contact lay at the heart of the cloak-and-dagger intrigue. They had identified the three Anotas impersonators who'd visited the hospital the previous evening. Their personnel records indicated all three worked for a mining corporation and were currently on off-world job assignments.

Chosant, Liam and Sean sat around the table in the hospital security center enjoying an afternoon cup of tea. "Clearly they are **not** off-world, and they're not working with Anotas." Chosant said thoughtfully. "If they're actually collaborating, why would they need replica uniforms?"

"Good point," Sean agreed.

"Yeah, and if those gentlemen are working for a small company like RareEarths Minerals Corp., I'll lick your shoes," Liam added. "I'm not sure what's going on, but I am sure your patients in 579 are in trouble. We need to get them out of here."

"Yes we do," Sean agreed. "And we're gonna need some smoke and mirrors to make that happen."

CHAPTER FOURTEEN
A GIANT PROBLEM

KADEYA HAD PREPARED a plan for work in the laboratory during their acclimatization process. This seemed to tamp down her qualms about what was happening to the sapiens of Ghrain-3. The plan also gave Ramuell something to focus on for 120 days.

They began not at the beginning but rather at the end and worked backward. They autopsied a nefilim specimen that had recently been culled by a security team on the planet's surface. Ramuell was assigned to do a comparative study of the giant's anatomy with the early anatomical studies of unmodified sapiens and hybridized sapiens. Kadeya instructed her grandson to pay particular attention to the endocrine and central nervous systems.

Using the extraordinary array of technology available in the lab, Kadeya sequenced the nefilim's genome. She focused on identifying anomalies in the specimen's nucleotide sequence, non-coding DNA, and RNA viruses.

They were enthused with their work and often wandered back to the lab after dinner. They talked about almost nothing else. After the second undecim they realized that their single-mindedness was not healthy, especially given the physiological stresses their bodies were undergoing with the incremental shortening of each day, decreasing atmospheric humidity, and increased fluid intake. The acclimatization process was proving more taxing than either had expected. They agreed to a self-imposed rule of not returning to the lab after dinner. In lieu of non-stop shoptalk they read books, explored the various toruses of the orbiter, and watched videos.

Toward the end of the third undecim, the Serefim Presidium Chief Science Officer, Dr. Durela, scheduled an appointment. On the day of the visit, Durela arrived promptly at the appointed time accompanied only by her administrative assistant. Kadeya was surprised. She had envisioned the Chief showing up with a small entourage, which was the modus operandi of the bureaucracy supporting the science community on Domhan Soil.

As they walked through the lab Durela greeted the technicians. She made a point of asking everyone she met a question pertaining to their specific work duties. Her questions were about making the staff feel valued as well as demonstrating her own familiarity with the work being done in the lab. Kadeya realized the visit was not about acquiring new information. *She's a scientist, probably a good one, but foremost she's a politician – and she has an agenda.*

Indeed she did and it was for Kadeya's ears only. After the walk through, Durela asked if they might have a private word in the office. Both Durela and her assistant accepted the proffered cup of tea and took seats on the couch. Kadeya seated herself in an armchair on the opposite side of a tea table with a high gloss terrazzo surface. The stone chips in the terrazzo were minerals from the mines of Ghrain-3. Durela commented on the table's beauty, pointing out some particularly striking stones and speculating which mines were the likely sources. "... which in a way brings me to the topic I want to discuss. Kadeya, as I'm sure you're aware, our interest in Ghrain-3 has expanded from the initial effort to enhance the sentience of an indigene species. Ghrain-3 is a rich world. It has a diversity of life that we have perhaps never seen elsewhere. It also has a wealth of minerals, including gold and silver found close to the surface and rather easily extracted."

As much to make this meeting a conversation rather than a lecture, Kadeya interjected, "I'm sure that fact hasn't escaped the notice of our mining corporations and their Business and Industry Council friends."

"Indeed it has not," Durela replied. "At the present time there are over twenty operational mines on the surface. They're located in the southwestern region of the largest continent, the far northeast and the extreme south of the largest southern hemisphere continent, and very recently mines have been opened in the western highlands of the smaller southern hemisphere continent."

For a moment Durela studied Kadeya's expression, but it was unreadable. "These operations are primarily focused on extraction and production of gold and silver. Interestingly many of the sapien-hybrids have shown an interest in these efforts and have proven to be helpful."

Again she watched for Kadeya's reaction to this cryptic piece of information. Kadeya looked down at her teacup and watched the tiny ripples she was creating by swirling the cup ever so slightly. Durela decided to wait for a more discernible reaction.

After a moment Kadeya looked up and said, "Helpful?"

Durela forced herself to make eye contact, though it seemed to Kadeya that she'd rather look away. "Uhm, yeah. The sapien-hybrids seem to be quite curious, and they learn quickly. In numerous ways their strength and frankly their courage have proven beneficial—perhaps even essential to our mining efforts."

"I see." Kadeya paused. "And they're being cared for?"

"Of course. They are well-fed. We provide reliable dwellings. And our medical care is so far beyond their comprehension they consider it magical."

"Oh I'm sure they do. I'd guess they consider us magicians—or angels—or perhaps even gods," Kadeya said.

"I haven't heard anything to indicate that's the case. It's not likely they've developed intellectually to that level of abstract conceptualization."

Again Kadeya affected an unreadable expression.

Realizing Kadeya was not ready to provide feedback, Durela chose to veer the conversation in the direction of a supervisor speaking with a subordinate. "Getting back to the issue of the sapiens' strength and courage, there are those who are particularly worried about the ramifications of the gigantism mutation. Have you had a chance to review any of the field reports regarding their behaviors?"

Creasing her forehead, Kadeya answered, "Yes I have—volatile would be an understatement."

"To be sure!" Durela exclaimed. "What is equally concerning is how rapidly the mutation seems to have spread. It appears that the clans with the mutation routinely force themselves on their smaller and weaker neighbors."

"And the powers-that-be are afraid of a world populated by powerful, fearless, combative giants," Kadeya surmised.

Durela acknowledged the truth of this statement with a slight nod.

Kadeya continued, "And just who are the powers-that-be?"

"Kadeya, they are powerful. They're far more powerful than the people back home have ever imagined. They know how to play the powerbroker game, and they play for keeps."

Kadeya drew in a deep breath. "What does that mean—play for keeps?"

Now it was Durela's turn to stare at her teacup. With a short forced sigh, she looked up and locked eyes with Kadeya. "It means you have one of the sapiens' generations, perhaps two, to make this mutation go away. If you don't, the Presidium will." She paused for a moment to let this bit of information sink in. "Kadeya, you need to do your job. Do it well and be careful. Be careful about making enemies out here—and even more careful when making friends."

At that, Durela stood and extended her hand for a palm-tap. With a quixotic expression she studied Kadeya for a long moment, then nodding slowly said, "All right, I guess that's about it. Kadeya, thank you for your time." In four steps she was at the door, opened it and left without looking back. On the way out, Durela's assistant did give Kadeya a brief glance over his shoulder.

Upon departing from the lab, Durela turned to her assistant, "Does she look well?"

Shaking his head, "Not at all. She'll not be able to acclimate for long-term assignments on the surface."

Still walking, Durela said, "Perhaps that's just as well."

CHAPTER FIFTEEN
EXIT PLAN

Danel and Rebecca had been field agents with the Law and Order Directorate for almost a century. They respected and liked each other and had even vacationed together on several occasions. First Rebecca and somewhat later Danel had become Liam's confidants; members of his elite cadre of eyes and ears spread all over the planet.

Both were in the air within an hour of Liam's call asking them to come to Nexo de Mando. Danel arrived at the Directorate central office first and Rebecca was less than an hour behind.

Sean summarized Egan's and Althea's situation and played the videos Liam had received on the flash-dot. After bringing the agents up to speed, Sean turned the meeting over to the boss. Liam explained the need to extract the couple, unseen, from the hospital and get them to a safe house. He asked Rebecca and Danel to brainstorm possible exit scenarios.

Simultaneously the agents rolled up their shirt sleeves. They studied the hospital's floor plans; considered ways of fooling electronic surveillance; proposed options for transporting Althea and Egan once out of the hospital. Only occasionally asking questions, Liam and Sean sat back and let Danel and Rebecca do what they did best.

By midnight they had a plan. Early the next morning, after too few hours of sleep, Liam and his entourage called Captain Chosant and reviewed the plan. The captain was dumbstruck by the fact that agents could be flown in from far afield and a detailed plan developed on such short notice. He was perhaps a bit uneasy with the resources the Law and Order Directorate had at its disposal.

Chosant's only suggestion was to use a different exit from the building. He informed them of the hospital's sub-basement utility corridor, which he was certain would go unnoticed when disconnected from the surveillance system.

"That's a **much** better option!" Rebecca enthused.

Liam and Sean exchanged a quick glance, conveying their shared relief that the Security Chief had been able to incorporate an important recommendation before the plan was finalized.

That evening when Althea removed the cover from her dinner plate she found a note:

Call food services at 23:00 – request a sleep-aid tea and an order of biscuits.

Egan likewise received a note instructing him to spill a drink on his pillow and call laundry services after dinner to request a replacement.

At 23:20 Agent Rebecca, disguised as a laundry worker, arrived at room 579 carrying Egan's replacement pillow. She handed it to him making certain he saw the note written on the pillow case. Egan read the message while Rebecca made some ado of tidying up the room and making small-talk with Althea. About three minutes later Agent Danel entered with the tea and snacks.

Rebecca and Danel greeted each other as friendly colleagues. They had rehearsed some conversational topics and encouraged Egan and Althea to join in the banter. Egan tossed the pillow to his wife with the comment, "This may not be quite firm enough for me, what would I have to do to get you to trade?" Althea peered at the pillow as if sizing it up while she read the note:

Agents Danel and Rebecca have come to help you leave the hospital without being detected. Danel will activate a device that will disrupt visual, audio, and all other electronic signals to and from your room for two minutes. During that time you are to exchange clothes with them. They will give you additional instructions verbally. AFTER YOU HAVE EXCHANGED CLOTHES KEEP YOUR HEADS DOWN AND DO NOT SPEAK.

After chatting for a couple more minutes Danel made eye contact to be certain Althea and Egan had read and understood the note. Deciding that they were at least nominally onboard, he nodded and reached in his coat pocket to activate the disrupter. Immediately Rebecca and Danel began stripping out of their clothes. The flurry of activity conveyed a sense of urgency.

Rebecca took the lead, "We know you don't know who we are. We know you're confused and probably a bit frightened. Please believe that the Anotas Agents' threat to inject you with psychotropics is serious. We need to get you out of their reach. For now you must trust us and do exactly as you're told. When we get you out of here, you'll have a chance to have your questions answered."

Rebecca's approach was so diametrically opposed to that of

the Anotas agents that it inspired at least a smatter of confidence.

"Put on our uniforms quickly and then assume the exact positions we were in when Danel activated the disrupter. We were both looking down at the floor when the signal was blocked. You should do likewise. Do not look up and do not speak. When you exit the room you'll turn right keeping your heads down. Dr. Leeza, your radiologist, will be waiting at the elevator. She'll have additional instructions for you." Rebecca turned to Danel and asked, "How much time do we have?"

"Twenty-five seconds." He took Egan by the hand and spotted him in the correct location. Looking him in the eye, he said, "You're good."

He turned to Althea and guided her to her spot. "Everything is going to be okay. When you turn to leave, walk casually out of the room and down the hall, but don't dawdle." With a reassuring nod he said, "You're good too!"

Rebecca and Danel assumed their positions and Danel turned off the disrupter device.

Rebecca walked over to the bed only a metre from Althea and began smoothing the sheets. While keeping her face averted from the cameras she said, "I suppose we should let you drink your tea before it gets cold." Her proximity to Althea would confuse the directional listening device. This ruse was likely to work, at least for a while, given that voice recognition scans would identify the voice as hers rather than Althea's.

Understanding the ploy, Egan and Althea wordlessly offered palm-taps with their doppelgangers and exited the room. Immediately upon their departure Rebecca picked up the remote control and turned out the lights. She grabbed Danel's hand and pulled him on top of her on the bed she had just been straightening. He whispered in her ear, "I assume this is for the benefit of the thermal imaging cameras?"

She bit his earlobe gently and whispered, "I don't think I'm that good of an actor."

Feeling an arousal beginning between his legs, Danel said, "Oh my!"

Rebecca began fondling his promising erection and replied, "Oh boy!"

Watchers at Anotas-Deithe Observation and Monitoring (O&M) Stations were assigned twenty-four screens to monitor. Every O&M Hub housed at least three dozen stations with live Watchers manning each station all day, every day. Their operations were covert, and the exact number of Hubs scattered around the planet was a carefully guarded secret.

On this night, the camera in room 579 at the Nexo de Mando Hospital was being monitored at an O&M Hub just two kilometres away. There had been nothing out of the ordinary observed all day and the Watcher had received no alerts that would have warranted an elevated level of vigilance.

The monitor went dark when Rebecca turned out the lights earlier than normal. This drew the Watcher's attention. He activated the thermal imaging camera and saw what he thought was Althea and Egan engaged in coital coupling. Sexuality had become a less important aspect of Domhanians lives as their species had pushed the limits of their mortality from a few decades up to several centuries. Naturally, there was a period during youth when sexual relations seemed quite enthralling and that was understood to be a hormonal artifact of their species' evolution. As Domhanians aged into adulthood, sex almost always ceased to be a primary behavioral motivator. That is not to say they never engaged in sexual relationships. Most adults, even as old as six hundred annum, enjoyed intercourse occasionally. But the libido was simply not as compelling after the age of about 150.

Nevertheless, the culture retained rigorous mores and taboos related to sexuality. Coupling on Domhan-Siol was pretty much just that – coupling. Any form of group sexual activity was virtually unheard of, as was voyeurism. This stricture was so deeply inculcated in the Watcher that his finger hovered over the infrared camera switch. *I could just turn this off and when the lights come back on the visual cameras will automatically activate – but my orders were to monitor all their activity – what if they decide to use the cover of darkness to exit the room?*

Realizing it was prudent to keep the thermal imager activated, he decided there was no need to watch the couple in bed. Their activity would only be of interest when they got out of bed. That he could monitor with occasional glances at the screen.

Danel felt a slight quiver begin deep in Rebecca's core which built to a whole body shudder. This was accompanied by a moan that began deep in her chest, rolled over her vocal cords, blew through her clenched teeth and out her lips. She giggled, nuzzled her nose into Danel's neck and said, "Yum!"

Danel put his index finger across her lips but was unable to suppress his own chuckle. He whispered, "Do you think we put on quite a good show?"

Rolling off of him, Rebecca slapped Danel's chest. "That's disgusting!"

Rebecca heard in Danel's whisper the grin she could not see in the dark, "So what do you want to do now?"

She leaned in and kissed his chest. "Now we buy our friends some time. They won't be looking for Egan and Althea as long as the Watchers think they're here enjoying a post-coital snuggle."

"And that sounds like a pleasurable deceit, but we should cut bait and run in two hours tops," Danel replied.

The six fingers of Danel's right hand entwined with Rebecca's left. They took turns dozing, but one or the other always stayed awake as if on some intuitively arranged watch duty.

CHAPTER SIXTEEN

CLOAKS OF INVISIBILITY

THE WAFT of steeping tea greeted Ramuell when he opened the door. He was surprised to find a stranger sitting in front of the computer. His grandmother had pulled up one of the dinette chairs and was sitting on the man's right. She was drumming her fingers rhythmically on the desktop – a sign that usually conveyed her frustration or impatience or both.

Ramuell pulled up short, concerned that he was intruding. Both the adults hesitantly tore their attention away from whatever they were studying on the screen. Gathering his composure, the stranger stood and offered his hand. As Ramuell tapped the upturned palm, he shot an inquisitive glance at Kadeya. Her tone was intended to put her grandson at ease, "Ramuell, this is Lector. We've known each other since childhood. We grew up in the same neighborhood and went to school together. It's been a century since last we saw each other."

Lector tilted his head, "Ohhh, it's been longer than that."

Kadeya replied, "Yeah, I suppose you're right. Anyway, you

can imagine my shock when I learned he's the Mission's Chief Librarian and Records Custodian."

"I'm sure that was a pleasant surprise," Ramuell commented cordially, though he was certain he'd sensed some tension. Masking his concern, he tossed his bag on the sofa and asked, "So what are you up to? Trying to find the whereabouts of your childhood sweethearts?"

Seizing the opportunity to lighten the mood, Lector joked, "We're way too old to know what to do with them even if they could be found!" As they laughed, Ramuell noticed Lector tapping the computer's power switch.

Kadeya clapped her hands and said, "Hey, it's time for some sustenance. I missed lunch and am starving."

"The galley is offering a dinner of fish and vegetation harvested from Ghrain's oceans. If you haven't had any yet, you're in for a treat," Lector replied.

"Actually we had seafood soon after arriving. We were true believers by the second bite. You'll be joining us I hope—we have so many memories to refresh."

Lector raised one eyebrow and said, "We may have stories you'd rather Ramuell not hear."

Ramuell responded to the banter, "Oh come on, I'm seventy-one annum—can't imagine your stories will be **too** shocking."

Chuckling, the three made for the door. As they exited Ramuell gave a furtive glance at the powered-down computer. Kadeya noticed her grandson's expression and with an almost imperceptible shake of her head, she puckered her lips as if to say 'shh.'

At dinner, the old friends reminisced nonstop. They spoke of family members whom Ramuell had never known; of friends and school pranks; laughs and loves and losses. Clearly they'd been more than just casual acquaintances.

Though he tried to be attentive to the conversation, Ramuell's mind wouldn't lay still. His thoughts kept wandering back to the scene he'd walked in on when entering their cabin. Since the lab visit by the Chief Science Officer, Kadeya had seemed aloof – no aloof wasn't quite the right word – perhaps distracted. At work she was spending more time behind her closed office door. Something was askew. Ramuell was relieved when the dinner conversation began winding down.

With a sigh Lector said, "This has been such a treat. I had not thought of these things for centuries. Thank you, my friend."

"Oh, the pleasure has been mine," Kadeya replied. Then casting a look in Ramuell's direction, "Though I fear we may have bored my grandson to tears—and tomorrow is another workday." With that, the three stood and offered each other upturned palms.

Ramuell said, "It's been a pleasure meeting one of my grandmother's old friends. Actually, I found your shared memories—uhm, enlightening."

"Uh oh, I fear we've given him a whole book full of excuses I'll be hearing." Affecting a falsetto voice, Kadeya teased, "But Grandma, you and Lector did such and such, blah, blah, blah." They all laughed, tapped palms again and parted ways.

As soon as they rounded the bend of the circular corridor en route to their cabin, Ramuell turned to Kadeya, "What's going on?"

She led her grandson out to the observation deck. They strolled along the seven-metre-wide walkway paying little attention to the spectacular views. Speaking in a low tone,

Kadeya told Ramuell how she had found Lector holed up in the library.

"After Chief Durela's visit to the lab, I decided to learn more about the Serefim Presidium. I started with their information site. Their Charter and Mission is a relatively straightforward statement of purpose, loaded with boilerplate language giving the Presidium a great deal of latitude. But the lack of language specifying restraints on their power is troubling.

"When reading the biographies of the Presidium members I became concerned by the oblique appointment process: how members are nominated, vetted, and ultimately who has the authority to appoint." Pinching the bridge of her nose she added, "The info regarding each member's background and experience is mostly pabulum.

"Quite by accident I stumbled across Lector's personnel record and learned he was on the orbiter. This morning I went to the library and found his office door ajar. When I peeked inside Lector looked up, took a couple of seconds to process what he was seeing, then jumped to his feet and rushed across the room to welcome me. It was sweet.

"We spent half an hour catching-up and laughing. But when I tried to turn the conversation to the Presidium, Lector became decidedly guarded. Late this afternoon he showed up at our cabin with a computer from the Records Resource Center. He logged in with an untraceable code that gave us top-level security clearance.

"Even before opening the computer he handed me a note explaining that his office is under constant surveillance. The note also said it's possible our apartment is likewise bugged with hidden microphones.

"At that point, I wondered if Lector was making much ado about nothing. Then he pulled out an electromagnetic signal jammer. It seems he genuinely believes we have reason for concern. I harkened back to Chief Durela's admonition, 'Be careful about making enemies out here, and even more careful when making friends.'"

Kadeya stopped walking and peered out at the moon. "Now I'm not certain if his apprehensions are justified or if he's just being paranoid."

"Grandmother, even if he is paranoid, that begs the question what made him so?"

"Exactly! What does he know that has his anxiety ratcheted up to the point of living in fear of hidden microphones?" After a few silent paces she added, "And even more troubling—if the Serefim Presidium is employing Watchers, why?"

CHAPTER SEVENTEEN
ESCAPE

When Egan and Althea rounded the corner outside their room they saw Leeza holding an elevator door. She gestured for them to join her with a twitch of her head. When the elevator arrived at the 22nd floor, Leeza waved them across the hall into the janitor's closet. After closing the door behind them, she opened the electric panel and tapped in a code on a small keypad. Egan and Althea stumbled as the closet turned elevator lurched downward.

While descending into building's sub-basement Leeza explained that they would be met by two men who would escort them out a utility corridor to a getaway vehicle. The Deputy Secretary of the Law and Order Directorate had arranged for their transport to a safe and comfortable place to recover from their ordeals. Almost as an afterthought Leeza added "You'll be meeting him by the way, and there'll be no big needles or threats of injections with truth serum!"

They exited into a long corridor with a smooth concrete floor. The walls and ceiling were almost completely hidden behind pipes, conduit and cables. Leeza gestured toward the two men and said, “Hasp and Toth are on the hospital’s security team, and you can trust them.”

Toth said, “Hello Dr. Althea – Professor Egan. I’m sure this is all very confusing.” Laughing he added, “Hell, even I’m confused. But as Dr. Leeza said, we’re going to take care of you.” Reaching into Hasp’s backpack Toth pulled out a bundle of garments. “Right now you should change out of Danel’s and Rebecca’s uniforms and into these clothes.”

As soon as Egan and Althea were changed, Toth said “Folks it’s quite a hike out of this tunnel. The vehicle will start making passes by the pick-up location in about ten minutes. It will stop when the driver sees the little flag I place beside the road.” He pulled a tiny yellow flag attached to a wire stake out of his coat pocket.

Hasp gave Leeza a quick hug, an uncommon display of affection to be sure, clapped his hands together and said, “Okay—let’s start making tracks!”

Leeza offered the couple both hands extended palms up and said, “You’re in good hands. Everything is going to be fine.” First Althea then Egan tapped Leeza’s palms.

As they moved off toward the utility corridor’s exit, Leeza retreated in the opposite direction. Before entering a stairwell, she glanced over her shoulder at Hasp and the retreating foursome.

Walking rapidly down the corridor, Althea asked, “Are you the gentlemen who arranged for us to see the videos in our room.”

Hasp lifted this chin slightly and said, “Yes, we thought that was a pretty clever way to communicate with you. By the way, you folks were wonderful and so was Leeza. And tonight your performance with Danel and Rebecca was so good the Watchers still think you're asleep upstairs."

Egan estimated they had walked over a kilometre when they arrived at an ascending stairwell. The thirty steps ended abruptly at a short ladder. Toth climbed up first and opened the polymer hatch cover. He leaned out and stuck the flag in the dirt.

Hasp said, "Okay, let's get ready to go quickly when Toth signals. Dr. Althea, climb up the ladder and wait just behind him. Professor Egan and I will follow you."

About a minute later Security Chief Farris pulled an ambulance onto the dirt shoulder of the road. Toth said, "Let's roll!" All four scrambled up the ladder and into the vehicle. Upon exiting, Hasp grabbed the flag and swung the hatch cover closed. He pressed a key fob and heard the locking mechanisms click.

They exited the ambulance in front of a tea house. Farris remained inside the parked ambulance on the off-chance there might be need for a hasty departure. Hasp and Toth seated themselves at an open table while Althea and Egan made their way toward the restrooms in the back. There they saw a woman wearing a yellow sweatshirt holding the backdoor open. Without a word they walked out and stepped into a personal use vehicle.

After engaging the vehicle's auto-drive, the woman turned to her passengers and said, "You're almost home. I've programmed the car to take a rather circuitous route so I can be certain we're not being followed. After all the feints and turns, a safe-house lies at the end of our ride."

After a couple of hours Rebecca and Danel decided it was time to depart the hospital. Just at that moment the Watcher at the Anotas O&M Hub glanced at the screen. When the couple opened the room door, he switched to the cameras in the hospital's 5th floor corridor. Both people were wearing the appropriate clothes, but it seemed they were intentionally keeping their faces averted from the security cameras. The Watcher was puzzled when they rounded the corner and entered a service elevator. He quickly accessed the elevator's camera and saw they were silently holding hands and still looking at the floor. He became alarmed when they exited the elevator at the basement level. The couple walked down the corridor and entered a stairwell without operational security cameras or microphones.

The Watcher grabbed his communicator and hit three digits. "Our hospital guests are on the move!"

The dispatcher at the other end of the call said only, "We're on it." She called Agents Chelt and Dyer, who were both asleep. Agent Chelt thanked the dispatcher and said he'd go over to the hospital immediately.

Agent Dyer responded in almost panic mode. "Have you dispatched an apprehension team?"

"No sir, the protocol is to contact the agents assigned to the case."

"Why the hell didn't you also deploy our apprehension team?" Dyer demanded apoplectically.

The dispatcher was having none of it. "Sir, with all due respect, this is a 'monitor only' assignment. These people are not being detained and have been charged with nothing. I'm not authorized to dispatch a team to subdue them. If they have actually left the hospital without being discharged we **might** have the authority to return them to the facility."

"What a pile of bison crap! These people are a threat."

The scolding angered the dispatcher, but she kept her voice steady, "In which case the assigned officers should have secured the appropriate information to document the need for an Order of Detention. Since we don't have that Order, we don't have authority to apprehend. I'd recommend you get out of bed and get down there as soon as possible." With that she disconnected the call. Dyer threw his communicator on the bed and began yanking clothes from his wardrobe.

Agent Chelt intentionally did not called Chief Melanka to update her on the unfolding situation. In his anger, Agent Dyer forgot to do so.

———

When Danel and Rebecca arrived at the sub-basement they found the hospital staff uniforms Egan and Althea had shed in front of the elevator. They hastily put them on and boarded the secret janitorial closet/elevator and rode it up twenty-six floors. Three huge grins greeted them when they exited into the hospital's security center.

"So far, so good," Chosant beamed.

Sean added effusively, "You guys are the best!"

As Liam slowly shook his head his grin morphed into a chuckle. "I suppose it's time for the four of us to make our own exits."

Turning to Chosant, he said, "Your assistance has been beyond valuable—and it will not be forgotten, my friend."

Casting his eyes downward the captain responded, "Yeah, uhm, all in a day's work I suppose."

A few minutes later Sean and Liam sauntered across the

foyer trying to blend in with the hospital's normal comings and goings. A couple dozen steps outside of the main entrance they were met by the trio of Anotas impersonators who had been staking out Althea's and Egan's room two nights prior.

Closing ranks the three men blocked the sidewalk. Liam straightened to his full height and calmly said, "Excuse us gentlemen."

"Where are they?" demanded the man standing in the middle.

Sean asked, "Who exactly are you talking about?"

The man spoke again while his companions assumed more combative stances, "You know exactly who I'm talking about! Where are they? Where have you taken them?"

"As you can see, we're standing here in front of you. How could we possibly have taken anybody anywhere?" Sean replied.

Being less coy, Liam added, "Perhaps you're referring to the patients in room 579. If so, I'm quite certain their present location is none of your business. Now if you'll excuse us, I have an appointment in a few minutes."

Liam turned his body to a 45° angle and shouldered his way through the muscular barrier blocking the sidewalk. The man on the right reached out, grabbed Liam's hand and growled, "Maybe you're going to be a bit late!"

Sensing how quickly this could go sideways, Sean stepped off the walkway. With strength and quickness, Liam twisted his hand out of the man's grip and took a long step forward. Fixing his balance on the ball of his left foot, he executed a lightning-fast spinning kick. His right heel flew less than two centimetres below his assailant's chin and landed a crushing blow directly to the throat. With a strangled gasp the man crumpled. Both of his comrades were so shocked they jumped back rather than trying to catch their partner as he fell.

Landing hard on his elbow, his face whiplashed into the sidewalk snapping the nasal bone.

Taking advantage of the momentary flabbergast, Sean scampered around the right side of the kerfuffle giving wide berth to the two men who remained standing. Liam was already making a hasty retreat from the scene. They absolutely did not want to be recognized by any of the passersby.

Moments after Liam and Sean rounded the corner onto the ramp into the train station, Agents Chelt and Dyer trotted across the lawn toward the gathering crowd. They noticed two rather formidable looking men pushing their way out of the middle of the squash and walking hastily toward the parking lot.

Chelt and Dyer looked at each other quizzically. Chelt said, "We'll check out the video at the O&M Hub."

Liam and Sean boarded the first Nexo de Mando Autorail car that arrived at Hospital Station. They didn't care which line they were boarding. All that was important was putting distance between themselves and the scene in front of the Hospital. When the doors shut, Liam discreetly tucked his shirttail back into his pants. Sean looked up at his friend and said with a combination of awe and amusement, "Where in all the galaxy's frozen-hells did that come from?"

"I don't know! It's been over a hundred annum since I've even practiced Bonn Sabaid. I used to be pretty good though." Liam said with a hint of embarrassment.

"Riiiight—pretty good!! As I recall you were ranked among the top five in the world for your weight class."

"Yeah, I was rather passionate about the sport. I just got too old—too many aches and pains." Looking at his reflection in the window he added with chagrin, "I suppose a couple centuries of muscle memory trumped my frontal lobe during that little incident."

Sean opened his mouth as if to say something, paused to collect his thoughts, then said, "All we can do is hope what just happened was not recorded and remains a 'little incident'—though I rather doubt the fella' you kicked in the throat will think of it that way."

Captain Chosant had been monitoring the security cameras as his colleagues exited the hospital. He was astounded when he saw Liam's devastating kick. Chosant's stunned inaction lasted for only two seconds before he initiated a pixilation corruption of all the hospital's security camera recordings. If by some chance he received a request by a law enforcement agency for the footage, he could act surprised by the system-wide failure. A failure that resulted in unusably distorted images.

Even though he was certain the Watchers at the O&M Hub had already saved their download of the camera feed, Chosant understood that Anotas would never go public with the video. In addition to the likely political fallout from trying to embarrass Deputy Secretary Liam, release of the video would expose the O&M Hubs to public scrutiny; something the Anotas leadership wouldn't allow.

As Chosant thought through the plausible scenarios, the unknown variable again was the arrival of the three men who tried to stop Sean and Liam. He suspected they were working for the Business and Industry Council, but their interest in the return of two long-lost surveyors eluded him. Clearly the Council had an equine in the race, but Chosant just couldn't imagine what their stake might be.

CHAPTER EIGHTEEN
THE SAPIEN-SPHERE

By the sixth undecim it was clear Kadeya was not acclimatizing well. On her seventy-fifth day she had an appointment with the physician. The two had become friends and were sitting in the doctor's spartanly appointed office sipping tea in companionable silence. Setting his cup down, Doc said, "Kadeya, you're a scientist and I'm certain it comes as no surprise that I'm pulling the plug. You must discontinue the Surface Preparation Protocol."

"No, I'm not surprised," Kadeya sighed. "Disappointed? Sure. But my body just has too many annum on it to adapt—Ramuell seems to be doing well though."

"Absolutely! His acclimatization is one of the easiest I've ever monitored. As for you, nobody wants to risk your health trying to hammer a wooden peg into a metal post. There are too many important things for you to do your labs. Now understand that this doesn't preclude occasional short-term assignments on the surface."

"I get it Doc. I'm assuming you don't just pull me out cold-turkey."

"No, definitely not! In fact we start moving you at the same pace in the opposite direction. Beginning tomorrow your day will be lengthened by one minute, the humidity in your cabin and laboratory will be increased incrementally, you'll begin drinking slightly less fluid, etcetera."

"So, this becomes a logistical logjam for Ramuell and me."

"Not really. For the next forty-five days Ramuell can move into the Ghrain-3 Atmospheric Simulation Torus. The G3AST houses staff who are between assignments on the surface. The atmospheric conditions in the torus mimic those on the surface. They have their own living quarters, fitness facilities, and galley," Doc explained.

"You know, even though Ramuell may seem older, he's still just a lad."

Doc nodded, "Kadeya, I understand, and this is your call. If you want to delay his surface deployment nobody would hold it against you. Because Ramuell just turned seventy-two annum this is something you alone must decide."

"So it may seem," Kadeya replied with an amused expression. "But in reality Ramuell would never forgive me if I pulled him out. He'll be okay—it hasn't been easy on him growing up without his parents. I've tried to be a good surrogate, but it's just not the same. And hey, he is so gifted he'll be able to do us a lot of good down there."

"No doubt—and it's not like you'll be unable to see him. In the meantime, there's no reason he cannot continue to work in your lab."

"Really! How do you arrange that?" Kadeya asked in a pitch one octave higher than usual.

Patting Kadeya's forearm, Doc said, "I'll rig up a breather he can wear that will provide the dryer air of Ghrain-3 while we slowly increase the atmospheric humidity in the lab. Now each day his work hours are going to decrease incrementally while your schedule will be lengthening, but with a little massaging of schedules you'll still be able to work together quite a bit."

"That makes me feel better. And we can still have daily contact while he's on the planet. I might have to pull rank and insist that the supervisors down there aren't bovines about allowing him extra telecom hours."

Doc stood and offered his palm, "No doubt you have the clout to reserve as much time as you want. No one would dream of fussing with Dr. Kadeya about that!"

Kadeya tapped Doc's palm and said, "Now I've got to go explain all of this to the kid. I'm not much looking forward to that." Then laughing at herself, "Who am I kidding? He'll think it's a big adventure to be rid of his old grandma for a while!"

Ramuell was excited about moving into what was facetiously called the "sapien-sphere." Because he wasn't yet fully acclimatized, he had to remain in a special tent-size cabin and wear his breather while in the facility's common areas. Both his room and the breather were programmed to continuously make the incremental atmospheric adjustments necessary for completing the acclimatization process.

Everyone else in the G3AST were acclimatized and would be returning to duties on the planet's surface. Walking around with a breather apparatus made Ramuell stand out like a five-fingered hand. He was called "Newbie." Though not fond of the nickname, he realized the advantage of anonymity. Because most of the surface veterans didn't bother to learn his name, they failed to make the connection that he was Kadeya's grandson. This suited him, fine as he desired no special treatment.

Conversations on the G3AST made Ramuell aware of the gulf between the people serving lengthy tours on the surface and the Serefim Presidium administrators, most of whom rarely left the orbiter. He wasn't sure if Kadeya, being a famous scientist, was viewed as one of 'them' or one of 'us' by the folks in the sapien-sphere.

While the folks in the G3AST were not outright disrespectful, he sensed their comments and expressions implied something like, 'Kid, you have no idea what you're in for!' His efforts to engage his more experienced colleagues were often met with cryptic responses. Nevertheless, he persevered. After a few days in his new digs, Ramuell's doggedness ingratiated him to a couple of the "old-timers." Azazel and Semyaza took him underwing and always invited him to join them in the galley at mealtime.

Ramuell learned that Semyaza and Azazel were Area Directors at two of the nine Scientific Study Projects scattered around the planet. Each area was staffed with 250 to 300 scientists and support personnel. Their research was focused primarily on geology, paleontology, biology and anthropology.

"The two western hemisphere continents have no indigenous humanoids," Azazel explained. "So there's only one Scientific Study Project on each of those continents. There are three projects on the largest southern hemisphere continent. Semyaza is the director of the NWA-1 project in the northern portion of that continent."

"And you are the director of which area?" Ramuell asked.

"I'm posted at SWA-1. Our headquarters camp is almost exactly eighteen hundred kilometres north of NWA-1. We are only about four hundred kilometres south of one of the continent's ice sheets," Azazel answered.

"And there's no way we'd trade our balmy weather with SWA-1," Semyaza teased.

"I'd been thinking the equator had been making you a bit soft," Azazel said pointing at his friend's stomach.

Though they only spent fourteen days together in the G3AST, Ramuell came to consider these two men as both mentors and friends. One morning in Kadeya's laboratory, Ramuell mentioned the prior evening's conversation. "At dinner we were talking about the nefilim. Azazel shared that gigantism spontaneously manifests in clans that have had no prior contact with the mutation. I was not aware of that."

"Even though we haven't seen demographic dispersal data, I had feared that might be the case," Kadeya responded.

"What made you think so?"

"Actually, you did. When you confirmed traces of *neandertalis* DNA in a large swath of the largest continent's sapiens. I had a feeling the spontaneous expression of gigantism was a distinct possibility once the sapiens with *neandertalis* DNA were exposed to our retroviruses or interbred with sapien-hybrids. I suspect the mutation of the cell cluster in the pituitary gland is a recessive trait and manifests occasionally among populations with traces of *neandertalis* and retroviral altered DNA."

Following his grandmother's train of thought, Ramuell said, "Ahh, so it's only when carriers of the genetic mutation mate with each other that the trait becomes dynamic."

"Correct, and from what our observers have reported, the nefilim are both hyper-sexualized and hyper-aggressive. When they force themselves on other clans, they spread the mutation."

"Perhaps that's why Azazel considers the nefilim such abominations. He has not said we should exterminate them, but I suspect he'd endorse that course of action. Semyaza's not quite so adamant."

"Hmm—and how do they feel about the individual nefilim who appear spontaneously in other clans?"

"They agree that culling would be most expedient. It seems the nefilim behaviors are simply atrocious, particularly when there are significant numbers of them within a clan. If what they tell me is accurate, I can understand their attitude."

"'If what they tell you is accurate'...therein lies the horns of our dilemma." She paused, rubbing her temples with both hands. "We must make sure your surface assignment is in a position where you can study the nefilim firsthand. Chief Durela made it perfectly clear that our number one assignment is to get a handle on the gigantism mutation with all its ramifications."

Two undecim after Azazel returned to the surface, Ramuell received a message from his friend.

Hello Ramuell – I trust this finds you well. If my calculations are correct, you are within just a few days of completing the acclimatization process. You should be proud – it's not easy and from what I've heard you've done remarkably well. Congratulations!

I'm writing to ask if you would be interested in joining my team on the surface. If so, please schedule a video-com by contacting SurfaceCom@StationSWA-7. We'll discuss the details of your assignment face-to-face. One thing you should know in advance, I envision a real job for you. You'll not be a go-fetch-it errand boy.

Looking forward to visiting with you soon.

Azazel

Operations Director, SWA-7

While he read the message Ramuell's bouncing knee jangled the miscellany cluttering his desk drawer. He was so excited he forgot to grab his breather as he bolted from the G3AST to find his grandmother. At this hour he figured she'd most likely be in the galley or having tea in the lounge. She was in neither place. Remembering that she had just rented a new apartment, Ramuell called up the station schematic on his foliopad. The map suggested the two most expedient routes.

The cabin door was slightly ajar at his grandmother's new digs. Knocking lightly, Ramuell stepped tentatively across the threshold. "Grandma, are you here?"

"Yes, come in Ramuell."

Kadeya and Lector were hanging a large framed photograph of Ghrain-3. "Since these are going to be my permanent quarters, Lector and the library staff gave me this picture as a housewarming gift. What do you think?"

"It's stunning!"

"So to what do we owe the honor?" Then with a mock sternness Kadeya added, "And where's your breather?"

Ramuell gave a one-shoulder shrug and dug the foliopad out of his satchel, "I just got a message from Azazel. He's asked me to join his team on the surface."

Kadeya clapped her hands, "That's **great** news!"

As he handed the foliopad to his grandmother, Ramuell noticed an inscrutable expression flit across Lector's face.

She read the message and said, "You know SWA-7 is tracking clans with high rates of gigantism. This is exactly the type of assignment I was hoping to arrange for you. So, you move out and don't even need your old grandma's help anymore!"

Ramuell laughed, "You know that's not true! And anyway, if this turns out to be the kind of assignment we discussed the other day, I'll be needing your help more than ever."

Gazing intently at her grandson, "I think we'll be reliant on each other more than ever."

When she turned to look at Lector she too sensed that he didn't fully share their enthusiasm. "What?" she prodded.

Lector narrowed his eyes considering how much to say. "I believe this is a remarkable opportunity. It's a huge honor to receive this invitation from Azazel. He's the most respected of the Area Directors within the scientific community. He's also the most politically connected of the bunch. For that reason, there are those among the Presidium who consider him a threat—including the Grandmaster."

"Elyon doesn't trust Azazel?" Kadeya asked incredulously.

"It's not a matter of trust," Lector explained. "I'm sure you've sensed the rift between the scientific community and the Presidium. In general, the Presidium and Elyon incline toward our business interests on Ghrain-3, rather than the scientific aspects of our mission." Lector exhaled loudly. "Those interests have been out of alignment for some time now. Because of Azazel's leadership position, he often challenges the Presidium. Azazel has considerable clout both here and on the homeworld—and Elyon doesn't like sharing power."

"So are you saying Ramuell shouldn't accept the offer?" Kadeya asked.

"Oh no, I think he should! But because he will be at SWA-7, **all** of your communications will be monitored. You will need to be exceedingly discrete."

Kadeya looked at her grandson and said, "We can do that."

"We can," Ramuell concurred.

Kadeya added, "This is too good of an opportunity to turn down—I am so, so proud of you."

As he walked back to the G3AST, Ramuell had a niggle of worry that Lector's concerns just might be prescient.

CHAPTER NINETEEN
SAFE HOUSE?

THE DRIVER OPENED the front door and told Egan and Althea to wait on the porch while she secured the house. A couple minutes later she returned and with a flourish waved the couple inside. “Please make yourselves at home. There’s tea in the pantry and beer in the refrigerator. I’ve got to get back to town, but someone from the Directorate will be out here shortly. You might enjoy sitting out on the deck. A pleasant breeze is blowing in across the lake on the back of the property.”

An hour later the doorbell chimed. When Egan opened the door he was shocked to see Liam and Sean standing under the porch light. “We were told someone from the Directorate would be showing up, but I didn’t expect the Deputy Secretary.”

Liam chuckled and introduced Sean, “Here’s the guy who really runs the show. We’ve had a long, long night. With your permission I’m going to put on a pot of café. We’re needing a bit more jolt than a cup of tea.”

“With our permission—it’s your place isn’t it?” Althea

asked as she walked into the den.

Sean answered, "I suppose you could say we're all guests of the Law and Order Directorate."

They were drinking their café at the kitchen table when alarm lights began flashing in each ceiling corner. A startled cat jumped out of Liam's lap as Sean sprang to his feet. "Follow me —**now**!" he commanded.

Liam, Althea and Egan fell in behind Sean as he ran into the laundry room. He opened a large clothes dryer, which was not a dryer at all. He entered feet first and slid down a three metre shoot to a soft landing on the floor of a hidden room.

Liam motioned urgently for Althea and Egan to follow. Althea whispered, "Good gods!" and hopped into the mock dryer. Her husband and Liam followed. Sean flipped on the lights illuminating an impressive array of electronic equipment crammed into the small room. Monitors lined the walls, and all manner of other apparatus were neatly arranged throughout the house's nerve center.

Tapping icons on a computer screen Sean pulled up heat images of the intruders. Six individuals were widely spread out and approaching the house from the north and west sides of the property.

"How did they find us?" Egan asked.

With a tight lipped grimace Liam said, "I have an uncomfortable hunch."

Concern furrowed Sean's brow. "If you're right, we need to deal with that immediately." He opened a knee level drawer and pulled out an old-fashioned radionuclide sensing device. He ran the sensor over Liam's body. When he arrived at Liam's hand the device began humming loudly. Turning the dial he studied the bluish lit display. "Xenon 133, probably bonded to some kind of inert powder—no real danger, but you need to wash it off. It's still emitting plenty of energy for them to track."

"What's going on?" puzzled Althea.

"Well, not long after you made your exit from the hospital we had a run-in with some thugs who seemed to be trying to prevent our departure—or so we thought. The boss dredged up a bit of his former martial arts glory. When one of the interlopers grabbed Liam's hand as we passed by, the boss delivered a devastating pirouette heel kick to the man's throat. No doubt he's now a patient in the hospital. It's now obvious they weren't actually trying to stop us. They created the confrontation in order to smear a radioactive tracking material on Liam. That's how they found us—we led them here!"

Liam flipped open a hand-sized greyish control panel mounted above the tube they had just slid down. He tapped in a code and turned to the screens displaying the front yard. With the heel of his hand he smacked a red button protruding just left of the keypad. The thermographic images showed all six individuals grabbing the sides of their heads as they dropped and writhed on the ground. Liam walked over to a deep sink and said, "I set the sonic blast on wide-field—no time to waste with targeting."

No one spoke while Liam scrubbed his arms and hands with a hand brush and liquid soap. When he turned back around he glanced at the monitor screens. The intruders were slowly climbing to their knees. With an unreadable expression, he walked back over to the wall and slapped the red button again. Again all six of the individual stumbled. With a sideways nod of his head, he motioned Sean toward a large round vault door in the south wall.

Sean said, "It's time to take our leave. If you'll follow me..."

The vault was equipped with an old-style turn knob combination lock. He twisted the dial to the correct combination of five digits, grabbed the handle, rotated it left and pushed the heavy metal door open.

Liam stripped out of his clothes and put on pair of overalls that were hanging on a wall hook. Being the last person to leave, he pushed the vault door shut and spun a dial to reset the lock.

They had entered a tube over three metres in diameter. It was an aqua color and appeared to be made of a lightweight cellulose material treated with a waterproofing agent. Every two metres it was braced with egg-shaped supports. Trotting along Althea calculated their location. She reckoned they were somewhere south of the house – under the lake!

At about four hundred metres the tube made a noticeable upturn. They arrived at a second vault door and again Sean dialed in the combination and pulled the door open. He waved everyone into a dimly lit shed. Sitting in the middle of the shed was a six-seat quadcopter. Sean walked over to a power terminal mounted on a wall post and flipped a switch that began rolling up the retractable roof.

While boarding, Liam explained that the copter was equipped with stealth and remote piloting technologies. "I'll be piloting this leg of our journey."

They rose so rapidly Egan felt his stomach had been left on the ground. Thankfully, the ascent was shortlived. Liam leveled the aircraft off mere metres above the trees and they zipped at full throttle toward the earliest blush of dawn. An hour later Egan tapped Althea's hand and pointed down. It was light enough to make out the froth of surf as they sped out over Darna Mar, one of the planet's fourteen saltwater seas.

Once over the water, Liam descended even lower. About half an hour later he initiated a long arc to the north. "Folks, in about twenty minutes we'll be arriving at the third largest island in the Dragon's Back archipelago. We'll make a water landing in a beautiful little cove on the island's south side. Now the people who will meet us there may look a bit rough about the edges, but they are our friends.

"And they know how to keep secrets," Sean added.

"So will we be staying here awhile?" Egan asked.

With an enigmatic expression Sean replied, "Hopefully for a helluva lot longer than you were able to stay at the lake house!"

Liam looked askance at his friend, "This place is a good deal more remote, which has its pros and cons."

"Meaning...?" Althea asked.

He turned back from looking out the side window. "To begin with, the main benefit of being on this spit of land in a remote island chain is that we're very difficult to find. With that said, should the bad guys find us, it may be more difficult to extricate ourselves unseen."

"Can't we just make a quick getaway in the quadcopter?" Althea asked.

"Actually after we disembark, our folks in the aviation office will take over the controls and remotely pilot this bug back to Nexo de Mando."

As Liam hit the switch to inflate the water landing pontoons he added, "We will not be staying here with you indefinitely. After you've had time to get some rest and a chance for some unmonitored conversations with each other, the four of us need to have a talk. If we're going to be able to help you, we need to know what you know; why you're being hunted and by whom."

Egan and Althea exchanged a sad look just as Liam settled the quadcopter on the water's surface so lightly it hardly made a splash.

CHAPTER TWENTY

TRUTHS, HALF-TRUTHS, AND UNTRUTHS

As Captain Chosant had anticipated, Anotas-Deithe had instantaneously grabbed the images from the hospital's surveillance cameras. His pixilation would prevent other prying eyes, but Anotas already had the footage of Liam's shockingly effective take-down in front of the hospital's main entrance.

After studying the videos, Agents Chelt and Dyer determined the man and woman who had coupled in room 579 were not Egan and Althea, which raised several questions: Who were they? When had Egan and Althea departed? Where had they gone?

The agents were watching the incident in front of the hospital for a third time when Melanka arrived, shouldering her way between them without a word. After watching the tape, Melanka removed the pipe from her mouth, tapped out the burned herb in an ash receptacle, then slapped her thigh and laughed out loud. "What in the name of everything holy was that?"

Dyer was so taken aback by Melanka's response, he stood

almost at attention and said nothing. Chelt, on the other hand, relaxed and took in a deep breath. He snickered and said, "Can you believe that? The B&I Council goons sure didn't see that coming!"

Melanka spun around to face Chelt. She snapped, "Play the video again!" As they watched, Melanka demanded, "So are those the same men who were staking out room 579 a couple nights ago?"

Dyer, who had regained his composure, answered, "Yes ma'am."

Melanka jerked her communicator from her pocket and smacked the keys to call the Business and Industry Council. "So Mr. Chairman, have you had a chance to get over to the hospital to console your rent-a-cop yet?"

"What the hell are you talking about, Melanka?"

With faux concern in her voice, "Oh, you haven't heard? Well, Deputy Secretary Liam took out one of the boys you sent to stop him from leaving the hospital last night. I'd estimate it took him less than, what would you say Agent Chelt, three seconds?"

Melanka held the communicator out toward Chelt, who beamed and played along, "Oh, less than two seconds!" He covered his mouth to muffle his laughter.

"So it took the five-hundred-annum-old Deputy Secretary just a couple of seconds to flatten one of the B&I Council's muscle-bound thugs—my, my." Now her tone took on an edge of threat, "Regan, the last time we spoke I warned you not to interfere with my investigation. It looks like I need not have been concerned, given how easily Liam and Sean dismantled your team of incompetents. Nevertheless, the only reason I can imagine for you to disregard my warning is because you know something that I need to know."

Hiding fluster with bluster, Regan responded, "I'm sure I have no idea what you're talking about."

Melanka responded menacingly, "I see. Perhaps a face-to-face meeting will jog your memory. You'll be receiving a summons within the hour." She disconnected without waiting for a response. Agent Dyer was already placing the call to order a hand-delivered summons to Chairman Regan's office.

Regan understood from that moment on he would be under constant surveillance. There was nowhere for him to go – nowhere to hide. He instructed his assistant to clear his schedule for the remainder of the day. As soon she left his office, Regan placed his communicator on the desk and tapped in the com-code used exclusively for conference calls with the Business and Industry Council's Executive Committee.

Chairman Regan knew Anotas could only hold him for a couple of hours without delivering some kind of formal charge to his solicitor. He also knew if he appeared to be cooperating and strung the interview out, it would buy time to implement the B&I Council's plan.

Regan spent the entire afternoon spinning a mélange of truths, half-truths, and untruths for the Anotas interviewers. He never complain about the extended interrogation, nor did he ask for his solicitor. Almost five hours after his interview began, Regan walked out of the Anotas headquarters believing he'd woven an unfathomable obfuscation that would have Anotas investigators chasing their tails for an undecim. He seriously underestimated Melanka's intellect.

Soon after Regan was released, Melanka placed a call to the Law and Order Directorate. When Liam's administrative assistant explained that he would be incommunicado for an unspecified period, Melanka rasped, "I'll just bet he is! I need you to tell him to contact me—and there is absolutely no acceptable reason for delay. Is that understood?"

The administrative assistant explained there would be some delay because she was not able to contact Liam either. Melanka seethed, "Don't bullshit me! You contact him. Play him the recording of this conversation that I know you're making. You have him call me immediately. I'm not one of the B&I Council oafs; I **can** find him, but no one will be happy if you make me do that!"

CHAPTER TWENTY-ONE

TERRA FIRMA

RAMUELL'S HEART was pounding when the transport's doors slid open, and he took his first steps on the surface of an alien world. It was the most exciting moment in his young life. Azazel met him in the rock bunker just south of the landing pad. Naturally occurring unhewn stone was used for all landing and take-off control bunkers on Ghrain-3. At some point Domhanians would disassemble the control bunkers and scatter the huge stones asunder, leaving no trace of their existence to be found by future generations of sapien archaeologists.

Azazel swatted aside Ramuell's proffered palm and pulled his young friend into an embrace. He noted the surprised expression on Ramuell's face and said, "You're on Ghrain-3 now. You'll find our customs have evolved to fit the environment."

With no hint of judgment Ramuell asked, "Is that a good thing?"

Azazel tugged his earlobe. "I'm not sure, but it's a real

thing." He paused for a moment before changing the subject, "Down here it's lunch time and I'm hungry. Can you eat?"

"Actually I was eased into your schedule over the last five days. So I'll probably be hungry when you're hungry and tired when you're tired."

Leading the way down the path to the basecamp, Azazel said, "Great, this will be a good time to introduce you to some of your colleagues."

"About that, I think it's probably best not to mention who my grandmother is."

Azazel furrowed his brow. "I understand and appreciate that you want to plant your own row of beans. We won't introduce you as 'Kadeya's grandson,' but we won't hide that fact either. There will be questions about your age. It will be asked 'how did a seventy-two-annum-old kid get out here?' We'll just say you were raised by your grandmother and came to Ghrain-3 with her."

"And then they'll ask who my grandmother is..."

"Some will and we aren't going to lie," Azazel replied. "There simply is no reason to keep that fact a secret. Soon enough you will prove yourself and people will see you as Ramuell, rather than Kadeya's grandson."

Azazel's first assignment for Ramuell was literally to wander around, meet people, observe the flora and fauna, drink water from the streams, tag along with colleagues on day trips."

One morning Ramuell and Gadrel, SWA-7 chief geologist, were sitting at one of the outdoor tables near the kitchen dome soaking in the warmth of the sun while drinking tea. Gadrel explained there were 33.2 eleven-day undecim in the 365.24 day annum of Ghrain-3. "But don't start thinking that means we'll have a longer summer. In fact, you arrived during a warm spell. We've not had weather this warm for several annum."

"This is warm?!" Ramuell was wearing three layers of microfiber clothing.

Chuckling, Gadrel responded, "Yes, by this planet's standards at this latitude it is. Ghrain-3 is in one of its cold cycles. There have been times in the past when this area was covered with tropical plant and animal life. Not far north of here there's an area now covered with ice that was once at the bottom of a salt water sea."

"That explains why so much of the planet's water is captured as solids and liquids rather than gaseous," Ramuell observed.

"Correct. As you know our home world also has long-term warming and cooling trends. Here on Ghrain the temperature changes are more dramatic. We've found evidence of repeated cycles of glacial and interglacial periods. This glaciation began about sixty thousand Ghrain annum ago," Gadrel explained.

"How long do you think it will last? I'd sure like to warm up a little!"

"Yeah, newbie!" Gadrel teased. "Actually we've all experienced what we call 'the chill.' That's one reason new people arrive in what we euphemistically call summer." He grabbed a handful of the microfiber sleeves covering his arms and said, "During the cold kuuk we wear more layers of clothes and shelter up a good deal more. But even then we're able to venture out on some days.

"To answer your question, we don't know how long this glacial period will last, mostly because we aren't certain about the cause. It's likely there's no single cause. Volcanism, solar output, changing ocean currents, meteor strikes, the planet's wobble on its axis all seem to play a part. The problem for us is figuring out how these factors relate to each other. That's one of the things I'm studying." Gadrel chuckled, "Which seems a helluva thing for a geologist, huh?"

"Actually it seems awfully important in terms of understanding Ghrain-3," Ramuell replied.

They were looking at the mountain range north of the SWA-7 complex. Though Gadrel had been on the planet for several decades, he remained awed by the vivid colors made possible by the sun's white light and Ghrain's dry atmosphere. For Ramuell the views felt like sensory overload. He had been told he'd become accustomed to and soon love the vibrancy of the planet's surface.

Gadrel glanced at Ramuell and said, "Tomorrow I'm headed out to one of our excavations for a few days. I know geology isn't your field, but if you're interested in joining me, I'd be happy to talk with Azazel."

"That would be great!" Ramuell enthused. "Azazel told me I should tag along with colleagues on daytrips."

With a puzzled expression Gadrel asked, "Oh! So you haven't slept under the stars yet?"

"No, not yet; I've been sleeping in the dome I share with Tamel and Luke."

"Hmm, that might be an issue. I'll speak with Azazel and see if something can be worked out," Gadrel replied cautiously.

Much of the trail to the dig site was too treacherous for Rough-Terrain-Vehicles, and due to topography the wind currents were too unpredictable for quadcopters. The group, led by Gadrel, labored up and down the rocky, brushy terrain for over four hours. They arrived at Dig #421 just after mid-day. When Ramuell's pack was lifted off of his shoulders he felt like he might float. He expected to be quite sore by morning. This thought was of no real consequence, given how excited he was about this first adventure afield. He knew he was going to learn a lot – he had no idea.

The staff at the Dig were expecting their visitors and had planned a rather elaborate picnic lunch. Watching the deference afforded Azazel informed Ramuell just how extraordinary the Director's visit actually was.

After the buffet table was cleared and the left-over food returned to cold storage, Owan, the site's senior scientist, gave Gadrel, Azazel and Ramuell a guided tour. They began with a walk through the cordoned-off dig areas. Owan explained the painstaking process of removing and recording each fragment of interest found at every level within each of the two metre by two metre grids. Not only were the scientists studying the geological record, they were also finding fossilized remains of creatures that had lived and died millions of annum earlier.

Owan said, "Let's walk up to the artifacts tent—that's where we're keeping the really good stuff!"

Ramuell was amused at Owan's unabashed enthusiasm. The tent was something of a museum with thousands of artifacts stored in hundreds of carefully labeled crates. With a sideways glance at Ramuell, Gadrel nudged Azazel and said, "When it's time to shut this dig down we're going to need some strong backs to carry all these boxes out of here. Do you know any young guys who might be up to the task? It'll probably only take a few dozen roundtrips to move it all to SWA-7."

Ramuell rubbed his sore shoulders and said, "Yeah, uhm, I'll do my part—for as long as my not-so-strong back lasts."

Chuckling, Owan said, "With a few more fieldtrips you'll get used to carrying the backpack. Anyway, when moving day comes we'll have a quadcopter landing platform on a ridgetop only a couple of kilometres away. It'll still be a hard haul, but a two kilometre carry sure beats the eleven kilometres back to the basecamp."

Dinner that evening was more haphazard than the picnic lunch had been. People wandered into the cook tent when the mood struck. They pulled frozen bags of food out of the various coolers and lowered them into pots of boiling water. The only rhyme or reason Ramuell noticed was that no one helped themselves to more than three bags.

Owan insisted on choosing the meals for each of his guests. Ramuell was surprised by the food's quality and tastiness.

"Do you like it?" Gadrel asked.

"Yes! It's good."

Gadrel explained the meat was taken by judicious hunting of local herbivores. Most of the vegetables were harvested from local plants and seasoned with spices from the homeworld. The sweet, high-carbohydrate dish was made of products imported from Domhan-Siol.

After dinner Azazel, Gadrel and Owan sauntered over to a table at the edge of camp. They sat talking quietly while Owan smoked a pipe filled with a pungent herb. Ramuell sensed he'd been intentionally excluded and also suspected he was the subject of their conversation. When they returned, Azazel said, "It's been a long day and since you haven't slept under the stars yet, perhaps for this first night you'd be more comfortable taking a cot in one of the sleeping tents."

Ramuell said only, "Point me in the right direction—I'm having a hard time holding my head up." He slept the proverbial sleep of the dead.

When he crawled out of the sleeping bag the next morning his shoulders, back, and hips were quite sore. He hoped to limber up as the day passed. At the dining tables he found Azazel, Gadrel and Owan huddled around a foliopad screen.

"Good morning," Owan greeted. "Hope you slept well."

"Indeed I did! The exercise facility on the orbiter is good, but I never had a workout that compared to yesterday's hike." Pointing at the foliopad, Ramuell asked, "What's so fascinating?"

Azazel answered, "Oh we're considering location and design options for the quadcopter landing pad Owan mentioned yesterday. This would bore you to tears, so Owan has arranged for you to work with a paleontologist at the dig."

"That sounds great! When do I get started?"

"The teams have already headed down there," Owan replied. "After you've grabbed some breakfast, just follow the path to the site. Alicia will recognize you and show you the ropes." Teasingly he added, "Though she's a few annum older than you, she's awfully cute—be careful there."

Rolling his eyes, Ramuell stepped into the cook tent.

It was a great day! Ramuell and Alicia hit it off from the get-go. One tiny chip at a time they made progress extricating the fossil of an extinct birdlike creature from its eons of capture within the massive layer of limestone. As they worked, chatted and teased each other, Ramuell could not help but notice Owan had been right – Alicia was awfully cute.

Ramuell was cautious, as per his acclimatization training, to consume adequate fluids throughout the day. But he hadn't eaten enough food to replenish the calories burned by two consecutive days of high activity. He was famished when they traipsed back into camp. After a quick hand and face wash he made a beeline to the cook tent. A more thorough bathing could wait until after he'd woofed down a mound of sustenance.

Azazel and Gadrel were asking about Ramuell's day when Alicia walked over and took a seat between Azazel and Ramuell. To say the least, Azazel was impressed with the young paleontologist's poise and confidence.

After about an hour the conversation around the table began to die down. Ramuell eyes were at half-mast when Alicia said, "You look like you're about to drop."

"Yeah, you're right. The food helped, but I'm foot-draggin' tired. If you'll excuse me, I have to get washed up and hit the sleeping bag." He noticed the furtive glances around the table.

"Perhaps you'd like to join us sleeping under the stars," Azazel suggested. "We don't have night skies like this back home."

"Now that's an understatement! When I was aboard the orbiter I spent hours looking at the moon and the trillions of twinkling stars."

Alicia told Ramuell, "You go get cleaned up. I'll haul your cot and sleeping bag out to the clearing where we sleep."

Looking into Alicia's jade-green eyes Ramuell teased, "I'd already decided to sleep outside given the beauty of the night sky, but if I'd been on the fence, your offer would have tipped the balance!" He didn't get the giggles he'd expected. Rather, his four tablemates looked at him with expressions he could not quite discern.

That night, lying under the stars of Ghrain-3, was the first time in Ramuell's life that he dreamed.

Ramuell heard the others rouse and dress. Not wanting to talk to anyone just yet, he waited in bed until they departed for the kitchen tent. He had never experienced anything like the preceding night. He had no context to understand the thoughts and visions he'd experienced.

He'd read that people with certain types of neurological disorders occasionally had hallucinations. He couldn't tamp down the fear that perhaps he was developing a mental illness, though he knew those disorders usually manifested at a younger or much older age – usually, not always. But his nocturnal experience just did not seem pathological – it seemed, well, he didn't know what...

When he finally crawled out of his sleeping bag and made his way down to join his friends he was greeted with expressions of insightful concern. Azazel spoke first, "Good morning. How did you sleep?"

"Okay, I guess," he said hesitantly.

Alicia said, "The stars were beautiful weren't they?"

He looked at her and immediately turned his gaze to his teacup and mumbled, "Yeah, like I said, I spent a lot of time looking at them from the observation deck on the orbiter."

Recalling her own bewilderment the morning after her first night under the Ghrain-3 sky, Alicia took no offense at her new friend's testiness.

Ramuell instantly regretted his tone. *The thing is, she had been there; she'd been in his night visions – nothing untoward, but a level of intimacy that was well outside his comfort zone.* He didn't understand why he should feel embarrassed, but he did. He was confused and couldn't bring himself to look directly at this young woman with whom he'd so enjoyed working the day before.

Gadrel arrived at the table carrying several plates of food for the group. Sensing the tension, he understood its source. There was not even a word to describe these kinds of nocturnal insights in Domhan Standard. The local sapien clans called the experience "*sen*." Endeavoring to ease the tautness, Gadrel said, "So Ramuell—Azazel, Owan and I are going to hike up what we call 'fly-it-out-ridge' to scout the location for the copter landing pad. You're welcome to join us, or if you'd prefer I'm sure Alicia would welcome your assistance at the dig again today."

Ramuell glanced up at Alicia. When their eyes met, he quickly looked away like an awkward schoolboy. He hated himself for it. Trying to recover a modicum of composure, he replied a tad too robustly, "Yeah, I'd like to hike up there with you guys." He forced himself to look up at Alicia and said, "If that's okay with you?"

She responded gently, "I will miss your company." Scanning the thickening overcast she added, "But if you gentlemen are going to climb that mountain Owan euphemistically calls a ridge, you should get going and take your rain gear."

Ramuell wanted to be alone with his thoughts and lagged a bit behind the group. His companions understood exactly what he was experiencing. They remembered their own first *sen* experiences – it was not an experience anyone from Domhan-Siol ever forgot.

The protocol was to allow a person to have the experience and process it for a few days before having a discussion with the new *sen* initiate. Azazel had misgivings about the wisdom of this approach, but it was established hundreds of annum before his arrival at Ghrain-3. He had read reports about earlier efforts to prepare Domhanians for the experience that had likely done more harm than good. Mission psychologists had settled on the protocol now in place, but still Azazel believed there had to be a better way.

As they made their way up the trail, Azazel called out over his shoulder, "How're you doing, Ram?"

"Fine," came the cryptic reply.

Owan removed his hat and wiped his brow. "We'll be topping out soon and the hike home is all downhill. So, when we get up there we're really more than halfway done for the day."

"That sounds good," was all Ramuell could muster.

As it turned out, Owan's optimism was not well placed. The sky went from overcast to heavy cloud cover during the two hours it took the group to shoot the photographs and gather the level data. A third of the way back down the trail Alicia's weather forecast proved accurate. Footing grew precarious as the rocky path became slick in the drizzling rain.

The northern polar icecap extended in some places to below the 50th parallel. Even summer storms could be quite cold. About twenty minutes later graupel ice pellets began to mix in with the rain.

Though the trekkers had put on parkas when the drizzle began, they were becoming cold. Owan removed four microfiber body wraps from his backpack. "Slip these under your parkas and wrap them around your torsos. Pull them snug and fasten with the hook-and-loop strips."

"I'm not really that cold," commented Gadrel, who was a bit heavier than his companions.

"Good! Put on the wrap anyway. Given the footing, we're going to have to slow our pace, which may require another hour to reach camp. Hypothermia is something **we do not want**," Owan emphasized.

As they progressed carefully down the treacherous path Azazel commented, "Guess we won't be sleeping under the stars tonight."

"Oh you could sleep out, if you want to be wet and cold, but I doubt you'd be seeing many stars," Gadrel teased.

Chuckling, Owan replied, "Yeah, uhm, no thanks on the wet and cold. The excavation teams can't work when the soil is wet, so they've called it an early day. They'll have moved our cots into the sleeping tents before anything got too wet. We'll be comfortable enough."

For the first time all day Ramuell initiated a comment. "After dinner I know I'll be looking forward to a good night's sleep—warm and dry."

"That's understandable," Azazel concurred. "It's been three physically demanding days in a row. We'll be tuckered out by the time we get our boots off."

The Dig staff were holed-up in tents. Some were writing, some reading, and others playing a game on a board with dice and small stones. Ramuell found it fascinating. All such games he'd ever seen were played on foliopads. After watching the six players for a few minutes he trotted through the drizzle to the kitchen tent.

Alicia had laid out a meal for him and his comrades. She'd begun preparing it when she saw them round the switchback in the trail about a kilometre away. She joined the four of them, though she'd already eaten.

Ramuell didn't feel nearly as uncomfortable as he had at breakfast. Alicia didn't sit next to him, but they did engage in conversation. He was able to make eye contact with her when they talked. He understood what she was doing and appreciated her effort.

When Ramuell took a swig of tea he winced as the hot liquid hit a sensitive tooth.

"Are you okay?" Alicia asked.

"Oh, it's nothing. I've just got a bad tooth."

"Ugh!" Owan groaned. "I had one abscess on a remote field assignment, and that's damn sure no place for a tooth to blow out. You need to get that taken care of—soon!"

When the table was cleared, the four men stumbled to the tent and tumbled into their warm, dry beds. The last thing Ramuell saw before drifting off to sleep was the glow of Owan's pipe. The next thing he knew dawn beginning to brighten the tent.

The storm intensified during the night but had broken in the early morning hours. Because of its almost constant cloud cover, sunrises were seldom seen on Domhan-Siol. Ramuell heard a rustling at the tent door then Alicia gently put her finger on his lips. She motioned for him to follow her.

Upon exiting the tent, Ramuell's mouth flopped open. Never had he seen or even imagined a sky painted with such brilliant splashes of pink, red, yellow, and gold. Thunderstruck is the only word to describe how he felt as he stood transfixed by a post-storm sunrise.

Delight dancing across her face, Alicia whispered, "Bet you've never seen anything like that before."

"When Grandmother told me we were coming to Ghrain-3, I looked at a lot of photographs and saw bunches of sky, clouds, sunrise and sunset photos, but nothing..."

"Right, photos just do not—cannot—do this justice," Alicia agreed. "The enormity of it cannot be caught by a camera lens; no matter how good the photographer and camera may be."

They continued to stare at the gradually changing hues extending across almost half the sky. Ramuell said, "It's more than that."

"What do you mean?"

"It's more than just the lens aperture or the camera's

ability to capture the colors and light—it's—well, it's the emotional impact of standing here and really seeing it. I mean seeing it here and now, in real-time rather than as an image from the past."

Narrowing her eyes, Alicia turned to Ramuell and said, "Perhaps you've just realized one of the most important things about this place."

Without shifting his gaze, "Which is?"

"We cannot really describe Ghrain-3 to the folks back home." Gesturing expansively with both arms, "Even our best photos are but pale imitations of this reality. I suppose we don't have the language to describe this place because our people simply don't have a common frame of reference. Heck, that applies to a mere sunrise and there are many, many things here that are a great deal more complex than dawn's light bouncing off of the bottom of a cloud layer."

Tearing his eyes away from the eastern horizon, Ramuell faced Alicia and was staggered by what he saw. Like the clouds, her skin and hair reflected the color of the sky; she glowed. Ramuell had never seen a more beautiful creature. Struggling mightily not to gawp, he stammered, "Uhm, yeah—I'm beginning to get a sense of the planet's mysteries."

They could smell café brewing in the kitchen tent. As Alicia turned to go she said over her shoulder, "The **magic** and the mysteries, my friend—magic and mysteries."

CHAPTER TWENTY-TWO

SEN REUNITED

Being too wet for excavation work, the staff at Dig #421 were enjoying a leisurely morning. They sat at tables talking, sharpening knives, repairing tools, and patching torn clothes. A lot of tea was being drunk and the pipe smokers had claimed a table at the east end of the camp where they sat amiably puffing away.

Azazel, Owan, and Ramuell hiked down to a creek and managed to net over fifty fish. That evening the camp was treated to the freshly caught feast. As they ate a dessert of wild melons, Azazel waxed nostalgic for the days when he spent more time afield.

Owan mentioned that the Crow Clan was in Blue Rock Canyon. "They've pretty much taken up permanent residence in the caves."

With a sideways glance, Azazel said, "And your point is?"

"Oh, nothing really...they're probably catching some whoppers out of the big river right about now."

Scratching the back of his neck Azazel grunted, "Um hmm."

Ramuell sensed that the two men were sharing an unspoken secret.

Without anyone saying, 'let's clean up this mess,' people began clearing the tables. Others departed for the sleeping tents. They removed cots and placed them outside for a night under the stars. Ramuell busied himself with the latter group, moving his, Owan's and Azazel's cots. He considered bringing Alicia's out as well but was reticent about doing so. Half an hour later he noticed, with a mild pang, that she had pulled her cot outside but had not placed it nearby.

Unlike the previous night, when sleep had settled on him as a luxurious oblivion, over the next several hours the *sen* enveloped him completely with its extrasensory awareness.

Ramuell froze mid-stride when he saw them walking toward him. Then he bolted into his mother's arms. His father stepped forward gathering both wife and son in a group embrace. Ramuell knew they were not on the homeworld, though he didn't understand where they were. He was not a little kid, but he wasn't seventy-two annum either. So odd!

His parents looked exactly as he remembered; handsome and physically fit. "I've missed you! Where have you been?" he asked.

"Not a day goes by that we don't think of you and talk about you and love you," Althea replied. "If we could get home we would. We are prisoners of beings from another world. They treat us well, force us to do nothing except travel with them and observe what they show us. We are healthy and we're not being hurt."

Ramuell took a step back. "What do you mean you're prisoners!?"

Althea waved a hand dismissively. "No. No. I misspoke. Prisoner doesn't really describe our relationship with the Beag-Liath. They're a highly advanced humanoid species. They've been nothing but kind to us. They seem to believe there are things we must be shown. We aren't free to return home because we don't have access to our 4D-

ship. We believe they've promised to return us to Domhan-Siol, but because they use an entirely different space travel technology, we really don't have any sense of the timeframe for our journey."

"Where are we now? How is this possible?" Ramuell asked.

Egan replied, "Those are questions we cannot answer. We just don't know. It's my sense we only have a short time together. We should make the most of it."

Althea took both of Ramuell's hands in hers. Tears pooled on her eyelashes. "I've missed you so, so much—but your father is probably right. We likely don't have much time together and there are some things you must see."

Suddenly they were standing beside a pumping station with enormous pressurized gas storage tanks. Ramuell didn't understand how they got there. They'd been joined by a small grey bipedal being with an oversized head and longish arms and hands. The four of them watched the hive of activity. The people coming and going around the worksite seemed completely oblivious to their presence.

The overseers spoke Domhan Standard to each other and a different language with the non-Domhanian workers. The extraterrestrials were doing all of the heavy lifting, but none were using any of the mechanized equipment.

The Domhanians wore expressions of fatigue tinged with something akin to aggressiveness. Whereas the laborers trudged slowly about their respective jobs and seemed sullen or cowed or both. Many had open sores and other visible injuries.

Ramuell looked at their companion, whom he assumed was one of the Beag-Liath his mother had mentioned. It gazed at Ramuell for a long moment, then shook its head. Ramuell understood this as a rebuke.

The four of them walked some distance away from the worksite and took seats resting their backs against the shady side of a boulder. Completely bewildered, Ramuell turned to his parents and asked, "Who are they? What is this place about?"

The alien creature stared at Ramuell. After an uncomfortable moment, Althea reached over and took Ramuell's right hand in both of hers. She gazed at their coupled fingers.

Egan cleared his throat and began, "We've been taken to several such sites by the Beag-Liath. Our ability to communicate with them is limited because our sensory and communication modalities evolved differently. In most other ways, we're almost identical. It seems to me they're showing us these places to enlighten us, or shame us, or perhaps to warn us."

Ramuell interrupted, "I—I don't understand. What are they showing you?"

Exhaling loudly, Egan continued, "This is a rather small operation. Judging by the equipment, they're likely extracting subterranean helium. The non-Domhanians you saw are slave laborers. They are sentient creatures from some other world. We believe they've been genetically modified for the purpose of meeting the labor needs of our extraterrestrial industries."

"Slave laborers?!"

Althea did not release Ramuell's hand when she looked up into his eyes, "They aren't here of their own volition. They're highly evolved beings from very primitive cultures. As slaves, their entire lives are work, eat, sleep—then do the same thing again the next day. We believe they're never returned to their home planet. Some are stationed on asteroids or planetoids without atmospheres. Those unfortunate creatures live and work in low-gravity environments with artificial atmospheres. They usually die within three annum."

Stunned, Ramuell implored, "How is this possible? How can this be legal?"

His parents just looked at him. When Ramuell looked at their Beag-Liath companion, he saw a flicker of emotion pass across the being's face before it stood and walked away.

Ramuell began smelling the delicious aroma of bread baking. "Do you smell that?" he asked his parents.

His father shook his head sadly, "It's time for you to go. There are no smells in the sen. *We love you. We will always love you."*

His mother could no longer hold back her tears. They flowed freely down both cheeks. "I believe we will see each other again. Until then, be well my dear, dear boy."

Ramuell awoke desperately needing to empty his bladder. He climbed out of the sleeping bag and struck a hasty pace down the latrine trail. Glancing over at the kitchen area, he saw several people watching dozens of loaves of bread baking in large hemispheric-shaped, wood-fired ovens.

After attending to his urinary urgency, Ramuell's mind returned to the visit with his parents. For a second time something had happened while he slept that he simply could not understand. Where had he gone? How had he gotten there? What had he experienced?

Azazel and Owan were sitting well away from the group crowded around the ovens. Steaming cups of tea sat on the table and a tendril of smoke wafted upward from Owan's pipe. As Ramuell approached Azazel asked, "Did you sleep well, Ram?"

"Did I sleep? Is that what it was? I don't know." He paused for a moment. Azazel and Owan watched him expectantly but neither spoke. "Okay, I can see you know something. Just what in every frozen-hell was that?"

Owan waved Azazel off with a quick motion of his pipe. He said, "Tell us what you mean."

"I saw my parents. I spoke to them. I was with them on a hot, rocky world. How is that possible? My parents haven't been seen for over sixty annum! Was I hallucinating?"

Having confirmed that Ramuell had experienced the *sen*, Owan nodded at Azazel who replied, "No Ram, you're not crazy and you were not hallucinating. You were sleeping under the stars of Ghrain-3."

"What does that mean?" Ramuell pleaded.

"I wish I could tell you. I wish we knew more about what the local sapiens call the *sen*," Azazel replied.

"*Sen*? That's a word my father used last night. I didn't understand what he meant."

Azazel and Owan exchanged a startled look. Azazel asked, "What have you read about this phenomenon?"

Ramuell answered, "Nothing. I've seen nothing in the research about this—uhm, *sen*"

With a quizzical expression Owan asked, "Then how could you have known the word?"

"I didn't know the word. My father used it," Ramuell replied.

Azazel grunted, "That seems impossible!"

"Why impossible? What is the *sen*?" Ramuell asked.

Tapping the burned ash out of his pipe on the heel of his boot, Owan tried to explain, "We've been studying the phenomenon since our early days on the planet. It's always been a controversial decision to classify the research. Virtually all Domhanians who spend time on the surface of Ghrain-3 have nocturnal *sens*. The range of our experiences with this alternative consciousness is so broad as to almost defy understanding. A few of us never experience the *sen*, whereas some Domhanians continue to *sen* while aboard the orbiting station and in rare cases even after returning home."

Half-jesting, Ramuell said, "That's probably why it's classified. Anyone talking about it on Domhan-Siol would be locked up in a psychiatric facility and force-fed psychotropics."

"That may be closer to the truth than you want to believe," Azazel replied. "In the early decades of our work on Ghrain the *sen* experience was so mysterious, so exotic, that many people were unwilling, perhaps even afraid to talk about it. Those who were less circumspect often found career advancement opportunities suspiciously foreclosed."

"So people just quit discussing it, at least with the folks upstairs," Owan said pointing his pipe stem skyward. "Oh, the diggers on the surface compared notes, but there was nothing to be gained by being too forthcoming. Some people found the experience so exotic they developed anxiety disorders and our clinics filled with people who believed the *sens* were hallucinations. That's what finally led to our scientific research of the phenomena."

"So what have we learned?" Ramuell asked.

"Quite a lot actually." Azazel fiddled with the spoon in his teacup for a moment, then amended his statement, "I should say we've learned enough to know how little we know."

"Which means what?"

Azazel looked up and said, "We know so much—but we understand so little. We know our brains' neuro-electrical activity goes through cyclical changes during the course of a night's sleep. We know our brains seem to be fully activated during the *sen*. Likewise our heart rate, breathing, and other autonomic functions are engaged as though we're awake. At other times during the sleep cycle our brain activity slows almost to the level of coma. During those periods certain glandular systems become hyperactive producing a host of hormones essential to our health.

"As you know, we have sleep cycles on the homeworld and in the orbiter. We have changes in neuro-electrical activity whether we're sleeping under the stars of Ghrain-3 or in environments where we typically do not *sen*. But here's something we don't understand; when we have a *sen* experience our eyeballs are activated though our eyelids remain closed. Whereas when we're sleeping elsewhere our eyeballs remain essentially immobile all night."

"Our eyes behave almost as though we're seeing a video on a panoramic screen," Owan added.

They paused to watch a small rodent dash across the yard. In a tableaux of fits and starts the little critter ran, nibbled on a crust of bread then ran on. Smiling at the animal's antics, Azazel pivoted back to the conversation, "A significant number of people report having a modicum of control over the *sen*. They claim to be able to consciously alter the course, location, or even the outcome of a *sen*. Most of us can't do that. Some people report clairvoyant *sens*. I personally have had several *sens* that came to pass within a few days. It's eerie when you realize an event is unfolding as it had during a *sen* only a few nights earlier."

"I didn't know you had prescient *sens*!" Owan exclaimed. "I've never had that experience, but I have shared *sens* with other people. Occasionally I communicate with another person during a *sen*. When I check in with that person later, sometimes they remember the conversation from our shared *sen*. The persons with whom I've communicated were always sleeping nearby, but I've heard of people having *sen* conversations over great distances."

Just then a man walked up to their table with a steaming loaf of sliced bread and a container of a high-protein nut spread. He set it down on the table and said, "Compliments of the chef."

Owan looked over his shoulder toward the ovens and asked, "Who's the baker this morning?"

With the slightest smile the gentleman pointed both thumbs at his own chest then turned and walked away.

Owan called out to the retreating chef, "Thank you! You're a good man Mr. Zeke!"

Zeke waved his right hand over his shoulder but didn't look back.

They each grabbed slices of the freshly baked bread and slathered on the nut-base pâté. "God, I've never tasted bread this good!" Ramuell exclaimed.

Azazel took a bite, closed his eyes, and chewed slowly savoring the flavor. After swallowing he took a swig of tea.

"Some *sen* experiences are truly terrifying," Owan continued. "Others are extraordinarily pleasant. People report sexual encounters during the *sen*. Some people report flying during their *sens*. People have actually been able to describe geographical features they've never seen. Many of us problem-solve during *sens*."

"The thing is, most of our evidence is anecdotal." Azazel shrugged, "So to say we know these things about the *sen* is probably a misstatement. We believe these things to be true because of the vast amount of consonant self-reported data. But how can we test a consciousness that exists in a non-corporeal reality?"

Waggling his finger he added, "But there's one thing we do know for sure. Those of us who have robust *sen* experiences on Ghrain-3, must have those experiences. When deprived of *sen* sleep we develop mood disorders, and some people even have psychotic episodes."

Looking deadly serious, Owan said, "Ram, the boss is not being melodramatic. You're a person who can *sen* and therefore you **must**. You must get your sleep, and you must make sure you get sleep that regularly incorporates *sen* experiences. We've seen people who neglected this part of their lives on Ghrain-3—it's not pretty."

Azazel licked his finger, picked-up the bread crumbs on his plate, and popped them in his mouth. "Semyaza told you one evening in the G3AST galley that nothing down here is simple, and the *sen* is an example of that. In the end, I'd not be surprised if Ghrain-3 changes Domhan-Siol as much as Domhan changes Ghrain."

Standing and brushing crumbs off his pants, Owan said, "You may have never spoken truer words."

CHAPTER TWENTY-THREE
A CHANCE TO BREATHE

Moments after landing on the lagoon's calm water, two canoes nudged in against the quadcopter's inflated pontoons. Liam and Egan disembarked into the canoe at the left pontoon while Althea and Sean slid into the one on the right. With three smooth strokes the bow and stern paddlers glided the canoes away from the aircraft. When the boats were clear of the four rotors, the pilot, sitting hundreds of kilometres away in the Nexo de Mando Law and Order Directorate office, restarted the quadcopter's electro-motors. Lifting only a few metres above the water the copter banked sharply to the left, reminding Egan of a bumblebee as it buzzed away.

Liam's comment about "a beautiful little cove" was an understatement. The water was as clear as the blue-green glass used to bottle the beer produced in the breweries of Domhan-Siol's northwest highlands. Fish could be seen swimming all around the canoes. A beach of fine bluish-grey sand surrounded the lagoon. A stunning waterfall cascaded through a notch in the cliff at least sixty metres high and splashed rhythmically as it tumbled into the sea.

As they were paddled toward the back of the cove Liam's politician persona emerged. He smiled broadly and waved at the couple dozen people who had gathered on the dock.

Sitting on the canoe's woven cane seat, Althea drank in the beauty of her surroundings. She noticed the entire cliff face was speckled with hundreds of windows of various shapes and sizes. Each opening was enclosed with what appeared to be glass treated with a non-reflective coating. They blended almost seamlessly with the surrounding rock walls.

When the boats docked Sean recognized most of the people in the welcoming party. He made introductions as Liam greeted every person. Egan and Althea were introduced only as guests who would be staying on for a while. The island's mayor greeted the couple warmly and gestured toward the main entrance into the cliff village.

The entrance was a natural cave at least six metres high and eight metres across. It was framed in and enclosed with large glass doors surrounded by glass side panels and a transom that were cut to fit the cave's curvature. In the lobby potted plants were strategically hung in various locations to take advantage of the natural light pouring in through the southwest facing windows.

Althea, Egan, Liam and Sean were escorted to a bath house where they found deep tiled tubs filled with natural hot springs water. After the harrowing ordeal of the preceding days they all needed a bath, food and sleep – in that order. The tubs were separated by two metre high privacy screens. They could hear each other's sighed, "Ahhs!" as they slipped into the water. This produced a couple minutes of fatigue-punchy laughter.

After about half an hour a couple of young people arrived pushing a food cart. The smell of the spices and hot food drew all four out of their liquid luxury. They dressed in the loose-fitting tunics and pantaloons that were provided. The couple served their guests a meal of locally produced foods on brightly painted terracotta dishes. The almost simultaneous pronouncements of "Yum!" again caused them to laugh at themselves. This time hunger superseded hilarity and the laughter lasted only a few seconds.

After eating, Althea and Egan were shown to comfortably appointed quarters. Just as their bodies had craved cleaning and nourishment, they now required sleep. They fell onto the mattress made of a dried sea grasses. It combined softness with a springy support that created the sensation of floating – and float they did almost immediately into a deep, dreamless slumber.

About ten hours later they roused. When Althea began stroking the inside of Egan's thigh they became aroused. The lovemaking was a slow, delicious interlude leading to a release they needed psychologically more than physically. They had not left their contented comfort when the doorbell chimed. They were perplexed by the unfamiliar sound. After a moment they heard a light knock and Sean saying softly, "It's me—are you awake?"

"Yes we are, just a moment," Althea called out. Begrudgingly they climbed out of bed and dressed in the cloths they'd been provided the night before.

At the door Althea found Sean holding two bags woven of sea grass. He handed her one, "Here are your clothes. Our gracious hosts have laundered them." Reaching for the bag, she waved Sean in. He walked over and placed the second bag on the table in the kitchenette. "I stopped by the village repository and picked-up some groceries."

Offering Sean his palm, Egan said, "Thank you. You are a gentleman, and we've not encountered many gentlemen since our return."

"Yeah, I suppose that's true enough. We hope to make amends." Sean retrieved what appeared to be a pen from his coat pocket, "Starting with this. This is the EMT disrupter Danel used to block the communication signals from your hospital room, uhm..." He frowned, "Was that really only two days ago?"

Egan thought for a moment, "Yes, though it seems like an undecim."

"Anyway," Sean continued, "we understand before you'll want to talk with us, you need to have the chance to speak privately with each other. And you haven't had that chance since returning from the gods only know where. I can assure you there are no observation devices secreted around this room, but you really have no reason to trust me. So, I'm providing you with this device. You also have no reason to believe it's not disabled. If that's what you think, please understand you're free to come and go as you wish. A walk on the beach or a swim in the cove will be totally private."

"You say we have no reason to trust you, but actually we have," Althea replied. "You got us out of the hospital where we were being monitored constantly and treated like criminals. You got us away from the so-called 'safe house' when it was under attack. You and Liam have expended a great deal of energy getting us here." She paused for a moment holding up her index finger as if placing a bookmarker between thoughts. "With that said, we know who the bad guys are, but we aren't yet certain about the good guys." Her lips trembled slightly and there was an audible catch in her throat, "We've had a **very** frightening return to Domhan-Siol." Exhaling loudly, Althea gathered herself and said, "You're right. We do need some privacy. We need to talk. After that perhaps we'll feel more comfortable having a frank conversation with you and Liam."

Egan looked at Sean and said, "You know she's right."

Sean's eyes smiled as he tapped his six finger tips on the table beside the bag of groceries. "Hope you enjoy the food." Turning to go he said over his shoulder, "I'll check in with you later to see when you'd like to go to the repository to stock up on any other necessities."

Melanka had decided to give Liam some time to contact her before dispatching a covey of agents on a seek-and-find mission. At mid-morning her administrative assistant stepped into her office holding his communicator. She knew from the expression on Cubra's face that Liam was calling. She nodded and signaled for him to transfer the call. "Mr. Deputy Secretary, I'm relieved to hear from you. I was just getting ready to sic the hounds on you and your new friends."

"And I'll add that to the list of reasons we are holed up," Liam replied dryly.

Melanka coughed and continued more cordially than was her wont. "Liam, I don't know what you've learned from Dr. Althea and Professor Egan, but they know something that has scared the shit out of the big money guys. We spent a whole afternoon with Chairman Regan. I'm sure you've figured out it's his goons on your tail. If my agents had been so incompetent they'd be looking for new jobs this morning."

"Yeah, we had figured that out, but we're not clear about their motives. Are you wanting to enhance our understanding?"

"In fact I am," Melanka replied. "Chairman Regan spent half his time with us lying through his teeth. But I have to give him some credit—he's a pretty damn good liar."

Liam clicked his tongue, "And...?"

"And, as you know, the best lies are laced with truth. The trick is figuring out what in Regan's diatribe is actually true. I've had some ideas. Given the company you're keeping, only you and Sean will be able to confirm my suspicions."

"Are you going to tell me what you think we should be looking for?" Liam asked.

"Yes. We believe our long-lost surveyors may have encountered another race of galactic explorers. We believe they learned something during their time off-world that could be very damning for the corporate elites and their sycophants. We need to know what they know."

"Melanka, they're tired. They are beyond tired—they're at a breaking point. Given what your guys put them through at the hospital, coupled with being chased by the bungling B&I thugs, their exhaustion is completely understandable.

"If you're right about their off-world experiences, we have no way of knowing what kind of strain they've been under for decades. We're not going to push them. We aren't trying to break them. We believe we'll get better information by winning their trust."

After a moment Melanka said, "I can understand that. You may not want to go too slowly though. We have reason to believe the Business Council rats are already scurrying. Regardless of what you learn, you and I will have different responsibilities in this unholy mess. But Liam, believe it or not, we're going to be partners in the hunt. You know I'm not a fearful person, but I am genuinely afraid of the damage we may find—not only here but on the other side of our interdimensional jumps."

Liam responded cautiously, "If your inklings are correct, it would be a monumental mistake to underestimate the forces that may be allied against us. Corporations have been out there managing entire planets for centuries. The resources they can bring to bear are colossal."

"I trust you'll keep me informed," Melanka said before terminating the call.

Over the next two days, Egan and Althea took Sean at his word. They explored the village that was carved into the many naturally occurring caves and gas pockets of the igneous rock. The design and activity within the cliff-village reminded Egan of an ant colony. Everyone seemed busily moving about their tasks, but the activity was not frenetic.

They toured the marina with its dozens of boat slips. They strolled along the beach around the cove and waded in the surf that crashed into the shore beyond the inlet. Twice they shared meals with Liam and Sean. Those dinner conversations were lighthearted, in no way resembling an interrogation. Mostly, they just walked and talked.

"We must tell them about the Beag-Liath."

"Yes, and at least some of what they showed us," Egan agreed. "Depending on how they react, we decide just how much to share about the abuses we observed."

"And we say nothing about our extrasensory meeting with Ramuell," Althea added.

"Agreed, not a word about that, not yet—perhaps never." Egan paused for a moment, then asked, "So do you want to invite them to breakfast tomorrow?"

"Let's make it brunch."

Reaching in his pocket for the communicator he did not

have, Egan remembered for the dozenth time that their digital signatures had been scrubbed. Looking up at Althea he simpered and shook his head at the remarkable power of habit.

Althea teased, "You might need to walk down to their room to extend the invitation."

CHAPTER TWENTY-FOUR
A SHARED SHAME

THE NEXT MORNING while Althea filled four mugs with café, Egan pulled a casserole out of the oven, added the last bits of garnish, and placed the pan in the middle of the table. Sean wasted no time in dishing out a serving for himself. Liam shot a raised eyebrow at his partner for not awaiting their host's 'go-ahead.'

"What? I'm hungry and this smells terrific!" Sean said.

Laughing, Althea gestured toward the food, "And that's why you should help yourselves. You'll find it tastes as good as it smells. It's one of Egan's specialties."

After taking a bite, Sean and Liam looked at each other with mirrored expressions of appreciation. Liam said, "Obviously sixty annum off-world didn't dull your culinary skills."

Althea and Egan exchanged an enigmatic glance.

Liam said, "It seems something I said burned a nerve. I meant no offense."

"Oh, you said nothing offensive. It's just..." Egan trailed off.

Not looking up from her plate, Althea said, "You see, we're heartbroken to have missed our son's childhood and stunned to learn that he and my mother had jumped across the galaxy only days before our return."

Egan said, "The whole damn thing is so bizarre."

Seeing the couples' distress, Liam said, "We can understand that. So, let us start by telling you some things we know." Althea looked up and nodded. Egan, who had been pushing his food around on his plate, forked a bite into his mouth.

"While it may be difficult for you to accept, given the way you were treated, Anotas-Deithe is not the bad player in all of this. Overzealous perhaps, but not the bad guys. Dyer and Chelt are Anotas agents. They are by nature and training given to suspicion."

"As is their leadership!" interrupted Sean.

"Indeed. I suppose suspiciousness is both a prerequisite and an occupational hazard. As you've probably figured out, Chelt concluded early on that though you were keeping secrets, nothing about your off-world activities smacked of criminality. Dyer, on the other hand, is a bit more fervent.

"To be sure, Anotas didn't want you to leave the hospital. But the thugs who tried to prevent it, and the ones who assaulted us at the safe house, were not from Anotas. They are mercenaries who provide security for various Business and Industry Council entities—and that's a rats nest you can hardly imagine."

Egan shook his head and said quietly, "Actually sir, you are the ones who cannot imagine the B&I Council rat nest."

Sean glanced sideways at Liam then said, "We've had our suspicions. Some of the things you've said have heightened our concern. Pfft—'our concern'—that's the devil in this situation. By virtue of the Law and Order charter what occurs off-world is, strictly speaking, **not** our concern."

"But what happens when the off-world activities are so illegal..."

"And so immoral!" Althea added.

"Yes, illegal **and** immoral...What happens when the profits and ethos of those activities bleed back into virtually every commercial transaction on the homeworld?" Egan asked.

For a moment no one spoke. Althea broke the silence. "We invited you here to tell you some things about our off-world experiences. It's time to cut to the chase."

Egan reached over and patted Althea's forearm gently. A wan smile flashed across her face.

"Gentlemen, this is a long story and it's going to take a while. When we made the 4D jump we realized almost immediately we had not arrived where or perhaps when we had expected. We're not certain what went wrong. We found ourselves on a planet about half the size of Domhan-Siol orbiting a red star. It was survivable with the right protection but too cold for liquid water.

"During our second sojourn in the ship's rover we had a complete power failure. Our vehicle shut off as did our suit warmers and breather pumps. We worked frantically trying to get the breathers restarted but passed-out fairly quickly.

"We awoke lying on stainless steel tables. Obviously, we weren't on our own ship. There were several small greyish colored beings bustling around the room. They were bipedal, hairless, and had long hands with four digits including an opposing thumb. Though their legs were short, they moved with a quickness and grace that's difficult to describe."

"What was going through your mind?" Sean asked.

"I was terrified!"

"Me too," Egan agreed. "In fact, I felt much the same way when we woke-up naked in the woods. We didn't know we were back on Domhan-Siol. Because we were so cold and so dehydrated I believed our situation was life-threatening. When we awoke on the Beag-Liath vessel we were horribly frightened, but at least we were receiving medical attention."

"Beag-Liath?" Liam asked with a quizzical expression.

"Oh, that's just what we decided to call them. It's a term meaning 'little greys' from one of our long-dead languages," Egan explained.

"Actually, I was frightened **by** the medical attention," Althea said. "We had no idea what they intended. I worried perhaps we were just lab rats. But as I watched it became clear that they weren't trying to hide anything from us. In fact, they were making an effort to communicate."

I remember thinking the same thing," Egan said. "But communication was difficult. Their vocalizations sound a bit like our speech, interspersed with clicks and yaps. They also seem to use a gestural language."

"These were our first fearful impressions," Althea continued. "Over the next couple of undecim we realized much of their communication is what we'd call 'extrasensory.' They have distended, creased foreheads. They used a hologram to show us that they possess sensory organs in the frontal lobes that can detect bioelectrical transmissions. They have evolved a neurologically sophisticated system of interpreting information received by their frontal lobe organs. It seems they're actually able to communicate many things with each other by projecting thoughts."

"We came to believe telepathy is their primary form of communication. Sounds and gestures just augment information exchanges," Egan added.

"That's right," Althea agreed. "Getting back to those first few hours, I sensed the metal tables were cold, but I wasn't cold. There were no physical restraints though we couldn't move. They were using some kind of technology that blocked our efferent neural pathways. I'm almost certain this was not done chemically, but I don't know what the suppressor mechanism was.

"They took at least a litre of blood from each of us and turned our heads so we could watch what they were doing at worktables a couple of metres to our left. They ran various tests similar to what you'd expect to see in any medical lab on Domhan-Siol. They used droppers, centrifuges, and microscopes, though all of these things differed somewhat in appearance from our own.

"We were given an intravenous drip that must have had the fluids and nutrients we required. Minutes after they began the drip I no longer felt hungry.

"Over the next several days we observed what looked like the use of our blood samples to incubate dozens of dishes of live cultures. By that time we'd been released from the tables and were allowed to walk around. The room was locked, but it had windows into the adjacent lab. We were able to watch them working with our blood.

"During these early days they provided us with some bars of an utterly tasteless sustenance. We understood we had to eat it in order to survive. When they brought us those bars they deployed no extraordinary security measures. One of them would just open the door, look at us carefully and hand us the food.

Althea wiped her mouth with a napkin and said, "Trying to overpower it and attempting to escape never even crossed our minds."

"I don't know whether we realized the futility of such an effort or if they telepathically muted any such consideration," Egan added. "We knew something was up one day when several of them entered the room. They'd given a good deal of thought to how they might communicate with us.

"One of them had a large foliopad type device. It called up a series of images of living cells. They showed us an animation of pathogens killing those cells. A second animation featured an autoimmune response. Clearly they reckoned we were technologically advanced enough to understand those videos."

"They were explaining that they'd tested us for what would likely be pathogenic in their environment," Althea continued, "and they'd developed vaccines to protect us from those pathogens.

"We agreed to take the injections willingly rather than being immobilized on their treatment tables again. We understood the inoculations were probably necessary if we were to live on their ship. At that point we had no sense of how long they planned to keep us."

Egan looked at Althea. They held each other's gaze for a moment. "...and we still don't have any sense of that," Egan continued. "Let me ask you a question. How long were we actually gone?"

Liam glanced at Sean, rolled his shoulders and said, "I don't recall the exact date of your departure, but you were gone for over sixty annum."

"Sixty-one annum and eighty-three days," clarified Sean.

Althea's expression melted into sadness, "We've heard that numerous times since our return but still find it almost incomprehensible. By our reckoning, we were off-world less than an annum."

Liam's eyes shot open, "What?!"

Egan took a moment to gather his thoughts. "According to our own clocks, as well as our internal sense of time, we were gone not more than fourteen undecim." He cleared his throat. "So, uhm, yesterday Althea accessed the medical lab —kinda uninvited. She ran cellular ageing tests on both of us."

Everyone turned to Althea. She said matter-of-factly, "We have aged less than six kuuk since our departure."

Sean immediately understood the implication. "So the Beag-Liath aren't using 4D-Initiator technology."

"That seems to be correct," Egan replied. "We don't know if they understand the concept of a multiverse, but Sean your comment implies what we've surmised. If they're not jumping through dimensions, they must have mastered space warp technologies."

"...and the downside of that kind of travel would be the time distortion effect," Sean added.

Liam asked, "So as a practical matter, you spent about a hundred forty days with the Beag-Liath?"

"That's about right," Althea answered.

Egan looked down at his half empty cup and said wistfully, "Though we were only with them for a short time, we learned a lot of things; more about our own species than about them—and we're ashamed of what they showed us."

"We learned a great deal about how our extraterrestrial corporations are behaving out there." Althea sighed. "From childhood we've been told lies about the noble purposes of our galactic endeavors."

With the pedantic vocal affectations of a politician, Egan said, **"We are seeding the cosmos with sentience**...What a bucket of bison crap!"

Althea bit her lip. "The big question is how many of our people know? How many of our leaders know that our better angels have been prostituted to feed corporate greed?" She turned to Liam and asked, "You are the Deputy Secretary of the Law and Order Directorate. Do you have any idea how our off-world industrial activities are being managed? Do you know how the corporate overlords have resolved their long-standing labor shortages in our off-world extraction industries?"

Liam puffed his cheeks and blew out a breath. "Judging by your tone, I suspect I do not—I could use the excuse that the Law and Order Directorate's responsibilities are limited to the homeworld." He paused but the others knew he hadn't finished his thought. Looking at Althea, "I could use that excuse, but that would beg the question Egan asked earlier. What happens when ill-gotten gains and the related ethos return home to infect Domhan-Siol? When we have to tell our children lies about the nobility of our galactic endeavors, I suppose the excuse that what happens 'out there' is not within our jurisdiction rings rather hollow."

Turning to stare out the window, Althea saw nothing of the beautiful scenery beyond the glass. "The first place they took us was a mining colony on a Domhan-Siol size planet. It had a breathable atmosphere, but the oxygen content was only 12.4% with very little water vapor. We saw an enormous mining operation. Most of the workforce was not Domhanian. There were hundreds..."

"Thousands," Egan interrupted.

"Yes, thousands of workers; bipedal hominids with round heads. They have more body hair than we do, especially the males. Their hands and feet have only five digits. Other than that, they resemble us even more so than the Beag-Liath." She paused, her brow knitted with dismay. "All of the Domhanian overseers wore a breathing apparatus, which I'm sure was providing the correct mixture of gasses and water vapor. None of the alien workers had those devices. Their skin, particularly their lips, showed signs of dehydration. They were performing only menial tasks—always under Domhanian supervision."

Egan turned to Liam and added, "The overseers were armed with electric stun-guns and charged-particle weapons."

Shaking her head sadly, Althea continued, "After visiting

an open pit mine, we were taken to a huge ore smelting facility. Corporations have made colossal investments on that world.

"As you know, one of the biggest cost cutting benefits of off-world mining is the non-consideration of ecological impacts and environmental rehabilitation. It seems likely most of the planets and planetoids where our mining facilities exist are devoid of life. But this world did have emerging primitive life forms. What we saw at the smelter was appalling. Toxic waste was being dumped in mountains of slag. All Domhanian overseers were wearing protective hazardous materials suits."

Althea's eyes clouded with tears. She took her napkin out of her lap and set it neatly on the table. Clearing her throat she added, "The alien workers were wearing nothing but rags. Many had open sores and I saw several with bone growths and swollen necks."

"There's no question they were being exposed to lethal doses of toxicity," Egan said. "The last place the Beag-Liath took us on this planet was to a facility where bodies were being cremated. While we were there, two vans arrived each carrying three bodies. We saw open lesions on every corpse."

Sean said, "I'm baffled. How you were able to observe all of these things without being seen yourselves."

"Oh my! We need to backup and explain something important about one of the Beag-Liath technologies. They've developed a cloaking technology that allows them to observe from relatively close proximity." Looking toward her husband, "what would you say...?"

"We got within a hundred metres," Egan answered.

Althea continued, "The cloaking device is a concave dish with six to eight posts or rods attached equidistant around its periphery. In the center there's a cone approximately one-fifth the diameter of the entire dish. These devices are mounted on all Beag-Liath vehicles including their ships. They vary in size from dozens of metres across to hand-held paraboloids a half metre wide.

"We don't understand how it works, but it disrupts all energy signatures associated with their presence; visual, auditory, radio, heat, electro-magnetic; literally everything on the energy spectrum that would make it possible for an observer to identify their presence."

"Good lord!" Liam exclaimed. "That means for millennia we've been searching the galaxy for technologically advanced species, and they may have been right under our noses."

"Exactly," Egan replied. "Perhaps they've been watching us from the very beginnings of our space exploration efforts and just didn't want to be seen. We've been so obsessed with finding energy signatures of advanced technologies it never dawned on us they could be using a technology to cloak the very signatures we were seeking."

Liam just shook his head.

"We don't know when they began observing us, but it would be fair to say they do not appreciate some of our exploits," Althea added. "In fact, we believe they finally became so dismayed they decided to make themselves known to us. We have no idea why we were chosen for this glimpse at our species' misbehavior."

"And all they wanted was for you to see what is happening?" Liam asked.

Shaking his head Egan replied, "No, that's not all they want. I cannot explain how we know, but we came to understand there is an implicit threat. Perhaps they were able to insert thoughts or feelings directly into our minds, but it's clear they were warning us that our species needs a course correction, or one might be imposed."

"And what do you think that means?" Liam asked.

"We don't know," Althea answered. "But from what we saw, they have ample reason to intervene."

Egan got up and brought over a bowl of salted sea grass chips. "Would anyone care for something to drink?" he asked as he opened a bottle of a light sour beer produced on one of the other islands in the Dragon's Back Archipelago.

Sean said, "Yes, I'll have one of those."

"I have a feeling I may need more than one before this story is over," Liam said.

The skin around Althea's beautiful half-moon shaped eyes crinkled sadly. "Mr. Deputy Secretary, you really have no idea."

Egan put the bottles of beer on the table. "Well, let me continue and we'll pass the story-telling baton back-and-forth to fill in our memory gaps."

At that moment Liam's communicator trilled. He tapped in an access code and waited a few seconds for the text-com to pop-up on the screen. His forehead furrowed as he read the message. He handed the communicator to Sean. After studying it for a couple of minutes, Sean looked up. "Professor Egan, Dr. Althea, we've had reason to believe you were telling the truth, or at least your understanding of the events that occurred during your absence. But it's also possible your perceptions of the encounter with the Beag-Liath were altered. Thoughts and perceptions may have been planted.

"It's also clear some faction associated with the B&I Council wants you silenced. That fact alone supports the notion that your extraordinary experience provided you with a glimpse of sensitive secret information."

Liam grimaced and said, "The message I just received erases any lingering doubts about the veracity of your stories."

"What have you learned?" Egan asked

"Our field agents have just confirmed that the Executive Officers and Board of Director members of at least a dozen major corporations have, with their families in tow, jumped on privately owned 4D-Initiators and gone on unscheduled holidays. I use that word euphemistically. Furthermore, their destinations haven't been logged as per 4D flight protocols." Liam narrowed his eyes, "It seems the rats are jumping ship."

Sean snorted. "Yeah, and the ship they're abandoning is our homeworld, which makes me think the information you two have is incredibly damning!" He paused for a moment and studied Liam, who was unconsciously tugging at the loose skin on his neck. "And if it's dangerous enough to cause a mass exodus among the most powerful Domhanian families, it's even more dangerous for the two of you."

Liam said, "Sean's right. For the moment, the best course of action is to stay put. They clearly haven't figured out where we are. I, however, must return to Nexo."

As Liam rose, Sean gestured for him to wait a second. "Before you go Mr. Secretary, I believe it would be wise for us to retire to a more secure facility for the remainder of our stay on Cascata."

Both Althea and Egan stared at Sean quizzically. Egan asked, "Why do you think that's necessary?"

"In addition to the information Liam just shared, we also learned that Secretary Elom was found dead this morning in his transport vehicle."

"Dear gods! That's awful!" Althea exclaimed.

"There were no signs of struggle or violence, but Elom was the picture of health." Sean continued. "He had not been ill for many annum. The timing of the Law and Order Directorate Secretary's sudden death is certainly mysterious. It would be wise for us to move to rooms deeper in the cliff village."

Althea looked wistfully at the beautiful view outside the picture window and said only, "Alas."

Turning toward the window Sean agreed, "Yeah, goodbye

to the views, at least for now." He paused and pinched the bridge of his aquiline nose, "Uhm, I hate to even bring this up, but should the unimaginable happen, it would be wise for us to record the rest of your testimony. The recording can serve as a video-affidavit."

Alarmed, Egan asked, "Do you believe we're in real danger of being murdered?"

"If it turns out Secretary Elom's death was the result of foul play, then we know assassination is a tool they're willing to use. So yes, the danger may be real. However, it's more likely an affidavit may become necessary not because you're dead, but because you've had to seek refuge off-world."

"Now wait a minute—we've been off-world quite enough," protested Althea.

Sean replied, "I realize that and I'm sorry. But remember we didn't choose this for you. The Beag-Liath did."

Egan silently put his arm around his wife's shoulder and pulled her to him. Never taking her eyes off of Sean's face, Althea laid a hand on Egan's chest as a single tear rolled down her cheek and fell on his lap.

Upon returning to Nexo de Mando, the first thing Liam did was authorize continuous satellite surveillance of the Dragon's Back Archipelago. He also assigned seven of his best special agents to accompany an aqua-ag work crew to Cascata.

When his communicator trilled, Liam wasn't surprised to see the Anotas Security Chief was using a secure frequency. "Hello Melanka."

Not one for small-talk, she dove straight to the point, "Liam, I have some information about Secretary Elom's death. It's not evidence, but it is credible."

Masking his curiosity, Liam asked casually, "And your information is?"

"I'm sure by now you've identified the toxin used to assassinate your predecessor," Melanka replied.

"Actually the autopsy found two different toxins, but we didn't identify the means of ingestion. The medical examiner listed the death as suspicious. What have you got for me?"

"Tell your medics to check under the toenails," Melanka answered. "Elom had a fungus treated at a local Red Shield MediCorp facility about three undecim ago. I'm sure you're aware your late boss wasn't a fan of the cultists. As it turns out several employees at Red Shield are adherents of the cultist codswallop. One of them injected a second treatment under the toenail when Elom returned for a follow-up the morning before he died."

Liam, who had been pacing around his den, sat down. "Are you still there?" Melanka asked.

"Yeah—I'm, uh, just trying to put all this together."

"Let me help with that. On several occasions over the last few annum Elom nixed requests to hire members of various cults. He did so solely on the basis of their cultist beliefs. Given that the positions required SA9 level security clearances, he had the authority to approve or disapprove employment for any reason. You have a mole in your house and he or she was sharing this information with the cultist groups waging a covert campaign against Elom."

Liam responded, "Yes, I was vaguely aware that was going on, but frankly their efforts seemed so feeble I never gave it much thought." He paused before adding, "It strikes me we must have more than one mole for you to know these details about our internal personnel matters."

Without acknowledging Liam's observation, Melanka continued, "Their efforts may not have been as feeble as you think, but they were a far cry from murder. I don't believe for a minute the cultists contrived this assassination."

Liam said, "So you believe some corporate heavyweight instigated the plot and used an antagonized or gullible cultist to do the dirty work."

"Perhaps more than one heavyweight; perhaps even the B&I Council itself. This is in your jurisdiction Liam, and you're going to have to chase it down. You may want to start with the corporation closest to the scene of the crime and work out from there.

"Dr. Camal, the CEO of Red Shield, was among the mass exodus of bigwigs. Here's something you may not know, Camal sits on the boards of two mineral extraction corporations in addition to his medical products manufacturing corporation," Melanka said.

"No, I did not know that."

"Yeah, what I can't figure out is why he or any other CEO would have believed Secretary Elom, rather than you, actually managed the Directorate. By now they may have figured out who's actually been in charge all along. You need to be cautious, and I mean much more cautious than normal."

"So do you think we need to start surveillance on all the cultists working at Red Shield?" Liam asked.

"That's where I'd start. Now it's possible the person treating Elom wasn't even aware the antifungal serum had been tampered with. It's also possible the med-tech was in on the entire plot. We know she's a cultist, and we know at least three of Camal's top-level administrators are also holy book thumpers.

"Liam, I wish I could provide you with some rock-solid evidence, but this is all I've got. Given the enormity of the galactic chase we're involved in, I don't see Anotas committing resources to investigate your predecessor's death. Actually, we weren't investigating his death. We stumbled on this information while investigating Dr. Camal's sudden exodus.

"Now I want to urge you to hurry Althea and Egan along. I'm absolutely certain their information will make our jobs much easier."

Noting the stress in Melanka's voice, Liam replied, "Our relationship with the long-lost surveyors is progressing well. We've earned a bit of trust, and they're recording a video-deposition. When I'm certain it's appropriate **and** legal for me to share that information with you, I will. And Melanka, thank you for this call and the information about Elom."

CHAPTER TWENTY-FIVE
THE CROW CLAN

Azazel decided to return to basecamp via the Blue Rock River trail. Samael and Rarus, two members of the SWA-7 security detail, would join the group for this leg of the journey.

When Ramuell studied the maps he realized this route would add two days to their trek. He thought this a somewhat curious decision but remembered Azazel had seemed nostalgic about the days when he spent more time afield. He also remembered the rather unusual byplay between Owan and Azazel when the Blue Rock Canyon clan had been mentioned. For some reason Ramuell felt it best to keep his own counsel regarding the director's decision to lengthen the trip.

After hiking over rolling hills for almost five hours the group finally arrived at the canyon rim. Ramuell was struck by the vibrant colors of the canyon's vegetation offset by the deep blue of the sky above. The clarity of Ghrain's dry air distorted his sense of distance. Though he could easily see the tendrils of smoke rising from the sapiens' campfires, it still took over an hour to reach the canyon floor via a long switchback trail.

On the way down the trail Owan told the story of how this group of sapiens became known as the Crow Clan. Domhanian observers noticed the clan had ingratiated itself to a murder of crows by sharing tidbits of food scraps with the birds. Several of the crows had become so tame they would fly by and tap a clansman on the head, begging for treats. This amused the people and the tradition of sharing with the birds had been passed down for at least three sapien generations.

As the hikers approached the clan's camp crows roosting in nearby trees squawked their warning caws, which Ramuell noted was quite a reliable alarm system. In this case it was hardly necessary, as several members of the clan already stood in a clearing watching the five Domhanians descend into the canyon.

A group of seven adults and a clutch of children met the arrivals. The adults knew both Azazel and Owan. One of the men approached and extended his palm in the Domhanian greeting style. As Owan tapped the proffered palm the man laughed and grabbed Owan in a full embrace. They rocked each other back and forth with a level of familiarity that would have been shocking on Domhan-Siol. Azazel joined in the laughter. Even the two security guards allowed huge smiles to crease their faces as they watched the affectionate greeting.

Just then a woman stepped forward. Instead of the almost ball-shaped skull of most sapiens, this woman had the beautifully elongated Domhanian parietal area. This made her quite striking in appearance, and members of the clan were subtly deferential toward her.

She walked directly up to Azazel, took both of his hands in hers and looked into his eyes. She spoke briefly. Azazel understood her comments and responded with words of the clan's language. The woman smiled more with her eyes than her mouth. Stepping forward she rested her face against Azazel's chest then turned her nose into the hollow of his neck for several seconds. Ramuell was simultaneously stunned and fascinated by the intimacy this greeting implied. He was unable to tear his gaze away from his boss and the clanswoman.

Noticing Ramuell's dilated pupils, Rarus coughed quietly. This alerted Ramuell that he was staring, which would have been considered quite uncouth back home. Looking around he saw a couple of children also shared the attractive head shape of the people of Domhan-Siol. He made a mental note to investigate the anomaly.

As the last rays of sunlight reflected off the canyon's high rims darkness poured into the canyon, filling it from the bottom up. Stars twinkled to life while the clanspeople stoked their cook fire and assembled in the primitive kitchen area. Ramuell counted thirty-six sapien adults and two infants being held by parents or older siblings. He could hear several children playing just out of sight.

There was an air of excitement among the clan. Ramuell assumed this was because they were unaccustomed to visitors. He was partially correct, but there was more to it than that. Dr. Durela's belief that sapien-hybrids had not developed intellectually to a level of sophisticated abstract conceptualization was inaccurate. In fact, clans of hybridized sapiens had begun to view their world's Domhanian visitors as supernatural beings. Among some sapien clans this perception resulted in a kind of veneration bordering on reverence.

Ramuell, Owan and Azazel were seated near the man who had first greeted them upon their arrival. He was called Ru Ta, which Azazel explained meant 'clear day' in the clan's language. Ru Ta was a person of some authority within the clan. The companionable exchanges among these three men implied, in Ramuell's mind, many annum of friendship. Owan, being somewhat conversant in the clan's dialect, tried to include Ramuell in the conversation by explaining what was being said.

Ramuell noticed Ru Ta had three feathers woven into a tight three-strand braid in his hair. Ru Ta spotted Ramuell studying his feathers and reached around to flip the braid in front of his chest. He held it out for closer inspection. Ramuell was taken aback by the gesture.

Owan noticed and said, "No reason to be embarrassed. Ru Ta is probably flattered by your attention. He asked if you understand the feathers woven into his hair."

"No I don't. Is there some significance?" Ramuell asked.

Ru Ta held his braid and studied the feathers for a long moment before beginning to speak. Owan translated as best his mastery of the language allowed. "Birds have much power. They fly. We cannot. They have great spirits." Starting with the top feather and working down the braid Ru Ta explained, "This is a feather of the crow. I carry it so I might have the intelligence of the crow. This is a feather of the hawk. I carry it so I might have the strength of the hawk. This is a feather of an owl. I carry it so I might have the wisdom of the owl." Now Ru Ta looked at Ramuell. "These things are good."

Ramuell wasn't sure what to make of this. Was this belief in spirits part of the planet's mystique or was it just primitive superstition? As if sensing his protégé's thoughts, Azazel said, "No matter what you may think of what Ru Ta just told you, his comments are anecdotal evidence that our retroviruses have become endogenous, and the mutations are having a remarkable impact on this species. We don't know if sapiens were able to entertain that level of allegorical thinking prior to our interventions. But we do know that if pre-hybridized sapiens had complex symbolic thoughts, they were not able to share those thoughts with such linguistic sophistication."

Ru Ta smiled and nodded emphatically, almost as if he'd understood Azazel.

Before the cook fire died, clansmen set several long sticks in the glowing embers. The sticks quickly ignited and were used to light fires in smaller pits all around the camp. By the light of multiple fires the clanspeople laid out their fur bedding.

As Ramuell watched this activity with fascination, the young woman who had hugged Azazel approached the three visitors. She smiled warmly, said "come" in Domhan Standard and gestured for the three to follow her. She led them to a blazing hearth. Rarus and Samael were already sitting on the beds laid out for the clan's distinguished guests.

Samael was one of those people who exuded an almost unremitting air of amusement. It was never mocking and did not manifest as a smile. Rather, it evinced with an alertness and a crinkling around his eyes. People were almost always drawn in by his disarming charisma.

As Sam pulled off a boot he noticed Ramuell looking dubiously at the furs. With a low chuckle he said, "To not use the bedding would be considered quite an insult, but your reticence is understandable. Among the inoculations you received before leaving the orbiter was one that makes our bodies smell awful to lice, ticks, and even mosquitoes. It's not likely you'll feed too many parasites tonight."

"Righto, we sure wouldn't want bugs distressing your sweet *sens*," Rarus teased as he snuggled into the furs. It was too dark for him to see Azazel's disapproving glare. He decided not to chide Rarus's tactlessness for fear any further comment might only heighten Ramuell's anxiety.

Actually Ramuell was not dreading the *sen*. He was almost looking forward to sleeping under the sliver of stars visible between the canyon's high walls.

———

During the night a heavy cloud layer rolled in. By sunrise the sky was an ominous grey and held the threat of an imminent storm. The Crow's camp was abuzz with activity that was neither frenetic nor chaotic. The clanspeople were packing their belongings in bags made of animal hides. They were moving from the river's edge up to the caves on a ledge that ran along the north canyon wall some five metres above the canyon floor.

Hearing the clanspeople, Azazel understood what was happening with the weather. He rolled out his bed, woke Owan and the security officers. They discussed the situation and agreed it would be unwise to depart for SWA-7 given the likelihood of a strong storm.

With that decision made, Samuel woke Ramuell and the two of them began stuffing backpacks while Owan filled all of their bottles with river water.

Azazel and Rarus discussed the need to communicate with the staff at SWA-7. "Sir, when I get to the rim, regardless of the weather, I should have no trouble bouncing a satellite signal to headquarters. It's also possible I can contact you on a frequency modulation channel. All we need is to establish a line of sight. Once I've linked to SWA-7, I'll contact you on FM19. Then I can relay any questions and instructions you may have."

"Excellent. We'll keep an eye on you with magnifying glasses. When we see you've unfolded the Sat-Com dish I'll move out into that clearing." Azazel pointed toward the north side of the canyon. "I'll set out a flag just this side of where the path starts up to the caves."

"Alright, that should work, if it's not raining too hard to see you."

Azazel studied the sky and said, "Hopefully the downpour will hold off for a while. Be careful Rarus, the trail is likely to be treacherous by the time you start back down. Did you pack boot-cleats?"

"They're in my pack. I'll be okay and back as soon as I can."

For the next two days rain mixed with graupel fell heavily. The caves provided dry and surprisingly comfortable shelter. The FM radio/Sat-Com relay had worked well, and Azazel was relieved there were no crises brewing back at SWA-7. That relief only served to reduce a modicum of the stress he felt about the work that was surely piling up while he was on this extended field trip.

He wondered about the wisdom of his decision to traipse off with Owan and Ramuell in the first place. He had no such doubts about the decision to drop in on the Crow Clan. He **knew** that had been impulsive.

For hours at a time various members of the clan delighted in teaching Ramuell words in their language. In these impromptu language lessons he was learning mostly nouns via the point and say method. Some verbs also lent themselves to that pedagogy: run, walk, sit, look, listen, etc. Ramuell had a linguistic gift. Learning and remembering the vocabulary came easily. The lessons also provided an opportunity for him to become friendly with many of the clanspeople.

Ramuell was mildly disappointed on the third morning when he awoke and realized the storm had passed. They began the hike back to SWA-7 immediately after breakfast.

The morning was cool with the canyon floor shrouded in a dense fog. Ru Ta escorted the Domhanians to a wide shoal where the river could be forded even though the rains had swollen the river significantly. The fog was so thick all they could see after crossing was a smudge on the opposite bank waving farewell.

As the Domhanians began their ascent out of the canyon they could hear the clan moving back down to the riverside camp. They had climbed out of the fog layer and were about sixty vertical metres above the canyon floor when they heard frenzied caws from the crows in the trees below. Rarus, who was leading the group, stopped and listened.

Sam remarked, "The crows sound excited about seeing their clan back outside." Then suddenly came shrieks and bloodcurdling screams.

Dropping their packs on the trail, the five Domhanians charged back down to the canyon floor. The fog had lifted slightly, but visibility was still limited. They were just barely able to make out the silhouettes of giant humanoids attacking the Crow Clan's riverside camp.

As members of the Clan tried to run away, the nefilim used long hooked tree branches to snare a retreating sapien's foot. This wouldn't have worked had the clanspeople turned to face their assailants. Two or three sapiens confronting a single nefilim would have more than evened the odds, as the giant humanoids were slower and somewhat clumsy. It seemed the size intimidation factor simply precluded contemplation of this tactic. The Crow Clan did not stand in to fight; instead, they fled like a flushed covey of quail.

As the five Domhanians inched closer to the one-sided combat they could see the nefilim bludgeoning males and dragging females away from the camp. Several clansmen lay writhing on the ground.

Azazel growled at Samael and Rarus, "Take 'em out!"

Immediately the security guards unslung their sonic-blasters and began targeting the nefilim. When hit by a blast the giant would grab his ears, drop to his knees, and keel over flopping like a fish. Targeting individual nefilim in the dense fog was difficult. Agonized screams made it clear their assault was continuing.

Motioning for Rarus and Samael to follow him, Azazel trotted toward the battle scene. At about fifty metres he dropped to his knees beside a body. Ramuell and Owan were following a couple dozen metres behind. As they approached, Ramuell recognized the body of the little girl with the Domhanian shaped head. The first thing he noticed was her snapped tibia protruding from the front of her shin. Drawing closer he saw that her spine had been broken in the middle thoracic area and her back was bent at a sickening angle.

Azazel stroked the girl's face almost frantically, then rocked back and let out a tortured scream. He stood and snatched the blaster out of Samael's hands. He flipped the targeting switch to wide-field and started pressing the trigger button repeatedly as he slowly turned from right to left – seven, eight, nine blasts. When at last he stopped every living thing around the Crow Clan's camp lay on the ground twitching. He was not done. His fury crackled like the fire of some hell's inferno. He dropped Sam's blaster and charged into the midst of the squirming bodies.

Approaching the first of the downed nefilim, Azazel picked

up a stone at least a half-metre in diameter and slammed it into the giant's face. Azazel snatched the wooden club the giant held and swung it with all his might into the head of another nefilim man lying nearby.

Ramuell pulled up short when he heard the popping sound of the giant's skull splitting like a melon. Azazel turned and smashed the club into the back of the head of the next nefilim. Ramuell saw the giant's eyes pop out of their orbits. When Azazel heard another groan of pain, or protest, or both, he slammed the bloody piece of wood into that giant's temple; blood spurted from the dispatched man's ears.

With each vicious stroke Azazel ended the lives of one nefilim after another – at least a dozen in all. Ramuell stood transfixed by the carnage. In his seventy-two annum he'd never seen violent bloodshed. Suddenly he found himself sprinting toward his friend. From about two metres away he launched himself into Azazel's torso. Azazel let out a loud "Ooph!" as they tumbled to the ground. He struggled to free himself from Ramuell's grasp. The youngster locked his fingers together and held his grip tenaciously. After about twenty seconds Azazel's body went limp. Slowly he began to shudder and silently weep.

When Ramuell released his grip, he saw the front of Azazel's garment was covered with bits of bone, brain, and blood. Ramuell pushed himself to his hands and knees and retched violently.

Samael and Rarus had chased fleeing nefilim down canyon and Ramuell could hear the occasional discharge of their sonic-blasters. After vomiting again he rocked back on his haunches and slowly looked around, taking in the pandemonium of his surroundings. Many of the clanspeople were injured. Some were already dead, and others had wounds that were surely fatal. Ramuell watched in amazement as Owan moved from person to person doing quick triage assessments. For those beyond help, he quietly and seemingly without emotion made a quick slit in their carotid artery with the sharply honed titanium folding knife he always carried.

One of the nefilim had somehow avoided Azazel's onslaught. As the effects of the sonic blasts began to wear off he groaned and rose to hands and knees. When Owan noticed the reviving giant's efforts, he strode up behind the man, calmly reached down and sliced from just below the left ear to the center of the throat. The giant jerked around and looked up at Owan in total bewilderment. He grabbed at the gaping wound in the side of his neck, blood spurted between his fingers, his eyes glazed, and he crumpled face first into the dirt.

Struggling to regain a modicum of emotional control, Azazel stood and approached Owan, who was tending an injured adolescent female. He asked, "What do you need me to do?"

"First aid kits—we have two in our packs."

Azazel turned and began sprinting up the switch-back trail. A few minutes later he returned with a first aid kit in each hand. After dropping the kits beside Owan, who was treating an injured male. Azazel dropped to his knees. His panted gulps for air were ruptured by an agonized moan as he gripped the sides of his head with both hands.

Though unable to intellectually or emotionally process the atrocity's horrors, Ramuell saw the first aid kits as a call to action. He grabbed a kit and went to work on a young boy who had been pitched against a tree. Ramuell cleaned and used topical disinfectant on the boy's wounds. Fortunately, no major arteries had been severed and the bandages he applied staunched the bleeding.

The sounds of sonic-blaster discharges had ceased, but an occasional scream could still be heard from down canyon.

Ramuell struggled to block out mental images of the source of those cries. He looked up and saw Rarus walking back toward the ruins of the Clan's camp. He was leading a group of at least a dozen women and children, most had minor wounds that would require attention.

Ramuell rose to his feet, as did Owan, and together they approached the women. Several were not members of the Crow Clan. When one of the women saw the battered body of a nefilim man she calmly put down the young girl she had been carrying. The woman cautiously approached and knelt beside the dead body. She rocked back-and-forth with tears streaming down her face. Abruptly she shrieked and began clawing the giant with her fingernails. She sobbed as she beat the dead man's torso so viciously everyone watching took a step back. She stood and ripped off the garments covering him from the waist down and began stomping his genitals. As the woman's wails subsided she crumpled to the ground beside the corpse.

Owan approached cautiously with what he hoped would be interpreted as kindness. Suddenly the woman screeched and grabbed an obsidian blade that was tucked into the giant's garment. She thrust it into her gut. The other women in the group let out a collective gasp and several ran to their sister's aid. They were too late. After stabbing herself she completed the abortion by yanking the blade ferociously left and right several times. Blood gushed from her wound. When she flopped on her side a fetus, not even ten centimetres long, spilled from the eviscerated womb onto the blood soaked sand.

Owan, with almost unfathomable detachment, walked over to the woman, studied her for a few seconds. Determining she'd be dead within minutes, he turned and walked directly to one of the Crow women who had returned with the group. She sat on the ground holding her forearm, rocking in agony. Her shoulder was obviously dislocated. Ramuell watched as Owan kneeled beside the woman and stroked her hair. They exchanged a few words. She looked up at Owan and nodded.

He gently helped the woman lie flat on the ground. He sat down beside her injured arm and slowly raised it to a 90 degree angle from her body. Then placing his foot against her rib cage he took her wrist and firmly pulled the arm directly away from the body. Ramuell heard the shoulder pop as the humerus slid under the shoulder blade and back into its socket.

The woman screamed. She then opened her eyes wide, smiled, and reached up with her other hand and gently stroked Owan's cheek. He gave her a tight-lipped smile, but his eyes betrayed a deep, deep sadness. He looked around, stood and walked off toward the next wounded person.

Ramuell, having been so transfixed witnessing the suicide and Owan's ministrations, hadn't moved for several minutes. Hearing a child's cry shook him out of his inertia. He saw that the whimpering child was likely the daughter of the woman who had just killed herself and her fetus. As he hesitantly stepped forward, the little girl pushed herself to her feet and reached up. Tears rolled down Ramuell's cheeks as he swooped the child up into his arms. She clung to his neck and began to sob in short gasps.

As Ramuell patted her back soothingly, he saw Samael walking back toward the camp with no hint of the amusement that normally etched his face. He carried the woman who had so affectionately embraced Azazel. Her beautiful elliptical head flopped unnaturally with each step. When Sam passed by Owan they made eye contact. In that instant they shared a crippling sense of grief for their friend.

Samael laid the woman down near one of the fire pits. Azazel, who had been sitting almost catatonically, crawled over to the dead body. He let out the most pathetic moan Ramuell had ever heard. Stretching his legs out straight, Azazel picked up the woman's head and laid it on his lap. In a low voice he repeated over and over, "No, no, no..." as he stroked that lovely woman's curly chestnut colored hair.

CHAPTER TWENTY-SIX

A TALE OF THREE WORLDS

EGAN AND ALTHEA began recording the deposition by retelling the stories they had shared over brunch the previous day. Then they launched into the next chapter of their extraterrestrial adventures.

Their second stopover with the Beag-Liath was an asteroid where ore extraction and smelting was done in near zero-gravity environments. The slaves were a dark skinned species, rather small in stature, with copious head hair and shallow eyes.

The Domhanian overlords only worked two hour shifts due to the health impact of long-term exposure to low gravity. Upon completion of a shift on the asteroid or in the ore processing vessel, they returned to the artificial gravity of the single torus revolving around the cargo cylinder of their main ship.

Though the Domhanians were not unkind to the all-male work crews, there was little consideration given to the workers' long-term health. The Beag-Liath snuck Egan aboard one of the work stations in a pilfered flight suit. He observed a group of new émigrés being given powerful anti-nausea medications. Absent that debilitating sensation, the new arrivals seemed almost giddy with their weightlessness.

The extraterrestrial laborers were assigned only non-technical, repetitive tasks. Because everything was weightless, strength was not an issue, stamina was. The slaves worked eight to twelve straight hours in zero-gravity. Althea estimated their health likely began to fail within two annum. She believed the workers were being dosed with mood elevating stimulants, thereby modestly extending the duration of their productivity.

Althea explained that on their last day at this site they watched a group of eleven ailing extraterrestrials loaded on a transport vehicle. "The individuals were no longer capable of doing physical labor. The Domhanians who guided the slaves aboard the vessel treated them gently. With the Beag cloaking technology deployed, we followed the Domhanian ship for a few minutes. When the ship began a long arc, turning back toward the asteroid, they opened the bay doors, and all eleven bodies of the extraterrestrial laborers were jettisoned into the near absolute zero degree temperature of deep space."

Egan shuddered. "Though we had expected this, the shock of actually seeing sentient creatures being disposed of like garbage shook us to our cores. One of the Beag-Liath stood nearby studying us carefully. I'm almost certain it was using the bioelectrical sensory organ to gauge our emotional responses."

Thrumming her fingers on the table, Althea said, "It seems the Beag-Liath had shown us a couple of our corporate mining operations to impress upon us the immorality of subjugating an alien species for slave labor. They were also showing us our corporations' disregard for the lives of those unfortunate beings. Perhaps our next stops were intended to show us why our fellow Domhanians behave with such indifference."

"Indifference? I think contempt is a better word," Egan said in a low, sad voice.

Althea rubbed her eyes with both hands, looked back at the camera and continued, "We spent almost six undecim at the Domhanian colony on the planet Froitas. By that point, the Beag-Liath trusted that we understood the reason for our abduction. On Froitas we seldom utilized the Beag-Liath cloaking technology, nor did they accompany us everywhere. Rather they transported us to different locales, provided the appropriate attire, and encouraged us to mingle with other Domhanians.

"Froitas is actually quite a breadbasket world. At certain latitudes there are enormous swaths of arable land where all kinds of crops are produced in abundance. We also saw aqua-ag facilities on the shores of both fresh and saltwater bodies.

"The Domhanian settlements on Froitas range from a few hundred people to tens of thousands. Almost without exception, Domhanians living there are affluent and their lifestyles opulent. They have extraterrestrial servants doing all manner of menial labor. They work the fields, the food and fiber processing plants, and the grounds surrounding lavish estates. In urban areas most alien laborers work on cleaning crews and in food preparation services.

"There are many thousands of alien servants living on the planet. Their living quarters are austere concrete structures. They seem to be well fed, but when their health deteriorates to the point of diminished productivity, they're generally discarded rather than treated. Chronically ill or weakened individuals are taken to facilities where they're put down by lethal injection."

"No one ever leaves these 'termination facilities' alive,"

Egan added. "But they do leave. The remains of the terminated individuals are desalinated, mixed with acidic chemicals and sold as lawn and garden fertilizer." He hunched his shoulders sadly, "The fertilizer actually works rather well. Purchasers may have some notion of its source, but that information isn't advertised or acknowledged." Egan looked away from the camera shaking his head slowly.

Seeing that Egan was overcome with anger or sadness or both, Sean hit the stop button on the videorecorder. "It's time we take a break. Understandably, this process is bringing back vivid recollections that are difficult to process. It seems many of the things you are sharing produce a sense of shame.

"I can't begin to fathom the callousness you observed. I didn't see what you saw. To the best of our knowledge no other Domhanian has ever had a similar experience with the Beag-Liath. But I want to stress this is not **your** shame. Rather, it's a feeling of ignominy for our whole species." Sean paused for a moment gathering his thoughts. "And I can understand that. But it's important to recognize that the Beag-Liath had an agenda."

Picking up the thread of Sean's thought, Althea said, "And that was to show us the worst of ourselves."

"Exactly! But we must remember that Domhanians also have wonderful character traits. We have achieved a remarkable civilization. We live on a world that does not make war with itself. I can take you to dozens of places in Nexo de Mando to show you the most incredible works of art and literature—places where learning and science are put to work in ways that boggle the mind—places where acts of kindness save lives, and make lives meaningful, and help individuals and families as they deal with the end of life."

Sean looked down at the camera's remote control. When he looked back up, his eyes were moist, and he had a catch in his voice. "We are an extraordinary species. We are intelligent. We are caring, and we **can** cleanup this mess. It's going to require a values renaissance led by people like you. I understand you had no choice about becoming involved in this imbroglio. But now you are. You've been given a role to play in reshaping our culture's morality." Sean leaned forward and glancing back-and-forth made eye contact with both Althea and Egan, "I am glad the Beag-Liath chose you. It will be my honor to follow your lead as we redefine what it means to be Domhanian."

After lunch there was a new emotion present in the recording studio. All three understood this was no longer just a retelling of experiences – no longer just about recording a deposition as a source of evidence. What they recorded, and how they comported, would likely be the genesis of a worldwide discussion on Domhan-Siol. They realized what was recorded in this little room, on this little island, would impact their culture's evolution for centuries.

Sean turned on the recorder and began, "In our last session you told of how extraterrestrials are being deployed and treated in our corporate off-world enterprises. You mentioned that there are several hundred thousand Domhanians living on Froitas. I'd like for you to share what you observed among the Domhanians—their lifestyles, where they came from, what kind of work they do, how they fill their days."

Without hesitation Egan began, "It would be a mistake to consider the Domhanian population on Froitas homogenous."

Althea laughed, "No, there are the wealthy, the very wealthy, and the obscenely wealthy."

Egan rolled his eyes and turned back to the camera. "Actually, she's not that far off. The estates and mansions are owned by corporate elites from the homeworld. Many even have private 4-D Initiator facilities.

"Froitas is a beautiful world. There are mountains, valleys, lakes, and seas that make it an extraordinary place to visit and live. Members of our corporate aristocracy come and go frequently. Some families reside in the mansions for extended periods of time.

"The estates are themselves entire industries. The overseers are Domhanians who stay more or less permanently on Froitas. In fact, many of the overseers were born there. Froitas, not Domhan-Siol, is their homeworld. These people live in splendid homes, though not as extravagant as the main mansions. Each estate has a village of slave hovels. There could be as many as sixty to a couple hundred workers quartered in those primitive communes."

Althea gestured toward Sean, "You asked how the Domhanians fill their days. Of course, there's no single answer. The estate overseers attend to the daily duties necessary to maintain the homes and grounds, feed the people and slaves living on the estates, deal with medical and other kinds of emergencies, plan the construction and demolition of facilities as needs change.

"Among the owners and their families there's great diversity in how they bide their time. We saw and spoke to people who are engaged in academic and scientific research. Others spend time in various artistic endeavors—writing, painting, sculpting, making music—you get the idea. Many spent a portion of each day involved in sporting activities—usually outdoor sports.

"It would be a mistake to assume these lives of luxury are without meaning or intellectual pursuit. But we also saw a whole lot of well-heeled idleness. Some people never lift a finger on their own behalf. Everything is done for them by alien servants."

Sean cocked one eyebrow and asked, "Everything?"

Looking down at the table Egan nodded, sighed and said, "Yes, in the case of some of our younger people 'everything' includes sexual services."

Clearing her throat, Althea went on, "Yeah, well...we also met people who were just so stunningly uninformed. People who probably haven't read a book in many annum, if ever. They live lives of pampered self-indulgence."

"Now the lifestyles of Domhanians living in more urban areas differ from those living on the rural estates," Egan continued. "Perhaps more bourgeois than aristocratic. It's fashionable to be out and about. When a new exhibit opens at a museum the who's who show up for stimulant beverages and lavish buffets of exotic hors d'oeuvres. Almost nightly there are theatres, concerts and sporting events. For many, the main reason to attend these events is to be seen."

Althea knitted her brows, "I suppose that's true." She shook her head slightly with a hint of dismay, "And slave laborers were just everywhere. They clean the restaurants and theatres. They tend the grounds of the parks. Often families have servants preparing the picnic lunches and even watching the young children while the older kids and adults play games. It just seems the entire Domhanian culture of Froitas is reliant on alien laborers to do almost everything. The kinds of things we, on Domhan-Siol, do for ourselves without a second thought."

Sean asked, "How many hours per undecim would you estimate the laborers work?"

"I don't need to estimate," Egan answered. "I had conversations with people in both rural and urban settings. I pretended to be playing with various ideas to enhance labor efficiency and longevity. My ideas were scoffed at in every single one of those conversations. I was told our slaves were too slow-witted to be any more efficient no matter what we did. I was told that improving housing, work conditions, or reducing the number of hours worked would have no effect. I was told they don't feel the same things we feel; they don't feel pain, fatigue, hunger, or emotions as we do. I was told that trying to enhance longevity was a waste of time since their lives are so short anyway; at best I'd only get another five annum of work out of them.

"So, to answer your question, Domhanian overseers expect the alien slaves to work ten to twelve hours per day. About half are given one day off per undecim. The others work every single day of their short lives."

"And when they get sick?" Sean asked.

"If our veterinarians determine the health problem is short term, they're given appropriate treatments and some recovery time," Althea replied. "If, however, the health issue is chronic and results in frequent absences from work, they're taken to a termination facility—and in their deaths they continue working as fertilizer."

Frowning, Egan said, "We estimated the aliens' average lifespan on Froitas is about thirty-six annum. They begin working at around age ten. So they only have about twenty-six annum of productivity, it is a **high** turnover workforce."

"The whole system is monstrous!" Althea's exclamation dripped with anger. "A monster that requires continuous feeding." She made eye contact with her husband, and something passed between them. "And I suppose that brings us to what was for me the most distressing thing that we observed during our travels around Froitas. For our last stop the Beag-Liath took us to a reproduction facility—a kind of factory really."

Egan interrupted, "Al, I'm tired. I'm sure you're tired too. Perhaps we should hold this part of the story for tomorrow."

"You're right," Sean agreed. "It's hard enough listening to your testimony; I can't imagine the distress you must feel recounting these events. Let's call it a day." He slid his chair back and asked, "Would you like to come to my place tomorrow for breakfast? Roe quiche is one of my specialties."

After breakfast in Sean's apartment, they returned to the studio. They took their respective seats at the round table, Sean leaned over and patted the back of Althea's hand. "So when we quit yesterday you were getting ready to describe, using your words, 'the most distressing thing we observed.' Are you ready to resume at that point?"

Glancing sideways at Egan, who closed both eyes briefly and nodded slightly, she answered, "Yes I'm fine—we're fine."

Reaching for the remote control, Sean said, "All right, then let's get started."

Althea inhaled and exhaled deeply, looked at the camera and began, "Through Egan's conversations with several overseers we learned a good deal about how often the slaves have to be replaced. The turnover is frequent and ongoing. Some are brought directly from their homeworld, but it was found that they were—hmm, how do I put it? I suppose they're more feral than members of the alien species who are born as a result of couplings on Froitas. About a hundred annum ago Benestar Pharmaceutical Corp. funded a reproduction center on Froitas."

She looked down at her folded hands and sighed. "If natural breeding and childbirth could produce more malleable servants, imagine how much more efficient an artificial insemination, gestation, and birthing facility would be. Actually, we don't need to imagine—females consigned to these facilities produce two point two times more children per five annum period than do female servants by way of natural coupling. Women in the reproduction centers have approximately twenty-five undecim gestations periods. They are allowed to nurse their babies for about six undecim. The females are again inseminated about three undecim after they quit nursing."

Doing a quick calculation Sean said, "So, the females can produce about four offspring every five annum."

"That's correct."

"How many annum are they fertile?" Sean asked.

"With proper diet, hormone therapy, and medical treatment they could be fertile for over fifteen annum," answered Althea.

Sean whistled. Althea realized where the math had taken him. "You're thinking each female in those baby factories have about a dozen offspring. But they don't. After the forth or fifth infant is taken away, the females just seem to fold in on themselves. When they're impregnated they find ways to abort, or they refuse to nurse their babies, or they commit suicide, sometimes assisted by their brood-sow sisters." Anger etched her face, and her words were taut. "I use that term literally. These women are treated like livestock. It is simply horrifying!"

"But here's the reality, even if they only average four babies per female, the profits are sizable," Egan interjected. "They raise the offspring in nurseries where the focus is on preparing them to work in some particular service. By the time they reach ten annum they're ready to be placed in jobs. They will perform that same job for the rest of their lives. These bred, born, and raised-for-labor creatures fetch a premium price. Slaves from the brood farms sell for double the price of slaves brought directly from their homeworld."

Hesitantly Sean asked, "And I assume the females who become uncooperative..."

"Retired to the termination facilities," Egan replied.

Sean slumped, "What in all the frozen-hells are we doing?"

Althea leaned forward, put her elbows on the table and rubbed her eyes.

When Sean's communicator trilled he shut-off the video-recorder.

"Aww dammit!" Sean exclaimed after reading the text. With a combination of frustration and anger he said, "I'm sure you're getting sick of this—I certainly am, but we have to go."

"Go?" both Egan and Althea questioned simultaneously.

"We've got to leave Cascata. There's no huge rush, but to be on the safe side, we should not tarry."

"But I love this beautiful place," Althea whined. "What if we just say no? We've done nothing wrong and we're not running anymore."

Sean shot Egan a glance. He turned to his wife and said, "Al, it's not what we've done. It's what we know; staying to face the B&I Council goons is not an option. These guys killed the Secretary of the Law and Order Directorate."

Sean added, "What you know is so dangerous to these people they're acting like cornered predators."

Althea rubbed both temples. "Yeah. I know—and they have a lot of resources."

Sean said, "That's for sure. Unfortunately, our pursuers have dispatched a team in this direction." Turning his attention back to his communicator, Sean tapped in a couple of numbers and said to whomever answered the call, "It's time."

"Okay my friends, go pack your belongings. I'll pick up some boxed lunches. Can you be ready to go in an hour?"

Snorting, Althea said, "We arrived on Domhan naked. The only things we have are the clothes you gave us to escape from the hospital and the few things we picked-up at the repository. We can be ready to go in ten minutes."

Egan scowled with disgust, or perhaps it was sadness.

Sean led Althea and Egan down two flights of stairs ending in a high ceilinged cavern. In the middle of the floor was a large, irregular shaped pool with a mini-submarine nestled snugly against a small mooring.

A man was sitting at the controls doing a systems check. Seeing his three passengers enter the grotto he waved and laughed at the shocked expressions on Egan's and Althea's faces. He reached over his left shoulder and snapped open a couple of latches then hit a button on the control panel. Almost silently the entire left side of the transparent aluminum oxynitride cockpit slowly opened 120 degrees.

With boyish exuberance the pilot hopped out onto the dock. He greeted them by extending both palms at once. With a warm smile he introduced himself. "My name is Donaldo, but most folks call me Captain Don, or just Cap."

Sean said, "And our guests are Dr. Althea and Professor Egan."

"Yes, I know who they are and why they're here." Turning serious, Donaldo said, "I'm sorry you have to leave our island on such short notice. But it will be a safe, beautiful and quite fascinating journey."

Half an hour later Donaldo piloted the boat through a 238 metres-long underwater fissure and dove to a depth of twenty metres in the open sea.

The boat's passengers shared exclamations of awe as they stared out the portholes at masses of fish, mammals and seaweed. After several minutes of this enchantment, Sean said, "I'm puzzled by something we didn't get to during our taping sessions."

Egan cast a concerned glance at Donaldo in the boat's bow.

Sean noticed, "Ah, there's nothing to worry about there. Captain Don has worked with the Directorate for a long time. I suspect he's privy to secrets even I know nothing about."

"You bet I am!" Donaldo called back over his shoulder. "And for both our sakes, it shall remain thus."

"Yep, we can agree on that," Sean teased.

"So what's troubling you?" Althea asked.

"Your return. Not **that** you were returned, but rather **how** —dumped unconscious and naked on cold ground in a Nexo de Mando park. I just don't get it. Why would the Beag-Liath have done that to you?"

Scratching his jaw Egan said, "It does seem a bit unceremonious, doesn't it? You'd think after all that time together we'd have been given a soft landing with a formal fare-thee-well and hugs-all-around."

Althea shot 'the look' at her husband. "Are you going to tell the story or shall I?"

With a gesture he beckoned Althea to proceed. "Okay— there were no 'hugs-all-around' because they weren't touching us. They were avoiding us like the plague."

"Which we probably were!" Egan interjected.

"That's correct. We think we know how we came to be carriers of a contagious pathogen and why they, as you said, 'dumped us naked.' You see, we believe the Beag-Liath made quite a big mistake."

"A scientifically unsophisticated blunder," Egan added.

Althea said, "Or naïve because they're probably novices in

the abduction business. Do you remember we told you about the regimen of vaccinations we were given soon after our abduction?"

"Yes, of course."

"I don't think we told you that they were also preparing vaccines for themselves. They seemed to be determining what kind of microorganisms we carried that might be pathogenic to them. We saw them giving each other inoculations."

"I hadn't thought of it, but of course that makes sense," Sean said. "So did they infect themselves with a live-cell vaccine?"

"Nope," replied Egan. "It's not what they gave themselves, but rather what they didn't give themselves that created the problem."

Puzzled, Sean leaned forward and wrinkled his forehead.

"We believe when we were roaming around Froitas we were exposed to something the Beag-Liath hadn't anticipated," Althea explained. "We didn't knowingly interact with anyone who was sick. The Froitas vaccination protocols are essentially the same as on Domhan-Siol. People come and go between the planets almost daily. Any infectious illness from Domhan-Siol would show up on Froitas and vice versa absent appropriate immunization.

"The day after our last visit on Froitas we came down with a very uncomfortable stomach bug—gas pains and diarrhea."

"And your last visit was the extraterrestrial's reproduction center," Sean recalled.

"Whoo boy!" Donaldo exclaimed from the pilot's seat.

Althea had forgotten he was listening and startled slightly. Looking into the cockpit she said, "It sounds like the captain has figured it out—so tell us what you're thinking."

"I think if you folks were exposed to an extraterrestrial species, one that is very similar to us, it's possible you contracted some kind of microorganism that's endemic within that species. Heck, it might not even make them sick. But we may lack the natural defenses to fight it off," Donaldo surmised.

Althea nodded appreciatively. "Very good! Actually we think that's pretty much what happened. We probably have some natural immunity as we were sick for only about a day. It seems the mistake the Beag-Liath made was assuming all they needed to do was immunize against Domhanian illnesses. When we returned to the ship carrying an exotic disease they were defenseless. Even with their advanced medical technologies, it's our belief at least some of them became extremely ill; perhaps even died."

"Much of what happened after the disease outbreak is a blur," Egan continued. "We were placed inside of a sealed shower stall, and they mimed for us to strip. We sealed our clothing in a vacuum tube in the shower wall.

"Then they turned on the showers and we were soaked in what smelled like a mild astringent. It was warm and cleansing. Not at all uncomfortable. After the shower was turned off, nozzles in the floor began emitting what we thought was steam, but it wasn't. We found it difficult to breathe and I wondered if we were being gassed."

Althea said, "Actually, we were being gassed, but not with a toxin. The Beag-Liath had expended too much energy on us. Their entire effort would have been for nought if we didn't survive to carry the story back to Domhan-Siol. We were conscious for a few minutes, and even though it was difficult to talk..."

"The gas triggered our cough reflex," interrupted Egan.

"Right, but we were able to croak a bit and concurred that we were likely being sterilized."

"Sterilized?" Sean asked.

"The Beag-Liath have some highly advanced medical practices," Althea replied.

Donaldo grunted, "Humph, that's why they let you folks infect them with some kind of contagious organism."

"You make a good point," Egan said, "but the fact that we became vectors doesn't negatively reflect on their technology. Rather it's an indictment of their judgment."

"Or perhaps their experience," Althea surmised. "You see, that they didn't anticipate the likelihood we'd be exposed to an unknown pathogen while traipsing around Froitas probably indicates they have very little direct contact with alien species."

"Even though they've perfected a hide-and-watch technology," Egan added.

"Which makes sense," conceded Donaldo.

Althea said, "Back to the question about what I meant by the word sterilized, we think the gas was likely some kind of antibiotic/antiviral/antifungal substance that was being fast-forwarded into our blood streams through our lungs. Three Beag-Liath wearing hazmat suits stood outside of the shower chamber watching us, probably for any sign of an allergic reaction.

"After a few minutes there was a slight change in the odor. Soon after that we became very drowsy. That's the last thing we remember until we woke-up on Domhan-Siol."

"They anesthetized you," observed Sean.

Egan said, "So it seems. They probably put us into some kind of cold stasis for our journey home. It's possible they had no further physical contact with us whatsoever, which would explain why we were naked and why our core temperatures were so low when we were found by the stream."

Shaking his head Sean said, "I'm guessing that's an ordeal neither of you would want to repeat."

"To be sure," Althea replied.

Twenty-three minutes later Captain Don nudged the mini-sub underneath a kelp harvesting barge. Sean squeezed Donaldo's shoulder, "Cap, as always, it's been great seeing you. When all of this has calmed down a bit, I'm going to come down here to do some diving with you."

A smile crinkled the crow's feet around Donaldo's eyes. He said, "I'll keep a regulator and some tanks ready for ya." He paused and with a bit of regret added, "But from just the little I've heard, I don't think this is going to calm down anytime soon."

The captain's observation turned out to be more prophetic than anyone in his little boat could have ever imagined.

CHAPTER TWENTY-SEVEN

HELPFUL HARM AND HARMFUL HELP

AFTER HOURS of administering first aid, Ramuell wondered what his grandmother would think of this debacle. This thought brought to mind their assignment from Chief Science Officer Durela.

"We must figure out a way to halt the passing of the gigantism mutation—the alternative is just too horrible to contemplate..."

Though exhausted, Ramuell removed the scalpel and box of surgical gloves from a first aid kit and tottered toward the body of the nearest nefilim. He took his multi-tool from a zippered pants pocket and used it to pull away shattered chunks of the giant's scalp and skull. With the scalpel he dissected the brain to remove the hypothalamus and pituitary gland and placed the organs inside a surgical glove, which he sealed with three knots.

Rarus came over and offered to assist. They measured the corpse's height, length of legs and arms, torso girth, and estimated the man's weight. Ramuell taped his notes to the glove.

The two of them repeated this process with each of the

nefilim corpses. Rarus worked alongside Ramuell almost silently. As they neared the end of the gruesome task he asked, "Will this help with your research?"

Staggering to his feet, Ramuell said, "My god Rarus, I am so sorry. I should have explained what we were doing here. I suppose I'm in shock. Please forgive me."

"Oh Ramuell, there's nothing to forgive. Of course you're in shock! I have seen bloodshed before, but I've never seen anything like this." He paused looking around at the gory scene. "The fact you can function at all says much about you. That you somehow remembered your mission speaks volumes."

"Thank you. That means a lot to me."

As they turned to leave Ramuell explained, "To answer your question, what we've got here are the glands that regulate sapien growth. We'll try to keep these samples as uncontaminated as possible. Removal in a non-surgical setting ensures some level of contamination, but if we can get these up to my grandmother's lab quickly enough, she'll be able to tease out some valuable information. She's a genius."

"So I've heard."

Approaching what had been the clan's river camp Ramuell said, "Oh shoot, I left my multi-tool back there. I'll catch up with you in a minute." Using this pretext, he returned and took tissue samples from the mouths of the girl and woman with Domhanian shaped skulls. He suspected they were the progeny of a Domhanian-Sapien union. Some instinct inclined him to say nothing about this part of Kadeya's research.

It was now almost three hours after the battle and Azazel had regained his composure. He had waded fully clothed into the river's cold water and washed most of the blood and pieces of tissue off his uniform. He was standing in front of a roaring fire, hands on his hips, discussing matters with Owan and Samael. When Ramuell approached he noted that Azazel's eyes were clear and his speech lucid.

"Even though it's past midday, I need you to hike out and call the basecamp," Azazel was telling Samael. "Have them send RTVs to meet us at Sawgrass Plateau and to get as close to the canyon as possible. Don't share any details about what's happened. The five of us need to debrief before I write up my report."

"Yes sir. You realize it will be well after dark when they arrive."

"Yeah, I understand your concern," Azazel replied. "But Ru Ta has already approached Owan and asked us to, hmm..." looking over at Owan, "What would you say he's asked us to do?"

Owan thought for a moment, "I suppose take them into protective custody."

"We simply cannot allow ourselves to be drawn into that kind of a relationship. We need to beat a retreat before the Clan has a chance to regroup and press their demands."

"You're right," Samael replied.

As Sam turned to walk away, Azazel added, "We'll be following you within the hour. We're going to drag the nefilim bodies out into the river's current and let nature take its course." He paused looking at the river, "I regret we can't build pyres to burn the bodies, but cremation of that many nefilim would take days."

Sam nodded his understanding. "I'll have our folks dispatch vehicles immediately."

Owan blew out an exhausted breath and said, "It would be nice to have a pot of tea when we get up there."

"Yes sir, it'll be brewed." Samael slung the sonic-blaster

across his shoulder and walked away. The communication equipment and his backpack were still on the trail where he'd dropped them early that morning.

Watching him go, Ramuell said, "I don't understand."

Azazel looked down. "I lost my head. I've seen the results of nefilim atrocities on four occasions, but this was the first time I've witnessed an attack. I lost control and I've probably made a pile of trouble for myself..."

"No, no! I understand that completely," interrupted Ramuell.

Azazel flinched and looked up. "So what don't you understand?"

"I don't see why we can't protect the Clan."

"I suppose the easy answer would be that kind of relationship with sapiens is not within our protocols." Owan looked askance at his friend. Azazel held up a hand in a 'wait-a-second' gesture. "That would be the easy answer, and it would be true. But that's not the real reason.

"Our relationships with the various clans are situational. To be sure, we could protect the Crow Clan from further nefilim attacks. But we cannot protect the clan living in the scrub forests some thirty kilometres north of here. We simply don't have the resources. And if we did protect them from the nefilim should we also intervene in conflicts between sapiens and *neandertalis*? Should we protect *neandertalis* from nefilim incursions?"

Ramuell said, "It just seems that since we created the nefilim problem, well, it's..."

"...it's ours to fix," Owan completed the thought.

Azazel had been facing the fire. He turned to warm his backside and let the heat dry the back of his clammy clothes. "It **is** our problem to fix, but we haven't figured out how to do that. In the meantime, some things we might do could make matters worse—perhaps much worse."

Ramuell stared into the fire's orange flickers. With a resigned shrug, he said, "I guess I can see that...things on Ghrain-3 are never simple."

Over three hours later the four men, huffing and puffing, topped the canyon rim and saw the smoke of Samael's fire. The next twenty minutes of mostly flat hiking led to a fifteen metre climb straight up a slot in the escarpment that rimmed the Sawgrass Plateau. Physically and emotionally drained, they flopped on the ground near the stone fire ring.

Sam handed out cups of tea and said, "I was starting to worry."

"It took us longer to move the bodies into the river than we'd expected. They're heavy!" Rarus replied.

"Man, that's the truth," Ramuell agreed. "We need to revisit the weight estimates we made earlier."

Samael stepped into a thicket of trees and returned dragging a log. "Here, you'll be more comfortable sitting on this."

The makeshift bench was more comfortable than the ground. Staring into the flames, Owan asked Azazel, "You mentioned earlier we need to talk before you write the report. Do you want to have that conversation now?"

"No! Not yet." Azazel gazed into the teacup he was holding in both hands, "...not ready to talk about it yet."

Sam grabbed the teapot sitting at the flame's edge and refilled Azazel's cup. Owan reached over and gently squeezed the Area Director's shoulder. Without moving his body Azazel turned his head and looked into his friend's eyes. Something passed between them that Ramuell could not decipher.

The group lapsed into a morose silence. Realizing it would be more than an hour before the vehicles arrived, Owan broke the tension, "Ramuell, earlier you questioned the decision to abandon the Crow Clan without providing additional protection, which raises all kinds of questions."

"Yeah, I've been thinking about that and must admit I'm not smart enough to see that far into the future," Ramuell replied.

Still staring into his cup, Azazel said, "None of us can tease out all the possible scenarios. I suppose that's why we have a nefilim problem."

Owan removed his fleece cap and vigorously scratched his scalp. "We didn't leave any kind of antibiotic with the Crow Clan, and here's their reality—most of the individuals with open wounds will develop infections. Some of those infections will become serious and some of the clan will die from the complications.

"As heartless as it may sound, those individuals need to die. They don't carry the genetic predisposition to aggressively fight off infection. For the long-term health and survival of the Clan's descendants, it's best that those individuals are weeded out of the gene pool."

Gloomily Ramuell nodded, "You're right, it does sound heartless."

Owan added, "And given that the sapiens' lifespan is so short, gene pool modifications occur with amazing rapidity. In just three or four centuries, less than a single Domhanian lifetime, a population can develop immunity to some particularly nasty organism; or conversely, they might develop a mutation that dooms them."

"I get it—don't like it, but I understand the biology," Ramuell responded quietly.

Samael groaned. His sore muscles protested as he stood to throw several pieces of wood on the fire. “You may want to move back some. It’s getting dark and we need a roaring fire our people can easily see. They should be rolling in here pretty soon.”

CHAPTER TWENTY-EIGHT

THE HEROES?

THE GROUP MET in Azazel's office after breakfast. Sitting almost motionless behind his desk, he instructed each of them to write a detailed account of their recollections; beginning with the first sounds of the ruckus in the fog-shrouded canyon until they had disposed of the last giant's body in the river. They were told not to discuss the incident with each other or anyone else.

Azazel's assistant scheduled appointments for each of the men beginning the next morning. The meetings with Officers Rarus and Samael preceded Ramuell's. When Ramuell entered the office, Azazel stepped over to the credenza under one of the geodesic dome's triangular windows and poured a cup of tea for them both.

Twice Azazel and sought clarification as he read Ramuell's report. After finishing he asked several questions trying to draw out Ramuell's emotional reactions during the battle and in its aftermath.

They discussed Ramuell's flying tackle that brought Azazel's tirade of butchery to an end. An aggressive intervention by a juvenile directed at an authority figure was beyond extraordinary among Domhanians. It seemed Azazel harbored no hard feelings. In fact, he was most interested in what Ramuell was seeing and feeling in the moments leading up to his decision to act.

The following morning Azazel gave each man a draft of his report. He asked them to read it carefully; comment and edit as they felt necessary. He dismissed them with the instruction that they would reconvene for lunch in his office.

That meeting went on for hours as they discussed differing perceptions and recollections. Ramuell was most forthcoming. Rarus and Samael were more circumspect. They understood the implications of what had happened and the possible consequences for Azazel. Owan was most succinct, commenting only on matters of fact. Ramuell felt certain Owan would be called upon to assist with drafting the final report.

When Ramuell read that report it was clear that Azazel had stated the facts from the collective points of view of everyone involved. He didn't try to justify his behavior and offered only a brief explanation for his actions.

Only Owan understood the whole truth about his friend's visceral reaction to the nefilim attack on the Crows. He also understood Azazel would **never** share that 'whole truth' with the Serefim Presidium.

Two days later the group was summoned to the orbiter. Azazel had little doubt that his bludgeoning of a dozen stunned nefilim would be considered so egregious that disciplinary action was in the offing. At the minimum he expected a reprimand, but believed it was possible he'd be discharged from service.

He even worried their transport ship might be met by a security detail at the docking port with the five of them escorted to their cabins and held under guard. He was more than a tad surprised when they exited the decontamination lock to find only Ramuell's grandmother and the Deputy Administrator for the Serefim Presidium awaiting their arrival.

Kadeya's anxiety washed away the instant she saw Ramuell. In an effort to appear professional Ramuell offered his grandmother an upturned palm, which she swatted away pulling him into a full embrace. After a few moments Kadeya pushed her grandson to arm's length and held his shoulders firmly while looking him up and down.

A handsome man, in a bookish kind of way, offered a greeting that seemed genuine. "Welcome back aboard Director Azazel. It's always a pleasure to see you." The man turned toward Owan, Samael, and Rarus and offered his palm. "Welcome. We may have met before, but at my age memory seems to fail me from time to time. My name is Trace."

Seeing that Trace was not going to elaborate of his own accord, Azazel interjected, "Trace is the Deputy Administrator for the Serefim Presidium." This comment both acknowledged the man's authority and alerted his colleagues that they needed to be cautious.

Tapping Trace's palm, Owan said, "I'm Owan and actually we have met, but it's been a few annum since we last saw each other."

"Yes, I recall. You're the chief paleontologist at SWA-7. Paleontology is one of my fascinations. I'd even go so far as to say it almost rises to the level of a hobby." He snorted and added, "...as if I have time for a hobby!"

"We should plan to get together for dinner," Owan replied. "We've recently made some fascinating fossil discoveries."

Beaming, Trace said, “I’ll contact you tomorrow and we’ll set something up.”

After a couple minutes of small-talk, Trace said, “If you’ll follow me I’ll show you to your cabins. You’ll be staying in the G3AST. Of course you can spend a few hours outside of the sapien-sphere, but not too many. You wouldn’t want to have to go through the acclimatization process again.”

A glance flickered between Azazel and Owan. *What’s he telling us?*

Though there was no security detail assigned to the G3AST, the five men remained on edge. They agreed to meet for lunch in the galley after getting settled in their temporary quarters.

Several people approached the SWA-7 team the moment they entered the buffet area. “Glad to see you guys are all right.”...“When did you arrive?”...“Let me know if there’s anything I can do.”...“Everything’s gonna be fine.”

A few people even said things like, “Good job!”...“You did exactly what needs to be done!”...“Hell, I wish I’d been there!”

They were surprised and somewhat embarrassed by the effusiveness of the greetings. Wisely, they followed Azazel’s example. He offered his palm to everyone, smiled at the welcoming comments, affected a stoic expression in the face of the more bellicose comments, and said very little.

When the last of the greeters departed, Samael scanned the expressions of his colleagues and quietly asked, “What in a pile of marsh bison dung was that?”

“I don’t know,” Azazel replied under his breath. “The greetings we’ve had so far this morning have **not** been what I expected.” He paused for a moment playing with the pasta in his bowl. “Remember, the people in the G3AST are stationed on the surface. They’re only here on temporary assignments.”

Owan understood. “Meaning they likely despise the nefilim.”

"Precisely," Azazel agreed. "They may think our actions were heroic, but probably none have ever witnessed an actual attack. It's easy to be gung-ho about something like that until you've stood in and smelled the blood and excrement."

"You're right!" Ramuell said stirring his soup. "Grandmother and I have been assigned to figure out how to stop the spread of the gigantism mutation. If by genetic manipulation we can prevent more births, mortality should resolve the problem long-term." Shaking his head, he added, "It's one thing to sit here and talk about attrition through natural mortality, and it's quite another to be standing in a canyon watching nefilim mutants grab children by the heels and bash their heads into trees."

Rarus leaned forward placing his forearms on the table's edge. "When you were dissecting the giant's brains..."

"...removing the hypothalamus and pituitary glands," interrupted Ramuell.

"Right—when we were doing that, you explained that you and your grandmother are working on this problem. I certainly hope your efforts are a success, but for the survivors among the Crow the idea of a 'long-term' solution is damn small solace."

Azazel tilted his head back and narrowed his eyes. "From whom did you get this assignment?"

Suddenly Ramuell realized Azazel had not been made aware of the assignment. He stammered, "Oh—uhm—a few undecim after we arrived the Chief Science Officer..."

"Durela," Azazel filled in.

"Yes, Durela. A few undecim after we set up shop she visited the lab. Afterward she and grandmother met privately in the lab office."

"Interesting—and do you know if Durela's assignment was given to Kadeya in writing?" Azazel asked.

Rubbing the back of his neck, Ramuell answered, "I don't.

Grandmother only told me about it after I began living in the sapien-sphere."

Shaking off a bit of annoyance at being left out of the loop, Azazel said, "Perhaps we can talk with Kadeya about this work sometime while we're here."

With an imperceptible relaxation of his shoulders, Ramuell said, "Oh, I think she'd be thrilled."

The men ate quietly for several minutes. Azazel cleared his throat and said, "Gentlemen, after you were shown to your quarters Trace came by my cabin." Owan leaned forward, tilting his head inquisitively. "He thanked me for what he called the 'Incident Report' and said within the next few days interviews will be scheduled for each of us with a Committee of Inquiry."

Owan frowned. "Committee of Inquiry?"

"Frankly, he gave the impression it's just a formality—that our battle with the nefilim is not commanding much attention from the Presidium."

Samael asked, "What's the Committee likely to ask?"

When Azazel hesitated, Owan took a stab at answering. "They'll likely ask each of us the same questions about specifics within the report. Then they'll ask some opened-ended questions like 'Is there anything missing from the report?' or 'Do you remember anything else?'"

"So they'll try to trip us up," Samael said. "Thinking we might give different answers to the same question. Will they try to make it appear the boss reported falsely?"

Azazel replied haltingly, "I don't think so—but I'm not sure why I feel that way. Now you can be certain we won't get the same kind of reception from the Committee that we got in here," he said gesturing around the galley. "But remember, tell the absolute truth. Don't try to protect me with even the slightest fabrication. If you do, the next person on the interview list won't know what you said, and it will become obvious someone is lying. If that's the case, they'll want to know why we must lie."

"The boss is right," Owan agreed. "We can no more change the consequences for what happened in Blue Rock than we can change what actually did happen down there. Our best strategy, our only strategy really, is the truth. Everyone needs to study the Director's report before we're interviewed."

"Will do," Samael said as he stood, clearly ready to leave.

After two days they still had heard nothing about the Committee of Inquiry or an interview schedule. "Perhaps we've been summoned a few days early just to make us sweat," Owan suggested.

Whatever the Presidium's reasoning might have been, Azazel had little patience with idleness. He asked Ramuell to set up a meeting with Kadeya. She invited them to her cabin for drinks and hors d'oeuvres that very afternoon.

Upon entering his grandmother's den, Ramuell was struck by the attractive upgrades in furnishings and décor. "You've made some improvements."

"I have. Since I'll not be on the surface much, I figured I should make my little suite a home. I also won't be returning to Domhan-Siol anytime soon. The gigantism problem won't be solved quickly."

"Actually, that's what we want to talk about," Azazel said.

Kadeya gestured toward the seats at an oval tea table that stood on copper legs with a striking greenish patina. Kadeya set a tray of cheeses, crackers and a tea service on the glass tabletop. She sat on the loveseat next to Ramuell and slung her arm on the back of the seat behind her grandson's shoulders. "I suspected that's what was on your mind. But before we get to the nefilim, tell me about how you've been received on the orbiter."

"Frankly, I'm bewildered," Azazel replied.

Ramuell said, "Walking over here, people stopped us three times with comments of support. It's almost been like a hero's welcome."

"Yes it has," Azazel agreed. "Which is rather troubling when you think about it."

"Can't say I'm surprised, but you're right, it **is** troubling," Kadeya agreed.

Azazel said, "I can't fathom what people think is happening down there. It seems they believe we did something wonderful—if so, they're being completely obtuse about our interventions with the planet's indigenes."

Tilting her head slightly, Kadeya said, "To begin with, I sense a fairly cavalier attitude. Most people up here consider the sapien-hybrids to be creatures of our own creation rather than indigenous."

"So do they believe we own them?" Azazel asked.

"I suppose there are quite a number of people who think exactly that. Which would explain the mindset that if you had to kill a bunch of mutants, so what!"

Ramuell stared incredulously at his grandmother.

Kadeya held up her hand, "I'm just reporting an attitude I sense among many people. I'm not predicting a largescale attack on the nefilim. If Durela is to be believed, we'll be given time to solve this problem without intervention by our security forces and a lot of bloodshed."

"Is Durela to be believed?" Azazel asked. "My question isn't to impugn her character, rather I'm asking about her authority and influence with the Presidium."

Kadeya made a squeaking noise as she sucked her teeth.

"That's the question isn't it? I've heard nothing that would lead me to think she's lost any clout. But...something strange is going on. I don't think your Blue Rock Canyon incident is going to rise very high on the Presidium's list of priorities right now."

Ramuell leaned forward, "Something's going on? What do you mean?"

"I wish I knew. There have been a lot of comings and goings among the Presidium's top echelon, and I don't mean to and from the surface. They are doing 4D jumps, they're gone for several days, then reappear on the orbiter." Kadeya tugged an earlobe. "There's also been a frenzied increase in gold shipments. We've built a large docking facility on the smaller continent in the southern hemisphere. Transport ships are being loaded there every couple of days."

Azazel said, "I'm assuming the facility is completely mechanized since sapiens aren't indigenous to that continent."

"The docking facilities aren't the kind of temporary structures we've built elsewhere. While we have placed a lot of machinery at the site, we've also imported sapien-hybrid laborers. I assume the smelting is almost all mechanized, so the sapiens are probably loading metal ingot on anti-grav pallets for stowage on the cargo ships."

Azazel twisted his lips. "And where are these sapien-hybrids coming from?"

"I don't know."

"This is **not** what I signed up for. I came here with the idealistic notion that giving sapiens an evolutionary nudge was a righteous and honorable enterprise. The use of hybrids as laborers has always troubled me. But their relocation to a far-off continent smacks of involuntary servitude. Perhaps I'm overreacting—but my gut tells me the corporations funding our efforts on Ghrain-3 are more interested in cheap labor than enhanced sentience." Putting both hands across his stomach Azazel said, "I almost feel queasy."

Ramuell exhaled loudly and said, "Grandmother, as you know, my first encounter with the sapien-hybrids was just a few days ago. Before our traumatic departure, we spent three wonderful days waiting out the storm in the Crow Clan's caves.

"What I learned during those days is that these are very smart people. They think symbolically. They are kind and gracious. They care for and about each other. They're not beasts of burden. If our corporations are treating them as such, and if it's condoned by the Presidium, then we need a course correction."

At that moment, the doorbell chimed. Kadeya said, "Pass."

The door slid open, Semyaza stepped in and was met with three astonished expressions. "What? What did I do?" The creases beside Semyaza's eyes crinkled deeply, though he managed not to laugh.

"What are you doing here!?" exclaimed Azazel.

"Oh, I ran into Owan and Rarus in the commissary. They told me you two were over here visiting Kadeya."

"No, I mean why are you upstairs?" insisted Azazel.

Semyaza's almost-smile melted, "Oh, I figured my friends might be needing some moral support."

"How did you even know that we're up here?" asked Azazel.

Semyaza rolled his eyes. "Everybody on the surface knows you're up here. Everyone has heard about your adventure."

"Misadventure—and I doubt they know the facts," commented Azazel.

"Most assuredly they do not, nor do I. So what is happening? What's going on with the investigation?"

Ramuell grunted.

Semyaza turned toward him and said, "And how are you holding up my young friend?" Then looking at Kadeya, "And how is grandma doing with all of this? Seriously, are you folks okay?"

"We honestly don't know," answered Azazel. "We've been here over two days and haven't heard a peep from the Committee of Inquiry. Kadeya was just telling us something odd is afoot. She thinks our incident, and my unfortunate behavior, may be little more than a blip on the Presidium's radar."

Casting a quizzical look at Kadeya, Semyaza asked, "So what are you hearing?"

"Not much. But there's been a flurry of unusual activity among the power-elites," Kadeya answered.

"And what about down below? Are you seeing anything unusual happening on the surface?" Semyaza asked.

Kadeya studied Semyaza's face, wondering what he knew. "Yes, downstairs there are some—well, I suppose you'd say curious goings-on."

Semyaza sniffed, "And...?"

Kadeya told Semyaza about the docking facility that had been built in the southern hemisphere. "I don't have any specific data, but we know they're shipping a lot of metal—mostly gold."

Ramuell added the more troubling information. "And they've imported sapien-hybrids as a workforce."

Kadeya stood and stepped into the kitchen for another mug. She filled it with tea and handed it to Semyaza. Staring at the dark brew, he pouted his lips.

Noting his friend's expression, Azazel said, "I see this doesn't come as a surprise."

Semyaza sat up straight and scanned the room. With both

index fingers he pointed at the ceiling and walls. “Are we alone in here?”

Ramuell and Azazel startled. The idea that perhaps the room was bugged hadn’t occurred to them.

“Oh, quite,” answered Kadeya. “When I moved into these quarters I **insisted** that all observation devices in this room be disabled.” She opened the drawer built into the front of the loveseat and pulled out an electromagnetic signal jammer. “No one can see or hear us. We’re good.”

Semyaza nodded. “Okay, you are correct. We are moving sapien-hybrids around to various worksites.”

A mask of wintery disapproval dropped across Ramuell’s face.

Noting the youngster’s dismay, Semyaza faced Ramuell and said, “What I have to tell is likely worse than what you’re imagining.

“Recently a nomadic clan we’ve been studying for a couple of centuries expanded overnight. We dispatched a team of researchers to investigate. As we had suspected, they had adopted the remnants of another clan. We were concerned that the other clan may have lost many of its members due to some kind of die-off, but we learned there had been no deaths. Their fellow clansmen had simply disappeared. The only ones left were those who had been away from their camp foraging. One person was filling water skins at a nearby spring. She heard the commotion and crested a hill in time to see members of her clan boarding a transport ship.

“Naturally, she couldn’t comprehend what she was seeing. Though her descriptions were muddled, we pieced together that at least half a dozen Domhanians were involved in the operation. It seems coercion rather than force was their modus operandi. None of the sapiens were dragged aboard the ship. They entered the shuttlecraft of their own volition.”

"I wouldn't jump to that conclusion. They may have been tranquilized," Azazel suggested.

"We thought that possible and can't conclusively rule it out. But it's more likely the Domhanians just cast themselves as angels, and the sapiens never really considered refusing." Semyaza waved his hand in front of his face, as if shooing the image away. "Anyway, we started looking at flight plans and transport records into and out of NWA-1."

Looking at Azazel, Semyaza said, "As you know, all of that information is within our purview as Area Directors, though our business and industry partners aren't always forthcoming. So I didn't pull any punches about my authority. After some heated exchanges, they finally acquiesced. It turns out a diamond mine in the far south needed a couple dozen laborers."

Turning toward Kadeya, Azazel explained, "We've known for a long time that sapien-hybrids are working in various enterprises. They're fed, clothed, and sheltered, but let's face it, these sapiens aren't laboring for compensation. They're working for our corporations because they believe they're doing the work of the sky-gods."

Kadeya pushed herself up a little straighter and said to no one in particular, "I'd bet somewhere in their evolving lore the notion that being chosen to work for the gods is an honor so enormous it cannot be refused."

With a thoughtful glance, Semyaza said, "I'm not aware of any research supporting that, but it wouldn't surprise me. Anyway, to the best of my knowledge the corporate guys are generally careful to collect from remote areas where hybridization has occurred through crossbreeding among clans, rather than directly from the retroviruses we've introduced. This actually makes sense; taking individuals from isolated clans wouldn't interfere with our research."

A wisp of cynicism flickered across his face, "But my more jaded view of this tactic is that the collection of untracked individuals limits conversations about the ethics of using this kind of workforce. In this case I believe the shuttle crew got sloppy. Their first mistake was abducting a group of sapiens living too close to the NWA-1 research area. They coupled that gaffe with an even bigger one; they took too many. They didn't leave enough individuals for a viable clan." With a forlorn look Semyaza added, "At least I hope that action was a matter of clumsiness rather than intentional."

Kadeya leaned forward, "I'm hearing some doubt."

"I fear they may have intended that the remaining clanspeople not survive. Abandoned on that grassland, the tiny group would die off from starvation or predation. If that was their intent, they didn't consider the possibility that the remnants would be taken in by another clan—a clan we've been studying."

"And you smell a rat," observed Azazel.

"A whole shipload of rats my friend—a whole shipload!"

Semyaza looked over at Ramuell and said, "Now here's the part you're really going to hate. Often the jobs performed by the imported sapiens are short-lived—perhaps five to ten annum. When their labor is no longer needed at a given site, they cannot be repatriated to their native areas."

"Cultural contamination and maybe even fratricidal warfare being the concern?" Ramuell asked.

Semyaza swallowed hard and said, "Exactly—when we allow sapiens to work at our industrial sites, they can never return to their clans or even be allowed to interact with non-exposed sapien-hybrids."

"So what happens to them?"

Semyaza grimaced. "Sometimes they're relocated to a different worksite. Almost certainly those being imported to work at the docking facility you mentioned are reassigned workers from elsewhere."

Curling her lip, Kadeya said, "So in our godlike omnipotence we're moving sapiens around the globe to work in inhospitable environments on continents where they didn't evolve."

"Oh, it's worse than that." Semyaza drew in a long breath, "Many are being loaded on 4D-ships and sent off-world."

"**What?!**" Kadeya exploded.

"Where are they being sent?" Azazel growled.

"I don't know," Semyaza replied. "But this is going on right under the noses of Anotas-Deithe. They may not be orchestrating the abductions, but it stretches credulity to believe they're unaware."

"Which means they're choosing to look the other way," Ramuell observed.

After a moment's silence, Kadeya said, "There is another plausible explanation for their hands-off. It's possible there's nothing they can do. Our legal codes don't contemplate this issue."

"So we don't consider slavery illegal?" Ramuell asked waspishly.

"Oh I'm not saying that. We've had laws for thousands of annum forbidding involuntary servitude."

"Well, then?" Ramuell pressed.

Azazel connected the dots. "Our laws apply to Domhanians; not to livestock." He turned to Ramuell, "Or to use your term, 'beasts of burden.'"

"Just so," replied Kadeya. "If Anotas tried to intervene, corporate solicitors would file Judicial Orders-to-Stay, claiming sapiens are not afforded the protection of our laws. In essence, they would claim the hybrids are domesticated animals."

Ramuell looked at his grandmother, "And that strategy

would work without definitive proof that the sapiens are a closely related species, warranting legal protection."

Out of the corner of her eye, Kadeya noticed a sharp glance exchanged between Azazel and Semyaza. She had an inkling what their nonverbal exchange might mean, bud did not want the conversation to veer in that direction. She slapped her hands on her thighs and said, "This has given me a lot to think about—a heck of a lot."

Semyaza, Azazel, and lastly Ramuell rose to their feet. Azazel said, "Kadeya, thank you for your time and hospitality."

Glancing at Semyaza, Kadeya chuckled, "I honestly can't say it's been a pleasure, but it has been enlightening."

Just then the door to the cabin opened and Lector stepped in. "Oh, sorry—I didn't know we had company."

Though he'd suspected as much, until that moment Ramuell had not been certain the chief librarian and his grandmother were living together. He was delighted with this development and said, "Hello, Lector. This is a pleasant surprise."

"It's good to see you, Ramuell. Pardon my intrusion. I left my new hearing aid on the charger. This old one's squealing is driving me crazy."

Azazel and Semyaza knew Lector and exchanged palm-taps. "It's not a problem. We were just on our way out," Semyaza explained.

As Kadeya escorted her visitors to the door, Lector made his way to the charger and furtively checked the recording chip he'd installed in the hearing aid. To his relief it had been recording for several hours. He put it in his ear and would remove the chip when he got back to his office. Kadeya's electromagnetic signal jammer had no effect on the micro-recording device, as it neither generated nor transmitted EM signals.

CHAPTER TWENTY-NINE

DEPOSITIONS AND SERENDIPITY

MELANKA PUFFED on her pipe as she listened to the recording Lector had sent of Kadeya's conversation with Azazel, Semyaza and Ramuell. Her assistant, Cubra, stuck his head in the office, "You have an encrypted message from the Law and Order Directorate."

Setting her pipe in its holder she said. "Let's see it."

He crossed the office and placed the communicator on Melanka's desk. She gestured for him to close the door and pull up a chair beside her.

She was reasonably certain the message was from Secretary Liam, but it said only:

We need to meet.

Melanka responded:

When would you like to come over?

The response was cryptic:

We need to be more inconspicuous.

Cubra said, "Be careful Chief—until we're absolutely sure it's Liam."

"Mm-hmm." She murmured then typed:

When would you like to meet?

A few seconds later Melanka and Cubra read:

It's important – today if possible.

She replied:

Where – when?

After a several second delay:

Where the Butterfly pilots fell? Two hours?

Melanka grinned, "It's Liam."

I'll be there.

Liam responded:

Our old friend will be with me.

Melanka signed off with:

My friend will also join us – see you in two.

"Where the Butterfly pilots fell?" Cubra asked.

With a glint in her eye, Melanka answered, "The old dog is shrewd. The 4-D ship Dr. Althea and Professor Egan departed in all those decades ago was named *The Butterfly*. He wants to meet at the creek where they were found."

As he stood to leave, Cubra felt the tiniest twinge about being considered 'the friend' accompanying Melanka. "I'll get a vehicle. It'll take almost an hour to get out there."

"We should leave the building separately. Where do I meet you?"

"To keep things simple, let's just use exit protocol three," Cubra suggested.

"Got it. I'll meet you in an hour," she said between draws as she relit the pipe.

Only four minutes after exiting at the basement food services ramp, Melanka was picked up by Cubra in front of a flower shop on Buenavis Street. An hour later they walked over a knoll and saw Liam and Sean sitting on a boulder beside the creek. Glancing around casually, but in reality taking in every detail of their surroundings, Cubra whispered, "No security detail."

As they approached, Melanka said, "Mr. Secretary, are congratulations in order?

"Given the circumstances of my appointment, congratulations are certainly not warranted. Secretary Elom was a good man," Liam replied.

"Indeed." *Never had any problem with his integrity, dealing with his limited intellect was a challenge though.* After a respectful pause, she asked, "So what have you gentlemen got for us?"

"We've decided it would be wise to share Dr. Althea's and Professor Egan's video-deposition," Liam answered. "Are you willing to take a ride?"

Melanka and Cubra looked around. "A ride? In what?" Cubra asked.

Pointing to the rise on the other side of the stream Sean answered, "We have a quadcopter right up there."

Melanka smiled, "Of course you do. Lead the way."

The six seat quadcopter sat in a clearing on the hill's crest. Its pilot was reading an old-fashioned paperback book. He looked up and after getting a nod from Sean slipped the book into his seat's side pocket. When his passengers had boarded, the pilot cranked the motors and let the four rotors idle while everyone buckled their harnesses.

As soon as it cleared the trees the aircraft canted at a low altitude bearing due south. Ten minutes later they emerged from above the forest to hover over a rolling pasture speckled with livestock. They saw a large corrugated metal barn sitting in the middle of the pasture. The pilot made a soft landing in the barnyard and shut off the electric motors.

Sean led his colleagues down an aisle between stacks of massive hay bales. The corridor ended at a wooden staircase that dropped into a basement excavated below the barn floor. At the bottom of the stairs was a handleless steel door. Sean tapped a code into his communicator and a second later they heard the clacking of the lock's tumblers. Sean pushed the heavy door open and with a flourish said, "Welcome to the fanciest barn basement you'll ever see."

Plush seats were arranged around a huge flat screen video-viewer.

In the kitchenette Liam heated a pot of water for tea and Sean inserted a video-card into the viewer.

"Melanka, I've been thinking about our last conversation," Liam began. "Right before we signed off you said having access to any information we gleaned from Egan and Althea would make your job easier. While Sean worked on recording the deposition, I ran through every scenario my feeble old mind could postulate.

"It seems clear that even though we have different responsibilities, we are allies in this unholy mess. You proved as much with the tip about Secretary Elom's assassination. Your informant was correct, the poisonous cocktail had been injected under his toenails during a fungus treatment."

"It was actually a rather sophisticated murder for amateurs," Melanka observed as she reached for the cup of tea Liam offered.

"I suppose it was," Liam said as he held the tea tray out to Cubra and Sean. "You trusted us with that valuable information and now we're going to trust you with what we've learned. I don't know if you're going to be surprised by what they have told us, but I'm quite sure you'll not be pleased."

Several times over the course of the next few hours Melanka asked Sean to playback some particular portion of the video. She listened intently, eyebrows knitted together in an expression of concentration and consternation.

When the recording was finally over Melanka pushed her head back into the chair's plush headrest. "Actually, I'm both surprised and saddened by Althea's and Egan's story. I'm surprised at the audacity and scope of the corruption, and I'm heartbroken by the betrayal of Domhanian values." She squirmed a little and asked, "Do you gentlemen believe in serendipity?"

The three men exchanged puzzled looks. "I suppose serendipity is possible, but I don't really believe in some according-to-a-god's-will grand design," Liam replied.

"Well, I've come to believe the cosmos is stranger than we can fathom," Melanka said. "As you know, their son and Althea's mother took an off-world assignment and were dispatched just days before the couple was so strangely dumped over there by the creek. Dr. Kadeya and her grandson were sent to Ghrain-3, a planet where our scientists have been working on the hybridization of a sapient species. When Egan and Althea were identified I had my folks track down their families as well as former colleagues, friends and associates. Since that time we've been monitoring several of these individuals."

Sean leaned forward, "Monitoring?"

"Yes. We have an agent embedded at the orbiting station where Althea's mother is working. As it turns out, our agent and Kadeya were good friends growing up. They've rekindled their old friendship, which has some advantages."

Creasing his brow Liam said, "You said the station where Althea's mother is located. Is Ramuell not with Kadeya?"

"They were together, and both began the acclimatization process for long-term assignments on the planet's surface. Kadeya was not able to make the physiological adjustments, but Ramuell was. He's now stationed at a research facility on the surface. I'm given to understand they video-com almost daily."

"Since you have eyes on them, I'd assume the Business and Industry intelligence service does too," Sean said.

Melanka snorted derisively, "To call their security staff an 'intelligence service' is being overly generous. It's our belief the B&I thugs have not put the pieces together. I'd say in terms of intelligence gathering their tradecraft is wanting, for lack of a better word.

"Now there's a reason I asked you about serendipity. If Althea and Egan are to be believed; **if** false memories weren't implanted by their abductors; **if** they're not suffering from some sort of brain dysfunction; **if** they're not under the influence of a long-lasting drug, then Domhanians are waist deep in swine dung. Frankly, I'd be pretty skeptical about this video-deposition were it not for the fact that just yesterday I received corroborating information."

Narrowing his eyes, Liam said, "Reeaallly! Now that's either an extraordinary coincidence or serendipitous indeed."

"What have you learned?" Sean asked.

"Now our long-lost surveyors have told us what we would have to consider a fantastic tale about corporations enslaving thousands of hybridized beings. According to them, these creatures are literally used up and discarded when they're no longer able to work. They would have us believe Domhanians on Froitas have created breeding facilities to more quickly reproduce these expendable laborers."

Looking at Sean she continued, "So what have we learned? Well, we've known for a long time about the extravagant planetary playgrounds the bigwigs and their families go zipping off to when they get bored with their opulent lives on Domhan-Siol. We also know that more than one world has been colonized for the rich and powerful."

Melanka took a deep breath, "But here's the clincher; why I'm inclined to think the video-deposition is for the most part true. We've received information from a completely reliable informant about the source of the slaves on Froitas."

Liam and Sean leaned forward in unison.

"And believe it or not, Kadeya and Ramuell are smack dab in the middle of this brouhaha—innocently to be sure, but in the middle none-the-less."

Melanka had not brought the flash-dot Lector had secretly recorded of the conversation among Kadeya, Ramuell, Azazel and Semyaza. But she was able to recite the gist of the conversation, often quoting exact statements.

Though he had worked with her for decades, Cubra remained in awe of Melanka's ability to recall even minute details of information. He realized this ability was part of the skillset that made her so formidable. One would think he would have been the last person to underestimate her.

After conversing for another hour, Liam sat back in his chair and said, "So, to cement my understanding, let's summarize. Over six decades ago a technologically advanced alien species hijacked a husband and wife survey team. They took the couple to several Domhanian mining sites and a planet that has been colonized by and for wealthy Domhanians. At these locations, our surveyors were shown at least one primitive alien species being exploited as slave laborers. They also witnessed Crimes-of-Barbarism, though it's likely our judiciary would rule that Domhanian criminal code is not applicable to extraterrestrials."

Nodding, Sean said, "Perhaps the judiciary would see it that way. Nevertheless, Althea and Egan believe they were snatched by the Beag-Liath with the express purpose of showing them how our species is misbehaving. They feel it's their responsibility to bring Domhanians' regretful behavior to light. They also believe that if our species doesn't take corrective action, the Beag-Liath will intervene—and the gods only know what that might mean!"

Liam looked at Sean and said, "So, we have two intelligent, accomplished, and now famous people who believe they've been chosen to bring to justice some pretty bad players among our society's most powerful people. Then, as if to reinforce the notion that some kind of unseen cosmic forces are in play, their son and Althea's mother find themselves on the planet that's at the vortex of this fecal-fuss. Am I missing anything?"

"Nope, that about sums it up," Sean replied.

Frowning, Melanka said, "It's no wonder the corporate elites consider Egan and Althea so dangerous. Where have you hidden them?"

Liam scratched his temple while deciding how to answer. "Actually they're in an apartment at our Nexo de Mando office building."

"That's **not** okay! You cannot leave them there."

"You're right, but it's been harder to find a safe house than we'd expected. The B&I Council's hired-guns have managed to track us down twice," Sean said.

"Given how clumsy they are, they didn't manage that without inside help," Melanka observed.

Cubra's eyes widened momentarily.

With a sideways glance at Liam she added, "You probably rue the day you snatched them from at the hospital."

Liam stared blankly at Melanka and said, "No, actually we don't."

Returning his stare, she replied, "Fair enough. So, where are you going to put them?"

"We don't know," Sean answered. "The pressure of life-on-the-run is getting to them. They are scientists; they're not suited for a life of clandestine pirouettes. We need to settle them somewhere for more than just a few days. At this point we're even considering off-world locations."

"I hope that's way down on your list of options," Melanka replied. She turned to Cubra and asked, "What do you think about the Lodge?"

Stroking his chin he said, "That just might work. I'll have to do some checking. If it's booked, we can clear the reservations by claiming the facility needs security upgrades that will require several kuuk. Then it's just a matter of moving our guests in." Cubra looked at Liam and added, "That would buy you time to come up with a longer-term solution."

"Now the Lodge isn't a fancy resort," Melanka added. "It's rustic but also comfortable and quite remote—a beautiful property located at the foot of a steep plateau in the southern highlands. Cubra can send you photos, maps, and anything else you might need to make a decision."

"Great. We appreciate the offer and will give it some thought." Slapping the chair's armrests, Liam stood. "This has been good. I want to thank you both for agreeing to meet with us."

"No, we need to thank you gentlemen for trusting us with the deposition. Our combined information is more than the sum of its parts. We have a much, much better understanding of what we're up against—not that I know what we're going to do about it..." Melanka trailed off.

CHAPTER THIRTY

EXONERATION, DENTAL IMPLANTS AND A GRANDCHILD

Kadeya's assessment turned out to be accurate. The Blue Rock Incident, as it had come to be known, was not high on the Presidium's list of priorities. In fact, it seemed to be getting almost no attention whatsoever. On their fourth day aboard the orbiter Azazel contacted Deputy Administrator Trace about "getting this damn thing over with." Azazel just wanted resolution, though he still believed it would likely be punitive.

A day later the SWA-7 team was informed that the Committee of Inquiry had been appointed. Azazel was surprised to learn his entire team was scheduled to meet with the Committee together rather than for separate interviews.

He was even more surprised that no Presidium members were actually on the Committee. In fact, Trace was the only top-tier staff person assigned to serve. The other six members were mid-level functionaries from the Personnel, Enforcement, and Policy bureaus. Interestingly, Trace didn't serve as the Committee's chairperson. Azazel was flummoxed.

The atmosphere during the initial meeting was cool but

not hostile. The Committee had studied the Incident Report and each member asked two questions regarding specific items in the report. Individual interviews were scheduled immediately after the group meeting and lasted about an hour each.

The next day the SWA-7 team was summoned to appear before the Committee. The Chairwoman asked if any of them had additional thoughts or recollections they would like to share. Azazel was sitting in the middle chair at the semi-circular table. Each of the team members turned to look at their Operations Director.

Speaking slowly he said, "Our people on the surface, especially those who have developed any kind of relationship with sapien-hybrid clans, loathe the nefilim, though we acknowledge that the gigantism mutation is of our own creation. Many surface workers advocate extermination as the way to resolve the problem. I do not. I believe that resolution would be so contrary to our core values it would create a tear in the moral fabric of what it means to be Domhanian. I shudder to even contemplate the long-term consequences."

Azazel swallowed, as if tasting his next words before continuing, "Yet I was the one down there smashing the skulls of those monsters. I cannot justify my actions. I cannot even explain them. I regret my loss of control but cannot promise that given identical circumstances I would react differently in the future." He inhaled deeply and added, "One last thought, Ramuell should in no way be condemned for intervening as he did to stop me." With that he looked down at his folded hands and nodded, indicating there was nothing else to be said.

The Chairwoman made a show of gathering the Committee members behind the dais and conducting a whispered conversation. When they returned to their seats she read a statement that had obviously been written in advance.

"Your engagement with the nefilim was intended to

protect an experimental clan of sapien-hybrids with whom we have invested decades of time and effort. Had you not intervened those efforts and even more clan members' lives would have been lost. Once you engaged the mutants your actions and reactions must be viewed through the lens of self-defense. While the Serefim Presidium cannot condone all of what transpired during that frightful encounter, the Presidium does not condemn your decisions. Nor does this Committee of Inquiry condemn the actions you took in the midst of what was perhaps the most challenging circumstances anyone might ever encounter while working on the surface."

Owan, Samael and Rarus grinned with relief. Azazel stared at the Committee Chair in stunned silence.

The Chairwoman looked to her left then to her right at each of the Committee members. Trace gave her a slight nod. She said, "On behalf of the Serefim Presidium we want to thank you for your service. You are free to return to your duties on the surface as soon as practical."

With that, the Committee stood in unison and exited the room through the door on their left. As they filed out, Trace, who was the last person in line, looked down at the SWA-7 team and winked. When the door slid shut, Rarus and Sam let out muffled "whoops." Owan reached over and patted Azazel's shoulder.

Ramuell turned to Azazel and asked, "What in a frozen-hell was that?"

"Something is seriously askew," Azazel said quietly to his young protégé. "That was proof that the powers-that-be don't have any real understanding of what's going on down there—or they just don't give a damn."

Overhearing the comment, Owan speculated, "There's another possibility. Perhaps we don't understand what's going on down there. Maybe we've never understood what the Domhanian efforts on Ghrain-3 are really all about."

The following day Azazel, Owan, Sam and Rarus returned to SWA-7. Ramuell requested leave for a few days. His grandmother had arranged a dental appointment for him to have the tooth replaced that had been bothering him. With bone growth accelerant, the jaw bone could adhere to an implanted titanium screw within three to four days. Being Ramuell's second implant, he had no concerns about the procedure.

After Ramuell saw his teammates off he dropped by the G3AST galley for a beverage. As he was leaving he looked up and saw Alicia standing directly in his path. Her lips were parted halfway between laughter and silence.

"Alicia! What are you doing here?"

She strode up to him, took his cheeks in both hands and kissed him, slowly and sensually. She leaned her head back a few centimetres, locked eyes with Ramuell, smiled and said, "I scheduled my annual physical exam, but I'm really here to check on you."

Her smile morphed into a chuckle when she realized Ramuell was utterly speechless. She took his arm, turned him around and led him to a table. "I haven't eaten. I'm gonna grab a tray of food. Is there anything you'd like?"

He looked down at his drink and said, "Uhm, I suppose not."

"I'll be right back."

They talked nonstop. They talked of everything and nothing. After a couple hours Alicia sighed wistfully. "Ramuell, I have to go. I really do have a physical exam and I'm booked on the supply transport back to the surface." As they stood to leave, Alicia's enticing expression was shaded with a hint of shyness. She asked, "May I kiss you again?"

When his eyes shot wide open, a laugh rose from deep in Alicia's throat. This time it was Ramuell who leaned in and did the kissing. Over the course of his life Ramuell would never be able to remember what was said during those hours, and he would never forget how those forgotten words had made him feel.

Ramuell stopped by the lab the day after his dental surgery. He was curious about Kadeya's analysis of the DNA samples from the slain Crow Clan females. "You kept the fact that you'd taken these samples secret from your colleagues. Why?" Kadeya asked.

Ramuell peered out the window of Kadeya's office into the adjacent lab. He furrowed his brow slightly and said, "I'm not really sure—I just had this sense it was best to say nothing."

"Did you get to know these two females while you were with the Clan?"

"Not really. I watched them and we interacted some, but not being able to speak their language..." Ramuell shrugged.

Kadeya picked up one of the jars and stared at the tissue sample as if trying to divine its secrets. "While you were observing them, did you notice any atypical behaviors?" Tutting at herself, "Now that was a dumb question—let me try again—did you see any behaviors that differed from those of other clanspeople?"

"I did," Ramuell answered. "When we first arrived in the canyon, we were met by a group of clan members. Ru Ta was the first to greet us. After palm-taps, he and Owan grabbed each other in an embrace. They rocked back-and-forth laughing and jabbering. Then the woman with the normal shaped head..."

"Normal? Really, Ramuell?" Kadeya teased.

"Okay, okay—the Domhanian shaped head—is that better? Anyway, she walked up to Azazel and hugged him. As they spoke she rested her head on his chest, and she put her nose right here," Ramuell pointed to the jugular notch hollow just below his neck.

Kadeya startled. "Did she really?! And how did Azazel react?"

"He accepted the gesture as perfectly natural. He held her for a long moment."

"That **is** interesting. Did you notice anything else?"

"Nothing extraordinary," replied Ramuell. "It seemed the other clan members were somewhat deferent with her, but not fawning. There were two young girls with Domhanian shaped heads. I watched them quite a bit. They seemed to fit right in with the other children." He looked away, trying to visualize his recollections. "Perhaps the adults were a bit more attentive with those two kids."

"Or did it just seem that way because you were watching them more closely?" Kadeya asked.

Tilting his head, Ramuell replied, "That's entirely possible." He paused for a moment, "There is one other thing. It's not about their behavior, but rather Azazel's. It was when he came to the mangled body of the little girl that he completely lost control. He knelt beside the child, touched her face and screeched. He snatched the sonic-blaster from Samael and just started firing, at least a dozen blasts. Everyone on the canyon floor in front of us was lying on the ground flopping around—nefilim and Crow Clansmen alike.

"There's one other thing that might be important—the pretty woman, the one who hugged Azazel, was snatched by the nefilim. Sam and Rarus chased them down canyon, but the giants killed her. When Sam carried the body back into the camp and laid her down, Azazel crawled over and put her head on his lap. He stroked her hair and moaned 'no, no, no' over and over."

Kadeya reached out and touched her grandson's arm. "That's a sad, sad image. I'm so sorry you had to see that."

"I'm okay—really, I am." Ramuell smiled tightly, and Kadeya knew the conversation was over.

As Ramuell had expected, Kadeya was able to work her magic with the tissue samples. She removed many of the contaminants and performed DNA tests. Without discussing it, they both knew what had to be the next step. Kadeya pulled the bio-records for Azazel and Owan.

On Ramuell's last day aboard the orbiter, they met for lunch. After they had gotten their food Ramuell made his way toward a table and said to his grandmother, "Well?"

Kadeya frowned slightly and shook her head. Holding the tray with both hands, she pointed with an uptick of her head toward a table out of earshot of the other diners. After seating themselves Ramuell stared at his grandmother inquisitively.

"I can say with absolute certainty the woman was **not** Azazel's daughter," Kadeya began.

Ramuell cocked an eyebrow. "Oh?"

Kadeya held up a finger, "I can also tell you with at least a .85 degree of confidence that she was his granddaughter."

Rocking back in his chair, Ramuell again said, "Oh!" He paused to do the math. "But, given the sapiens' lifespan that means..."

Wrinkling her forehead and nodding, Kadeya completed

Ramuell's mental calculation. "That means Azazel had a sexual relationship with a sapien-hybrid woman about two decades after he began his surface assignment."

Ramuell took his first bite and chewed thoughtfully. After a swig of water he said, "A child, really."

Kadeya narrowed her eyes, confused by the comment. Gradually her face cleared, and she looked up at Ramuell. "Ahh, so you're thinking he had sex with a girl perhaps only about twenty annum of age, which on the homeworld would be considered pedophilia."

Kadeya waved her hand back-and-forth; not chastising her grandson, more as a cautionary gesture. "That's an ethnocentric way of thinking and it's a deep, dark hole for a scientist to fall in. You're applying the biological and perhaps even ethical norms of Domhan-Siol to a world a couple thousand light-annum from home."

"Actually my first impulse was to apply our ethical standards to a person from home—Azazel. But grandmother, that's totally unfair. Something happens to us down there. That planet, and maybe its inhabitants, are doing something to us —psychically."

"Explain that to me."

Ramuell wiped his mouth with a napkin. "I wish I could. But it's possible that what happens to our psyche defies explanation."

Though Ramuell remained reticent about discussing the *sen* with Kadeya, she'd actually read a great deal about the phenomenon. She had access to scientific logs and reports classified at the highest security level. She understood that reading about a phenomenon did not necessarily impart an understanding. Some things had to be experienced and even then may not be understood. But she knew enough to be a little worried about her grandson. “Ramuell, are you all right? You don’t have to go back down there if you’re not ready.”

Ramuell replied quickly, “Oh no, I’m fine! I **must** return to the surface!” He didn’t realize it in that moment, but his vehemence was borne of a fear of ever again living without the *sen*.

CHAPTER THIRTY-ONE

BETRAYAL

When last they met, Melanka's parting comment to Liam and Sean had been, "We have a much, much better understanding of what we're up against." She'd been wrong! She had no idea how deeply the tentacles of corruption had dug into Anotas-Deithe. She was about to find out.

After hours of stops and starts, jukes and feints, Althea, Egan, and their driver finally arrived at the bottom of the mountain where they would leave the car. The "road" to the Lodge was far too rough for a highway vehicle. They would travel the rest of the way in the enclosed Rough-Terrain-Vehicle that was parked in a locked garage on a small graveled parking lot.

Sitting atop a ridge overlooking a shallow north-south canyon, the Lodge was nestled in a stand of enormous old-growth conifers. A hundred metres downhill a cold creek gurgled over stones and around boulders. To the north two massive granite outcrops punched skyward at least six hundred metres high.

"This place is beyond beautiful!" enthused Althea. "It'll be easy to stay here awhile."

The driver handed her the door key and grabbed the bags from the back of the RTV. Althea and Egan walked up the four rustic split timber steps, followed by their driver carrying a suitcase in each hand. As Althea placed the key card on the reader, the door swung open a few centimetres. In that instant the hairs at the nape of Egan's neck stood on end. He shoved Althea away from the threshold and kicked the door open as he dove to the porch's wooden floor.

A man standing in the middle of the room fired his charged-particle gun. Discharging it at chest level he missed his intended targets, who were both sprawled prone on the deck. Instead the energy slammed into the Anotas agent walking up the steps with the luggage. It lifted him off his feet and threw him backward. He landed on his right shoulder, which snapped loudly. The agent did not suffer the pain of a broken shoulder; he was dead before he hit the packed gravel walkway.

Althea slid catlike under the rail surrounding the portico. Egan commando crawled swiftly along the porch toward the side of the house. He saw his wife scurrying toward their driver's body. In his holster she found a sonic-blaster and flipped the safety switch off as she rolled away from the body. Unable to see the ground beyond the steps leading to the front door, the assailant had no idea Althea had availed herself of their driver's weapon. For the second time in less than ten seconds he underestimated his prey with a slapdash exit from the house. Lying flat on her back, the moment Althea saw his hat she aimed and pushed the trigger switch.

Her target crumpled to the porch with a scream. Worried there may be others inside, Egan signaled for Althea to scoot under the raised deck. He went the opposite direction and quietly eased himself under the rail and onto the ground beside the corner of the house. He crept around the Lodge peeking in each window and listening carefully for sounds coming from within. He heard nothing. By the time he circumnavigated the building and returned to Althea, they were reasonably sure their would-be assassin's overconfidence had resulted in an undermanned ambush.

When the stunned man moaned they sprung to their feet and rushed up the steps. Egan squeezed the assailant's throat hard enough to restrict the carotid arteries. The man slipped back into unconsciousness. As Egan rolled him onto his stomach, Althea stripped polyurethane coated fishing line off a rod and reel propped in the corner behind the front door. They used the line to tie the man's wrists and ankles behind his back. Then they lashed the ankle and wrist knots together with the man's belt.

As the adrenalin rush began to subside, they crumpled to their butts on an area rug in the middle of the den. With their backs against the sofa they sat staring at their captive who lay just outside the open front door. Though she made no sound, tears welled up and fell from Althea's eyes. Egan reached over and put his arm around his wife's shoulder. "He was going to kill us—they are trying to kill us. His weapon was..." Althea's voice broke.

Egan hesitated for a minute before saying, "We were betrayed, but by whom? Who can we trust?"

"And even if we knew who to trust, how would we contact them?"

"I don't know, but I know we have to get away from here," Egan replied as he stood-up.

"Now wait a minute, let's think this through," cautioned Althea.

Egan sat down on the sofa, "You're right. It's likely

whoever our friend here is working with is monitoring our vehicle's location."

"Do you know how to disable the tracking device?"

"No, but we want the tracking device on our RTV to remain functional and parked here at the lodge."

Nodding, Althea said, "Of course. They'll think we're lying here dead."

"Exactly!"

"They're probably expecting him to call to confirm the kill, but we can't allow him to speak with his cohorts. He probably has a code word to alert them things have gone awry."

"That's likely," Egan agreed. "It seems the best we can do is buy some time by letting them think we're still at the Lodge and that their man has departed."

Their captive had regained consciousness. Althea studied him carefully as she spoke. "In that case it would be wise to use his vehicle for our escape. They would see it leaving the scene. Perhaps they'll assume that his communicator isn't operating." *His pupils dilated. I hit a nerve.*

"Go see if you can find his RTV and I'll keep an eye on him," Althea said as she picked up their assailant's weapon.

Egan said, "Okay, I'll be back in a few minutes."

"Take the sonic-blaster and set it on wide-field. He might have collaborators out there in the woods." This time Althea noted their captive's eyes and expression gave away nothing. She walked over to the doorway and pointed the charged-particle gun at his head. "Where's your vehicle?"

He craned his neck to glower at her.

"Do you have the key?"

His pupils flickered ever so slightly.

"He has the key. Search him. I'll keep this gun pointed right here," Althea said as she held the charged-particle weapon a few centimetres from the man's temple. Squatting down to make eye contact she added, "You had this weapon set to kill. I haven't changed the setting."

Egan cautiously reached down and found the key card in the right shoulder pocket of the man's jacket. Surprisingly, that was the first place he checked. "I suppose that's a good omen."

He picked up the sonic-blaster and left through the back door. He began walking in a spiral working out from the cabin. Within fifteen minutes he found the Rough-Terrain-Vehicle sitting in a thicket of brushy, waxy-leafed trees. It was a brand new six-wheel-drive with an enclosed cab and an open cargo box tail. *Whoever he's working for isn't worrying about expense.* Egan slid the key card into its slot. When he touched the accelerator the vehicle lurched forward powerfully. The electric motor and drive mechanisms were so silent the only noise was from the knobby tires crunching brush and gravel.

When Egan drove the vehicle around to the front of the Lodge he was confronted by the ugly reality that their driver had died there just minutes earlier. *He died because of what we know and for no other reason.* When he stepped out of the cab Althea called to him, "Did you find his communicator?"

"No. I didn't think to look."

"He doesn't have it on him, and he's not talking. If we are supposed to be dead, we obviously can't use ours."

"Of course." When Egan found their assailant's communicator in a pocket sewn under the passenger seat he called out, "Got it. In order for our subterfuge to work, I'm going to click it on and off a few times and rub the speaker on the seat fabric. Whoever is on the receiving end will hear the static and assume the communicator has malfunctioned." As soon as he was finished with the ruse he popped the batter pack out of the device.

Pointing the gun at their captive, Althea asked, "What are we doing with him?"

"I'm throwing him in the bed of his RTV and we're taking him with us. We need to know what he knows," Egan answered.

"Yeah, and if we run into some of his friends down the mountain, he might be a bargaining chip," Althea observed.

"Let's hope it doesn't come to that."

Egan grabbed the belt strung behind the man's back between the wrist and ankle ties. As he started to drag their captive, Althea said, "Wait a minute. Help me move our driver's body."

After they slid the corpse aside, she jumped in the RTV and backed it up to the porch. Egan slid the hogtied captive to the first step then rolled him over into the vehicle's open bed. "We need some rope."

"Will that do?" Althea asked, pointing to a couple of garbage barrels lashed with heavy-duty straps to a tree at the corner of the house.

"Perfect!" He fed the strap through the wrist and ankle bindings and tied it around the vehicle's back bumper. Looking at their captive menacingly, Egan said, "If he decides to jump out the back, we'll just drag him the rest of the way down the mountain."

Althea looked over at their lifeless driver lying beside the porch. She felt queasy. "They planned to kill him. There's no way they'd allow a witness to live."

Following his wife's eyes to the body, Egan's shoulders drooped. "We have to do something with him before we leave."

"We haven't time to dig a grave. Let's just lock him in the house so scavengers won't get to him," Althea suggested.

It took both of them to carry the body up the steps and into the house. They silently rolled him in the entranceway area rug. For the second time in an hour Althea brushed tears from her cheeks. It seemed to Egan that his wife's moan just sucked all the air out of the room.

On the drive back down the mountain, Althea and Egan agreed the only person they felt certain they could trust was Sean. "But how do we contact him?" Egan asked.

"I know his communicator code," Althea replied.

"How did you get that?"

"Do you remember the afternoon Liam stopped by our apartment at their Headquarters?" Althea asked.

"Yeah."

"Well, when his communicator trilled I looked over his shoulder and saw him enter, 'Hello Sean.' I memorized the sender code displayed at the bottom of the screen."

Stepping out of the RTV Egan said, "You, my love, should have been an agent."

He walked around to the vehicle's bed and demanded of the assassin, "Where's your vehicle?" The captive just glared sullenly.

Egan pulled the communicator battery out of his pocket and tossed it to Althea. "Call Sean."

Not recognizing the contact code from the incoming call's source device, Sean answered cautiously, "Yes?"

"Sean, it's Althea. We were ambushed at The Lodge. Our driver is dead."

"What?! Where are you?"

"We found the assassin's RTV and came back down to our vehicle—Uhm, we captured him and have him tied up in the back."

"You what?! How did you manage ... oh, never mind. What communicator are you using?"

"His. We left ours powered-up back in The Lodge."

"Good! That's good! Get back in the RTV and drive into the woods. Get out of sight of the road and hide. I'll call you in exactly five minutes."

"He won't tell us where his vehicle is hidden. Should we just use ours and get out of here?" Althea asked.

"No! Get away from the road. Go now! I'll call you in five."

Sean and Liam were both on the next call. "Are you well hidden?"

"Yes, we're in a thicket of brush and trees." Egan replied.

"Okay—we're only going to talk for one minute so listen carefully. Look on the inside of your captive's wrist in the hollow between the flexor tendons."

The assassin was lying on his side still hogtied with the fishing line and belt. Egan lifted the man's arms a bit. "Okay, what am I looking for?"

"Do you see a small scar, a bump or a dark spot of any kind?" Sean asked.

"Yes, actually all three," Egan answered.

"Okay, that's an Anotas tracking chip. You have to cut it out."

"Cut it out?" Egan asked squeamishly.

"Yes, right this minute. Dr. Althea, this should be no problem for you."

"No problem at all," she responded flatly.

"Try not to damage it. Leave it sitting on a log or something. Then drive the RTV cross country for ten minutes, stop and wait for our call."

Just before Sean cut the connection Liam said, "Remove the communicator's battery before you start driving."

Egan handed Althea the sharply honed pocket knife he always carried. Though he had heard the conversation, the traitorous Anotas agent remained stoic when she twisted his wrist around for better access. With a quick 'V' shaped incision Althea had the tracking device out in less than twenty seconds. She took off the scarf she'd been wearing as headgear and tied the wound tightly.

They only drove about seven minutes when Egan saw an ideal spot to hide.

About a minute later Sean called. "Did you get the device out of his wrist?"

"No trouble at all. I don't think it was damaged. We put it in the crotch of a tree branch—not easy to see," Althea answered.

Sean said, "Okay, good thinking. We have a bead on your general location, and we've dispatched a quadcopter. Are you in good cover?" Sean asked.

"Yes, I found a spot where we're completely hidden by trees and brush," Egan replied.

Liam came on, "Have you seen any clearings where our copter can make a safe landing? As you know it doesn't have to be huge, but there must be enough room for the rotors and a few metres to spare all the way around."

"Oh sure, we've seen several grassy knolls and meadows," Egan answered.

Liam spoke to Sean, "How long should they wait before making their way to one of the clearings?"

Sean said, "Take the battery pack out now. Stay where you are and replace it in ten minutes. We'll call you."

Althea could see their captive was in extreme discomfort. He had been tied in the same position for over two hours. This man was a trained Anotas agent and had been assigned to kill them. For good reason she was afraid of him and refused to loosen his ties. She leaned over the bed of the Rough-Terrain-Vehicle and held her water bottle to his lips.

When Sean called again he instructed the couple to lay low

for an hour. Then make their way to an area free of trees and brush in a swale rather than on a ridge crest; a low spot being less visible to any possible pursuers.

Melanka answered the incoming call, "Good afternoon Liam. I haven't heard from our guests at The Lodge."

"It was a set-up. They were ambushed."

"What are you talking about?" she rasped. "Nobody other than the driver knew they were going up there. And we absolutely trust him."

"Somebody else knew," Liam said. "Melanka, your driver was killed. Somehow Egan and Althea escaped. They even captured the assassin! That's all we know right now. We've dispatched a quadcopter to pick them up."

Melanka's brain was processed the information Liam had provided and spun out every possible scenario in milliseconds. "Liam, I may be in trouble. If you don't hear from me in ten minutes, assume I'm out of commission and do not trust **anything** you hear from Anotas."

Concerned, Liam asked, "Is there something we can do?"

"Yes. Keep Althea and Egan safe—and perhaps pray to hear from me in ten minutes." Just seconds after she tapped the disconnect icon on the communicator screen her office door whooshed open.

Cubra, who had been eavesdropping, walked into Melanka's office. She looked up and said, "Well, my old friend, it seems we have quite a problem."

CHAPTER THIRTY-TWO

BACK TO BLUE ROCK

UPON RETURNING to SWA-7 Ramuell requested permission to return to Blue Rock Canyon to check on the Crow Clan. He expected Azazel's enthusiastic support, but the Director denied the request. Assuming a return visit was a foregone conclusion, Ramuell was stunned.

Azazel explained, "I've got three primary misgivings. First, another nefilim attack is always possible. Next, you haven't been here long enough to be familiar with the ambiguities of Ghrain-3. And finally, Ru Ta was not happy that we left them unprotected. The Clan's reception is unpredictable."

Ramuell excused himself to give the matter more thought. After several hours he arrived at counter-arguments for each of Azazel's objections.

The next morning he asked to meet with the director and was able to get in to see him just before lunch. Ramuell made his points in order. While Azazel was impressed with his protégé's reasoning, he remained unswayed. At that point Ramuell became even more adamant.

"Why do you feel so strongly about this?" Azazel asked.

Ramuell ran a hand through his hair and sighed. "Because I've had three extremely distressing *sens* about the Crow Clan."

"Distressing?"

"They're in danger. If my *sens* mean anything, I am certain the threat is real."

With a tightlipped frown, Azazel asked, "What is that danger?"

"The threat is not from the nefilim. I haven't seen a single giant in my *sens*. **We** are the danger. I've seen security forces seizing the Crow Clan."

"Anotas security?" questioned Azazel.

Narrowing his eyes, Ramuell answered slowly, "No—they weren't wearing Anotas uniforms—perhaps some kind of paramilitary force."

Azazel leaned back in his chair. Ramuell remained silent as his boss stared at the ceiling for a full minute. Azazel blew out an exasperated exhale. "Okay Ram, I'm going to reconsider. But I want to call Owan before we decide what to do."

———

"The whole time we were upstairs I had the feeling something was seriously amiss," Owan said. "The administrators and even the Committee of Inquiry were just too cavalier about what happened. Hell, they even referred to it as an 'incident.' An Incident Report is what we file when someone runs an RTV off in a gully and breaks an axle. You and I were in Blue Rock Canyon, and we know what happened there was whole orders of magnitude more than just some incident.

"Now we must wonder if Ramuell's *sens* are telling him something. Did he hear something while at the station that registered subconsciously and his *sens* are explaining what an offhand comment may have meant? Or might he be having clairvoyant *sen* experiences? Either way, Azazel, we have to take this information seriously.

Azazel sniffed and said, "I know you're right. I just can't shake the sense that there's something else going on. I don't know what it is, and Semyaza hasn't been able to root it out either. Even if they are planning to take out the Crow Clan, that can't be the only reason we were let off without so much as a rap on the knuckles."

"If you and Semyaza figure it out, let me know. And boss, be sure Ramuell has your best interpreter and security detail."

Dr. Lilith was the chief of the anthropology group assigned to SWA-7. The middle-aged woman of 266 annum was highly respected by her colleagues. Because Lilith was unequaled in her mastery of the Crow Clan dialect, Azazel assigned her to join Ramuell on his journey back to Blue Rock.

Though he would have preferred not sending Samael and Rarus back so soon after the traumatic events, they were Azazel's go-to security officers. They also knew and trusted Ramuell.

Azazel told the team he wanted them to check in three times each day. When the foursome arrived at the canyon's rim, Samael set up two communications relay dishes. One would receive signals from the canyon floor and the other would bounce those signals off a satellite to SWA-7.

As they neared the canyon floor the crows began their cacophony. Rarus studied the camp area and saw no smoke rising above the trees. Pushing up his sleeves he said, "We better be cautious."

"You're right," Samael agreed. "But we've been friendly with this clan for a longtime. I think the likelihood of aggression is minimal—though we're probably in for a more subdued welcome than on our last visit."

He was correct. When the party reached the trail's end only Ru Ta and one other man came out to greet them. There were no overt displays of affection and Ramuell picked up what he thought was a sense of betrayal or perhaps disappointment from Ru Ta. The other man projected an obsequiousness seemingly borne of fear rather than fondness.

After Ru Ta and Dr. Lilith spoke for a couple of minutes she turned and explained to her companions, "I cannot say Ru Ta's invitation into the camp is begrudging, but I can't say it's enthusiastic either. Let's tread lightly."

"Maybe we should set up our camp some distance from theirs," Rarus suggested.

"Actually they're still staying up in the caves."

"That's understandable. They were traumatized—perhaps as much by our sonic-blasters as the nefilim."

Sam grunted concurrence.

Late that afternoon the clanspeople began gathering their fish and other belongings. Single file they meandered toward the caves in the north canyon wall. Ru Ta waved for the Domhanians to follow.

As they approached, a little girl charged out of one of the caves and launched herself at Ramuell. He dropped down to one knee and gathered the child in his arms. He rocked her back-and-forth as his colleagues and the clanspeople looked on. Slowly Ramuell pushed the little girl back and looked her over carefully. Clearly the clan had adopted her. She was being attended to, fed, and washed.

"You seem to be acquainted," Lilith commented, a smile crinkling her eyes.

"Her mother killed herself while performing a self-abortion with an obsidian blade after the battle." He shook his head sadly. "I saw this child squalling beside the dead body and tried to comfort her."

Lilith's smile melted into trembling lips.

Rarus noticed and reached over to pat Lilith gently in the small of her back.

The little girl shadowed Ramuell everywhere he went. The clan had named her Shiya, which Lilith explained meant 'left' or perhaps 'left behind' in the clan's language. When Shiya couldn't keep pace with Ramuell, he would scoop her up and carry her slung across his shoulder the way farmers haul sacks of tea. She giggled and waved at people as they passed. Amused, the clanspeople laughed and waved back.

The connection between Shiya and Ramuell was the ice-breaker. Over the next couple of days the SWA-7 team members and the clanspeople were able to restore a modicum of the warmth that had defined their longstanding relationship.

Ramuell and Rarus inspected the wounds of everyone who'd been injured during the nefilim attack. A plant, ash and mud salve had been applied to all open sores. Only one clansman had a significant infection.

"I just don't get it," Ramuell said. "We're missing something."

They were indeed. The people of the clan weren't sure what to make of what had transpired and were reticent about sharing the information. Lilith finally coaxed Ru Ta and a couple of other adults to recount the events. Two days after the attack the clan was visited by some other "sky-people." They were grey, had large heads, small bodies and four digits on each hand.

The Domhanians were quite suspicious of this tale until a women explained how the little grey beings had treated their wounds. She was clearly describing treatments that required advanced medical technologies. Rarus looked at Ramuell and said, "**That** explains a lot."

"Yep," Ramuell agreed. "I just didn't believe that a mud salve could possibly be so effective in preventing infection."

"But who were the physicians?" Samael asked. "Could they have been Natharians?"

"I doubt it. Why would Natharians make contact with a primitive species when they know we've been watching them for centuries, and we too have developed 4D technologies?" Lilith's comment was more of an anthropological observation than a question.

Suddenly Ramuell flashed on the being who'd accompanied his parents during their *sen* meeting at the worksite with slave laborers. The sky-people Ru Ta described precisely matched his recollection of that alien.

For the first time he connected that *sen* experience with the conversation in his grandmother's apartment with Azazel and Semyaza. He couldn't believe he'd not already put all this together – that he'd been so obtuse. He said only, "Something strange is happening here."

CHAPTER THIRTY-THREE
THE BARN

Even before she disconnected the call with Liam, Melanka had removed her pipe from its holder and replaced it with one that she kept in the desk's lower right drawer. As Cubra approached she repeated, "Yeah, it seems we have quite a problem."

Cubra halted directly in front of her and replied, "I think **you** have even more of a problem than I do."

Melanka reached over and picked up the pipe and looked down thoughtfully as she tapped it lightly on the desktop. Heartbroken, she looked up into Cubra's grey eyes; normally calm pools of intelligence and humility but now salted with arrogance. The lump in her throat felt like a fist. "Oh Cubra, I don't know about that." As swiftly as a viper strike, Melanka whipped the pipe up and squeezed the bowl. A compressed gas cartridge blasted a small nail size projectile directly into Cubra's forehead.

His eyes squeezed shut then opened wide in astonished terror. His hand automatically reached for the wound in this head as he keeled over backward. The seizure lasted for about a minute before he was dead.

After checking for a pulse, Melanka called Liam. "The immediate threat has been neutralized, but I don't know how deep the betrayal runs."

"Are you safe?" Liam asked.

"I doubt it."

"We should extract you until you've had a chance to sort things out," Liam urged.

"I'll call the landing-pad operator and tell him I'm expecting a Law and Order quadcopter in a few minutes. How long will it take you to get one over here?"

"Sean has just authorized a remotely piloted craft. It will be in the air in two minutes and should be there in about..." Liam looked at Sean.

Sean said, "About twelve minutes."

"I'll be waiting in the pad's weather shelter," Melanka replied.

"We'll meet you on our roof, but you won't be staying here —and Melanka, I'm glad you're okay."

Melanka picked up her valise and walked over to her long-trusted assistant's dead body. Kneeling down she went through his pockets, removed his communicator, the pencil size recording device he carried clipped to his shirt, and the solid-projectile weapon that was holstered at his ankle. She dropped these items into the valise then checked all the buttons on his clothing for microphones and cameras.

She strode into Cubra's office and removed every electronic device she found in the desk and credenza drawers. By the time she'd finished her valise was bulging. She returned to her office, grabbed a rarely used attaché case, and dumped some of Cubra's items in it.

When she exited the office she locked the sliding metal door behind her using a security code known only to herself and Cubra. After hearing the locking mechanism click, she dropped the attaché and valise on the floor.

Melanka slumped back against the door and pressed her eyes with the heels of both hands. After a couple of moments she rubbed her face vigorously. Looking at her feet she moaned as a grieving mother might for a lost child. With a deep inhale she straightened, brushed the front of her jacket, picked up the cases and made her way toward the stairs.

Liam and Sean were at the barn standing in the aisle between the massive hay bales when Althea and Egan arrived. "Thank everything holy you're safe!" Sean exclaimed.

Again Althea cut loose with her frustrated rant. "I've had it. You've tried to hide us at a Safe House, on Cascata Isle, and The Lodge. Each time we were found. Each time we had to run for our lives. I've just had it! I'm not running anymore!"

Calmly Liam asked, "Up there at The Lodge, what was your assailant's weapon setting?"

Althea looked down at her feet and said quietly, "Kill—it was set to kill."

Egan looked over at Althea. With a forlorn expression he said, "We hide and run when we must—we have no choice."

Rebecca, the agent who had helped the couple exit the hospital, tapped Althea's forearm sympathetically. Turning toward the flight of descending wooden stairs, Rebecca removed a communicator from her pocket and tapped in the code to unlock the steel door at the bottom of the stairwell.

Hoping to break the tension, Sean said, "Let's go down-stairs and have a cup of tea or perhaps something stronger. We can discuss our options after we've relaxed a bit." He stopped at the top of the stairs and with a flourish beckoned his companions to lead the way.

The instant Rebecca stepped inside the basement she saw Melanka squatting against the wall to her left with a sonic-blaster pointed at the door. "Whoa Chief Melanka, it's just us —Secretary Liam, Sean, Althea and Egan."

Lowering the blaster, Melanka blew out her held breath. "You have the advantage on me. I recognize you from the videos of your hospital escapade but don't know your name."

With the flicker of a self-satisfied smile, Rebecca walked across the room and offered Melanka her upturned palm. "My name is Rebecca. I've worked for Liam and Sean as a field agent for several decades."

"It's good to meet you."

Rebecca gave Melanka a slight bow before turning to the kitchen. "I'll brew a pot of tea."

Sean pulled a bottle of a distilled stimulant out of his satchel and said, "Or maybe something with a bit more kick?"

Althea flopped in a chair and announced, "I'll have some of that."

Egan sat on the padded arm of the chair and massaged Althea's neck. Looking at Melanka he said, "So it seems you're on the lam too."

Melanka snorted with disgust. "Yeah. Apparently I've been the unwitting source of your betrayals. **Unwitting**!" She turned to Liam. "Can you believe that? Can you even imagine it? After all these decades, I'm making unwitting mistakes! It must be time to retire."

Liam said, "Melanka, you trusted a young man whom you practically raised. No one can hold that against you."

She grunted derisively, "Humph, the family of the dead agent lying up at the Lodge damn sure can."

Jutting her chin out toward Egan and Althea, "These folks

can too. Professor Egan, Dr. Althea, I am sorry—genuinely sorry." She studied the couple for a moment, "There is one thing I have to know. Just how the hell did you manage to overpower and capture a highly trained Anotas agent?"

Holding up a hand Sean said, "Whoa, there will be time enough for rehashing the adventure at The Lodge; first let's relax and have a drink." Sean wanted a drink, but he also wanted to delay that conversation until after the traitorous agent was delivered to the holding cell in the barn's basement. He wanted to question the man before getting drawn into a 'where do we go from here' discussion.

Sean put the clear glass bottle on the table and popped open the cap while Rebecca made the rounds offering tea as an alternative to the stronger libation. Sean looked at Melanka and said, "As for your retirement plan Chief, I'm afraid that mare has left the barn."

Melanka blinked rapidly and asked, "Meaning...?"

"Meaning you've seen Althea's and Egan's video-deposition—you know too much. The traitors are never going to let you retire. In fact, you're going to be hunted. We're all going to be hunted."

Sean handed Melanka a glass half-filled with a golden colored liquid. She took it with a nod of thanks and watched the rich beverage ride up the side of the glass as she swirled it gently. "So you're saying the only thing left for us to do is fight—fight until we win."

"Or die trying," Liam said dryly.

CHAPTER THIRTY-FOUR
MOTHWINGS AND PHEROMONES

DURING THE EVENING call to SWA-7 Dr. Lilith informed Azazel the about the alien species the Crow Clan claimed had visited them. He instructed the team to climb out of the canyon at first light and return to the basecamp. He wasn't sure what to make of the strange story, but sensed danger might be lurking.

The day after their return, Ramuell met with Lilith, Samael and Rarus to discuss their visit with the Crow Clan. He prepared a detailed written report and submitted it to Azazel late that afternoon. After dinner he received a text-com from the boss.

Reading between the lines, I sense there are controversial matters that you didn't included in your report. Do we need to meet privately?

A few seconds later Ramuell replied:

I believe we do, sir.

Azazel:

I'm flying over to inspect our seafood processing facility tomorrow morning. Please plan to join me. Let's meet for breakfast and we'll head out after we've eaten.

Ramuell:

I'll be there.

At breakfast Azazel described the seafood processing plant. He explained how some foods were being cultivated in self-contained saltwater tanks and how other foods were being naturally harvested. They didn't discuss Ramuell's report in the dining module where they might be overheard.

After buckling themselves into the quadcopter that would whisk them down to the coast, Azazel turned toward Ramuell and said, "Well?"

Taken aback by the abrupt launch into the real reason he'd been invited to join the director, Ramuell hesitated a moment, "Well, uhm...I need to tell you more about the *sen* I had when I met my parents. We talked about it briefly with Owan one morning at the dig. It was only my second *sen*. Though I've had many *sen* experiences since, none have been like that one."

Ramuell explained that he felt certain his parents were still alive. "They've been traveling with an alien species they call Beag-Liath. These aliens have taken them to observe Domhanian extraterrestrial outposts at several locations.

"In that *sen* the little grey being showed us a pumping operation. Dad thought it was likely they were extracting helium. The people in charge were speaking Domhan Standard, but the people laboring at the site had round heads and spoke quite differently. Only after our visit with the Crow Clan did I realized the people working at the facility were sapien-hybrids."

"Oh my! Did you record your recollections of the *sen* before our trip to see the Crow Clan?"

"Unfortunately, I didn't, and I know what you're thinking. But the *sen* was so new to me, and this one was so peculiar I just didn't think about making notes."

Azazel nodded and said, "Completely understandable."

"Yeah, but an opportunity lost." Ramuell said shaking his head.

"We can't do anything about that now, so just let it go," Azazel counseled.

"You're right, and anyway there's more. The four of us walked up a hill and sat in the shade of a boulder to get out of the extremely bright sunlight. While we were sitting there, Dad explained that the non-Domhanians were slave laborers; sentient beings from another planet. They'd been genetically modified for the purpose of filling our extraterrestrial industries' labor shortages."

Azazel turned to look out the side window for a long time. He finally spoke just moments before the quadcopter crested a hill and began its descent toward the seafood facility. "You had an extraordinary *sen* experience. The clarity and details of your recollections make me think you were shown something in a *sen* that could explain an awful lot."

"Yes sir—a lot about what we discussed in grandmother's apartment and a lot about the improbable wound healing we saw among the Crow."

After the copter touched down Azazel reached over and lightly gripped Ramuell's arm before he could unbuckle the safety harness. "So I'm supposing this *sen* experience is what you left out of your report." Ramuell's eyes darted away from Azazel's face. "Ahh—I see. So we have more to discuss on our return trip."

Stepping out of the copter Azazel said, "Now, however, our food production responsibilities require my attention. Come on, you'll find this operation fascinating."

Azazel's inspection was not one of his regularly scheduled visits. Rather it was the result of a mishap. He wanted to inspect the repairs and make sure appropriate safety protocols were being implemented.

Once those duties had been attended to, the plant manager took Ramuell and Azazel on a tour. While the entire facility was interesting, the enclosed aqua-ag complex intrigued Ramuell the most; particularly the filtration systems. Water being returned to the ocean was filtered at .015 micrometres; far smaller than the size of any known virus, bacteria or parasite.

Ramuell was excited about the fishing boats off-loading their wild catch, even though the amount of blood made him a bit queasy. He was relieved when Azazel turned to the plant manager and offered his palm, explaining it was time for them to return to the basecamp.

When they were buckled in Azazel asked, "So what did you think?"

Enthusiastically, "That was fun—and interesting. I'd never really thought about how much food is required to feed all the Domhanians working on and orbiting around the planet."

"Many hundreds of thousands of kilograms per day. This facility produces almost eighteen percent of all the food consumed by our Expeditionary Mission personnel," Azazel said. He waited for the copter to get airborne then turned to his protégé, "And you have access to some additional information you wanted to share?"

Azazel's sudden pivot toward the sensitive topic again jolted Ramuell. He wanted desperately to equivocate but took a deep breath and gathered his composure. "As you know I removed the hypothalamus and pituitary glands from the brains of the dead nefilim after the battle."

"Yes, I knew that," replied Azazel.

"After Rarus and I completed the dissections, he returned to the Clan's camp. I lagged behind and took tissue samples from the mouths of the two females with Domhanian shaped heads."

Knowing what was coming, Azazel glanced sideways at Ramuell. "And..."

"Grandmother did the DNA testing and matching. The beautiful woman who hugged you was not your daughter."

Azazel's eyes glazed with a sheen of moisture. "No, she was not my daughter. She was my granddaughter—but you already know that. And I loved her—as I loved her mother who was my daughter."

After spending time on the planet's surface, after experiencing the *sen*, Ramuell had become much less judgmental about relationships between sapien-hybrids and Domhanians. When his grandmother first told him about sexual liaisons between the species, Ramuell had dogmatically asserted it was "...completely unacceptable—completely unethical!" Kadeya had cautioned that if they were to figure out how and why it was happening, they would need to suspend their ethical certainties.

Sitting next to Azazel in the quadcopter and thinking about how to proceed, Ramuell realized he'd come full circle – scientific inquisitiveness had replaced his moralistic certitude. He turned to Azazel and asked, "How? How did it happen?"

Azazel was aware that Ramuell was watching him closely. Looking at the instruments Azazel said, "It's a long story." He looked up at the Estimated Time of Arrival clock. "We'll be landing soon. Let's continue this conversation in my office."

After landing they grabbed a plate of food and retired to the director's office. Seating themselves on either side of the desk, they took a few bites in silence. Azazel began, "I'm sure you noticed there's something about the sapien-hybrids that fosters rather strong feelings of affection."

"To be sure," Ramuell agreed. "During my brief encounters with the Crow Clan I saw displays of affection that we would consider unseemly. We just want to hug them."

"Mmm, not all of us, but they do have that effect on many Domhanians, especially those of us who have spent much time with a clan." Azazel considered his next words carefully. "We didn't expect that reaction when we first began meddling with their DNA. Nor did we expect their reciprocation of our affections."

Ramuell mulled this for a few seconds before asking, "Do you know who fathered the child killed by the nefilim?"

Azazel twisted his lips to one side, "Perhaps."

"Grandmother said the DNA sample must have been too contaminated to find a match among the Domhanians serving on Ghrain-3."

Azazel exhaled loudly. "Or maybe she couldn't find a match because she was looking for a Domhanian father."

It took a moment for that statement to sink in. Ramuell jolted upright, **"Females**! You mean Domhanian females are engaging in intercourse with hybrid males?"

Cocking his head slightly, Azazel returned Ramuell's gaze. "Do you think Domhanian females are incapable of sharing feelings of affection with the hybrids?"

Looking down at his plate Ramuell said, "Uhm—no, I just..." He paused. "There's a lot of distance between the affection I saw with the Crow Clan and actually copulating with one of their kind."

Azazel was impressed that Ramuell's tone had not sounded judgmental. "You're right about that, which brings us back to your question, 'how did this happen?' We've done some research, though our laboratory resources down here are limited. As you can imagine we dared not kick this issue upstairs."

"Yes sir, I can certainly understand that."

"But we have learned enough to have plausible hypotheses." Azazel stood and said, "Follow me."

He led Ramuell outside to a woodpile covered with a thin waterproof tarp. Azazel lifted the tarp and pointed to a few insects clinging to its underside. He picked one off and held it cupped in both hands. "Let me show you something."

Back in his office, Azazel rubbed the insect's wing between his index finger and thumb. He placed the insect under a clear shallow dish beside a microscope mounted to the workbench. He patted his finger on a glass slide and placed it under the microscope. He flipped on the power switch and the microscope automatically resolved to a 1000 power focus. "Okay, now take a look."

Studying the microscopic image, Ramuell asked, "What exactly am I looking at?"

"These insects are moths. There are thousands of species on Ghrain-3. This particular species is very common. You're looking at the insect's scales. The scales' color is what makes the pattern on their wings."

Ramuell looked at the moth beneath the dish. It had dramatic striations along the edges of the wings and a pattern in the middle of each wing resembling an eye. "Alright, that's interesting, but I'm not seeing how this relates to sexual relations among Domhanians and sapiens."

"Sapien-hybrids," Azazel corrected. "To my knowledge there have been no couplings with non-hybridized sapiens. Anyway, that substance is psychoactive. It's hallucinogenic to our species."

Ramuell jerked his head away from the microscope and took an involuntary step back. Azazel laughed, "Not **that** hallucinogenic! You'd have to inhale a **lot** more than what's on the slide. We estimate the altered state of consciousness threshold is about fourteen milligrams ingested nasally."

Ramuell took a seat on the stool at the workbench. "Okay, and..."

Azazel smiled. "Well, my impatient young friend, we don't understand exactly why, but every few annum these moths experience a huge but short-lived population explosion. When that happens hundreds of millions of insects hatch. They can be found clinging to everything. If you brush against a bush, a cloud of moths take flight in such profusion the swarm almost blocks your vision. With that much exposure, we quickly inhale more than the critical threshold of the powder. We are able to protect ourselves primarily by staying indoors."

"Dust masks don't work?" Ramuell asked.

Azazel pulled a couple of stools up to the workbench and motioned for Ramuell to join him. "They're marginally effective but only if the exposed person can get back inside and wash all exposed clothing. It's intriguing that this substance has no psychoactive effect on sapiens or sapien-hybrids. There are substances they consume that do affect them, but moth scale is not one of them.

"Now I can imagine what you're thinking, and this substance is not a sexual stimulant. My first exposure occurred when I was on a field trip. I was studying the diet of sapien-hybrids and had been with a clan for almost two undecim when the moth hatch occurred." With a slight reddening of his cheeks, Azazel pushed his stool back a few centimetres. "I was with one of the clan's adult females. We were gathering grubs from under stones in a moist grassy area near a creek, We were putting them in hollow gourds. It was a beautiful sunlit day, and the moths were swarming. Every time we brushed a shrub or tree, hundreds of the insects would take flight swirling all around us. My companion thought it was funny and would intentionally shake bushes just to watch the explosion of moths. I was aware of a mild sense of euphoria and some visual sensory distortions but certainly not a full blown hallucination."

At this point Azazel's blush colored his ears, but he was determined to soldier through the telling of his story. "We were on our hands and knees and occasionally we accidentally touched each other. Then we began touching intentionally and more frequently. Ahh well, one thing led to another and soon enough we were engaged in intercourse." A kindly expression swept his blush away. "This was not a frantic coupling. It was gentle and affectionate. After the deed was done we probably laid together in that meadow for an hour."

He turned back to Ramuell and back to the present. "That's how it happened. I didn't see her for several kuuk. When I did see her again she was pregnant. Naturally, I wondered if I might have fathered the child. When babe was born, there was no doubt."

"What happened to your daughter?"

"As you know, sapien-hybrids have very short lifespans. She died twenty-nine annum later, I assumed she had not inherited our longevity. However, my granddaughter, the one those bastards killed in Blue Rock Canyon, was the oldest member of the Crow Clan. She was more than twice the age of the next oldest clan member."

"What?! She looked like an adolescent!" exclaimed Ramuell.

"Like a sixty-annum-old Domhanian," Azazel replied.

Ramuell drummed his fingers on the workbench thinking. "Let's back up—you said the mothwing scale is not a sexual stimulant..."

"More accurately, in and of itself the scale doesn't cause sexual arousal. Several annum ago a group of us who had experienced sexual encounters with sapien-hybrids began an anecdotal study of the phenomenon. It was obvious the mothwing scale was somehow a catalyzing factor, but every single person in our group had experienced exposures to the hallucinogen without becoming aroused. The only times sexual arousal seems to occur is when we are in close proximity to sapien-hybrids."

Ramuell narrowed his eyes and said, "That **is** fascinating—actually it's astounding. There has to be some other biochemical or bioelectrical factors in play."

"Yes, you're likely right," Azazel said. "As I'm sure you've learned in school, mammals on Domhan-Siol evolved to have sexual intercourse primarily when the female is within a few days of ovulation. Understanding the female's arousal is fairly simple. She undergoes certain hormonal changes that produce sexualized ideation and arousal. But why did males only seem to become aroused when their female partner was fertile?"

"I don't really know," Ramuell replied.

"Well, take a look at this." Azazel called up an anatomy site on his foliopad and scooted his stool over beside Ramuell. "This is a magnified image of the inside of our nasal passage. Do you see these three indentations?"

Ramuell nodded.

"We have three pheromonasal receptors in each nostril. They're highly specialized sensory organs. Throughout most of our biological history, they were quite important. Beginning about two days before ovulation and ending about three days after, certain hormonal changes in the female triggers the release of a chemical, mostly through sweat glands around the nape of the neck.

"Have you ever wondered why so much of our foreplay involves nuzzling around the neck?" Suddenly realizing it was likely Ramuell had never had a sexual encounter, Azazel tried to cover his faux pas, "Never mind that. The point is, in our distant past we were able to sense the female's chemical discharge and that led to sexual thoughts, encounters, intercourse and procreation.

"Now I'm speaking historically; before our medical technologies so dramatically lengthened our lifespans. Our arousal mechanisms don't work that way anymore. It's the current scientific consensus that these sensory organs," pointing at the photo, "are an evolutionary artifact and no longer functional in our species. As it turns out that's probably not accurate."

Jumping ahead Ramuell blurted, "The psychoactive agent in the mothwing scale potentiates the pheromonasal receptors."

"You're one sharp young man. But we also have to consider one other factor. Sapiens and a few other species on Ghrain-3 do not mate exclusively during the period of female fertility. They seem to be copulating all the dang time!"

Ramuell snickered. "So does that mean their females are always releasing the sexually stimulating chemicals?"

"That's a good question. Maybe so. At this point we've been unable to isolate exactly what chemical or cocktail of chemicals are sexually stimulating to the sapiens. There's ample anecdotal evidence that sapien males also discharge pheromones that cause arousal." On his foliopad Azazel pulled up a photo of a sapien nasal passage. "You see this structure—we're almost certain it's an organ that performs the same function as our pheromonasal receptors did millennia ago."

"But if they're copulating even when females aren't fertile, how could it have the same function?" Ramuell asked.

"Another good question—and we don't know the answer," replied Azazel. "We believe sapien-hybrids probably discharge a palpable miasma of pheromones, and we become susceptible to those chemicals when coupled with the psychoactive effects of mothwing scales. But that raises the question, why is it that our interbreeding with hybrids almost always results in fertilization?"

Ramuell didn't seem to understanding the gist of his question. Azazel said, "Okay, let me try to explain. We know sapiens as well as their closely related cousins, the *neandertalis* and *denisova* species, copulate often. The vast majority of those couplings don't result in fertilization. Yet among the informal study group I mentioned earlier, almost three-fourths of our group's sexual liaisons with sapien-hybrids produced viable offspring."

"Every single one of those children were born with Domhanian shaped skulls. Other than that, they looked much like their sapien-hybrid siblings and cousins. As you saw in my granddaughter, that head shape prevails at least into a second generation." A gust of wind whipped by loudly. Azazel looked out at the swaying trees, sighed, and wiped away the tears that had pooled on his eyelashes.

Ramuell reached over and patted his mentor's shoulder. He decided it was not his place to tell Azazel that Kadeya had been assigned to study the Domhanian/sapien-hybrid interbreeding issue. Instead he proposed, "Why don't we have a talk with Grandmother? Perhaps we can even arrange for her to come down here and you can show her what you've shown me."

This suggestion seemed to instantly wash away Azazel's sad thoughts. "That's a great idea! She hasn't been to the surface yet. I'm sure she's itching to make some tracks on Ghrain-3. And being down here will help her understand why this research is important."

"I think you might be right," Ramuell agreed. "One thing though—protocols be damned—we must talk with her in advance about how she wants to handle the *sen*."

CHAPTER THIRTY-FIVE

CUSTODY AND PROTECTIVE CUSTODY

When the aerial-cam alarm indicated an approaching aircraft, everyone in the barn's basement crowded around the video-screen. With its blackened out windows, it was identical to the quadcopter that had delivered Melanka to the barn several hours earlier. The moment its rotors stopped kicking up dust, two passengers jumped out.

Agent Danel hooked a hand around Faltor's elbow and escorted toward the barn. The prisoner's wrists were secured behind his back, and his ankles were shackled with metal cuffs tethered by a half metre long cable. When the men were several steps away, the remotely piloted copter shot skyward banking sharply to the northeast.

Agent Rebecca pulled a charged-particle weapon from the holster that fit snugly under her right arm. Setting the weapon on stun, she ascended the stairs and met her partner and his prisoner at the first row of hay bales. She fell in behind Faltor training the weapon on the middle of his back.

Althea, Egan and Melanka were startled when Sean tapped a code into his communicator opening the steel wall on the right side of the stairway landing and revealing a room with a single bed bolted to the floor, a sink, and a toilet.

On the wall near the stairwell door, Liam slid open a panel that hid another video-screen. Sean stepped into the cell while Liam booted up the cameras. Within a couple of seconds Sean appeared on the screen.

"Is it working?"

"Yep—crystal clear," Liam answered.

"Okay, turn off the lights."

Liam pushed the light switch and Sean's heat image glowed on the screen. "That's working fine too. You can place Agent Faltor inside and lock it up."

Melanka muttered, "Agent—my ass. Traitor Faltor is more like it."

Danel cut the plastic cord binding his prisoner's wrists. He didn't remove the ankle bands and cable. Rebecca gave Faltor a gentle push into the cell. Once inside, he turned and glared at his captors as the door slid closed.

When Rebecca reentered the basement's main room Melanka rasped, "Please take him some food and water."

Behind the steel wall on the opposite side of the landing was another much more accommodating bedroom with a kitchenette. When Liam showed the studio apartment to Melanka he invited her to make use of it for as long as she needed.

"Thank you, Liam. There's a lot to sort out; I've got to figure out who at Anotas can be trusted and who are the traitors. This is a good place to start that sorting."

"And it's a good deal safer place than most," Liam added.

"No doubt." With her thumb, she pointed toward Faltor's

cell and said, "And my investigation begins with breaking him."

Liam scowled.

Without so much as a twitch she said, "There will be no torture—but the use of some chemical inducements to lubricate his tongue is likely."

Remembering the Anotas agents' threats when they were in the hospital, Althea and Egan exchanged a look, but said nothing.

Melanka turned to Sean and said, "I'm going to need assistance contacting some people at Anotas whom I hope are trustworthy." Melanka's ramrod-straight posture slumped as she said, "But having fostered the agency's worst traitor right under my nose, my judgment needs to be double checked."

Sean said, "I'll do..." he stopped and gestured toward Rebecca and Danel, "rather, **we** will do what we can to help."

Liam said, "Now we don't know where the Anotas skeletons are buried, and we'll follow your lead." He turned to Althea and Egan, "We also need to figure out your best options. That, in no small measure, may depend on what we learn from your would-be assassin."

"How long do you think that will take?" Althea asked.

"And what do we do in the meantime?" Egan added.

Sean replied, "With regard to your question Althea, I don't think we know." Looking at Egan he continued, "In the meantime—if you two will follow me." He led them upstairs to the ground floor.

Mounted on one of the barn's corner posts was an old-fashioned hydraulic lever. Sean pushed it up and one of the five hundred kilogram hay bales began to rise from the floor on a four prong forklift. Below the lift was a cuboid cage roughly one metre by one metre wide and two metres high. Sean stepped inside and turned to look at Althea and Egan expectantly.

Egan, looking dubious, asked, "You believe all three of us can fit in there?"

"We may have to synchronize our breathing, but it's a short ride. Come on, we'll be fine." When they had squeezed in, Sean pushed down on the lever mounted inside the lift door. The elevator descended only about three metres. Sean stepped out into a plushly appointed apartment. He raised his arms and did a half turn. While not top-of-the-line, the furnishings and kitchen appliances were only one notch removed.

Althea stepped out of the elevator and walked over to three pieces of art hung beside a large bookcase. She studied them for only a few seconds before turning to Sean and exclaiming, "These are original pencil portraits by B.S. Quade!"

"Oh? Are they valuable?" Sean asked innocently.

Althea shot him a narrow-eyed glare.

Amusement flitted across Sean's face as he waved them into the bedroom. He entered the walk-in closet and opened an invisible door in the closet's left wall. "This is an emergency escape. A short tunnel leads to a staircase into the pump house."

Studying the hidden exit Althea said, "I suppose since we've been found everywhere else, it's likely to happen here too—sooner or later."

"You're understandably worried and I can't honestly say, 'Oh that won't happen here.' We'd be foolish to rule out the possibility." Sean formed a steeple with his index fingers and held them against his lips. After a moment he said, "Look, we know you're sick of this hide and seek. We're sick of it too. Please believe we're going to figure out somewhere safe for you to go."

Althea looked at the man she'd come to think of as a friend.

"Sean, we were shown a planet colonized by slave owning industrialists. They consider themselves a master race and believe they're completely entitled to champion a kind of galactic imperialism. With 4D technology they could have outposts all over the galaxy. Nowhere is safe—not for us."

Egan added wistfully, "And probably not for you either, my friend."

CHAPTER THIRTY-SIX

ENCRYPTIONS, HOSPITALS AND BODY BAGS

After closing the apartment door, Melanka tottered into the kitchenette and collapsed on a dinette chair. She stared at nothing for a few minutes before picking up her valise and dumping its contents. She knew Cubra's devices were protected by passwords and biometric identifications. She stirred the gadgets around aimlessly as she considered how to bypass the security measures.

An epiphany had her on her feet and at the apartment door. "Gentlemen, you had the help of a technologist when your folks sprung our guests from the hospital."

Liam glanced over at Sean then evasively said, "I really don't recall all of the details about the plan, but..."

Melanka interrupted, "Liam, that was a statement not a question. I'm not asking **if** you had that help. I want to know who it was."

Sean said, "You have Cubra's communicator and..."

"...and of course it's protected by layers of encryption," Liam completed the thought.

Melanka waved the two men over and pointed at the table. When they peered into the room, Liam whistled.

"Yeah, uhm, more than just his communicator," Sean observed.

"There are decades of information stored on those devices. We should be able to piece together a history of the Anotas betrayal and identify many of the perpetrators." Melanka paused and added, "Which will probably not make me feel one iota less miserable."

Liam scratched the back of his neck. "No doubt you've got a cornucopia of information there, but I don't want to bring any outsiders to the barn."

Melanka pinched her lips together tightly, "And these devices are too important for me to surrender possession."

Sean said, "Outsider? Are you thinking of Officer Toth?"

"What do you think?" Liam asked.

"He's good," Sean recalled.

"I should call Captain Chosant," Liam said almost to himself.

"Ah, the hospital security chief," Melanka recalled.

Sean said, "He'll be curious about why we're not using an Anotas techie to crack the codes."

Melanka sniffed then said, "You're probably right, and I'm not sure how I want to answer that question. When will you call?"

"This afternoon."

Melanka glanced once again at the devices piled on the table. "I need to shut my eyes for a few minutes. Let me know when you get hold of Chosant."

Taking the hint, Liam and Sean stepped out of the apartment's doorway, and Melanka pressed the closure switch.

Realizing Melanka was probably on the verge of collapse, Liam put off calling Chosant for a couple of hours. The Captain had just finished working out in the hospital's gymnasium and was sitting down for a snack at his desk when his video-com buzzed.

Chosant exchanged greetings with Liam and even though Sean could not be seen on the video screen, he said, "Hello Sean. How are you doing?"

"About as well as can be expected, given what the Secretary is going to explain to you," Sean replied.

"How can I help?"

Liam described some of what was happening at Anotas. When he finished there was dead silence for several moments. At last Chosant said, "Whew—so is that all—nah, what am I saying? Of course that's not all. Liam, this is a potential crisis isn't it?"

"Anotas-Deithe has been the backbone of public governance for millennia. They have their tendrils in almost every aspect of society. They have for the most part been a benevolent overseer of Domhanian society, but we've always known that much power could be misused—could be used against the citizenry with only a quarter-turn in a wrong direction."

"And with disastrous results," Chosant added. "Have either of you ever studied the military history of the old nation-states before the Unification?"

Sean grunted, "Now that's a frightening thought." He swiveled toward Liam and said, "They poured almost half of their nations' wealth into building militaries. The civil authorities honestly believed those militaries would never use their power to seize control. It was mindless, absolutely mindless."

"I don't believe we're anywhere near that far along yet, but we must get a handle on the renegades before the unthinkable happens." Liam looked into the camera and said, "Captain, we are going to need your help sorting this out."

"I understand," Chosant replied. "I left public sector work a longtime ago, but if you guys say you need me, I'll damn sure do what I can."

With that, Sean went to wake Melanka. When she joined the three gentlemen a few minutes later, Liam thought she looked more composed.

Liam and Sean sat back and let her carry the conversation. They were surprised at how much detail about Cubra's betrayal she was willing to share. Chosant agreed that Toth probably could be helpful, though there were no guarantees he'd be able to break through the encryptions.

Liam explained that Althea and Egan had been tracked down three times already. For that reason he was unwilling to allow outsiders access to the secret location where they were currently holed up. They decided the best way to arrange a meeting with Toth would be for Melanka to check into the hospital using an alias.

"We can put you in a room on the 22nd floor. You'll have easy access to the janitor's closet," Chosant explained.

With a perplexed frown, "Janitor's closet?"

Sean laughed and said, "We'll explain later." Turning back to the camera he said, "Captain, we need to make this happen quickly."

Chosant's main concern was getting Melanka into the hospital without being seen by the security cameras, which he knew were monitored by the Anotas O&M center. He leaned back in his chair, tapping his chin with an index finger. The solution he hit on was quite obvious. Melanka would arrive at the hospital zipped in a body-bag as a 'dead-on-arrival.'

Ten hours later Melanka laid down on the bed in room

#2237. She was exhausted and the hospital bed was surprisingly comfortable. She was soon sound asleep.

Althea was not handling waiting nearly as well as her husband. She understood there was nothing they could do and little they could plan without the information locked in Cubra's electronic devices and inside Faltor's head, but she hated being at the mercy of two traitors.

The couple spent much of their time studying the history of the Ghrain-3 Expeditionary Mission. What they learned convinced them that Ghrain was the likely source of the slaves they had seen while with the Beag-Liath. And the more they learned the more zealous they became about the need to expose the slave trade.

Egan believed at some point they would have to go to Ghrain-3. Althea enthusiastically supported this notion in large part because she wanted so desperately to see her son and mother. They understood a trip to Ghrain-3 would require a labyrinth of smoke and mirrors, as well as the full support of the Law and Order Directorate and the uncorrupted elements of Anotas-Deithe. They were not at all certain that support would be forthcoming.

CHAPTER THIRTY-SEVEN

NOT THE ORIGINAL SEN

AZAZEL HAD BEEN CORRECT. Kadeya was thrilled about a trip to Ghrain's surface. "I won't even need to invent an excuse. I really do need to observe nefilim clans in their habitats."

"SWA-7's security team tracks the movements of many clans and probably know the locations of several groups of nefilim," Ramuell explained. "I've become friends with a couple of the officers and will ask them about the best places for observation."

"Now we'll need at least three days to observe the clans with nefilim."

"No doubt Samael and Rarus can find a way to make that happen," Ramuell assured.

"Sounds good! On this end I'll go see Doc to get my medical clearance for the trip. That should be no problem. I'll also check weather forecasts before packing." She paused for a moment, "Do you think I should bring a few items from the lab we might want for field testing."

"Yes, I'll send you a list of what we might need, and I'll tell Azazel you're on your way."

Kadeya had been overly optimistic about the ease of getting medical clearance. Doc insisted she have a full medical exam. Unfortunately, there was a three-day delay in making that appointment because he was tied-up with a contagious outbreak of dermatitis among the staff in the food supplies torus.

When Kadeya finally did get in to see the doctor, he found no lingering health concerns related to her failed attempt at acclimatization. Doc approved a surface visit for Kadeya not to exceed eleven days, which would be ample time as she didn't intend to stay on the surface for a full undecim anyway.

In close-knit communities a great deal of information is always folded into little pleats of "common knowledge." The SWA-7 staff knew Kadeya was Ramuell's grandmother. When Director Azazel led the renowned scientist and her grandson into the dining dome, the room fell silent with gazes turned toward the new arrival.

Kadeya raised her hand and waved. "Really folks, I don't bite—or haven't for at least a century."

Everyone laughed even though the joke wasn't all that funny. Kadeya understood self-effacing humor, especially when served up by a famous person, almost always won over the room. After selecting their meals from the buffet, they took a table by themselves. Gadrel soon came over and joined them. Samael and Rarus came over to introduce themselves and a few others stopped by to pay their respects.

Taking advantage of a lull in the action Kadeya stuffed in a few bites of food. While she was chewing a mouthful of an algae called saltwater grapes, Alicia sauntered up. An enchanting almost-smile played across the spray of freckles on her nose and cheeks. Ramuell rose to his feet, and she greeted him with a hug and a kiss on the cheek. Kadeya had noticed the charismatic young woman as she approached and was unable to veil her surprise at Alicia's affectionate greeting. When Ramuell introduced his grandmother, Kadeya stood and offered a palm.

Alicia said, "Your grandson has been through the icicle gates of hell since he and I first met at the Dig site. Hopefully, your time with us will be, how should I say it...a little less exciting."

Kadeya acknowledged the comment with a knowing smile and nod.

Glancing at Azazel, Ramuell said, "Yeah, it hasn't all been fun, but we're still here."

Alicia fixed her eyes on Azazel and said, "Perhaps this is a bit too bold, but given what you've been through, Director, you look good."

"Given what I've been through, I look good." Azazel turned to Kadeya and teased, "Now I'm not sure if that's a compliment or not, what do you think?"

Kadeya eyes danced as she waved off the question.

Alicia's cheeks bloomed with color, "Okay, let me try that again. My comment was more misspoken than bold. You look **very** good. How's that?"

"Better."

Alicia turned back to Ramuell and placed both hands on his forearm. They lingered there as she said, "And you look good too—excuse me, very good too."

"Well, then..." Ramuell said as if he was going to say something more. Alicia smiled as if he had.

Kadeya motioned toward an empty chair and asked, "Would you like to join us?"

"I would. I haven't even had a chance to say hello to Gadrel."

Faking a pout, Gadrel said, "Yeah, I noticed."

"Aww..." as she patted his shoulder, "Let me grab a plate. I'll be right back."

After dinner Ramuell and Alicia escorted Kadeya to an enclosed log lean-to used as sleeping quarters for visitors. Before parting company Kadeya said, "Okay, I don't need to be sleeping under this shelter. I'm ready to get on with this *sen* thing."

Ramuell startled at his grandmother's comment and shot a sideways glance at Alicia.

Alicia took Kadeya's cavalier attitude in stride and chuckled, "Now you don't hear that every day." She looked down for a second while gathering her thoughts. "Dr. Kadeya, I'd suggest you take it slowly. It would be good to give yourself a bit of time to settle in."

"Grandmother, you should heed Alicia's advice."

Again with that almost-smile, Alicia added, "Trust us. We've had a lot of experience with this. Yours will not be the original *sen*."

The next morning Rarus and Samael presented Kadeya with a plan for observing nefilim clans. They had topographical maps and information about recent movements of three different groups.

Rarus explained that there were significant behavioral differences among clans with only a couple nefilim members as opposed to clans in which the gigantism mutation had expressed more frequently. Kadeya was enthused about the chance to observe these different manifestations.

It was late morning when Azazel was able to break away from other duties and join the group. Sam and Rarus shared their surveillance plan. At the conclusion of the presentation Azazel told Kadeya, "There's no way an undertaking like this can be risk-free. It's always best to do a risk assessment in order to minimize the dangers and to have back-up plans for when Plan A fails."

"You said 'when' Plan A fails, rather than 'if.' Do you expect Plan A to fail?" Kadeya asked.

"Yes. Not because it actually will, but on Ghrain-3 we've learned to expect the unexpected. That's why we anticipate Plan A's failure and always have a Plan B, C, and D." Samael and Rarus nodded their agreement. Azazel continued, "Gentlemen, thank you for the efforts; well done. Let's meet back here after breakfast tomorrow morning to finalize timeframes."

Samael said, "That works for me."

"One more thing, Kadeya. I understand you are aware of the *sen* phenomenon. Before going out in the field, you need to experience the *sen* at least once or perhaps twice to see how you react."

Rarus added, "The Director is right. You do **not** want to have a bad first *sen* experience in the backcountry."

CHAPTER THIRTY-EIGHT

THE CHIMERA WITH A THOUSAND HEADS

LIAM DEPARTED for the Law and Order Directorate headquarters as soon as Melanka was safely ensconced at the Nexo de Mondo Hospital. Sean stayed at the barn and met Melanka when she returned three days later.

It was a muggy day. A flush painted Melanka's cheeks even though her skin was a few shades darker than most Domhanians. Sean said, "You look like you're roasting. Come inside, it's cooler downstairs."

As soon as the basement door was closed Melanka wilted into a lounge chair. The heat pump was both cooling and dehumidifying the air. "Ahh, it feels good in here," she said fanning herself with her right hand.

Sean returned from the refrigerator and offered her a drink poured in a frosty mug. She sipped it hesitantly. "Just citrus and berry juice mixed in roughly equal portions," Sean explained.

Melanka looked at the mug with the murky purple liquid and puckered her lips appreciatively.

"Well?" Sean asked.

"Well, we weren't able to break the encryptions on all the devices. Captain Chosant has assigned Toth to continue working on the code breaking pretty much fulltime. Chief Farris is also helping, mainly with an hour of brainstorming each afternoon."

"Good for him. Liam knew Chosant would come through for us," Sean said.

Melanka took another long swig of her juice and watched the glass as she clinked the ice balls around. "But we did learn a lot. Sean, it's bad; worse than I imagined. I cannot believe this has been going on right under my nose. I was so blinded by loyalty to Anotas that I didn't see the twin rots of avarice and power-lust eating at our core. Thousands of our staff at every level are on the take. What the hell are they thinking?" She snorted. "A disproportionate number of the corrupted staff are cultists. Perhaps they believe the additional credits are some form of manna from heaven."

Sean said, "Cultists huh—maybe the payments are a reward for doing some god's work."

Melanka's expression betrayed such aching sadness Sean had to look away. She continued, "If that's the case, the gods are using corporations to bankroll their enterprise, and they're funneling the manna through the Business and Industry Council. I suppose that's why Chairman Regan always felt he could just call and tell me what I ought to be doing."

"As of this morning Regan still hasn't left the planet. Should we pick him up?" Sean asked.

"Nah—he's always thought of himself as a kingpin, but we learned from Cubra's memoranda that Regan is a bigshot only in his own mind. He's never really called any of the shots."

Sean startled slightly. "Really! He's served as the Council's Chairman for so long. How do you explain that?"

"He's simpleminded and malleable. Both attributes have

been manipulated by the true powers. It's easy to trick him into thinking the Council's initiatives are his own ideas. Sean, the man has probably never had an original thought in his life."

"But he comes off as being quite a competent administrator."

Melanka held both hands up, "Oh, I'll give credit where credit's due. He is the great communicator. Remember he used to be an actor. He knows how to read the script he's handed." Almost under her breath she added, "...and dumb enough to think he actually wrote it. Anyway, getting back to the point, he's such small fry with a big ego it's better to leave him where he is. Since he considers himself some kind of very stable genius, he'll unwittingly give away a lot of information with his incessant cryptic communiqués to his adoring throng of dimwitted followers."

They sat thinking for a couple of minutes. Their glasses were empty but neither seemed desirous of a refill. Sean broke the silence, "So who do you trust, and what help do you need?"

"I don't yet know who we can trust. What I need is some help figuring that out. I'd like to bring an agent out to the barn in order to assist with debriefing our friend here." She pointed with tilt of her head toward the wall between the main room and the cell holding Faltor. "You've had experience with the man I want to invite to help us, and if you veto my request I'll understand."

"Who are you considering?" Sean asked.

"I'd like to bring Agent Chelt out here."

"And you trust him?"

"I do. In fact, if you check with Althea and Egan they'll likely confirm Chelt realized early on something was askew with our investigation of their absence and return." With a note of humiliation Melanka added, "He understood that before I did."

Closing her eyes she inhaled and exhaled deeply. "We can also trust him because we found information on Cubra's communicator indicating Chelt was considered quite a threat to the B&I/Anotas partnership."

"That's promising. Now Liam will insist we confirm Chelt's loyalty before he'll give his approval. It seems the barn is about the only place the bad guys haven't found yet, and the Secretary is determined to keep it that way."

"His caution is justified," Melanka agreed.

Sean did follow-up with Althea and Egan. Althea described the meeting she'd had with Chelt the day she and Egan were threatened with "truth" drugs. She explained how he'd used an electromagnetic transmission disrupter to block the audio signal from their hospital room for a few seconds in order to assure her that no matter how things might appear she had nothing to fear from him. "I knew from the sincerity in his voice and eyes that I was safe. He was not going to punch a syringe of the green goo into my veins."

Sean drew in a deep breath. "Well, Melanka wants to bring Chelt out here to help with her investigation. What you've told me indicates he smelled a rat and wasn't buying into their game plan. **But** if either of you are uncomfortable having him know your whereabouts, I'll nix Melanka's request in a heartbeat."

Egan and Althea looked at each other and shrugged.

Sean smiled and said, "Look guys, I need someone's advice."

"I'm okay with this," Althea said. "Not only did he put my

mind at ease by promising not to use the drug, he also alerted me, without actually saying so, that Anotas suspected we'd been in contact with an alien species. I think we can trust him."

"I'm with her," Egan said.

Sean stood up and said, "All right! I have a couple more things to check before making a decision. I just wanted to give you folks veto power before moving on to the next steps."

Sean asked Rebecca to check on Chelt's tender institution transactions, income sources, purchases, etc. He had Agent Danel look into Chelt's living arrangements. Did his home, furnishings, dining, travel seem congruent with his income? For Agents Rebecca and Danel these were not difficult investigations. They reported their findings within a day.

Finally, Sean called Liam. "You know Sean, I had considered recommending to Melanka that she needs some trustworthy help from the inside. Agent Chelt had actually crossed my mind. In retrospect it seems clear he wasn't playing their game." Sean knew Liam well enough to visualize his boss leaning back in his chair and looking at the ceiling while gently pulling at the loose skin under his neck. Liam continued, "I didn't feel comfortable making that recommendation because Chelt is partnered with such a gung-ho ass."

Sean chuckled, "We certainly agree about that."

"Partner, I'll back whatever you decide. One thing though, anyone brought to the barn must be scanned for trackers and delivered in a windowless quadcopter."

Faltor's interrogations didn't produced a trove of information. After a few days Chelt said to Melanka, "Chief, Faltor didn't have access to the heavy hitters. He's not going to be much more use to our investigation."

"You're right," Melanka agreed. "He's just a hired gun. I'll ask to have him put on ice elsewhere."

Sean arranged to transfer Faltor to the bowels of the Law and Order Directorate headquarters. There he would remain in custody for over an annum awaiting trial for murder.

———

The day after Cubra's body was discovered, the Anotas-Deithe Enforcement Bureau identified Melanka as a "hypothecant" in the investigation, but over an undecim later she still hadn't been labeled a "suspect." Liam and Sean took this to mean she probably retained powerful allies within the Anotas hierarchy. If that were true, Liam reasoned there was likely a cut-throat stab-'em-in-the-back war going on within every nook and cranny of the ancient organization. On one side would be those who had refused to sell themselves, and on the other side those who'd been bought by the Business and Industry Council's overlords.

"I'd guess the notion of a clear-cut dichotomy is an over-simplification," Sean suggested while sipping tea and relaxing in the den of the home they had enjoyed infrequently of late.

"What are you thinking?" Liam asked.

"Well, before Melanka invited Chelt to join her, she asked him about payments people at the agency were receiving from the B&I Council. He responded that the practice is so prevalent many employees consider it a perquisite of employment."

Stunned, Liam said, "He actually said that!"

"Yes, those are his words. Melanka asked why he hadn't accept the payola offered by the Council. He replied, 'Remuneration!' He said something like, 'I'm paid pretty dang well by

Anotas for my skills and services. I just couldn't see any way the Business Council would be gifting all that money. The disbursements had to be remuneration, in abeyance, but remuneration none-the-less. I did not want to have a quid pro quo relationship with the likes of Chairman Regan and his bootlicks.'"

"Chelt is an interesting character, isn't he," Liam observed.

"Yeah, the guy is quick on the uptake. The next thing Melanka asked was why he didn't report the bribery, given his personal feelings about the payments. Chelt is clearly conflicted on this matter. He said he didn't report it because he hadn't observed any change in the performance or quality of work among the people he knew were receiving the Council's money."

With a little snort Liam said, "That's probably because the B&I bosses hadn't called in any chips yet."

"That's almost exactly what he said," Sean replied. "It's likely his circle of colleagues were not receiving specific assignments from the corporate overlords, at least not yet. But he was certain a day of reckoning was coming. He called himself a fool for not acting on his instincts. He knew at some point B&I would start asking their off-the-books employees to help facilitate unethical and perhaps illegal schemes.

"He's pretty depressed both about his partner, Dyer, as well as his own failure of nerve. That's why the Anotas situation is likely even more chaotic than just two sides warring it out."

"So you think there are a lot of Anotas staff like Chelt. They disapprove of their colleagues' arrangements with the B&I Council but are complicit by their silence?"

"I do," Sean replied. "And given the sheer enormity of Anotas, it's a mess from the ninth realm of hell."

Liam sat thoughtfully for a moment before tacking in a

new direction. "It's my understanding Melanka has been pretty well frozen out in her efforts to investigate Anotas employees' tender institution transactions."

"That's correct. She has allies on the inside, but not enough clout to get investigation warrants issued."

Liam sighed. "We're not having that problem. The team we have looking at our staff's tender accounts haven't had much problem accessing transaction records. Sadly, we are finding a significant problem within our own ranks."

"Significant...meaning?"

"Perhaps ten percent of our employees," Liam answered.

Sean whistled.

"Yeah, ten percent is bad. Nowhere near as bad as—well, let's just say I'd rather not be the Secretary at Anotas-Deithe."

"And perhaps that's the real problem. They don't have a secretary. Anotas a chimera with a thousand heads—and a hundred thousand eyes," Sean observed.

Several hours after Sean had gone to bed, Liam stayed up thinking about the information and observations his partner had shared. Sean's last comment articulated too much truth to be considered hyperbole. Anotas was like the batting of a quilt. It undergirded the disparate pieces of an ancient, complex society. Since the advent of 4D technologies Domhan-Siol had evolved into an interplanetary society, which added even more layers of complexity.

Domhanians did not have a tradition of governance by ballot, nor did they expect that all decisions would be achieved through consensus. Since the Unification, their world had not known open warfare. That's not to say there were never conflicts. Down through the ages communities had taken actions they deemed in their own best interest, knowing that those actions might disadvantage another community in some way. When these kinds of conflicts resulted in bellicosity, Anotas-Deithe had always been able to step in and mediate or, as necessary, impose a resolution. The institutional power of Anotas was so widely respected the notion of centralized authority through a chief executive officer was not even contemplated.

At times Anotas even interjected itself into conflicts when corporations found themselves at loggerheads over business dealings or personnel management issues. Naturally, the corporate elites preferred to resolve their own conflicts; thus the evolution of the Business and Industry Council. Though the B&I Council's conflict resolution efforts were reasonably effective, Anotas had never ceded authority to intervene should they determine intercession necessary.

Decision making processes within the organization were arcane to say the least. '...a thousand heads and a hundred thousand eyes' indeed! Yet Anotas-Deithe was the strand of gold thread that had woven stability into the fabric of Domhanian society for thousands of annum.

Now things were changing. Perhaps the complexity of permanent Domhanian colonies on far-flung planets; perhaps the growth of power-lust within corporate hierarchies; perhaps the emergence of materialistic avarice among the general population; or most likely some combination of all of these factors had pushed Anotas and all of Domhanian society to the brink.

The brink of what? Liam wondered. What he knew was with Egan's and Althea's return, Anotas had rapidly devolved into a gurgling, crackling cauldron of conflict. He would soon learn the conflicts were not just inside the institution, they spanned the Domhanian corporate empire.

———

Sean was up early. He'd made a pot of café and had a plate of sliced fruit, cheese, and toasted rolls laid out on the counter. Liam entered the kitchen and looked at the breakfast then at Sean appreciatively.

"A long night Lee?" Sean asked.

As he swiveled one of the barstools to take a seat, Liam replied, "Yeah. After our conversation I couldn't turn off my brain. Your last comment about Anotas being a chimera got me thinking about that behemoth; how it's been a stabilizing force for good throughout its history—though the potential for misuse has always lurked just under the surface."

As Liam blew the steam off his café, Sean said, "Now that I've thought about it some more, perhaps the fact Anotas doesn't have a secretary is actually a strength rather than a weakness. Maybe because of the thousand heads it has achieved a byzantine kind of equilibrium."

"Perhaps," Liam replied. "It is remarkable the institution has functioned as well as it has for as long as it has. But now Anotas is facing an existential crisis like none other in its history."

"And if that's the case, Domhanian society may be in for a level of tumult we've not seen since the Unification," Sean added.

"That's what kept me awake until after midnight—playing out various scenarios and contemplating how the Law and Order Directorate might mitigate a possible firestorm." Liam took a bite and chewed slowly. "I'm going to announce the appointment of a Special Investigator today. You need to come to the office for the announcement—to be one of the guys standing with me in front of the cameras."

Sean grunted but understood the theatrics the media and

public expected to accompany major announcements by high ranking officials. He said, "Ahh well, that'll be fine. I need to check in at the office before heading out to the barn anyway." He studied Liam's face for a moment. "Who are you planning to appoint?"

"Judge Cartan, if he'll agree to take it on."

"Oh—he's a great choice. The venerable old Judge timed his retirement perfectly, at the apex of his career."

"Right," Liam agreed. "His credibility is uncontested and his reputation beyond reproach. I suppose the trick will be convincing him to say yes."

"If you explain what we know, his sense of duty will trump any reticence." Thinking about what was on his things-to-do-list Sean continued, "Lee, we've got to meet with Althea and Egan to start forming a plan for their safe relocation. I've been putting it off because the situation seems so fluid."

"You're right," Liam agreed. "Look, with everything that's going on I'm not getting out to the barn anytime soon. So, after we make the announcement, let's do a video-com with Melanka and Chelt. We need to talk with them before you meet with Egan and Althea."

CHAPTER THIRTY-NINE
FRIENDS OF MELANKA

Shortly after midday Sean got the principals together on a video-com. Melanka began, "Liam, remember some time back I shared our suspicion that corporate elites have developed resort type colonies on three planets? It turns out that estimate was wrong. There are more—several more. We caught a break yesterday when Officer Toth broke the encryption on one of Cubra's files. It's massive and we haven't waded through everything yet, but it contains a lot of information about our extraterrestrial outposts."

"So, what have you got for us?" Sean asked.

"Quite a lot," Melanka answered.

She gestured for Chelt to continue. "Some of the colonies are quite populous. We think Froitas is the largest at over two million. We also learned that the colonies are not of one mind regarding slavery. There's a colony on the planet Realta-Gorm 4 that adamantly opposes the industrial hybridization of sentient creatures for labor. We need to deploy someone to gather information on Realta-Gorm to get a more complete picture."

Sean looked at Liam and asked, "Are you thinking what I'm thinking?"

Meeting again with the group three days later, Sean reported, "When approached with the proposal of an off-world assignment to Realta-Gorm 4 Althea and Egan were surprisingly enthusiastic. They understand this mission is about gathering intelligence on the colony."

"Understanding a mission is one thing, being equipped to accomplish it is something else entirely," Melanka observed.

Though smart and well educated, Egan and Althea lacked training and experience in covert operations tradecraft. Melanka was skeptical about the prudence of this assignment.

Liam pointed out that the couple had managed to give the B&I Council hired-guns the slip on three occasions.

"Yes, but they had you and your teams orchestrating their escapes," Melanka countered.

"Not always. Up at the Lodge they not only managed to avoid being murdered, they actually captured the would-be assassin—a highly trained Anotas agent," Liam reminded the group.

Seeing she was in the minority, Melanka relented. "Okay, but I can't in good conscience support sending them on this mission without backup. One of your officers should accompany them—Agent Rebecca," Melanka stated matter-of-factly.

Liam responded, "Oh—well yeah—we can consider that. They do know each other."

"And more importantly they trust each other," Melanka added.

Looking at the ceiling and rubbing his chin, Sean said, "You know, teaming those guys up just might be a good idea. Would we want to also consider adding Danel to the mix?"

Melanka said, "Perhaps. I know Rebecca and Danel worked together on your little hospital escapade, but have they partnered on other missions?"

With the tiniest smirk Liam raised an eyebrow and looked a Sean.

Sean grinned and said, "Let me put it this way. They have a decades old relationship that includes many joint missions and, uhm, a personal friendship."

Melanka grunted and said, "So he'd be a perfect addition to the team."

The group sat quietly thinking for a couple minutes. Liam drew in a deep breath and closed the meeting with a piercing observation. "What we're dealing with is a cultural malignancy. Gathering intel on our colonies will help us figure out to what extent it has metastasized."

Over the next three undecim Danel, Rebecca, Sean, Egan and Althea devised a plan code-named Blue Star. The cover story would be that of two couples on holiday looking for an adventure on Realta-Gorm 4.

Unfortunately, media coverage following Althea's and Egan's mysterious return had often included photos. It was likely some of those stories had made their way to Realta-Gorm. This would necessitate haircuts, hair dying, eye coloring contact lenses, glasses, and other cosmetic procedures to alter their appearance. Danel assured the couple that these procedures were quite effective.

Given what they'd been through since being returned to their homeworld, Althea and Egan came to see this assignment as something of a vacation – at least a vacation from pursuit by would-be assassins.

While their colleagues were planning the mission to Realta-Gorm, Melanka and Chelt got busy identifying a cadre of Anotas staff loyal to her and the institution's traditional values. This was a tedious and painstaking process.

Those who had been beneficiaries of corporate largesse were easy to weed out. The accept/reject decision was not so easy for many others they considered. It would have been Melanka's instinct to automatically exclude anyone who had silently acquiesced to the B&I Council's secret payroll, but for the fact Agent Chelt was the charter member of the FOM (Friends of Melanka).

From this she took two lessons: 1) Be cautious in judging those who were not the direct recipients of ill-gotten gains; and, 2) The tentacles of corporate corruption within Anotas were so extensive no one, not even the most honorable and vigilant, had escaped exposure. After all, her most trusted colleague and long-time assistant had been at the vice-storm's vortex.

The Friends of Melanka numbered thirty-one field agents, five finance experts, eight support staff, and half a dozen technologists (she counted Toth among this group though he was not Anotas staff).

Melanka understood rebuilding the credibility of Anotas-Deithe was absolutely essential for Domhanian culture. She also understood it would be a decades-long process. This core group was where that process began.

Melanka convinced Liam and Sean that they also needed to send someone to Ghrain-3 on a covert fact-finding mission.

She proposed dispatching Sean and initially he was enthusiastic about the prospect. However after a day's reflection he vetoed the idea.

"Look, there are just too many photographs of me standing with the Secretary."

"Yeah, I'd arrived at the same conclusion," Liam agreed. "The fact is, you're just too old."

Sean blew out a breathy, "Oh, thanks a lot."

Chuckling, Liam tried to smooth the rough edges off his statement. "Okay, not too old, but you've been around too long. A lot of people on Ghrain-3 would recognize you and a few probably even know you."

"You're right. Melanka shared a personnel roster with me. In a quick scan of just the first few pages of the file I saw at least a dozen people with whom I've crossed paths. As much as I'd relish an off-world assignment, this is not the one for me."

Tapping her chin, Melanka said, "Another person has come to mind. Evander is not our typical field agent. He has a doctorate in history, which seems a strange background for an Anotas agent, but he's known within the agency as a get-the-job-done kind of guy—without all the trappings of ambition. He's been promoted through the ranks, but he never applies for the promotions. It's almost a point of pride with him... 'If you want me for that job, you're going to have to recruit me.' He's also extremely cordial. I don't know anyone who dislikes him."

"What would his cover story be?" Sean asked.

"I'm thinking he would be sent to deliver restricted materials to the Ghrain-3 library. Because the material is classified Level 4, we have to assigned an agent to oversee the download. The chief librarian, Lector, will be his contact person. Because Lector already works for me there will be no need to fool him with a cover story."

"Excellent—actually a better cover than the Realta-Gorm vacationing couples," Sean observed.

Melanka picked up her pipe and stared into the bowl, then hesitantly said, "Yeeaahh, with one glitch. Gentlemen, I'm tired—and perhaps a bit emotionally ragged. Anyway, I slipped up a couple of days ago, a mistake I'd never have made three kuuk ago. One evening while dining with Chelt, Althea and Egan I let slip that I wanted to send an operative to Ghrain-3. The second the words were out of my mouth I realized my blunder. When I looked up, Althea's eyes bored through me like drill bits."

"Let me guess," interrupted Liam. "She wants to go, or she insists your man inform Kadeya and Ramuell that they are alive."

"Actually the latter, she understands why it would be dangerous and foolhardy for them to traipse into the Ghrain-3 hornet's nest. But she does insist on getting word to her mother and son," Melanka explained. "The best I could do was promise that our agent would be authorized to contact Kadeya and inform her, should he decide it is safe to do so. Initially this assurance did not appease Althea. But with Chelt's assistance we played out several scenarios whereby providing that information might actually endanger Kadeya and Ramuell."

"And with that she relented I suppose?" Liam asked.

"She did, but I'm still very unhappy with myself for opening that can of worms."

"Melanka, how long has it been since you were able to go home and sleep in your own bed? Since you've been able to set foot in your office? Since you were able to meet a friend in Nexo for dinner or a cup of tea?" Liam asked in rapid fire succession.

"You know exactly how long. Since the day you flew me out here, I've only been off this property once—my clandestine trip to the hospital." Looking down she added almost inaudibly, "I haven't been home since the day I killed Cubra."

Liam and Sean sat silently for a moment. Then Liam said, "Melanka you need to be gentle with yourself. Never in our history have we had to deal with a situation like this. We are going to get tired, emotionally and physically. We will make mistakes."

Because of its "official business" nature, Dr. Evander's trip to Ghrain-3 was easier to arrange than the foursome's trip to Realta-Gorm. As Evander was walking out of the barn Althea approached and pressed a note into his hand. She said, "I beg you, if it's possible, if it will not put them in danger—please, please find a way to let them know."

Rather than offering her his palm, Evander pulled Althea into a quick embrace, but said nothing as he turned to walk toward the waiting quadcopter. Egan, standing several paces away, never took his anguished eyes off his wife as she watched Evander climb into the cockpit.

CHAPTER FORTY
THE SENSE OF SENS

Kadeya was somewhat disappointed with her first *sen*. Most Domhanians were frightened, mystified, or excited, but rarely disappointed. "Perhaps I've studied it too much and had unrealistically elevated expectations." She looked across the table that held cups of tea and a plate of freshly made biscuits.

Ramuell shifted uncomfortably on the bench seat and stared at his grandmother with an expression of incomprehension. For him, the *sen* had been a life altering experience.

Kadeya cleared her throat and said, "Maybe it's like watching a movie that's been over-hyped, or one poorly adapted from a favorite book." She paused hoping for an inkling of comprehension. "You remember how you felt about the movie based on your favorite children's book, *A Time of Magic*?"

'Yeesss, I suppose I can see what you're getting at," Ramuell replied dubiously. "So, what did you see in your *sen*?"

"I'm not sure. It didn't make a lot of sense." She paused, trying to remember details. "It was about your parents, or at least partially." Ramuell's eyes widened expectantly. Kadeya hurried to quash her grandson's excitement, "They weren't in the *sen* per se, but some other man was there. He was from the homeworld, but I didn't know him." Kadeya scrunched her eyebrows, "Or I just can't remember who he was. Anyway, he told me your parents want to come to Ghrain-3, but they can't because sapien-hybrids are being sold as slaves. I asked him 'How do you know that?' and he said 'You know.'"

Seeing his grandmother's befuddlement, Ramuell recalled, "I was bewildered and frightened by my first *sen*. I thought I was losing my mind! I expected your experience would be different because you had so much foreknowledge. I'm surprised your experience didn't seem more profound."

"I was not at all frightened, just confused—someone from Domhan-Siol coming here to tell me my daughter and son-in-law want to visit, but they can't because of slavery. What does that even mean?" Kadeya shook her head quickly and grinned at her grandson. "Don't worry. I'm still looking forward to my next nocturnal adventure."

Without their noticing, Alicia had walked up. With a sympathetic smile she said to Kadeya, "Now that sounds promising." Hiking up her pants, she hurdle-stepped across the bench and took a seat beside Ramuell.

Upon his arrival Dr. Evander stuck to the script of his cover story. He installed the classified files in the research library's information retrieval system. He was friendly with everyone, observed everything and gave away nothing, not even to Lector. Melanka had assured him Lector was on the side of the angels and could be trusted. But Evander was a good agent, which means he was careful.

By the end of his second day Evander had decided Lector

was just as Melanka had described. It was at that point Lector entered the office Evander was using and closed the door. He said, “Dr. Evander, please turn off the computer and your communicator.” Evander looked at him quizzically and Lector continued, “I’ve shut off all recording devices in this office.”

Evander picked up his communicator and flipped open its power pack. He reached over and shut off the computer.

Nodding, Lector said, “Thank you. Now, let’s cut to the chase. What is your real assignment—and how is Melanka doing? I’ve been receiving confusing reports from home.”

Evander sighed, “It’s more than just confusing.”

“Melanka?” Lector asked again.

“In trouble. We’re all in trouble. There’s a deep rooted betrayal among our ranks.” Evander looked away considering how to proceed – how much to say. He turned back and studied Lector’s face carefully. “Melanka says you’re one of the good guys—that you are one hundred percent trustworthy.”

With faux humility Lector smiled and said, “Well...”

Evander locked eyes with Lector and asked, “Well—are you?”

“Yes, I am.”

No look-away. He’s telling the truth, or at least he thinks he is. Evander began by filling Lector in on the mess with Anotas employees and the Business and Industry Council’s payola. He told of Cubra’s death and how that came about. He explained the role taken on by the Law and Order Directorate. When Evander was finished, he took a breath and said, “And that’s about it.” *If he’s good he’ll realize I’m leaving out a key piece of information.*

Lector had listened intently, not interrupting or asking questions. He sat quietly for a long moment looking at the table. “This is all very interesting, tragic, and frightening really —but nothing you’ve told me can explain how or why we’ve gotten to this point." He shifted his gaze from the tabletop to Evander. "That either means you don't know what's happening or you're not telling me everything. Now I've been known to gamble occasionally and being a betting man I'd bet it's the latter.

"I know Melanka well. She would not have sent you here if you weren't privy to the deep background. I understand it's possible you've been instructed not to share that information. If you tell me that's the case and give me a dispatch from Melanka explaining my assignment, I'll do whatever I can to help you accomplish your mission. And I'll ask no further questions. So, what's it going to be?"

Amusement tugged at the corners of Evander's mouth. "Okay, it's going to be the whole truth. That was just a little test to see if you're as competent as Melanka seems to think. She said you're good, and indeed you are." With that Evander told of Dr. Althea's and Professor Egan's return after sixty-two annum in space. He conveyed the story about their time with the Beag-Liath and the things they'd been shown. He told about the numerous attempts on their lives by agents acting on behalf of the B&I Council. Finally he told of the exodus from the homeworld by whole hosts of the corporate power-elites and their families.

When Evander was finished, Lector's forlorn expression spoke volumes. "And that brings us full circle doesn't it? That's why you're here. You need to know what's going on with the hybridization of sapiens, and if Ghrain's hybrids are the source of the slave laborers Professor Egan and Dr. Althea claim to have seen."

"That pretty much sums it up—so where do we start?" Dr. Evander asked.

Pointing roughly in the direction of the planet's surface, Lector said, "Down there."

Three days later when Kadeya, Ramuell, Rarus and Samael rode the Rough-Terrain-Vehicle back into the SWA-7 base-camp, Lector's broad smile met them as they pulled into the garage. After introducing everyone to Dr. Evander, Lector asked, "So how are the nefilim observations going?"

Rarus rolled his eyes. Sam spit.

Kadeya said, "I must admit, and I'm not proud of this, but my feelings about what we need to do to resolve this problem are evolving."

Lector looked at her quizzically.

She shrugged and said, "The giants are, simply put, bullies without a shred of empathy or remorse. They routinely throw tantrums when they don't get their way and bludgeon those who antagonize them. Observing those creatures' belligerence forces me to contemplate more immediate solutions."

Ramuell cringed slightly. He turned to Lector and Evander and said, "It's probably too early for dinner, but we had a light lunch on-the-go and I'm starving. Perhaps you'd like to join us for a snack."

"I'm hungry too." Kadeya said. Taking Lector's arm she urged, "Do join us. We'll tell you about our observations."

When they were all seated at the wooden outdoor table, Kadeya launched into an animated description of what they'd observed among the three clans with nefilim.

"So, what are you hoping to accomplish? What exactly is your mission?" Evander asked.

"Chief Science Officer Durela made our assignment clear soon after we arrived at Ghrain-3. We have a couple of the sapiens' generations to make the gigantism mutation go away."

"And how long is that?" Evander asked.

"Their lives are very short. I'd estimate that we only have about fifty annum."

"And if we're not successful," Ramuell added, "the Presidium will deploy more direct measures for eliminating the nefilim. At the time, we were both aghast at that suggestion."

"And now?" prodded Rarus.

Ramuell said, "And now, it's complicated."

"We still believe in our mission," Kadeya answered. "Ultimately the only way to eliminate the mutation is by disrupting the genetic transmission. The thing is, after observing their remorseless brutality, I'm finding it very difficult to surrender one or two sapien generations to entire lives of torture, humiliation and fear. The way the non-giant members of these clans are forced to live is deplorable."

Samael said, "If it were up to me, and if Director Azazel said we needed to take care of this problem quickly, I'd be happy to start at sunrise tomorrow. But that's not likely to happen and right now I've got three days of reports to write. I'd better get started before my memory fails or I fall asleep."

"Right you are," Rarus said. He turned to their guests and said, "Dr. Evander, it was good meeting you, and good to see you again Lector. I hope our attitude hasn't been too shocking."

Evander replied, "Before we came down I read the account of the Blue Rock Canyon incident. So, your attitude isn't a surprise, though I hadn't understood just how volatile the nefilim are."

After Rarus and Samael excused themselves, Lector led the conversation in a new direction. "We need to share some news with you, but first I have to get something off my chest. I'm not who you think I am—or rather my job isn't what you think it is. You think I'm a librarian. Well, I am and I'm a pretty dang good librarian, but that job is just my cover. I'm an Anotas agent. I report directly to Security Chief Melanka. I'm so deep undercover nobody at Ghrain-3 knows I'm an agent."

Kadeya rolled her eyes. "Uhm, perhaps you're not quite as good as you think. I've had my suspicions."

Lector coughed, looked down at the table and said, "Uhm, do I talk in my sleep?"

Kadeya cocked an eyebrow then turned toward Evander, "And you are?"

"I too work for Melanka." He paused considering how to explain. "It's my understanding you've sensed something out of the ordinary is going on, and you're right. There's been quite a dustup within the Anotas ranks. We've been betrayed by tens of thousands of our staff."

"Wha'...what's going on?" Kadeya stammered.

"As it turns out the Business and Industry Council has been...hmm, guess there's no way to sugarcoat it, they've been the conduit of corporate bribery for decades. At least half the Anotas staff are on the take," Evander explained.

"That can't be!" Ramuell exclaimed.

"But it is. The bribery is so pervasive it's become part the institutional culture. Somehow it became acceptable for Anotas staff to receive generous tender-deposits from the B&I Council."

"Why hadn't this come to light before now?" Kadeya asked.

Lector cleared his throat. "Let me take a stab at that. Before now there had never been a massive quid pro quo demanded by the B&I Council's corporate overlords."

Kadeya looked at Evander. "And the fact you've been dispatched to Ghrain-3 means Melanka believes the Serefim Presidium is involved. Gold and silver are the corporations' bread and butter exports from Ghrain, but there's nothing controversial about that."

"So, there must be another more provocative export," Ramuell posited.

"And the first place you came was to the surface." Scratching her chin distractedly, Kadeya turned to Ramuell, "We're sending a lot more hybrids off-world than we had previously thought."

Ramuell squeezed his eyes shut and massaged his temples.

"So, how bad is it back home? And what brought all this to a head?" Kadeya asked.

Evander and Lector exchanged a troubled glance. "To answer your first question, it's a disaster. Melanka had to kill her long-time administrative assistant. As it turns out, Cubra had for many annum been at the heart of B&I Council's scheme to purchase Anotas-Deithe. He was outed by a failed covert operation that resulted in the murder of an Anotas agent."

"And what's happened to Melanka?" Kadeya asked.

"She was forced to seek the protection of the Law and Order Directorate," Evander replied. "She's operating out of a secret Directorate facility and has daily contact with Secretary Liam.

"To answer your question about why this is happening now..." Lector closed his eyes and pinched the bridge of his nose.

Evander coughed and said, "It's an exceedingly strange story." He told Kadeya and Ramuell of two people who were mysteriously found naked on a creek bank just outside of Nexo de Mando. They were taken to the hospital and identified as the team that had been dispatched on a survey mission over sixty annum ago. They had been missing ever since. Cellular ageing tests indicated the long-lost couple had aged less than six kuuk during their sixty annum absence.

Ramuell raked his fingers through his hair. "Now wait a

minute! So you're telling us Mom and Dad are alive, but they didn't age while they were gone. How is that even possible?"

"We're not sure," Evander replied. "And you may be even more skeptical after you hear what your parents had to say in a video-deposition."

Evander proceeded to tell of how something had gone wrong during their 4D jump. No one was certain if they had been kidnapped or rescued by another spacefaring species. Althea and Egan called them the Beag-Liath whom they described as a smallish, grey colored, bipedal species.

Ramuell's jaw dropped. Not only was Evander describing the creatures who had visited the Crow Clan, but Ramuell had actually seen one of these beings with his parents in his *sen*. For some reason he'd never told Kadeya about that *sen* experience.

While Ramuell was becoming more convinced, Kadeya's skepticism ratcheted up as Evander described the misadventures that had befallen her daughter and son-in-law upon their return. She couldn't believe people were actually willing to commit murder just to silence them.

When Evander came to the story's end he looked quizzically at Lector. "Is there anything you'd like to add?"

Lector raised his hands and shook his head. "I suspect they're overwhelmed enough for one evening."

Kadeya took off her colorful beret and slapped it down on the table. "Now that is quite an incredible story. So incredible I'd swear you two have been reading too much science fiction in your off-hours.

"Wait a minute Grandmother," Ramuell interrupted. "There are some things you don't know."

"Actually there are many things none of us know," Evander agreed. "But I'm telling you the truth, and I want you to believe that." He reached in his coat pocket and took out a sheet of paper and laid it on the table between Kadeya and her grandson. They read the short note scrawled in Althea's handwriting.

> *We are alive. We were with the Beag-Liath for almost an annum, which turned out to be over sixty-two of your annum. Since returning we have been in trouble. There are people who want us dead. We will find a way to get to you as soon as we can. We love you beyond words.*

At the bottom of the sheet was a picture of Egan and Althea standing in front of a quadcopter. Tapping his finger on the picture Lector asked, "Do you know what that machine is?"

Kadeya sucked in a sharp breath, "That's a Personnel Transport 220-R4!"

Ramuell studied his grandmother's face, not understanding the significance. Kadeya said, "That model first came off the assembly line only thirteen or fourteen annum ago?"

Lector nodded, "Right—decades after they disappeared."

Ramuell looked back down at the picture and covered his mouth with both hands.

Kadeya whispered, "They **are** alive!" Staring at Evander, she said, "In my first *sen* a man from the homeworld brought us word that Althea and Egan are alive."

CHAPTER FORTY-ONE
OPRIT-ROBIA

THE 4D-INITIATOR SHIP settled gently at the terminal just outside the city of Saorsa on Realta-Gorm 4. When the doors hissed open, Egan took Althea's hand and Rebecca hooked her arm through Danel's as they disembarked. In an effort to look the "tourists" they were pretending to be, all four donned blue-block sunglasses and full brim hats. These were recommended for Domhanians to protect themselves from the blue star's more harmful rays; electromagnetic radiation with wavelengths shorter than 350 nanometres.

Before leaving Domhan-Siol they had spent scores of hours studying everything they could anonymously access about Realta-Gorm through the cyber-library. Rebecca and Danel had been adamant that their research leave no traceable digital trail.

Their studies had led them to believe Saorsa was a lovely little backwater colony nestled along the northern edge of Realta-Gorm's vast hill country. Danel doubted the idyllic picture painted by the information and literature. "If the place is as heavenly as it sounds, it would be overrun by the families of the corporate aristocracy. They'd have ruined it by now." Danel's skepticism was justified, but his reasoning was flawed.

Because there were only fourteen people on their small 4D-ship, there was little greeting hubbub when they disembarked. This gave the four of them an opportunity to hang back and look around before making their way to the security checkpoint.

The Saorsa terminal was not what they had expected. Armed men and women in black uniforms were patrolling both the personnel and cargo docking areas. Rebecca pointed out that all import cargo containers were being opened and inspected.

While they ambled around, a flurry of activity in front of a large 4D-ship caught the foursome's attention. When the vessel's doors opened a group of about thirty extraterrestrial beings hesitantly disembarked. Their heads were round, and the males had hairy faces. Clearly, they were stepping onto this new world with a combination of anxiety and awe.

A contingent of eight Domhanians, or perhaps Realtans would be more accurate, approached the extraterrestrials calmly and gently. They offered earthenware cups of water and tidbits of cooked meats and vegetables that the aliens recognized as food. This resulted in a lot of smiling and animated nodding among both species.

After several minutes, the greeters began ushering the extraterrestrials through a gate and onto a bus. When the aliens had departed Egan, Althea, Rebecca and Danel circled back toward the queue in front of the security office.

The identification and verification process took over two hours. Travel documents were reviewed thoroughly, and luggage was inspected. All arriving travelers also had to undergo a physical examination at the terminal's clinic.

Arranging ground transportation was painless compared

to the security clearance ordeal. They had been issued Planetary Pass Cards, which were scanned by the rail-service vending machines. The appropriate credits were auto-deducted from the tender accounts they had each been required to open with a minimum deposit of 18,000 Domhanian Standard Credits.

As the foursome rode toward the city they saw through the train's clear acrylic walls that Saorsa was not a metropolis by Domhan-Siol standards, nor was it a sleepy little hamlet. The streets bustled with purposeful activity. It was almost as if the Realtans were on a mission of some kind. What exactly that mission was couldn't be easily discerned, but it exuded a sense of something vaguely militaristic.

Upon entering the hosteller condominium, they were struck by its quaint, attractive floor plan and furnishings. The foursome made their way to the kitchen and were impressed with the well-stocked refrigerator and pantry.

When someone knocked on the condo's ornate wooden front door, Danel told his companions to act as though they were preparing lunch. He cautiously opened the door; keeping it between himself and the unexpected visitors. Two women stood on the stoop and introduced themselves as "greeters" from the Saorsa Bureau of Tourism. After the initial hellos, it was clear from the ladies' body language they expected to be invited in. Assuming that might be the planet's cultural norm, Danel hesitantly bade them enter.

When the door was closed, the shorter of the two women called into the kitchen, "Dr. Althea, Professor Egan, Agent Rebecca, would you mind joining us?"

Rebecca popped the screen off her foliopad and removed a

tiny solid-projectile weapon, which she stuffed into her pants pocket. She led her two companions through the swinging door into the condo's den.

The group stood on a beautiful woolen area rug that covered much of the den's hardwood floor. Danel said, "Obviously you know our names and probably why we're here, but we have no idea who you are." He scratched his cheek and added, "And I don't really believe you are 'greeters' from the Bureau of Tourism."

The shorter woman answered, "In fact we are greeters, but we don't work for the Bureau of Tourism. We are members of an interplanetary task force committed to the manumission of non-Domhanian laborers."

Egan and Althea exchanged a glance.

The other woman said "My name is Imamiah and my colleague is Nanzy." Standing at over two metres, Imamiah's appearance was striking and not just because of her height. In fact, one would be hard pressed to articulate why she was so stunning. Looking at Althea and Egan, she continued, "We cannot begin to tell you how honored we feel to have you with us."

Rebecca released the weapon and removed her hand from her pocket. She said, "I'm sorry, but I'm totally confused. We don't know you or what you're doing here. How is it you know who we are?"

A smile flashed across Nanzy's face. "We'd heard you, Agent Rebecca, would not mince words—and that's a good thing." Looking over at the chairs and sofa she suggested, "Perhaps we could sit down, and we'll tell you our story and try to answer your questions."

Althea gestured toward the seats while Egan went into the kitchen to retrieve an assortment of beverages and snacks.

Rebecca leaned forward in the hardwood armchair she had chosen, slapped her hands on her knees and said, "Well...?"

"Okay, obviously we know too much about you to be the kind of greeters one might expect from a Bureau of Tourism," Imamiah began. "We are members of Oprit-Robia. It's our organization's leaders whom you would have eventually wanted to meet. I believe it's safe to say your supporters on Domhan-Siol have learned of our people's disapproval of the slave trade."

"By 'our people'—you mean your organization?" Danel asked.

"Not just Oprit-Robia. There are more than five hundred thousand Domhanians on Realta-Gorm. Of that number you'd be hard pressed to find dozen who support the notion of hybridizing and breeding a species in order to feed our corporations' appetites for cheap labor. Oprit-Robia is our—hmm, how should I describe it?"

Nanzy said, "Oprit-Robia is an aggressive expression of our opposition to the breeding and selling of sentient beings."

"And what does that mean?" Althea asked.

"Most Oprit-Robia members are or have been Anotas employees," Nanzy continued. "When Anotas first dispatched scientists and engineers to study the feasibility of colonizing Realta-Gorm 4, it was believed this planet might be a bountiful addition to our agricultural production programs." She gestured toward the lush greenery outside the window, "Plants thrive in the light of the blue star. Early explorers identified large swaths of fertile areas where food and fiber crops could be raised in ways that were both ecologically sound and profitable. Not long after the initial research reports were submitted two medium size agricultural corporations arrived and began tilling soils and building processing and transport facilities. That development was expected and welcomed.

"However, both corporations soon began importing extraterrestrial laborers. The workers were not provided with the protections from the harmful rays of the blue star that we consider minimally necessary. As it turns out, these beings are not as susceptible to the negative effects of this star's shorter wavelengths as are Domhanians, but they're not immune either. Within a few annum, the incidence of malignancies among the workforce began to alarm our medical professionals. Our administrators asked for maps of the aliens' genome. The corporations responded by clamming up.

"It became apparent the farms were using these laborers while young and productive, but when they became too feeble to work they were discarded and replaced." She held up both hands, "Now understand, at that time we didn't know their life expectancy. Heck, we didn't even know where they were coming from."

"But what we did know was that this arrangement was just wrong!" interrupted Imamiah. "Within a decade our administrators began trying to take action, but the complaints they lodged with the powers-that-be on the homeworld fell on deaf ears.

"By the time we tried to implement regulatory control of all immigration, including extraterrestrials, there were four agricultural corporations operating on Realta-Gorm. When access to the Saorsa 4D terminal was limited, the corporations simply expanded their own 4D facilities and sidestepped our efforts."

"Sounds like a difficult situation," Althea observed.

"It was," Nanzy agreed. "And a resistance movement emerged among the Anotas rank and file. Most of the activists were engineers and scientists, support staff and maintenance workers. But almost without exception Realta-Gorm's Anotas administrators supported our efforts.

"What pushed the movement past the tipping point was when the corporations began beefing up their security teams with paramilitary units. That crossed an invisible line. Public interest in our principles and our efforts exploded, and Oprit-Robia was born."

"Our early endeavors were rather feeble," Imamiah added. "We liberated some sapien-hybrids and disrupted the transport of some products. But it was our administrators who came up with a plan for more meaningful action.

"Now this is an important point, given your mission. What we did next was violent, but it was not insurrection. Rather it was a legal use of force to reassert Anotas-Deithe authority over transports to and from this planet.

"Nine annum ago Anotas forces raided every single 4D-Initiator facility on the planet at exactly the same time. We jammed all communications—and I mean all! That was the most controversial aspect of our plan because we knew it would result in some injuries and perhaps fatalities."

"Quadcopter crashes and the like," Danel observed.

"Correct."

"And?" Danel asked.

Imamiah sighed, "There were nine incidents resulting in sixteen deaths and a score of injuries; several were quite serious. This was worse than we'd anticipated, and it was not our proudest moment."

"But you were able to secure the facilities," Egan observed.

Imamiah sat up straighter and replied, "Yes we were. Our troops suffered only one fatality, and a couple hundred minor wounds and injuries.

"We immediately destroyed some parts of all of the docking facilities to prevent any landings by paramilitary reinforcements. We dismantled some of the infrastructure for other uses, but even if our need for haste hadn't been an issue, recycling or reuse of their equipment was impractical—in the end, we just blew-up their 4-D ports."

"What about the corporate employees?" Rebecca asked.

"Interrogated, but no matter how contrite they may have seemed, not a single one was given the option to remain on the planet," Nanzy answered. "Over a four kuuk period we allowed the corporations to deploy two ships per day to our docking facility in Saorsa to retrieve their personnel."

Althea asked, "And what about the sapien-hybrids?"

"They were a dilemma—no, that's a misstatement. They **are** a dilemma." Nanzy replied. "After exposure to our culture and technologies they couldn't be returned to Ghrain-3." She bit her lip. "They have been relocated to large swaths of land near the southern pole where the sun's rays are not nearly so harmful."

"But these beings should never have been removed from their homeworld," Imamiah interjected.

The group sat quietly for a few moments. Danel asked, "May I change the subject?" Everyone looked at him expectantly. "I'd like to ask how you knew about us. Clearly we were expected. Minutes after we arrived, you showed up at our door and knew our names."

Nanzy gave Danel a tight lipped nod before answering. "Over the last six annum we've had several opportunities to transfer Oprit-Robia members to jobs on Domhan-Siol and Ghrain-3."

Turning toward Althea and Egan she added, "We've also placed people on other planets, including Froitas. Though only a small cadre of people are involved, our information gathering network is rather sophisticated. We know the two of you went missing for over sixty annum and during that time you traveled with another spacefaring species. We also know you have been hunted relentlessly since your return, which can only mean you have information that is utterly damning for the slave traders."

Rebecca said, "So, you have access to classified information."

Nanzy groaned quietly and said, "It's our mission to disrupt the slave trade. Toward that end we gather all the information we can about the corporations involved with the industry. Obviously, in that effort we frequently come across classified information. In your case, it was a woman working at a corporate office on the homeworld who passed information to our agent about your trip to Realta-Gorm. Our agent arrived here with that information just four days ago."

Althea gasped, "So the corporate thugs are already on our tail, or may already be here!"

Holding up an open hand, Imamiah said, "Now wait a minute. A corporate employee had access to that information and shared it with our agent. We can therefore assume it's likely some of those thugs, as you so aptly call them, know you're here. But because we so tightly regulate all traffic through the only operational 4D terminal on the planet, the chances are nil that any arrived here before you. Now, are they going to try to pursue you? The answer to that is probably yes. Thus we've redoubled our scrutiny of everyone arriving at Saorsa."

Egan scoffed, "So they find some way to bribe one of the dozen people on this planet who support the slavery business —they pay one of those folks an assassin's fee."

Imamiah chuckled, "My reference to the dozen slavery supporters was facetious, but I get your point. It's more likely they'd try to dispatch a small 4D craft that doesn't require a terminal."

"Even if they try that," Nanzy interjected, "we have thousands of energy tracker satellites orbiting the planet. **All** 4D energy signatures to and from our world are identified and tracked. But if you'd feel more comfortable, we will assign you a security detail."

Egan looked at Althea then back to Nanzy and said, "Not sure I want to give up that much privacy but let us think about it."

"The point may be moot anyway," Imamiah said. "When we first learned of your journey here, we decided to just let your visit play out as you intended. In other words, we were going to let you find us rather than initiating the first contact with you. That plan changed the next day when one of our people from Ghrain-3 arrived here with rather startling news."

Althea blanched. "Are Ramuell and Kadeya okay?!"

"Melanka recently dispatched an agent on an information gathering mission to Ghrain," Imamiah replied.

"Yes, we know him," Egan said. "Dr. Evander."

Imamiah nodded. "And we have reason to believe that his cover may have been blown. If so, Kadeya might be implicated through her relationship with Lector."

Now the color drained from Egan's face.

Nanzy quickly added, "We believe there's a way for you to help, but it would mean going to Ghrain-3 rather than returning home."

"What can we do?" Egan asked.

Imamiah looked down at her bottled drink then back at Egan and Althea. "It seems your friends, the ones you call Beag-Liath, have intervened on Ghrain-3." Noting the couples' puzzled expressions she added, "Oh, on the side of the angels to be sure. We need them to know they have many Domhanian allies, and you are our most logical emissaries given that you two are likely the only Domhanians they know."

CHAPTER FORTY-TWO
BOOGEYMEN EVERYWHERE

RAMUELL AND KADEYA wanted privacy to discuss the revelations shared by Drs. Evander and Lector. Ramuell asked Azazel if they might drag cots into his office and spend the night in there. Azazel was a bit confused by the odd request but sensed it would be best to ask no questions.

After settling in their temporary bedroom, Ramuell and Kadeya took seats on the workbench stools. They stared at each other in disbelief. Naturally, they were thrilled beyond words that Althea and Egan had returned, but they were also mortified by the assassination attempts.

Ramuell told Kadeya about how extraterrestrials had visited the Crow Clan and used sophisticated medical technologies to treat the clanspeople's wounds. Kadeya asked several questions and agreed that the beings who had treated the Crow were almost certainly not Domhanian.

They moved over to the cots and sat down. After removing their boots Ramuell said hesitantly, "And there's more." He launched into the story of his *sen* meeting with his parents. He told of the slave labor at the mining facility and that the slaves were likely from Ghrain-3. He reminded Kadeya that this *sen* had occurred before he'd laid eyes on any sapien-hybrids of Ghrain-3.

Ramuell slid his boots under the cot. "And I'm not done yet. In my *sen*, Mother and Father were accompanied by a grey colored being. It had big eyes and a head that was quite large in proportion to its body. Live births are not likely among that species. They probably gestate in an egg of some sort. Their bodies are too small and thin to have a birth canal large enough to accommodate those heads. My parent's companion had long arms and long thin hands with three fingers and an opposing thumb. Mother explained they had been traveling with these beings she called the Beag-Liath."

"And you remember her using those exact words in your *sen*?" Kadeya asked.

"Yes ma'am. It's the same..."

"...the same name your mother wrote in the note," Kadeya said. Knowing each other so well, Kadeya and Ramuell often finished each other's sentences.

"When I told Azazel of my *sen* experience, he had me prepare a written report. In it I stated that my parents had called these beings Beag-Liath. Obviously, I hadn't seen Mother's note at the time I wrote that report."

Kadeya flopped back on her cot. When Ramuell stood to undress Kadeya said, "Impossible."

"What's impossible?" Ramuell asked.

"It's impossible that all this is a matter of coincidence. These beings manipulated your *sen* in some way in order to arrange a meeting with your parents. There simply is no other plausible explanation."

Both of them lay awake for a long time before sleep finally laid its claim.

The next morning Ramuell and Kadeya met Evander and Lector at the kitchen dome for a late breakfast. Ramuell retold the story of his last visit with the Crow Clan and how the clanspeople's injuries had been treated by beings who matched his parent's description of the Beag-Liath.

"For whatever reason, it seems they have chosen to intervene," Lector observed. "We don't know what their sense of time might be and it's possible they've lost patience waiting for your parents to resolve the slave trade issue."

"You might be right," Kadeya said. "They seem to have a special interest in the sapiens of Ghrain-3...and if they have a stake in this game, it seems they've upped the ante."

"So it seems," Evander agreed. "And since I'm on an intelligence gathering mission I believe I must visit the Crow Clan."

Ramuell explained that Blue Rock canyon was inaccessible by ground or air transportation and the hike in and out was strenuous.

"Ahh, so you're worried about us old folks," Kadeya teased.

In fact he was, but he hedged, "No, no—just want you to understand that you'll need your best hiking boots and several pairs of socks."

Azazel was not happy about their proposal to trek back into the canyon; especially given that Rarus was the only security officer he had available to accompany them. He argued against the trip for at least an hour. After meeting privately with Kadeya that afternoon, Azazel relented on the condition that he would be joining the party – though he absolutely did not relish the prospect of revisiting the scene of his granddaughter's death.

Azazel knew he was not fluent enough with the Crow language to serve as Evander's interpreter, but he was unwilling to expose Dr. Lilith to the dangers of another trek into the canyon.

Soon after they arrived in Blue Rock his ear grew accustomed to the clan's dialect. He was able to understand what was being said when the clanspeople spoke slowly and directly to him. *My imperfect mastery of the language is just going to have to be good enough.*

The sun was almost at its zenith on their second day in the canyon when they heard the clatter of falling rocks. Using his binoculars Rarus reported four Domhanians were descending the northside trail.

Azazel was worried about the unexpected visitors and kept a close watch on their progress.

Kadeya was also watching the Domhanians' with her handheld telescope. Suddenly she said, "Oh my gosh! Durela is with them."

"Really!" Azazel exclaimed. Borrowing Kadeya's telescope he studied the descending group. "The three men accompanying her are armed."

"What the heck is going on?" Kadeya wondered aloud.

"I have absolutely no idea, but if they bear us ill will, we don't have the fire power to take them on. Rarus, go find a hiding spot with a good view of that clearing." He pointed to the meadow just upstream from the path leading to the Clan's caves. If you see me take my cap off, blast us with wide-field sonic stun. Knock us all out! Ramuell, you go with him. If we have to resort to that, Rarus will need help disarming and binding our guests before they awaken."

"How long should we stay holed up?" Rarus asked.

"Not sure—if everything's okay, how should I signal you?"

"Uhm—dust the knees of your pants off with both hands. We'll be able to see that clearly."

"Good, that'll work, it'll be obvious but not too obvious," Azazel agreed.

Rarus said, "Boss, we're smart to take these precautions, but this isn't an ambush. If it were, they would surely be more stealthy coming down the trail." Just then another rock was kicked loose and came crashing down the steep wall of the canyon.

Azazel chuckled, "Yeah, I see what you mean."

Half an hour later Azazel and Kadeya met Durela and her three escorts in the middle of the meadow. "Durela, I'm shocked and worried about seeing you here." Azazel said as they approached.

When they were face-to-face, Durela tapped Azazel's palm and with a little smirk said, "It's always a pleasure to see you too." Then a darkness flitted across her face. She turned to Kadeya and offered a palm. "Kadeya, I hope your adventure has been going well."

"Very well. We're learning a lot," she said gesturing toward Lector and Evander, who were sitting in the shade of trees at the meadow's edge.

Durela waved her escorts up and introduced them. With each introduction Ipos, Trey, and Marc offered their palms to both Azazel and Kadeya. "That's a good sign," Rarus whispered to Ramuell as they watched from their hideout. "Everything is probably fine, but we'll sit tight until Azazel gives us the signal."

After the introductions Durela turned back to Azazel and said, "You're right to be worried." Shifting her eyes to Kadeya, "In fact, both of you should be—but even more so your friends over there in the shade."

Without even inquiring about the nature of the threat, Azazel asked, "How much time do we have?"

"You probably have a good deal of time. That may even be the case for Kadeya and Ramuell, but the good Doctors need to be ready to go within an hour."

"So we have enough time for you to fill us in on what's happening?" Azazel asked. He noticed two of Durela's escorts exchange a nervous glance. "Or maybe an hour isn't enough time."

"Not even close, but I can provide enough information for you to make whatever decisions you must to get yourselves to safety. After you're out of the canyon you'll need to think through what course to pursue long-term," Durela said.

To jog Azazel's memory Kadeya said, "I hope Ramuell and Rarus will be back soon."

"Oh yeah, I'd forgotten they were gone." Azazel reached down and brushed the dust off the knees of his pants. "They should be back pretty quickly."

He looked back up at Durela, "I take it a horde of demons has broken loose."

"That's why we're here."

"Let's go over to our camp and get you folks something to eat and drink. Lector and Evander can pack their gear while you give us an abridged version of the situation."

Ramuell and Rarus waited until the group had seated themselves before walking into camp. Ramuell said, "Chief Durela! It's a shock seeing you way down here. What's going on?"

"I was just getting ready to explain," Durela replied.

As they stepped over to take a seat on a log, Rarus and Ramuell noticed that Lector and Evander were stuffing clothes and gear into their packs.

Durela said, "I don't even know where to begin. Anotas-

Deithe has imploded. People are choosing sides, but it's not a bifurcated situation—more like a hexagon." Shaking her head slightly, "There's not enough time to get into all the different factions. In my opinion we're tacking on a very dangerous course. It's also my opinion Grandmaster Elyon has gone completely rogue. Unfortunately, most of the Serefim Presidium are so enthralled with him they can't seem to see what's happening."

"He's made most of them extremely rich," Azazel observed.

"Well that might explain the infatuation, but he's ordered a slew of detention warrants with wording that could be interpreted to mean 'dead or alive.'"

"Why would he go to such extremes?" Kadeya asked.

"As you know, the Serefim Presidium was for centuries more or less owned by the corporations profiting from the Ghrain-3 ventures," Durela explained. "Several decades ago Elyon began a process of turning the tables. Now the Presidium owns the corporate interests. A business plan cannot be implemented on Ghrain without the Presidium's approval."

"Is the flashpoint the use of sapien-hybrids as laborers?" Azazel asked.

"Yeah, that's the crux of the matter. They probably could've gotten away with breeding a species of slave laborers had they not gotten greedy; had they just kept them on Ghrain-3. But no! They had to export their working pets all over the damned galaxy. The slavers have been exposed and a lot of people back home are hopping mad. But there are a lot of other people who actually support the idea of using non-Domhanians as slaves."

"The slavers have been exposed?" Azazel questioned.

"I don't know the details about how that happened. I do know it has something to do with your parents' return," Durela said looking at Ramuell.

"I also know that Anotas employees have formed a manumission paramilitary organization on at least one of our colonized planets. They have dispatched raiding parties to rescue sapien-hybrids from numerous worksites. If the worksite security forces resist, the raiding parties respond with overwhelming force. It seems they're well-armed and well-trained."

Kadeya asked, "Did the raids push Elyon over the top?"

"The raids coupled with what's happening back home." Durela looked at Evander and Lector and continued, "As you gentlemen know, Security Chief Melanka is leading a coalition of Anotas personnel who have taken a decidedly anti-Business and Industry Council position. Elyon and the corporate bigwigs here on Ghrain are certain Melanka is orchestrating the efforts of the raiding parties."

"That's just not true," Evander interjected. "Things on Domhan-Siol are far too chaotic for that."

Durela said, "It doesn't matter if it's true or not. Grandmaster Elyon and his supporters are seeing boogeymen everywhere. They've learned Melanka dispatched you to Ghrain-3." Turning to Lector, "And because you were his primary contact it didn't take Serefim Security long to chase down your connection with Melanka. This information was taken to Elyon early yesterday and he immediately began issuing Warrants of Detention. The list is pretty long, and your names are at the top.

"A Serefim Security squadron has already been dispatched to SWA-7. No doubt they've learned where to find you. It wouldn't surprise me to see them begin their descent into the canyon at any time."

She turned to Kadeya and continued, "It will be learned you came to Blue Rock with these gentlemen, so it's likely you'll all be painted with the traitor's brush and accused of rebelling against Serefim authority."

"And Ramuell?" Kadeya asked.

She tilted her head and said, "He is a minor—I'm just not sure. Because they have vilified his parents, whom they blame for most of these problems, it's possible he isn't safe either."

"And what about you, Durela?" Azazel asked.

"It's already known the four of us are on the surface."

Ipos interjected, "But we've tried to keep secret what we're doing down here. We filed a false flight plan and en route reported a problem with our global positioning locator."

Durela pointed at Lector and Evander and continued, "However, given that you two gentlemen are going to escape their clutches, the seeds of doubt about my loyalties will have been sown. I suspect a whole bunch of us will become persona non grata."

"Perhaps even cast out by the Grandmaster," Azazel observed. He had no idea just how prophetic his words were.

When Azazel went to speak to Ru Ta, he endeavored to controvert the Clan's widely held belief that all "long-heads" were "good angels." He tried to impress upon Ru Ta and the clanspeople who were listening that a group of "bad angels" were coming to the canyon.

After several attempts to explain the situation, Azazel realized that even if his facility with the Crow language was far more advanced, he'd still be unable to help Ru Ta apprehend the notion that some long-heads were bad. Ru Ta just laughed and waved his hand back-and-forth, acting as though Azazel was making a joke. At least Azazel was able to convince the Clan to move back to their caves.

While Azazel was speaking with Ru Ta, Ramuell played

nearby with Shiya. He understood at some level their bond was in part because he was with her at the moment she was orphaned. But he also felt there was something more to their connection than just that, though he did not embrace the notion of destiny.

After he had done his best, Azazel walked over to stand by Ramuell. They watched the Clan's half-hearted departure from the river camp. Shaking his head, Ramuell said, "I don't have a good feeling about this."

"Me neither, my friend, me neither," Azazel said as he turned and walked away.

———

The north canyon trail was steeper and more difficult to traverse than the southside trail. Lector and Evander were both in good physical condition for men their age, but they were over four hundred-annum-old. The security team members lightened their load by carrying some of the older gentlemen's gear. Still, the steepness of the slope and the treacherous footing necessitated frequent rests.

Ipos, the team leader, kept a close eye on the southside trail. As they neared the rim, he pulled-up short and yanked the telescope from its case attached to his backpack shoulder strap. He scanned the opposing trail some eight hundred metres across the canyon. "There's a squad of at least a dozen people making their way down the south trail. Trey, Marc, your eyes are younger than mine. What do you see?"

Marc and Trey pulled their own scopes and studied the group. Without taking the scope away from his eye Trey said, "I cannot make out insignias, but I don't think the uniforms are standard Anotas issue. They are all armed."

"Do you think they've seen us?" Durela asked.

"They don't seem to be looking across the chasm," Trey said. "They're focused on the trail at their feet, and when they stop walking they're looking down into the canyon, not over here."

Ipos removed his hat and scratched the scalp hidden beneath his mane of thick, curly hair. "Okay, we're almost out —I'd estimate about thirty more vertical metres. We need to move very, very quietly the rest of the way; no stumbles; no dislodged stones. We need to be absolutely certain of our footing with each step. We want to allow about twenty metres space between each of us. It's much more difficult to spot individuals than a moving group." He slid his telescope into its carrying case and said, "Trey, you take the lead, Marc you follow him, and I'll take the sweep. Everyone else spread out between us."

When they emerged from the canyon, Trey led Marc, Durela, Lector and Evander well away from the rim before stopping. He wanted to be certain they were beyond the line of sight of anyone in the canyon below.

As Ipos approached the last few metres of trail before emerging from the canyon he felt the hair on the back of his neck bristle. He unslung his weapon and ducked behind the cliff face just below the trailhead. Hiding, he cautiously studied the open area where his team had gathered. Though he saw nothing untoward, he couldn't shake the sense of menace.

Marc and Trey were looking back down the trail, aware that he hadn't topped out of the canyon yet. Suddenly people came crashing through the brush shouting, "Drop your weapons! Drop your weapons!"

In less than a second, Marc and Trey had taken defensive positions in front Durela, Lector and Evander; just as they'd been trained to do. They did not drop their weapons. Out of the corner of his eye, Ipos saw one of the charging assailants shoulder a blaster. He ducked. She fired. In an instant the sonic blast leveled all five people. Ipos was far enough below the escarpment for the disabling wave of energy to sail harmlessly over his head.

The cliff's caprock was harder than the layers it sheltered. Numerous caves had eroded into the softer stone beneath the rim. Ipos backtracked down the trail a few metres then shinnied laterally across the cliff face, not caring about the noise of the scree he kicked off in the process. The commotion coming from the activity above masked the sounds of the falling stones. He found a shallow grotto with a flat floor.

Soon he heard people on the canyon rim talking. A couple of men walked at least a hundred metres down the trail before turning back. Ipos was able to back far enough into the little cave to remain hidden. As they walked back up the trail they seemed to stumble over every other stone in the path, sending showers of pebbles tumbling downward.

They did not try to search the caves on either side of the trail. Clinging to a rock face and trying to scurry mouselike into the caves was an intimidating maneuver, especially for people who had been living in the artificial gravity of a spinning torus in outer space. Ipos was thankful for his pursuers' lack of confidence or ineptitude, whichever was the case.

As their voices receded, Ipos heard the sounds of people being dragged away. He had no doubt what that meant, but knew he was so outgunned there was no possibility for a successful rescue. He sat, listened, and worried.

About ten minutes later he heard shuttlecraft motors warming up. His frustration boiled as he listened to three shuttles launch themselves into the heavens.

For at least fifteen minutes Ipos strained to hear every sound. What he would have given for an amplification device. His team had brought one with them, but it was in Trey's backpack. Slowly and cautiously he crept back out of the cave toward the trail. About halfway across the span his foot slipped and dislodged a couple of paddleball size stones. To him they sounded like explosions each time they hit and bounced off the cliff face below. He scampered back into his hideout.

Again he sat silently trying to stretch his auditory senses out to the edge of his innate ability. After a few minutes of this intensely focused energy, Ipos realized he might be hearing head noises – tinnitus. He became uncertain about whether what he was "hearing" was real or not.

Exhaling his irritation, Ipos cinched his weapon on firmly, and peeked out of the cave. This time he studied the footing and hand holds more carefully before setting out on the perilous fifteen-metre journey. When he reached the firm footing of the canyon trail he wiped nervous sweat from his forehead.

Cautiously he climbed the last few metres to the top and peeked out across the plateau. He watched for several minutes and saw no movement other than a few birds. In a low crouch he crept away from the trailhead. After a few steps he stood and dashed across the clearing to a nearby copse of trees. Slowly, Ipos turned 360° searching for anything that looked even slightly out of the ordinary.

There was no sign of the armed force that had absconded with his party. He was distressed to see they had come in two shuttlecraft but departed in three. They'd taken his shuttle. He was stranded.

He had studied the area maps well enough to know which direction he needed to hike to get to the SWA-7 basecamp. That entailed the long hike back down into Blue Rock canyon and the arduous climb out the southside trail. Far more vexing was the armed force that lay between him and the canyon's southern rim.

When Ipos searched the area he marveled at the quick wittedness of his teammates. In the seconds between being ordered to drop their weapons and being disabled by the sonic blast, Trey and Marc had managed to unclip and drop their water bottles. Both bottles were a bit over half full. He also had about half a bottle. With careful usage, he had enough water for a day and a half. *By then surely I'll find a way to reach the river and replenish.*

———

Azazel, Ramuell, Kadeya and Rarus had broken camp before the Serefim Security squad began their descent into Blue Rock. Perching their telescopes on boulders in a rockslide that fanned halfway across the canyon floor, they focused on three points along the southside trail. They saw the squad arrive at the rim. When the force arrived at the second focal point, Rarus counted fourteen well-armed people. Each carried both shoulder and handheld weapons. "That doesn't look like a hospitality party sent with friendly greetings from the Grandmaster."

"Yeah, and fourteen people with that much firepower seems like a tad bit of overkill just to detain Doctors Evander and Lector," Azazel observed.

Seeing Kadeya's face blanch white as the soapstone on the river's edge, Ramuell asked, "Grandmother, are you all right?"

"I'm worried sick about Lector," she said gazing up at the canyon's northside trail. She had an overwhelming sense of foreboding.

When she leaned down and put her hands on her knees, Ramuell thought she was going to vomit. He rubbed her back gently.

After about a minute she stood up, took a deep breath and said, "I suppose we better be making our way to the hideout."

Azazel and Rarus exchanged worried frowns. Rarus said, "Kadeya's right. It is a bit of a hike."

Rarus led them to the shallow ford they had crossed several times in the last day and a half. The banks were blazed with numerous sets of boot tracks. They waded a couple hundred metres up-stream on a shallow shoal. At that point they turned north up a small, rocky side stream. They hiked up the bottom of the creek for almost a kilometre to the point where the rivulet had initially forked away from the river's main channel.

Being careful not to leave tracks, they exited the stream where the riverbank was strewn with sizeable boulders. After hopping from rock to rock for almost a hundred metres, they turned up an animal trail that ascended steeply from the river bank to a hunting blind clansmen had made by piling flat stones. The rocks enclosed an 'L' shaped notch at the foot of a fifteen metre high cliff. Even game animals, with their sharply honed senses, could not see hunters hiding behind the low wall. Azazel and Rarus felt confident a security team from the orbiter some four hundred kilometres overhead would lack the skills necessary to find this hidey hole.

Sitting with their backs against the cliff, Azazel said, "Look, we don't know who they are or anything about their mission, except that they intend to detain Lector and Evander. We need to get a look at them before deciding our next move."

Of the four people holed-up in the blind, Rarus had the best skills navigating the planet's wild country. He would, using all his stealth, sneak the one kilometre back down canyon to observe the armed force.

Two hours later Azazel was worried. He had hoped Rarus would return before dark.

When Kadeya heard a splash she pressed her finger to her

lips, quieting her companions. A couple of minutes later Rarus climbed over the blind's rock wall and said, "Well that was enough noise to wake the dead."

"I didn't hear anything, but grandmother did," Ramuell said.

"Ahh, as I was pulling myself out of the creek I slipped and fell on my butt in the water."

Azazel said, "I'm sure we're too far away for them to have heard anything."

"Oh I'm not worried. If they heard me they'd not be able to distinguish the noise from a river mammal or a fish splashing —just glad I wasn't so sloppy when less than a hundred metres from their camp."

"So what did you learn?" Azazel asked.

"That they're not friendlies. They have Dr. Lilith with them, and she's not here willingly. They have a cable hobble around her ankles, and she's wearing a tracking device."

"That means they've seized SWA-7. I've got to get back there—somehow," Azazel worried aloud.

Kadeya added, "It also means they need Lilith's language skills. They need a translator, which implies they're here for the Crow Clan, not Lector and Evander."

"Or maybe the Crow Clan in addition to Lector, Evander, **and** Durela," Azazel suggested.

As the nighttime temperature dropped they activated two chem-heat sticks. They'd been huddled around the heat sticks for several minutes when Rarus said, "There's another south-side trail several kilometres downriver. But topping out at that point puts us so far from SWA-7 as to be an impractical exit plan."

"Perhaps we should call for pick-up by RTVs or a quad-copter?" Ramuell suggested.

"Nope!" Rarus replied immediately. "We know the basecamp has been compromised and at least one person taken hostage. We cannot communicate with our staff until we have a better sense of their situation."

"Which means our eyes on them before they have eyes on us," Azazel observed.

"Right."

Kadeya rubbed her forehead. "Given this turn of events, we cannot be certain Lector, Durela, and the others got away cleanly."

"And even if they did, where could they have gone?" Azazel wondered.

After a moment Rarus grunted and said, "Uhm, there's one more thing boss."

Azazel turned slowly to look at the security officer.

Returning the director's gaze he said, "Ru Ta didn't exactly take your advice."

"Dammit, I knew he wasn't taking me seriously!"

"Nah, he was laughing and waving you off," Ramuell said. "So what's the clan's situation?"

"It looks like most of them are still up at the caves, but several, including Ru Ta are at their river camp." Rarus paused, thinking about how to describe what he sensed. "They aren't being held hostage. There are no physical restraints, but I have a gut feeling these guys are planning to march the Clan out of here."

"And their weapons?" Azazel asked.

"They're making no effort to hide or secure them. In fact, they're laid out as if on display," Rarus explained.

"So, they're already using them," Ramuell stated flatly. "The Clan knows how powerful those devices are. They saw and felt the sonic blasts' devastating effect. Those weapons are magical wands. They're god-sticks." He paused thinking for a moment. "The Clan will do as they're told, and our kinsmen will never need to press a trigger."

Azazel rubbed the side of his face as he looked up into the night sky. His companions could almost see thoughts pulsing at his temples. "We have one thing going for us."

"What's that?" Kadeya asked.

"The language barrier; the soldiers can't communicate with the Crow Clan. As you said, that's why Lilith was forced to come."

Kadeya said, "Ahh, which also means they don't know how faithfully she's interpreting what's being said."

"We need to get a message to her somehow."

Rarus said, "But how? I didn't recognize any of the militia. I've been in T-Taxiarch torus often enough to be familiar with most of the security personnel assigned to Ghrain-3. I'm almost sure these guys are recent arrivals. I don't even think they went through the acclimatization process. They're too fatigued and lethargic. Now we don't know how many days they've been down here, but heck Dr. Kadeya, you're doing better than they seem to be."

Startled, Ramuell asked "Grandmother, how many days has it been?"

She blew a lip-trill. "Today was my tenth."

"And you were cleared for an undecim?" Azazel asked.

"Yep. Doc would want me back upstairs tomorrow," Kadeya admitted.

Azazel sniffed and said, "You understand that's not likely to happen."

"Of course, but I'm feeling fine. I've been taking the supplements Doc gave me and have felt no ill effects of having to urinate so much. I've taken naps every day except today. I think I'm good for several more days—as if we have any choice."

Ramuell and Azazel glanced at each other and knew in an instant they were sharing an unspoken thought. *Because of her connection with Lector, she might already have been charged with conspiracy. In order to survive, Kadeya may have to surrender herself to incarceration on the orbiter.*

Azazel looked away and said, “It’s clear these guys have been authorized to completely bypass my authority.”

“If that’s so, we have to wonder why?” Kadeya worried.

“And we have to wonder what the hell is going on up there?” Rarus said, pointing skyward.

Meanwhile, Durela and her companions had regained consciousness cuffed to a steel table bolted to the floor of a cell on the orbiting station. They were not gagged. As each person awoke Lector asked about their condition.

When Durela tried to initiate a conversation about their ordeal, Evander shushed her with a soft, “Shh, shh, shh.” He leaned over and whispered to Trey, who was cuffed next to him, “We aren’t gagged for a reason. They’re listening.” He pointed with his nose for the agent to pass the message along to the next person bound to the table’s tie-downs. By remaining silent, the group gave away nothing to their Watchers.

CHAPTER FORTY-THREE
THE DISTRACTION

IT WAS A LONG, fitful night in the hunting blind. At first light, Rarus broke a couple of chem-heat sticks and warmed water for four cups of tea. With enough sweetener the tea made the protein breakfast biscuits almost palatable.

"Each time I woke-up last night I had these nagging doubts about Ru Ta," Azazel said after taking a sip.

"Me too," Rarus grunted. "Since he didn't accept your explanation about bad angels, he may think nothing of saying something about the other long-heads camping just a short way up-canyon."

"Don't you think Lilith would realize what that meant and intentionally misinterpret?" Ramuell asked.

"Probably," Azazel answered. "But Ru Ta might insist on introducing the two groups of angels and lead them up here anyway. We can't hike out in the light of day. It's almost certain someone would see us."

After a few seconds Rarus said, "Been thinking about that, and I'm not sure that matters much. If we could get halfway out before being seen, they'd never catch us—unless they've made a miraculous recovery from the fatigue they were showing last night."

"Okaayy, but how do we get that far up the trail without being seen?" Azazel asked.

"Distraction," Rarus replied.

Within the hour they'd packed their gear and moved to a location about a hundred metres from where the southside trail exited the canyon. They hid behind a couple of huge boulders.

"A billow of smoke should draw the soldier boys' attention," Rarus explained. "When you see them moving toward the river, the three of you need to make haste up the trail. The fire should be big enough, and baffling enough, that it'll hold their attention for a good while. Heck, you might get lucky and make it all the way out without being seen. These guys don't seem well organized. They may not even have sentries watching the trail."

"What about you?" Kadeya asked.

"I'm going to try to follow you out—hopefully catch-up with you by the time you reach the crest." Rarus held up a finger, "But if it's not safe, I'll hide down here and climb out after nightfall. Either way, I'll hook up with you at the top of the canyon. Don't worry, I'm not going to get caught."

"How much time will you need?" Azazel asked.

"Not sure—I'm going to set an island ablaze."

"You're going to what!?" Azazel exclaimed.

"Yesterday as I was sneaking toward their camp I noticed an island about halfway across the river caught a mountain of driftwood during a flash flood. It's high and dry now and it'll make one roaring, smoky fire!" Rarus explained. "Since it's in the river the fire won't spread."

Soon after Rarus began creeping across the canyon floor, two armed Domhanians walked by talking casually. *Crap!* He hid in a thicket of brush for a couple of minutes. Deciding more stealth was in order, he began scooting snakelike toward the river. He'd freeze firm at any sense of something awry. It took fifteen minutes to cover the last eighty metres to the river.

Realizing the current was pushing strongly, Rarus slid into the water and worked his way upstream underneath the tall river grass that arched away from the bank and draped gracefully into the water. Tucked into the two metre wide tunnel of vegetation, he was invisible from either side of the river.

He estimated he needed to be about thirty metres upstream of the island before launching away from the bank. He was able to walk on the gently sloping gravel bottom for several metres before needing to launch prone and swim. He miscalculated the power of the current and in a moment of panic thought he was going to wash out below the island. Turning himself at a sixty degree ferry angle, he swam as hard as he could. He grabbed the sturdy root of a tree overhanging the river at the island's most downstream point. He pulled himself out of the water completely spent and lay gasping for a couple of minutes.

It was easy to stay hidden on the brushy island as he clamored toward the four metre high pile of driftwood. Gauging the light breeze, Rarus found the best spot to light the fire. He needed the breeze to blow the blaze into the tangle of dry sticks.

When he had a mound of tinder set to his satisfaction, he

pulled out his waterproof ditty bag and was flabbergasted to find everything inside soaked. He'd punctured the bag as he'd slithered toward the river. *This is a cursed enterprise! Perhaps it's a sign from the gods to abandon the plan...superstitious nonsense.*

Rarus didn't know how long it would take his lighter to dry enough to strike, or even if it would strike after being so thoroughly soaked. He pulled out the small telescope and scanned the riverbanks. After assuring himself he'd not been detected, he began hacking the telescope tube with the saw blade on his multi-tool. Soon he managed to open the telescope enough to pop the lens out.

He had planned to have the fire lit earlier in the day but having the bright sun higher in the sky was now helpful. He held the lens at a distance above a powder dry pile of grass so as to focus the sun's rays. He was surprised at how quickly the grass smoldered, but that's all it did. It just wasn't heating to kindling temperature. *So I need something that kindles at a lower temperature.*

Looking around at the flammable materials, Rarus had an epiphany. *Perhaps I don't need something that catches fire at a lower temperature, maybe I just need more heat.* He piled up several more handfuls of grass and covered it with a single layer of hand-sized dry leaves. Again he focused the sun's rays through the telescope lens. Within seconds a hole burned through the leaf. Rarus held the focal point steady as it powered a pinpoint of light and heat through the tiny hole. Smoke began to billow out around the edges of the leaves that were containing the heat. Suddenly there was a whoosh of ignition. Dropping the lens he began feeding the flames with twigs. Within five minutes the flicker had become a blaze and soon it was the size of a campfire.

He laid a lattice of sticks from the fire onto the heaped driftwood then scurried back into the water. This time he used the current and his body angle to ferry himself back across the river to the south bank. This was much easier. He was barely winded when he arrived downstream of the Domhanian soldiers' camp. Unfortunately, three of the soldiers were standing on the bank just above where Rarus emerged. Even more unluckily, he'd surfaced at a place without thick underbrush draping into the water. Flattening himself against the steep drop off, he remained as still and silent as possible. With half his body submerged he felt progressively colder as the river sucked away his core temperature.

A down canyon wind was blowing a cloud of smoke past, yet Rarus still did not hear any hullabaloo. *Where are these people from? Are they too dumb to understand a burning island is rather implausible?* He worried again that this entire effort was cursed and wondered if he should try to get to Azazel and call off the plan to exit the canyon.

Finally, Rarus heard Crow Clansmen shouting upstream. The three men on the ledge above him took off at a trot toward the smoke's source. He dragged himself out of the water. His feet and lower legs were so cold and numb he couldn't stand. Lying in the sunshine waiting to warm up was not an option. He knew the exertion of moving, even as painful as it was, would begin to warm his body. Using his arms he was able to scoot himself into a thicket of brush. With all of the commotion up canyon, he wasn't concerned about the noise of breaking sticks and twigs as he dragged himself away from the river.

After about seventy metres Rarus managed to pull his legs up under him and crawl. He was making good progress when he saw the clearing to his left that housed the troop's campsite. He dropped prone and lay silently for several seconds scanning the camp. From his brushy lair he saw Lilith bound to a tree. He crawled to the edge of the clearing and tossed a stick in her direction. When she looked up Rarus shook a branch of the bush he was hiding under.

Lilith's eyes widened when she saw her colleague. Rarus touched his lips with an index finger, and she nodded. He mimed that he planned to climb out of the canyon and would come back to rescue her. Again she nodded understanding. He gave her a thumbs-up sign, and she shot him a big smile in return.

Rarus thought about the serendipity of having made contact with Lilith. *Finally something breaks our way!*

As he warmed up, the numbness in his feet was replaced by a thousand pricks of pain. Nevertheless, he was able to get his feet under him and trot in a crouch toward the boulders where Azazel, Ramuell and Kadeya hid. When Rarus came around an enormous tree trunk that had folded itself across the house-size boulder he was stunned to see a Domhanian soldier holding a weapon on his comrades.

Rarus pulled his handheld sonic-blaster and flipped the switch to the narrow-field setting. He spoke just loudly enough to be heard, "Raise your hands, turn around slowly, and drop your weapon." The man raised his hands. Just as he turned around a second soldier stepped out from the other side of the boulder. Rarus spun in his direction and pushed the sonic discharge trigger. Though water resistant, these weapons were not designed for several minutes of full submersion. It buzzed, crackled and failed to fire.

The man who had been the intended target dove to the ground. The other soldier had not yet dropped his weapon. A fiendish smile flickered across his face an instant before he lowered his charged-particle gun and pressed the trigger. Rarus dropped instantly; first to his knees then he flopped face first onto the rocky ground.

The two soldiers looked at each other for just a second. It

was a second too long. Azazel pulled a solid-projectile weapon from his cargo pants pocket, stepped directly toward the man who had shot Rarus and fired a peanut size ball bearing into the back of the man's head.

The second sentry had dropped his weapon as he'd thrown himself prone. He now scrambled to pick it up. Azazel took four lightning fast steps toward him and stomped hard on the soldier's wrist. Before the man even had a chance to cry out, Azazel pushed the discharge button again and another pressurized-gas powered spheroid blasted into the man's skull.

Kadeya ran to Rarus and kneeled at his side. She searched his neck for the carotid pulse. There was none. "What in the name of god? They killed him!"

Azazel picked up his first victim's weapon and held it out toward Ramuell, pointing to the discharge setting. "I saw he had it set to kill when he raised his hands."

Kadeya walked over and inspected the other weapon lying just centimeters beyond the second dead soldier's reach. "It's also dialed to the kill setting. What in the name of god?" she said again, this time her voice cracked.

Azazel shuddered, as if hitting a cognitive reset button. "Okay, we've got to get these bodies hidden and get ourselves out of here. If we're caught, they'll kill us!"

Ramuell looked around and pointed, "There's a bunch of brush growing beneath that cliff overhang."

Azazel gritted his teeth and said, "Goddammit!" at the thought of abandoning Rarus' body to scavengers.

"I believe we probably have at least half an hour of diversion. Look at that!" Kadeya said pointing toward the roaring driftwood fire. Flames could be seen above the tree tops licking the blue-green sky.

Raised voices of confusion and awe were still coming from the crowd gathered at the river's edge after Kadeya, Ramuell and Azazel had hidden the bodies and begun the trek up the canyon's southside trail.

Meanwhile, Ipos had descended over two-thirds of the way back into the canyon and stayed the night in a shallow cave. From that vantage point he'd watched Rarus set the driftwood bonfire ablaze and realized a diversion was afoot.

Though he'd been unable to see where Rarus emerged from the river, he had seen the shocking encounter at the boulders. He estimated the entire shootout lasted less than three seconds. In those few instants many hundreds of annum of life were just snuffed out. He was horrified. *This is **not** the Domhanian way. Something has gone terribly wrong.*

Witnessing these slayings after watching his compatriots' captured by Serefim Security Forces the preceding afternoon, filled Ipos with a peculiar combination of sadness and apprehension. As he watched Kadeya, Ramuell and Azazel hike out of the canyon he feared, as bad as this was, things could get much, much worse.

CHAPTER FORTY-FOUR
FAILED JUDGMENT

Grandmaster Elyon's sumptuous living quarters were located on Torus-1 adjacent to the Serefim Presidium's lavish offices, gymnasium and dining hall. Elyon infrequently left Torus-1 and was rarely seen by the thousands of Domhanians employed at Ghrain-3.

The Grandmaster's aloofness added to his carefully cultivated air of mystery and invincibility. He expected a certain kind of deference from the staff and Presidium members with whom he interacted. People stood when Elyon entered a room.

He had only a handful of personal relationships that weren't predicated on some form of homage. Those few people could speak frankly, give candid advice, and tactfully tell Elyon when he was off-course, but only in private.

Though he was seldom seen among the rank and file, he insisted his deputies be out and about daily. They were to be seen as competent, knowledgeable, hands-on administrators. Elyon recognized the cosmetic value of grooming that perception. Of equal importance was for those individuals to serve as his sources of first-hand information. All staff who reported directly to Elyon submitted daily briefings. They filed Activity and Accomplishment reports (the A&A) each kuuk. He read every word of the daily briefings and at a minimum the executive summaries of all A&A reports.

When he did put in a public appearance, it was almost always before a large group gathering. He never overtly indicated he expected exaltation from the audience. He left the creation of that dynamic to Administrant Pravel and her Strategic Communications staff. They choreographed every aspect of Elyon's visits to the lectern; a job that was made easier by virtue of the fact that he was a spellbinding elocutionist. His handlers' task was to assure that the atmospherics made Elyon look as inspirational as his oratory. Pravel and her staff were good at their jobs. Usually by the end of Elyon's time on stage, the devotion of his audience had been so manipulated as to verge on veneration. The fact that he had made almost everyone in his audiences quite wealthy didn't hurt.

Elyon had expected some blowback about the decision to utilize sapien-hybrids as laborers in the mining operations, but it had been manageable while the workers stayed on Ghrain-3. Administrant Pravel and a few other trusted advisors counseled that the decision to sell sapien-hybrids to far-flung operations would lead to more vociferous opposition. The Grandmaster was intractable.

The reports of dissension among staff working on the planet's surface began as a trickle. However, within a decade Serefim Security was receiving daily reports of passive-aggressive opposition to all kinds of Presidium directives. The resistance came primarily from the Scientific Study facilities.

Elyon considered this rebelliousness among the science

personnel a nuisance rather than a real problem. This arrogant miscalculation led him to believe the Presidium could somehow hide the export of hybridized workers to off-world job sites.

One evening over a private dinner in his quarters, Elyon complained to three of his confidants. "Look, we've been here for over a thousand annum, but before I got to this chunk of ice we'd never turned a profit. Now we're depositing some serious credits in everyone's accounts. If the Presidium was of a mind, we could pool our money and just buy the damned planet. Actually, with just a couple of other investors, I could probably do that myself—and I just might!"

As had been the case among the corporate aristocracy for generations, the three men and a woman seated at Elyon's dining table spoke and acted as if the people serving their food and beverages were deaf. They were not!

Elyon's empire had always paid its taxes. At an outpost so far removed from the homeworld there were dozens of ways to hide profits. But why should he? Because he returned such enormous sums of wealth to Domhan-Siol, he enjoyed almost universal support from the Anotas-Deithe hierarchy and the Directors of second-tier government agencies. His administration of the Ghrain-3 Expeditionary Mission was unfettered; or at least it had been for most of his reign.

The sale of sapien-hybrid laborers started changing that. Because this business was potentially controversial, Elyon and the Presidium decided to hide its revenues off-the-books. The income did not flow through any of the corporations doing business on Ghrain-3. It was not reported, and taxes were not paid. In the beginning the amount of hidden revenue was a pittance. But when the sale of sapien laborers went interstellar the earnings exploded.

Elyon was quite right when he reckoned there were those on the homeworld who would take a dim view of the slave trade, and Melanka was among its most outspoken critics. Elyon considered her a moralistic ideologue.

Ironically, most cultists also had considerable disdain for Melanka because she had often been so outspoken about their dogmatic codswallop. Elyon understood that common enemies give birth to odd alliances. He reasoned the cultists' energy, albeit simple-minded and ill-informed, could prove valuable in bringing Melanka's faction to heel.

Elyon dispatched a team of covert operatives to Domhan-Siol to explore the idea of buying cultist support. He understood even if his agents determined that forging such an alliance was feasible, it could be several annum before the investment would pay dividends. This timeline was troublesome because the news from his intelligence reports just kept getting worse.

He received a message from his Security Director that Realta-Gorm zealots had staged another successful raid and carried off two dozen sapien-hybrids from a small moon-based mining operation. Upon learning this, he locked himself in his office and flew into a rage. He kicked over chairs and threw his communicator against the wall, as if to kill the messenger.

Only two days later Elyon learned that Melanka had dispatched one of her loyalists to Ghrain-3. His security staff went to work frantically trying to identify the covert operative. The investigation uncovered some tangentially related information that astonished Elyon and his confidants. They knew about the attack by the nefilim on the Crow Clan, but only as a result of their search for Melanka's spy did they learn that a heretofore unknown spacefaring species had medically treated injured clanspeople subsequent to the battle.

If that was true, it lent credence to the stories Professor Egan and Dr. Althea had told about the Beag-Liath. Further investigation led to the stunning revelation that Ramuell was Althea's son and Dr. Kadeya her mother. This cast a strange new light on Ramuell's involvement with the Crow Clan and the Blue Rock Canyon incident.

Several days later the Serefim Security Director received a report that a contingent of grey skinned beings had materialized out of thin air on the surface of Ghrain-3 and prevented a sapien-hybrid clan from boarding a Domhanian transport ship. The suddenness of the creatures' appearance so terrified the sapien-hybrids that they fled into the bush. The security detail assigned to the operation boarded their vessel and launched immediately. The commanding officer explained in her report that they had no idea what technology might be in play, and she did not want to risk her people or the ship.

It seemed to Elyon there were too many coincidences to be coincidental. He became convinced that Melanka's spies were traitorously collaborating with the Beag-Liath creatures. This mistaken notion proved to be the last straw; both his patience and his judgment failed. Elyon was in such a fury even his closest confidants feared challenging his bellicose, irrational decisions. One of those decisions was to use the Crow Clan to demonstrate to the Beag-Liath just who was in control of Ghrain-3.

CHAPTER FORTY-FIVE
HAM-HANDED

Semyaza communicated frequently with a cadre of his confidants on the orbiter. None of them knew much about the design, construction, or purpose of the new torus. Information about the project had been strictly classified. The coupling of the mysterious torus to the orbiting station had required only a single annum because of the huge workforce.

When the construction crews departed, hundreds of new arrivals took up residence. Their unknown work assignments added to the mystery. For Semyaza that mystery was solved late one evening when he received a clandestine communiqué from one of the Serefim Presidium food service staff. She informed him that two cohorts of armed forces were stationed in the now fully operational torus. At least thirty shuttle and attack craft were docked at its ports. This force strength made possible the simultaneous deployment of over nine hundred troops.

Upon learning this Semyaza began making emergency evacuation plans for NWA-1. His instincts were correct, but there wasn't enough time to implement a plan. Only four days after learning the purpose of the torus called T-Taxiarch, he received another message that assault craft were being supplied and boarded by several hundred soldiers under the command of Brigadier Migeal.

Within the hour Semyaza issued an order to abandon the basecamp. All NWA-1 personnel had been briefed on the plan to exit the basecamp, but they had not yet staged any drills. The evacuation was chaos! People scrambled to gather their gear but usually grabbed too much, not enough, or the wrong items. They rushed to their designated departure sites to find only about half the assigned vehicles staged at the correct locations. Nevertheless, by the time the armed force landed most NWA-1 staff had gotten away – many in the wrong vehicles headed to the wrong satellite research camps.

Two people who had failed to evacuate eluded capture by ducking into a subterranean pump house. They watched the commotion through cooling vents that protruded about twenty centimetres above ground level. Hovard and Ruth saw the soldiers roundup their colleagues and tether them to cables strung between trees.

Davad, a young zoologist, had been a three-time champion of the Ghrain-3 Bonn Sabaid foot-fighting tournaments. He took umbrage when one of the soldiers manhandled him and sent a vicious roundhouse kick smashing his heel into the aggressive soldier's ear. The soldier was unconscious before hitting the ground.

When Davad made a dash across the camp's central yard, one of the soldiers leveled his charged-particle weapon on the running target and popped of three quick blasts. The first blast knocked Davad to the ground, the next two shots were, simply put, spiteful. At that moment, the NWA-1 laggards understood they were in real danger.

Hovard gasped loudly and Ruth shot her hand over his

mouth. She studied the yard in front of them to see if anyone had heard the noise. Hovard nodded indicating he'd regained control and Ruth removed her hand. "Do you think he's dead?" she whispered.

"It seemed to me the weapon was set on stun, but the second and third shots may have been too much. If he's alive, it's because some god wishes it."

Ruth and Hovard waited until dark before emerging from their hideout. They sprinted to the fruit arboretum behind the communication center dome. Hiding among the trees, they caught their breath and searched the camp's perimeter for sentries. They saw only two, both of whom seemed quite casual about their duties.

Hovard crept over and looked in the open window of the communication center. He was thrilled to find the occupiers hadn't inactivated the equipment. He climbed in the window and with the ambient light from nearby buildings managed to stuff several pieces of portable equipment in a backpack.

When he returned and told Ruth that the invaders had not disabled the communication equipment she exclaimed, "What?! I'm no soldier, but even I would have thought to do that. These guys are amateurs!"

"Yeah, probably, and that might make them even more dangerous."

They made their escape toward the rolling hills north of NWA-1.

The ice-age world's early autumn nights were already quite cold. The couple only had the clothes they were wearing and wished they'd taken the emergency evacuation plan more seriously. They hiked into a narrow ravine and found a place reasonably sheltered by boulders and trees. They built a fire, fully aware this greatly increased their chances of being found.

They also knew without its warmth they would not be able to endure the cold temperatures of the night ahead.

After the fire was built Ruth booted up the "liberated" communication equipment. For two hours they listened to the chatter clogging the airways. Finally, they decided it was safe to report on the situation at NWA-1.

Semyaza had also been monitoring the frenetic communication activity. Upon receiving Ruth's message he replied via an encrypted text-com. First he inquired about their condition then about the captives being held at the basecamp. After receiving their status report, Semyaza gave Hovard and Ruth the coordinates where they were to meet a rescue party the next morning.

Though on the verge of exhaustion, Semyaza began trying to contact SWA-7. He finally gave up and dragged himself to his sleeping bag. The next morning he was thrilled to find a message from Samael. It contained only a video-com link. Semyaza took it to his technology specialist who hid their location by routing the call through three communication satellites.

"Sam, you have no idea how good it is to see you. Are you okay?" Semyaza asked.

"Yes, fine. We've been listening to the brouhaha."

"I assume SWA-7 was occupied too."

"Actually, no," Sam replied.

"What?!"

"A Security squad arrived here a couple of days ago with orders to detain some of our guests."

"Guests?" questioned Semyaza.

"Kadeya has been with us for several days. She and Ramuell have been observing nefilim clans. Then a few days ago Dr. Lector accompanied by a man from the homeworld arrived. Dr. Evander claims to be a historian, but if he's not an Anotas covert ops guy I'd eat your bootlaces," Samael said.

"So, what's happened over there?"

"When the Security detail learned Lector and Evander had gone to observe the Crow Clan, they commandeered a quadcopter and three RTVs," Sam explained.

"How many people did they need to arrest an historian and a librarian for god's sake?"

"Fourteen," Sam replied. "There were fourteen troops in the squad that departed for Blue Rock. Four others stayed behind. I assume to keep an eye on us, but they've been cordial and not at all obtrusive. That's why I was so shocked when we started hearing about the landings at all the other basecamps yesterday."

"Did Azazel go with them to Blue Rock?" Semyaza asked.

"Yeah he did, but with a shipload of misgivings."

"And I take it you've not heard from him?"

"No, nothing from either the Director or Rarus—we don't even know if the soldiers made it into the canyon, which worries me because they took Dr. Lilith with them as an interpreter. And I mean **took** her—against her will. They had to cuff her to get her in the quadcopter."

"Oh my, that's not good! Azazel is down in that big ditch with a potentially volatile group of gung-ho youngsters, **and** he has no idea what's happening out here." Semyaza paused, "Can you go to the canyon to check on them?"

"I can't, or rather I'm not supposed to leave. None of us are. It would be easy for me to slip away without our four new friends being any the wiser, but..."

"And your reticence is because...?"

"Rarus, Kadeya, and Ramuell are also in the canyon," Sam explained. "And Gadrel is over at the Dig. We don't know what orders our four-man occupation force has received from upstairs. Personnel at our study area camps have been warned off and won't be traipsing into the basecamp, but all the rest of our staff are here. I need to stay to keep a lid on things just in case the situation turns ugly. And besides, those were Azazel's orders."

"I understand. Well, it's chaos down here. Fortunately, most of our people got out of camp before the assault."

"Assault?" Sam asked, surprised at the word choice.

"Hell yeah, it was an assault! These guys charged out of their shuttlecraft brandishing arms, pushing people around and shackling them to cables strung between trees. Two of our people hid for a few hours before they were able to escape. They saw one of my scientists shot and likely killed."

"Whoa! I'm thankful that hasn't been our experience. Clearly these troops had a different assignment, at least when they arrived. The squad down in the canyon probably haven't even heard the orders to seize our headquarters facilities," Sam conjectured.

"All the more reason we must find a way to contact Azazel. I may try to commandeer one of our shuttlecraft and jump to Blue Rock myself. **If** I can abscond with a shuttle, I could be up there in a few of hours."

"Man, it would be great if you could make that happen."

"Let me see what I can do. One way or the other I'll let you know," Semyaza promised.

"Thank you sir—you're a good man."

With Ramuell leading the way, they climbed out of the canyon unnoticed by the soldiers who were engrossed with the belching smoke of the flaming island. Kadeya was able to maintain a reasonable pace. Her lack of acclimatization still didn't seem to be affecting her strength or stamina. Azazel's heart was breaking with each step of the trudge up the south-side trail. Even when they stopped to rest he remained silent.

Upon cresting the canyon's rim, they took cover in a thicket of squat conifers. Ramuell said, "I'll make a loop to reconnoiter the area."

Azazel said, "Thanks. And Kadeya you should rest and hydrate. You've probably not had enough water."

While Ramuell was gone Kadeya decided to try to pull Azazel out of the doldrums. She understood his leadership was essential if they were to survive this ordeal – and that's exactly what she told him.

Azazel sat silently for a couple of minutes before saying, "I know you're right. If what Durela told us is true, thousands of annum of Domhanian progress is on the precipice of an unfathomable collapse. I'm heartbroken about Rarus's murder, and what I had to do down there. The last two times I've been down in that god-forsaken trench I've killed people." He looked away, eyes not focused on anything. "I'm not a killer. This is not who I am!"

Just as Ramuell crept back into their little hideout Azazel rubbed his face, took a deep breath and said, "But you're absolutely right, Kadeya. I have responsibilities here and now. There will be time enough to wallow in grief and guilt later."

Ramuell wrinkled his brow and shot his grandmother a look. She shook her head ever so slightly then asked, "So what did you find?"

"I found their vehicles, or rather our vehicles atop the second shelf over there. I don't think they posted a sentry. I crawled a circle all the way around the vehicles and there are no tracks indicating anyone has been meandering around the area."

"What do you mean by 'our' vehicles?" Azazel asked.

"One quadcopter and three Rough-Terrain-Vehicles—all from SWA-7."

Azazel said, "They certainly made themselves at home, but at least we're not stranded."

"No you're not," came a voice from the other side of the trees.

All three of them jumped for cover even as Azazel recognized the voice. "What in nine levels of hell, Semyaza! You scared the crap out of us! What are you doing here?"

"Not sure how much you know about what's going on, but I'm here to save you from walking straight into one of those levels of hell," Semyaza said as he embraced his friend.

CHAPTER FORTY-SIX

4PLANS IN BENT TIME

ALTHEA, Egan, Rebecca and Danel were invited to breakfast at the Anotas headquarters their second morning on Realta-Gorm. Nanzy and Imamiah met their guests in front of the building and escorted them into a dining hall. "This morning we really are your greeters," Nanzy teased.

Eight Oprit-Robia leaders were standing around an oval table made of a dark grainy wood. All of them walked toward the room's entrance to welcome the visitors. When everyone was seated, the woman on Danel's right raised a finger to one of the staff. Soon platters of breads, fruits and nuts were being delivered to the table and served family style. Before they began to eat, a man rose and offered a blessing. This caught the four guests off-guard, but nothing about the prayer smacked of the cultists' zealous mindlessness. Three people at the table bowed and closed their eyes. Everyone else sat erect with what might best be described as respectful silence.

The breakfast had an optimistic feel. The Oprit-Robia leaders asked Egan and Althea many questions about their time with the Beag-Liath. They also drilled down for information about the Anotas situation on the homeworld. Danel and Rebecca handled those questions but were clearly evasive on some points.

One woman whom the other Oprit-Robia members subtly deferred to said, "We understand your reticence. You don't know us and being Law and Order Directorate officers you understand better than most how information can be misused. We respect that and won't push you to provide more than you're comfortable with. Hopefully, as we get to know each other, we'll earn each other's trust. Then perhaps we can have more guileless conversations."

Danel said, "Thank you. We appreciate your understanding."

"Okay folks, this conversation has gone on quite long enough." She folded her napkin, looked around the table at her colleagues, smiled and said, "There are extraordinary challenges and opportunities afoot, and these folks have a mission to plan." There was a bustle of palm-taps and side conversations as people mingled in a protracted exodus from the room.

Imamiah, Nanzy, and the contingent from Domhan-Siol agreed to meet back at the condominium in a couple of hours. For the next three days the six of them would spend almost every waking moment huddled in the condo's den planning their next moves.

"The best way to describe Elyon's role is to say he sits on the Serefim Presidium throne," Imamiah explained. "He doesn't approve everything happening within the massive network of Ghrain-3 projects. But in a macro-sense, he or his lieutenants know what's going on, and his disapproval amounts to a veto." A smug smile flashed across her face. "That was until we began our feeble little raids, which have made Elyon furious and paranoid. When he learned another technologically advanced species was intervening with the Ghrain-3 indigenes his response was completely over the top.

"It's our understanding he's convinced your Beag-Liath friends are collaborating with the scientists stationed on the planet's surface. We know the Beag-Liath have waylaid Serefim ships transporting sapien-hybrids, but our agents have not confirmed any Beag-Liath / Domhanian joint ventures whatsoever." She paused and looked from Althea to Egan, "In fact, you may be the only Domhanians to have ever had direct contact with them."

"What do you mean by 'over the top' response?" Egan asked.

"He ordered Serefim paramilitary forces to seize and occupy all of the Scientific Study Project headquarters," Imamiah replied. "It's clear those forces weren't trained for largescale military operations and their implementation has been erratic. It's not hyperbole to say his orders have created an unholy mess."

"And where in that mess would we find Ramuell and my mother?" Althea asked.

"Wanted for questioning at the very least, but not detained," Imamiah answered. "Your mother happened to be on a temporary surface assignment when the assault troops were unleashed. She was with your son at the time, but their exact location is not now known.

"Ramuell completed the acclimatization process and has been given a long-term surface assignment. However, the process was just too physically taxing for Dr. Kadeya."

Althea pinched the bridge of her nose, "Which means she's only able to stay on the surface for a limited period before she begins to have health problems."

Imamiah tilted her head and gave an affirmative nod.

"How many days has she been on the surface and how many days were medically authorized?"

"Althea, we just don't know," Nanzy answered.

After a long pause Egan said, "So do you believe our presence on Ghrain-3 would somehow draw the Beag-Liath out?"

"Perhaps," Nanzy replied. "We want to explore the possibility of an alliance but have no idea how to make contact. For whatever reason, they initiated contact with you. Maybe they will again."

Egan said, "There are two things you should know about the Beag-Liath. Both issues might be problematic, but they also might be advantageous. First, they have extremely sophisticated cloaking technology. They can alter virtually every wave length on the entire energy spectrum."

Pointing out the picture window Althea said, "They could be watching us right now and we wouldn't be able to see them, hear them, or even detect heat signatures."

"You believe they could avoid detection by our energy tracking satellites?" Nanzy asked.

"Pfft ... We don't have any technology that can detect them if they don't want to be seen," Althea replied.

Imamiah turned to Egan, "And you said there were two things."

"Yes. Now understand this is conjecture, but it's likely our temporal perceptions are dramatically different. They don't use 4D-Initiator technology."

Imamiah gave Egan a puzzled look.

Althea tried to clarify. "When we returned to Domhan-Siol people kept telling us we had been gone for over sixty-two annum. We were shown physical evidence of that time passage, but it just didn't jibe with our internal sense of time passage nor our time measurement devices. We were thoroughly confused and when we finally had access to a lab, I ran cellular ageing tests on both of us. We aged less than four kuuk between the time of our departure and the time of our return."

Imamiah's jaw dropped, "Whaaat?!"

"We don't understand it either," Egan said. "But without technology to jump across dimensions, the only way the Beag could travel the enormous distances across the galaxy would be using space/time warping technologies."

Imamiah said, "But I'm given to believe that's not possible."

Egan flicked a hand and said, "We can jump through dimensions of the multiverse. The Beag-Liath can warp energy. Both were impossible until someone developed the technology, then they weren't impossible anymore. What we know is during our absence you aged over sixty annum, and we aged about a hundred seventy days."

Imamiah narrowed her eyes, "So it's possible the Beag-Liath whom you met may not arrive at Ghrain-3 for hundreds of our annum."

"Or the Beag-Liath at Ghrain-3 have not yet even heard of our time aboard one of their ships," Althea conjectured.

"**Or**—they can bend time the way they bend energy, and the Beag-Liath at Ghrain-3 are many annum ahead of us," Egan offered.

CHAPTER FORTY-SEVEN
ANGST

A FAINT PREDAWN glow was seeping into the eastern sky when Ramuell quietly climbed out of his sleeping bag and stole into the camp's kitchen area. He lit Semyaza's tiny stove to heat water for tea.

After pouring himself a cup he made his way to the canyon overlook and took a seat on a boulder. There were no views anywhere on his homeworld that compared to this. Many Domhanians reported an agoraphobic response to the enormous vistas afforded by the dry atmosphere of Ghrain-3. Ramuell, on the other hand, reveled in the awesome beauty.

Semyaza approached and gestured toward the slowly brightening canyon, "No matter how much or how far I can see, it's never quite enough."

Ramuell smiled, "That's exactly how I feel about this place."

"I sensed that in you."

They sat in companionable silence sipping tea and drinking in the panorama for several minutes.

"You were mighty stealthy. I searched all the way around the vehicles and found no evidence of anyone coming or going after the Serefim squad hiked into the canyon," Ramuell said.

"Nah, not all that stealthy—Adair landed our shuttlecraft on a flattop knoll about two kilometres further south. We had just come over the rise when we saw you doing your crawled circumnavigation of what looked like an RTV parking lot," Semyaza replied.

"Oh, so you hadn't been to the vehicles yet—that explains it. I didn't sleep well, and I remember at one point during the night lying awake worrying about how I'd missed your tracks."

"I just hate that! You're lying there and know there's absolutely nothing you can do about those worries in the dead of night." Semyaza paused then added, "But Ramuell, you're too young to be having those kinds of sleep problems."

"Yeah, don't I wish—I didn't even *sen* last night."

Just then Semyaza saw some movement deep in the canyon. "Something's going on down there. I'm going to get our scope."

"We need to be careful with alignment, don't want them to catch any reflections off the lens."

"Right you are," Semyaza agreed. "Find a good flat rock. We can use my mini-tripod."

A couple of hours later the five Domhanians on the canyon's south rim were taking turns watching the Crow Clan and their soldier "escorts" climbing the trail on the opposite side of the canyon.

Azazel paced back-and-forth muttering, "Dammit, dammit, dammit."

"You couldn't have known," Semyaza said trying to reassure his friend. "It was logical to assume they'd exit this side of the canyon since the vehicles are here."

"Damn small consolation when Rarus lost his life implementing a plan to get us out on the wrong side of the canyon," Azazel retorted.

Semyaza exhaled loudly. "I understand."

Then he added, "We need to contact Samael. Maybe he can learn from the four soldiers who are still at your basecamp how many forces remain on the orbiter. From the chatter Adair and I listened to, it seems all of our basecamps have been forcibly occupied. Our best move might be for Sam to arrest the security detail if it can be done without bloodshed. SWA-7 is likely our only stronghold left on the planet's surface."

"But you're worried Elyon has another squadron held in reserve," Kadeya said as she stepped away from the scope.

"Exactly," Semyaza replied. "And if so, they could easily overwhelm the camp."

Kadeya faced Azazel and said, "I'm not a student of military history and know nothing of military tactics, but it seems to me until you have better information about the forces arrayed against you, you want to maintain the status quo. The status quo at SWA-7 is not that bad. In the status quo your staff is alive and reasonably free to come and go, which seems a lot better than the situation elsewhere."

Semyaza said, "Kadeya makes a good point. The situation at SWA-7 **is** a lot better than anywhere else."

Azazel said, "I hear what you're saying, and we need Sam to confirm that the camp's status this morning is the same as it was yesterday. Let's make the call."

"Sam's situation is already stressful enough," Kadeya observed. "I'd urge you to tell him only that Rarus arranged the diversion for our escape but hasn't made it out of the canyon yet."

Azazel twisted his lips to one side, "That's an obfuscation but not a lie."

Semyaza said, "When you do tell Sam he'll be incensed

that you withheld the information, but you can explain you wanted to share the heartbreaking news face-to-face."

Raking the dirt with his boot, Azazel said, "Which is absolutely true."

CHAPTER FORTY-EIGHT
CHASING CROWS

Ipos watched the soldiers discover and bury the three bodies Azazel and Ramuell had hidden in the brushy fissure. They didn't allow any of the Crow clanspeople to see the corpses. *Smart! They don't want the sapiens to realize we're mortal.*

An hour later he couldn't believe what he was witnessing. Without resistance, the Clan was abandoning their cave homes. Carrying some meager belongings, they were following the Serefim troops climbing the northside canyon trail. *That was their plan all along. They came here to abduct the Clan.*

Ipos was holed up about three-fourths of the way down into the canyon. He couldn't possibly climb out unobserved in front of the clan and their armed escorts. His best option, his only option really, was to hide in the small cave. Minutes after the long file of soldiers and clanspeople had passed his hide-out, Ipos scurried down to the river. He drank the cold clear water and refilled his bottles.

Looking up the southside trail he thought it was probably a less difficult climb than the steeper serpentine trail up to the north rim. He stuffed the water bottles in his pack, cinched his weapon's strap tightly, took a deep breath and set out at a controlled brisk pace. Traveling solo Ipos was able to reach the south rim well before the contingent of soldiers and clans-people topped out on the canyon's higher and steeper north side.

"They **must** be stopped," Ramuell insisted.

Ramuell and his companions had watched the transport ships settle gracefully on the opposite canyon rim. The Crow Clan parade and Serefim troops were still snaking their way up the northside trail. Though not moving fast, they'd probably arrive at the trailhead within a half hour.

"But how?" Azazel wondered.

"We have so many of our own to attend to; I'm not sure the Crow Clan is our priority," Semyaza said. "Perhaps we can turn this horror story to our advantage."

"What are you thinking?" Azazel asked.

"Well, if you return to SWA-7 and report the successful departure of the squadron with the Clan, maybe the four person security team would consider their mission accomplished and just leave."

Azazel thought about this for a minute, "That's a longshot and..."

"And it's never going to happen."

Startled, the five Domhanians crouched and swung their attention toward the unexpected voice. Adair, who had never met Ipos, pulled his weapon and demanded, "Stop! Hands up —get on your knees!"

Jumping between the two men, Azazel raised both arms with an open hands 'hold your fire' gesture. "Whoa, whoa, whoa! We know this man." Adair lowered his weapon as

Azazel turned and said, "Major Ipos, what happened? Why are you here?"

"I came as soon as I could to warn you," with both index fingers he pointed at Kadeya and Ramuell, "more specifically, you two. You shouldn't return to SWA-7." After Ipos was introduced to Semyaza and Adair, he went on to detail the entire episode of his team's exit from the canyon and subsequent capture.

Kadeya speculated, "So if Elyon ordered the detention of Durela, Lector and Evander, it's likely orders of detention have been issued for us as well."

"The more I thought about it, the more certain I became," Ipos agreed.

Semyaza said, "It seems Grandmaster Elyon has succumbed to some serious paranoia. I'd bet my last tender deposit the Major is right."

"So what do we do about that?" Ramuell asked, pointing toward the Crow Clan and Serefim troops who were just beginning to emerge at the north rim.

Looking across the canyon Ipos asked Adair, "Can you fly one of those big birds?"

"Yes, I'm qualified to pilot almost every aircraft that comes and goes on this planet. Those are P-24 shuttlecraft—they are virtually identical to the C-4MT cargo transports, which I've flown many times."

"Then there is something we can do—at least for a few of the sapiens." Everyone gathered around Ipos as he outlined a plan.

Because a quadcopter would be heard flying across the canyon's open air, Semyaza led the group back to the shuttlecraft Adair had "liberated" from NWA-1. It would make the canyon crossing almost silently. The two kilometre hike to the shuttlecraft took half an hour. It took less than a minute to fly across the chasm.

Adair landed the shuttle behind a low ridge about one kilometre away from where the Serefim troops and the Crow Clan had gathered. Half an hour after leaving the shuttle Ipos led the group to a hiding place in a dense thicket of brush.

Though the people of the Crow Clan had been cooperative on the trek out of the canyon, those who were reticent became more so upon seeing the first of the three shuttlecraft launch. Several clansmen appeared quite agitated about boarding the remaining two vehicles. "This is going to take some time. I know the Crow people, and some aren't going to board unless forced," Azazel whispered to the others.

Ipos responded, "Which plays right into our hands. We don't have the numbers to take on the crews of both shuttles. The most intractable will probably be the last ones coerced on the last ship. The crew will be distracted and all we'll need to do is make clean shots."

"Stun only," Azazel insisted. "We need the prisoners."

A quarter-hour after the second shuttlecraft finally launched, nine clanspeople were still refusing to board the remaining vehicle. Azazel could see Dr. Lilith pleading with them to get on the ship. "Judging by her body language, I think the soldier's weapons are set on kill."

"Which makes sense," Semyaza said. "From their point of view they want to quash rebelliousness right here."

Straining to hear, Azazel said, "I wish we had an amplifier."

Semyaza whispered, "We do!" He reached in his pack and pulled out the ten centimetre long listening device, unrolled the wire attached to an earbud, and handed it to Azazel.

After less than a minute Azazel said, "Lilith's command of

their language is way beyond mine, but there's no doubt she's telling them if they want to live they have to get in the sky-gods' bird machine."

Ipos said, "Okay, that does it! Adair is going to get on that shuttle and take the pilot out. Our job is to clear the field so he can do so. That means we have to immobilize all of the remaining crew.

"Go find a position where you have a clear shot at your target. I'll take the first shot and everyone else should fire immediately thereafter. I'll sweep the field to take any second shots, but hopefully they'll all be down with the first volley."

"We'll get 'em, Major," Ramuell said with excitement and fear in equal measure.

"I hope so, but they aren't stationary targets. One thing we absolutely do not want is an extended fire fight." Ipos looked at Adair, "Are you ready to make the run?"

"I'm good."

"Okay, you stay here with me. Everyone else fan out. We start shooting in one minute."

Sixty-four seconds later Ipos fired a charged-particle into the center of a soldier's back. He heard the discharges of the other weapons as he and Captain Adair jumped from the brush and dashed toward the shuttlecraft's door. Ipos scanned the area for any soldiers who hadn't been hit by the initial volley. One man had dropped his weapon and seemed slightly stunned as he lumbered on hands and knees toward a sonic-blaster. A charged-particle probably hit him in the forearm. *We lose the day if he gets to that blaster.* Ipos crouched to one knee and squeezed off a quick shot. It hit the intended target, who twitched violently. *Dammit, I hope that didn't kill him!*

Ipos rose and chased after Adair who had gained the open door, but just barely. The door made a hissing sound as it closed. The shuttlecraft's motors began to whir as the anti-grav mechanisms warmed up. Ipos scrambled away from the P-24 waving frantically for everyone to get back. Then he heard the motors powering down. A few seconds later the door reopened, and Adair stood radiating relief in the threshold.

Ramuell came crashing out of the brush with a "Whoop!" of adolescent braggadocio.

Semyaza scrambled toward the downed troops pulling plastic lashing cords from his back pocket. "Ramuell, help me get these guys tied up before they regain consciousness."

Azazel ran to Dr. Lilith who remained motionless where she'd dropped in a duck and cover position. He kneeled and brushed her hair back. "Lilith, it's me. It's all over. You're okay."

With one eye still squeezed shut, Lilith peeked up at her boss. Slowly she released her hands' vicelike grip on the sides of her head. Putting an arm around her shoulder Azazel helped her into a sitting position. "You're white as a ghost my friend," Azazel said.

"Small wonder!" Lilith leaned into Azazel who took her in a gentle embrace. She began to cry quietly. "I was so scared. I'm almost four hundred annum old and I've never actually witnessed violence. I didn't know who was shooting and who was being shot." She grunted, "For a minute I thought even if I wasn't shot I was gonna die of heart failure."

Azazel reached over and placed two fingers on her carotid artery. "Yikes, your heart is still hammering pretty hard. Just sit here. Take some deep breaths. I'm going to get you some water."

As Azazel approached Ipos, they grinned and surprised each other by exchanging a quick, muscled hug and slap on the back. Azazel said, "Well done Major—**well done**! Hey, I need one of your water bottles. Lilith said she felt like she was having a heart attack and her pulse is racing. Sipping some water should help."

"Sure. It's river water, but she's probably been drinking river water for the last couple of days."

Semyaza approached with a forlorn expression. "The last man we shot is wearing a lieutenant's insignia. He's not going to make it. His pulse is weak. And pupils are fixed and dilated."

"Crap!" was all Azazel said as he turned to take the water to Lilith.

Ipos yanked off his cap and rubbed a hand through his mane of thick, curly hair. "He was crawling toward a sonic-blaster and we couldn't risk that he'd get hold of it. My shot probably hit him in the head."

———

After the prisoners were cuffed, Ipos gathered his impromptu strike force. "Okay folks, are we ready for phase two? More importantly, are we sure we want to go down that road?"

Azazel answered the second question. "I want to go down that road about as much as I want to jump off that cliff, but...I just don't see that we have a choice if we're going to save this sad remnant of the Clan."

Turning to Lilith, Azazel explained, "You and I are going to escort the sapiens and our four captives back into the canyon. You can explain to the clanspeople that our prisoners are bad angels, and they want to hurt the Crow people."

Astonished, Lilith asked, "Just the two of us?"

"Unfortunately yes. The rest of our little rescue party are going to follow the other ships."

A puzzled expression slipped across Lilith's face as she looked around at the four men and Kadeya. "Where is Rarus? I saw him when I was tied up at the camp a couple of days ago. He signaled he'd be back to rescue me."

Azazel's head dropped and he kicked at small stone. The others exchanged furtive glances.

"Oh no! What happened?" Lilith demanded.

Seeing that Azazel was unable to speak, Kadeya answered, "Dr. Lilith, it must have been just minutes after you saw Rarus that he stumbled into the middle of a firefight. We'd been discovered in our hideout by two sentries. Their weapons were dialed to the kill setting. Rarus gave his life saving ours."

Lilith's hands shot up to cover her mouth. She gave Kadeya a wide-eyed stare then raked her gaze around to Azazel. "Are you all right sir? He—he was your friend."

Azazel looked up at Lilith. "No, I'm not all right. It's hard, very hard, to lose someone in your command. But to see someone give his life to save yours, well ... Nope, not all right yet. But Kadeya and I had a talk, and I understand that I'll have to deal with that grief later. Right now my energy is needed in this moment."

"So, you and I are going to escort these people back into the canyon. Then what?" Lilith asked.

"We were able to contact Samael. He's going to sneak away from the basecamp and meet us at the caves. Depending on what kind of transport he's able to filch, he may arrive as early as this evening. Tomorrow or the next day we'll take the prisoners to Dig 421. From there we'll plan our next move. There's a four person security detail at SWA-7. How we deal with that situation is not yet clear."

"And that may remain unclear for quite some time," Semyaza added.

Ipos said, "Okay folks, we need to get moving. If we're too far behind the other craft they may send someone back looking for their comrades."

Adair turned and strode into the shuttlecraft. When they heard the whir of the motors Kadeya, Ramuell, Semyaza and Ipos exchanged palm-taps with Azazel and Lilith.

"Director, keep them in front of you," Ipos said pointing a thumb at the bound prisoners. "Set the sonic-blaster on wide-field-stun and the particle gun on kill. Make sure they see the weapons' settings."

Azazel grimaced then sighed.

After their compatriots had departed, Lilith and Azazel dug a shallow hollow in the rocky ground. They covered the dead soldier with a layer of dirt then piled head-size stones on top of his grave. "He was just a kid." Lilith said quietly. "They all are."

"Just a bunch of kids following orders," Azazel agreed. "Perhaps the orders of a madman."

"Humph, a madman who fancies himself some kind of god."

Azazel walked over to the wrist bound captives, removed his cap and asked, "Would any of you like to say some words over your lieutenant's grave?"

The expressions the four men exchanged revealed their surprise at the kindness of Azazel's offer. The pilot looked up with his clear blue-grey eyes and said, "Yeah, I believe I would."

Azazel gave a tight lipped nod. He knelt in front of the men and laid his weapons on the ground. First he picked up the sonic-blaster and made a show of setting it on wide-field stun. Then he switched the charged-particle gun onto the kill setting.

The prisoners' wrists were bound behind their backs, and they were tethered to a six metre long cable. Azazel stepped behind the group and one at a time helped each man to his feet. With a hand wave he indicated the captives were free to approach their friend's grave; that he was allowing them thirty metres of privacy.

Seeing Lilith watching, Azazel turned away and blew out a long, sad exhale.

Adair engaged the energy signature tracker to ascertain if the hijacked ship's preprogrammed flight plan was on the same heading as the earlier shuttles. If the other two shuttlecraft were en route to different destinations that would scuttle their plans to retrieve the Clan.

The first two shuttles had risen to an altitude of over ninety kilometres, indicating their destination was perhaps half-a-world away. Once at altitude the tracking device and the ship's flight plan indicated all three craft had the same destination; a high plateau in the mountains of the southern hemisphere's smaller continent.

Ipos, Semyaza, Ramuell and Kadeya rummaged through a locker stuffed with dirty uniforms. They all found something that fit well enough.

"When we arrive only I will disembark," Ipos instructed. "Hopefully, the other soldiers in the squadron of kidnappers won't be at the docking facility. I'll learn where they've taken the Clan. Then we can plan how, **or if**, we can mount a rescue."

"Aren't they going to be curious about why we didn't bring the other hybrids?" Kadeya asked.

"Probably. If they ask, I'll explain that we dispatched the nine clanspeople who refused to board the ship," Ipos explained.

"Pretty flimsy," Semyaza observed. "Someone may ask why we didn't just stun them and haul them onboard."

"In that case, I'll say we received new orders. We were told to kill any rebellious sapiens."

Semyaza squeezed his lips together and nodded. "Mmm, that's pretty good. Given the chaotic conditions on the planet and the insane orders coming from the Presidium, that explanation is sadly plausible."

"But what if there are soldiers from the squadron at the landing site who realize you're not one of them?" Kadeya asked.

"That's our worst case scenario." Ipos replied. "I'll be wearing this collar-camera, so you'll see and hear pretty much what I see and hear. If my cover is blown, I turn and run like hell while you guys provide a line of cover fire. Do you know how that's done?"

Kadeya shook her head and looked at Ramuell. He said, "Nope."

Ipos spent the next twenty minutes demonstrating how to stay out of each other's way while laying down an arc of discharges that should keep their opponents ducked behind cover.

From the pilot's cockpit Adair called over his shoulder, "On low power these motors run almost silently. I'll keep them idling so if we have to, we can beat a retreat the instant you're onboard."

"That's good." Ipos narrowed his eyes and added, "We're going to need a lot of luck to retrieve even a few of the Crow Clan. To get them all, we'll need to be ridiculously lucky."

As it would turn out, they weren't, and they were.

CHAPTER FORTY-NINE

CRY "HAVOC!" AND LET SLIP THE CATS OF WAR

IPOS EXITED the ship onto an elevated platform assembled with enormous, precisely hewn blocks of silica-stone. The rest of his party remain in the ship riveted to the video-screens.

"I figured this was our destination," Kadeya said. Ramuell looked at her quizzically. "Remember I mentioned this facility when we met in my apartment before the Committee of Inquiry hearing. Our mining corporations discovered rich metal deposits in this mountain chain. They're shipping out unprecedented amounts of gold. The Presidium authorized building this terminal to accommodate 4D cargo ships. By loading the behemoths down here, we skip the step of routing through orbiting facilities."

"That explains the heavy-duty construction. This facility is designed to handle ships a lot larger than our anti-grav transports," Adair noted.

Semyaza said, "When you mentioned this place in our conversation I didn't envision anything this massive. We've always been so cautious to limit our footprint. How will we ever pulverize blocks of stone as huge as that?" He pointed at a slab on the video-screen with a surface area of about seven-metres by five-metres. "The slabs are almost two metres thick. What are they thinking?"

"They're thinking profits," Kadeya replied. "The sapiens' descendants **will** find this site, no matter what we do to scrub the scene."

They watched Ipos as he called, "Good Day," to an approaching Port Authority official.

"Hello sir. Your friends were beginning to get worried. We called over and told them you just arrived," the woman explained.

"Uh, where are they?"

"They're over at the small terminal on the south side of the lake. You've landed at the wrong facility," she explained.

"That's odd, we were on a pre-programmed flight plan," Ipos said.

"This was your original destination, but a flight plan change was sent to your ships."

Ipos pasted on a quizzical expression, "Maybe we weren't airborne when the message was sent."

She gave him an odd look and he realized he may have said something giving away his ignorance. Recovering quickly, he added, "So we'll find both of our other ships over there?"

"Yep."

Rubbing the back of his neck, "I suppose they've already unloaded their cargo."

"Cargo?" the woman snickered. "You mean the sapiens?"

"Well, I suppose this wasn't much of a secret mission," Ipos commented.

"I'd heard the Presidium's new soldiers were a bit green, but secret mission—really?" She laughed. "Moving *sapes* around is hardly a secret. Heck, we see three to six transports every undecim. I'm sure yours are already over at the mud huts."

Ipos looked away and drawled, "Okaaay..."

"Hey, I'm gonna need you folks to clear the platform. We have a cargo ship scheduled to land soon." She pointed at the other end of huge platform and said, "In fact, there are some of our *sapes* getting ready for the arrival right now."

Ipos followed her gesture and saw several sapien-hybrids wearing coveralls and positioning anti-grav pallets loaded with flat rectangular slabs of gold ingot. "Okay, then we'll be getting out of your way." Turning back toward the ship, Ipos called over his shoulder, "Sorry about the mix-up. Thanks for your help."

"So, the Clan isn't here," Kadeya said as the shuttlecraft door closed.

"Right. The other ships landed at a smaller terminal south of the lake."

"Did I hear her say the *sapes*," Semyaza rolled his eyes when he used the term, "have been moved to mud huts?"

"Yep, but I don't know what that means," Ipos replied. "The question is, do we think we can find these huts, wade in there and get the Clan out? Or, should we cut bait and run?"

From the pilot's seat Adair asked, "What do you want me to do, boss?"

Semyaza pointed up, "But go slowly."

The ship ascended higher than necessary for such a short hop, but not so high as to seem suspicious. From their vantage point a kilometre overhead they studied the terminal carefully.

Both of the ships from Blue Rock Canyon were stowed neatly at the eastern edge of the landing platform. Four other ships were packed tightly in front of a hangar on the terminal's west side. An enormous Anti-GravXL shuttle dwarfed the other aircraft on the platform.

Ipos asked Adair, "You're qualified to fly one of those monsters too?"

"I actually piloted an XL on about a dozen missions a few annum ago. We were transporting equipment to a new mine site. They're great ships, but so heavy when the anti-grav magnets are shut off they **must** be sitting on a flat, solid surface."

Semyaza was studying magnified images of the ground below. "There are people moving around the platform. They seem to be doing routine maintenance. None are wearing Security Force uniforms. I don't see any of the Crow Clan."

"Do you see any primitive looking structures?" Ipos asked.

"The hangars are cellulose buildings," Semyaza replied. "There are also a few hewn stone structures. I just can't get over how strange it is that we've used massive stone blocks... wait a minute...that might be it. There are four small buildings several hundred metres east of the docking facility. They have thatch roofs. Take a look."

Ipos stepped over to the viewer. "Yeah, that must be what we're looking for—and those may be sapiens milling around."

"That's good, isn't it?" Ramuell asked. "They're not locked inside."

"Yeeaahh, maybe," Ipos drawled. "But—I'm not seeing any soldiers."

"Which means they're probably inside the huts." Semyaza conjectured.

"We can't just hover around up here any longer," Adair

cautioned. "...at least not without raising questions with the Port Authority."

"Can you land near the huts?" Semyaza asked.

"Oh yeah. All we need is a semi-flat spot. Unlike that XL, flat stone platforms are a luxury for this bird."

Ipos inhaled deeply and said, "Alright, let's drop in close to the huts somewhere with a little cover."

When the P-24 made its characteristic humming noise on descent, the clanspeople looked up then scrambled into the huts. On their final approach Ipos said, "Set us down with the portside door facing the huts. Before I get out, you three exit the starside door. Hide behind the ship. Be ready to lay out an arc of cover fire at an instant's notice."

A moment later Adair eased the ship onto its landing feet. He swiveled the captain's chair around and hopped out of the cockpit into the passenger cabin.

Ipos handed Adair a sonic-blaster. "Stand just out of sight at the portside door. If things go bad, sweep the whole field with several shots. You'll probably have to drag us back onto the ship."

Looking at the girth of Ipos' torso, Adair cocked an eyebrow.

"Maybe adrenalin will kick in," Ipos said with mock hopefulness.

Ramuell bit his lip then said, "I don't think Grandmother should go out there. She should stay on the ship and if necessary shoot from the portside door."

Ipos nodded thoughtfully. Turning to Kadeya he said, "Ma'am, I'm not saying you're old, but Ramuell makes a good point."

With a mirthless chuckle, "You need not say I'm an old woman. Facts speak for themselves."

"Well, perhaps. I do know a firefight is challenging even for a young person—especially in the thin air of this altitude. We're almost four thousand metres above ocean level. If Adair has to lay us down with a sonic blast, you'll be here to help haul us onboard."

Adair added, "And if it goes that badly, someone's likely to be injured. Dr. Kadeya would be able to attend to wounds while I get us airborne."

Kadeya said, "The fact is I **am** too old to be running around out there. I might even endanger you. Everyone has a role to play, tending wounds makes sense for me."

Ramuell blew out a relieved breath.

"Okay, are we ready?" Ipos asked as he picked up his charged-particle gun and stuffed a solid-projectile weapon in his jacket pocket.

Semyaza told Ipos, "Pull your hood over your head to hide that bushy mane. Cinch it around your face. A bit of disguise may buy you some time. The soldiers won't fire on you if they're not sure who you are."

"One of the men we captured at the canyon actually was about your size," Ramuell recalled.

"Yeah, this is probably his uniform. Okay folks, let's do this. But remember, we don't die trying to free the Crow Clan. If we can't do it, we can't. We live to fight another day."

Ipos affected a casual stride in the direction of the four huts arrayed in a semicircle some two hundred metres away. His eyes darted around taking in everything. He saw no movement within the structures.

A four-metre tall slab of silica-stone lay on its edge a little less than halfway to the huts. One corner of the stone had broken off and was lying on the ground almost directly in his path. The triangular chunk was about two metres wide and well over a metre thick. As he approached the discarded quarry stones, a Domhanian voice called out a name Ipos didn't recognize. He stopped, waved, and resumed his approach.

This time the voice ordered him to halt. As he stood waiting, he studied the structures carefully. They were made of reeds and heavy grasses woven through a stick superstructure and chinked with mud. *They may be decent weather protection, but they don't offer much in the way of armor.*

As if the soldiers in the huts had read his thoughts, the heads of several clansmen appeared in each window. Terrorism was almost unheard of on Domhan-Siol. Ipos had never even considered the notion of using living beings as shields.

The voice came again, "Why did you land over here?"

Ipos had anticipated this question, "We hovered overhead for several minutes but there was a lot of activity on the landing platform. The pilot suggested we could just as easily land nearby."

Again there was a delay. "What's the pilot's name?"

Dammit we should have gotten their names. Ipos took two giant steps then dove for cover behind the broken-off wedge of stone.

When Ramuell saw a sonic-blaster emerge from a hut window, he shoved Semyaza behind the starside ramp and threw himself to the ground behind one of the ship's landing feet. The heavy hinged strut protected him from the concussion waves of two blasts. Squirming to his knees he peered around the strut and saw Ipos sitting with his back against the stone.

Ipos and Ramuell exchanged thumbs-up signs. Ipos pointed to his ear and drew a finger across his throat. The blaster had disabled his earbud receiver. He leaned over and spoke into his collar-microphone. Ramuell heard only static.

"Grandma, can you hear Ipos?"

"Yes, we can hear him fine."

Ramuell realized his earbud had also been fried. He stood just high enough for Ipos to see him. Cupping his hands beside his mouth, Ramuell hollered, "They can hear you." He pointed up at the ship. "I can't."

Ipos gave Ramuell another thumbs-up then ducked his head and began speaking into his collar-mic. "They made a show of standing some of the clanspeople in front of the windows; we can't fire on them."

"Those bastards!" Adair exclaimed. Kadeya relayed the message down to Ramuell, who held up his weapon for Ipos to see then waved his hand back-and-forth in a negating gesture. Ipos nodded.

"What about using sonic-blasters?" Kadeya asked. "We could grab the clanspeople, drag them aboard and get this ship in the air."

Semyaza had climbed back aboard the ship and was studying the huts with binoculars. "The walls appear thick enough to prevent a knockout punch with the blasters set on stun, but it's too risky to power them up."

Adair said, "Yeah, and we have another problem."

"Which is?" Semyaza asked.

"This ship's a P-24. There are at least thirty sapiens and five of us."

Semyaza slapped his forehead. "We could never squeeze in that many people."

They looked at each other for a moment then Kadeya announced matter-of-factly, "We have to steal the Anti-GravXL."

Gaping at the group's senior citizen, the two men realized she was right. It was either that or abandon the idea of rescuing the whole clan.

At that moment, the ship's motion detector alarms began to buzz. The motion sensor-camera zoomed to the west but didn't autofocus on anything. Adair switched the camera from visual to thermal imagery. It panned back-and-forth across the heat images of five people approaching the ship from the west. They were spread out in a two hundred metre wide arc, advancing in a squat-trot.

Semyaza said, "They've arrayed themselves widely, making it difficult to take them down with sonic blasts." After giving the situation a moment's thought he continued, "Adair, you have to stay here—only you can pilot the craft. Ramuell and I are going to go take out the two men on each flank. They're not expecting us. We should be able to ambush them easily enough."

"Stun?" Kadeya asked hopefully.

"Oh yeah, stun only. We've got no reason to kill anyone."

"And what should I do?" Kadeya asked.

"You're going to hide beneath the starside ramp and take out anyone approaching the ship," Semyaza answered.

Adair said, "Okay. And I'll stand just inside with the sonic-blaster."

"And you also have to keep an eye on what's happening with Ipos."

Ramuell slithered back from the landing foot where he'd been hiding and Semyaza explained the plan. Just before they began to crawl away Kadeya squeezed Ramuell's shoulder. He leaned over and they tapped foreheads gently.

The sun was setting and Semyaza knew they needed to get their shots off before it became too dark to see. The last thing he said to Ramuell before parting was, "When you have a shot take it. Then try to locate your second target as quickly as possible."

The assault team arrived only a couple of minutes after Ramuell and Semyaza had taken up their respective positions. Semyaza didn't take his own advice. He had a clear shot at the second man from the right but hesitated when he heard a noise further to the right. He looked but saw no movement. He'd reacquired the man in his sights when a woman standing behind him said, "Drop it!"

He did not. Instead he squeezed off the shot. The charged-particle felled his target like a sawed tree. Semyaza began his roll with a feint to the right then rapidly back to the left. The woman standing behind him was so stunned by Semyaza's unexpected disobedience and the sight of her fallen comrade that she froze for half a second – four tenths of a second too long. Semyaza had rolled onto his back and squeezed off two wild shots. The first charge hit the officer in the shin and as she crumpled, the second slammed into her sternum. Even with his weapon set on stun, the jolt of two charged-particles at such close range was too much. Her heart beat arrhythmically eight or ten more times in this life.

When she groaned, Semyaza heard the other members of the assault team dropping to the ground and scrambling for cover. He scurried on hands and knees toward his first target, arriving in time to see the light on the officer's communicator blinking. Snatching the device from the unconscious man's face Semyaza put it on. The commander was saying, "Gordone, are you there? Gordone, check in."

"Okay here." Semyaza held his breath and waited.

"Where did the shots come from?"

Rubbing the microphone to create static, Semyaza kept his words to a minimum, "Not sure—dove for cover—banged a knee."

There was a long pause. Semyaza snapped plastic ties

around the unconscious man's wrists and ankles and began crawling toward Ramuell's position.

The sun had now set, and daylight was giving way to the short grey twilight typical of this latitude. Semyaza sensed something big approaching the man he'd left bound behind him. Suddenly there was a roar and the man screamed wildly. Semyaza heard what sounded like the splintering of bones and instantly the screams fell silent.

The commanding officer began hollering, "Fall back! We've got a long-tooth cat. There will be more! Get out of here!"

Ramuell had kept his sights trained on the location where one of his targets had taken cover. When the man stood to run, Ramuell had a clear shot but chose not to fire. Scanning the horizon, he saw the silhouettes of three people running wildly back toward the smaller docking facility. It was then that he heard the low growl of a giant smilodon cat warning the younger cats in the pride off her kill.

Meanwhile, inside the mud huts the Serefim Security squadron's lack of experience, coupled with the fact that their commanding officer was lying in a shallow grave on Blue Rock canyon's rim, was taking a toll. Unbidden, one of the soldiers grabbed a grenade launcher loaded with a 2.5 kilogram impact projectile. He fired it at the shuttlecraft some two hundred metres west of the dwellings. Not having experience with the weapon, he failed to calculate trajectory. The hard polypropylene projectile fell short of the fuselage but slammed into one of the landing struts. The craft wobbled and groaned as its portside collapsed to the ground with the slow-motion twisting of metal.

The soldier who had fired the weapon whooped and ran some thirty metres into the yard toward the disabled shuttle. His comrades watched in horror as an enormous smilodon streaked toward him. The giant cat slammed the man to the ground with a single swipe of her gigantic paw. She gored him with her long teeth as she snatched him up; her powerful jaws snapped his spine like a twig.

The bewildering scene was so incomprehensible to the Serefim soldiers they stood rooted like trees as the cat carried their comrade away into the enveloping darkness. Whereas the clanspeople understood exactly what they'd witnessed and retreated to huddle against the back walls of the flimsy shelters.

The squad leader let out a delayed scream of fear, then gathering his wits punched the Emergency Alert code into his communicator. "This is Sergeant Kassim of SPSF Squadron 119. We're under attack. Our commanding officer is missing. We have in our custody a clan of sapiens from SWA-7. We were followed and are now pinned down by a troop of unknown hostiles. We've also lost one man to a long-tooth cat."

Communicators everywhere erupted! "What did you say?"... "Did he say a cat?" ...

After about a minute of radio bedlam, an authoritative voice came on the air. "Silence! Silence! Clear this channel. This is Commander Croga—Sergeant, what is your name again?"

"Sergeant Kassim."

"What is your location?"

"We're in the thatch shelters near the landing facility south of the lake."

"Okay, you're in the mud huts. How many soldiers do you have with you?"

"Eight—no, only seven," Kassim answered.

"Now listen to me, smilodons travel and hunt in groups. There may be as many as twenty in a pride. Do not, I repeat, **do not** leave those shelters," the Port Authority commander ordered.

"What about doing a sweep with a sonic-blaster?" the lieutenant asked.

"Absolutely not! Ineffective. You don't know where the smilodons are, what cover they're in, or how far away they are. Any people you might disable with the sonic blasts **will** be taken by the cats. You should shoot any cats that approach the huts with charged-particle weapons. You do have those, don't you?"

"Yes sir, we have six," Kassim answered.

"Good. Set them on kill and sit tight. How many hostiles are assaulting your location?" Commander Croga asked.

"Uhm, eight, maybe ten?"

"You don't sound sure. Did they arrive in one ship?"

"Yes, one ship—the other P-24 transport we had at Blue Rock Canyon."

"So there could be a lot more than eight or ten. They must have hijacked the ship after you departed and followed you here." Croga rubbed his brow as he thought through the exigencies; a pride of enormous carnivores and perhaps twenty or more armed assailants. "This is going to take some time. We're going to mount a rescue, but first we'll try to get some heat signature images to figure out what we're dealing with.

"I want everyone listening in on this conversation to stay the hell off of your communicators. I want this channel open—and I mean not a peep. My voice will be the next one anybody hears on this frequency."

As the shuttlecraft collapsed, Adair's main concern was for Kadeya. "Hey! Are you okay out there?" he shouted.

"Yeah, the strut buckled slowly—plenty of time to get out

of the way." After climbing into the ship, she scanned the area to the west in search of her grandson and Semyaza.

On the other side of the ship Ipos had watched the enormous cat tossing the Serefim soldier around like a toy. *This may be the most gruesome distraction of all time!* He rolled from behind the broken off wedge of stone to the large slab. Peeking around the corner at the huts he saw nothing to give him pause. Crouching he ran back to the crippled ship.

Kadeya jumped when Ipos popped up in the starside doorway. "Oh dear gods! You scared me!"

"Sorry," Ipos said. "So, what's happening?"

"An assault team was approaching from the west. Semyaza and Ramuell went out to intercept them. We heard shots, cat roars, and screams," Kadeya answered anxiously.

"Did you see what happened in front of the huts?" Ipos asked.

"No. The collapsing ship had all of my attention. But we've been listening to the communications chatter."

"It was the damnedest thing I've ever seen!" Ipos exclaimed. "I'll head out to look for Ramuell and Semyaza, but first I need to speak to Adair."

Just as Ipos pulled himself into the crumpled P-24, Kadeya saw her grandson and Semyaza crawling single file toward the ship. She gasped, looked thankfully toward the heavens, and saw planets beginning to glow in the darkening sky.

When everyone was safely aboard the disabled craft, they sat on the sloping deck sharing stories. "There must be several of those monsters out there," Ipos said. "We're gonna have to hole up in here for a while."

"We can't wait too long. The Port Authority commander is working on a rescue plan. He said something about getting heat images," Adair informed the group.

Thinking out loud, Semyaza mumbled, “They won’t get images of us in here—maybe a good thing.”

“Perhaps...” Ipos added hesitantly. “But if they determine we’re likely sheltered inside, they may just demolish the ship.”

“So we’ve got to take our chances with the cats?” Ramuell asked.

Ipos replied, “Not just yet. We sit tight for a few more minutes.”

CHAPTER FIFTY
REUNION

Some six kilometres east of the smaller docking facility, Imamiah, Althea, Egan and a dozen Oprit-Robia fighters exited their 4D transport as the sun was setting. The ship then hopped to a high mountain glacier just a short distance north.

Major Anso led the squad two kilometres down a small drainage. They found a hideout protected by a four metre high bank on the west side and a grove of waxy leafed trees to the east.

The squad had intercepted the Port Authority communications and couldn't believe what they were hearing. A tiny Oprit-Robia geosynchronous satellite had been monitoring all arrivals and departures at the main port for six days. "How could they get a whole clan of sapiens down there without us seeing them?" Althea asked.

"They didn't," Imamiah answered with disgust. "They offloaded them at the small port. We were buffoons and should have been surveilling both docks."

Anso said, "That's a bygone. The question now is who's trying to rescue the sapiens?"

"Who knows?!" Imamiah responded. "But I suspect Commander Croga is correct. The ship was probably hijacked at Blue Rock Canyon then followed the other ships here."

"Where is Blue Rock Canyon?" Althea asked.

Imamiah scrolled through global location data on her foliopad. "Humph, it's in SWA-7."

Althea sucked in a sharp breath. Egan shot his wife a nervous glance. Turning to Imamiah, Althea asked, "Have we intercepted any of the rescuer's communications?"

"Not a peep."

"So we have no idea who they are?" Althea asked.

"No, we don't," Imamiah replied.

Major Anso said, "Nevertheless, I don't think we have much time. If we're going to accomplish our mission, we've got to wade into the fray."

The communication silence was broken by Commander Croga's voice. "Sergeant Kassim."

"Yes sir."

"The cats are moving off to the south—eleven in all. There are no heat signatures outside of the ship. Which means the assailants are onboard—probably hiding from the smilodons. But we can't figure out why they're still grounded," Croga said.

"Sir, they can't takeoff. We blew out one of their landing struts."

"And you didn't think that might be something I needed to know?" Croga gritted his teeth.

"I...I'm sorry sir. I just, well I just..."

Croga took a purging breath and said, "No, no, I shouldn't blame you. These are extraordinary circumstances. I should have asked more questions. You've got your hands full over there. How are your sapes doing?"

"Sir, they're terrified of those cats—I suppose we are too."

"As well you should be," Croga replied.

After listening to the exchange between Croga and Kassim, Ipos opened a supply cabinet and pulled out a box of polyimide heat sheets. He popped the vacuum seal on each pack as he handed them out. "Wrap yourselves in these. The sheets will goof their heat signature equipment. Now that the Commander knows our ship's disabled, he'll likely order an attack."

Adair scooted down the precariously tilted metal floor toward the starside door and said, "Let's get out of this deathtrap and go steal a big ship."

"Right," Ipos agreed. "We need to spread out and zig zag our way toward the landing platform. Pull the heat sheets over your heads. I'll stay several metres behind to cover the rear. Hopefully, they won't send anyone out from the huts, but now that they know the cats are gone...who knows?"

"We know they only have seven soldiers in there. They probably have their hands full with a bunch of panicky clanspeople," Semyaza said hopefully.

The Oprit-Robia squad had also listened in on Commander Croga's and Sergeant Kassim's conversation. Major Anso said, "Okay team, squeeze in here close enough to see the map on the foliopad. It's only two kilometres from here to the grass shacks. We'll leave a four person team there." He pointed at the two women and two men standing to his left. "The remainder of us will cover the last kilometre to the landing facility. We'll assess the strength of their defenses before making any decisions about how to engage.

"Imamiah, Althea and Egan, I want you to move as quickly as possible to this position." He pointed to a small round top hill about four hundred metres south of the mud huts. "Put our two drones up and do a continuous search of the area between the two docking facilities. If you see anything, key your communicator, and say 'company' and give me a one word estimate of their number.

"Otherwise, we'll maintain complete communicator silence. If we make the decision to strike," looking at the four assigned to take the mud huts, "I'll signal you with three clicks, two seconds of silence, then two more clicks on the communicators. When or rather **if** you hear that, you should take the huts immediately. With the element of surprise, you'll only need a few seconds to take out the seven defenders.

"Imamiah, how soon will our transport ship return?" Anso asked.

She looked at her communicator's timer and said, "It'll be landing on the escarpment in about ninety minutes."

"Okay, that's good. Hopefully we can have this done and be out of here in a couple of hours."

As they moved cautiously toward the docking facility, Ramuell heard rustling brush to his left. He frantically waved his hands signaling for everyone to stop and drop. Semyaza turned and clicked his tongue twice. When Ipos saw his comrades lying prone in the grey light of the waxing half-moon, he also dropped to his stomach.

Soon everyone else was able to make out the sounds of people moving through the open field to their left. Ipos slithered forward to join the others under a more or less solid layer of the polyimide heat sheets. He whispered to Ramuell, "Can you tell who they are and where they're headed?"

Semyaza retrieved the amplification device from his pocket and handed it to Ramuell. After listening for a minute, Ramuell answered, "They're not speaking much, but I'd guess they're Port Authority security hunting for us. They're creeping slowly toward our ship."

"Then we lay here and wait for them to pass," Ipos said.

Within twenty minutes the Oprit-Robia fighters had arrived at the shacks housing the Crow Clan and their captors. The four assigned fighters took up positions behind the huts. The other eight began trotting toward the docking facility.

As they passed by, Adair whispered, "Now what the heck is all that noise?"

Still using the amplification device, Ramuell pointed to his right and said, "I don't know. They're over there and moving pretty fast."

The Port Authority security detail also heard the trotting Oprit-Robia fighters. Ramuell said, "Shh, shh," as he listened to a frantic conversation. "The guys on our left are **definitely** Port Authority security. Some of them are circling back to the dock. The others are going on toward our ship and the mud huts." He listened intently for a few more seconds. "They've been going so slowly because they're not sure if we are still in the ship or if we've surrounded the huts."

Ipos said, "Good! That means they think there are a lot of us."

"So what just went running by over there?" Kadeya asked. "More cats?"

Ipos answered, "Nope, those were boots. I'd guess about ten people."

"What do we do now?" Semyaza asked.

"For now we lay here and wait. Under these sheets we're dang near invisible to heat imaging devices," Ipos answered.

———

The four Oprit-Robia fighters had positioned themselves to rush each of the huts should they hear Anso's communicator clicks. Quite suddenly six Port Authority security personnel jumped out of a shallow trench less than a hundred metres to the south. When the Serefim soldiers guarding the Crow Clan heard the footfalls coming quickly toward the huts they believed they were under attack. Two of them stepped outside and fired sonic-blasters. Again their lack of training and discipline cost them. The soldier shooting from the northern most hut downed his comrade who was standing almost directly in the line of fire.

Three of the Port Authority servicemen saw what was happening and dove back into the trench just in time to avoid the blast.

Major Anso and the Oprit-Robia team dropped to the ground when they heard the sonic discharges. He grabbed his communicator and said only, "What?"

"Huts have been attacked!"

"Who?" Anso asked.

"Don't know." Anso heard a background voice, "Look like Port Authority uniforms."

Anso turned to his fighters, "Holy hell, these guys are idiots!"

Royan, who was lying next to him asked, "What should we do?"

Anso shook his head and snorted. "I suppose if they're fighting each other, we should take advantage of their stupidity." He tapped his communicator three times, waited two seconds then tapped it twice more.

Upon hearing the signal, each of the Oprit-Robia fighters at the mud huts rolled stun bombs into their assigned shelters. The sensory overload of a blinding flash and deafening bang was utterly disorienting to everyone inside. Stooping low, the Oprit-Robia combatants stepped inside each structure and stunned everyone wearing a uniform. They immediately bound their captives' hands and feet and also ran strips of tape across their mouths.

One of the Oprit-Robia fighters ran back into the yard and picked up the sonic-blaster dropped by the Serefim soldier who'd been hit from behind by his trigger-happy comrade. She set it on wide-field and started methodically discharging blast after blast; no creature within two hundred metres south of the huts would be moving for the next half hour.

The clanspeople inside the huts were disoriented, frightened, and hurt. Many had simply folded in on themselves. Long-tooth cats were terrifying enough; but angels using their magic sticks on each other...that was completely incomprehensible.

Less than two minutes after the assault began, everything at the huts fell silent. Anso spoke quietly into his communicator, "Report."

"Got 'em."

"Move the clan?" Anso asked

"Negative, we need pick up."

"Secure area—wait," Anso instructed.

Imamiah realized that scanning the area nearest the main docking facility first, rather than starting at the small site and working backwards, had been an amateurish mistake. By the time they saw the contingent of Port Authority personnel, they were deploying in defensive positions around the ships on the small landing platform. "Oh good gods!"

She switched on her communicator and said urgently, "Company!" They waited a moment but got no response. She repeated the warning, "Company!" Again no response.

"They're not hearing you. I'm sitting right here and didn't pick up your signal." Althea grabbed her communicator and said, "Company." Both Egan's and Imamiah's communicators emitted only static.

Egan snorted. "The sonic-blaster must have fried the microphones."

"Dammit!" Imamiah exclaimed. "This is my fault. I should have insisted we swap our personal devices with military grade communicators—just never occurred to me."

Althea asked, "So what should we do?"

"We **must** warn Anso."

"What if we downed one of the drones on top of them," Egan asked.

Shaking her head, Imamiah said, "Nah, he'll probably just assume it's malfunctioned. Let's use the drones to find their location. We can then run head them off."

Within a minute Imamiah and Althea had piloted their drones into the area east of the docking facility. Almost simultaneously they said, "There they are."

Egan leaned over and looked at the screen, "Yep, eight heat signatures, and they're not moving."

"Maybe they've seen the Port Authority security team on the dock," Althea said hopefully.

Imamiah said, "I don't see anything to worry about between here and there. We can circle behind the shacks then run directly to the squad."

"We should land the drones near their location and pick 'em up later," Egan suggested.

Imamiah led Egan and Althea across the open flat area behind the mud huts. The moon was setting, but there was still enough light to make out the disabled ship leaning awkwardly on the ground. They angled to the northwest and continued moving quickly, hoping Anso and the fighters were holding their position.

Still some two hundred metres from the Oprit-Robia troop's last known location, Imamiah caught her foot on something solid and tumbled hard on her shoulder. Suddenly what seemed to have been a mound of dirt sprang to life. People scrambled out in every direction from under the sand colored heat sheets. They pointed weapons at Egan, Althea and Imamiah.

It was too dark to make out facial features, but something about the way they moved seemed unnervingly familiar to Kadeya. "Hold your fire!" Hesitantly she said, "Althea? Egan?"

Several seconds of stunned silence followed. Her voice was so out of context – so totally unexpected – Egan and Althea were momentarily unable to identify this person they knew so well. Ramuell couldn't make sense of what his grandmother had just said. The hush was broken by Althea's squeal. She slammed her hand over her mouth and dove into her mother's arms. Kadeya caught her in a full embrace, and they dropped to their knees rocking each other back-and-forth.

"What the heck is going on here?" Ipos asked.

Neither Ramuell nor his father understood well enough to

answer. After watching Althea and Kadeya for a moment they turned and stared at each other. "Ramuell, it's you. It's really you!" Egan said at last.

Ramuell took one step then lunged into his father's embrace. "All these annum we thought you were gone—lost to us forever," Ramuell said with eyes squeezed tight to staunch his tears.

Althea released her mother, turned, and gathered her husband and son in a group hug. Tears flowed unchecked and she couldn't stop sniffing. Wordlessly they held each other for a long time. At last Egan released himself from the huddle and offered his hand to Kadeya. They exchanged a quick palm-tap then embraced.

Althea stepped back, gripped Ramuell by the shoulders and held him at arm's length, trying to give him a good looking-over in the semi-dark. Ramuell asked, "How did you get here? Where did you come from?"

Before Althea could answer they heard the pops of charged-particle weapons. The sounds were coming from the docking facility to the west. Imamiah exclaimed, "Aw hell!" as everyone dove to the ground near where she still lay, rubbing her shoulder.

A hundred metres further ahead, Major Anso and his team had seen that the ships berthed on the well-lit landing platform were heavily guarded. Having already taken control of the Crow Clan, they understood there was no choice but to "liberate" the Anti-GravXL. After studying the Port Authority defenses, one of the team members recommended a surgical strike to take out the four men armed with sonic-blasters.

"Yep, that's exactly what we should do," Anso agreed. He

assigned two of the Oprit fighters to target each of the four Port Authority soldiers armed with sonic blasters. He arrayed his squad in an arc around the northern side of the facility.

Anso fired first and the other marksmen fired within half a second. All four of the stunned soldiers dropped immediately, but two more emerged from deep servicing bays at the back of the platform and let fly a series of sonic blasts.

Egan, Althea and Imamiah had squeezed under the heat sheets with the others. Semyaza had reasoned the polyimide material would provide adequate protection from a sonic-blaster over three hundred metres away. He was right. Though their ears were ringing, they were not otherwise disabled.

Imamiah heard Semyaza's communicator crackle to life. The Port Authority defenders were reporting to Commander Croga. Still tucked under the heat sheets Imamiah asked Semyaza, "May I use your communicator? Ours were cooked earlier by the sonic blasts from the mud huts. I should be able to dial yours to our squad's frequency."

Semyaza handed Imamiah his device. "Have at it."

Thirty seconds later she was stunned to hear a distress call from the Oprit-Robia ship's captain. The ship had returned early to the escarpment above the mud huts. The pilot said, "We've got company up here."

Throwing the sheet off, Imamiah said to Althea, "We need to get the drones up."

Althea grabbed the remote control devices from her pack and handed one to Egan. "You fly one over the landing platform and I'll send one up to the ridge to see what's going on with our ship."

"Right!" Egan flipped the switches to power up the nearby drone. It only took him a minute to locate the prone bodies of four Oprit-Robia fighters who were felled by the sonic blasts. He soon located the unimpaired fighters as well. "Four of our people are on the move. It seems they weren't hit by the blasts. They're crawling away from the dock."

Egan elevated the drone some two hundred metres and scanned the platform. "It looks like we took out several of the Port Authority guys, but at least ten are still active."

Imamiah said, "Well, those aren't good odds."

"Nope, and reinforcements are probably en route," Ipos reminded her.

Althea sat cross legged on the ground studying the view screen in her lap. "Uh oh."

Jerking her head around, Imamiah said, "Uh oh, what?"

Althea turned the screen around and held it up for the others to see. The Oprit-Robia transport vehicle was surrounded by three tiny vehicles. Adair scooted over to Althea for a closer look. He studied the screen carefully. "What the heck are those things?"

"How many people?" Imamiah asked.

"I count six," Althea replied.

Imamiah stroked her forehead then picked up Semyaza's communicator and said, "Oprit Ship 1, this is Highbrows. Liftoff. I repeat, liftoff."

"Without you!?"

"Defenders down here shot a landing strut out from underneath our other possible evacuation ship," Imamiah explained.

The pilot replied, "Eyes in the sky." The ship lurched, sending the six Port Authority people scrambling for cover.

"'Eyes in the sky' meant she'll hover overhead keeping an eye on us," Imamiah explained.

While this was going on, four quadcopters arrived at the landing platform. A dozen armed personnel boiled out of the aircraft. The quadcopters swooped away at a low angle as soon as the passengers were clear of the rotors. Semyaza and Ipos sat close to Egan watching the deployment on the screen.

"Okay, those aren't trained security personnel," Ipos observed. "They don't carry themselves like soldiers."

"Yeah," Semyaza agreed. "They've given weapons to some dock workers and told them to come over here as a show of force. Actually, there's no way a facility like this should have more than a dozen, maybe fifteen, security personnel. There just wouldn't be any reason to have a hefty security team."

"Perhaps there is," Imamiah speculated. "Oprit-Robia's raids have become increasingly daring. The Presidium knows we're busy liberating sapien slaves."

Ipos grunted.

"The two people in front of us are beginning to move," Egan said excitedly as he watched the drone's video-feed.

Imamiah scooted over to look at the screen. After a few seconds she said, "That's Anso!" She tapped the screen with a fingernail.

"We've gotta go get him," Egan said. "He was out for a couple minutes. He has no idea what's transpired or even who among us are still alive."

"And we don't want to break communicator silence just yet," Imamiah said as she grabbed her weapon. "Can you crawl that far?"

Egan cocked his head dubiously.

"I can," Ramuell said.

"No!" Althea exclaimed.

Kadeya reached over and gently gripped her daughter's wrist. "You've been gone a long time. He's a young man now."

"And in the last few days he's been through a lot worse than a two hundred metre crawl," Semyaza observed. "If they have to drag an injured fighter back, well—dragging dead weight is a job for young guys."

"Thanks for the compliment," Imamiah said. Her grin was almost audible.

Ramuell slung a weapon across his back and together they lit out on hands and knees.

Though wobbly, neither Anso nor his partner needed to be dragged. They required a stop along the way but made it back under their own power.

When they returned, Althea introduced Anso to the group they had literally stumbled over. With an incredulous expression, Anso said, "You mean to tell me you've traveled all over the galaxy with an alien species, returned to the homeworld, were sent to Realta-Gorm, haven't seen your son and mother for decades, then stumble over them in the middle of a battle on Ghrain-3?"

"Actually it was Imamiah who stumbled over them," Althea replied.

Shifting his gaze back-and-forth between Egan and Althea, Major Anso said, "You do understand that's just too damn improbable to be coincidence, don't you?"

Quietly Kadeya said, "The cosmos is not just stranger than we imagine, it is stranger than we **can** imagine."

Anso twisted his nose to one side and said only, "Hmmm." With a little headshake he refocused on the urgencies of the moment. "We need to huddle. We probably need days to lay in a plan, but we have only minutes." Their expressions became increasingly forlorn as they picked through their options, discarding one after the other.

Egan, who had continued to pilot the drone, interrupted the strategy session to report to Anso, "Your fighters to the north have hooked up with each other."

"What about Royan and Kadi?" Anso asked.

Egan frowned, "Still no movement."

The Major sucked his teeth, "That's not good."

"Uhm, something's happening up on the ridge," Althea said hesitantly. "After our ship got away the six Port Authority personnel stood around talking. Suddenly they bolted for their vehicles. I couldn't see any threat, but they all stopped running at almost the same instant. Then there was a flash and the drone quit transmitting." Turning away from the darkened screen she looked at Egan, "What do you think?"

After a few seconds Semyaza said, "I sense maybe you two suspect something—but the rest of us are in the dark."

"Actually," Egan began slowly, "given the little we've seen and the little we understand, what Althea just witnessed is consistent with Beag-Liath technology."

"So you think they're intervening directly on the planet's surface?" Semyaza asked skeptically.

"Sir, they already have," Ramuell reminded the NWA-1 Director. "The Beag-Liath provided medical treatment to members of the Crow Clan after the Blue Rock Canyon incident."

"Blue Rock Canyon incident?" Althea questioned.

"Time enough for that story later," Kadeya said gently.

"And it's the Crow Clan back there in the mud huts." Semyaza paused. "They seem to have a special interest in this clan—I suppose we've seen stranger things in the last few days. Well, perhaps not stranger, but..."

"Awfully dang strange," Ramuell filled in.

Anso cleared his throat, "Yep! And right now I need to hear your ideas about our current situation." Everyone scooted into a circle around the Major. He spoke quietly, "Even if everyone here were soldiers trained in assault tactics, which is not the case, we don't have enough people to seize the Anti-GravXL and make a clean get away. By now the Presidium has surely dispatched a Security squadron from the orbiter. I'm open to suggestions, but we haven't time for much discussion. I'd estimate we have less than two hours before the Serefim reinforcements arrive."

CHAPTER FIFTY-ONE

BEAG INTERCESSION

A LOUD GABBLE of Clan voices interrupted Anso's impromptu planning session. Everyone turned an ear toward the mud huts. No one was fluent in the Clan's dialect, so it just sounded like a cacophony of gibberish. Reluctant to break communicator silence, Anso sent an encrypted text-com.

The communicators of the four Oprit-Robia fighters at the huts trilled simultaneously. They entered the password enabling a preprogrammed decipher.

Hearing a lot of racket – what's happening? (Anso)

Unexpected company – not Domhanian – never seen the like (Team Leader)

Explain (Anso)

People – not Domhanian – appeared out of thin air – not threatening us.

clanspeople know them and are happy to see these little grey guys (Team Leader)

Anso turned to Althea and Egan. "It seems your friends may have put in an appearance."

The couple collided as they leaned in to read the messages on Anso's communicator.

Send a photo? (Anso)

A few seconds later Anso, Althea and Egan were staring at a picture of a Beag-Liath surrounded by smiling clanspeople. Althea said, "Yes – he, or she, is Beag-Liath." Althea felt rather than saw her son staring at her.

Ramuell squeezed between his parents. "I was there. It was in the *sen*—I don't know how—but we were together with one of the little grey fellows."

Egan and Althea had come to believe the Beag-Liath had manipulated a hypnagogic state of consciousness to arrange the "meeting" with their son. They understood it had been a sharing of consciousness rather than physical space, but a subjective reality, nonetheless. They looked at Ramuell, then at each other. While on their knees, the three of them once again folded into a group hug.

Anso interrupted their moment of affection, "You're probably the only Domhanians to have ever had direct contact with these beings. So, I need you to scoot back to the huts and see if you can figure out what they have in mind."

Ramuell said, "I need to go too."

Anso deliberated for a moment, "Yeah, we're not going to mount any kind of an assault until we learn what the Beag-Liath are up to anyway."

Anso said to Ipos, "I'd like for you to accompany them." He looked at the charged-particle gun slung across Ipos' shoulder. "Ramuell, you should take that sonic-blaster." He pointed with his chin at the weapon leaning against a nearby bush.

"Yes sir. Stun only?"

"Correct," Anso replied with an 'off-you-go' wave.

The four of them trotted hunkered over until they arrived at the slab of silica-stone that had two hours earlier provided Ipos with cover from the Serefim troop's sonic blasts. They stood and walked slowly holding their hands out to their sides. After taking several steps into the yard, three of the Beag-Liath approached with their quick, short strides.

The person in the middle stepped forward and gently placed a hand on Althea's chest just above her breasts. It made eye contact and nodded almost imperceptibly. It then repeated this greeting with Egan. They looked at each other for a moment before the Beag stepped over and glanced back-and-forth from Ramuell to his parents. With both hands it clapped Ramuell on his upper arms. Finally, the Beag stepped before Ipos and inclined its head in a graceful salute.

The three Beag-Liath turned and led the group back toward the huts. As they approached a clansman recognized Ramuell and started chattering excitedly. Sapiens came boiling out the doors like a dug up nest of ants. When Shiya saw Ramuell she squealed and sprinted toward him. From two metres away she leapt into his open arms. He swung her around and squeezed her tightly. She giggled her delight.

Althea watched this unexpected welcome then looked over at Egan, who just stood grinning with amusement.

Ipos approached one of the Oprit-Robia fighters and asked her to send a message to Anso:

Arrived safely – cordial reception by extraterrestrials. No information yet regarding their plans.

Semyaza had taken over piloting the remaining drone. He

turned toward the mud huts upon hearing the Crow Clan's enthusiastic greeting of Ramuell.

Adair was the only member of the group who hadn't looked back toward the source of the noise. He was peeking over a berm at the landing platform. "Whoa, look at that!" Then raising his voice dramatically, "Uhm, I mean really, you need to come look at this!"

Surprised by Adair's adamant tone, Anso and Imamiah scooted up beside him. They raised their heads just high enough to peer over the berm. Three Beag-Liath were standing some forty metres apart on the stone slabs. "They just materialized out of nowhere!" Adair explained. "I was studying the platform—those little guys weren't there one second and the next second they were."

Each of the Beag-Liath were holding black tubes about one metre in length. Simultaneously the tubes fired projectiles that flew straight up about fifty metres, leaving wisps of white smoke in their wakes. At almost the same instant all three of the devices detonated with muffled pops. Instantly all of the lights blinked off and the ambient noise of equipment and motors around the facility died to silence.

"Hey, I just lost the drone," Semyaza said.

"Were you near the landing platform?" Imamiah asked.

"Yeah, fifty metres or so to the east."

Imamiah exclaimed, "I'll – be – damned!"

"What just happened, Imamiah?" Anso demanded.

"Those devices—I think they emitted an electromagnetic pulse."

"An EMP **weapon**! Why in some god's holy name would anyone invent a device that could produce an EMP powerful enough to use as a weapon?" Semyaza asked.

The peoples of Domhan-Siol had lived without warfare for thousands of annum. Culturally they treasured social stability.

Domhanians had committed enormous resources to develop technologies to limit the destructiveness of naturally occurring electromagnetic pulses. The notion of creating a device to intentionally produce an EMP, which would be so utterly devastating to a technological society, was simply unfathomable on their world.

Anso, however, was not from the homeworld. He had been born on Realta-Gorm 4 and was committed to an armed struggle against the slave trade that the people of his planet considered an existential evil. He quickly realized the purpose of the devices they'd just seen deployed. He turned to Semyaza and said, "I can understand why someone would invent an EMP weapon, and why they'd use it." He inhaled deeply and said, "Because those devices just won this battle."

Imamiah said, "So these gentle looking little creatures have a heritage of barbarity."

Anso pulled out his communicator and sent another message.

"Ipos, don't waste time trying to figure out what the Beag plan to do – just showed us."

The electromagnetic pulses were targeted in cones from the point of detonation straight down to the ground. After checking his weapons to be certain they were unaffected by the pulses, Anso broke communication silence with a message broadcast to all the Oprit-Robia fighters. "We believe the Beag-Liath just detonated three EMP devices over the dock. Check your weapons to determine if they're operational—report back."

One of the fighters responded immediately, "They did what?!"

"Set off three EMP weapons over the landing platform. Are your weapons functional?"

One of the fighters at the mud huts said, "Ours are fine,"

"Okay, good. I want you to move up to my position. Leave Ipos, Althea, Egan and Ramuell with the Clan," Anso instructed.

Within a few seconds a report came in from the four Oprit-Robia fighters northeast of the platform. "Sir, we don't know if our charged-particle weapons are operational. The display screens are flickering."

Imamiah said, "If their communicators are working their weapons are probably okay."

"Probably is not good enough."

Anso's communicator crackled again, "Sir, we have two solid-projectile weapons."

"Of course! No electronic components," Anso replied. "And Royan and Kadi?"

There was a long pause. When the reply finally came the voice cracked, "They're—they're gone sir."

Anso muttered "Goddammit!" before pressing his communicator's transmission button. "Understood. I want the four of you to move forward to where you have a clear shot at the platform. Hold your position and await my instructions."

Imamiah nudged Anso and asked, "What're you thinking?"

"We may need them to fire their weapons as a distraction, but in the dark solid-projectile weapons are pretty much useless," Anso answered.

When the four fighters from the mud huts arrived Anso explained his plan. The six of them would spread out with about twenty metres between each person. The two in the middle would carry sonic-blasters. The two on each side would use charged-particle guns. Semyaza and Kadeya were dispatched with a sonic-blaster to a position some hundred metres further to the south.

Captain Adair remained behind, armed with the last of the sonic-blasters.

Anzo said, “Okay, let’s go win the day.”

The fighters lurched over the berm toward their assigned positions. As if anticipating Anso’s strategy, the Beag-Liath launched an enormous flare bathing the dock in a bright yellow light.

CHAPTER FIFTY-TWO
FISH AND GRIEF

Back on Blue Rock canyon's north rim, Lilith had spent hours trying to calm the nine agitated members of the Crow Clan who had refused to board the transport ship. They were too disoriented and too leaderless to commence the trek back into the canyon. By mid-afternoon she'd made little progress.

"Azazel, they're lost. They cannot imagine angels would deceive them. They think it's possible the other members of the clan have been taken to some far-flung paradise. They worry that their reticence has condemned them to some kind of punishment by the sky-gods—they fear that they are recreants, for lack of a better word."

"So they're viewing this whole episode in metaphysical terms?" Azazel asked.

"It seems so," Lilith replied. "Our technologies are, in fact, supernatural in the truest meaning of the word."

"So let's play the cards we're dealt. You explain in hyperbolic terms that I am Azazel, a great and powerful watcher—an angel who speaks for the sky-gods. Tell them the people of the Crow are my chosen people."

Embracing the scheme Lilith added, “Then you speak, and I’ll translate that they must return to their cave homes in the canyon.”

“Exactly.”

Rubbing her hands together, Lilith said, “Okay, let’s do this.”

With word selection, tone of voice and gesticulation, Lilith emphasized Azazel’s power and importance among the sky-gods. When he spoke, her translation of his diktats was laced with just the right amount of embellishment.

When they had finished, the nine clanspeople demonstrated their obsequience by lightly touching Azazel’s arms and hands. He also managed to convince them that the four captives and the dead man were from a clan of wicked angels who wanted to harm the people of the Crow. The clanspeople gave the tethered captives wide berth as they gathered the meager belongings that they would lug back to their caves.

“That worked better than I had hoped,” Azazel said with relief.

Nodding, Lilith explained, “What we did was banish their fear of retribution from the gods for some imagined apostasy.”

Aware that something profound had just happened, Azazel frowned and said, “If they imagine Elyon and the Serefim Presidium as a godly pantheon, we’ve mislead them to be sure. Retribution may very well be in their future, and this day may be the genesis of a lost innocence.”

It was dark by the time they arrived at the caves. Only because the clanspeople knew the trail so well were they able to safely navigate the last kilometre.

Live coals remained in several hearths and soon the

women had reignited a couple of fires. As they scavenged the camp for edibles it became clear to Azazel they were going to be hungry. Azazel had six dehyd-food packets in his pack.

"Should we break out the emergency rations?" Lilith asked.

Azazel scowled as he looked into one of the fires. He groaned, "No—we should save them. We're hungry now, we may be starving later."

"You're right. And we've already contaminated this clan with exposure to our technologies. To pop out packets of instant food would be way too much.

Azazel cringed, "Yeah, they might quit hunting and fishing altogether—expecting packets of food to fall from the heavens."

Samael didn't sneak away from SWA-7 as early as he'd hoped. It was past midday when he finally absconded with a rough terrain bike. He pushed it several hundred metres away from the basecamp before starting the rather noisy 70cc hydrogen powered engine. When he arrived at the canyon's south rim and looked into the chasm, he knew he'd be unable to hike to the bottom by nightfall.

After dark he was able to make out two fires at the mouth of the caves. This worried him. Normally the clan would have at least six fires. He suffered a long, restless night, afflicted with anxiety tinged *sens*.

At first light he packed his gear and began the trek. Relief washed through Azazel when he saw his security officer descending the switch-back trail crisscrossing the canyon's south wall.

By the time Samael arrived at the caves, Azazel and a couple of the clansmen had managed to noodle a couple dozen fish from an undercut bank at the river's edge. Others had dug a white fibrous root vegetable and gathered a passel of water-cress. The banquet was laid atop a flat boulder. They ate the delectable feast with their hands. While they ate, Azazel explained to Samael what had happened since the time they saw the abduction of the clan by the Serefim Security troops.

After everyone had eaten their fill, Lilith, Azazel and Sam gathered the leftovers and took them to the four captives tethered at the mouth of another cave. They hand-fed each of the hungry men.

When they returned to the cavern with the cook fires, Azazel asked Sam, "Would you like to see where we caught the fish?"

"Absolutely, I'd be up for catching more for dinner—unless you planned to light out this afternoon."

Waving a hand Azazel said, "No, we need some time to discuss plans. Tomorrow or the next day will be soon enough."

"It would be best to know what happened to the others before settling on a plan," Lilith added.

"You're right, but we can't bide too long in hopes of their success." Turning to Samael, Azazel said, "Hey, let's take that walk down to the river."

When they arrived at the riverbank Azazel sat down on the trunk of a fallen tree. Time had stripped away its bark leaving an almost perfect bench of smooth grey wood.

Noting his boss's expression Sam said, "Uh oh, this looks serious."

"Please, have a seat. It is serious—serious and sad."

Sitting on that log Azazel told Samael the rest of the story. He told of their hiding from the Serefim Security squad in the hunting blind upriver; of how Rarus set the driftwood log jam ablaze on the island; and ultimately of his murder by the two sentries.

A moan of misery rose from somewhere deep inside of Samael. After sitting quietly for several minutes Sam finally said, “Can you take me up there where you hid—where Rarus spent his last night?”

“Of course. But before we go, look out there.” Azazel pointed to the charred island in the middle of the river. “That was where he set the diversionary fire that made our escape possible.” He paused, looked down at his feet and shook his head. “Sam, your friend gave his life saving ours.”

Samael stood and looked away. “He was a good man—he was a good friend, and I will miss him.” Silently, they walked the kilometre upriver to the site of Rarus’ last *sen*.

CHAPTER FIFTY-THREE
RESCUE

Seeing the platform bathed in startling bright light, Anso grabbed his communicator and gave the order to advance. As the Oprit-Robia fighters hustled toward the docking facility they could see its defenders attempting to discharge their weapons. When none fired, most of the men and women simply turned, ran to the back on the dock and leapt off. All vehicles were likewise disabled. They fled afoot.

The contingent of trained security personnel stood in and readied themselves for hand-to-hand combat. They were disciplined and prepared to protect the dock and ships. Anso realized the defenders probably assumed the Oprit-Robia weapons were also inoperative. He grabbed his communicator and ordered his fighters to halt. Rather than waste time negotiating, he shouldered his weapon and discharged one carefully aimed stun shot. The leader of the Port Authority's security squad collapsed. Anso hollered, "Our weapons are operational. Sit down. Put your hands on your heads."

The security officers on the dock hesitated, exchanging looks of disbelief. Two men ran to their downed commander, grabbed her by the armpits and began dragging her away. The others turned and ran toward the deep service bays notched in the landing platform. Anso roared, “Semyaza, fire one!”

It was actually Kadeya holding the weapon and she instantly squeezed off a wide-field sonic blast. Everyone on the dock crumpled.

Anso held no grudge against the immobilized security personnel. *They were just doing their jobs.* He was determined there would be no more deaths on this night. He bellowed, “Cease fire! Get up there and secure the prisoners.”

The ten surviving Oprit-Robia fighters rushed up the platform’s steps. They pulled plastic zip cords from their cargo pants pockets as they ran across the stone slabs. The dock’s defenders were not unconscious, but none were in any condition to offer resistance as their hands and feet were trussed.

“Should I call Althea and Egan to have them lead the clanspeople over here?” Imamiah asked Anso.

“Let’s get Adair up here to check out the XL to make sure it’s operational before we start moving people.” Then as an afterthought, “But call and let them know that we’ve secured the dock. Don’t tell them about Royan and Kadi yet.”

At the mention of their names, Imamiah bit her lower lip. “I’ll make the call.”

With his flashlight, Anso illuminated the scene of Royan’s and Kadi’s deaths. They had thrashed around wildly. Excruciating is too prosaic a word to describe the pain they must have suffered. The sonic-blasters had not been set to kill. They died because of numerous direct hits. In the end, they found each other. They were holding hands.

“Wrap them up and bring‘em over to the dock,” Anso

ordered. "They'd want their ashes spread on the highlands of Realta-Gorm."

It took Adair twenty minutes to complete a rushed but thorough systems check of the Anti-GravXL. Imamiah and Anso stood arms akimbo, surveying the scene. Adair trotted across the dock and reported, "It'll fly.

"So, the EMPs didn't fry the electronics?"

"No, everything in there is hardened for coronal mass ejections." Pointing with his thumb at the small transports on the other end of the platform, Adair added, "I doubt if those ships are hardened. They'll require some serious work before getting airborne again.

"Sir, we can launch with the entire clan, but if we're taking them back to Blue Rock, it's going to be tricky finding a place to land that beast. Landing areas on both rims are likely not level enough."

Semyaza joined the conversation. "It seems to me we've got no choice but to get loaded and get in the air. We'll figure out some place to land."

"You're right." Anso turned to Imamiah, "Make the call."

A moment later she was asking Althea, "Are they settled enough to hike over here and get onboard the XL?"

Althea chuckled, "If Ramuell asks them to I believe they'd jump out of a tree thinking they could fly to Blue Rock."

"So, they're a bit taken with him, are they?"

"I would say so!"

"Here's the thing, we've got less than an hour before reinforcements from the orbiter arrive. Have Ramuell lead the sapiens at a trot. We need to get airborne," Imamiah explained.

Kadeya pointed at the bound captives and asked, "What do we do with these guys?"

Imamiah said, "Nothing, they'll be rescued minutes after we depart."

Dawn was blooming pastel in the eastern sky. The high altitude morning air was quite cool – the coldest temperature of the day. One of the Oprit-Robia fighters ran up to Anso. "Sir, we have a problem! I've been watching the main facility with the heat imaging scope. A group of armed people are headed this way. They're on foot."

"That makes sense," Anso said. "They're walking rather than risk any more of their vehicles to another EMP." He paused for a moment concentrating, "They're almost certainly armed with solid-projectile weapons—no electronics."

"What's the plan?" Imamiah asked.

"We'll I'd damn sure rather be in the air than in a shootout," Anso replied. "Is there any way we can hurry our passengers along?"

"I'll check."

"Uhm, I hate to be a doomsayer, but the landing strut on our shuttle was knocked out with a large solid-projectile," Semyaza reminded everyone.

Anso slumped, then suddenly his eyes brightened. "Wait a minute, do we still have that weapon?"

Kadeya grabbed her communicator and called Ramuell, "Son, where are you?"

"We're about halfway."

"Do you have the large solid-projectile weapon with you?"

"No, we left it." Ramuell replied.

"Was there any ammo?"

"Yeah, there were several more shells."

When Anso gave her two thumbs-up, Kadeya said, "Ask your dad to go back and get that weapon. He needs to run it over here as fast as he can."

Egan was listening in on the conversation. "I won a lot of foot races in my day. My legs can still move if my lungs hold out."

"Pace yourself—very thin oxygen at this altitude," Kadeya cautioned.

Ten minutes later Ramuell, holding Shiya's hand, led the Crow Clan up the steps onto the docking platform. He walked up to Kadeya and gave her a firm hug. "I'm glad you're okay. We heard weapons."

Althea approached as Kadeya replied, "Yeah, it was scary. And it's not over yet. An armed force is approaching on foot from the main facility. We need to get everyone boarded and out of here."

Many of the clanspeople recognized Kadeya and walked up to tap her on the shoulders. She smiled broadly and gestured toward the open bay of the Anti-GravXL. At that, several exchanged dubious looks.

Ramuell saw the hesitation and knew they had no time for a repeat of the defiance they'd seen on Blue Rock canyon's north rim. He jumped on the ramp and started saying in the Crow language, "Come! Come! Home—go home."

The Clan knew Ramuell was a good angel. He'd fought the nefilim. He'd saved Shiya. He'd tended their wounds and shared their meals. Hesitantly at first some clanspeople began walking up the ramp. Ramuell continued to exhort, "Come—go home—go home." The first few aboard began chattering after passing through the doors. Whatever was said broke the dam. The others surrendered their reticence and began rushing onto the ship.

When they were all aboard Imamiah called the Oprit-Robia

pilot and instructed her to bring their 4D-ship in and land on the platform. Just as she said that, a solid-projectile slammed into one of the small shuttlecraft. "Belay that order! We're being fired on!"

All of the Oprit-Robia fighters except Anso dove for cover. He stood surveying the scene for a couple of seconds. "Lay down an arc of sonic blasts!" he hollered. The fighters armed with blasters took up positions in one of the service bays between the huge stone slabs. Three of them stood simultaneously. Each triggered two sonic blasts then ducked back into the trench's safety.

Almost immediately several solid-projectiles whizzed over the platform. A couple pinged off the XL. One of the Clan's adolescent girls screamed and fell. Althea turned and saw blood gushing from the girl's upper calf. Adair yelled, "I'm shutting the doors."

As he dove into a service bay with his fighters, Anso shouted at Imamiah, "Go! Go! Go!"

She stood frozen momentarily. Suddenly she understood and leapt for the ramp while it was swinging upward. Just seconds before the door locked and sealed, Imamiah screamed at Anso, "Meet the Oprit shuttle up on the ridge!"

Adair called back from the pilot's cockpit, "Get everyone seated—we're out of here!" Before launching, Adair saw six of the Oprit-Robia fighters dragging their bound prisoners to the safety of the service bays.

While the Domhanians were manhandling the clanspeople into seats, Imamiah called the pilot of the Oprit-Robia shuttlecraft. "We believe the Beag-Liath set off an electromagnetic pulse weapon after you launched from the ridge."

"Really!?"

"Yeah, if so, would that affect your ability to land there now?" Imamiah asked.

"No. There would be no lingering effect," she answered.

"Okay, go back there and wait for our squad. They'll extricate themselves from the fight and be there in about an hour. It's less than six kilometres."

"Yeeaahh," the pilot drawled doubtfully, "but it's uphill."

"True—it'll be a tougher trek than our downhill jog last night," Imamiah agreed.

"It's going to be **too** tough. I'll hover and set the ship down near the mud huts when I see them making their way across the open area in front of the buildings."

"Of course! That's much better. Uhm," trying to swallow the lump in her throat, "there's one more thing—Royan and Kadi won't be with them."

"Aww dammit!" The pilot wiped her suddenly wet eyes, "Okay Imamiah...good luck. Report your whereabouts when you can. I'll come get ya."

"Thank you my friend."

Projectiles continued to whiz past. Anso said through clenched teeth, "What the hell?" He yanked off his cap and rubbed the nape of his neck. "What kind of weapons are those? How far can they throw the projectiles?"

"I don't know sir. They make a lot more noise than any solid-projectile weapon I've ever used."

"Okay, let's try this," Anso said. "Put your blasters on narrow-field, full range. Each of you stand and pop off three blasts starting left and moving right."

One of the fighters pursed her lips and nodded. "That might work. Even if we only take out one or two, it'll give 'em pause."

At that moment, another fighter slithered into the service

bay. "We could try this." He held out the huge solid-projectile weapon Egan had carried back from the mud huts. He pulled a bag off his shoulder and opened it. All five heads leaned forward to peer inside. There were six twenty centimetres long cartridges. Anso looked up, his eyes wide, "How did you get these?"

"That man, the professor..." the soldier pointed to where the Anti-GravXL had been docked.

"Professor Egan," Anso filled in.

"Yeah. He ran across the platform just as the last few sapiens were climbing onboard. He tossed me the weapon and dropped the bag at my feet. He said, 'you might need these,' then ran up the ramp seconds before Imamiah."

"I didn't even see him. Damn, this is a good break." Twisting his lips sideways, Anso thought for a moment. "Yeah—hell yeah we can use this. We'll shoot one round right now, that is if anyone here knows how to use this weapon."

One of the men said, "I do sir. These are a type of miniature rocket. Otherwise the recoil would be too much to handle."

"Okay—I'll take your blaster. Can you take out that small tree that's about four hundred metres to the southwest?"

The fighter peeked up over the top of the stone slab. "It's easily within this weapon's range. I can try."

Looking down to check the blaster setting, Anso said, "Good! You go first. As soon as you've fired, the three of us will stand and let loose with sonic blasts—narrow-field, full range, stun only. Start left and move to the right; three shots each."

Everyone nodded. "Okay, let's go," Anso said as he gave the shooter a couple of claps on the shoulder. A moment later the slowly approaching Port Authority personnel must have thought demons from several hells had broken loose. And perhaps they had!

Just seconds after the Oprit-Robia fighters had discharged

their weapons, the gargantuan stone slabs of the main Port Authority facility began flying into the air and crashing back to earth. The ground trembled as the slabs tumbled willy-nilly in every direction.

The roar of the commotion was so loud it could be heard all the way over at the small dock. Simultaneously several of the Oprit-Robia fighters exclaimed, “What – the – hell?!”

“I’m not sure, but I’m guessing the Beag-Liath are demonstrating another one of their weapons.” Anso paused, “Well, whatever’s going on, we need to take advantage of the distraction. Let’s move!”

Everyone jumped from the service bay, dashed across the platform, and down the steps. They huddled behind the dock. Pointing at the weapon, Anso said, “Okay, we’re going to take one more shot with that monstrosity. Then we’re going to run like hell for the cover of the trees at the mouth of the drainage we came down last night. Our ship should be waiting where it dropped us off.”

Several turned to look at their fallen comrades’ bodies rolled in polyimide sheets. Anso coughed and said, “Yeah, we’re taking them with us—we’ve almost won the day. Let’s make Royan and Kadi proud.”

Seconds after the Anti-GravXL lifted-off, Egan stood and tore a strip of fabric from his shirttail. He tossed it to Althea, who had not taken a seat. She crouched beside the wounded girl who was writhing on the floor. “Someone find the medical kit. I need an antiseptic.” She tightened the strip of cloth around the girl’s leg just below the knee. Immediately the tourniquet staunched the flow of blood.

Imamiah dropped to her knees beside Althea and opened

the ship's medical kit. Althea grabbed a handful of fabric bandages, "Ramuell, come hold these on the wound—apply pressure, I've got to inspect it to see if the projectile is still in there."

"I don't think it is," Semyaza said as he picked up the crushed polypropylene projectile that had passed through the girl's calf and slammed into the pedestal of his seat. "When I buckled in I saw it lying at my feet."

Althea took it from Semyaza and squinted as she studied the slug. "It's possible there's still a fragment in her leg." She slipped on a pair of surgical gloves and scooted her son out of the way. She gently pulled the wound open and inspected it thoroughly. She pulled Ramuell's hands back into position to reapply pressure. "It didn't hit the bone, and I don't see any fragments. Has anyone found any anesthesia?"

Ipos held up a bottle between his forefinger and thumb rattling the pills with a slight shake, "I found this."

Althea read the label. "That's a strong sedative but ineffective for use as a local." She sighed contemplatively and looked around at the frightened faces of the Clan. "This wound is not a big deal. I can clean it, sew her up, and she'll be walking in an undecim. I'm afraid if we knock her out with this stuff the clanspeople will think she's dead, and if we don't she's gonna scream like death itself when we irrigate and stitch."

Semyaza walked forward, leaned into the pilot's cockpit and spoke quietly to Adair. He returned to stand beside Althea and Ramuell. "Let's move her up to the cockpit. There are four reclining seats. You can use one as an operating table."

"And we can put her to sleep without having a riot on our hands," Althea added.

Egan tapped Ramuell on the back and said, "Okay, you pick up her legs and I'll get her shoulders."

Semyaza said, "Ramuell, let me take her legs. You and your

grandmother should stay back here and try to reassure these folks that the girl is going to be fine."

And she was.

Brigadier Migeal had been in the T-Taxiarch Command Center on the orbiting station when he was informed that one of the transport ships from Blue Rock Canyon had been hijacked and had followed the other ships to the recently built docking facilities on the southern continent's western plateau. A couple hours later he was relieved to learn that the stolen ship had been disabled in a skirmish near the smaller of the two terminals. He ordered that if at all possible a few of the rebels should be taken alive and interrogated. He needed information about the rebel forces, their strength, and intentions.

Migeal was receiving a continuous stream of reports from the ongoing military operations all over the planet's surface. Assuming the Port Authority security Forces had their situation well in hand, he turned his attention to what seemed like more pressing matters. An hour later the Brigadier was completely flabbergasted when Commander Croga called to report the hijackers had been reinforced by a well-armed squad of insurgents.

"What are you not telling me?" Migeal demanded.

"I'm not sure," Croga replied. "The reports and video we're receiving are frankly unbelievable."

Becoming impatient Migeal raised his voice at least twenty decibels. "And what the hell is that supposed to mean!?"

Drawing in a deep breath, Commander Croga screwed up his assertiveness a couple of notches. "Brigadier Migeal, I believe the Domhanian insurgents likely include a squad from Realta-Gorm 4."

With that bomb dropped in his lap, Migeal exploded, "What the fuck are you talking about?"

The outburst angered Croga. "That is quite enough of that. You need to calm down. I need help and your vitriol is not helpful."

Migeal was unaccustomed to being spoken to so bluntly. He had to remind himself that he was talking to the Port Authority commander, not some subordinate in the Anotas Security apparatus. Though his ego prevented him from offering an apology, he remained silent while Croga continued. "We have some pretty good video. Using our face recognition application, we're 73% certain that Professor Egan and Dr. Althea are among the assailants. Their last known location was Realta-Gorm."

"Oh dear gods, I can't believe this," Migeal muttered to himself.

"And what's really unbelievable is we also have video of their heretofore mysterious Beag-Liath."

Again raising his voice but this time in shock rather than anger, "What? That's not possible!"

"There are smallish grey beings interacting with the sapien-hybrids. It appears they actually know each other. But what's more troubling," he cleared his throat, "...these creatures have detonated what we assume are electromagnetic pulse weapons over the smaller landing platform."

"Commander, I'm dispatching one of the two squads we held in reserve on T-Taxiarch. You need a show of force."

"Perhaps you should dispatch both squads," Croga suggested.

Migeal considered this for a moment, "No, can't do that without getting clearance from the big guy, and it's too early to report this turn of events to him."

"I get that."

The Brigadier flipped on his three-dimensional holographic map and in a moment realized luck was not on their side. "Commander, I'm looking at the Station's orbit location. We are one hundred and sixty-five degrees west and about sixty degrees north of you."

Croga did a quick calculation in his head. "So, it'll be almost two hours before your troops arrive."

"I've just transmitted the emergency deployment order. This very second the squad is running to the weapons room. They'll launch in less than ten minutes, but yeah, it'll be at least..."

"**Holy shit**!" Croga yelped.

"What?!"

"The slabs—the docking platform slabs are being ripped apart—they're just flying through the..."

Migeal could feel sweat trickle down the middle of his back and his pulse start to race as he stared at the communicator that had just gone silent.

CHAPTER FIFTY-FOUR

LAWS, TAXES, AND BULLION

The advent of 4D technology radically changed the Domhanian business model within just five centuries, a single lifetime. Their galactic footprint expanded to hundreds of worlds, moons, and asteroids; mitigating the need for almost all mining on the homeworld. The corporations that successfully utilized dimension jumping technology to exploit far-flung natural resources evolved into quasi-governmental entities.

Over those centuries Anotas convened numerous congresses to draft and amend the "Edicts of Codification" for governance of Domhanian off-world activities. Melanka found buried within those edicts a clause in the Taxation Code she thought just might trip-up Elyon and his Serefim sycophants.

> *Corporate* ***and personal [amended 6•38•23252]*** *income from all sources* ***whether originating on Domhan-Siol or elsewhere [amended 6•38•23252]*** *shall be reported on Quinquennial Revenue Reports. Profits shall be taxed at rates established by the decadal Anotas Assembly of Taxation and Regulation.*

After reading the citation twice, Liam tapped his index finger on the foliopad screen. "Melanka, this just might work. Walk us through the evidence."

Melanka was tired, her voice even more raspy than normal. "We began with subpoena orders for the tax records of all Presidium members. From those records we identified their Tender Institution Accounts."

"Or at least those they reported," Judge Cartan, the special investigator, surmised.

"Judge, your intuition is correct. We found many Presidium members had not reported all of their accounts."

Sean added, "Which doesn't constitute a violation unless those accounts are used to hide income. But listen to what else Melanka uncovered."

She leaned forward placing her forearms on the edge of the table. "We subpoenaed disbursement reports for all corporations operating on Ghrain-3. We also looked at disbursement reports for corporations and individuals whom we know have purchased significant numbers of sapien-hybrid laborers."

Liam leaned back in his chair, laid his interwoven hands on his chest and grinned ever so slightly.

"Per share income for members of the Serefim Presidium should be equal. But it hasn't been for decades. Let me amend that, they have not reported the same amount of income per share."

"They got sloppy," Liam observed.

"A better word is careless, in the truest sense of its meaning," Sean responded. "They literally came to **care less** whether or not anyone checked on this kind of detail."

Raising his bushy eyebrows, Judge Cartan asked, "They believe they are above the law?"

"Or perhaps beyond the law's reach," Sean speculated.

"Naturally, we looked at their reported revenue sources to

identify the discrepancies," Melanka continued. "Two of the Presidium members are probably clean as washed window panes. They reported income from labor contracts with several corporate entities. 'Labor contracts' is the euphemism they use to obfuscate slave sales."

"So, the corporations' disbursement reports didn't jibe with the Presidium members' reported income," Judge Cartan conjectured.

"Correct, but it's more complex than that. Elyon has been cagy with the off-world sale of Ghrain-3 hybrids. He's maintained complete control of those sales. All contracts are negotiated with his office and all income flows through him. The revenue for off-world sales is not equally disbursed among the Presidium," Melanka explained.

Liam asked, "So how is it two members appropriately reporting their income from this sordid business?"

"There's a vibrant market for slaves among the mining corporations on Ghrain-3 itself. All Presidium members have their fingers in that pie. Two of them, who receive no income from off-world sales, have consistently reported accurate receipts from the sale of slaves on the planet," Melanka explained.

Rubbing his temples with both hands, Liam asked, "What in the name of everything holy are we doing out there?"

Sean stood and walked to the credenza in front of the conference room's window. He stared out at the rain for a long moment before placing cups and a pot of tea on a serving tray. While setting the service down between Liam and Melanka he asked, "So where is Elyon hiding the income? The amounts must be astronomical."

"He's not taking payments as credit transfers. The man is stashing gold ingot somewhere."

"Really!" Liam exclaimed. "And your proof of that?"

"If I had proof, we'd know where to go collect the bullion."

Judge Cartan cleared his throat and said, "Okay, with regard to tax evasion, you **may** have enough evidence to file charges. Perhaps the charges could be beefed up sufficiently to actually issue an Order of Summons rather than just a citation. But I don't think you're going to get a detention, especially if Elyon escrows enough to pay off any back taxes and fines, pending an audit."

"Judge, you're right. This is going to require finesse that likely borders on entrapment," Melanka stated bluntly. She went on to describe her plan.

When she finished, the old Judge lowered his gaze and stroked his chin for several times. "Yep, he's got too big of an ego to let that slide. I'll sign off on it—you **might** just get him."

Sean, who'd been thrumming his fingers on the table awaiting the Special Investigator's take, blew out a relieved sigh.

CHAPTER FIFTY-FIVE

MELANKA'S GAMBIT

When Sean learned Elyon had ordered Serefim Security agents to detain Evander, Lector and Durela, he requested the record of charges. There was no record! The trio hadn't been charged with any illegal activity.

Sean decided to share this information with Melanka in person. They met at a tea and pastry shop not far from the Law and Order Directorate headquarters. The proprietor was a former enforcement officer for the agency and understood Sean's occasional need for a private parlor.

Sean was seated at the single table in the small room when Melanka was shown in. He stood and they exchanged palm-taps. Melanka studied her colleague's face carefully before saying, "You look like you're going to serve some poison with my tea."

Sean snorted and replied, "You might think so." He called up the document on his foliopad and slid it across the table.

Melanka read the brief about Elyon's orders to detain her two agents and Durela. She slid Sean's device back across the table, pursed her lips and reached into her coat pocket for the ever-present pipe. "What's your source?"

"Several of the food service people on Torus-1 work for us. They see and hear almost everything."

"So the report is reliable?"

Sean nodded.

Melanka slapped the table top with an open palm and broke into delighted laughter.

Sean was so stunned he blinked rapidly and leaned back in his chair. "Not sure what response I was expecting, but it certainly wasn't that!"

"Don't you see, he's already made the false arrests we wanted!" Melanka exclaimed.

Sean shook his head as if the opaque lenses clouding his vision had just fallen away. "Good grief! Of course. This is better than any false arrest we might have contrived."

"Not just better, much better! We can charge him with false arrest **and** imprisonment of a scientist, a librarian and a historian, all of whom are Anotas employees."

"Well, well—Elyon may have just served himself up well-poached," Sean chuckled.

Over the next two hours they discussed the upsides and pitfalls of numerous options and settled on a strategy.

"This is a good plan. Not foolproof," Melanka rasped, "but a good plan."

With a sardonic knit of his brows, Sean said, "As Liam often says, 'any time you think you've arrived at something that's foolproof, someone comes along with a more foolish fool.'"

Melanka chortled as she pulled her communicator out of her attaché and called the Law and Order Directorate Secretary. Sean and Melanka explained to Liam what they had in mind.

The 4D-ship's pilot had transmitted the Anotas identification information and the necessary docking codes. Melanka held her breath as she watched the screen over the pilot's shoulder and blew out a long exhale when she read: APPROVED FOR AUTO-DOCK – TORUS-1 – PORT-3.

"That's good," Melanka said. "You don't have to answer any questions, which might have aroused suspicions."

"Is the team ready?" Melanka asked Chelt.

"Yes. They're at the disembarkation portal. Let's go have a final word."

In addition to Agent Chelt the team included two Law and Order Directorate detectives and one uniformed officer from the Anotas Interstellar Enforcement Division (AIED). Liam insisted on adding an officer from AIED who could legally take command of the Serefim Security Forces and order them to stand down in the case of conflict. Colonel Uzza fit the bill. His rank and bearing added the right touch of gravitas.

Melanka greeted her team, "Good morning gentlemen. You look ready and eager."

Colonel Uzza replied, "Perhaps not eager but certainly anxious to get started and hopefully get this thing over with in short order."

Meanwhile, in the ship's recreation room, an eighteen person squad of the 83rd Anotas-Deithe Interstellar Enforcement Force, known as the Matzod, was pouring over the schematic of Torus-1 for the dozenth time. The Matzod were the most elite Special Operations Force within the Domhanian interstellar empire. The squad was double and triple checking their equipment and reviewing each trooper's role should they be required to storm the torus.

Engrossed as they were, they didn't noticed the slight lurch of the ship as it nudged and locked onto Port-3. When they heard the chime indicating the lock pressure was being equalized two of the Matzod troopers and their commanding officer, Major Amil, joined Melanka's team at the portal.

When the lock's doors hissed open Major Amil and the Matzod troopers were the first to enter the Port's receiving foyer. The troopers shouldered their weapons and aimed at the two Serefim Security officers. Without a word Major Amil stepped forward and removed the Serefim Officers' communicators. She took two long steps backward and said, "Please remove all of your weapons and place them on the floor."

As they reached for their holstered weapons, the simultaneous clicks of the Matzod weapon's safety switches was clearly audible. The Serefim Officers froze and raised their hands. Again Major Amil said, "Please remove your weapons and place them on the floor—slowly."

When they were disarmed, Agent Chelt and Colonel Uzza walked into the foyer. Chelt handed the Serefim Officers a paper printout of his orders. "This is not a hostile action," he explained. "We are law enforcement officers here to deliver a Court Order of Summons to a person believed to be present on this torus. No one will be injured and when the summons is delivered we will depart. Do you understand?"

When the two Serefim Officers had finished reading the document Col. Uzza said, "If both of you will please take a seat, hopefully we'll be in and out in just a few minutes. Then you can return to your business."

The Serefim Officers realized Col. Uzza's rank did authorize him to issue orders. They turned to each other, shrugged, and took seats behind the Identification Verification Counter. One of the Matzod troopers stepped in front of them and disconnected all of the terminals at the counter to prevent any possible communication with other Serefim Security personnel on the orbiter.

Uzza said, "All right! Thank you for your cooperation."

As the two Matzod took up positions at both of the foyer's doorways, Agent Chelt, Col. Uzza and the two Law and Order detectives exited into the corridor that ran around the circumference of the rotating torus.

Brigadier Migeal had just delivered the bad news to Grandmaster Elyon about the Port Authority battle and the Crow Clan's escape. Migeal was walking out when Agent Chelt and his team arrived at the Presidium's reception lobby. Elyon was giving his Administrative Assistant some instructions. He did not acknowledge the new arrivals.

The receptionist at the counter in the lobby's entrance asked, "How may we help you?"

Chelt responded with a slightly elevated volume, "We are here to see the Grandmaster." He gestured toward Elyon.

Even though Elyon had heard Agent Chelt, he refused to even glance at the group of visitors. When he had finished conversing with his assistant he turned to follow Brigadier Migeal, who was already in the zero-grav transport tube scooting toward the T-Taxiarch at the opposite end of the orbiting colossus. As Elyon walked past the counter the receptionist called, "Sir, these gentlemen are here to see you."

"They'll have to make an appointment."

Using his command voice, Col. Uzza stepped forward and said, "That will not be necessary."

Hearing this Elyon pulled up short and fixed Uzza with a haughty glare. "And just why might that be?" Looking at the badge indicating Uzza's rank, Elyon added in a tone dripping with disdain, "Colonel."

An amused quirk tugged the corners of Uzza's mouth as he gestured toward Agent Chelt. Stepping forward, Chelt read aloud the court's Order of Summons.

When Elyon realized what was happening, right there in the Serefim Presidium's reception lobby, he became livid. By the time Chelt had finished reading the order, rage had flushed Elyon's cheeks and his ears had become almost purple. He snatched Chelt's foliopad and slammed it on the floor. He hollered at the two person security detail stationed just outside the lobby doors, "Arrest these imposters! I have reason to believe they're Realta-Gorm terrorists. Take their communicators and show them to the brig."

As had been agreed upon earlier, under these circumstances Melanka's team would offer no resistance. Both of the Law and Order detectives raised their hands. One of them said, "Our only weapons are in our shoulder holsters." Colonel Uzza reached in his pocket and removed his communicator and an unloaded solid-projectile weapon. Holding them between the forefinger and thumb of each hand he slowly leaned over and placed both items on the floor at his feet.

Agent Chelt looked into Elyon's eyes, held out both hands touching at the wrists. "Would you like them to cuff us?"

Elyon was confused that the four men so willingly acquiesced, but his anger overruled his judgment. Fixing Chelt with a surly glare he answered, "Hell yes!"

The Grandmaster wanted the Anotas-Deithe team's exit from his inner sanctum to be humiliating.

CHAPTER FIFTY-SIX

HOMEWARD BOUND – ALMOST

WITH EGAN ACTING as surgical assistant, Althea irrigated the girl's calf wound and stitch it up within twenty minutes. By the time she had completed the procedure the ship was approaching the planet's northern equinox latitude. It was flying at an altitude of 21,500 metres as it traveled in a north-easterly direction toward SWA-7.

When the cockpit door hissed, Ramuell and Kadeya looked up anxiously. Reading Althea's expression they knew instantly all was well. Ramuell had observed the Crow Clan's animated celebration of good news one evening when a hunting party returned with slabs of fat scavenged from an enormous two horned mammal that had fallen to its death off a cliff. He rose to his feet, threw his hands in the air waggling them in rapid semi-rotations. He swayed back-and-forth slightly at the hip and chanted, "Ja, Ja, Ja!"

He got it right. Huge smiles emerged on the faces of all the clanspeople. Ru Ta approached Althea, took her hands in his and bowed touching her knuckles with his forehead. The girl's parents stood and joined Ramuell in the celebratory dance before approaching Althea and repeating Ru Ta's honorific.

They wanted to enter the cockpit to see their daughter. Althea led the parents to the door where they saw the girl's chest rise and fall with each breath. When they turned and beamed at their fellow clanspeople, the Domhanians sensed a collective, albeit inaudible, sigh of relief. Several more rose and did the "Ja, Ja, Ja!" dance. Egan and Althea looked at each other, giggled, and tried to imitate the sapien's jig.

Adair waited for the merriment to die down before calling Semyaza to join him in the cockpit. "Boss, I've been thinking about landing this behemoth. I don't remember seeing a good landing spot on the south rim. The clearing on the flattop knoll where we put down our shuttlecraft isn't big enough."

"What do you think we need to do?" Semyaza asked.

Adair scratched his head. "First things first, we can fly over both rims to see if there are any other possibilities. But I have a vague recollection of hearing that the SWA-7 folks were building a landing platform. Do you know anything about that?"

"Not really, but Ramuell might."

When Semyaza stuck his head out the cockpit he saw Ramuell sitting cross legged on the floor teaching Shiya and two other children a hand-clap rhythm game. The children's eyes danced, and their giggles amused the adults. He loathed breaking up the helpful diversion, but time was of the essence. "Ramuell, Captain Adair needs to have a word."

Puzzled, Ramuell pushed himself to his feet and made his way to the cockpit. When he stuck his head inside Adair motioned for him to have a seat.

"Ramuell, I seem to remember Azazel mentioning the building of a landing platform somewhere in SWA-7. Or is that just wishful thinking on my part?" Adair asked.

"So, I take it this thing is too big to set down on the canyon's rim above the Clan's caves," Ramuell observed.

"Probably. The clearings on the south rim are too small."

"The clearing on the north rim where we hijacked the PT-24 is quite large," Ramuell recalled.

"Yeah, no problem with trees and brush there, but I doubt if it's level enough. When the anti-grav devices on this beast are turned-off, the struts cannot support the ship's weight if the slope is more than two degrees," Adair explained. "Do you know anything about a new landing pad SWA-7 may have been working on?"

"Yes I do, but I have no idea if it's completed or if the work has even begun. When I visited Dig 421 Azazel, Owan, Gadrel and I hiked up to a plateau they called fly-it-out-ridge. They were scouting for the best location to build a landing for quad-copters."

"Oh, a quadcopter pad," Adair grumbled. Then, brightening a bit, "Well, maybe if they were building it large enough to accommodate four landings at a time..."

"I just don't know about that. I do remember they planned enough dock space to load supplies and artifacts from the dig."

"So it might be large enough to accommodate an XL. Do you think you can locate the plateau?"

"I can if you fly us over the Dig."

Adair tapped an inquiry into the ship's navigational computer. "Yeah, that's easy. The topography won't allow us to go low, but I can hover a couple thousand metres overhead."

"If the weather's clear enough to see the Camp, I'll be able to find the plateau. Whether or not a landing platform has been built, who knows?" Ramuell shrugged.

On the ledge in front of the Crow Clan's caves, Lilith sat beside Samael stroking his back. In the cook fire's light they discussed plans for the days ahead. Azazel said, "It seems we have only four options. We could stay put—wait this mess out in the safety of the caves. Or, we could go camp up on the south rim and monitor communications."

"Perhaps even hear from Semyaza and the others," Lilith said hopefully.

"Yeah, that's a possibility," Azazel agreed.

After learning of Rarus' death, the darkness of grief had descended on Samael. Without looking at Lilith he said, "We should prepare ourselves. Our comrades and the other clans-people might be dead."

Understanding Samael's pain, Azazel said, "Perhaps, or captured." He paused, rubbing the length of his jaw. "Another option is to head straight back to SWA-7 basecamp. But I think we need more information about what's going on before doing that."

"You're right," Sam agreed. "If Semyaza's efforts failed, we'd be walking into a certain trap."

"Which leads to our fourth option; we could go to Dig 421 and hole up there until we get better information. But what should we do with our four friends over there? We can't get seven people in our quadcopter up on the rim."

Sam said, "And if we decide on going to the Dig, the quad-copter isn't an option anyway."

"So we'd have to use the RTVs, but it's a long climb out of here with four men in shackles."

Lilith closed her eyes and rubbed her forehead, "Gentle-men, I have my doubts about these guys climbing that trail even without shackles." Sam and Azazel gave her a querulous look. "I'm almost certain none of our uninvited Security guests went through the acclimatization protocol."

Azazel narrowed his eyes and stared into the fire. "You know, Rarus said the same thing when he returned to the hunting blind after observing them on their first night in the canyon."

"What we're doing is crazy. I'm gonna talk to them," Sam said.

Looking at Samael out of the corner of his eye, Azazel asked, "Are you sure you want to do that?"

"Hey, those guys didn't kill Rarus. You dealt with those two. The men over there are just exhausted, sick schmucks doing what they're told." Sam looked over at them for a long moment. "Toward that end, we probably have a lot in common."

Azazel felt pricked by Samael's pejorative comment but knew to let it go. He just nodded and followed Sam to where the four men slouched uncomfortably around the cable tether.

Sam sat down only an arm's length away. Azazel stood silently more than a dozen metres behind the captives. Sam began the conversation by talking about food; how they planned to mimic the hunting and gathering of the Crow Clan. "We have a few dehyd-food packets, but the boss says we're only going to break those out in a dire emergency. We can hunt, fish, and gather enough edible plants to get by on."

One of the men said, "Get by on? Hell, that fish meal we had this morning was the best food we've eaten since being down on this icy globe."

Samael forced a smile. "Yep, it is a bit colder here than the homeworld."

The four captives groaned at the understatement.

"That's one of the reasons for the G3AST." Sam watched the men's response. *Just blank stares.* "You don't know what I'm talking about, do you? You didn't spend a hundred and twenty days in the Atmospheric Simulation Torus."

The man sitting to Sam's left said, "We have no idea what a G3 whatever-ya-call-it is."

"So, you were deployed directly to the surface from T-Taxiarch?"

Creasing his brow the man said, "Uhm—yeah."

Anger flashed in Samael's eyes. "Good gods! What have those bastards done to you?"

Two of the men asked simultaneously, "What do you mean?"

Samael explained, "If you did not slowly acclimatize to Ghrain's twenty-four hour day, your biorhythms are out of whack and you're going to get sick. If you haven't increased your caloric intake, regardless of these fancy heat retaining clothes, you're going to get sick. If you're not consuming two litres of water per day, you're going to get sick. And some of us get sick **because** we consume two litres per day."

Two of the prisoners affected the Domhanian emotional mask. Outrage etched the expressions on the faces of the other two men.

Sam said, "They probably thought your mission was going to be a quick in and out—probably didn't think you'd be down here long enough to require acclimatization."

One man said, "**Fuck that**! Have they killed us?"

Shaking his head, "No, they haven't killed you, at least not yet. But you're already feeling lousy, and that's gonna get worse. We need to get you back upstairs as soon as possible."

Sensing now was the time to pull out the stops, Samael continued, "Look, I know you're soldiers just doing your jobs—following orders. And I don't know what you've been told, but I'm telling you we're not your enemies here. Those sapien-hybrids over there, they're not your enemies either."

The pilot said, "So what are you saying? Now we should all be pals? You guys killed Lieutenant Korwin up on the ridge. I'm not ready to be your friend." His comrades exchanged nervous glances.

"No," Samael said looking down, "I'm not proposing we become buddies. I wasn't up there when your lieutenant was killed. I wasn't down here when my friend was killed. But I can tell you that up on the rim my comrades had their weapons set on stun. They didn't intend to kill anyone. I can only assume your friend was hit by two charged-particles." Without lifting his head Sam glanced around at the captives from under his thin eyebrows.

After a moment of silence one of the men spoke. "Actually, that is what happened. I was down but not unconscious. I saw Korwin go down. He started crawling toward his weapon and a second charge caught him right in the head."

Looking at the man who had spoken, Sam said, "And that's an image you're never going to un-see. I'm guessing he was your friend as well as your commander. The memory of seeing his death will stay with you for the rest of your days. So, no, I don't think we'll become chums. But as I'm sure you've sensed, things are sliding into some godforsaken abyss—with Anotas on the homeworld, with the Presidium upstairs, and for sure down here on the surface. People are choosing sides and fighting, and we don't even know who's on whose side."

Azazel stepped out of the shadows and picked up on Samael's train of thought. "Gentlemen, we're in survival mode here. As Samael said, you're not well now and you're going to feel worse in the days ahead. We need to get you guys to medical help—sooner rather than later."

With his thumb Azazel gestured over his shoulder toward the dark south rim. "Look, I suspect you're going to have a hard time making that six hundred metre vertical climb. The three of us can't help you if we have to keep you shackled and hold guns on you.

"If you are going to survive, you must work with us. Your only other options are we remove your shackles and you run away, or we leave you tethered to a tree." With a chilling expression he added, "Either way—the surface of Ghrain-3 would become your final resting place."

Azazel turned an inquisitive gaze on Samael, who nodded. With that, both men pulled out their multi-tools and began snipping the prisoner's plastic cuffs. "We're going to climb out of here tomorrow morning. If you plan to join us, you need to hydrate and sleep tonight. We can help you get to the medical attention you need—if you'll let us.

Adair piloted the Anti-GravXL over the canyon rims above the Clan's caves. He did a laser scan of the ridgetop and tapped a terrain inquiry into the ship's computer. "Nope. Not even close. The slope is almost four degrees."

"Fly-it-out-ridge?" Semyaza asked.

"Yep. Hopefully, the platform's been built and it's big enough."

As they hovered over Dig #421 Ramuell scanned the area below and recognized the direction he, Azazel, Owan and Gadrel had hiked. Though it had been over five kuuk, Ramuell remembered the day with stunning clarity.

On the way toward the ridge Ramuell told of his first *sen* experience the night before he trekked up the ridge. "You'd think such a transcendent experience would have left me addled. But I remember almost every detail of that day."

"Well, your sense of direction and distance are spot-on. Look down there," Adair said as he banked the ship slightly circling a stone landing platform.

It looked awfully small from a couple hundred metres overhead. “Will it work?” Semyaza asked anxiously.

“Sure it will. It doesn’t compare to the gargantuan stone slabs we launched from, but it’s big enough to accommodate our landing struts. I just need to ease her in gently.” Adair glanced at the magnetic levitator charge display. “We have plenty of power—we’ll glide in like a feather.”

Kadeya, who was listening in at the open cockpit door, sensed Captain Adair’s words overstated his actual confidence.

CHAPTER FIFTY-SEVEN

DEFIANCE

BRIGADIER MIGEAL WENT to Grandmaster Elyon's office to report the gist of his conversation with Commander Croga. As he exited the Presidium's reception area, Migeal saw but did not notice Col. Uzza and Agent Chelt.

While Magael's weightless body was being pushed by the directional air current in the transport tube toward the torus at the opposite end of the orbiter, Chelt was reading the court's Order of Summons to Grandmaster Elyon. When the Brigadier stepped onto T-Taxiarch's deck he immediately began issuing orders. "The Port Authority at WSA-1 is under attack. Our remaining squadron is to launch for WSA-1 at once. Two attack craft shall accompany the troop transport. Get me a report on every flight we've tracked into and out of WSA-1—I need that before our first squadron arrives. What's their time of arrival?"

The Security Forces in T-Taxiarch were already on alert. With the Brigadier's frenzied commands, the entire torus became a whirlwind of activity, which belied the physics of its graceful, artificial gravity producing rotation.

By the time the first Serefim troop transport ship arrived at WSA-1, the large docking platform had been completely torn asunder. The pilot and the troop commander stared at the demolished structure with a combined sense of confusion and foreboding.

"What in an unholy hell happened down there?" the lieutenant asked.

"And how?" the pilot added. "Those slabs weigh over fifty thousand kilograms—some of them much more! They look like tossed dice."

"Can you find a place to land?" the lieutenant asked.

"Sure, there's plenty of flat terrain. It should be no problem. Question is, how close do you want to be?"

Rubbing his brow the lieutenant said, "I don't know. There was fighting at the smaller platform. Let's make a reconnaissance fly-by."

"We can do that but remember some kind of electromagnetic pulse device was likely detonated over there."

"Yeah, I certainly remember hearing that tidbit," the lieutenant replied.

"I don't want to crash this bird, so we'll stay well above the fray. We also don't want to be on the ground and have one set off nearby. It could cook our electronics and we'd be stranded."

Flying over the battle scene they saw only a few people wandering around. There was no organized effort to do much of anything, nor was there any sign of ongoing combat.

"Not much happening down there," the lieutenant observed. "I think it's more important for us to investigate the destruction of the main facility. They may have wounded needing medical attention."

"Okay, I'll put us down three or four hundred metres from what was the landing pad."

As they flew over the platform again, the lieutenant said, "Good gods, it must have been a hell of an explosion. I'll be surprised if there are any survivors."

The lieutenant's observation was wrong on several counts. The Serefim Security forces found everyone had survived the facility's destruction. There were only a few minor injuries. As perplexing, they found no evidence of any kind of explosion.

The dock

had been ripped apart by a technology Domhanians had yet to even imagine. It was another bit of evidence the Beag-Liath had at one time been a warlike species. That they fastidiously avoided killing any of the dozens of Port Authority personnel implied they had abandoned their former barbarity, but not the technologies developed to facilitate the savagery.

When the second Serefim Security squad arrived they were directed to land and evaluate the situation near the smaller docking facility. There they found several wounded, all inflicted by weapons of Domhanian origin.

The mystery of what actually happened at what came to be known as "The Port Authority Battle" would remain controversial for decades.

Meanwhile on the orbiting station Colonel Uzza's badge was doing double-duty. It indicated his rank within the Anotas Interstellar Enforcement Force, and it hid a minuscule camera/microphone that was transmitting to receivers aboard the Law and Order Directorate's 4D-ship.

When Major Amil saw Grandmaster Elyon's temper tantrum then Uzza, Chelt and the two detectives being shackled, she barked, "Let's go! Let's go!" Her squad stormed through the Port-3 foyer. The two Matzod standing guard at the foyer doors remained at their posts as their comrades charged into the Torus-1 circumference corridor.

Two Matzod were assigned to each of the other three ports on the torus. Port-2 was unmanned and not operational. Port-4 had a ship docked and eight people were milling around the receiving foyer. The first Matzod trooper through the door ran directly into the surface-to-station transport vehicle. She made her way to the cockpit and began disabling the communication system.

The Port-4 security guard followed the trooper into the cockpit. The guard demanded, "What do you think you're doing?"

The Matzod responded dispassionately, "Disabling the ship's communication system."

"By whose orders?"

"My commanding officer—Major Amil." She continued disconnecting power feeds to the communications equipment.

The security guard pulled his weapon and told her to stop at once.

The trooper had anticipated this turn of events when she heard the guard enter the cockpit. With her back turned, she unholstered her charged-particle handgun. With only a half turn of her body she fired one quick stun shot. The guard's legs crumpled beneath him.

The ship's pilot walked into the cockpit just as the trooper was stuffing a wad of power cables into her pack. The pilot saw the stunned security guard twitching on the floor. She looked the Matzod in the eyes and backed out of the doorway. With upraised hands she indicated, 'you'll get no fight from me.'

The other Matzod trooper had closed and locked the exit from the Port-4 foyer into the circumference corridor. After placing a communication jamming device on the Identification and Verification counter, he panned his charged particle weapon around the room and said, "We are part of a team here to deliver an Order of Summons from the High Court of Domhan-Siol. We want no trouble and intend no harm. Your cooperation is required. Please take a seat with your backs against the wall. You're free to talk, but I'm not authorized to provide any additional information."

All of the people except one did exactly as they were told. One man, however, had more bravado than sense. "I'm not going over to that wall." When the Matzod trooper did not respond, the man continued with even more bellicosity, "I'm not going to sit down either—I'm going out that door and report this to Serefim Security!"

The trooper stepped in front of the door, raised his weapon, and pointed it at Mr. Testosterone's forehead. The man pulled up short less than two metres away. With the speed of a snake strike, the Matzod lowered the gun and lunged forward slamming the barrel directly into the man's solar plexus. Gasping, he dropped to his knees and curled into a fetal position. The trauma induced diaphragm spasm would last a couple minutes.

Out in the circumference corridor two other Matzod troopers had made their way to the zero-grav transport tube's access portal. A Serefim Security officer was stationed at the portal. One of the Matzod recited the mission authorization statement verbatim.

The security officer looked down at the Matzod's foliopad and with a gesture indicated, 'Okay, show me what you've got.' The trooper unclipped his foliopad and handed it to the officer. He checked the Matzods' identifications then read the Court Order. He pressed his lips together tightly for a moment then said, "Okay—what do you need me to do?"

Both of the Matzod blew out almost indiscernible sighs of relief. "Has anyone passed through here in the last few minutes?"

"Yes. One of the big bosses exited not two minutes before you arrived."

"Who was that?"

"Brigadier Migeal."

The two Matzod looked at each other. They were not exactly sure what to make of this information but knew it was significant. One grabbed his communicator, "Major Amil—Team 3 here."

"This is Amil—go three."

"We're at the portal to the zero-grav transport tube. The officer in charge checked our identification information and the Court Order. He told us that Brigadier Migeal was on Torus-1 but departed a few minutes ago."

"Do you know where he was going?" Amil asked.

The security officer held up a finger and said, "I might be able to check." He tapped several keys on the control panel, then looked up at the overhead schematic of zero-grav tubes and access spokes. "There was other traffic between toruses, but someone just entered T-Taxiarch"

Major Amil said, "That was probably Brigadier Migeal." She paused thinking about all the implications. "We know he wasn't present when the Order of Summons was delivered, so he's probably unaware of that situation. No one is to leave or enter Torus-1 until this operation is concluded. Is that understood?"

The Matzod trooper cocked an eyebrow at the security officer who replied, "I can lockdown the tube's access portal."

Amil said, "Very good! Please do so. Our number one concern is to accomplish this mission without anyone getting hurt. Your cooperation is appreciated officer—what is your name?

"Davel, ma'am."

"Officer Davel, today you're on the side of the angels. Thank you gentlemen."

Sean was on the Law and Order Directorate fleet's flagship. A total of 240 Anotas Interstellar Enforcement Division officers and sixty support staff were aboard the fleet's six 4D-ships. Their mission was to assume command of the Ghrain-3 orbiting station – by force if necessary. The fleet maintained an orbit 167° behind the Ghrain-3 station. In this way the planet hid the ships from the station's view. A network of tiny monitoring satellites had been deployed in an orbit 74° ahead of the fleet. The satellites were so small even if the orbiter detected them, they would appear to be space junk. They were definitely not junk; the cluster of seven satellites networked to create an extremely powerful tracking array.

The fleet's Comms-Technicians were monitoring the orbiter's internal and external communications, as well as tracking all ship arrivals and departures at the station. Suddenly a shrill alarm assaulted the senses of everyone on the flagship.

"Sir," one of the technicians called out, "We have a launch from the T-Taxiarch torus. It looks like one personnel shuttle-craft and two attack craft."

"Attack craft—really! What's their heading?" the duty officer asked.

"Not sure. I need to track 'em for a few minutes," the technician replied.

The Law and Order fleet could have been monitoring the

surface communications during the battle at the docking facilities some forty thousand metres below, but the array of mini-satellite tracking devices were focused on the orbiter. It hadn't occurred to the fleet commanders that momentous events might be unfolding on the planet's surface.

"They're headed in our general direction," he paused studying the data scrolling across his screen. "But they're on a course to drop out of orbit. At this time they're tracking toward the western edge of the continent directly below us."

"Can they detect us?" the duty officer asked.

"They can, but they haven't any reason to scan in this direction."

The duty officer turned and looked up at the fleet admiral, who was standing on the Command Mezzanine taking in the beehive of activity on the deck below, "Sir, I recommend we issue an Action Stations alert."

"Very well—laser transmit the message to the fleet. We are not to break radio silence and all craft are to remain in their present orbital configuration." Under his breath, Admiral Faxcil said to Sean, "If we start jumping around that might draw their attention. If we sit tight, they probably won't notice us." He turned his attention back to the monitoring and communications deck and said, "Turn our shipboard array toward the continent below. We need ears and if possible eyes on whatever situation called for the deployment of attack craft —and shut off that damn alarm!"

A couple minutes later the Comms-Tech monitoring the surface said, "Sir, there's been some kind of kerfuffle down there."

The duty officer walked over and plugged in his headset. He listened intently for a moment. With a perplexed expression he looked up at Admiral Faxcil and said, "You're going to want to listen to this. The people on the surface are talking all over each other. They seem to be in full-blown panic mode."

The technician clicked his tongue. "Right, they sound terrified. I'll try to filter the signals. Perhaps we can ferret out some distinct conversations."

The wristcuffed Colonel Uzza, Agent Chelt, and the Law and Order Detectives were led out of the Serefim Presidium reception lobby. The colonel's badge was still transmitting live audio/video, making it easy to track their whereabouts. Melanka and four of the Matzod were sprinting to intercept the group before they arrived at the zero-grav transport tube.

Though the Serefim Security officer at the tube had thus far been cooperative, Melanka wasn't certain how he might respond when approached by two of his peers escorting prisoners to the brig by order of the Grandmaster. Melanka's team intercepted the two Serefim Security officers and their prisoners just as they arrived at the tube portal.

One of the escorts told the guard at the zero-grav tube portal, "We have orders to escort these detainees to the brig."

Forcefully Melanka rasped, "And I am countermanding that order." She pulled her foliopad out of its pouch and presented it to the security officer. On it he saw her name and Anotas-Deithe rank. He was taken aback but decided to bluster. "Grandmaster Elyon has reason to believe these individuals are affiliated with a Realta-Gorm terrorist organization."

Taking her foliopad back Melanka said, "If you're talking about Oprit-Robia, none of these individuals have ever met a member of that organization nor have any of them set foot on Realta-Gorm 4." She scrolled to another screen and handed the device back to the security guards.

There they saw Colonel Uzza's identification information. "Colonel Uzza is here to take command of the Ghrain-3 Serefim Security Forces until further notice." She studied the expressions of the two guards. They were unaccustomed to anyone questioning Elyon's orders. Melanka sensed their loyalty remained with the Grandmaster, but she had gone too far to back down, "I'm ordering you to release your superior officer immediately."

Both of the security guards were distressed and uncertain. One guard keyed his communicator microphone and said, "We're at the transport tube portal and have a..."

With catlike deftness two of the Matzod pulled handheld charged-particle weapons from under their jackets and pointed the guns directly at each of the security officer's chests. The other two troopers grabbed the Serefim Security guards' communicators.

Seeing his fellow officers being maltreated, Officer Davel's cooperativeness waivered. Still standing by the locked portal he exclaimed, "Now wait a minute! What's going on here? I thought no one was to be injured."

"We intend that no one is injured," Melanka replied, "but we also expect complete cooperation."

Melanka turned back to the two arresting officers, "Release Colonel Uzza immediately or you will be shot and if I can't find the lock release codes on your unconscious bodies I'll cut the colonel's shackles off myself."

The eyes of the two security officers widened. They knew Melanka's reputation. Col. Uzza spoke up, "Now Chief Melanka, I don't think there's any need to resort to such drastic measures." He turned his attention to the two confused and frightened officers. "Gentlemen, you have seen my credentials and identification information. You can scroll down further, and you'll find the Anotas-Deithe Security Forces chain-of-command. As you know, Serefim Presidium Security is a unit within the Interstellar Enforcement Force structure. You also know I am your superior officer. If you will look at the Command Structure Organization Chart, you'll see I'm authorized to assume command of the entire Serefim Security Force in the case of an emergency." Uzza could see the officers' resolve was wavering.

"We are acting under orders of the High Court of Domhan-Siol. This is an emergency—now I need you to release my wristcuffs and follow my orders. You have my word I'll not leave you hanging. I will explain the exact nature of the emergency when we have the situation under control." He paused for effect, "But at this time, it's your sworn duty to be good soldiers and follow the orders of the officer in command."

At that point Officer Davel, who had served in various Anotas Security branches for over two centuries, spoke up. "Gentlemen, Colonel Uzza is actually right. We have no choice but to recognize his authority and follow his orders. You need to remove his cuffs."

With tremendous relief the two officers deferred to their more experienced colleague's judgment. One of the officers entered a three digit code on the fob he was holding. The wristcuff lock snicked open.

Uzza ordered the wristcuffs removed from Chelt and the detectives as well. As the group of eleven people turned to make their way toward the Serefim Presidium offices, Col. Uzza heard Officer Davel asking one of the two Matzod who remained behind, "What the heck's going on?"

The personnel transport and two assault ships did not scan for other ships in the neighborhood. Migeal nor anyone else among the ranks of the Serefim Presidium Security Forces were aware the Law and Order Presidium Fleet lurked nearby.

The Fleet's officers were listening to the hysterical chatter of Port Authority personnel about the violent destruction of the large docking platform. Given that there had been no explosions, Admiral Faxcil and his officers could not fathom what had happened on the planet's surface.

However, they did learn that a clan of sapien-hybrids had been "abducted" by a group of insurgents. (The Domhanians involved in the sapien slave trade were unable, or unwilling, to conceptualize the Clan's removal as a liberation rather than an abduction.) An Anti-GravXL had been commandeered and appeared to be en route to SWA-7. Another much smaller ship was also tracked departing from the area north of the destroyed docking facilities. It was heading almost due east when the ship's energy signature simply disappeared.

Perhaps most incredible, there was a mishmash of conversations about intervention by an extraterrestrial race of beings and something about an electromagnetic pulse weapon! Sean turned to Admiral Faxcil, "Perhaps Egan's and Althea's friends became impatient with our progress on the slave trade issue."

Faxcil just grunted.

Everyone in the reception lobby stood agog when Major Amil and the six Matzod who accompanied her strode through Serefim Presidium Administrative office entrance. They knew the Matzod were the elite of the elite security force and never deployed for protocol missions. The fact that seven of them had unexpectedly appeared at the Presidium reception lobby was disconcerting.

The murmurs of the Serefim staff in the reception area,

though not loud, had a certain sense of urgency. Many heads emerged from office doors to see what was happening in the lobby.

As she marched past the reception desk, Major Amil told the receptionist to buzz open the Grandmaster's office door. When he hesitated one of the Matzod stepped behind the counter, scanned the control panel then hit the correct touch screen key. A pleasant sounding chime accompanied the clicking sound of Elyon's office door opening.

With weapons drawn, two Matzod troopers sprung into the office. Grandmaster Elyon and Serefim Security Director Dantan leapt to their feet. "What's the meaning of this?" Dantan demanded.

Elyon already knew the answer to that question. Ignoring the Matzod and their weapons, he stepped away from his desk and squared on Major Amil. "How dare you?" he seethed. "You're going to live to regret this! Your career is over, you insignificant little whelp."

Though intimidated, the Major's expression remained wooden. "Grandmaster Elyon, I am here with a Court Order of Detention. You are charged with false arrest and imprisonment of three individuals working on behalf of Anotas-Deithe for the greater good of Domhan-Siol—namely Doctors Durela, Lector and Evander."

"Ha!" he barked. "We'll see which charges of false arrest stick—yours or mine."

Major Amil continued as if unfazed, though her stomach was spewing acid toward her throat. "You will also be charged with refusing a Court Order of Summons and the illegal detention of the four individuals who, acting at the behest of the High Court of Domhan-Siol, attempted to deliver said order."

"Where is my security detail? Get these traitors out of my office."

"Grandmaster Elyon, all of the Serefim Security personnel on this torus have been disarmed. All communications to and from this torus have been blocked. All of the external ports have been locked down as has the portal to the zero-grav transport tube. Colonel Uzza, would you please join us," Amil called over her shoulder.

The colonel and Agent Chelt stepped into Elyon's opulent office. Uzza looked at Director Danton and said, "Director Danton, I am under a court order to assume command of all Serefim Security Personnel associated with the Ghrain-3 Expeditionary Mission. As of this moment, I am relieving you of command."

Hearing this Elyon realized he had lost this round. His shoulders slumped ever so slightly. *This is just one little battle. This is not the end of the fight!* With that thought he pushed himself to his most erect posture and looked down on Major Amil who stood at least twenty-five centimetres shorter than him. "So are you going to cuff us?"

Amil blinked rapidly. The thought of how to deal with this situation had not occurred to her.

Melanka's raspy voice came from the open door behind Major Amil. "To answer your question, no, we aren't going to try to humiliate you. That's your tactic Elyon, not ours. You'll be escorted out without shackles."

By now a crowd of stunned onlookers had gathered around Elyon's office door. Some were grumbling. Some were cursing the irreverence of the Interstellar Enforcement Force intrusion. Most were standing by watching in dumbfounded silence.

The eight Matzod inside the Serefim office complex began to clear a path through the crowd. Officer Rafel approached Major Amil with a proposition. "You're going to need to secure the data files in every office. You'll need to keep this group under control until we have Elyon off the orbiter. Heck, you may even have to make additional arrests. I'd recommend Officer Barak, Chief Melanka and I escort the prisoner to our ship."

The Major thought for a moment and said, "That's a good suggestion. When you have Elyon secured on our ship, call me and we'll dispatch a team to free Evander, Lector, and Durela from the Torus-3 brig." She looked at Melanka who nodded her assent.

Upon exiting the Presidium office Rafel led the group to the left, which would take them past the zero-grav transport tube portal. When the Matzod troopers who had remained behind guarding the closed portal saw Melanka and the others approaching, they beamed. "Mission accomplished!" one of them said with delight. Officer Davel was flabbergasted when he realized it was the Grandmaster who had been taken into custody. He was also perplexed by the fact that Elyon was not wristcuffed.

Officer Barak returned their smiles and said, "Yeah, everything went according to plan." Then suddenly he pulled his handheld charged-particle weapon and pointed at Melanka. Everyone froze in complete astonishment; everyone except Officer Rafel who took a sonic-blaster from the holster hidden under his coat. He pointed it at the men guarding the portal.

One of the Matzod said stupidly, "Hey, that weapon's not authorized for this operation."

Elyon, who had already figured out what was going on, laughed and said, "I suspect that's the least of your problems young man." He turned to Officer Rafel and asked, "So what's the plan?"

One of the Matzod troopers had the presence of mind to stealthily press and lock his communicator microphone switch on transmit mode.

Motioning with his weapon toward Melanka, Rafel said,

"We're going to take her with us to T-Taxiarch. From there we'll mount a force to retake this torus."

Elyon shook his head. "Nope, we need another plan." Puzzled, Rafel and Barak stared at the Grandmaster. "Not five minutes before Melanka's flunkies came in my office we deployed our last cohort of Security Forces to the surface to put down an attack on one of our main shipping ports—we don't have enough people left in T-Taxiarch to take control of the galley, much less contend with a squad of Matzod."

Grasping at straws, Barak said, "Then we can use her as leverage to secure a 4D-ship."

Elyon replied, "No, we don't need to do that." He snatched the charged-particle gun from Barak's hand, flipped the weapon setting from stun to kill and raised it toward Melanka's head. A sneer flickered across his face as he said, "This self-righteous bitch has been a pain in my ass for long enough."

Realizing just how malevolently narcissistic Elyon truly was, Melanka's eyes shot wide open. Her terror lasted only an instant. Elyon discharged the weapon directly into her forehead. She melted into a lifeless heap on the metal floor.

The destruction of the Port Authority's docking facility had been so loud and shocking the Oprit-Robia fighters had needed no other distraction to cover their withdrawal. Commander Anso led the group to the mouth of the drainage they had emerged from several hours earlier. Dreading the climb up the escarpment, the squad was thrilled to hear the hum of the transport ship landing on flat ground a couple hundred metres away. In less than two minutes everyone was aboard and the ship was airborne.

At about ten thousand metres altitude the Oprit-Robia ship was intercepted by a peculiar looking craft. The odd ship nudged in much too close; less than a hundred metres. While the Oprit pilot stared at it, a dark solar shield opened and peering at her through the transparent aluminum oxynitride window were creatures like none she'd ever seen.

"Major, I need you up here—**now**!" the pilot shouted over her shoulder.

The cockpit of the Oprit-Robia ship was separated by only the narrowest of bulkheads and had no door. Anso leaned in and looked out at the other ship. He saw two Beag-Liath staring at him in their odd expressionless way. "Well I'll be damned!"

"What are they?!" the pilot asked.

"Those creatures are Beag-Liath. You're probably going to doubt my sanity, but we just met several of them down on the surface. They are apparently the species Dr. Althea and Professor Egan traveled around the galaxy with for all those decades."

The pilot studied the Major out of the corner of her eye. *He's serious!* "What do you think they want?"

Anso replied, "They helped us down there. In fact, we wouldn't have been able to steal the Anti-GravXL without their support. Can't say for sure what they want, but I am sure they're on our side."

One of the Beag pointed a long index finger at the pilot. It made eye contact and held her gaze for several seconds. It then pointed back at itself and repeated the back-and-forth gesture two more times. Turning to Anso the pilot said, "They wants us to follow them." Pushing hair back off her forehead she asked, "What do we do sir?"

Blowing out a loud breath Anso said, "Their technology is

advanced—and they certainly know a lot more about warfare than we do. Let's follow!"

Unbeknownst to Anso and the pilot, when they fell in behind the strange vessel the Beag-Liath deployed their energy bending stealth technology, completely cloaking both ships from all Domhanian tracking systems. The Beag-Liath ship then made a hard left turn, heading 22°30' north-northeast.

Horrified expressions were etched on faces that pivoted toward Elyon. He turned the weapon on Officer Davel and said, "Open that goddamn portal."

Davel was an erudite man who had long harbored doubts about Elyon. Having just witnessed the Grandmaster's cavalier taking of Melanka's life, dispelled those doubts. He was now certain that Elyon lacked any semblance of rectitude. Nevertheless, he was not going to throw his life away on a reckless and meaningless gesture of defiance. He looked Elyon in the eye, nodded and turned to enter the code that unlocked the transport tube's access portal.

Looking down at Melanka's body, Officer Rafel muttered with a hint of arrogance, "Cubra's revenge."

Barak did not share his fellow traitor's insouciance. *What in all the frozen-hells?! I didn't sign-up to participate in cold-blooded murder.* He hung his head and didn't make eye contact as Elyon handed the weapon back to him.

The Matzod scattered around Torus-1 were hearing everything through their comrade's open microphone. The notion of traitors among the ranks of the 83rd Interplanetary Enforcement Force created a cognitive dissonance that made what was happening incomprehensible. This was especially true for Major

Amil. Officers Rafel and Barak couldn't possibly be traitors. She'd known them for a dozen annum. How could she have so monumentally misjudged their character? *But I did!* She leaned over and clutched the reception counter feeling she might vomit.

Before they entered the tube Elyon pointed at Rafel's sonic-blaster and said, "Anyone who follows us will enjoy a blast from that."

"Sir, inside the tube even a stun setting blast would be fatal," Barak cautioned.

Elyon glowered at Melanka's crumpled body then back up at Barak and said, "That is correct." Barak's face froze into an expressionless mask. He said nothing. Elyon continued, "Now that we have that cleared up, let's get going gentlemen." He pointed at Barak, "I'll follow you and officer-sonic-blaster here will take the sweep position."

As soon as the three men entered the transport tube, one of the Matzod dropped to his knees beside Melanka and took her wiry body in his arms. He held her as though the embrace might somehow bring her back from the abyss that had yawned at her feet.

The other trooper unclipped the communicator from his belt. It was still transmitting through its open microphone. In a voice laced with grief and anxiety he called, "Major Amil, we have a situation at the zero-grav transport portal." He kneeled down beside Melanka's body and searched his comrade's face. The trooper bit his lip and shook his head. "Major, Chief Melanka is dead. Elyon has escaped."

The dreadful message jolted Melanka out of her stupor. She released the edge of the counter, spun around and pointed at two of her troopers, "**No one** and I mean absolutely no one is to leave this office or use any kind of communication device. If they try to do so, shoot them." As she ran into the torus's circumference corridor she called over her shoulder, "The rest of you are with me!"

The Comms-technician monitoring signals from the orbiter sputtered then turned to Admiral Faxcil, "Sir, I've just picked up a transmission on the Matzod communication frequency—Chief Melanka has been killed."

Faxcil's jaw dropped, and Sean blanched white as ovine wool. Turning toward Sean, the admiral realized his colleague was fainting. He grabbed Sean by an elbow and guided him into a chair. In those few seconds Faxil gathered his wits. He leaned over the Mezzanine rail and said, "Duty Officer, instruct ships two, three, and five to deploy at once for the orbiting station. Tell all ship captains we have a Strategy and Command videoconference on Channel-33 in fifteen minutes."

CHAPTER FIFTY-EIGHT

HARD CLIMB, HARD LANDING, AND A BROKEN HEART

AZAZEL AND SAM were sitting at their breakfast fire on the ledge in front of the Crow Clan's caves when the four erstwhile Serefim soldiers approached. The pilot acted as the group's spokesman. "We want to go out with you. We won't make trouble." He looked up at the switchback trail ascending the canyon's south side and snorted. "Actually I should say we'll offer no resistance. You were right last night. We are not well—none of us. Our lagging on the climb out may be trouble for you.

"That kind of trouble we'll gladly deal with," Azazel said with a very slight smile. "Anyway, I'm certain my appointment calendar has been cleared."

"Perhaps that's a good thing, yeah?"

Dr. Lilith returned from speaking with the nine remaining clanspeople. "They're shaken; worried about the Clan. They fear they may never be reunited, which likely leads to fear about their own survival." She paused for a moment, "But I'm an anthropologist, not a psychologist."

"I'd bet your assessment is correct. The question is, what should we do?" Azazel asked.

The six men looked to Lilith. Pursing her lips she said slowly, "Boss, I should stay with them—at least for a while. Our people caused their trauma. If we all just pull up stakes and leave, they're going to feel incredibly abandoned."

Azazel wasn't thrilled with the idea of leaving one of his staff alone in this canyon he'd come to consider a place of ill-fortune. He did, however, understand Lilith's concern. Rubbing his temples, he spoke hesitantly, "You're right—we'd also be leaving them vulnerable to another nefilim attack. We'll figure out some way to get a message back to you as soon as we learn anything about the situation with our colleagues and the clanspeople."

Samael added, "I'm not feeling nearly as pessimistic as I did yesterday. I haven't lost hope that they may have succeeded with the rescue."

"What makes you think so?" Azazel asked.

"Late yesterday afternoon a large transport ship made a pass over both canyon rims. Now it may have been another contingent of soldiers sent to retrieve the sapiens left behind, but that would be a helluva commitment of resources for nine potential sales."

Azazel scoffed, "Unless they're selling these people for a lot more than we've imagined."

"I doubt that. I've imagined quite a lot," Samael replied. "But I think it's possible the ship was carrying our friends."

Kadeya's misgivings about setting the Anti-GravXL down on the fly-it-out-ridge quadcopter landing platform proved to be prescient. Adair took the ship up and down three times before aligning the struts precisely over the small pad of level stones. When he cut power to the anti-grav devices the full weight of the ship settled in and cracked the stones under two struts. The ship groaned as it torqued beyond the limits of its design.

Several of the Domhanians gasped when they heard the creaking metal. This in turn frightened the clanspeople. Many of whom jumped to their feet, jabbering anxiously.

Matters were made worse by the fact that the twisting of the ship's frame, though only a couple dozen micrometres, was enough to seize the exit's hatch dog latches. While Adair and Kadeya disassembled and studied the door, Ramuell did everything he could to calm the clanspeople. It would be thousands of annum before their descendants would smelt metal. All this was supernatural magic in their eyes, and it was disconcerting to see angels confounded by their own creations.

Adair wedged the curved chisel end of the prisebar from the ship's toolbox between the door and the jamb. When he and Ipos leaned their combined weight into the bar's fulcrum, the frame moved enough for Imamiah to hammer the six hatch dogs open.

The bottom-hinged door flopped open and clanged loudly on the stone platform. Had it not offered egress, the noise would have caused the Crow people to panic. Althea noted that even though they were frightened and wanted out immediately, the clanspeople picked up the smallest children and carefully guided the other youngsters to the safety of solid ground. She also noticed how Shiya grabbed Ramuell's hand and almost dragged him off the ship.

The Crow, like all sapiens on the planet, were hunter-gatherers. This often led them far afield from Blue Rock Canyon. Upon exiting the ship the Clan's adults scanned their surroundings, recognized numerous landmarks, and knew exactly how to return to their canyon home. However, they had not eaten for almost two days. With his rudimentary vocabulary and a good deal of mime, Ramuell convinced Ru Ta that there would be plenty of food at the angel's camp; after eating and resting his people would be in better condition for the journey back to Blue Rock.

Two hours later Ramuell led over thirty sapiens and seven Domhanians into the Dig #421 camp. During the trek off the ridge he had envisioned his return to the camp as a moment of triumph. Alicia would run up and hug him fondly, perhaps even kiss him again.

The celebration and warm feelings he had anticipated dissolved into crushing heartbreak. Though Ramuell had only spent a few days at the Dig, he had a sense of the enthusiastic, even joyous camaraderie the staff shared. Now a malaise lay over the camp like the grey fogs that shrouded the wetlands of Domhan-Siol.

Owan and a couple of others came out to meet the group. When Owan offered his palm, Ramuell asked, "What's going on?"

The camp leader's eyes brimmed with tears he would not allow to flow. "They're gone..."

"Who's gone?!"

The lump in Owan's throat choked off any possibility of speech.

Zeke, the camp's quartermaster/chef, stepped forward and also offered Ramuell an upturned palm. "Alicia is dead. She and two others were killed."

With the previous night's combat fresh in his mind, Ramuell assumed they had been killed by Serefim Security forces. "The fucking bastards! Why would they send a squadron all the way out here?"

"Oh, it wasn't our people," Zeke replied hastily.

Owan's expression morphed from grief to seething anger. He croaked, "Nefilim."

Kadeya, who had walked up beside her grandson, staggered when she heard this. "Nefilim? Really?! How? Where?"

"At the dig site—we made a stupid mistake—and now they're gone," Owan answered.

Semyaza sensed where this conversation was going. He nudged Adair and together they stepped forward. In his despair Owan had failed to notice Semyaza among the group Ramuell led into the camp. The shock of realizing an Operations Director was present helped Owan regain a modicum of composure. "Semyaza! I'm surprised to see you. Of course, it's an honor to have you visit our camp—I wish it was under better circumstances."

"As do I, my friend. We have much to discuss, but right now we have most of the Crow Clan with us, and they've been through a mind-bending hell in the last two days. They need food and rest. Do you have enough to feed such a large group?"

"Food? That's one thing we have in abundance. After the inexplicable attacks by the Presidium's Security forces, we made a call to the Seafood Processing Facility. The plant manager and I go back a long way. Anyway, given that no one really understands what's going on, the folks at SWA-7 decided we should stockpile a hefty supply of food here. The landing we built on fly-it-out-ridge has already paid dividends."

Surprised, Semyaza asked, "So you've been in contact with the staff at the basecamp?"

"Yes sir. Things there are fine. I'll fill you in after we get these people fed."

Supplying food was a simpler matter than providing bedding. The camp didn't have near enough pads or blankets to accommodate some forty additional people. When Ramuell became aware that this was causing concern, he shook himself out of his doldrums and approached Owan and Semyaza. "Gentlemen, I've seen Crow Clansmen return from extended foraging expeditions with only the meagerest of creature comforts. They often don't carry bedding with them. I suppose doing so would limit the amount of food they could carry back. Anyway, if you can provide a few blankets, they'll huddle together and make do."

"Okay," Owan said. "And we should set them up in a separate camp."

"That would be wise," Semyaza agreed. "After they've slept we'll get them headed to Blue Rock first thing in the morning."

A wave of grief washed over Ramuell like an ocean surf. He turned and walked back to the table where his parents and grandmother were sitting. Althea reached over and gave his forearm a squeeze. Taking his hand she asked, "Do you want to talk about it?"

He did. Ramuell told them about how he'd met Alicia. How they had worked together his first day at the Dig. How smart she was. He described the adorably disarming 'almost' smile that framed her face most of the time; her laugh that was so radiant people actually stopped and stared. He even told them she'd been part of his first *sen* experience. He did not mention their encounter on the orbiter.

"You really liked her," his mother said.

"Everyone really liked her," Ramuell replied.

"You more than most," Althea observed.

"I had the chance to meet her," Kadeya recalled. "Hers was the kind of personality that had almost everyone smitten. She was, simply put, incandescent."

"She sounds like very a special lady," Egan said softly.

Ramuell looked at his father for a moment then turned away and squeezed his eyes shut, to no avail. Tears leaked out of the corners of each eye. He opened them and wiped his cheeks.

Kadeya said quietly, "Nefilim." She looked at Ramuell and with a forlorn shake of her head said, "Somehow we must fast-track our work."

"I know. I thought the same thing in the days after the Blue Rock Canyon incident." Looking at his parents, Ramuell said, "Yeah, that's the second time you've heard about 'the incident'—it is something we need to tell you about." His lip quivered, "But not tonight."

Althea reached over and pulled her heartbroken son down to her chest as if he was a child of ten – and there he wept.

Azazel, Sam and the four Serefim Security officers made the ascent up the southside trail, but just barely. Two of the unacclimatized soldiers dropped to their knees several times. They were able to climb the last four hundred metres only by clinging to Azazel's and Samael's shoulders.

While the others rested and hydrated, Samael inspected the available means of transport. He started all of the RTVs and chose the two with the best battery charge. Only an hour after cresting the canyon rim the six men mounted the mechanized beasts and began the long, rough ride toward Dig #421.

CHAPTER FIFTY-NINE
BANISHED

Administrant Pravel, the Serefim Presidium's strategic communications officer, had been kept in the dark during the decade it took to construct T-Taxiarch. She'd known a new torus was being built but was never informed of its purpose. She wasn't even brought into the loop during the annum required to attach T-Taxiarch to the orbiting station's hub. Only when the cohorts of armed forces and a fleet of troop transports and attack ships began arriving did she realize the torus's function.

Given the turmoil within the ranks of Anotas-Deithe, Pravel did not share Grandmaster Elyon's confidence about the loyalty of the new security forces. With the troops stationed so nearby, she hid a hand-held sonic-blaster in the recording studio adjacent to her office.

Pravel had just stepped into the Presidium office lobby when Agent Chelt began reading the Order of Summons to the Grandmaster. Pravel backed into the corridor leading to the recording studio, locked herself inside, and linked the video-monitor to the hidden cameras in the reception area.

She groaned and buried her face in both hands when Elyon commanded the detention of Agent Chelt, Col. Uzza, and the two Anotas detectives. After a moment she took a deep breath and began calling-up different camera views of Torus-1. She was flabbergasted to see Matzod troopers storming through the corridors.

Pravel felt nauseous when she saw Elyon kill Melanka. Nevertheless she was certain his reasons were just. She knew it was time to act when the Grandmaster escaped into the zero-grav transport tube. She sent a text-com on a special communication device tuned to a secure frequency for messages exclusively to and from the Grandmaster.

Hiding in recording studio – Matzod have troops posted all around the torus. Awaiting your orders – Pravel

Hold for further instructions - Stay hidden – Elyon

Sir, I have a sonic-blaster – P

Shrewd – E

Abruptly the monitors Pravel was watching went dark. The Matzod had either activated a signal jammer, or they had disabled the cameras at the security office control center. Hoping for the latter, she picked up her direct access communicator.

Are you still there? – Pravel

Where else could I be? – Elyon

Lost video-feed. Feared Matzod had activated signal jammer. Any instructions yet? – P

In a few more minutes - Sit tight – E

Sitting in the darkened studio, Pravel's stomach gurgled,

and her muscles twitched. She jumped when the communicator vibrated.

Tracking three large 4D-ships approaching from the other side of the planet - Not ours - Only have a handful of Serefim Security soldiers remaining in T-Taxiarch - Cannot make a stand - Must withdraw – E

Unable to exit offices without being seen. Shall I surrender? – P

No! Use sonic-blaster – E

What?! – P

Boarding 4D-ship now - will launch and dock on Port-1 in five minutes - Will send message when to discharge blaster - stun everyone in lobby then board our ship - Security officers will retrieve personnel loyal to Presidium – E

Using a flashlight, Pravel went to a cabinet and dug out the blaster. She dialed in a power setting certain to immobilize everyone in the lobby.

Port-1 was exclusively for use by Presidium members and high ranking officials. Access was through the Serefim office complex. The stunned loyalists would be dragged directly aboard the ship without encountering Matzod troops in the circumference corridor. Though this dramatically limited the risks, Pravel's heart was pounding ferociously – and her fealty to the Grandmaster never wavered.

Sean was so grief-stricken by Melanka's murder he was unable to concentrate during the Strategy and Command videoconference. Admiral Faxcil, on the other hand, was laser focused. By the meeting's end it was decided Ships 2, 3, and 5 would endeavor to prevent any arrivals or departures from the orbiting station. However, there were too many ports on too many toruses to actually blockade the facility.

Being conservative by nature, Faxcil held back Ships one, four, and six. They could be called on as reinforcements should an assault on the orbiter become necessary. After monitoring communications on the planet's surface, the Fleet's commanders knew that most of the Serefim Security personnel from T-Taxiarch were deployed below. Without that contingent of combatants, Faxcil could not fathom how the Law and Order Directorate forces would be unable to secure the orbiter. However, he understood that scenarios one cannot fathom are often the most dangerous.

The volatile conditions on the surface also factored into the admiral's decision to hold back half the fleet. He reasoned the Serefim Presidium's command structure was likely collapsing, and his forces might be needed for intervention and rescue missions on the planet. His assumption about the tumult aboard the orbiter was correct.

Docking now - Discharge blaster in exactly one minute - ***stun everyone****. We will retrieve our own – Elyon*

Yes sir. See you in two – Pravel

Elyon smiled to himself. Though furious about being driven from his throne, he was thrilled he'd evaded arrest; his nemesis, or at least one of them, was dead; he and his most loyal followers would soon be jumping across dimensions and would exit the multiverse portal at Froitas. There, with his allies, he would resurrect the Business and Industry Council. He would transform it into a collective corporatocracy – a force for good – a force with the military might necessary to protect the fruits of his creation. The refashioned B&I Council would assert control over Anotas-Deithe and Domhan-Siol's galactic industrial empire.

One minute later Pravel fired her sonic-blaster into the reception area. People collapsed instantly. Running at full-speed down the corridor she turned the corner and smacked into one of the Security officers who had charged into the lobby to extract Elyon's stunned allies. Pravel conked her head so forcefully with the officer's helmet she tumbled sideways. Instinctively she grabbed the reception counter to break her fall, which torqued her shoulder and snapped her left clavicle. Groaning, she rolled onto her right side holding her left elbow.

The sonic blast's pressure wave reverberated around the torus circumference corridor. Major Amil was kneeling over Melanka's dead body when the jolt shook her back into the present. Overcome with grief and anger, the Major wobbled as she rose to her feet. She crouched low, armed her charged-particle weapon, and began trotting as fast as her unsteady legs would carry her toward the Presidium office complex. Three Matzod troopers and Officer Davel fell in behind.

Colonel Uzza, Agent Chelt, and Serefim Security Chief Dantan were unaware of Melanka's murder and Elyon's subsequent escape. After the Grandmaster was escorted from the Presidium office lobby, the three men had closed themselves in Elyon's office to discuss the logistics for transferring command of the Serefim Security Forces. Chief Dantan was defiant on every point. Uzza, being the consummate professional, patiently and forcefully reminded Dantan that their conversation was **not** a negotiation.

Hearing the sonic discharge in the lobby the three men launched from their seats toward the office door. It slid open just in time for them to hear the snapping of Pravel's clavicle.

Upon seeing the Serefim Security officers grabbing certain individuals by the armpits and dragging them toward Port-1, Chief Dantan realized a rescue was underway. He shoved Agent Chelt out of the way and scrambled into the lobby. Pointing at Chelt and Uzza, he shouted "Those men are terrorists. Shoot them!" He then sprinted toward the ship docked at Port-1.

One of the Serefim Officers yanked a charged-particle gun from his holster, aimed and fired at Chelt. Anticipating the shot, Chelt dove toward the open office door. The charged-particle hit his right ankle.

Though it was only an extremity strike, the energy discharge depolarized neural pathways in his right leg and up to the lower lumbar spine. He was momentarily paralyzed. Colonel Uzza grabbed Chelt by a forearm and elbow and dragged him into the office. Uzza slapped the closure button an instant before a second shot slammed harmlessly into the closing metal door.

At that moment Major Amil peeked around the edge of the lobby entrance. She leveled her shoulder weapon and fired a charged-particle directly into the armed Serefim Security officer's back. He crumpled with a whimper.

Forcing himself to take a calming breath, one of the Matzod asked, "What do we do, Major?"

"Damned if I know! Perhaps Colonel Uzza has successfully taken command of the Serefim Security forces. For all we know they're acting at his behest."

"So why did you shoot that officer?"

"I'm not sure," Amil replied. Her subordinate shot her a look of complete astonishment. She continued, "Sometimes you gotta trust your gut, though I don't trust my gut enough to take any further action. We sit this one out—but no one leaves here until we say so."

Upon hearing their Major, the Matzod troopers spread out with backs against the circumference corridor wall; aiming their weapons at the lobby door.

———

A lightning bolt of pain shot through Pravel's shoulder every time she moved. She was addled, believing she must have fallen on a sharp object that stabbed her in the shoulder. As the cognitive cobwebs cleared, she saw Security officers checking photos and comparing them to the faces of people disabled by her sonic blast. Most people were being hauled toward the awaiting escape vessel.

It had been assumed Pravel would run aboard the ship under her own power, thus her photo was not among those loaded on the Serefim Security team's foliopads. With a voice made feeble by her agonizing injury, she croaked, "I'm with you guys. Take me with you."

When no one paid any attention to Pravel's pleas, she tried to drag herself toward the Port door. The movement fired a jolt of pain from her shoulder to the middle of her torso. She screamed in agony...and that hurt too. No matter what she did or said, the Serefim officers ignored her. She could not move herself. She could not make herself understood. She could not get help. *They're going to leave me here. The stupid bastards are going to leave me!*

Within less than three minutes the Security officers had dragged the last of the Presidium members and their loyalists into the awaiting ship. Pravel heard the chime indicating the pressure seal had unlocked. She felt the 4D-ship disengage from the port. They'd abandoned her. "Damn you!" she tried to scream and again a paralyzing pain shot through her body.

On the ship Elyon began looking around at the group who would be the alpha generation of his resurrected Business and Industry Council. His self-satisfied smirk slowly melted away. "Where is Pravel?" he asked no one in particular. Frantically he began scurrying around looking at the individuals lying on the deck who were now recovering from the sonic blast. "Where's Pravel?" he asked again. Then grabbing one of the officers detailed to the rescue team, "Have you seen Pravel?"

The young man was almost too intimidated by the Grandmaster to even respond. "I...I, uhm...I don't know who that is sir," he stammered.

Seeing the officer in charge of the operation, Elyon pushed passed the young soldier. "Lieutenant, uhm..." naturally he didn't know her name. "Have you seen Pravel?"

"Pravel, sir?"

"Oh holy gods—my Communications Administrant." Seeing the blank stare, Elyon's frustration boiled. "Goddammit she's the one who fired the sonic-blaster laying all these people out! She's the one who made this rescue possible! Now where the hell is she?"

The security officer's face blanched. She said, "I don't know her personally sir. But there was a woman lying on the floor pleading to be brought along." Turning her foliopad toward the Grandmaster, she added, "Her image was not among those in our photo file."

"So what, you just left her?!" Elyon screamed.

"Yes sir, we left her," the officer replied.

"And how many of these other people were begging to be dragged aboard?" Elyon's question dripped with sarcasm.

"None, sir, they'd been stunned by a sonic-blaster."

"And it didn't strike you as odd that one person among all

those scattered around the reception area was talking and asking for help? Praise the gods I'm surrounded by geniuses!" Elyon growled, "Turn this ship around! We're going back for Pravel!"

Screwing up all of her courage and understanding her next statement would probably end her career, the lieutenant said, "Sir, we can't."

Elyon glowered at the lieutenant, but he said nothing.

"We saw a squad of Matzod gathering in the corridor outside the reception area. By now they've taken control of the office complex and the docking port. It would be a blood bath."

Chief Danton walked over and stood beside Elyon. "Grandmaster, I believe they'd like nothing better than for us to re-dock. If they've figured out what we've just done, and it's likely they have, they'll just lock us to the port the instant the pressure seals make contact. They'll have us with no need to even risk forcing the doors open. They could just starve us into submission."

"Goddammit people! Goddammit!!" Elyon bellowed, "Get us out of here! The approaching ships are probably full of Melanka's traitors." Shaking his head and walking away he screamed one more "Goddammit!" for good measure.

On the Law and Order Ship #2, the Tactical Officer studied images on his computer screen. "Sir," he called to the ship's captain, "a large ship just launched from T-Taxiarch. It appears they used gas thrusters to move to the other end of the station and docked at Torus-1."

The captain grimaced and nodded at the duty officer. The DO called out, "Communications, report what we've seen to the other ships and to Fleet Command." He turned back to his captain, "It could be Col. Uzza has taken command and is redeploying some of the security personnel."

The captain replied, "I fear that's wishful thinking. If the colonel had succeeded in taking command we'd have heard from him. It's more likely troops loyal to Elyon are trying to retake Torus-1."

A few minutes later the Tactical Officer reported, "Sir, that ship has just uncoupled from the torus. It looks like they're charging up to initiate a 4D jump."

The duty officer said loudly, "Communications..." and pointed his finger at the officer manning the comm-center.

"On it sir," the Comms Officer said as he composed and transmitted this additional information to the fleet.

"How long were they docked at Torus-1?" the captain asked.

"About six minutes, sir."

The captain frowned and called out, "Navigation, what's our ETA?"

"We should be in their neighborhood in forty-three minutes, sir."

The duty officer ordered, "Comms, you've got to raise Colonel Uzza or Major Amil—even Agent Chelt. We **must** have more info before we try to dock."

"Aye sir; I'll do my best."

The duty officer looked up at the captain, shut his eyes, and pinched the bridge of his aquiline nose.

CHAPTER SIXTY

REUNION

THE SUN HAD JUST CROWNED the distant mountains east of Dig #421 when the Clan set out for Blue Rock Canyon. Walking at the rear of the long procession snaking its way up the steep incline, Ipos said to Ramuell, "They're already carrying four children. How much time will that add to the trek?"

"I don't know. The adults range fifteen, twenty kilometres afield and often return carrying considerable forage and killed game animals. Their stamina and strength are pretty impressive," Ramuell replied.

"So, how long is this hike to Blue Rock?"

"I've only done it once, and it took us about seven hours. I wouldn't be surprised if they're able to maintain that pace even with the kids riding piggyback." Ramuell snorted, "Heck, they may be waiting for us at the top of each ridge."

"Are there a lot of climbs?"

"Other than this first big ascent, I recall a bunch of ups and downs through a series of shallow basins. There are no big canyons except for Blue Rock, of course."

The two Domhanians had secreted a couple of litre bottles

of water in their packs but had not offered bottles to the sapiens. When Ramuell had asked about water, Ru Ta waved off any concern.

An hour and a half after departing from the Dig camp a man who was leading the group detoured onto a side trail. About four hundred metres up a shallow ravine the path came to a dead end at a limestone seep. Water dripped through a tangle of ferns growing out of the rock's face. The cold, clear water dribbled into a metre deep pool that had been dug out and lined with slabs of stone. Ipos and Ramuell looked at each other.

Ipos said, "Perhaps we worry too much."

Ru Ta was smiling broadly when he pointed at the pool, urging the Domhanians to drink their fill.

Under his breath Ramuell said, "Thankfully it looks like we won't be needing our bottles."

About an hour later the Clan was exposed to Domhanian technology whole orders of magnitude more complex than stainless steel water containers. One of the women heard them first. She began talking excitedly. Ru Ta made a hand gesture calling for the clan's silence. Several clanspeople cupped their ears to hear the unnatural noise. Seconds later Ramuell and Ipos identified the sound of RTV electric motors and the crunching of brush and rocks beneath knobby tires.

"What do you think?" Ramuell asked.

"We don't know who they are, and we don't have any recent information about Serefim Security Force activities," Ipos replied as he looked around anxiously.

Ru Ta picked up on the meaning of Ipos' visual survey of their surroundings. He cawed like a crow and started waving everyone toward a thick copse of waxy leaved trees growing against a low rock face. Both Ramuell and Ipos were astonished at how quickly and quietly the entire Clan melted into the cover provided by the dense branches.

"You're probably right; we may worry about them too much," Ramuell said seriously.

Ipos and Ramuell pulled handheld weapons from their packs as they scrunched under bushes growing near the trail. When the two approaching RTVs were still some hundred metres away Ramuell said excitedly, "It's Azazel and Sam!"

Ipos grabbed Ramuell's forearm in a vicelike grip. "And the other four men are wearing the Serefim's paramilitary uniforms." He squinted, studying the occupants of the approaching vehicles. "Those are the men we captured up on the north rim—that seems like an undecim ago."

With clipped words Ramuell asked, "What do we do?"

"You lie here. I'm climbing out on the trail to stop them. If you see someone going for a weapon, take them out." He turned and looked at Ramuell sternly, "Don't get excited. Take your time and aim carefully. You don't want to hit Sam or Azazel. Understood?"

"Yes sir!"

With that, Ipos lunged out of the brush, jumped to the center of the trail and lowered his weapon directly at the oncoming vehicles. Startled, Azazel released the accelerator and slammed on the brakes. He sat looking dumbly at Ipos for a few seconds before an ear-to-ear grin claimed his face. "I wondered if we'd ever see you again."

Sam pulled up several metres short of the lead vehicle and tumbled off the RTV. As he dove for the ground he unholstered his sonic-blaster. Azazel jumped up on his seat and waved his hands in a frantic 'don't shoot!' gesture. "It's Ipos! We know him—everything's fine!"

Sam climbed unsteadily to his feet, having banged his knee

when he hit the ground. "Dear gods, I almost peed in my pants!"

Azazel hopped off the RTV and turned to face Ipos. "You're alive!"

"Yes sir, and so is he." Ipos pointed down to where Ramuell was scrambling out of the thicket.

Azazel ran forward and threw his arms around Ramuell. They hugged for a long moment. "We have so much to tell you," Ramuell said as they released their grip and stepped away from each other.

He turned and tried to imitate the cawing sound he'd heard from Ru Ta just a few minutes earlier. Members of the Crow Clan began emerging from the grove like some kind of other-worldly apparitions. Unable to quite piece together what was happening, Sam and Azazel stood gaping at the approaching sapiens.

Turning to Ramuell, Azazel said, "Yeah, it seems you do have a lot to tell me." Then nodding in the direction of the four Serefim Security soldiers who had not moved from their seats in the RTVs, "These men are sick. They were not acclimatized before deployment. We need to get them back upstairs, and I need to know what's happening at SWA-7."

Ipos said, "We've got good news on that front sir."

Ru Ta approached Azazel with a happy expression. He said the Crow Clan word for 'water' several times and motioned for them to follow him. Little Shiya stepped up and took Ramuell's hand. She gently tugged him in the direction Ru Ta wanted to go.

Azazel told the four former captives, "We're going to leave the RTVs here. I'm not sure how far we're going or how long we'll be gone. But I promise we will return and get you guys on a transport back up to the orbiter."

Surprised by Azazel's comments, Ipos and Ramuell

exchanged a poignant glance. Ipos decided to weigh in. He said to the soldiers, “Obviously, you’ve made some accommodations we’re not aware of, but we do know what these clanspeople have been through since they were abducted by your comrades. They aren’t going to have a lot of love for you or your uniforms. I would strongly recommend that you stay here with the vehicles rather than join the group.”

Samael nodded and said, “Ipos is right. You’ll find dehyd-food packets beneath the seats. You’ve got at least six litres of water and there are blankets in the boot box.” He offered each of them a palm-tap and added, “As the boss said, we’ll be back as soon as possible. Hang in there and drink as much fluid as you can.”

Ru Ta led the group down a lightly traveled side trail. After walking a bit less than a kilometre, they arrived at a marshy seep, overgrown with tall grasses and reeds. The water from the marsh trickled over a natural dam of small boulders. Fifty metres below the little dam numerous rivulets had gathered into a shallow stream. Several large deciduous trees were rooted at the stream’s edge. The ground was flat beneath the trees that had lost most of their autumn leaves.

Ru Ta approached the couple who had all day been assisting their wounded daughter walk. They were sitting with their backs against a tree near the stream. Ru Ta squatted to talk with them quietly. When he arose it was clear a decision had been made. He nevertheless felt compelled to seek the angel’s permission to spend the night. He approached Ramuell and gestured toward the couple and the girl with the leg wound. He also pointed to the other children and spoke slowly.

Ramuell was able to understand a few words. He pointed to the stream and said the Clan’s word for water. Ru Ta smiled and nodded. When Ramuell mimed sleep and waved his hand around the area, Ru Ta reached over and squeezed Ramuell's shoulder.

Ru Ta turned and spoke rapidly to his clansmen. In minutes they were bustling about making camp. The whirlwind of activity was somehow oddly serene and purposeful. Slightly amused, Samael watched for a moment and said, "It seems we're staying here for the night."

With the flicker of a smile, Azazel said, "It seems so." He turned to Ramuell and Ipos, "As we said earlier, there's so much I need to know before proceeding; a layover here is probably a good thing."

Indeed, there were many things to tell: the pitched battle at the enormous landing facility in the southern hemisphere; the intervention of Oprit-Robia fighters; the deaths of Royan and Kadi; the reunion with Ramuell's parents; the Beag-Liath and their use of electromagnetic pulse weapons; the commandeering of an Anti-GravXL; the situation at SWA-7; the stockpiling of food at Dig #421; and on and on...but the first thing that came out of Ramuell's mouth as his face crumpled into an expression of absolute despair was, "She's gone—they killed her."

Samael's eyebrows shot up, "Who's gone?"

"Who was killed?" Azazel demanded.

"Alicia..." was all Ramuell was able to get out.

Ipos cleared his throat. "Alicia and two others stayed at the dig site for a few minutes after everyone else had left—uhm, that would have been three evenings past. They didn't have a weapon and were ambushed by nefilim—all three were killed."

Azazel groaned and buried his face in his hands.

"I never met her," Ipos continued, "She must have been quite a special person—I'm sorry sir."

As Ramuell wiped tears from his cheeks, Samael said, "Sir,

we've got to hunt these murderers down and get rid of them—get rid of them all!"

With a long mournful sigh, Azazel replied, "We have other things we must attend to first."

Ramuell inhaled deeply and stood up straighter. "I'm sure that's true, and anyway, getting rid of them all is a much bigger issue than hunting down and eradicating this one nefilim clan." Then with a ferocity that shocked his comrades, he added, "Finding and killing the bastards who killed Alicia is something I'll do myself." The burst of aggression left him drained. He plopped on ground beside Azazel. "The big picture problem with the nefilim population is something Grandmother is working on—if she can ever get back up to her labs."

Ipos and Sam pulled up logs to sit on and the four Domhanians spoke quietly for several minutes. Shiya came over and took Ramuell's hand brushing it gently with her fingertips. At that moment Ramuell's heart felt like it would burst with the love he felt for this little sapien-hybrid girl. She pointed to the open area between the men's feet and said the Crow word for fire.

Ramuell knew the word and nodding enthusiastically replied, "Yes, fire."

She jumped up and ran off to gather kindling materials. One of the adult women brought over an armload of firewood. Smoke was already rising from a couple of fire pits. Ipos shook his head and asked, "They don't have spark lighters. How do they start fires so quickly?"

"Ahh, they carried live coals with them from their fires last night," Azazel explained.

Ipos gave him an bewildered look.

"Did you notice the bovine horns several of the women are carrying?"

Ipos nodded.

"They pack the bottom of the horn with ash, then put in several pieces of live hardwood coals. They cover the coals with more light weight ash. The coals stay ignited all day inside of their horn carrying cases."

"Really! Were they doing this before we introduced the retroviruses?" Ipos asked.

"We don't know, but we've been unable to find archeological evidence of this behavior," Azazel answered.

Watching the woman blow on the embers to ignite the fire laid at their feet, Ipos said, "Man oh man—what have we started here?"

For the next hour, Ramuell and Ipos took turns telling stories about their adventures since leaving Azazel and Lilith on the rim of Blue Rock Canyon. Just before sunset Sam excused himself and hiked back to the RTVs. He wanted to check on the four men and let them know they would be staying put for the night.

When he returned, Azazel looked at him anxiously. "None of them are feeling too well, but they're not much worse either. If they rest, eat, and drink they'll be okay." Sam looked at his feet then back up at his boss. Sheepishly he added, "After hearing the stories about the nefilim and long-toothed cats, I gave them a charged-particle gun."

Azazel scratched his jaw, nodded and said, "Yeah, that was the right thing to do."

"Tomorrow morning I'll just approach cautiously with a sonic-blaster at the ready. But honestly, I don't think we have anything to worry about. They no longer see us as the enemy."

Azazel grunted and said, "I'm sure they don't. In fact, they probably see us as their best chance of surviving this ill-conceived blunderbuss."

Without the stimulants of anxiety and adrenalin, the exhaustion of the last few day's adventures was dulling their senses. Just before drowsiness became sleep, Ramuell's thoughts returned to their original topic. "We haven't yet figured out how to eliminate the nefilim." eliminate that one clan."

His companions stared at him as he rose to find a place to bed down.

CHAPTER SIXTY-ONE
CHANGING OF THE GUARD

As the three Law and Order ships drew to within two thousand kilometres of the orbiting station, they detected the energy signature of a 4D-ship initiating an interdimensional jump. A couple of minutes later the Comms Officer on Ship 2 finally made contact with Major Amil. He looped her in with the fleet's other ships.

"Major, what's your status?" Admiral Faxcil asked.

Amil's face was drawn, and her expression suggested a combination of anger, sadness and dejection. "Sir, I have failed. We were betrayed."

Struggling to maintain a professional demeanor, she momentarily looked away from the camera. "Two of my Matzod assisted Grandmaster Elyon escape after he had been arrested. We have video of Elyon taking a weapon from Trooper Barak and using it to murder Chief Melanka."

"Sadly, Major, we were aware of that," Faxcil said. "We were briefly able to monitor the audio transmission from one of your communicators. We lost that signal and have since had trouble contacting either you or Colonel Uzza."

"After Elyon escaped into the zero-grav tube we deployed communication jammers to prevent him from issuing orders to personnel in other toruses. It appears our jammers were not a hundred percent effective. It's our belief that Elyon, Brigadier Migeal, and a few troops loyal to the Presidium launched from T-Taxiarch, docked at Torus-1, and dragged several Presidium members and administrators onto their ship. They jumped a few minutes ago."

"Did you say Presidium members were dragged onto the ship? They didn't go willingly?"

"Sir, everyone in the Presidium office lobby had been incapacitated by a sonic blast. I stunned one Serefim Security officer with a charged-particle before they departed. Administrant Pravel, who is the Presidium's Communications Officer, was injured during the melee. We believe she had been communicating with Elyon and discharged the sonic blast. We don't understand why they left her and she's not talking. We're assessing damage and casualties at this time. Agent Chelt was hit by a charged-particle but was not badly injured. To be on the safe side, I sent him to the infirmary."

"And where is Pravel now?" Faxcil asked.

"Two Matzod and a few Serefim Security officers escorted Pravel and the man I shot to the infirmary. They'll stand guard while those two are treated."

"Did you say escorted by Matzod **and** Serefim Security people?"

"Yes sir," Major Amil replied. "The Serefim Security personnel in Torus-1 have accepted Colonel Uzza's command. This, in large part, is due to the leadership of Officer Davel. He has experience with various branches of Anotas Security and is respected by his peers. When presented with the documentation, he acknowledged Colonel Uzza's authority to take command."

Blowing out a relieved exhale, Faxcil said, "At least one thing broke in our favor. So what else do you have for us?"

"Col. Uzza and his team are at this moment headed for the brig in Torus-3. They'll release Doctors Durela, Lector and Evander."

"That may be tricky," Sean interjected. "Are they prepared for resistance?"

"Yes sir. We discussed that before they left. They have sonic-blasters and will stun everyone in the brig if need be," Amil answered.

"So Major, how should our ships proceed?" Faxcil asked.

"Sir, we've secured Torus-1. I'd recommend a ship dock here and deploy forces to Torus-2 through the zero-grav tube."

The captain of Ship 2 spoke up, "Agreed. Our ETA is twenty-one minutes. Admiral, which ship would you like to dock first?"

"Ship Five, proceed directly to Torus-1 and deploy your troops. Major, do you think we'll receive any additional information from Col. Uzza within the next twenty minutes?" Faxcil asked.

"Sir, we should be hearing from him momentarily. Then we'll have a better sense of the situation on Torus-3."

"Good. Ship Three, if the torus is secure, dock at the port nearest the brig. Your troops should disembark but hold them on Torus-3 until we get additional information about developments on the other toruses."

"Yes sir," the ship's captain replied.

"Ship Two, I want you to hover at T-Taxiarch. Without endangering lives, you need to try to prevent the docking or departure of any ships at that torus," Faxcil instructed.

"That might be a bit thorny, but we'll do our best."

"I'm sure you will, Captain. Okay, Major Amil, let us know the instant you hear from Col. Uzza. All Comms Officers, you need to leave this communication link active. As soon as possible I'd like to have Col. Uzza looped in as well. Okay folks, let's go take command of that row of doughnuts."

Believing the deployment of a communications jammer indicated something was amiss, the brig's duty officer activated the ID-Override-Verification system. This required him to visually identify anyone wishing to enter the brig.

One of the Serefim Security personnel accompanying Colonel Uzza had served as the brig duty officer in the past. She advised the colonel it would be best for him to act as if he'd been detained and was being escorted to confinement.

"Very well, that's what we'll do. Will there be other officers beyond the brig foyer?" the colonel asked.

"Yes sir, inside the cellblock. The last I heard there are seven prisoners, so I suspect it's likely only one guard will be posted back there."

Turning to the Matzod troopers, Uzza said, "The three of you stand ready outside the entrance camera's view." Looking at the two Serefim Security officers he continued, "You need to wristcuff me and proceed with the appropriate protocol to get us inside."

One of the Matzod held up a hand and said, "Sir, I'm not so sure cuffing you is a good idea."

"I appreciate your concern—but it's going to be fine." Uzza understood his willingness to trust these Serefim officers would make the rounds and engender more support than perhaps anything else he might do.

When they approached the brig door the security officer scanned her identification badge. As she had anticipated, the door did not auto-open. She looked up at the camera and awaited the face recognition software to identify her. A moment later the duty officer's voice came through the speaker. "Hello Officer Niko. Please state your business."

"We were ordered to detain this man in Torus-1 and bring him to the brig." She turned Col. Uzza around in order for the duty officer to see the prisoner was cuffed.

"What the heck is going on over there?"

Glancing back-and-forth conspiratorially, Niko replied, "I'd rather not talk about it out here. I'll explain when we get inside."

Uzza raised an eyebrow, impressed with Niko's quick wit. As the door hissed open, the Matzod troopers rounded the corner and all six people lunged into the brig's foyer.

The duty officer slammed his palm on the door closure button, which locked everyone inside. He also pressed the silent alarm button beneath the counter, alerting the guard in the cellblock that they'd been breached. When he reached for his holstered weapon Colonel Uzza stepped a few centimetres ahead of his escorts and with a kind expression said, "Son, you really don't want to do that."

With her multi-tool Officer Niko snipped the plastic cuffs off of Uzza's wrists. A bewildered expression crossed the duty officer's face as he took in the curious assemblage standing before him with their weapons drawn.

Col. Uzza removed a foliopad from a Matzod trooper's backpack. He opened the court order, held it out toward the duty officer and asked, "May I?"

The officer nodded.

Placing the foliopad on the counter, Uzza explained, "The court has found Doctors Evander, Durela and Lector were incarcerated under false pretenses. We are here to secure their release." After the duty officer read the document, Uzza added, "I'd also like to introduce myself. I'm Colonel Uzza of the

Anotas Interstellar Enforcement Division. I've been ordered to take command of all Serefim Presidium Security Forces detailed to Ghrain-3."

"As you say, sir." The duty officer again pressed the silent alarm button when he entered the code to open the cellblock door. When the doors slid open the guard standing inside fired a sonic blast into the foyer.

Karl, one of the Matzod, had been suspicious of the duty officer's immediate cooperation. A few milliseconds before the guard in the cellblock triggered the blaster, Karl hunkered below the countertop. Everyone else in the foyer crumpled as the weapon's energy wave addled their senses. When the guard crossed the threshold into the foyer Karl jumped up and fired a charged-particle into the man's ribs. The shot was at such close range it stood the man upright then in slow motion he fell over sideways clunking his helmet on the floor.

Karl unsnapped his communicator and called Major Amil. "We've been hit by a sonic blast. Everyone is down except me. Please send medics ASAP."

"Was the blaster on stun?" Amil asked.

"Yes ma'am, but it was in closed quarters at close range."

"Have you checked pulses?"

"I'm checking Colonel Uzza's right now." Karl paused a few seconds. "His pulse is strong but a bit erratic."

"Is the brig secured?" Amil asked.

"To my knowledge there were only two officers on duty. I will cuff them, check everyone's pulse, then sweep the cellblock."

"Very good. Medical help is on the way. I'm headed your direction as well. Don't release any prisoners until I get there to confirm identities," Amil instructed.

"Yes ma'am. I'll call you back after I've cleared the cellblock."

Within fifteen minutes the medics had revived the blast victims. Major Amil sat on the floor beside Col. Uzza. With their backs against the wall they discussed their next moves. She wanted to be sure he was clearheaded before looping him into the communication link with Admiral Faxcil and the fleet's captains.

By the time Amil initiated the video-com call, Ship 5 had already docked at Torus-1. The consensus among the fleet officers was that the resistance by the brig personnel didn't bode well for a smooth transfer of command. Nevertheless, Col. Uzza recommended that Ship 3 proceeded with docking at Torus-3.

It turned out the fleet officers' pessimism was unwarranted. The handful of Serefim personnel remaining in T-Taxiarch knew Grandmaster Elyon, Brigadier Migeal, and much of the Presidium's hierarchy were aboard the 4D-ship that had just made an interdimensional jump. When Col. Uzza opened a channel of communication with T-Taxiarch it was his impression that those who remained felt forsaken by their commander and the Presidium.

Ship 2 docked at one of the fourteen ports on T-Taxiarch. The ship's troops stormed into the torus prepared for combat. They were met by a contingent of five unarmed Serefim officers. Initially the greeting was stoic, but when it became clear there would be no resistance **and** no arrests the mood lightened. The Law and Order Fleet's troops were shown respect, even hospitality, in all of the station's toruses.

The three remaining ships moved into positions within fifty kilometres of the orbiter. From there they monitored communications and devised a plan to take command of the two cohorts of Serefim troops deployed on the surface. Here too the fleet's officers overestimated the amount of resistance they would encounter.

Most of the nine hundred soldiers arrayed around the globe were exhausted, weak, and ill. They had learned from the staff in the scientific research facilities that bypassing the acclimatization process had been an egregious dereliction. Many felt betrayed and abused by their commanding officers.

The soldiers' anger was exacerbated by their loss of communication with the orbiter. There were a few mutinies, injuries and even a handful of deaths during the two days before Col. Uzza began communicating with the stranded forces. The conflicts and ill will among former friends and comrades would taint relationships for decades.

CHAPTER SIXTY-TWO

SOLUTIONS THAT AREN'T

IPOS AND RAMUELL continued on to Blue Rock Canyon with the Crow Clan in order to escort Dr. Lilith back to Dig #421. They spent two nights with the Clan. On the morning of their departure, Shiya sensed this parting was different; that they might never see each other again. She snuggled close to Ramuell as he ate a breakfast of dried meat and fruit. Before putting on his pack he kneeled down and took her in his arms. She threw hers around his neck and clung fiercely. After several moments one of the clanswomen gently pulled the little girl away. She whimpered once and said "Ohhh," with a heartbreaking catch in her voice.

By the time Lilith, Ipos, and Ramuell returned to the Dig, Azazel had already sent the four Serefim soldiers back to the SWA-7 basecamp accompanied by Samael and a medic. Since there was still no communication with the orbiter, Azazel wasn't sure whether transport was even possible. The next best thing was to get them to the SWA-7 medical clinic.

Ramuell was anxious to begin the hunt for the nefilim who had slain Alicia and her colleagues. Ipos shared no enthusiasm for that adventure; Azazel had become more circumspect about the issue; and Kadeya made it clear that while she believed the nefilim must be eradicated "a murderous hunting party" was not a means to that end.

Their son's zeal for revenge distressed both Egan and Althea. Late one afternoon Althea saw him sitting alone at the edge of the camp. She decided to join him. "Alicia was clearly an extraordinary young woman."

Ramuell looked at his mother without responding.

"You must have had strong feelings for her."

"You should have met her, Mother."

"I wish I had, because you loved her."

"Everyone loved her." Ramuell drew a shattered breath and waited for the lump in his throat to dissolve. "Brightness—I cannot explain it—she had an aura that illuminated every room she walked into." He looked toward the horizon thinking of the spectacular sunrise they had shared not so long ago. "... illuminated everyone she ever met."

Having confirmed that her son had been in-love with the young woman, Althea's heart broke. She had no words of comfort. She leaned over and took Ramuell in her arms and rocked him gently as they sat beside each other on the smooth log bench.

With tears clouding his eyes, he leaned back and said to his mother as if pleading, "They must pay."

Althea pinched her lips together tightly then said, "And yet Alicia will still be gone."

That evening Althea shared the conversation with her husband and mother. Kadeya said to Egan, "Let me have a chance to talk with him before you do."

"Okay, with the understanding that when one peers into the abyss, it peers back." Egan paused, searching for the right words to express his thought. "Naturally, he must deal with his grief, but vengefulness will consume him. It's my sense Azazel won't authorize a search for the perpetrators anyway. He's come to see that mission as a fool's errand, a distraction from more compelling issues requiring our attention and energy in the here and now."

The next day Kadeya found Ramuell sitting in the autumn shade of a large deciduous tree. Red leaves covered the ground and made a soft cushion when swept into a pile. Sunlight flickered on the ground through the tree's few remaining leaves.

At Kadeya's approach, Ramuell looked up from his foliopad and said, "This is a beautiful time of annum in this hemisphere." Sensing Kadeya wished to talk, Ramuell raked up a pile of leaves, "Have a seat. We can watch the world for a while."

An appreciative expression deepened the creases around Kadeya's eyes. "I think I will. But when you get to be my age getting down on the ground is much easier than getting back up." She took a seat and shuffled around a bit trying to find the most comfortable notch in the tree bark for a backrest. After a moment Kadeya said, "This is nice." She looked down at her straightened legs and waggled her feet back-and-forth. "Yeah, this is nice."

"So, Grandmother, what's on your mind?"

"Ahh, you want to cut to the chase. The nefilim, that's what's on my mind. I understand you want to get those who killed Alicia."

"You bet I do," Ramuell responded so coldly the words seemed to freeze mid-air.

"As do I, but we're scientists. Grandmaster Elyon's mindless nonsense has not changed our mission one iota. We need to get back to the labs and work on a real solution."

Ramuell looked away toward a distant stand of conifers.

"And you're saying hunting down and killing those bastards would be no solution at all."

"Actually that's not precisely what I'm saying. That group of nefilim did assault and kill Domhanians. We know that's very uncommon. They tend to reserve their wrath for sapiens and sapien-hybrids. So, killing that group would eliminate any chance they would ever again kill our people."

"Exactly!" Ramuell exclaimed, slapping his thigh.

"Mm-hmm, but your hunt might take several undecim. As you know, I cannot join you, nor can your parents. None of us are acclimatized and I've already exceeded by several days Doc's authorization for temporary surface duty."

Ramuell felt as though his life was tumbling in turmoil, so caught up in an extraordinary sequence of events that he had literally forgotten about his grandmother's situation. Looking at his hands, he counted on his fingers, "You're past the approved undecim by at least five days. It's been sixteen or seventeen days since you first arrived."

Puffing her cheeks, Kadeya said, "Sixteen days—it seems like a kuuk."

Still with their backs resting against the giant tree trunk, Ramuell turned his head and studied his grandmother, her skin color, her eyes, her weight. "I am **so** sorry! I should've been paying closer attention."

Waving a hand, "You've had a lot of other things on your mind—we both have. And there's nothing either of us could've done anyway."

Still studying Kadeya's physical appearance, he asked, "So how're you feeling?"

Turning toward her grandson she said, "Please don't tell your mother, she'll worry needlessly, but it's wearing on me. I'm having some urinary tract issues—not severe yet, but bothersome and uncomfortable. And fatigue—let's just say my energy levels are on the wane."

"We **must** get you back upstairs."

Sensing this was the opening she had sought, Kadeya said, "We both need to get back up there." Hearing that his grandmother thought he should also return to the orbiter caught Ramuell by surprise. Kadeya continued, "Not only for my health. We need to get back in the labs. I've had some ideas about the nefilim, and I'll need your help."

"Ideas? What are you thinking?"

Kadeya asked, "Do you recall in addition to pituitary mutations we also noticed differences in their thyroid glands? We didn't think much of that finding as it seemed superfluous to the gigantism."

"Yes, we noted a higher incidence of hyperthyroidism. We even talked about the possibility it might be a contributing factor to their aggressive behaviors." Ramuell jolted a bit more upright, "Oh! Is that the issue more than the gigantism?"

"No, I don't think so," Kadeya answered. "But it might be part of the solution. What if we engineer a gene that would cause thyroid failure among those predisposed to hyperthyroidism?"

Ramuell rubbed his jaw thoughtfully, "Perhaps we could."

Kadeya said, "This is a research tangent worth exploring. It's clearly a different approach than engineering infertility, but it just might offer a quicker solution."

"The quicker we eradicate those bastards the better," Ramuell replied.

They sat silently for a couple of minutes, each with their own thoughts. Kadeya reached over and patted her grandson's knee affectionately. "Ramuell, I understand you're heartbroken. I met her. She was extraordinary!" Kadeya waited for Ramuell to meet her eyes before continuing. "But your desire to hunt down her killers does nothing about the real problem. As I said, we need to get back to the labs. The reality is there will never be a **final** solution to the nefilim question. Bullies and tyrants carrying this monstrous mutation are going to crop up from time to time. They will bedevil and haunt the creatures of this planet for generations—no, for millennia to come. We cannot totally eliminate but we can limit the damage we've caused by our careless mucking with this planet's DNA."

Again they sat without speaking, this time for at least ten minutes. At last Ramuell said, "I know you're right. But will we be safe among the Presidium's henchmen up on the orbiter?"

CHAPTER SIXTY-THREE

THE HIGH GROUND

Unlike every other Scientific Study outpost, SWA-7 had come through the Presidium's aggression relatively unscathed. Samael was warmly received upon his return and the Serefim Soldiers who had remained at the basecamp were elated to see the arrival of their four comrades.

After Samael got his charges checked in at the medical clinic, he gathered the staff at the outdoor dining tables. Everyone was anxious to hear about Azazel, Ramuell, and the Crow Clan. Sam gave an abbreviated account of his adventures. He shared the sad news last. Looking away, his voice cracked as he told of Rarus's and Alicia's deaths. Turning back to the group he saw several people wiping at tears. A heavy, angry pall settled over the camp.

After Azazel receiving Samael's report about the situation at SWA-7, he informed Semyaza, Adair, Imamiah, Althea, Egan,

Ramuell, Kadeya and a few others that they would journey back to the basecamp the following day.

Azazel was most concerned about Kadeya. He instructed Sam to send a medic at first light. They would meet her on the trail, and she'd accompany them back to the basecamp. He explained to Dr. Althea that he was taking this precaution in case Kadeya needed medical attention. Althea stared at Azazel but said nothing.

"I know, I know!" he said holding up his hands. "You're probably more qualified than anyone on my staff. But she **is** your mother. If I had a medical emergency, I wouldn't want my child to be my physician."

Althea's expression softened, and she said, "You're right, of course. I appreciate your concern. If, heavens forbid, Mom needs help I'm sure your medic will be more objective than I could ever be."

When the group from Dig #421 trudged into the basecamp the next afternoon they found the place abuzz with a dam-burst of news. Azazel and Semyaza were gobsmacked to learn the Law and Order Directorate had deployed a fleet to Ghrain-3 and had arrested Grandmaster Elyon. They were further stunned to learn that Elyon had managed to escape with Brigadier Migeal and several others aboard a 4D-Initiator ship.

Semyaza paced back-and-forth. "Absolutely unheard of! By what authority did Liam order intervention in off-world Anotas affairs? I'm glad he did mind you, but by what authority?"

Hanging on every tidbit of news, a group of at least twenty-five people were squeezed inside the communications dome. Azazel preferred a bit more privacy and signaled for his confidants to follow him. Eight of them gathered in his office and continued monitoring the pandemonium being broadcast over the Ghrain-3 communications networks.

Azazel fired up his sat-com and tried to contact Deputy Administrator Trace. Trace was "unavailable" but Azazel did speak with his assistant. She explained that the situation on the orbiter was chaotic and she sadly confirmed Melanka's death.

Althea and Egan were stricken by that news. Althea squared on Egan and gathered both his hands in her own. For a long moment they stood silently with their foreheads lightly touching. Releasing his wife's hands, Egan took a deep breath and began telling the story of the horrors they had witnessed while with the Beag-Liath.

When Egan finished speaking, Semyaza said, "Of course we'd heard of the upheaval within Anotas-Deithe, but we didn't understand just how bad things had become. I'm glad you're safe and reunited with your loved ones. At one level I'm also glad your return has served to catalyze change, but your story is troubling—I am feeling both ashamed and fearful."

He frowned before continuing. "What you have described is not the Domhanian way. Ours is an ancient culture that evolved slowly over many thousands of annum. We are ill equipped for rapid, cataclysmic change. Upheaval is simply not built into our individual or societal DNA. I fear we may have a tumultuous road ahead."

"Though your fears are well-founded," Althea replied, "the fact is our culture's evolution took some wrong turns along the way. When we began exploring the galaxy we were driven by the desire to find other technologically advanced species. When we developed 4D technologies, we undertook a noble endeavor—seeding sentience for its own sake. We believed that was a destiny worthy of a great species." She stopped and looked down at her hands. "Ahh but we strayed—we bred sentient slave laborers! And when those slaves are unable to continue producing a profit, we simply discard them. You're right Semyaza—that is not, or rather that **should not be** the Domhanian way."

"We didn't know. We just didn't know," Azazel said almost to himself.

Althea blew out a puff of air, "Of course we didn't. Almost no one knew. The Beag-Liath showed us that our exploration efforts are no longer about science and sentience. The Serefim Presidium is interested in generating massive profits for a tiny sliver of Domhanian society." She snorted, "Many of whom no longer even live on Domhan-Siol. They've insulated themselves on slave-made heaven planets." She turned her back on the group, placed her hands on the workbench and stared at her reflection in the darkened window pane.

Kadeya spoke softly, "And now the upheaval is upon us, as inevitable as it is unsettling."

After their impromptu homily, Althea and Egan excused themselves and retired for the evening. When they exited Azazel's office dome they faced each other. Haltingly Egan said, "I—I just can't believe it—can't believe she's gone." Althea buried her face on his shoulder and sobbed. Melanka's persona had grated much as her voice rasped; hers was not exactly a lovable personality, but they had come to love her anyway.

The next morning Egan told Ramuell and Kadeya, "A giant intellect has been lost—an advocate and a voice for the moral high ground. Melanka was the spearhead of a movement to return sanity and morality to Anotas. I really don't know where they will turn for leadership."

"A more immediate concern is your safety," Kadeya said thoughtfully. "It's my sense from conversations with Lector and Evander that Melanka was both your benefactor and protector within Anotas. Without her it'll be difficult to know who can be trusted among their ranks."

"What will you do?" Ramuell's voice betrayed some fear for his parents.

Althea's eyes were pools of sadness. "We'll find Anso and hopefully return to Realta-Gorm—at least for now. We know we can trust our safety to Oprit-Robia."

Kadeya looked at her grandson, "Ramuell, perhaps you should join them for a while."

Althea jumped to her feet, "Yes! You should do that!"

Though enthused by his grandmother's suggestion, he said, "But what about our work? What about the nefilim?"

"I'll stay. Though I'll miss your company and assistance in the lab, I can do the work. I'll call you back the minute we have a plan. As you know, you'll have to take the lead with implementation. After this fiasco, Doc's gonna be loath to approve surface visits for me."

"Oh boy—can't wait to go through the one-hundred-and-twenty-day acclimatization again," Ramuell moaned.

Kadeya shrugged, "We'll do what we must."

A palpable relief flooded Anso when he finally heard from Imamiah. He'd received intelligence that the Crow Clan had returned to Blue Rock, but didn't know how Imamiah, Althea and Egan had fared. "We've been so worried about you. Just last night we decided to stay holed-up for a few more days hoping you'd make contact."

"The Beag-Liath have established an underwater settlement just off the western coast of a huge island. There's no way the hull of our ship could withstand the pressure at a depth of two hundred metres, so they hid us on the island. It has a mild, moist climate and we're not suffering too many physical challenges."

"Still I'm guessing you'll be happy to get home," Imamiah surmised.

"Oh, you bet we will!"

Althea spoke up, "There will be a fourth person joining us—our son Ramuell—and that's not negotiable."

"I had a feeling that might be the case," Anso replied.

Althea blew out a relieved breath, reached over and hooked her arm around Egan's waist. He smiled as she sidled up against him.

CHAPTER SIXTY-FOUR

THE SHOW MUST GO ON

ELYON AND MIGEAL had begun laying plans for reestablishing Serefim control of Ghrain-3 even before their 4D-Initiator ship docked on Froitas. The resources they could bring to bear were staggering. They had deposited colossal sums of Domhanian Standard Credits in various tender institutions. Though many of those accounts would later be identified and confiscated, they also had tonnes of precious metal ingot stashed in far-flung locations all over the galaxy.

Elyon and his entourage were welcomed on Froitas by many Business and Industry Council members who had escaped Domhan-Siol just hours ahead of being served Warrants of Detention. Because those warrants were pending, a sizable percentage of the corporate aristocracy were fugitives from justice and would face arrest should they return home. However, exile had little effect on their ability to oversee their corporate empires.

Though rumors swirled about Elyon's role in Melanka's death, he dismissed these stories as fake news. A masterful manipulator, Elyon easily curried favor among the Business and Industry expatriates. From afar, he also began dog whistling Domhan-Siol's cultists about the "godless" agents of change within Anotas-Deithe.

———

Meanwhile a Domhanian exodus from Ghrain-3 had begun. Most Serefim Security soldiers who had been dispatched to the surface, without benefit of acclimatization, felt utterly betrayed. In droves they requested reassignment. Colonel Uzza approved almost all transfer requests knowing full-well some Elyon loyalists would slip through the cracks, but absent evidence of criminal activity there was little he could do.

The second wave of Ghrain-3 emigrants were primarily scientists and their support staff. Many Domhanians who had served for decades on the planet's surface were disgusted and disillusioned when details of the slave trade came to light. Intimidation and fear were also factors; most personnel on the surface considered the Serefim Security action an illegal and unjustifiable armed assault. Resignations and transfer requests were tendered by almost half of the Scientific Study Facilities' staff over the ensuing two annum.

———

Sean returned to Domhan-Siol after serving at Ghrain-3 for over an annum. His departure did not leave Ghrain-3 without a Law and Order Directorate presence. Many of the fleet's officers were assigned to the Expeditionary Mission.

Revelations about the Business and Industry Council manipulation of Anotas-Deithe and the Judiciary set off a sea-change sequence of events on Domhan-Siol. The enabling charter for the Law and Order Directorate was rewritten expanding the Directorate's authority to enforce legal codes on Domhanian colonies and outposts throughout the galaxy.

However this enabling legislation was not accompanied by a significant increase in funding. The Directorate did not have the level resources necessary to deploy galaxy-wide law enforcement assets.

While his legal authority had been expanded, Secretary Liam understood the limits of that power. He also understood he needed to tread lightly on Froitas lest the Directorate instigate a severing of the Domhanian galactic empire – possibly even leading to civil war.

While tumult reigned elsewhere throughout Domhanian civilization, Ramuell and his parents spent almost three annum on Realta-Gorm 4 getting to know each other. For them it was a joyous interlude. After a period of time they were able to let go of their grief about the many annum they had lost as a family.

Realta-Gorm was a world replete with recreational opportunities, which the family enjoy immensely. They also continued to work. Althea and Ramuell used a laboratory at the University of Saorsa to continue research on the nefilim genome and gigantism mutation. Egan spent much of his time doing anthropological research on the populations of Ghrain-3 sapien-hybrids that had been rescued and relocated to remote reservations on the planet's southern hemisphere.

One day a 4D transport delivered a cryptic message from Kadeya:

> *We've run into snags – technical and with personnel – I need your help – all three of you.*

Althea and Egan were delighted about the opportunity to join Kadeya's research team.

Vacant apartments were plentiful on the orbiter. They chose comfortable, though not posh, accommodations. After signing the occupancy agreement, Egan commented, "At these bargain basement prices we could afford more, but several of the larger units seemed a bit too, uhm, too extravagant for my taste."

"Yeah, I have no desire to emulate the avarice of the Business and Industry aristocrats," Althea agreed.

"Oh, I dunno, I kinda liked the spa in that one suite. Like that matters...Grandma will probably have me in the G3AST in just a few days." Ramuell shrugged and sighed. "While you two get settled, I'm going over to the lab."

When Ramuell walked in, Kadeya looked up, smiled and pulled off her goggles.

"So, are we saying bye-bye to nefilim thyroxin?" Ramuell asked teasingly.

"Nope," Kadeya replied. "That approach is just not practical."

"Tell me."

"Well, the development of thyroid dysfunction happens too slowly," Kadeya answered.

"How slowly?"

"Ten to fifteen annum."

"Ohhh—a slow, lingering death." Ramuell shook his head. "That's not okay. So, what are we going to do?"

"We write-up the results on this dead-end then proceed full-bore with infertility. You and your parents will be up here in the lab rather than traipsing around on the surface for quite a while," Kadeya answered almost apologetically.

It didn't take them long to settle on two infertility producing retroviruses. One triggered a genetic mutation resulting in an extreme form of hyperandrogenism; females producing male sex hormones far in excess of normal, thereby preventing ovum release. The other retrovirus targeted male fertility through hypogonadism; almost eliminating the production of viable spermatozoa.

One evening Kadeya and Lector invited Althea and Egan over for dinner. They were talking shop and Kadeya realized Lector was being left out. She tried to explain their work. "Developing a method to produce these mutations has not been problematic. Our challenge is finding a way to attach the artificial retroviruses to the genetic markers that produce gigantism. From our computer modeling data, it's my sense that's where we may run into a wall."

"Or," Lector interjected, "a solution may just fall in your lap."

Egan looked at Kadeya, "And you call me an optimist!" He turned and winked at Lector.

As it turned out, Lector's optimism was prescient. One morning over a cup of tea, Kadeya and Althea had a collective epiphany. They could create the desired linkages by tinkering with the hypothalamic-pituitary-ovarian axis, which would make it possible to attach the retroviruses to the DNA sequence that produced the gigantism causing pituitary dysfunction.

Almost exactly one annum later, Ramuell rather wistfully made an appointment with Doc for the physical exam required before beginning the one-hundred-and-twenty-day acclimatization process.

INTERLUDE #3

November 2018
Lake Norman, North Carolina

We had been working on this project for over a year. Admiral Cortell had seemed more fatigued in recent weeks. His naps were longer, and his eyes danced less than they had when he first began telling the story. The cadence of the story telling had changed. There were longer pauses between sentences while he searched his memory. Carla and I were a little worried about him.

The always attentive Frank Williams had observed the same things. One morning during breakfast at the Lake Norman house Frank suggested we retire to the farm in Puerto Rico. Looking across the table at me he said, "That place always seems to recharge our batteries."

"I'm game," I said. "It's mid-November. The hurricane season's behind us."

The admiral pushed his half eaten plate of scrambled eggs

aside. "These need green chile. Carla, I'm addicted. I almost don't want to eat eggs sans chile."

She smiled and said, "So, we've made that much of a New Mexican out of you."

"Just so." He paused for a moment. "Puerto Rico you say. All right. If that's what you folks want to do."

Later that day as Frank and the housekeeper packed some essentials for our southerly migration, Cortell, Carla, and I went into the library. We sat in three overstuffed leather wing-back chairs. (I loved those chairs.) Cortell looked from me to Carla and narrowed his eyes. "I've been having more and more trouble recalling the details of that life. I know you've noticed. I also know you're worried."

Carla drew her eyebrows together but said nothing.

I set aside my clipboard and plopped my hands on the chair's arms. "I've noticed—and yes it's worrisome. The biggest change I've seen in the last few weeks is you've included more narrative and summary. Early on, much of the story was told as dialogue."

He closed his eyes and nodded slowly.

"Are you feeling okay?" Carla asked. "Are you having some memory issues?"

"Oh I'm a bit tired. This is a taxing undertaking and I'm not so young anymore. With regard to my memories, yes there are issues." He shook his head ever so slightly. "But the memory problems aren't in this life. My memories of what happened last week, last year, four score and seven years ago are as good as ever."

"I'm having trouble remembering that other life. I'm not sure whether it's slipping away, or whether it was never firmly fixed to begin with. Perhaps I woke-up from the coma too soon!" He clapped his hands on his knees and barked a laugh.

"So where do we go from here?" I asked.

"Frank thinks we need to go to Puerto Rico." With a hint of amusement, he added, "He'll be a lot easier to get along with if we go down there—that is, as long as he thinks it's for my benefit."

Carla chuckled, "Yeah, I can see that."

The admiral added more seriously, "And if he's happy it will be a helluva lot easier to convince him we need to go to Romania."

"Romania!" Carla exclaimed.

"Yep, that's where we need to go. But Frank's not going to like it."

"Why Romania?" I asked.

"I'm almost certain modern day Romania is where SWA-7 was located. I'm struggling with remembering what happened to Ramuell, Azazel and a handful of others who were involved in the nefilim project." He paused, "I have these flashes, more emotion than memory, that the whole affair became quite distasteful, but Ramuell and the others remained committed to the project. They understood just how debauched the nefilim mutants were. But the details of their activities seem to be floating just beyond my grasp. It's as if I never really had direct access to that information—or I've repressed those memories in this lifetime—all these thousands of years later. If that's the case, it's a bit alarming."

I said, "But in order for your story to really mean anything, in order for it to make some kind of sense to twenty-first century readers, we've got to have more."

"Yes, I understand that."

"And that's why you want to go to Romania," Carla observed.

Looking down at his hands, "Have you ever heard the story about how Paul Simon wrote the song Graceland? He was collaborating with a group of South African musicians, and they hit on the musical mix. Simon's last task was to write the lyrics. For some reason the words, *'Graceland, Graceland, Memphis Tennessee, I'm going to Graceland'* kept running through his mind. He couldn't turn off the replay. He decided his perseveration on those words must mean something. So he and his daughter drove up to Graceland, and he wrote the most popular song of his career.

"That's how I'm feeling about Romania. Something he could not explain drew Rhymin' Simon to Graceland. Something I cannot explain is drawing us to Romania."

We sat quietly for several minutes sipping our coffees. I broke the silence, "In the meantime, let's keep talking about what you do remember. Sometimes we just have to write, even if it's crap. We just keep writing and hope the truth emerges."

"That's what we should do. You know, there's something buoyant about the truth. Given enough time it tends to rise to the surface."

"Wow, that's an interesting observation," Carla said.

"So, let me ask a question."

The admiral gesture in my direction.

"Do you remember whether Elyon returned to Ghrain-3?"

"Oh God yes, I remember that! He returned with a vengeance." It almost seemed a shadow fell over Cortell's face. "And vengeance is mine sayeth the Lord."

CHAPTER SIXTY-FIVE

I HAVE RETURNED

Admiral Cortell continues his story:

IT HAD BEEN over a decade since Melanka and her allies had exposed the Business and Industry Council's ubiquitous bribery schemes. That scandal, coupled with the sapien slave trade, made a large swath of corporate executives decidedly uneasy.

Not all corporate leaders were corrupt. In fact it's likely a majority of directors loathed the notion of breeding a species of slave laborers. Nevertheless, even the scrupulous got caught up in a tide of public revulsion. The revelations of Judge Cartan's Special Investigation team had a profound impact on the Domhanian psyche. It didn't take long for public revulsion to turn to anger.

However, most Domhanians did not understand just how much of the material abundance they enjoyed was the result of raw materials imported by extraterrestrial enterprises. Without slave laborers, many interstellar extraction industries were downsized or abandoned. It was virtually impossible to recruit Domhanians to work in off-world mining operations. The health risks were simply too daunting.

What had begun as a sense of betrayal and righteous indignation at corporate excesses, morphed over a dozen annum of collapsing economies into a reactionary nostalgia for the good-old-days. It was easier to be incensed about the slavery of some primitive species half a galaxy away when it didn't impact one's own financial fortunes and lifestyle.

A decade of discontent played right into the hands of Elyon's operatives on Domhan-Siol. His agents shamelessly bought the leadership of society's most reactionary elements. They found fertile soil among numerous cultist sects. Elyon and Brigadier Migeal understood how any restiveness they stirred up on the homeworld would tie the Law and Order Directorate up in knots.

Several dozen Serefim Security personnel who had returned to Domhan-Siol after Elyon's ouster had remained fiercely loyal to their former Grandmaster. Many had been transferred into various positions within Anotas-Deithe. From that foothold they actively recruited among the cults. Hundreds of their most promising recruits were reassigned to the security forces stationed at Ghrain-3.

When a critical mass of Elyonists (a moniker they coined for themselves) were stationed on Ghrain's orbiting station, the Serefim Presidium reconquest fleet was launched from Froitas. Migeal arranged to have Elyonists on duty at every port in every torus of the orbiter when his fleet of 4D-ships arrived. Serefim vessels simultaneously docked at each of the main toruses and two docked at T-Taxiarch.

Eighty of Elyon's paramilitary troops poured off of each ship and were enthusiastically waved through the ports of entry by their onboard conspirators. They immobilized and disarmed all security personnel who were inclined to resist. So thorough had been the Elyonists' infiltration of Ghrain's orbiting station, the number of resisters was shockingly small. Within an hour every nook and cranny of the station had been seized. Only one person was killed, and that by the discharge of a weapon accidentally dialed to the kill rather than stun setting. Three others sustained minor injuries in verbal altercations that had escalated into brawls.

A half hour after the orbiter was secured, the fleet's flagship docked at Torus-1 Port-1. Elyon strode into his former offices and announced, "The **good** people of Ghrain-3 are hereby liberated from the oppression of the traitorous radicals. The Serefim Presidium is reconstituted forthwith. Together we will return to the values and beliefs that embody the true greatness of Domhanian culture."

Virtually everyone aboard the orbiter, save the Elyonist conspirators, were stunned by the audacity and immediate success of the incursion. As Colonel Uzza listened to Elyon's liberation announcement he thought – *The devil in that statement is who Elyon perceives as the* ***good*** *people of Ghrain-3.* Uzza would not be counted among that number. Minutes later he was detained and escorted to the brig. Doctors Durela and Evander soon joined him.

Having the Ghrain-3 managerial triumvirate incarcerated gave Elyon and Migeal some breathing room. Intelligence officers were assigned to pour over the personnel records of everyone on the orbiting station as well as those assigned to duty stations on the planet's surface.

Fortunately, Althea and Egan had departed from Ghrain-3 a couple of undecim before the coup d'état. They had finally decided to act on their long dormant plans to return to Domhan-Siol. They'd even made arrangements with Sean and Liam to be their houseguests.

Kadeya had remained at Ghrain-3 rather than join her

daughter and son-in-law on their trip home. The introduction of the infertility causing retroviruses had only been underway for four kuuk.

Ramuell was leading the teams responsible for staging the introduction of the retroviruses among populations of nefilim. He had returned to the surface just four days before the arrival of the Serefim fleet from Froitas.

The moment Kadeya realized what was happening, she transmitted a message to her friends and allies on the surface. She warned that a hostile takeover of the orbiter was underway; that they should not initiate communication with the station until they heard from her again; and, they should cancel any planned transports to the station. After sending the message she pulled the memory chip from her communicator and dropped it in a solution of sulfuric acid.

Kadeya was on her way to check on Lector when she saw Serefim security officers escorting him out of the library. They made eye contact but said nothing. After they had passed Kadeya slumped against the wall and watched her wrist bound partner being hauled off to the brig.

Staring at the floor, Kadeya tottered back toward her lab. There she found three members of the Serefim Science Council waiting. After a two hour discussion, it was obvious to the Serefim scientists that Kadeya's work was on the right track. They reported to their superiors that her continued leadership of the project was critical. The need to eradicate the gigantism mutation was one area of consensus among all factions involved with Ghrain-3.

Reluctantly Elyon acquiesced to his scientists' advice. Kadeya did not join several dozen of her colleagues behind the brig's electric grids.

———

A storm blew in during the pre-dawn hours. The wind-hurled crystals of ice bit into Ramuell's face as he made a dash for the kitchen dome. When he stepped inside he threw back his jacket hood and shivered. Azazel looked up and they exchanged a friendly half-wave as Ramuell made his way to the table where most members of his team were assembled. Ramuell had called the team back to SWA-7 to ride out the blizzard in the geodesic shelters. Before reaching his team's table, communicators all over the room trilled simultaneously.

As he pulled his communicator from the oversized coat pocket Ramuell scanned the room and saw Samael, Lilith, Azazel, Buer, Forcas, and Vapula all reaching for their devices as well. It only took seconds to read the cryptic message from Kadeya. As the recipients finished reading they exchanged looks of bewilderment. Azazel rose and said, "Everyone who just received that message follow me." As an afterthought he looked around the room and said to those who hadn't received Kadeya's text, "I promise to let the rest of you know what's going on as soon as we have more information—hopefully within the hour."

After the group gathered in Azazel's office he told everyone to remove the power packs from their communicators and any other devices that might be used to track their whereabouts. As they began shutting down their devices, Azazel sent a message to Semyaza:

Did you get that? - Azazel

Yes. - Semyaza

Are your people pulling their power packs? - Azazel

They are now. - Semyaza

Good. You and I need to leave ours powered up for a few more minutes – at least until we have a plan. - Azazel

Right – Let's talk in 5. - Semyaza

When Azazel looked up he saw seven wide-eyed stares. "We need to go completely dark until we know what's going on upstairs. All communication needs to be face-to-face."

"We can't all shut down," Ramuell observed. "Grandmother needs to have someone to communicate with."

"Yes, and I'm the logical person," Azazel replied.

"Why not me?" Ramuell questioned.

"Because you were at the Port Authority battle."

"You think Elyon is back?"

"I don't know. But that would be my guess. Either Elyon or a group of his loyalists," Azazel answered.

"In which case..." Ramuell began.

"In which case you may not be safe," Lilith finished the thought.

"So, we need to meet with Semyaza and his folks, but we need to send the location of the meeting in code," Azazel added.

"What do you mean?" Lilith asked.

"If we're all going to assemble in one place, we need to share that location in terms that no one upstairs will be able to understand," Azazel explained.

Immediately Ramuell said, "The place of Alicia's last smile."

"Yes! Very good—the actual dig site outside the #421 camp —Semyaza will understand that," Azazel agreed as he reached for his communicator:

Meet – place where Alicia last smiled. - Azazel

Got it. - Semyaza

When? - Azazel

The people crammed in Azazel's office had to wait a couple

of minutes. "He's probably consulting with Adair," Azazel said to fill the silence.

Hourly weather storm tracker–storm departure from said site +14 hrs. - Semyaza

"Oh that's clever," Azazel said as he responded.

See you then & there. - Azazel

"He coded the time of our meeting by suggesting we meet fourteen hours after our weather tracker predicts the storm will clear Dig #421," Azazel explained to the group.

Nodding, Vapula said, "You're right—that **is** clever! How many people will Semyaza have with him?"

"For sure Adair and Davel. Others at NWA-1 may also have received Kadeya's message—I just don't know."

Azazel dismissed the group who returned to the kitchen dome, though without appetites. He waited a little over an hour before messaging Kadeya:

Elyon?

The three Serefim scientists were still visiting Kadeya's lab when she received Azazel's message. With foresight she had muted her communicator. When her guests departed about half an hour later, she closed and locked the door.

Yes, Elyon and Migeal with 550+ troops – just met with three of their scientists.

Azazel had been as anxious as a beaver in a flashflood while awaiting Kadeya's reply. He responded:

Are you okay? The project?

Kadeya answered at once:

I'm fine. All seems good with nefilim project. Ramuell needs to lay low.

Azazel:

Thanks for the heads-up my old friend. All gone dark down here except me.

Kadeya walked back into the lab and again pulled the memory chip from her communicator and dropped it in the beaker of sulfuric acid. "Damn, that one was brand new!"

CHAPTER SIXTY-SIX

PLANS, THREATS AND DEMANDS

WHEN WORD of Elyon's incursion at Ghrain-3 reached Liam, he pulled together a task force to develop a law enforcement response. He appointed Admiral Faxcil, Dr. Althea, Professor Egan, Agent Chelt, and several Law and Order Directorate staff to the group.

Egan and Althea believed it unlikely that the Beag-Liath would react to Elyon's return to Ghrain-3. "They may not even care," Althea opined. "However, if the Serefim Presidium reboots the slave trade the Beag might respond militarily."

Liam said, "Of all the unholy outcomes that could be the worst. Do you think they'd limit their actions to Ghrain-3?"

"We don't know," Egan answered. "They would probably track the off-world shipment of sapiens, in which case they might target other Domhanian outposts."

"And how would we fare?" Admiral Faxcil asked.

Egan thrummed his fingers on the table. "I'm making some assumptions, so bear with me. They have weapons and technologies that suggest a warlike history. At the Port Authority battle they deployed weapons we've never even dreamed of developing."

"And they probably didn't show us their most powerful or technologically advanced capabilities," Faxil observed.

Nodding, Egan said, "That would be my guess."

Althea added, "It's my sense their culture has turned away from the warrior ethos, but they have retained the technologies from that era in their history—cloaking devices, EMPs, anti-grav weapons, and the like. I believe we'd have zero chance against them in a military conflict."

Leaning into the table, Sean scooted his chair forward. "Look folks, war with the Beag-Liath would likely be catastrophic."

Liam stared at Sean for a moment. "So how do we impress upon Elyon and his ilk that this is a real concern?" He looked around at other members of the group. "Given his ego driven power-lust, he may never have even considered this scenario. So, within two days I want each of you to send me your ideas. We must come up with a plan that will help Elyon see the light."

Turning to Faxil, Liam said, "Admiral, as much as I hate the notion, we need a military option for retaking Ghrain-3, with the understanding that the use of force is not our first choice."

Clutching his teacup with both hands, Faxcil nodded. "You're right Mr. Secretary. We don't want bloodshed, but we must have a way of dealing with the Serefim Presidium if their actions could lead to war with the Beag-Liath."

Liam received dozens of proposals from the task force. He brought the flash-dots home and Sean loaded them on the computer in their basement vault. The vault, a five metre by eight metre metal room, was probably the most secure place in Nexo de Mando. In addition to an office workstation, it was outfitted with a large video-screen, a conference table, and eight plush chairs.

After a dinner of six legume stew, Althea, Egan, Faxcil, Sean and Liam retired to the basement and began their review of the documents. They would take only necessity breaks for the next nine hours. As the next morning dawned, the group emerged with a multi-pronged strategy:

First, the Law and Order Directorate would make some arrests on Froitas. The Directorate had a few operatives on the faraway planet who had covertly identified the routines of several individuals with outstanding warrants. Small teams of agents would be assigned to swoop in and arrest several of the fugitives at times when they were most isolated; taking walks, going for runs, fishing, etc. The detainees would be hastened to secure launch facilities, boarded on 4D-ships, and returned to face justice on Domhan-Siol.

It was understood this amounted to little more than a scratch in the veneer covering the house of corruption on Froitas. Nevertheless, even a dozen arrests of Elyon's supporters would send a powerful message: *There is nowhere you are completely beyond the reach of justice.*

Second, the group agreed Admiral Faxcil should begin putting together an armada to blockade the Ghrain-3 orbiter. This operation was to be "top secret," with the caveat that Faxcil would arrange for plans to be leaked to sources certain to get back to Elyon. They wanted the Grandmaster to understand that the Law and Order Directorate had military options.

Third, Althea and Egan would return to Realta-Gorm 4 to discuss strategy with the Oprit-Robia leadership. These meetings were to be kept absolutely secret.

Forth, Sean would return to Ghrain-3 to hand-deliver a list

of demands to Elyon. The three ships in his fleet would be outfitted with communications jamming equipment as well as the weapons necessary to destroy ships attempting to dock or depart from the orbiting station. These capabilities would be harmlessly demonstrated. A drone launched from one of the fleet's ships would be molecularized within view of the orbiter. Likewise, all of the orbiter's internal and external communication systems would be blocked for several minutes.

After these not so subtle displays, Sean would demand an immediate audience with Elyon and his top lieutenants to convey the Directorate's demands:

1. Release to the Law and Order Directorate all detainees in the Ghrain-3 brig;
2. Offer reassignment opportunities to all Ghrain-3 Expeditionary Mission personnel (Law and Order Directorate to review all requests);
3. No resumption of the sale of sapien laborers;
4. Provide full and unqualified support to all nefilim project personnel.

Two kuuk later Sean walked onto the deck of Torus-1. He was accompanied by Agent Chelt and a security detail of seven Matzod, more for show than security. Sean's personal safety while aboard the orbiter was all but assured by the earlier demonstrations of his fleet's combat capabilities.

The meeting with Elyon and the Serefim Presidium's top echelon was a prickly affair. Elyon fervidly resented any effort to meddle with his authority. Vitriol dripped from his every pronouncement. However, the Law and Order Directorate's groundwork had been effective. Word of the arrests on Froitas and the leaked information about Admiral Faxcil's blockade fleet preparations had the expected chilling effect.

In the end, Elyon agreed to the immediate release of prisoners. Durela, Evander, Lector, Col. Uzza, and a host of other detainees whom Elyon had deemed subversives were escorted to the Law and Order Directorate ship.

Elyon also agreed that the scientists, technicians and security personnel working on the nefilim project would have free rein to continue their work. What was not said was that he actually had reprehensible plans for Azazel, Semyaza, Ramuell, Lilith, Kadeya and several others once the project was wrapped-up. He didn't comprehend that "wrapping-up" was not possible in the near-term. He simply had no scientific understanding of the long-term commitment required to introduce infertility as the means of eradicating the gigantism mutation.

The Presidium dug in their heels about Ghrain-3 personnel being given the opportunity to request reassignment. They argued that many staff were mission-critical and should not be allowed to transfer. Sean promised that reassigned personnel would be replaced by equally qualified individuals as determined by authorities on Domhan-Siol. Elyon half-heartedly acceded to this demand, but in reality he intended to stymie transfer requests at every turn.

With regard to the slave trade, the Grandmaster acquiesced much too readily. Sean understood that Elyon's promise was smothered in duplicity, but there was little he could do except warn his colleagues on Domhan-Siol and Realta-Gorm.

Sean's instinct on this matter was correct. While the Presidium would keep a lid on the nefarious business for a while, they would not relinquish the lucrative enterprise long-term. The sale and use of slave laborers was just too profitable. In fact, Elyon's industrialist supporters on Froitas had already begun pressuring him to kick-start the flow of workers.

In a Serefim Presidium meeting several kuuk later Brigadier Migeal cautioned that reviving the slave trade might result in renewed conflict with Oprit-Robia, but he was certain that their ragtag efforts would be little more than nibbling around the edges. It's not clear whether Migeal failed to consider or just grossly misjudged the prospect of an alliance between Oprit-Robia and the Beag-Liath.

CHAPTER SIXTY-SEVEN
ENOUGH

Following their meeting at Dig #421 the group of twelve, or "G12" as they came to call themselves, continued their work and tried to ignore the brouhaha upstairs. Though they'd been led to believe the Presidium was supportive of the Nefilim Project, Azazel advised the group to remain "...ever so cautious, particularly those of you who were at the Port Authority battle."

For the next six annum the G12's work progressed unimpeded. Then one day during early summer Vapula and Davel returned from a trip afield and made a beeline to the NWA-1 Director's office. Semyaza looked up from the microscope and greeted them with a warm smile; a smile that melted when he saw their expressions. He motioned for them to take a seat at the table in the kitchenette. After putting the teapot on the stove Semyaza joined them.

"Sir, two days ago we were en route to the camp of the GIG14 clan," Vapula began. "We observed a hunting party of sapien-hybrids making camp just upstream from the N1A1 river confluence."

"They were camping on the smaller river. There were eight men and three women," Davel added.

"It wasn't just an overnight camp," Vapula continued. "They had setup meat drying racks. Clearly they intended to work the area for several days. We did our observations of the GIG14 for a day and a half then made our way back to the Rough-Terrain-Vehicle. We camped at the vehicle that night and left the following morning. When we neared the sapien hunter's camp we parked a kilometre beyond the ridge east of the confluence. We crept up to the ridge crest to view the camp and saw it completely abandoned."

"But all of their possessions were still there," Davel explained. "Meat was drying on the rack and a young antelope was hung to bleed out. The people were just gone!"

Semyaza stared at Davel for a moment, glanced over at Vapula, then said, "Dammit! Dammit all! Dammit! They weren't just gone..."

Vapula shook her head. "No sir, they were taken."

"We found the footprints of a transport ship a couple hundred metres downstream," Davel said. "It was either a P-24 or a C-4MT."

Semyaza sat back in his chair and let his head flop back against the headrest. He stared at the ceiling and blew out a groan. "So he's already begun. That brazen bastard!"

Semyaza sent an encrypted message to all members of the G12 calling an emergency meeting. At that meeting Lilith and Buer reported there had been a similar abduction of a hunting party in the mountains of SWA-6. It was decided Ramuell would return to the orbiter to see what he could learn. In the meantime the others would continue their work, acting as if they knew nothing about a resumption of sapien abductions.

———

While aboard the orbiter, Ramuell learned there had been a modest number of sapien "relocations" to various worksites around the planet. Kadeya believed "relocation" was just a marketing ploy. She conjectured that sapiens' work was being video-recorded for showing to potential off-world customers.

Kadeya had no proof of this and her access to information was severely limited with Lector and Evander back on Domhan-Siol. "Ramuell, I don't know how long I can keep going. I don't even know if I **want** to continue working under these circumstances."

"By 'these circumstances' you mean Elyon and the Presidium?" Ramuell asked.

"Exactly! They're crazy! They are mean-spirited crazy—driven by avarice and power-lust. Thank whatever is holy that Trace was appointed the Presidium Administrator. I don't understand how or even why he works for them, but at least he's sane."

"Yeah," Ramuell responded thoughtfully. "I remember how he handled the Committee of Inquiry after the Blue Rock Canyon Incident all those annum ago. He impressed me as a smart and reasonable man."

"Which makes his connection to Elyon all the more perplexing," Kadeya observed.

"Perhaps they have something on him," Ramuell suggested.

"Or perhaps he's just a good, honest Domhanian trying to limit the damage," Kadeya said waving hand in front of her face as if swatting at unwanted thoughts.

Kadeya's speculation about the reason for relocating sapiens on the surface was correct. The "worksites" were akin to vocational evaluation and training centers. They were stage one of a marketing grand plan.

When word got out that the Ghrain-3 sapien labor shop was once again open for business the demand for workers exploded. The Serefim leadership coyly explained they had to progress slowly with the development of next generation laborers. Many orders for servants would not be filled for several annum. This allowed the Presidium to jack-up the prices for job-ready sapiens.

The Group of 12 and many other Anotas staff assigned to Ghrain-3 watched with horror as the slave trade reemerged. Realizing there was nothing she could do to disrupt the misuse of the sapien-hybrids, Kadeya became increasingly depressed. When Ramuell received a message from his grandmother to come back upstairs, he knew what was likely in the offing.

After closing her apartment door and activating the electromagnetic transmission disrupter she'd hidden in a kitchen cabinet, Kadeya announced, "Ramuell, I can't do this anymore. I just can't. It's immoral. What they're doing is immoral and I want no part of it."

"But grandma, we really don't have any part of it," Ramuell countered.

"Oh, I understand that on an intellectual level. I understand you and I are working to rectify a mistake made by our predecessors." Kadeya stopped and stared at Ramuell. "And it was a mistake, or better said, a miscalculation. We didn't intend to create a race of giants to terrorize the other beings on the planet. But I can see now that we **did** intend to create a species to be sold as slaves all over the damn galaxy."

She curled her lips into a morose frown. "It's time we went home."

Ramuell looked away and rubbed his jaw for a long

moment. "I can't go. Not yet. I can't leave until I'm certain we've succeeded in preventing nefilim reproduction."

Kadeya's shoulders slumped. "I know. It's just that we've been together so long, you and I. I can't imagine getting on a 4D-ship and leaving you to who knows what." She sniffed, "But I understand—I understand your memory of Alicia demands that you see this project through."

Her eyes welled with tears. "I just don't know how I'm going to be able to leave you, but I can't stay here any longer."

Over the next six kuuk Kadeya and Ramuell orchestrated an enormous stockpiling effort on behalf of the G12 and those working with them on the nefilim project. The scale of the effort required a multilayered cloak of subterfuge. Supplies of every imaginable type were secreted on food and personnel transports. Usually additional supplies were added to requisitions; a case here and a case there didn't raise eyebrows among the logistics and shipping personnel.

Most of the additional supplies were stockpiled at Dig sites rather than Area headquarters. This required a great deal more effort by the people on the surface. Many dozen crates had to be hand-carried down fly-it-out-ridge to the Dig #421 campsite. Semyaza and Azazel both reasoned that storage in these locations was worth the additional effort. Should Serefim Security Forces once again try to project a military presence on the surface, the dig sites would probably go largely unnoticed.

The day before her departure for Domhan-Siol, Kadeya and Ramuell sat reminiscing in her laboratory office. They laughed. They cried. They talked about the future. "In fifteen Ghrain annum the retrovirus should be widely enough distributed to all but assure the ultimate demise of the nefilim," Ramuell predicted.

"Though we'll never completely eradicate the mutation, I too am optimistic," Kadeya said. "What we can't predict is what the Serefim Presidium is going to do in the annum to come."

"Hence our supply stockpiles."

"Yep, your teams should have enough to see you through," Kadeya said. Wistfully she added, "Ram, I'll be back in a dozen annum to check on your progress. No matter what happens, I'll find some way to check in on you."

They felt certain the nefilim project was stocked with what they would likely need for at least a dozen annum. In fact, they had done much better than that. The supplies would be enough to last more than a quarter of a century. During that last supper together neither of them could imagine what was to transpire that would require stretching those supplies for decades.

CHAPTER SIXTY-EIGHT

TO ARMS!

Over the next annum it became clear that the Serefim Presidium's strategy had evolved. Instead of coaxing entire clans onto transports, the Security Forces used smaller shuttlecraft to hunt more isolated groups of sapien-hybrids, generally foraging and trading parties. These groups usually numbered six to ten.

This strategy made sense for several reasons: The disappearance of a few individuals could be explained as the result of some catastrophic event; The traveling groups usually did not include the clan's alpha males or females, who had occasionally proven problematic in the past; And perhaps most importantly, the abduction of only a few clanspeople left a breeding stock to replenish the clans' numbers, thereby assuring a future source of slaves.

The number of sapien seizures around the globe increased with each passing kuuk. One morning Azazel and Ramuell received a report of two separate EMP detonations in the SEE-2 region during abduction attempts. Within an undecim a similar report came in from the mountains of SWA-6. The reports were sketchy, but apparently the Serefim abductors were left stranded and had to be rescued by ships from the orbiter.

Ramuell, Semyaza and Azazel met to discuss the implications of these attacks. “There can be little doubt about what devices are being used,” Semyaza observed. “But who’s deploying them?”

“And given that many hundreds of kilometres separate the attack sites, we can safely assume there are multiple perpetrators,” Ramuell added.

“Good for them. It’s about damn time!” Azazel’s belligerence was out of character and surprised both Ramuell and Semyaza. They did not reply.

The following day Samael found three crates some six hundred metres from the SWA-7 headquarters. Each contained six EMP devices and two launch tubes.

An undecim later Buer and Forcas sent a cryptic message from a site in the SEE-2 area:

Abducted=7 Dead=4

Ramuell forwarded the message to all G12 members and added:

Emergency meeting: Adair’s parking place – three days.

The Group of 12 met on the flattop knoll above Blue Rock canyon where Adair and Semyaza had landed their shuttlecraft the day before the Crow Clan abduction all those annum ago.

Baur and Forcas told the group that they had witnessed Serefim troops simply kill four sapiens who would not board their shuttlecraft. Azazel and Samael were the most bellicose.

They argued for intervention and use of the mysteriously provided electromagnetic pulse weapons.

Ramuell's focus remained on the nefilim project. He questioned whether the abduction of sapiens was their fight. Would their involvement bring down Elyon's wrath, thereby preventing them from completing their mission? Now perhaps more than ever Ramuell missed his grandmother's counsel. It was Semyaza who stepped into the breach.

After listening to the differing points of view for over an hour, Semyaza weighed in on Ramuell's side. "Ours is a mission only we can accomplish. We're the only ones on the planet who have the viral cultures in deep freeze. We're the only ones who have the expertise to effectuate the spread of the retroviruses. And we're the only ones with the necessary training to track the efficacy of the infertility efforts. We alone can tweak the process in order to ensure success."

By the meeting's end Ramuell's and Semyaza's point of view held sway, though not everyone was convinced that the Serefim's atrocities could be ignored long-term. The more aggressive members of the G12 were somewhat mollified by accounts of attacks on Serefim forces attempting to abduct sapiens.

Over the next four annum the G12 received a steady trickle of reports about how groups all around the planet were successfully opposing Serefim forces engaged in the slave trade. All the while G12 members kept their heads down and their efforts focused on the nefilim project. Nevertheless, every time the group met the fight against Elyon's slave trade topped the agenda.

Through Egan's and Althea's efforts, Oprit-Robia had negotiated an alliance with the Beag-Liath. Use of Beag cloaking technologies allowed Oprit-Robia many opportunities to strike at sapien-hybrid training facilities with impunity.

After Oprit fighters successfully executed several dozen liberation raids, Elyon ordered that sapiens be transported directly to off-world sites after capture. In turn, the Beag-Liath began engaging Serefim shuttlecraft attempting to snatch sapiens. Direct involvement in combat was a **major** escalation by the Beag-Liath.

One day the SEE-2 Director called Azazel and Semyaza and shared that three Serefim shuttlecraft had been attacked moments before landing. The ships were destroyed, and all troops aboard had died in the crashes. Both Semyaza and Azazel slept not a wink the following night.

Meanwhile up on the orbiter, Elyon had become a maniacal inferno of fury. Brigadier Migeal counseled that it was highly unlikely any of the nefilim project personnel had been involved in the lethal attacks. The Grandmaster was unwilling to listen to reason. He was convinced that **all** of the "eggheads" working in the scientific research facilities were collaborating with Oprit-Robia and the Beag-Liath to undermine his authority. The idea that the food servers in Torus-1, in collaboration with Administrator Trace, were actually the source of information enabling the attacks on Serefim ships never even crossed Elyon's mind.

He ordered the conscription of several thousand more troops from Froitas. He didn't imagine this would be problematic, but the sons and daughters of Froitas were not eager to surrender their gilded lifestyles for dangerous, dirty duty on a frozen world several hundred light-annum away.

Elyon felt betrayed by the failure of the people of Froitas to answer his call to arms, which made him even more volatile. In a fit of pique he ordered Serefim Forces to occupy all scientific outposts on the planet's surface. Even though undermanned, Brigadier Migeal followed his orders and launched the invasion.

The final assignation of the Group of 12 was a heartbreaking affair. They met at Dig #421 to divvy up the stockpiled supplies. They mapped out the regions where nefilim clans were known to range and divided their assignments geographically.

When they adjourned, each member of the group understood their one mission had essentially became twelve. They also understood it was possible they might never see each other again. They laughed, they hugged, they cried, and they departed for their new duty posts with heavy, heavy hearts.

Two days later Ramuell began the descent into Blue Rock Canyon.

PART THREE

CHAPTER SIXTY-NINE
INTERLUDE #4

June 2019
Lake Norman, North Carolina

Admiral Cortell furrowed his brows, "That seems to be where my memories end."

Taken aback by his abrupt announcement, I stammered confusion, "But—but we **can't** just leave it there—'Ramuell walks into Blue Rock Canyon—The End!'"

I leaned forward, as if proximity might scare a bit more story out of him. "Don't you remember what happened to anyone? Readers are going to want some kind of closure—no, not want, they'll **need** to know what happened to at least some of the people. Otherwise they're going to think the tale is nonsense and we are utterly mad!"

Frank Williams shifted in his seat. Cortell stared at me with a bewildered expression. Gradually his expression transmuted into a grin and then a chuckle. He looked over at Frank, rapped his knuckles on the table several times as the chuckle spiraled into a guffaw.

Soon Frank joined in the hilarity. The contagion of their laughter enveloped me as well, though I remained so confused.

When we at last stopped laughing, the admiral removed his reading glasses and wiped his eyes with a tissue. He looked at me, still amused, but trying to be serious. "Gary, what did you think this story was? Some kind of novel? A neat little book where everything gets wrapped up all nice a tidy? All the characters in their place; living happily ever after? Justice prevails... the good guys win?"

He pointed at the newspaper folded on the table, "In case you hadn't noticed, the good guys didn't win. Only the names of the rogues in charge have ever changed. Our story doesn't arrive at some terminus all tied up with a pretty pink bow. That, my friend, is just not how it was—and that's not how it is."

It was an unsettling thought I'd have been happy to leave dormant. I didn't want to think too deeply about the present day implications of the admiral's observation.

"I don't remember what happened to Ramuell, Semyaza, Azazel and the others after I returned to Domhan-Siol."

Only rarely had the admiral used a first-person pronoun when speaking about his "memories." But this time his use of the word "I" rocked me to my core. My face must have gone ashen as I pushed myself back from the table. Frank rose from his seat, poured a glass of water, and brought it over. Setting it down in front of me he asked, "Gary, are you all right? You look like you might faint. Do you need to lie down?"

I looked down, rubbed my face with both hands then looked up at the admiral. "But, I—I've thought all along this was Ramuell's story."

The concern on his face was slowly replaced by the disarming glint that made the motes of gold in his irises appear to be shining. "In a way I suppose it is. It's probably more Ramuell's story than anyone else's. But the memories are Kadeya's."

I picked up the glass and took several gulps, set it down, and stared at the water trying to process what I had just learned. *How could I not have figured that out? What had I missed? What was I missing still? How could Kadeya have known about all of the disparate events? There are whole chapters of the tale where she wasn't even present.*

I must admit this was the moment I most doubted the admiral's story and his state of mind. Cortell and Frank were silent while I mulled these thoughts.

Frank cleared his throat and said, "Perhaps we should call it quits for the day. I'll go fix us an early dinner." As he rose he had another thought. "Or, we have all the fixin's for some of Gary's famous tacos."

Frank was looking at me expectantly when the admiral announced our decision with a slap on the arm of his chair. "Yeah, that's what we want! And while Gary's whipping that up, Frank, maybe you'd be so kind as to mix us a martini, or maybe two?"

A young couple with a teenage daughter and son lived a quarter mile up the lakeshore from the admiral's house. We'd become friends with the family during our visits over the preceding year and a half. They'd invited Carla to join them for an afternoon on their ski boat. Rheumatoid arthritis had ended her skiing days, but she still loved riding in the bow with the wind blowing through her hair as the boat skimmed across the lake's riffles.

They were laughing when the boat nudged up against the mooring poles. One of the kids jumped out and gave

Carla a hand as she stepped over the gunwale onto the modular floating dock, which was attached to the back of the house by an elevated plank boardwalk, some forty yards long.

When Carla stepped onto the porch she turned to wave as our friends drove away.

"You missed Gary's tacos," Frank teased.

"What?!"

"Just kidding, there are three in the oven. I'll go grab them...and to drink?"

"I'd love some iced tea."

Frank set the plate and glass of tea on the porch table. I joined Carla there. Sensing something was amiss she kept glancing at Frank and the admiral sitting in their reclining deck chairs. After a couple of minutes she shot me the "What's up?" idiom in American Sign Language.

I responded with the one motion sign for "later."

After cleaning-up the kitchen we bid our hosts goodnight and retired early. The guest cottage is attached to the house, but the entrance is separated by a tiled courtyard adorned with several potted plants. The moment we shut the door when Carla rounded on me. "What the heck is going on?"

I explained what I'd realized from the admiral's use of the pronoun "I" in reference to Kadeya. Carla was almost as shocked by this revelation as I had been. She too had believed the "memories" were those of Ramuell.

"If he was Kadeya, there are a lot of things that don't make sense. I guess I'm having more than my normal doubts."

"Are you doubting the admiral's integrity, or his mental capacity?" Carla asked.

"I don't know. Since the beginning, I've felt the story could be the memory of a bizarre encephalitis coma dream. But what if they have just been playing us all along? What if we are some kind of research project? The title might be, 'How Gullible Can People Be?'"

Oh, I don't think so," Carla replied. "That would be mean, and meanness is not in their nature. They're both very kind. Of course the memories could be the result of some odd kind of brain damage, but the admiral believes they are real."

"Yeah, you're right—and the level of detail—that's what's kept me thinking just maybe he really does have memories of some past life. But now that he claims they are Kadeya's memories—well, hundreds of those details no longer fit."

We stayed up two hours past our normal bedtime reviewing notes and identifying anomalies. "You know, many of these enigmas were here all along," Carla observed.

Confused, I asked, "Meaning?"

"Meaning even if the admiral's memories had been those of Ramuell, we would still have to wonder how. How could Ramuell have known all those details about events when he had not been present?"

"You're right," I replied. "I suppose we were just too enthralled with the story to realize we were missing something important."

"We need to make a list of questions," Carla suggested. "We'll go over the list with the admiral first thing tomorrow."

"This afternoon when he was laughing at my bewilderment, he asked if I thought this was just some novel where everything gets wrapped up all nice and tidy; all the characters in their place and living happily ever after." I shrugged, "Perhaps his story is an elaborate fiction."

From the list we decided to limit our questions to a few specific areas. His answers and explanations would be telling; enough so we would probably know if he was actually relating memories of a life lived thousands of years ago, or memories of a dream born of his bout with encephalitis.

After we cleared the table of our breakfast dishes, Frank returned with a fresh pot of coffee, and Dorie loaded the dishwasher. Admiral Cortell and Frank sat looking at us expectantly.

I began, “Frank, soon after we met at the farm you said something that stuck in my mind and has almost been my mantra ever since.”

“Refresh my memory.”

“You said, ‘in order to take on this project one must be open-minded enough to embrace the unbelievable and agnostic enough to ask the right questions.’ I believe I...” shaking my head I pointed at Carla, “I believe **we** have been open-minded. But now it’s time for the agnostics to ask a few questions.”

Cortell rubbed his hands together enthusiastically. “And it’s high time, too!”

“Okay, we’ve assumed all along this was primarily Ramuell’s story and therefore his memories. Then yesterday you told me the memories are those of Kadeya. If that’s the case, a lot of things don’t seem to fit.” I waved the tablet with the questions we’d written just prior to midnight. “But we’ve only listed a few.”

His eyes gleaming, the admiral gestured in our direction and said, “Have at it.”

“Okay, most of the first part of your story is about the adventures and misadventures of Egan and Althea after their return to Domhan-Siol. But Kadeya and Ramuell had already left the planet. How could Kadeya have known any details about that part of the story?”

“I want to point out the same question should be asked

regardless of whether my memories are those of Kadeya or Ramuell," Cortell began. "And it's a fair question."

"I've actually wondered about that as I read and edited notes," Carla said.

"As well you should." He took in a deep breath. "I'm not sure exactly how it is I can remember all those events. But I do remember some things. First, because Domhanians lived for centuries, many of them kept detailed autobiographical journals. My family, or rather Kadeya's family, was passionate about that practice. They devoted at least an hour each day to recording their experiences and their thoughts and feelings about those experiences. When at last Althea, Egan and Kadeya had a chance to catch up, after all those annum apart, they spent hundreds of hours sharing stories. They also shared their journals."

He held up an index finger. "That I clearly recall, but this part is entirely conjecture. The way memory works in the Domhanian brain and the way our human memories work are likely quite different. Humans like to say 'hindsight is twenty-twenty,' which is nonsense. Eyewitness testimony is notoriously inaccurate. So much so it amazes me that it's still considered a cornerstone of evidence in judicial proceedings. Whereas, I believe Domhanians had an almost eidetic memory for events they'd experienced and in many cases even events they had only heard or read about.

"We humans, or at least some of us, seem to have an extraordinary ability to evaluate data and extrapolate complex meanings and implications. Even as extraordinarily advanced as their technologies were, Domhanians had never conceptualized Edward Lorenz' formula for Sensitive Dependence on Initial Conditions—the Butterfly Effect."

He paused then added wistfully, "Perhaps that's why we blundered so badly on Ghrain-3."

Carla stared at the admiral and said, "Wow! That's an interesting answer. And it begs the question why do you believe that you, of all the people on earth, have access to the memories of a Domhanian?"

Cortell scratched the back of his neck. "Carla, as you can imagine I've spent decades thinking about that very question... and not just idle thinking either. I've done a lot of research. On April 14, 2003, it was announced that we had successfully mapped the human genome. I clearly remember thinking, '... and so it begins.'

"So what begins?" Carla asked.

"When mapping of the human genome was announced, what they really meant was that geneticists had sequenced of over forty-six thousand base pairs of protein-coding genes. While we certainly don't understand the implications of all of those couplings, having a map of the sequence changes everything. Scientifically speaking, it's the equivalent of splitting of the atom, launching sputnik, and the moon landing all rolled into one."

Cortell looked over at Frank then turned his gaze out the window. "But here's the problem—as huge as that scientific accomplishment was, less than two percent of human DNA codes protein sequences. Ninety-eight percent of our DNA is non-coding."

"You asked me about 'junk DNA' on one of our first walks around the farm in Puerto Rico," I recalled.

He turned to me and said, "Yes, I remember, and you had the correct answer. Junk DNA is a terrible misnomer—it's not junk at all, it's just that we are staggered by the complexity of non-coding DNA. Human and chimpanzee coding DNA is almost identical. It's the stuff swimming around in the so called 'junk' that distinguishes us from other species."

He looked back to Carla, "So to answer your question,

Domhanian scientists were also playing around with non-coding DNA. I believe Kadeya's memories have been living in our junk DNA for tens of thousands of years."

Staring back at him, Carla said, "And it was your bout with encephalitis that opened a door for her to walk through."

"So it would seem."

"Sheesh, I don't even know where to go from there." I paused looking at our notes.

Carla said, "Okay, let's change the subject. Do you understand how the 4D technology worked?"

"Ahh, you're really asking if I can alter humanity's future by revealing a technology that will continue to elude us for many hundreds of years. Did Kadeya understand the technologies involved in interdimensional jumps? Not really. She was a renowned scientist, but that was not an area within her realm of interest or expertise."

I gave him a puzzled look.

"Okay, you're wondering, how could she have jumped all over the galaxy and not been interested in the technology making that form of travel possible? Well, we're always fly agriculturalist, biologists, and geneticists to and from the farm in Puerto Rico. Most of them have only a vague notion of the aerodynamics that keeps those planes and helicopters in the air. It's not surprising that Kadeya didn't understand the workings of 4D-Initiators. So no, I'll not be jump-starting our galactic explorations."

"Next question?" I asked.

"By all means."

"You told us of how Domhanians initially inched their way across their solar system and then zoomed out into the galaxy, intending to seed the cosmos with sentience. Why was that so important to them and how did their mission become so distorted?"

The admiral thrummed his fingers on the table. "Now that's a tough question...interesting, but tough. To begin with, you have to remember all of that occurred centuries before Kadeya was born. So, my comments aren't recollections but rather interpretations of what Kadeya understood about Domhanian history. When they first became galactic explorers they were intent on finding other technologically advance species. Perhaps they just didn't want to feel so alone.

"Their early explorations were frustrating. Of course, they were aware of the Natharians but never had a close encounter with them. Domhanians came to believe the reason they were not finding the preponderance of advanced life forms they'd expected was because entropy and perhaps cataclysmic events were more dynamic variables than originally assumed."

Carla kind of halfway raised her hand and said, "Can you explain that? What does entropy mean in that context?"

"Hmm, what I mean is that species and civilizations rose to the height of their technological development and collapsed more rapidly than the Domhanians originally theorized.

"Do you remember way back when we first started this project I explained that Domhanians had developed mathematical formulas for predicting the likelihood of technologically advanced civilizations. The formulas included variables such as the rate of star formation, the fraction of planets per solar system with an environment suitable for life, the fraction of suitable planets on which sentient life and technologically advanced civilizations actually emerged, and so on and so forth. What the Domhanians came to believe was the length of time such civilizations released detectable energy signals into space was surprisingly short."

"Do you believe that was due to natural cataclysmic events," I asked. "Or were the collapses more often the result of self-inflicted wounds?"

"I just don't know," the admiral answered. "I don't think Kadeya had access to any definitive evidence one way or the other."

"Well, if we look at the way we humans are managing our existence on this planet," Frank interjected, "self-inflicted wounds might be a safe assumption."

Cortell nodded. "Frank may be right, particularly if we include the production and release of pathogenic microbes, either malevolently or through carelessness. Anyway, Domhanians came to believe it was likely their own DNA had at some time in the distant past been engineered or at least tinkered with. They embraced the notion of finding promising species and altering their DNA in ways that would enhance the likelihood those species would advance intellectually and technologically."

"Now the second part of your question is about mission drift. You politely used the word distortion, but it wasn't distortion. It was perversion, and I have a simple but sad explanation—power-hungry avarice. Perhaps whoever engineered the Domhanians left some remnant of a 'greed code' in their DNA. Perhaps the Domhanians left it in ours."

Carla said, "Okay, let's circle back for a second. In the last few weeks you've been telling us about things that happened with the Group of 12, Oprit-Robia, and the Beag-Liath on Ghrain-3. Ramuell was there but Kadeya wasn't. How could she have had those memories?"

The admiral looked down at his empty coffee cup, rubbed his jaw slowly and shook his head. "That confounds me. Althea and Egan had returned to Domhan-Siol. They were not privy to what happened to the Group of 12 anymore than Kadeya was. But—it's just—I don't know. There's something else I feel like I should be able to remember—it's right on the edge of my consciousness."

"Like a dream you try to recall an hour after waking up," Carla suggested.

"Exactly!" Cortell squinted out at the glare reflecting of Lake Norman. "Althea, Egan and I returned to Ghrain-3. I had not kept my promise to Ramuell. I told him I'd find a way to return and check on him in a dozen annum or so. I did not. But decades later..."

He looked at us with an unsettling sadness in his eyes. "I cannot remember why I didn't keep my promise, but I didn't." He twisted his lips to one side, "I know we finally returned—I just can't remember what we found."

Frank combed his long black fingers through his wiry white hair. "And I know what comes next."

Cortell looked at him almost apologetically, "We have to go, Frank. While I'm still able, we must go."

Admiral Cortell had first announced his decision to go to Romania when we were in Puerto Rico several months earlier. At the time I thought Frank might have a cerebral apoplexy. But the boss's mind was made up. He was undeterred by Frank's protestations.

Frank did prevail in having the trip deferred for five months. Winters in Romania can be tough. A summer trip made more sense. During the interim, the two men spent hundreds of hours doing research. On their laptops they bookmarked dozens of webpages describing all kinds of archeological sites.

Carla decided to forego the trip to Eastern Europe and returned home to Santa Fe. Frank insisted that the admiral's daughter, Kelsey, join us. He discretely explained to me that females had more success talking the admiral out of his risk-taking instincts than did males.

Kelsey walked into the room carrying a tray with four cups of coffee. She scowled looking for a clearing on the table. As I scooted books and papers aside, she said, "Yep, maps and pictures—but what Daddy really wants to do is crawl around in some caves."

She was right, of course. We all understood our trek to Romania was really about the admiral seeing something that might jump-start some long, long lost "memories."

One day after studying the best routes to various caves, Frank suggested it would be better to fly into Belgrade rather than Bucharest."

The admiral looked at him expectantly. Frank said, "All right. I'll make the arrangements."

Cortell nodded and said, "Perhaps we should invite Señor Roibal to join us."

Frank pulled up short. "That's a heck of a good idea. Having Chris along would give us the option of leasing a small plane and puddle jumping from site to site rather than driving everywhere. Romania is as big as Colorado and almost as mountainous."

Because we were booking flights on such short notice we had to settle for a late night departure. Chris flew us from Charlotte to Atlanta in the Admiral's King Air 250. Our flight to Paris departed at 11:00 p.m. Eastern Daylight Time. We enjoyed a leisurely dinner in the Delta Sky Club.

Carla and I had met Kelsey on a couple of occasions, but we didn't know her well. She pulled me aside after dinner and suggested a walk to stretch our legs. "So, is this trip going to be too hard on Daddy?" she began.

"I don't think so. His health and spirits seem to be great." I shrugged, "But he isn't a young man. We're going to have to make sure he paces himself, particularly during the first couple of jetlag days."

"That may be quite a trick," Kelsey sighed.

We walked in silence awhile then she stopped and turned to me to ask the question that was really on her mind. The concourse was noisy. When she started to speak I waved her off, "We're going to have to find a quieter corner, unless you know sign language."

She actually signed "OK" and walked over to the double doors of the Interfaith Chapel. She opened one and peeked inside. "There's no one in here. I suppose given Daddy's story about fallen angels, a chapel is as good a place as any to have a talk."

I grinned, pulled the door open, and gestured for her to enter.

We sat down beside each other. She turned her knees slightly in my direction. "Mr. Beene, I've wondered for a while if you're just playing my father for an old fool."

My jaw dropped, but I said nothing. My silence forced her to continue.

"It's my understanding he's made some financial arrangements with you. So, naturally I wonder if this is just a cushy gig, and you actually think Daddy is a bit crazy—or even crazy as hell."

This was **not** the conversation I had expected. Kelsey had just served up a whole trough full of thought fodder, and I couldn't decide if I was more shocked or insulted. Her eyes didn't wandered from my face. "You do know your father called me. I didn't reach out to him. I would never have even dreamed of contacting him. Who would ever guess he'd have such a story to tell?"

"That may be part of what's bothering me. Not even my sweet mother knew about these memories Daddy claims to have."

"Frank knows and you know."

"Oh, but that came much later. Daddy had been retired seven years before he shared a word of this with me. I don't think he would have even then had Frank not insisted.

"They told me on a road trip to view the fall foliage of New England. In the car I was a captive audience. As I listened it became clear that Daddy believed the memories were absolutely real." Kelsey turned her gaze toward the pulpit and continued, "Even though Momma never knew the story, she did believe something inexplicable happened to Daddy. I suppose she just decided not to pry.

"Naturally, they swore me to secrecy. I've always been a bit ashamed that I've never even told my husband and daughters... So, can you imagine how I felt about him sharing the whole dang story with a couple of strangers? You know more about his so-called memories than any other living soul. More even than Frank and certainly more than me."

I looked down at my feet, rubbed my mouth and beard then turned to Kelsey and said, "No, actually I can't imagine. I've given no thought whatsoever to how that might have felt to you." I took a deep breath. "I didn't know you'd never shared this family secret with your own family—which I suppose makes Carla's inclusion in the admiral's telling of his story even more painful."

"Painful is probably too strong a word. I'm more perplexed than hurt."

"And probably more tempted to share the story with your husband and children, right?"

“Oh no! Not after so many years.” Kelsey replied. “When a secret has been kept this long, sharing it becomes more hurtful than keeping it.”

“Interesting. You’re probably right about that... Uhm, regarding craziness, I absolutely do not think your dad is crazy. He’s brilliant. Well, I suppose a lot of brilliant people are crazy, but your dad’s not one of them.”

“So you believe his story?”

I frowned, “It is hard to believe, but as you said, it’s clear he believes. Now, if you asked me if it’s possible the memories are an artifact of the encephalitis coma or the subsequent use of LSD, I’d have to answer yes. But there are also some things that argue against that interpretation. Most compelling is the consistency of detail. I’ve listened to recordings he made fifty years ago and when he retells those events during our writing sessions the changes are primarily adjectives, adverbs, and prepositions.”

I studied her face to be certain she’d understood my point. “Kelsey, it’s astounding that there are no substantive differences between the stories he recorded five decades ago and the stories he tells today. That’s just not how human memory works—at least not under normal circumstances. That’s why I remain open to the possibility that just maybe these memories are not human.”

She cocked an eyebrow, “And now we’re going to fly halfway around the world to literally chase Daddy’s dreams.”

I think a hint of a grin flitted across my face. “It should be quite an adventure.”

———

I 'm a poor boy and had never flown business class before. I felt spoiled rotten. Alas, the downside is that it will be extremely difficult to ever fly "economy" again.

Admiral Cortell sat in seat 6B, and I was in 6A. It seemed that just boarding the plane rekindled some of his memories. About a half-hour out of Atlanta he began telling me things he'd overlooked or perhaps was only then remembering.

"When she returned to Domhan-Siol, Kadeya secured a beautiful little property not far from the safe house where Egan and Althea had been taken after escaping from the hospital. The house was certainly not posh. It was cute and comfortable and had gorgeous views. It overlooked the lake that hid the escape tube used by Liam, Sean, Althea and Egan. We could see the fog rising off the lake's surface almost every morning."

Again I noticed Cortell's use of pronouns. "You said 'we.'– 'We could see the fog...' Who were 'we'?"

"Althea and Egan—when they returned to Domhan-Siol—I don't really remember how many annum they spent on Realta-Gorm, but when they returned we lived together." He paused for several seconds, "It sure was a nice place," he said wistfully.

Creasing his forehead he added, "And there was somebody else living with us." He shook his head, folded his hands across his tummy and let his chin droop down to his chest. His eyes were closed but he wasn't asleep.

About fifteen minutes later he started into an upright position. "Lilith! Dr. Lilith somehow managed to get off Ghrain-3 and return to the homeworld. She lived with us for a while—but she didn't stay at the lake house much." He squinted as if trying to make out his illusive memory through the lake's fog. "Althea had fallen in love with Cascata Isle when they were holed up there. She and Egan got a suite on the island. It had glassed-in cave windows with a view of the cove." He smiled contentedly and nodded. "Yeah, we split our time between the two places, but Lilith stayed out on the Isle most of the time. Rarely did she venture into Nexo de Mando."

He lowered his seat into the bed position and soon had drifted off. I hoped he was dreaming of those happier days in Kadeya's life.

Since all the connecting flights from Charles de Gaulle to Belgrade had five or six hour layovers, we decided to spend a couple of days in Paris. We did some sightseeing, drank a lot of coffee, and ate the best pastries and baguettes in the world.

Chris Roibal researched our travel options while in Serbia and Romania. At our last dinner in Paris he sat between Frank and Cortell. "Gentlemen, I've looked into plane rentals, and I'd have no trouble qualifying to rent a small Piper. But I'm looking at the places we're scheduled to visit. Public airstrips are limited and quite some distance from the sites. We might arrange access to some private strips, but then we have the problem of arranging ground transport. As much as I hate to say it, I don't think tootling around in a plane makes much sense."

"So, what do you suggest?" Frank asked.

Chris pulled up a site on his laptop with an impressive inventory of rental motorhomes. "We could go smallish and rent the Adria Twin 640. It would be comfortable. It has a kitchen, bathroom and can sleep five very friendly people. But I'd recommend we go with the Adria Coral XL Access. It's larger and can easily accommodate all of us if we need to use it for sleeping someplace without a nearby inn."

Chris looked back-and-forth between the admiral and Frank. Cortell grinned and said, "As usual, Captain, you make too much sense to deny, and of course we defer to your judgment about flying. If you're not comfortable with the landing facilities we've got no business getting in an airplane, regardless of how good the pilot and weather conditions might be."

Chris knuckled the underside of his nose and said, "You make another good point. If we run into ratty weather we could be grounded for days. With a motorhome we move on down the road—more slowly perhaps, but we can keep moving."

Chris arranged to have the motorhome delivered to Hotel Constantine the Great, where we spent the night in Belgrade. The 24' Coral XL was quite posh. After stepping inside, standing to his full height, and doing a 360° look around, Frank announced, "Yes, this will do. This will do nicely."

Frank and the admiral had decided we should begin our journey through Romania's prehistory at Peștera cu Oase. The "Cave with Bones" is a system of twelve caverns in a limestone formation just outside the southwestern Romanian city of Anina. This is the site of some of Europe's oldest early human remains. Part of the Peștera cu Oase appears to have been a Cave Bear den at one time. When discovered in 2002, mammalian skeletal remains were displayed in locations throughout the cave in ways suggesting human placement of the bones.

Perhaps most interesting for our purposes was the discovery of early modern human skulls that were enigmatic in terms of DNA. "Now look at this," Admiral Cortell pointed excitedly at the caption describing the photograph of a skull:

Oase 1 belongs to an extinct Y-DNA haplogroup and an extinct mitochondrial
DNA haplogroup.

"Could this be consistent with the long-term effects of DNA altering retroviruses? We may now consider those haplogroups extinct, and in a way perhaps they are, but what if the retroviruses just put evolution on a fast track?" Frank asked.

Nodding, the admiral said, "That's something we're going to want to research."

Of course that research had to be deferred until we returned to Puerto Rico. The trip to The Cave with Bones was all about getting our boots muddy. When Chris eased the motorhome into the Belgrade traffic the excitement in the vehicle was palpable. We were off on an adventure; headed toward our first and one of the most promising Paleolithic sites.

One thing I was to learn while traveling with a retired admiral, a former member of the Joint Chiefs of Staff, and former U.S. Senator was that when abroad they have a lot more support than the average tourist.

Cortell had been an adviser at the North Atlantic Treaty Organization's Prague Summit in 2002. During that summit he infuriated the President of the United States by advising against a military intervention in Iraq by a "coalition of the willing" to "disarm" Saddam Hussein. At the same time he endeared himself with the civilian and military leadership of Romania by strongly supporting their application for membership in NATO. Many of those leaders remembered and appreciated Cortell's advocacy on Romania's behalf.

I suppose it was not all that surprising when Romanian Army Captain Croitoru and two Military Police officers met us at the Peștera cu Oase trailhead just off highway 57B. Even with their support, Kelsey was anything but enthusiastic about her father attempting the hike down to the caves. The trail passes through some fairly rough and heavily wooded terrain. Once while his daughter was clucking her dismay, the admiral looked at me and rolled his eyes.

"I saw that! I'm serious, Daddy, this is probably not a good idea!" Kelsey chided.

Actually I concurred with her sentiment. I'd hiked a few hundred yards down the trail and back to the vehicle and knew this was going to be nothing like our strolls around the farm in Puerto Rico. But this was a family matter. I kept my own counsel.

It was a moderately strenuous hike to the actual site. We understood from the get-go that cave-diving through a five meter deep sump, climbing a seventeen meter high shaft, then crawling through a narrow squeeze made access to the caverns all but impossible for an eighty-nine-year-old man. Nevertheless, the admiral insisted on "...getting the lay of the land."

Captain Croitoru's English was flawless, which must have been one factor in his assignment. He coupled his English mastery with expertise in spelunking as well as considerable knowledge about the history of this site. He had been inside these caverns on numerous occasions and was able to describe in detail what lay beneath our feet.

The admiral was fascinated and walked all around the area above the subterranean formations asking questions. After sitting and eating a high energy snack, Cortell slapped his thighs, stood up and said, "This is all just so interesting, but this is not the place."

I suppose all of us were slightly disappointed, but no one was crestfallen. When we returned to our vehicles we gave our thanks and made our farewells. I made a move toward my wallet to offer a tip to our guides. The admiral caught my eye and with an anxious shake of his head waved me off that notion. He must have had some other way of expressing our appreciation to the Romanian soldiers that didn't involve cash.

Kelsey and Frank were thrilled when the admiral was securely buckled into one of the motorhome's plush captain's chairs. He was a bit tired but animated. He seemed happy to be moving on toward our next destination.

We drove north on Highway 58 to the industrial city of Reșița. After World War II the area became a steel production hub. The population grew from around 25,000 to over 90,000 by the time the Iron Curtain collapsed in the early 1990s. Romanian's Communists sure did love concrete buildings.

Eschewing the Communists' preferred architecture, we checked into the charming Hotel Rogge near the city's center, just a block from the Barzava river walk. Only Chris and I ventured out for that stroll. The others had had quite enough exercise for one day.

The next morning we arose and continued north to the town of Chișcău. The route took us along the western side of the Southern Carpathian mountain range. In my youth I hiked, fished and climbed the high terrain of the Colorado and New Mexico Rockies. Though not nearly as high in altitude, the Carpathians are a formidable range that would challenge even experienced hikers and backpackers.

One other travelogue note, Google maps indicates the drive from Reșița to Chișcău requires four hours and twenty-two minutes. While we were not trying to break any land-speed records in a rented motorhome, I'd advise adding at least an hour to that travel time estimate.

When we arrived in the village of Chișcău we made a beeline to Casa Otilia, a delightful cottage where Chris had reserved rooms for the admiral, Kelsey, and Frank. Chris and I were happy to use the motorhome for our overnight accommodations.

After getting settled in and refreshed, everyone returned to the Coral and we drove ten kilometers to the police station in the town of Pietroasa. There had been a scheduling mix-up and the police officer who was to act as our guide to the Coliboaia Cave was not going to be available the following day. Learning this Kelsey exclaimed, "That's a good thing! We can use a day of rest."

Admiral Cortell gave me a sideways glance and winked. He understood Kelsey really meant **he** could use a day of rest.

The policeman at the duty desk assured us Officer Hoferescu was scheduled to guide us to the cave on Tuesday. Though I didn't say so, I actually agreed with Kelsey. A relaxing day would be good for the admiral, and perhaps the rest of us as well.

The next morning Chris and I cooked omlettes after we'd downed a second cup of coffee. We didn't have New Mexico red chile, so we substituted a Romanian hot pepper (Capsicum annuum) and Cașcaval cheese. They worked quite well. As other members of our intrepid little band wandered out to the motorhome, we turned out breakfast omelets as individually served brunches.

When everyone had eaten, we decided to visit the local museum, La Fluturi Etnographic Muzea. It's not exactly what most Americans would call a museum. It is an eclectic assortment of memorabilia from the 18th, 19th, and early 20th centuries. For Eastern European antique enthusiasts, the La Fluturi Ethnographic should be on the 'must-see' list. It was intriguing but offered no insights about the region's prehistory.

We returned to Casa Otilia and spent the afternoon studying websites and satellite maps of places we planned to visit on our itinerary. Around 4:30 Kelsey and I went out for a walk to a church monument just a few hundred meters up highway 252.

"Your father seems particularly intrigued and optimistic about the Coliboaia Cave."

"I've noticed the same thing," Kelsey said. "I'm not sure exactly why. He may not even know why, but the more he studies the photos and the maps, well..."

While walking back toward the cottage Kelsey hooked her arm through mine as if she were taking a sibling's arm. To confirm this notion she said to me, "Daddy is very, and I do mean **very**, fond of you." We strolled along in companionable silence for a couple of minutes. Then she continued, "They tried to have another child, but Momma had two miscarriages and they just decided it was probably not a safe proposition. Now I never had any doubts about how much they loved and cherished me. Daddy would not in a thousand years have replaced me with a son. But I could always tell that both my parents wished for a second child—a boy."

"So you think I'm a surrogate?"

"No...not at his age. Perhaps a long-lost nephew." She paused for a moment then added, "And between you and me, he's a bit smitten with Carla."

"Why that ol' coot!" I laughed as we entered the wrought iron gate in front of the cottage.

The next morning Officer Hoferescu arrived at Casa Otilia a few minutes after 9:00. He lugged a cardboard box over to the motorhome. Hoferescu had a sizable English vocabulary, but he'd never mastered putting all those words together in grammatically correct phrases.

He pointed to the box and said "Boots!" and gave me the thumbs-up sign. He popped open the box for me to see inside. It was full of waist high rubber waders.

I did a double-take, "The cave has water?"

He nodded excitedly, "Yes, yes—much water—not high," he explained, marking the depth by swiping his open hand across his mid-thigh.

Now it was my turn to give him the thumbs-up.

He laughed, clapped me on the shoulder and said, "One box more." This one was already open, and I could see an assortment of Soviet era miners helmets, the flashlights lashed on with straps. After setting the box in one of the motorhome's storage compartments he said, "We go now."

I wasn't certain if that was a question or an instruction. I held up a 'wait a minute' finger and walked into the cottage to gather the rest of our party.

As the crow flies, the Coliboaia cave is only three or four miles from the cottage. However, the road to the trailhead has to circumnavigate Valea de Jos and Valea de Sus. The sixty kilometer drive took over an hour. The hike from the parking area down to the cave was only about a mile and nowhere near as strenuous as the hike into Peștera cu Oase.

Officer Hoferescu, Chris and I each carried two pairs of the waders slung over our shoulders. The closer we got to the cave the more excited Cortell became.

The mouth of the cavern was at least fifty feet high. Steel stairs with handrails led from the mouth down into the bowels of the cavern. In addition to the lamps on our helmets we also carried high power flashlights, which made me wonder what the cavern must have looked like in the dim light of torches used by prehistoric peoples.

The ceilings in most of the galleries were quite high. Admiral Cortell kept shining his flashlight upward and I noticed a steady dampening of his enthusiasm. We donned our waders when we arrived at a series of pools. To no one's surprise, Kelsey announced "Daddy, I don't think this is a good idea."

"But the main panels of artwork are just beyond the water," the admiral insisted. "These cave paintings are the oldest known artworks by Homo sapiens in central Europe, at least as old as the masterpieces in the Chauvet Cave in France. If I can get there safely I really do want to see them."

Sensing what was going on, Hoferescu said, "It be okay. Water low. You watch to me—it okay."

He waded out into the pool and rubbing his palms across each other several times he said, "Bottom flat smooth. I hold arm, admiral."

He waded back to where we stood and without waiting for Kelsey's permission, took Admiral Cortell by the arm and they launched into the water.

"Let's go," Frank said as he took Kelsey's arm. "It'll be okay. We'll stay right with them."

Chris and I looked at each other, shrugged and followed the others into the waterlogged depths of the cave. We had to pass through three swamped areas to get to the main art gallery. The first two pools were short and shallow. The final one was almost hip deep and approximately fifty meters long. About halfway through I began to share Kelsey's anxiety. It was a relief when I sensed the cave floor's ascent.

While not as spectacular as the photos I've seen of the drawings in the Chauvet-Pont-d'Arc Cave, just knowing what we were looking at inspired awe. After a few minutes of walking around shining our lights on the various works of art, Chris whistled, "And they're at least thirty-thousand-years-old."

The admiral said, "Oh, it's likely they're older—perhaps much older."

"Why do you think so?" Chris asked.

"Contamination," Cortell replied. "Radiocarbon dating is a remarkably precise system of measurement unless there has been some kind of ex post facto contamination. This is a spectacular cavern for habitation by early humans. There were likely people living in here off and on for tens of thousands of years." He pointed back at the pool we had just waded through. "There were times when this cave was probably almost completely dry. People have accessed and looked at this art for millennia. I can't imagine that at some point, perhaps on several occasions, someone looking at that bison or rhinoceros decided they'd faded and required some touchup. The moment they touched their charcoal to the image, voila, the radiocarbon clock was reset."

We remained cautious on our hike out, but our safety concerns were diminished by having already waded the pools – knowing exactly what to expect. As Officer Hoferescu locked the gate at the cave's entrance, Admiral Cortell and I began a leisurely stroll back up the trail toward the motorhome. The boyish jubilance that had put the bounce in his step on the way down to the cave was gone. He said, "I had such high hopes."

"Yeah, I could tell. Why did you think this might be the place?"

"Three things," the admiral answered. "First, this cave has a nearly perfect orientation. Its mouth opens almost due south. The sapiens understood the value of solar gain. They also learned to shade the entrances with various kinds of portals, pergolas and canopies during the summer months. Second, I have some vague recollection of a cave that was on a small drainage rather than a large stream or river. Finally, I believe the cave we are looking for is near a canyon floor. From the photos it appeared the Coliboaia cave met those three criteria."

I said, "But you seemed to realize soon after we entered the cavern, even before we got to the second gate, that this was not the place."

"That's very observant, and you're right."

"What gave it away?" I asked.

"The cave's height. At the mouth of the cave I thought there could've been multiple collapses over the millennia. But as we went deeper inside, I realized that the ceiling of the cavern is at least four times higher than in my vague memories."

"So, it's on to our next destination," I replied jauntily.

He looked sideways at me then back up the trail. His eyes danced as he said, "So it is my friend. So it is."

The following morning we loaded the motorhome and thanked our hosts. I saw Admiral Cortell slip the landlady a generous tip. Smiling, she took his hand in both of hers and gave it an animated shake. She stood at the front gate and waved as we drove off toward Peştera Muierilor.

Even though we only stopped for petrol and to stretch our legs, the three hundred kilometer journey took almost six hours. We stopped and made lunch at Cetatea Devei, a thirteenth century fortress sitting atop a small volcanic mountain just outside the town of Deva.

Kelsey pulled out her Pentax K70 with a 55-300 telephoto lens and took several shots of the restored structure. We even lined up for the obligatory group photo with the tower's bulwark in the background.

By the time we checked into Vila Nico Hotel we were tired and ready for some quiet time in our rooms. After dinner I saw the admiral standing on the parking lot studying the cliffs and ridges on either side of the hotel.

It was a gorgeous evening. I was lounging on a bench under one of the gazebos. As he walked back toward the lobby he noticed me and waved enthusiastically. The spring was back in his step.

Peştera Muierilor has a visitor center and museum. It's only a few hundred feet of well maintained trail from the hotel to the cave entrance. Guided tours are available and access is not an issue. It was, therefore, surprising when Captain Croitoru met us in the hotel restaurant the next morning. When he saw us he stood, smiled broadly and waved.

"What are you doing here?!" the admiral asked good-naturedly.

With a shy smile he said, "Oh, I told my commander I like you. He did not make me beg."

Actually, it was good to have the captain's assistance inasmuch as none of the tours were offered in English. A guide led us through about six hundred meters of the cave. After we finished the tour, Croitoru approached a woman who seemed to be in charge of the guides. He greeted the lady cordially, removed a letter from his uniform's coat pocket and presented it to her. She read it then stepped outside the cave's entrance. After a brief conversation on her walkie-talkie, she returned and handed the captain his letter and a detailed map of the entire cavern.

He'd received permission to lead us through several

portions of the cave that are off-limits to the public. When he explained this to us, Cortell beamed. The woman called and waved us over to a metal trunk filled with spelunker helmets.

For a couple of hours we poked around in the depths of the cavern lit only by our helmet lights. When we emerged into the sun's welcome rays of light and warmth, I walked up beside Cortell and said quietly, "This is the place, isn't it?"

He took me by the elbow, as much as a show of affection as to steady his fatigued gait. "Not quite, but we were here!"

"So where is it?" I asked.

"I'll be danged if I know." He sucked his teeth and said, "If only I could remember exactly what it is we're looking for." He chuckled, "We're kinda like the Knights of the Round Table. They knew they were searching for the Holy Grail, they just didn't know what it was."

When we returned to the hotel Cortel and Croitoru approached the desk clerk and asked if there were any other interesting caves nearby. The clerk affected a somewhat stunned expression and gestured toward Peştera Muierilor as if to say, 'What more cave could you possibly want?'

They returned to the porch where we were enjoying an Ursus beer. Both men wore amused expressions and ordered coffees.

Cortell laughed quietly and said, "The desk clerk seems to think Peştera Muierilor is the only cave that could possibly be of any interest in the entire area."

Frank suggested, "Tomorow let's drive over to Peştera Polovragi. It's only about fifteen kilometers east of here. I'd also like to stop and see the Polovragi Monastery."

"Sure, that should be interesting," the admiral replied without much enthusiasm.

Later the two of us were sitting under the larger of the

hotel's two gazebos and I asked why he was only half-hearted about exploring the Polovragi cave.

He explained, "The mouth of the cave faces north and it's too wide and high for much use by Paleolithic Homo sapiens. While the cave has quite a history, much of it seems more applicable to the vampire folklore of Transylvania than Oltenia. But hey, it'll be interesting and as Frank said it's close and worth taking a look at."

"And what about the monastery?" I asked.

"Oh, that's a must-see! It's over five-hundred-years-old. It's an Orthodox Church monastery rather than Roman Catholic—should be interesting."

That evening we could not have imagined the discovery that awaited us there.

Captain Croitoru was assigned to remain with us during our visit in the Oltenia region. Again he joined us for breakfast in the Vila Nico diningroom. The captain's expression shouted enthusiasm about our planned visit to Peştera Polovragi.

We were in high spirits as we piled into the motorhome for the twenty minute drive. Peştera Polovragi is in a drainage that is geologically almost identical to the canyon where Peştera Muierilor is located.

Peştera Polovragi is a complex of caverns over ten kilometers deep. Only the first half kilometer is open to the public. Though the numerous stalactite and stalagmite formations were beautiful, five hundred meters was enough. What we sought was definitely not there.

"Okay, that was both pretty and interesting," the admiral commented as we exited the cave. "It would be fun to trek deeper into the closed off areas, but this cave has been so heavily used by humans over the last few thousand years any Paleolithic remains have long since been removed or contaminated beyond the point of meaningful study."

"So is it back to the monastery?" Kelsey asked.

"By all means!" Frank answered enthusiastically.

The Polovragi Monastery now houses an order of nuns. Both the artwork and the archetecture differ significantly from most structures and ormamentation of the Roman Catholic tradition. Walking around the beautiful grounds I realized that this is one of those places where one just feels at peace. For the most part, we did very little talking as we meandered about. Kelsey must have taken at least fifty photos.

Several times I noticed the admiral staring at the limestone cliffs northwest of the monastery on the opposite side of the creek. When we returned to the parking area he studied the bluffs carefully for several minutes using Kelsey's telephoto lens, even snapping a few photos. Handing the camera back to his daughter he said, "Captain, how difficult do you think it would be for us to get permission to hike over to those cliffs?"

"Let me go talk to the Prioress. I think something can be arranged," he said with a wink.

"Daddy, you are not, and I repeat **not,** going to climb up to those caves!"

The mouths of several tiny caves near the top of the grey cliffs were visible from the monastery. "Sweetheart, that's a **huge** climb to the top of the bluff. We'd need a helicopter! Then we'd have to rappel down into the caves—uhm, I do know my limits," he teased.

With faux sternness Kelsey replied, "Sometimes I wonder."

"Me too," Frank agreed lightheartedly.

About ten minutes later Captain Croitoru returned bearing an enigmatic expression. "She said if we promise to just hike to the base of the cliffs that would be fine. The caves have been looted over the years and have nothing of archeological significance. Anyway, she will not permit us to explore the caves. She said she has no interest in mounting an emergency rescue because someone fell off the cliff."

Days later I would remember that comment.

"Oh, I don't have any interest in those caves. It's actually the rockslide that fascinates me—you see it there—the light colored stones just to the left of the bluff." Cortell pointed it out to Croitoru. "Please thank the Prioress and tell her we promise not to do any rock climbing."

We drove about a quarter mile up the road to a pullout beside an old rectangular building foundation. The hike across the streambed and up to the rockslide was difficult because it was so brushy. Croitoru moaned, "I have a machete back at the base!"

Though it was only a few hundred meters, it took us over twenty minutes to reach the foot of the rockslide. Kelsey had insisted we remove any obstacles that might trip her father. We happily obliged – a broken hip would not have been anyone's idea of an adventure.

When we arrived we sat, rested and drank some water. The admiral rose and began poking around the base of the slide and nearby cliff. We hovered nearby as he studied the immediate area and frequently turned to study the views from numerous vantage points.

He was particularly interested in a deep crevasse in the stone face that was obscured by the tumble of rocks. With an expression of awe, the admiral turned to us and announced, "I believe this is it."

"What does 'this is it' mean?" Kelsey asked.

"What we're looking for is behind those boulders." Pointing at the rockslide he said, "Not buried—behind.

Captain, how hard would it be to hire some help to move a few rocks?"

"I can get a detail of soldiers from the fort," he offered.

"No, no. That would draw too much attention. If we find what I think we're going to find, this place will become a madhouse soon enough."

Like many multiple language users, Captain Croitoru had difficulty with idioms in other languages. Furrowing his brows, "Madhouse—what is madhouse?"

"Oh, sorry—there will be a stampede of people. It will be like a running of the bulls," Cortell replied.

"Oh! Why do you think so?"

"Every second-tier professor and journalist will rush to the site trying to make a name for themselves. Amateur archaeologists and anthropologists will swarm in here, certain they have some tidbit of knowledge that will be absolutely essential. And those are the good guys. There will also be treasure hunters, grave robbers, con artists and people selling sodas, tee shirts and balloons...like a circus."

Noting Croitoru's concern, Cortell raised both hands in a 'hold on a second' gesture. "Captain, it can be controlled. But **if** we find what I think we might, you're going to want a squad of your Military Police friends out here. They'll need to secure this place twenty-four hours a day until locking gates can be built into the mouth of the cave.

"I don't know what Romanian Department of Antiquities procedures are, but your scientists and universities will need to have this place sealed in order to prevent disturbances and contamination, either accidental or malicious.

"So, do you think we can round-up some local workers —**trustworthy** workers?" Cortell asked again.

"Many young men around here would be happy to have an extra payday," the captain answered confidently.

"And it will be a good payday," Frank added. "We'll definitely make it worth their while."

The admiral seconded Frank's statement with two enthusiastic thumbs-up.

That evening Captain Croitoru went out on the town to recruit some strong looking, reliable young people to help with the project. When he described the essentials of what the dig would entail his recruits promised to bring picks, shovels, crowbars, and three come-along hand winches with five-ton load capacity.

He also made a call to his commander and requested the deployment of his two Military Police friends. There were myths aplenty about ancient stashes of religious icons in caves all over the area. Captain Croitoru didn't want to take any chances and planned to have guards posted as soon as the dig began.

The admiral and Frank made a run into the Baia de Fier shopping area. They stopped at Salon Fuxia, a beauty salon, and bought a box of plastic gloves, a dozen shower caps, and the few facemasks the shop had on hand.

The next morning everyone gathered at the monastery where Admiral Cortell and Captain Croitoru went inside to discuss their plans with the Prioress. Fortunately, she was a person with a lively sense of curiosity. She approved of the plan to do a limited excavation and even asked if she might stop by later to inspect the progress. Her one condition was that one of the convent's sisters accompany the group and be present during all aspects of the dig.

Cortell promised to make a sizable donation to the

monastery which the Prioress dismissed as "not at all necessary."

"Nevertheless, you will be receiving some financial support as our way of thanking you for your cooperation," the admiral insisted.

As it turned out, additional support from the Prioress was required sooner than expected. After arriving at the crevasse we realized we needed several more meters of cable and chain in order to effectively use the come-along winches. Croitoru, Chris, and I returned to the monastery to inquire where those items might be purchased.

The Prioress explained that we didn't need to purchase anything. They had several lengths of chain and steel cable in the toolshed. She also loaned us a wheelbarrow to haul them to the dig.

Much of what had to be removed around the periphery of the slide ranged in size from scree to softball size stone to rocks the size of a person's head. This was for the most part shovel and hand work. There were many stones the size of an automobile tire which required the use of crow bars, and a few boulders ranging from the size of a coffee table to that of a refrigerator. Some of them weighed several tons.

During the first day's work we removed most of the rubble that wedged the large boulders in place. By midafternoon it was clear the admiral was pushing the edge of his physical limits. Frank called a halt to work for the day and paid the laborers, securing promises they would return tomorrow. Given that he had paid at least double the normal day-rate, their return was all but assured.

"Ugh," Chris said. "I suppose we have to haul the chains, cables and tools back to the monastery."

Captain Croitoru said, "No, that won't be necessary." When

he whistled the two MPs emerged from a truck parked on the other side of the creek.

Admiral Cortell shot the captain a questioning look, "What's this all about?"

"Admiral," Croitoru began seriously, "I am sure we can trust our workers. But they are going home for dinner then probably to the café or pub. We don't know their brothers, cousins, or friends. We cannot trust that someone will not come up here during the night and try to finish the dig."

Cortell narrowed his eyes and nodded.

"Officers Bodiu, Florescu, and I will be staying here tonight," Croitoru explained.

"Yeah—that probably makes a lot of sense. Do you need us to bring you any food?"

Captain Croitoru translated Cortell's question. Both officers laughed. Florescu responded at length in Romanian.

The captain turned to Cortell and said, "He says they loaded up enough gear to bivouac here for about a month!" He added teasingly, "Perhaps that is their wish."

Chuckling, the admiral shook hands with all three of the Army officers. "In that case gentlemen, thank you and we'll see you in the morning."

On the drive back to the Vila Nico hotel, Cortell lay down on the bed in the back of the motorhome and promptly fell asleep. In a quiet, subtly chastising voice Kelsey announced to the rest of us, "We let him **way** overdo it today. We cannot allow that to happen again tomorrow!"

At least she included herself in doling out shares of blame.

The next morning we arrived at the dig site just before 9:00. The workers were already rigging chains around two enormous tree trunks. They attached the come-alongs to the chains and ran cables around the large boulders. We only needed about five feet of displacement to allow us to get behind the boulders to dig out the detritus blocking the mouth of the cave – a cave only the admiral was certain existed.

Moving the boulders proved to be a challenge. The cables kept slipping and losing purchase. The workers decided to chisel grooves in the boulders with pick axes. Once they had done that, they were able to cinch the cables more tightly. A couple of times we had to use three different come-alongs secured to the boulders at different angles. We'd move the boulder a few inches to the right, then a few inches to the left, then straight ahead; thereby rocking them back-and-forth until they were in positions that made it possible to move them straight downhill.

This took the better part of the day. By late afternoon we were able to move smaller stones by hand and crowbar. The workers shoveled gravel and sand into buckets and dumped it on the downhill side of the rockslide. We were tuckered out by four o'clock and called it quits. No one was disheartened. It appeared from the way the notch at the top of the crevasse had sloughed, there probably was a hollow behind the remaining stones and scree.

"Same time tomorrow?" Frank asked and Captain Croitoru translated.

All of the workers nodded enthusiastically. There was not a light at the end of the tunnel, but several of us had come to believe there just might be a tunnel. Even the sister from the monastery, who had been our constant companion, clapped her hands excitedly.

Before we left the admiral asked Captain Croitoru and the two Military Police if there was anything they needed.

Croitoru chuckled his reply, "Yes, we need three liters of beer."

"We'll go into town and bring it right back to you." Cortell offered.

Slapping the admiral affectionately on the back of his shoulder Croitoru said, "No, my friend. I've already arranged for one of the boys to fetch them for us."

"Who's making the beer run?" Cortell asked.

Croitoru motioned to one of the workers. The admiral reached in his pocket and pulled out a hundred Leu and handed the bills to the young man. He pointed to everyone on the work crew then mimed drinking a bottle of beer. They all beamed, and several said, "Da! Da!"

Captain Croitoru looked the admiral in the eyes and said earnestly, "Thank you. That gesture means a lot to those young guys."

"I just hope they don't show up tomorrow with hang-overs," Cortell replied.

"Oh do not worry; they will be fine. You will see."

The air crackled electric as the workers, the sister, and even the Prioress gathered at the rockslide. Kelsey scowled when she saw her father slipping on work gloves. "Oh no you don't!" she said.

"Oh yes I do," Cortell responded with a timbre in his voice that brooked no objections. "I promise I'll take it easy," he added to allay his daughter's concerns. He didn't keep that promise.

It wasn't that he tried to lift stones that were too heavy or too awkward, he just threw too many. After about an hour Frank noticed the admiral's flushed face and heavy breathing.

With a sideways nod of his head, Frank alerted Kelsey they needed to team up on the old gentleman.

"Daddy, what do you think you're doing? You're gonna pass out if you don't sit down. Let the young guys do their jobs."

As she scolded, Frank took the admiral by the elbow and led him to sit on a boulder. This worked for about twenty minutes. Soon enough he was up wandering around the crevasse picking up softball size stones and tossing them aside.

We all stopped dead in our tracks when we heard the hollow echo of stones tumbling inside. About fifteen feet above ground level a small dark hole had opened at the top of the rockslide. One of the workers scrambled up the sloping debris and shined a flashlight inside. He studied it for a few seconds and said, "Prăfuit."

"It's dusty," Croitoru explained.

"Let me have a look!" the admiral exclaimed, rushing toward the base of the slide.

Frank and I each grabbed a forearm. "Whoa!" Frank said. "It's too dusty to see anything and the men need to open the hole up some more anyway."

"Admiral, this is one of those times when patience is a virtue," I added.

"Oy, este o pestera. Este profundă," the man with the flashlight shouted.

"He says it is a cave and it's deep!" Captain Croitoru interpreted. A huge smile etched his face.

The Prioress and the sister took each other's hands and did a little jig.

The workers' enthusiasm soared and the pace of shoveling accelerated. As they tore into the top of the rockslide the admiral said, "Captain, please tell them to be careful not to let stones fall into the cave. We don't want to carelessly break a fossil or damage an artifact."

As the captain relayed the admiral's instructions, Cortell turned to Chris, "Roibal, run down to the motorhome and bring back the plastic gloves, face masks and shower caps." Looking at Frank, Kelsey and me he said, "Only the five of us will go inside. Even by opening the cave we have contaminated it. We must limit how much of our own DNA we scatter around. We'll cover as much of our skin and hair as possible."

"So should we shake out our shirts and pants?" Kelsey asked.

The admiral slapped himself on the forehead and said, "Oh good grief! No, that won't do much good. We need to change into clean clothes before entering the cave."

"I'll run to the motorhome to get long sleeve shirts and pants for everyone," I offered.

"Yes, do that," Cortell said. "We're going to have to let these guys look inside. They might lynch us otherwise. Or worse, start rumors about hobgoblins and vampires or some such nonsense."

"Oh for sure—vampire rumors would be worse than lynching," Kelsey sassed.

He grinned, "Okay, perhaps I misspoke. Anyway, we'll have to explain they can only look around from the top of the slide with their flashlights."

Frank said, "Captain Croitoru is a spelunker. He understands contamination issues. He'll keep a lid on it."

Within an hour the workers had prised an opening about four-feet wide. They had also built a stairway, of sorts, by wedging and leveling flat stones into the scree pile leading some ten feet up to the fissure. No one wanted to see the admiral stumble and slide down an embankment of knifelike shards.

It was almost one p.m. when we guided the admiral to the cave opening. He studied the cave floor for a quarter-hour. Kelsey climbed up beside her father and took several dozen photographs. For the next twenty minutes we took turns shining our lights inside the hollow and discussing an entrance strategy.

There was a rockslide fanning into the cave almost identical to the slide on the outside, except the cave floor lay only about six feet below the opening. We decided I would step through the hole first, make sure of my footing, then the admiral would place both hands on my shoulders as we descended to the floor. Chris would follow with his arms looped under the admiral's armpits. Kelsey would follow Chris and Frank would bring-up the rear. Captain Croitoru would stay at the mouth of the cave with a rope that he'd throw in for us to use as a handhold on our climb back up the interior fan of rocks and scree.

Our plan worked flawlessly, but once inside, the admiral again seemed to be having some trouble breathing. I believed this was likely the result of excitement rather than over-exertion. No one could imagine what he must have been experiencing. Kelsey told him, "Daddy, take a deep breath. Relax. Breathe."

The cave was everything we had hoped it might be. There were human remains laid out all around the periphery. The admiral's instructions had been clear. Once inside we were not to walk around. We estimated the chamber was about thirty yards wide by forty-five to fifty yards deep.

Admiral Cortell began to speak in an almost otherworldly tone of voice, "The remains of these people have been lying here unseen and undisturbed for tens of thousands of years. Undisturbed is the key. They were placed here, and the cave mouth was intentionally closed. Otherwise scavengers would have scattered the bones."

"Do you think they were all placed in here at the same time?" Chris asked.

"I doubt it. This was some kind of burial vault. These people's clansmen opened and closed the entrance with the placement of each body."

It was then that Frank's light shown on something that reflected brightly. "Hey, look at that. What do you suppose it is?"

We all looked where Frank was shining his light. Admiral Cortell said, "Oh! Oh my!" He stared for several seconds. "Okay folks, I'm going to break my own rule. I'm going to step very carefully over to those remains and take a closer look."

He moved slowly and purposefully. He looked down at the remains of a man with an elongated skull. Again he whispered, "Oh my."

To our shock and horror he reached down and picked up the jawbone. The admiral staggered slightly.

"Daddy, what is it?"

"It's Ramuell! My dear, dear boy—my friend—after all this time, I've found you at last."

"Oh my God, Daddy! It's always been true."

When the admiral looked up and saw tears streaming down Kelsey's face, he staggered sideways and began to stumble. One step, two steps, three, and his legs just melted like butter. He crashed into the powdery deposit covering the cave's floor. When his shoulder hit the ground his head snapped downward, and his helmet slammed into the ground. Unfortunately, the miners' helmets we wore did not cover our ears. The admiral's mastoid thumped one of the many fist size stones that were strewn about.

Any concern about cave contamination evaporated in that instant. Kelsey screamed and rushed to his side.

Chris and I yelled simultaneously, "Don't touch him!"

Kelsey had already laid her hands on her father's face and jerked them back in response. Chris explained, "We need to get his neck stabilized and we need to get him out of here on a spine board."

Captain Croitoru was already on his phone.

Frank was the most stoic of us all. Perhaps he was the only one of us who had not harbored doubts about Kadeya and her memories. He dropped down prone beside Cortell and was shining his light on the mastoid. "It's bleeding a little bit, but it looks very superficial."

"So why is he unconscious?" Kelsey asked almost hysterically.

Croitoru called in, "An ambulance is coming. The Prioress has gone to the road to meet it. I will stay right here Kelsey, with my phone in hand."

Still kneeling beside the admiral, Frank reached over and embraced her. "It's going to be okay Kels. We're going to get him out of here as soon as the ambulance arrives."

With Kelsey sobbing Chris pulled her to her feet. Frank motioned for me to look at the jaw Cortell had dropped. It was cleanly broken in two places. At each fracture, our lights reflected off of titanium screws capped with zirconium crowns.

Throughout the entire project I had naturally harbored doubts. How could I not? It was at that moment, when Frank and I were looking at tooth implants in a prehistoric jaw, that I knew this story was much more than an old man's coma dream.

Frank reached down, picked up all three fragments of the jaw and stuffed them in the oversized front pocket of his cargo pants. My bulging eyes surely betrayed what I was thinking. *What in the hell are you doing, Frank?*

He looked at me and quietly said, "Shh, shh, shh—later."

I wasn't happy about it, but I bit my tongue and said nothing.

Captain Croitoru had called a small hospital about fifteen kilometers from the Polovragi Monastery. Within twenty-five minutes we heard the ambulance siren approaching on Highway 22. The captain had done a good job describing our situation. Not only did the Emergency Medical Technicians come running up the trail with a spine board, they also carried an eight-foot aluminum ladder.

When they arrived at the cave's opening there was a rapid fire conversation between the EMTs and Captain Croitoru. The EMTs put on surgical gloves and masks before entering the cave. First they checked the admiral's breathing and vital signs. Captain Croitoru had also donned gloves and a facemask and followed the EMT's into the cave. He told Kelsey, "They say his breathing, pulse and blood pressure are good."

Kelsey put a hand over her facemask trying to stifle her sobs.

The EMTs expertly stabilized the neck with a cervical collar. When the Velcro straps were secured, one of the men held the admiral's head while the other EMT and Captain Croitoru used the lift and slide transfer technique to move Cortell onto the spine board. One of the workers at the cave's mouth slid the aluminum ladder down the interior scree slope. The EMTs lifted and placed the spine board on the ladder.

The two EMTs, Croitoru, and Chris lifted the ladder with the admiral's body and spine board on top. With adrenalin fueled strength they heaved it above their heads. With the ladder sloping slightly down toward the cave's opening Frank and I slid the spine board along the ladder's side rails. Two of the workers, who were positioned at the mouth of the cave, grabbed the board and slid it off the ladder.

The EMTs, Chris and Croitoru scrambled up the rockslide and out of the cave. I arrived at the opening just in time to see the workers using the ladder to lower the admiral down the outside slope to ground level. By the time Frank and Kelsey emerged the admiral was laid out on a flat spot at the base of the slide.

The EMTs re-cinched the straps securing him to the board. Four of the workers took a corner of the board and the two EMTs grasped the middle handles. The six of them hauled the board down the brushy trail and across the stream. The admiral was lashed to the gurney and pushed inside the ambulance within a minute.

Kelsey and Chris climbed into the ambulance. Frank and I would follow in the motorhome. Just as we were getting ready to leave Captain Croitoru trotted up. "A squad of Military Police will be here in a few hours. The cave will be secure. My Commander will call the Ministry of Culture to report the find."

"Yes, very good," Frank said. "I assume they'll take over administration of the site."

"Probably...I'm not sure how that works."

As Croitoru turned to go, Frank said, "Wait a sec." He reached in his pocket and pulled out a roll of Romanian currency. "Will this be enough?" he asked.

"Oh! I had forgotten about payment. The boys probably forgot too. This will be plenty, but they will not be happy until they hear that Admiral Cortell is okay."

We climbed in the motorhome and Frank saw me glance at the bulge in his pants pocket. "Look Gary, there are hundreds of thousands of people who believe the earth is only six-thousand-years-old. There are people who still deny evolution for God's sake!"

I started driving and gave him a sideways glance. He rubbed his chin and continued. "Yeah, there's just so much we don't understand about our origins. I don't know a lot of things, but I am certain that the people of this planet are not ready to see a Paleolithic jaw bone with titanium tooth implants. Not yet—maybe someday—maybe even someday soon, but not yet. So, should I have desecrated a Paleolithic find? In this case, the answer is yes—a resounding **yes**!"

I nodded, not sure if I agreed, but I did understand.

The hospital was a rural government facility in the village of Novaci. The attending physician seemed every bit as competent as the ambulance EMTs. The clinic was equipped to set broken bones, perform appendectomies, and stitch up wounds. The admiral needed a head/neck CT scan and an MRI of the brain. Those diagnostics were not going to happen in Novaci.

Within a few minutes Captain Croitoru had correctly assessed the situation. He and Frank exchanged a nod and the captain called his commander about a medevac helicopter.

An IAR-330 was dispatched from the Romanian Air Force base at Câmpia Turzii. It has a cruise speed of 250 km/hour and a range of well over 500 km. The flight distance from Câmpia Turzii to the Novaci Hospital is less than 200 kilometers. The moment the orders were received the pilot began the preflight check. He had his machine and crew in the air inside ten minutes. They landed on the hospital's parking lot about fifty minutes later.

Kelsey, Frank and I joined the admiral and the helicopter

crew on the flight back to the airbase. Chris drove the motorhome back to Belgrade. He would catch a commercial flight from Serbia to the Saarbrücken Airport the next day.

Even before the helicopter arrived in Novaci, Frank had succeeded in getting through to the U.S. Air Force Base Commander in Ramstein, Germany. The Base Commander notified NATO Command that he was authorizing the emergency medical evacuation deployment of a C-21 twin turbofan jet to Romania's Câmpia Turzii Air Force Base. He reported this decision up the chain of command. Because an iconic figure in American military and political history was in trouble, the President of the United States was briefed on the situation.

It took over an hour to get all the authorizations and approvals before the C-21 was actually taxiing to the runway. At a cruise speed of 531 miles per hour, the jet was on the Câmpia Turzii tarmac just two hours later.

By the time the admiral was secured on the plane's gurney, and we were buckled in our seats, Frank was limp with exhaustion. I was operating on caffeine and adrenalin. Kelsey's wakefulness was surely fueled by anxiety. Nevertheless, all three of us nodded off within twenty minutes of takeoff.

The ambulance ride from Ramstein Air Base to the Medical Center only takes about fifteen minutes. Upon our arrival at the hospital the admiral had still shown no sign of regaining consciousness. A CT scan was ordered first. He was hooked up to an EEG and an ECG while a radiologist studied the CT results. Soon thereafter the admiral was carted away for an MRI. The three of us collapsed in a waiting room and dozed fitfully.

It was there the attending physician and radiologist found us after two a.m. "Admiral Cortell is back in his room," the doctor began. "He has not regained consciousness, but he doesn't seem to be uncomfortable or in any kind of pain."

"Why is he still unconscious?" Kelsey pleaded.

The physicians looked at each other. The radiologist rubbed a hand across his forehead and said, "We don't know. We don't see any kind of hematoma nor any bleeding in the brain. He does have a **very** tiny concussion where his head hit the rock. But the mastoid is the hardest bone in the human body. That injury is simply not causing his unconsciousness."

Again she asked, "So why is he in a coma?"

"He's not," the attending physician replied. "We are frankly baffled by his neurological condition."

Kelsey gave the doctor a confused look. He explained, "If he were in a coma we'd expect to see an EEG pattern of theta and delta waves, perhaps some alpha and mu waves depending on the depth of the coma." He paused and shook his head, "Instead, what we're seeing are beta and gamma waves interspersed with brief periods of alpha. Then for a couple of hours he produced only delta and theta waves."

"Which means what?" Kelsey asked.

"It means his brain is awake most of the time and then it seems to take a short nap before turning itself back on."

Hearing this, I disguised my gasp as a cough. This was almost verbatim what Cortell had described to Carla and me about his neurological condition when he was at Mayo Clinic back in 1954. I didn't know if he had shared that information with either Frank or Kelsey. *Should I say something about this or not?* I was flummoxed. I needed to talk to Carla. I hadn't spoken with her since the night before we opened the cave, which I realized had only been about thirty hours earlier.

As soon as the doctors left, Frank and Kelsey made a beeline for the admiral's room. I excused myself explaining I needed to call Carla.

Naturally, she was worried sick about our friend, but when

I told her about the admiral's current EEG pattern all she said was, "Oh – my – God!"

"Should I get on a plane and get over there?"

"Yes," I replied. "The sooner the better."

Frank walked up just as I was saying, "Look, we have plenty of points on the Visa Card. Get an upgrade to Business Class so you can have a fully reclining seat."

When Frank heard me he started waving his hand and said, "No, no, no. Here, let me talk to her—Hi Carla... Yep, we're pretty wiped out...I dunno, it's hard to say. We believe he's gonna be fine, but...Hey, just I overheard what Gary was saying about flying over here. I have an idea. Can you get to Baltimore-Washington International by early Tuesday morning? ... Okay, check on that and let me know. If you can get there I'll arrange to have someone from the USO meet you at your arrival terminal and escort you to the AMC terminal. There you'll board either a C5 or C17...They can install all kinds of seats in those huge planes; even hospital beds...Yeah, I suppose that would be a bit much. Anyway, I'll be sure you're accommodated with a reclining seat, but you're going to want to bring your own light blockers and whatever kind of earplugs or white noise device you like...Good, looking forward to seeing you in a couple of days. Do you want to speak with this husband of yours—whom you are way too good for by the way?" He laughed and handed me the phone.

"I guess you know you've arrived when they're going to mount a reclining seat in a military transport plane just for you," I teased.

After Frank had walked away I asked Carla, "What do you think I should say about the admiral's EEG?"

She advised that I pull up our notes about Cortell's stay in Mayo Clinic and share them with Kelsey and Frank. They can decide whether or not to share that information with the medical staff. As usual, her advice was spot-on.

In fact, the admiral had told Frank about his anomalous EEG readings at Mayo, but Frank didn't remember the details. After Kelsey and Frank read our notes I found it interesting that they agreed it would be best to not share that information with the Landstuhl medical staff just yet.

Chris Roibal arrived at the Medical Center Monday evening looking haggard and tail-draggin' tired. He was dismayed the admiral hadn't regained consciousness, but intrigued and relieved that he wasn't actually in a coma.

Kelsey had secured a block of three rooms in the nearby Schloss Hotel Landstuhl. She handed Chris a room key and said, "I didn't think I'd ever hear myself say this Chris, but you look bad!" He let out a little half grunt/half chuckle. She continued, "You should go over to the hotel, take a soak and get some sleep."

Taking the key he said, "Thanks Kels. I'll see you in the morning. Call if his condition changes."

It did not. Tuesday morning the admiral remained in a bizarre state of mentally alert unconsciousness.

Carla arrived at the Ramstein Air Base in the wee hours of Wednesday morning. Chris and I drove his rental car over to the Air Base to pick her up. We waited for her at the Visitor Control Center while she went through the military's passport and travel credentials review process. By the time a shuttle brought her to the West Gate, we had been waiting for almost forty-five minutes. As we drove away to the west, the sun was crowning over the horizon in the rearview. Adjusting the mirror to keep the glare out of his eyes, Chris said, "I suppose the roosters are crowing and it's time for breakfast."

"Oh, please! I'm famished," Carla replied.

"Except for McDonalds, the restaurants around here are pretty much lunch and dinner only. The café at the hotel is actually pretty dang good and their coffee is excellent," Chris explained.

"Let's do that." Carla agreed. "I'd like to jump in the shower before heading to the hospital anyway."

"It's all good," Chris said as he turned onto avenue L363.

As the three of us walked into the Medical Center's entrance lobby we heard Frank's resonant voice from way down the corridor. "Hurry, you need to come quick!"

Alarmed I asked, "What's happened? Has he taken a turn?"

"Yeah, he's awake!"

We rushed into his room and saw the admiral had his bed raised into a sitting position. His eyes were twinkling. He didn't look a day older as a result of the ordeal. In fact, I'd even say he actually looked younger. "Come here sweetheart," he said to Carla.

As she crossed the room the admiral laid a yellow tablet and pencil down on the rolling bedside table. Carla gave him a hug and said, "I've been worried sick about you."

His eyes fluttered a little and he said, "I'm fine—really." Then he looked around at the rest of us, "I remember—I remember it all!"

CHAPTER SEVENTY

NEW OLD MEMORIES

WHEN KADEYA RETURNED to her homeworld she realized a day of reckoning had arrived for the people of Domhan-Siol. They had to come to terms with how their culture had drifted so far off course and what they had become. With the best of intentions Domhanians had paved an interdimensional highway to hell.

The chaos on Ghrain-3 was mirrored and in some ways magnified on Domhan-Siol. The economy that was initially staggered by the turmoil within Anotas-Deithe, had since stumbled badly. This was exacerbated by the tumbling fortunes of the extraterrestrial extraction industries. To make matters worse, most of the profits the extraction industries managed to produce were being funneled into off-world investments, particularly on Froitas.

Resentment grew. It was directed at the industrialists who had fled to Froitas; it was directed at Anotas-Deithe; it was directed at the Business and Industry Council. A sizable portion of the population also began to resent the influence of the cultists.

As corporations failed, families lost multiple generations of investments in those businesses. People were forced to withdraw most or all of their Domhanian Standard Credits from their Tender accounts just to live. This in turn led to the collapse of numerous Tender Institutions.

There were demonstrations for and against almost everything. Violence broke out between protesters and counter-protesters in places all around the globe. Often the cultists would instigate the confrontations and ultimately pay the price when the counter-protesters exacted revenge.

Liam and Sean believed Anotas was actually evolving in a constructive direction. It was regrouping around what had once been seen as Domhan-Siol's traditional values, but the process was excruciating. Maintaining some semblance of order within Domhanian society while Anotas rose from its own ashes became the primary focus of the Law and Order Directorate.

The military option to blockade and reclaim Ghrain-3 from the Serefim Presidium had, due to a lack of resources, been abandoned.

During all this turmoil the people on Domhan-Siol continued to be fed an almost daily ration of increasingly distressing reports about the war on Ghrain-3. Early on there was a great deal of jingoistic support for the Serefim Presidium, particularly among the cultists. As the war became a stalemate and the slave trade no longer economically benefited the people of Domhan-Siol, a war-fatigue malaise set in.

Brigadier Migeal's simultaneous abductions of sapien-hybrids had been a strategic success, keeping the slave trade alive, albeit a pale imitation of its prewar pinnacle. This second iteration of the ghastly business remained possible only because the Beag-Liath seemed reticent about bringing the full weight of their military superiority to bear. However, after almost four decades of the tit for tat warfare, Elyon instigated a colossal escalation. He ordered the abduction of several thousand sapiens in an operation euphemistically called "Hybrid Harvest."

Up to that point the Beag-Liath and Oprit-Robia had been satisfied with their efforts to make sure the Serefim Presidium overlords could not enjoy a deific existence. But operation Hybrid Harvest proved to be the last straw for the Beag-Liath. They began destroying Domhanian transport ships en route to "harvest" sites. This was not done as a slow step by step escalation. It was a massive coordinated assault. Over a three day period twenty-eight Serefim ships were destroyed. These attacks resulted in 100% crew fatalities.

The Serefim paramilitary forces on the orbiting station rebelled. They refused orders to continue the harvesting efforts. All hell broke loose when Elyon had four transport ship pilots executed for refusing to fly.

Within days, people throughout the Domhanian Empire learned of the devastating turn of events on Ghrain-3. Domhanians realized the Beag-Liath had been toying with the Serefim forces for almost half a century; that the Beag-Liath in fact had an enormous military and technological advantage. With the exception of a few diehard cultists, support for Elyon and the Serefim Presidium evaporated overnight.

Elyon and almost all members of the Presidium scampered to safe havens on Froitas. Many of the Serefim administrators and Ghrain-3 industry executives did likewise. A few people among the lower echelons trickled back to Domhan-Siol and a few even made their way to Realta-Gorm 4.

So it was that a decades-long war effort collapsed in just a couple of undecim. It had been almost four decades since Kadeya left her grandson on Ghrain-3. With the war's end she began at once making plans to return. Althea and Egan couldn't have been kept off of that mission by a herd of stampeding marsh bison.

Some thirty annum earlier, when Elyon had ordered the military occupation of Domhanian outposts on the surface, it was already clear the nefilim project was going to be successful; the retroviruses would in time render virtually all nefilim infertile. At that point, Elyon issued an Order of Excommunication. The assiduousness of the Group of 12 was rewarded by complete abandonment on the surface. They received no support or supplies of any kind. All communication with the group was terminated. They had only each other and some friends among the hybridized sapiens. Like fallen angels, they were cast out for their perceived rebelliousness.

At one point after the excommunication, three people on the orbiting station orchestrated a subterfuge resulting in Dr. Lilith's retrieval from Ghrain-3 and return to Domhan-Siol. An investigation identified the perpetrators, and Elyon summarily sentenced them to death for treason. Their execution was accomplished by placing them in one of the docking ports and opening the external hatch. They were instantly frozen as their bodies were blown out into the icy abyss. There were no further efforts to rescue any remaining nefilim project castaways.

When the war ended so abruptly, no one on Domhan-Siol knew if any other members of the G12 remained alive. Burdened by the guilt that the conspirators who helped her escape had been executed, Dr. Lilith had a shipload of emotional misgivings about returning to Ghrain-3. Nevertheless, she felt a strong obligation to search for and hopefully rescue any of her colleagues who may have survived. She asked to join Kadeya, Althea, and Egan on their quest to find Ramuell.

Althea and Egan reasoned the place to begin the search for Ramuell would be at the Crow Clan's last known home. The pilot landed their ship on the same knoll Adair and Semyaza had used all those decades ago.

There had been rumors of a catastrophic event at Blue Rock Canyon, but the Serefim Presidium had never provided any details. Kadeya set up a powerful telescope to search several kilometres of the canyon both upstream and down. It was clear something truly awful had happened. Vines overgrew the charred remains of long dead trees and many thousands of saplings had sprouted, but not a single old-growth tree could be found. They saw some animals on the south facing canyon wall, but no sign of sapien activity.

The search party returned to their ship and flew west until they got well beyond the enormous burn scar. When the pilot slowed the craft they began searching for evidence of sapien habitation. They at last spotted a sizable nomadic clan's camp.

"We should land a few a few kilometres away," Lilith advised. "Given decades of abductions by Serefim forces, there's no way to predict how the sapiens might react to seeing a Domhanian shuttlecraft."

The pilot remained with the ship while Kadeya, Egan, Althea and Lilith found some good cover to set up telescopes for observing the clan. They remained hidden and watched the clan for the rest of the day. They returned to the ship and informed the pilot they would try to make contact, but it might be a tedious process requiring several days.

"Be careful! Let me know if you need assistance or emergency evac," the pilot urged.

The group set up camp in sight of the sapiens but didn't try to initiate contact.

The sapiens were curious. Several wandered nearby to investigate the Domhanian camp but likewise didn't instigate any kind of communication.

The following day there were no actions by either group that could possibly have been interpreted as hostile. At last two men and a woman meandered within a hundred metres of the Domhanian camp. Lilith approached them cautiously with gestures of greeting. She employed the gesticulations she had remembered from the Crow Clan. Egan and Althea kept sonic-blasters handy but out of sight.

The sapien-hybrids seemed to be surprised and somewhat amused at Lilith's greeting gestures. They spoke and used made-up sign language for several minutes. When the conversation was over they parted cordially.

"So what did you learn?" Kadeya asked as soon as Lilith returned.

"Interesting—first, they don't speak the language of the Crow Clan. But the dialect is similar enough for us to have something like a conversation." Lilith paused for a minute organizing her thoughts. "If I understood correctly, the Crow Clan, per se, doesn't exist anymore. I believe they were telling me they know where to find the 'Two-Rivers-People' whom I assume are Crow Clan descendants."

"Where is that?" Althea asked excitedly. "How far?"

"I believe it's near the mouth of two small river canyons emerging from the mountains northeast of here. How far is hard to say given how they describe distance. It's my guess these 'Two-Rivers-People' may be living about a hundred kilometres away. I doubt we could find them without using sapien guides. And I'm damn sure we don't want to try to load any of those people on our ship."

"That was rather emphatic," Egan observed.

"There are a few things I'm certain I understood. First, it's clear these sapiens no longer deify us long-heads. They have bifurcated the 'sky-people' into groups of good and evil."

Kadeya said, "Most of us falling into the latter group I suppose."

"Precisely—they suffered at the hands of the Presidium. On more than one occasion they lost hunting parties to Domhanian abductors." Lilith shook her head with disgust. "Toward the end of the wars, they began fighting back, but encounters without support from Oprit-Robia or the Beag-Liath—well, wood and stone weapons against sonic-blasters and charged-particle guns..." She sighed.

"So what do we do now?" Althea asked.

"We wait. This clan seems to have a fairly egalitarian decision making process. The three people I met with are going to discuss our search for Ramuell with the clan. Tomorrow morning I predict the camp will either be gone or they're going to come offer help."

"You talked to them about Ramuell?" Althea asked excitedly.

"Yes and they don't know him," Lilith explained. "But I'm pretty sure they knew his name. I suspect he has quite a reputation among the sapiens of this entire region. I also suspect he is one of the good sky-people. These people have not seen a nefilim for a dozen annum. They credit the good sky-people with that blessing. When I was finally able to get them to understand who you three are and why you're searching for Ramuell, there was a subtle attitude shift."

"Attitude shift?" Egan questioned.

"Yeah, I sensed they became more interested in trying to help. But like I said, we're going to have to wait until morning to see if my perceptions are accurate."

Lilith's intuition had been correct. A couple of hours after sunrise five clanspeople approached the Domhanians. They made gestures of greeting as they approached. This time the three people whom Lilith had spoken with the day before were joined by a man and woman. Lilith surmised these were likely the alpha male and female of the clan, though neither wore any extraordinary clothing or accoutrements indicating elevated rank.

Lilith explained to Althea, Egan and Kadeya, "This is requiring all of my attention. I'm not going to be able to interpret. I'll summarize at the end in case you have questions."

"Of course—do what you must," Althea replied.

They spoke for about twenty minutes when at last Lilith turned to her companions and explained. "They do want to help, but they're nomadic hunters and going all the way to the mountain foothills is outside of their range and well beyond their intended route."

Dejected, Kadeya grunted.

Holding up a finger Lilith continued, "Now hold on. These three are willing to lead us to another group north of here whom they know trade with the Two-Rivers-People. They may even be related in some way through couplings."

"That's good news isn't it?" Althea asked.

"Potentially very good news. This man," she pointed to the older male, "believes Ramuell at one time lived with the Two-Rivers-People."

Egan nodded and smiled at the sapiens. He said, "If Ramuell is not there now, it's likely the clan may know where we can find him."

"That seems very likely," Lilith agreed.

Althea raised her hand as if sitting in a primary school classroom. When the others turned toward her, she stepped over beside the woman who was to be one of their guides.

Althea gently patted the young woman's tummy noting the first bloom of pregnancy. Looking at Lilith, Althea said, "Ask her if it's safe for her to lead us on this journey. She's with child."

This was not hard for Lilith to say, but the nomadic sapiens seemed bewildered by the question. They went back-and-forth with Lilith trying to understand. Finally the pregnant female looked at Althea, pointing to herself, the four others with her, and with a sweep of her arm the entire clan. She said something that was only a few syllables.

Creasing her forehead Althea looked at Lilith for an interpretation. Lilith explained with a slight smile, "The woman said simply, 'We walk.'"

Kadeya understood instantly. Snickering she said, "They are nomads. Pregnant females of this clan likely walk until the day before they give birth. This woman probably can't even fathom your concern."

Althea smiled broadly, grasped the woman's forearm and bowed slightly; hoping that might mean 'I understand and thank you.'

Soon after sunrise the next morning Kadeya, Egan, Althea, and Lilith packed up their tiny camp and awaited their guides. They waited for over an hour. Apparently certain traditional ceremonies were conducted by the clan before hunting and foraging parties journeyed forth.

The pace set by the three guides was brisk but not brutal. They understood the connection between caloric intake and energy rationing. They snacked, drank water, and rested frequently. Late afternoon they stopped to make camp.

Eagan wore a locater beacon in order for the ship's pilot to track the group's progress. Each evening, under the cover of darkness, he flew the shuttle to somewhere within four kilometres of his comrade's camp.

Late on the second day they encountered a group of eight young adults and a few children. Kadeya hypothesized they were possibly a subset of a larger clan because there were no infants, toddlers, nor any elderly among the group.

When the guides explained the Domhanians were looking for Ramuell, the members of the group became decidedly circumspect. Lilith explained, as best she could, that Althea and Egan were Ramuell's parents, and Kadeya was the grandmother. The clanspeople simply didn't understand this.

"I'm not absolutely certain, but I believe these people consider Ramuell to be much more than an elder; so old he has outlived at least two of their generations." She listened intently for a couple more minutes. "They cannot imagine how Ramuell's parents could possibly still be alive."

"Much less his grandmother," Kadeya speculated. "Their doubts are perfectly reasonable. We live fifteen to twenty times as long as the average lifespan of a sapien-hybrid."

The next morning, the three nomads approached the Domhanians in single file. It was much like a ceremonial reception line. In turn each of the sapiens took both hands of each Domhanian, squeezed them gently, bowed slightly, and repeated a brief statement to all four Domhanians.

Perplexed, Egan asked Lilith, "What are they saying?"

"I'm almost sure they're saying, 'Be well. Walk in beauty.'"

With that the three guides picked up their scant gear and simply walked away. They stopped as they topped a low rise about three hundred metres south and each gave a wave that began at the waist and extended to the tips of their outstretched fingers. Althea thought the rhythm of those big waves was both lovely and somehow wistful.

The four Domhanians turned to look at each other. They had no idea what was supposed to happen next. Lilith approached the clan's cook fire and bowed several times standing just outside the seating circle. After only a few seconds she was waved over and invited to sit beside one of the young adult women.

They spoke at length. Lilith was more fluent with the dialect spoken by these people than the nomadic clan. Kadeya, Egan and Althea watched the interaction carefully. On more than one occasion Lilith seemed surprised by something she was told. She returned to her colleagues with a gleam in her eyes.

"So what's next?" Althea asked anxiously.

"Well, I think it's all good news. Many of the Two-Rivers-People are descendants of the Crow Clan, but all were born after the exodus from Blue Rock Canyon. Two of these adults grew up with the Two-Rivers-People and do know Ramuell. They have since coupled with persons from other clans, but I don't really understand the relationships."

"So, is Ramuell with the clan they're leading us to," Egan asked before Althea could.

"No," Lilith reached up and scratched her ear. "This might be shocking but the reason we're being taken to the Two-Rivers-People is because Ramuell's daughter is the clan's leader or perhaps holy woman."

With wide eyes and a soft voice Althea said, "Daughter—you said daughter?"

"Yes," Lilith replied. "They say she has an elongated head. I feel certain the woman they are taking us to see **is** Ramuell's daughter."

Beaming, Althea said, "Our granddaughter! And surely she will know where Ramuell is!"

Holding up both hands in a 'whoa, let's slow down' gesture, Lilith said, "That I don't know. And it was not at all clear to me if these people don't know where Ramuell is, or just aren't saying."

For the next four days they hiked up a narrow flat river valley. The main slowdown came from the frequent need to ford the small river. Given that this was a larger group, with children, the pace was not as vigorous as that set by the guides from the nomadic clan.

The topography made the pilot's job simple. He could hop their ship from site to site in about five minutes, landing well out of view of the sapiens' camps.

Though the sapiens' wariness had almost completely evaporated, the Domhanians were not invited to share the clan's camp. On the fourth night two of the sapiens walked into the Domhanian camp. They were relaxed and unfearful while the squatted by the fire and spoke with Lilith. When they rose to leave they each clasped both of her hands and bowed slightly, just as the three guides had done with the Domhanian group at their parting a few days earlier.

After they walked away Kadeya said, "Something about that gesture is sweet and respectful, isn't it?"

"Yeah," Althea agreed. "Likewise with the way our guides turned and waved to us with their whole torso and arms." With an affectionate smile she added, "They're much more animated than we are—and I suppose that's a good thing."

"So what were they saying?" Egan asked.

"They were explaining that by mid-day tomorrow we'll arrive at the Two-Rivers-People's cave," Lilith replied. "The clan we're going to meet is probably much more like the Crow Clan; not particularly nomadic. They seem to live most of the annum in caves and supply their needs by dispatching hunting, foraging, and fishing parties."

"Do you think maybe they're beginning some forms of agriculture?" Egan asked.

Kadeya answered, "No. Not yet. That's probably many thousands of annum in the future...unless Ramuell or others in the Group of 12 jumpstarted that aspect of their evolution." Then with a little laugh, "And if they did, I swear I'll choke 'em!"

Egan and Althea both smiled at Kadeya's rebuke.

When the travelers came into sight of the large cave they heard gleeful shouts. Adults and children emerged from the cave and seemingly a dozen other places along the stream. Many came running up and offered happy, laughter-filled greetings. When the four Domhanians followed the group into the clearing between the cliff ledge and the stream the joviality came to an abrupt halt.

Egan scanned the gathering of sapiens arrayed before them. He studied the men carefully trying to measure the possibility of hostility. He subtly gripped the blaster in his pocket. Within a few seconds he determined the sudden silence was not the result of fear of anger. Rather the cave dwelling clan was shocked. It must have been a long time since they had seen sky-people.

During these few moments, the four Domhanians had instinctively inched closer together. Althea and Kadeya tried to mimic the gestures of nonaggression they had seen exchanged by members of the nomadic clan. Egan noted this brought subdued smiles to a few faces as the clanspeople inched closer to the foursome.

Then without a spoken word the crowd parted just enough to allow a tall woman to step through. She strode boldly up to the Domhanians. Her hair was pulled back in a loose braid. Her eyes were a stunning green with a bright halo of gold flecks around each pupil. But it was not the color that was so remarkable, it was the appearance that they were actually clear; the green hue seemed to shine from somewhere inside of her head rather than her irises. It was actually rather disconcerting.

As she stood studying the four visitors, Kadeya noticed the occipital area of her skull was a good deal larger than a typical sapien-hybrid, though not as elongated as that of a Domhanian. She also noticed the young woman had a sixth finger on each hand. Then with almost perfect Domhan Standard inflection the woman said, "Kadeya." She turned to Althea who had thrown her cupped hands over her mouth in complete amazement. The woman said to Althea, "Mother." Slowly she turned to Egan, pointed and with a little laugh said, "Dad."

Without another word she took Althea by the arm and led her up the path toward the cave. At once the crowd's joviality returned full force. There was laughter, slapping of backs, running and squealing of children. The still fully feathered game birds that had been taken by the guides over the previous two days were unstrung from the pole they'd been tied to. Cook fires were stoked. The clamor of voices exuded excitement and happiness.

Throughout the afternoon and evening Kadeya's great-granddaughter, whom the clan called Enepsy, regaled the Domhanians with stories about her parents. Her mother had aged and was very old when she died, but Ramuell seemed to age not at all. As she said this, her guests exchanged glances understanding the genetic dynamics involved.

Enepsy told stories of how even as her mother's health failed and her life faded, Ramuell attended to her with adoration. At that point something seemed to pass between Egan and Althea. They exchanged a poignant glance and Egan said with a question in his tone, "Shiya?"

Enepsy's astonishing eyes almost seemed to explode with excitement and joy. Laughing she exclaimed, "Eo, Eo, Shiya!"

Althea's lower lip trembled just before tears gushed from her eyes. This emotional response baffled Enepsy. She stopped laughing and looked mortified at what must have been her appalling faux pas.

Althea reached over and took her granddaughter's hands in her own and said, "No, no dear child. We are not angry. We are not sad. We are just so shocked. We knew your mother. We met Shiya when she was just a little girl. It was a horrible time. There was a battle with evil sky-people in a place far, far away. We brought your mother and the Crow Clan back home." Althea's eyes seemed to become unfocused, or perhaps she was staring into that time so long ago. "She was such a sweet little girl—and she so loved our Ramuell."

All this time Enepsy had been speaking an understandable pigeon Domhan Standard, relying on Lilith only when she got stuck on a word. But she had not understood Althea's last comments. She turned to Lilith who interpreted those last few sentences, word for word. When Lilith finished the translation, Enepsy looked at her three Domhanian ancestors. She squeezed her eyes together tightly, but it was not enough. Tears leaked out of the corners and down both cheeks. She made no effort to wipe them away. They rolled off her jaw and dropped onto her leather leggings.

Later that evening Egan asked, "Your emotional reaction was not just that we had known Shiya as a young child, was it?"

Looking into the cook fire's flames Althea answered, "No—it was more than that. You see, Ramuell embraced our most core value—our original purpose and real reason for coming to Ghrain-3."

Egan's eyebrows drew together, "Meaning?"

"He fathered a child," Althea answered. "It seems to me having a child is the creation of another consciousness—the essence of spawning sentience."

Early the next morning a wiry looking young man and Enepsy showed up at the Domhanian's camp beneath a deciduous tree. She explained they needed to take a walk. It was not a long walk and there would be water enough along the way. She handed each of the Domhanians a couple of dried meat strips.

When the Domhanians had laced on their boots they joined Enepsy on an oft trod path to the east. The young man leading the way was armed with a well-made stone tipped spear. As they walked, Enepsy began to talk. Lilith moved up beside her to help translate should the need arise. Occasionally Lilith would interrupt to clarify some point and then Enepsy would continue.

She told several humorous stories about Ramuell. Enepsy was about thirteen annum when her mother died, which wasn't unusual given the sapiens' lifespan. Ramuell on the other hand had been around well into Enepsy's adulthood. About six annum ago he began having difficulty breathing. Actually Enepsy said she had seen signs of problems even earlier, but it became worse rather suddenly. He was unable to walk far and could no longer hunt. He did sometimes go to the stream to catch fish, though often he only returned with watercress.

Even as his health failed he remained funny and happy. All of the clan's children loved Ramuell. They would climb all over him while evening meals were being prepared. He would play handclap games with them, show them tricks, tickle them and tell stories. Enepsy narrowed her eyes, "Sometimes the stories were too scary. But they loved my father as I had when I was a child." She turned and looked at her Domhanian family and said, "As I still do."

The group stopped and drank from a stream then walked a few hundred metres up a slope toward a south facing bluff. When they arrived at a crevasse the young man laid down his spear and began removing flat stones that had been carefully stacked in the mouth of a cave.

Enepsy ran her tongue across her upper lip as she tried to think of a way to explain. With a slight shake of her head, she decided it was better to show than tell. She began removing stones from the mouth of the cave. After looking at each other for a moment, the four Domhanians joined in the labor. The stones were large enough to be formidable but not too heavy to handle. They had been fitted together precisely to make intrusion by hungry scavengers all but impossible.

When they'd opened the cave, Enepsy led the foursome inside. The cave was a tomb. Several corpses were naught but skeletons. Others were in various stages of desiccation. They were arranged around the periphery of the cave, and all had their arms folded across their chests.

Enepsy pointed to the right and led her family to the remains of a man with an elongated skull. A necklace of bears teeth strung on a leather thong encircled his neck. A foliopad lay on his chest. Enepsy knelt down and gently slid the device out from under the folded arms. She stood and with a bow handed it to Kadeya.

Althea dropped to her knees beside Ramuell's body. "No! No! This can't be Ramuell!" She turned and looked almost pleadingly at Enepsy.

Enepsy pinched her lips together tightly, gazed back at Althea and silently nodded.

Althea cupped her son's jaw in her hands. "Oh no. Oh Ramuell, my son! We had so little time together, but you were always the light of my life. Did you know that? Were you happy? Did you know how much we missed you? Did you know how much we loved you?"

With tears streaming down her cheeks, Kadeya knelt beside the body, laid her hand on Ramuell's chest and added in a whisper, "How much we will always love you—until the end of our time."

Althea moaned between almost silent sobs.

As Egan's frozen disbelief melted, he drew in a ragged breath and lowered himself to his knees behind his wife. Wrapping his arms around Althea, he began rocking her back-and-forth as he gently pulled her hand away from their son's leather-dry face.

Lilith sidled over and stroked Kadeya's shoulders.

After a few minutes, Enepsy knelt at Ramuell's head and ever so gently removed the bear-tooth necklace. She moved beside Althea and tenderly slipped the necklace around her grandmother's neck and adjusted it, so the teeth hung just right. She then leaned forward and placed her forehead between Althea's and Egan's, lightly touching both of her grandparents' heads simultaneously.

The young man outside the cave coughed. Enepsy let out a sad sigh, leaned back and pushed herself to her feet. She stooped over to brush the dust off her leggings. Her movements and body language said, 'It's time to go.' When Kadeya stood, Enepsy stepped forward and placed her cool hands on her great-grandmother's cheeks. Slowly and gently they touched foreheads—a moment of the purest love.

As Enepsy stepped back she saw Kadeya still clinging to Ramuell's foliopad—a technology her species would not even contemplate for some 50,000 annum. Yet somehow she understood it was incredibly important. She gave Kadeya a melancholy smile.

To prevent any disturbance of the hallowed hollow, the group reclosed the entrance, meticulously restacking the stones that had been flattened and chiseled to form fit the cave's mouth.

INTERLUDE #5

July 2019
Landstuhl Regional Medical Center
Rhineland-Palatinate, Germany

No one had said a word during the admiral's recitation of these "new" memories. He looked up at us and whispered, "Oh, my Ramuell."

He pushed his head back into the pillow and squeezed his eyes shut. We stood around his bed in stunned silence. I had a fist size lump in my throat. Kelsey was dabbing tears from her eyes.

Carla shot Kelsey a sympathetic glance then turning to the admiral asked, "So what do you think sickened Ramuell? He wasn't old for a Domhanian was he?"

Cortell opened his eyes, rubbed his face with both hands and cleared his throat. "Oh no, he wasn't old. By my calculation he'd lived about 155 Domhan-Siol annum—a kid by their standards.

"I really doubt the harsh living conditions got him.

Ramuell was tough. He sailed through the Ghrain-3 acclimatization process numerous times. He'd lived on Earth for decades before he got sick."

He closed his eyes and blew out a long exhale. "Althea collected swab cultures from several members of Enepsy's clan. Later back in our lab she found a bacterium we hadn't seen before. Domhan-Siol and Ghrain-3 did not share the same bacteria. Of the hundreds of thousands of identified species, there were many similarities in structure and function among the bacteria of both worlds, but to my knowledge there were no DNA doppelgangers ever found.

"The early Domhanian explorers on Ghrain-3 always wore sealed biohazard suits with self-contained breathing apparatuses. They didn't breathe the air, drink the water or even touch anything. They tested for and identified thousands of potential pathogens. In their labs they produced vaccines, antibiotics and antitoxins.

"We were astounded to find a new species of bacteria that appeared to be pathogenic." The admiral raised both hands in a gesture of surrender, "We never understood what we were looking at. But as a human, all these thousands of years later and considering the symptoms Enepsy described, I would not be surprised if Ramuell died from what humanity would many millennia later call consumption."

Astonished, I said, "Really! You think he had tuberculosis—some fifty thousand years ago?"

"I do. Or more likely some early iteration in the bacterium's evolution. Hell, for all I know, the way Domhanians played like gods with the planet's DNA, they may have accidentally engineered the organism."

We stood for several moments thinking about the implications of that cautionary tale. Kelsey said almost as an aside, "Her eyes—Enepsy's eyes were like yours."

The admiral looked at his daughter with a bewildered expression.

"You really don't know, do you?" she said.

"Know what?"

Several of us exchanged glances, surprised by the admiral's apparent lack of self-awareness. Kelsey unzipped her purse, which was slung across the back of a chair. She pulled out a mirror and handed it to her father. He looked at his image and blinked several times. There, staring back at him, were two bright green eyes with gold colored motes haloing each pupil. He gasped and quickly looked away. His hand trembled as he passed the mirror back to Kelsey.

He said nothing. No one else knew what to say.

After several uncomfortable seconds, Frank broke the silence. "Do you remember what you saw in the cave at Polovragi?"

"Yes I do—an elongated skull and a jaw with two dental implants." Hesitantly he asked, "What did you do with them?"

Frank looked at me and grimaced. "I did what I thought was best. I picked up the whole jaw, took it to the motorhome and put it in a zip lock bag."

Cortell stiffened, stared wide-eyed at Frank, then he exhaled and nodded slightly. "As much as I hate it, you did the right thing."

I looked at Frank and said, "I've thought a lot about what you did, and I agree with the admiral. It's kind of an X Files meets the Holy Bible thing."

"Whaat?" Frank drawled.

"Well, Fox Mulder was correct, the truth **is** out there. But the Apostle John got it wrong, the truth will not necessarily set us free."

"Humph, at least not yet," Cortell agreed. "For now this

little slice of truth is beyond our horizon...and where's the jaw now?"

Frank glance anxiously at the room's open door. "For now, it's in a safe place."

After a moment of silence I said, "I suppose that leads to the next question."

Looking at me the admiral asked, "Which is?"

"The foliopad—Ramuell's foliopad, the one Enepsy gave to Kadeya. Was it functional?"

"Functional? Ah yes, it was functional all right and packed with unfathomable amounts of information." He squinted at his own thoughts. "Ramuell had recorded an extraordinary amount of detail about the nefilim project. But perhaps even more important, his journal described and analyzed the war with astonishing clarity—I suppose he recorded the only definitive history of this planet's first world war. So you see, we have a lot more work to do," Cortell said with an enigmatic smile.

Just then one of the physicians walked in. Chris coughed and we fell silent instantly. The admiral scooched up a bit straighter in his bed.

Realizing he'd interrupted something, the perplexed doctor glanced around the room. "Nope, nope, this won't do—won't do at all. The patient needs his rest, folks." Pointing at Kelsey he said, "You may stay. The rest of y'all need to git out. Go do somethin' fun—there'll be time enough later for y'all to be about," he stopped, looked around at us again, "for y'all to be about whatever in the heck it is y'all're about."

The admiral said, "I don't know doc. I'm not such a young guy anymore and we've got a lot to do—you see, I remember.

"Yep, that may well be, but as long as you're in my care, you're gonna by-God get some rest."

Looking down at the shiny brown cowboy boots peeking

out from under the doctor's scrubs, the admiral sighed and said, "And I don't suppose it's going to do us any good to argue with an Army doc from Texas."

With a smirk, the doctor turned and gestured the way toward the door.

"But before you go..." the admiral reached over and picked up the tablet from his bedside table. He tore off the top yellow sheet, folded it with a crisp crease, and handed it to me.

Again the doctor waved toward the door. This time we filed out like a little brood of ducklings.

EPILOGUE

CARLA, having given the admiral one more hug, was the last to emerge. The doctor closed the door and under knitted eyebrows gave us one more befuddled look. He shook his head, shrugged, and walked away. Over his shoulder he called back, "Don't even think about sneaking back in that man's room."

Chris whispered, "That man? Does he not know who **that man** is?"

"Ohhh, he knows! Everybody in this hospital knows 'that man' is here," Frank replied.

When the doctor rounded the corner, I unfolded the sheet of paper. Frank, Chris, and Carla crowded around to read what the admiral had written.

Ramuell of Domhan-Siol: Son of Althea and Egan

Grandson of Kadeya
Journal - Final Entry
Date: 24212-7-38

SEN-TIME

Lying on the cold hard ground
Under a bright night sky
Nuclear orbs lit our heaven
As we tumbled by.

The dust of a trillion stars
Pounding all around
Lying in that fallout was
A peace I'd never have found.

A rapturous sound of beauty
From tiny specks of light
Across the fathomless distance
Came the music of the night.

From within the depths of time
Songs of hope and songs of fear
An eternity in the making
The sen-time was here.

Stories will be written
The bards will have their say
But no one will remember
The sen-time of these days.

Digging in their holes
Bits of pot and bone they'll find
But ne'r a shovel will turn
The psychic dances of this time.

Now I lay me down to sleep
Never to awake
Surrendering up this sentience
To the boundless cosmic lake.

ACKNOWLEDGMENTS

Foremost a debt of gratitude is owed to my spouse, Carla. She took incalculable hours away from her own writing to critique, consult, and edit this book. She placed one hand between my shoulder blades to push me along and the other hand in front of my chest to catch me when I stumbled. I must thank my four long-time friends (Stuart Gustafson, William McGonigle, Bill McKinney, and Ralph Vigil) who agreed to be beta readers of the ridiculously long manuscript. They saw things I never would have seen. Their observations added a year of work to the final product, and because of that it is a much better book. My editor, Sharon Ammen, earned my colossal appreciation and respect. Though this book is not of a genre she typically reads, she did a deep-dive, line by line edit and taught me things about the English language that I would never have known. If this is a good book, it is because Sharon made it so.

ABOUT THE AUTHOR

Gary Beene is a native New Mexican. *Alien Genesis* is his fourth book. He lives and writes in Santa Fe, New Mexico with his wife, Carla. Two cats and a dog have agreed to let Carla and Gary share their living space.

To learn more about Gary Beene and discover more Next Chapter authors, visit our website at www.nextchapter.pub.

Alien Genesis
ISBN: 978-4-82414-266-5

Published by
Next Chapter
2-5-6 SANNO
SANNO BRIDGE
143-0023 Ota-Ku, Tokyo
+818035793528

16th April 2022

Lightning Source UK Ltd.
Milton Keynes UK
UKHW010246090223
416650UK00002B/582